Maxim Jakubowski is a Lo̶... was born in the UK and educated in France. Following a career in book publishing, he opened the world-famous Murder One bookshop in London. He now writes full-time. He has edited over twenty bestselling erotic anthologies and books on erotic photography, as well as many acclaimed crime collections. His novels include *It's You That I Want to Kiss, Because She Thought She Loved Me* and *On Tenderness Express*, all three recently collected and reprinted in the USA as *Skin in Darkness*. Other books include *Life in the World of Women, The State of Montana, Kiss Me Sadly, Confessions of a Romantic Pornographer, I Was Waiting for You* and, recently, *Ekaterina and the Night*. In 2006 he published *American Casanova*, a major erotic novel which he edited and on which fifteen of the top erotic writers in the world collaborated, and his collected erotic short stories as *Fools for Lust*. He compiles two acclaimed annual series for the Mammoth list: *Best New Erotica* and *Best British Crime*. He is a winner of the Anthony and the Karel Awards, a frequent TV and radio broadcaster, a past crime columnist for the *Guardian* newspaper and Literary Director of London's Crime Scene Festival. He edits Constable & Robinson's digital Modern Erotic Classic series, and recently translated Emma Becker's *Monsieur*.

THE MAMMOTH BOOK OF

Quick & Dirty
EROTICA

Edited by

MAXIM JAKUBOWSKI

ROBINSON

RUNNING PRESS
PHILADELPHIA · LONDON

ROBINSON

First published in Great Britain by Robinson in 2013

Copyright © Maxim Jakubowski, 2013
(unless otherwise stated)

A CIP catalogue record for this book
is available from the British Library.

UK ISBN: 978-1-78033-791-3 (paperback)
UK ISBN: 978-1-78033-792-0 (ebook)

Printed and bound in Great Britain by CPI Group (UK) Ltd., Croydon, CR0 4YY

Robinson
is an imprint of
Constable & Robinson Ltd
100 Victoria Embankment
London EC4Y 0DY

An Hachette UK Company
www.hachette.co.uk

www.littlebrown.co.uk

3 5 7 9 10 8 6 4 2

First published in the United States by Running Press Book Publishers in 2012
All rights reserved under the Pan-American and International Copyright Conventions

Books published by Running Press are available at special discounts for bulk
purchases in the United States by corporations, institutions and other organizations.
For more information, please contact the Special Markets Department at the
Perseus Books Group, 2300 Chestnut Street, Suite 200, Philadelphia, PA 19103,
or call (800) 810-4145, ext. 5000, or email special.markets@perseusbooks.com.

US ISBN: 978-0-7624-4813-5

US Library of Congress Control Number: 2012942539

9 8 7 6 5 4 3 2
Digit on the right indicates the number of this printing

Running Press Book Publishers
2300 Chestnut Street
Philadelphia, PA 19103-4371

Visit us on the web!

www.runningpress.com

Introduction

For the many years that I have been assembling the red hot volumes in *The Mammoth Book of Erotica* series, I have been selecting stories from all provenances and covering a wild variety of themes in the process.

Apart from quality and inherent sexiness and the fact the hundreds of stories I featured in the anthologies all connected with me in a very personal way and answered to my often generous and all-encompassing definition of what is actually erotic, what the tales I've been privileged to edit have had in common is their length.

In my crusade to make erotic writing not only respectable but appreciated, my greatest sin has been so far to prefer longer stories in which characters and plot were properly developed and I've been reluctantly turning down on a regular basis many stories where the length was too brief to accommodate those factors. Not that any of them weren't erotic. They were sizzling, close to the bone and wonderfully arousing. Like fires of lust caught in amber, all too often.

So I'm particularly pleased to now be able to devote a whole volume to shorter length erotic tales, "quickies" if you will. Ably demonstrating that, to use an analogy from another trade altogether, it's not the quantity, but the quality that counts.

Many of the regular contributors to *The Mammoth Book of Erotica* series make welcome returns together with an invigorating injection of new names, all demonstrating that you can, over the space of a few short pages, evoke lust, desire, love, romance and, most of all, emotions in myriad ways, all touching, surprising, oft shocking but always exciting.

Two-thirds of the 120 stories in this bumper collection were specially commissioned to showcase the breadth of talent in today's erotic writing field, and the remaining third were selected from the many stories already available in a variety of sources, so a particular big vote of thanks goes to Clean Sheets online magazine, the Erotica Readers and Writers Association Treasure Chest where many of the existing stories originated, as well as to some of the authors who were generous enough to recommend tales or writers of which I was previously unaware.

So, if you will forgive me a cliché that is just too much of a temptation not to use, enjoy these tales and agree with me that it's not how long a story it is but how good it is that counts at the end of the day.

I hope you enjoy all these sizzling tales of lust at first sight.

Erotically yours.

Maxim Jakubowski

Contents

Contents

Acknowledgements

All stories © 2013 by the respective authors, with the exception of:

"Gravity" © Helen E. H. Madden, 2008
"Pattern Passion" © Remittance Girl, 2009
"Scars" © R. V. Riment, 2012
"Flowering" © Valentine Bonnaire, 2011
All appeared first on the Erotica Readers and Writers Association website.

"They Plan Bunch" © Bill Noble, 2002
"Barbados Bound" © Lily Lick, 2003
"Kissing on Concourse C" © Susannah Indigo, 2003
"Mad Ida Loved the Wind" © Lily Lick, 2001
"Strange Fruit" © Shanna Germain, 2003
"At Liberty" © Sacchi Green, 2004
"Joining the Mile High Club" © Rachel Kramer Bussel, 2004
"Engineers and Astronauts" © Jacqueline Applebee, 2008
"The History of her Tongue" © Shaun Levin, 2008
"The year of Fucking Badly" © Susannah Indigo, 2008
All appeared first on the Clean Sheets website.

"The Room After She Left" © Maxim Jakubowski, 2002. First appeared in *13*, edited by Mare Atkins.
"Like A Virgin" © Maxim Jakubowski, 2002. First appeared in *Down and Dirty*, edited by Alison Tyler.
"In The Empire of Lust" © Maxim Jakubowski, 2008. First appeared in *Open for Business*, edited by Alison Tyler.

Violet Sex

Kristina Lloyd

I've always enjoyed violent sex but then John lost our letter "n", and sex turned violet. It was filled with the colours of love: rose-pink, mauve, lilac and wine. At its most intense, usually on Sunday evenings, our designated "special time", it was the deep blue-purple of violets.

"John," I said, as we got kissy in the kitchen. "I'm not so sure about this. Do you think we could put a little 'n' back into it?"

He moved to strike me but his hand turned lavender, his fingers stroking bruise-hued streaks across my cheek.

"Harder!" I hissed.

He slammed me against the counter but his strength dimmed in an indigo puff, sparks of firework-purple shimmering to the floor.

I lunged for his crotch and he was stiff inside his jeans. "Fuck me!" I urged. "Fuck me like a filthy, filthy beast."

"Sweetheart, I don't think I can," he replied. "I'm feeling kinda off-colour. I don't want to hurt you. I'm sorry. It's not you, it's me."

"I know," I replied grimly.

We hunted high and low for our "n": behind the sofa, under the bed, in the dog basket. We even searched the garden, paying particular attention to the heliotrope, the buddleia (made a note to cut that back), the romping clematis and baskets of lobelia, both of us alert to signs of unwarranted botanical aggression. It was to no avail. Our "n" was lost.

As time slipped by, our lovemaking became increasingly gentle and purplish until one day we stopped altogether. In the emptiness, I grew randier than a sailor's wife. I considered taking another lover and John said he wouldn't mind but I could see from his eyes he didn't mean it. I didn't much care for the idea either. At night in bed, I would trail my hand over his back, swoop over his hips and, as I kissed his shoulder, I would reach around to test how he was feeling. Nothing. His cock was palest mauve. I would watch him fresh out of the shower as he towelled his hair, beads of water coursing down his torso and glinting like rain in the black bush of his pubes. I'd forgotten how much I wanted that body until our misplaced "n" had rendered it off-limits.

The worst times were when he was hard, his cock jutting up to his belly, his tip a fierce blood-violet and filmy with moisture.

"Let me," I would plead. "Let me suck you, let me get on top, let me have it inside me."

Oh God, I'd never wanted anything so much in my life. My cunt was wet and ready, his cock was massive and eager. But no: "Darling, I'd love to, you know I would, but let's just have a cuddle, eh?"

One night, I got up to masturbate. It always seemed rude to do it with him there and anyway, my fear of waking him would have put me off my stroke. I went into the kitchen, looking for a suitable vegetable. I hadn't bought a vibrator, fearing plastic would imply permanence, choosing instead to fuck myself with green and orange perishables. On the kitchen table, a small bowl of plums gleamed in the moonlight, a whitish bloom dusting their skins like a soft, quiet frost. I took one and ate it, and then another. Juice trickled down my chin and strands of flesh got stuck in my teeth. I was reaching for a greedy third when I saw it, nestled among the fruits, our much-loved letter "n".

"John!"

But John was fast asleep. Hurrying carefully, I carried the "n" in the palm of my hand and clambered onto the bed. I didn't know how John had lost it so I didn't know how to return it. Force-feed him? Squash it in his ears? Up his butt? In the end, I wiped it on his cheek, although I suppose you could say I slapped him across the face. He woke with a jolt.

"What the . . .?" He glared at me, a hand pressed to his cheek, dark sleepy curls tumbling around his face. "You insane fucking bitch!"

"Bitch" made me moist.

John flung the covers aside and sprang at me. I lurched back and he grabbed my hair. "You hit me!" he exclaimed. I tried to resist him, hair follicles stinging as he pulled my head to the mattress, pinning me there, angled down on all fours. I caught a glimpse of his cock, rearing up and ready for battle.

"Apologize!" he barked.

"No way!"

He yanked my hair.

"Ouch, no."

My cunt was plump and slippery. John swivelled behind me, grabbed my hips and, before I even realized we were about to end our purple period, his big, strong cock was rushing inside me.

"Greedy bitch." He yanked back my arms, making me half wheelbarrow, half woman, and hammered away at me. "Teach you a lesson," he gasped. "Teach you to wake me up, you slut. Always wants fucking! Wakes me up so I'll fuck her."

I groaned into the bedclothes, biting at fabric, shoulder sockets pulling, wrists hurting where he clutched. But the pain was nothing compared to the pleasure of him fucking me, his end rubbing over my sweet spot then bumping deep and good.

"Whore. Filthy little whore."

He reached for my clit, fretting me there. "Come on!" he said. "If you want it so bad, come. Show me what a slut you are. Come for me, you dirty, greedy bitch."

Before long I did. He quickly followed suit, weeks of distance ending in an eruption of crazy, colourless cries.

"Ohhhhh."

"Oh God."

We flopped onto our backs, panting heavily before edging together for kisses and cuddles. My cunt was throbbing with the impact of his thrusts, and my arms and shoulders ached. We fell asleep, united in bliss. In the morning, my wrists were tender. In the evening, I checked them. Bruises were forming where his fingers had gripped, moody purple patches, bluish-plum like a storm gathering at dusk, the colour of violent beauty.

Sniper's Song

Robert Buckley

I could've drunk a lake. It was the damned wind. It wasn't just cold, it was so damned dry it cracked my skin and drew the moisture right out of my throat. My nostrils burned.

Still, I managed to sleep, if only fitfully. 'I'm too old to be doing this,' I chuckled to myself, but it was true. Climbing goddamned mountains and sleeping in thorny scrub on a cliff face just a few yards from eternity – that was for younger guys. Like my spotter.

Bogs ... short for Bogdan, a Polish kid. He went straight from Gdansk into Uncle Sam's Army. One of the best spotters I ever worked with. He seemed to be happy to be teamed with this old fossil too.

I heard Bogs tapping away at the laptop. A false dawn was beginning to reveal the contour of the peak across the chasm. Neither of us wanted to have been sent up here on a wild goose chase.

I began to doze again, and dream of Linda. Always the same dream, always about the last night we were together. I never thought I'd be reactivated. Not in this century. Maybe they'd called me back to be an instructor. That's what I had told Linda.

"They'll keep me stateside to teach young kids coming up. They aren't going to trust a pair of eyes that are nearly fifty years old."

"Those eyes never age," she had said, smiling through tears. "They look the same, since the day they caught me skinny-dipping."

I didn't stay stateside, thanks to Willard. Damned company man put in a special request for me. He probably thought he was doing me a favor. He was always a pain in the ass.

Willard was in charge of this mission and that meant he got to handpick his team, whether they wanted to be picked or not.

Willard's prune face receded and again I dreamt of Linda, naked, eyes glistening from fresh tears. I had never felt such a powerful need to fuck a woman as I did that night before I left. I was relentless and she responded fiercely and recklessly, screaming and crying ... even drawing blood. It was as if she felt it would be our last time.

Bogs shook me awake. "Camel is on the move."

Camel was the code name of our target. He had returned to this mountaintop twice, a foolish mistake. We expected him to return a third time, a fatal mistake. Intelligence had tried to divine what attraction this godforsaken place had for him in this entire shithole of a country. In the end, it was enough that he returned at regular intervals.

His movements were tracked by satellite. They could have taken him out with a Predator, but Willard demanded absolute confirmation of a kill. That meant death had to be made by personal delivery, with a bullet.

A natural arch spanned the chasm and provided access to the opposite peak as it had since the days of Alexander the Great. Camel's vehicle would traverse the arch to our right, turn left and disappear behind a jagged formation of rock, and then stop on the small, sloped plateau outside the rude hovel we'd been spying on since we arrived. There was no sign the hovel was occupied.

Bogs efficiently set up equipment and attached cables to the riflescope that fed into a small black box that itself connected to the laptop.

In a moment, the whine of a struggling engine caught our attention. A beige Range Rover made its way gingerly over the natural bridge. Once it had attained the opposite peak, it stopped and dislodged five armed men, Camel's bodyguards.

The engine began to whine again and we could hear the stubborn clutch as it popped into gear. The vehicle disappeared behind the rock formation and then entered the unobstructed plateau. I already had the driver fixed in my sights as he emerged from the Range Rover. I zoomed in. Everything I could see was being fed via satellite to Willard, wherever the hell he was.

I fixed my earpiece and waited for Willard to confirm the target and authorize the shot.

"Hey," Bogs said. "He's got company."

I raised the scope a bit to the left. From the hovel emerged a small woman. She was dressed in the garb of the mountain people from this region, but her face was uncovered. As her features became clearer I surmised she was in her twenties. As she got closer to Camel she broke into a run and threw herself into his arms. He spun her around, and as he did he revealed his face.

Less than thirty seconds later Willard's voice crackled through my earpiece. "Target is confirmed – repeat – target is confirmed. Looks like he had a yen for a little poontang. It'll get 'em every time. Take your shot – repeat – take this fucking prick out."

It was perfect. The moon lit up the area like a ballpark during a night game. Camel was dead. He just didn't know it.

Camel and the girl kissed. He had to bend down to her. Her hands gripped the material of his shirt in tight fists as his hands roamed gently over her body. They broke the kiss and he stepped away to the vehicle from which he retrieved blankets and other loose bedding and tossed them on the ground.

The girl's hands moved deftly over her garments, which fell away in ribbons and billows in the wind. She ran to Camel and began to help him shed his own clothes.

Bogs's voice was insistent, yet questioning. "They repeat – take your shot. They'll lose satellite in thirty seconds."

Willard's voice crackled again. "What's happening? Looks like a clear shot."

"I'll take it when I'm ready," I whispered into the microphone set.

"We're losing satellite video for thirty minutes. What are you waiting for?"

"I'll take it when I'm ready and confirm he's down. You stand by with Predators when we need to book it out of here."

There was a second or two of hesitation before Willard said, "Roger that."

I yanked the cables off the scope. They couldn't see what was happening now anyway.

Camel and the girl were all arms and legs rocking on the

ground. And when the wind blew just right, I thought I could hear their moans and sighs as they made love in one of the most loveless places on the planet.

Bogs said nothing. He knew enough to trust me not to let the target slip away.

Now we both heard the cries of urgent passion, and a sweet, sad girlish voice waft across the chasm. Camel sat up with his back toward us. The girl sat in his lap, her breasts to his chest and her legs clenched tightly around his hips. Through the scope I saw the ripple of his muscles as he rocked himself up deeply inside her. Her small hands traced his shoulder blades and the three shrapnel scars about midway down his back.

The girl's chin rested on his shoulder. Tears running freely down her cheeks. Her face – like Linda's – a profound mixture of passion and sadness. It was as if she knew this would be their last time.

He shuddered and her eyes rolled back. Then they fell back on the blankets and curled together.

Bogs nudged me. "It'll be dawn soon."

I nodded. I wondered about the girl, and about Camel. I wondered if she knew how many arms were left empty because of him, how many cunts were left empty because of him, how many hearts were empty because of him.

Even as I watched him fill her legs and fill her womb, my thoughts turned to Linda. Linda liked to fuck like that, breasts to chest, in my lap, with her thighs clenched around my waist. Strong little thighs. My ribs hurt after we were done.

The sky was becoming pink. Camel rose and lifted the girl to her feet. Tenderly, he swathed her in a blanket against the cold. She handed him a piece of red cloth that fluttered like silk. One tender kiss and he took his leave.

"We have satellite back," Bogs said.

I reattached the cables to the scope. "Tell Willard to have the Predators target the arch bridge," I said.

The Range Rover left the girl standing in a swirl of dust and disappeared behind the rock formation. It reappeared and stopped at the arch. Camel's men tumbled into the vehicle as he moved over into the passenger's seat. I trained the scope on him through the windshield.

The vehicle again moved gingerly over the ancient formation. At about halfway across, I watched him lift the red fabric to his nose and breathe deeply. It was the last thing he knew before my rifle coughed and his chest exploded all over his companions.

They tumbled out of the Range Rover like a clown act pointing their AKs in all directions. They didn't have a clue where the shot came from. Two glints like welders' torches in the sky shot over the peaks. The missiles launched by the Predators hurtled into the stone arch. Then the entire formation, which had stood since before the time of Alexander the Great, broke into blocks of granite and plummeted into the chasm below.

"Confirmed, Camel down – repeat – confirmed, Camel down." Willard's voice crackled again. "Nice shot, excellent . . ."

Bogs broke the connection. In his thick Polish accent he said, "Time to boogie, boss. Gotta make the LZ in twenty minutes."

I nodded. Bogs had already packed the equipment and was humping it down the slope. I lifted my glasses to the opposite slope. The girl stood, looking at us. I focused in tighter. Her face was wet. I looked for a sign of hate in her eyes, but saw none. Just sadness.

I turned and stumbled down the slope. I was going home to Linda. Nothing, or no one could stop me.

The Swimming Pool

Vina Green

I have always loved the water.

My family is religious.

I grew up near the sea, reading the Bible.

As a child, one of my favourite stories was the biblical account of Moses leading the Israelites through to the Promised Land by parting the Red Sea. In pictorial reproductions of this story, I always thought that Moses seemed unreasonably terrified, holding his staff aloft as if that stick alone might hold back the walls of water which in a short time would sweep away the Egyptians.

I was never particularly impressed by Moses's miracle. The ocean and I were good friends. Given the right motivation, I thought, I could convince water to part. It was just a matter of asking nicely.

I often fantasized about how the Egyptians must have felt as the sea came tumbling down on them. I thought that the illustrators of my children's Bible story book had it wrong. The pictures were full of screaming soldiers with wide white eyes clinging to the backs of horses with legs kicking high into the air as if running against the waves. I thought that it might feel wonderful to drown. When I swam laps with my high school swimming team, I angered my coach by neglecting overarm and back stroke and breast stroke and instead travelling from one end of the pool to the other in a single dive, holding the air in my lungs until I felt my chest would burst into flames without another breath, and then bursting out of the water in one heady gasp, like a whale emptying its blowhole.

The first time I ever discovered pubic hair and the natural secretions of a woman's sex, I was in a swimming pool. I was lowering myself into the water, easing a severe sunburn, when I found a thick strand of coarse black hair, curled up and stuck to the side of the pool.

"What's that?" I asked my older and wiser friend.

"Ugh," she said in disgust, "it's a pube."

"What's it got on it?" I asked again, pointing to a thick, luminous droplet that had gathered on one end of the hair.

"It's come," she hissed into my ear, pushing off from the pool side with a splash to signal that the conversation was over.

That explained a few things, I thought, tying together strange words overheard in schoolyard conversations and remembering the shock I had felt when I had looked down at the small mound between my legs one day and noticed a few long strands of silky hair gathering in a place that I was too ashamed and too afraid to talk about.

I gave up swimming in school clubs, as I was always too independent to turn up on time and to swim drills, which I hated. I continued swimming, but always on my own, and always when and where I wanted to swim.

Years later, when I was married, I shocked my husband by taking off my clothes and diving into the water naked when we were on holiday in Brighton one November.

"Someone will see you!" he hissed, kneeling onto the pier and flailing his arm in the water, as if to grab me by an errant limb and pull me out again.

"I don't care!" I yelled back, the cold weight of the water rushing against my skin with all the hard comfort of a steel blanket.

When we returned from holiday, he filed for divorce.

I still swim, nearly every day, at a pool around the corner from my office. Of course, the other executives presume that I do it out of some kind of dutiful attempt to stay slim, because having the long slender legs and the strong muscled shoulders that come from regularly pushing through water is good for business. But I couldn't care less about that. I swim for the feeling of swimming, the cool brush of liquid against my skin, the heady freedom of nearly passing out in the water with a foolish too long holding of breath. I swim because it's the only chance that I have, that I have ever had, to do whatever I like with my own damn body.

There was a boy who swam around the same time of day, and I could tell by the way that he glided through the water that he swam for the same reasons I do. He was about half my age, perhaps twenty, perhaps twenty-two. He had milky skin that glowed in the water and the firm chiselled body of someone who is both very young and very careful with their diet. I was glad, watching him, that I didn't have a son of my own, so I felt no rush of guilt at my voyeurism, despite his youth.

Sometimes we swam laps alongside each other, in adjacent lanes if the pool was quiet, or in the same lane, if it was busy. I imagined as we passed each other that the rush of water that lapped my skin was an extension of his skin, the wave instigated by his body like a cool hand running from the tip of my feet to the top of my head.

I felt that he looked at me too, that it was no accident he appeared at the pool more and more frequently at the time that I swam. I noticed that he would join my lane, rather than swim alongside one of the other swimmers, though their pace was often more suited to his own.

On one occasion, I had stepped out of the pool and was rinsing off the pool water under one of the two shower heads alongside the pool. The showers were unisex and accessible from the poolside, but blocked off by a concrete wall to give occupants a sense of privacy. The boy stepped under the other shower head, next to me. I watched the water running down the lines of his muscles, like streams running over rocks.

He soon noticed that I was staring, and caught my eye. I felt a flush run across my cheeks, and glanced down as if to avert my eyes, noticing that the bulge in his trunks had grown, his cock now hard and straining at the seam of his shorts. Water ran down the bulge like a waterfall. He blushed too, and turned to the wall, hiding his hardness from me and breaking our gaze.

"Would you like me to give you a hand?" I whispered to his back.

He turned around again. "Sure," he said.

His voice had the strange, almost American sound of someone who had grown up somewhere foreign, but had been schooled in an American school. His hair was thick and dark, his eyes almost black, and I imagined that outside of the pool he was the kind of boy who would look good wearing anything, but would look best wearing something expensive and Italian, perhaps a designer leather jacket, and weaving dangerously through cobbled streets on the back of a Vespa. He should have some pretty young thing sitting behind him with her arms wrapped gracefully around his thick waist and her long hair flying back into the wind, not someone twice his age in a one-piece swimsuit offering to grope his cock in the local swimming pool.

But never mind what should have been, here he was, this marble statue brought to life in front of me with a still-grown member standing to attention and waiting for my touch. I peeled down the elastic band of his shorts, so small and tight I had to reach in and pull his cock free from the wet fabric. It sprung out of his trunks, grazing my stomach as it filled the space between us. It was perhaps the most beautiful penis I had ever seen. I've always been a big fan of cock. And, attached to the right man, I was willing to work with a multitude of penile idiosyncrasies, knowing that I had my own imperfections, which were still enjoyable in their own way. I'd seen purple cocks, cocks stretched all the way over to one side like a banana, cocks no larger than my thumb, even when fully erect. My husband's cock was the strangest I'd ever seen, short and stumpy with a thin shaft and bulbous head, like a doorknob.

But this boy's penis, it was something to be revered. Long, but not so long that it would hit the end of my cervix uncomfortably if we were to fuck, thick enough that my fingers just met as I wrapped my hand around it, completely straight and evenly coloured, as pale as the rest of him. I ran my hand gently up and down the shaft, and then knelt, my knees hurting immediately on the concrete floor of the pool. I gave the head a couple of gentle licks. His skin was silkier than anything I had felt before. I looked up to admire the full length of it, then bent my head to take the whole wondrous thing into my mouth.

I forgot he was there, if I'm honest, so lost was I in the gentle rhythm of my mouth sliding up and down his shaft. He gave a low moan, within minutes – he was young after all – and he placed his hands on my head, motioning that I should move away, as he was about to orgasm. I clamped my mouth down around his cock and put my hands on his arse, pulling him into me, and felt his hot liquid shoot into my mouth. I gently removed my lips, careful not to knock his private parts at their most sensitive time, as he shrivelled against me.

Cocks aren't the same when they're flaccid. Still nice, of course, but without an erection not nearly as beautiful a thing to my mind. His was no different in this respect, seeming somehow less brave as it shrank.

I stood and helped him pull his trunks up.

"*Merci*," he said, into my ear, and I understood what he meant. It wasn't a very English thing to do, and perhaps for the occasion, a French word was best.

We saw each other again regularly after that, though never outside the pool, and never for sex. I didn't once remove my bathing suit. We were nearly caught, once or twice, but the pool wasn't very popular, and most people showered inside the changing rooms rather than by the poolside. I must have worshipped that cock of his about a hundred times, until he eventually did get a girlfriend, and, I like to imagine, a leather jacket and a Vespa. After one final day, I never saw him again.

Photos for My Husband

O'Neil De Noux

My husband, who has been in the Army in Afghanistan for seven months, asked me to email pictures of myself to him, sexy pictures. He said he missed me terribly. He wanted pictures of me in the new red negligée he had sent me. He suggested I look up someone we could trust, his old photography teacher here at LSU, where my husband and I met. I remembered Professor Lupo and set up an appointment.

Craig admired Professor Lupo and wanted to be a photographer himself before he went into the Army. They had become friends. It sounded fine to me, but I must admit, I felt a little apprehensive and a little excited about it. I guess every girl has a naughty desire to be a centerfold.

I'm not *that* good-looking, but with the right make-up, I can hang in there with the rest of the hot chicks. What I do have, and what my husband always told me I had, was a great body. You see, I'm Craig's Miss Boobs. So I fixed myself up, put on some nice make-up, fluffed my dark brown hair and wiggled into a short, tight black dress.

It was July, no classes and no students, and Professor Lupo's studio sat along a cul-de-sac on the sprawling campus. He was a good-looking man in his mid-forties with greying hair and said Craig had sent him an email about what poses he wanted. My photographer's smile was warm and friendly.

The shooting parlor had a skylight and a line of windows facing a closed-in courtyard. Bright sunlight streamed into the room where there was a red sofa on a black rug. He turned on a stereo and I walked around the sofa to the windows and back again. He grabbed one of his cameras and began snapping pictures.

He waved me to the front of the sofa and said, "Stand here. Put your hand on your hip. Move this way. Bend over. Roll your hips. Run your hands through your hair."

I was getting a little turned on, especially when he had me lie down on the rug. Moving around me and snapping pictures, I could see he got some good shots up my dress. I was wearing extra thin pink panties. Well, Craig wanted sexy.

After, I went into the bathroom and changed into the red negligée. Checking myself out in the mirror, I felt a rush of excitement. My large breasts were plainly visible through the sheer material and the matching panty did little to hide my mat of dark pubic hair. Stepping out of the bathroom, I felt my face flush when the professor's eyes gave me the once-over. But his warm smile put me at ease as I posed for him, standing and moving around. He draped me across the sofa.

I felt the camera's lens as if it were a caressing hand. I was getting wet and breathing heavier, especially when Professor Lupo began posing me seductively. Each time he touched me, I felt a rush. He moved my arms around and then my legs, until I was lying on my back, my knees open. He took close-ups between my legs. *Craig wanted sexy.*

Smooth as hell, the professor said, from behind his camera, "Now take off the top, slowly."

I gulped, sat up and did as I was asked, letting the top fall from my shoulders.

"Now cup your breasts in your hands."

My nipples were hard and incredibly sensitive. I offered them to the lens – for my husband, I told myself. But I was wet as hell then and it wasn't for my husband, it was for the camera. I was getting real turned on.

"Take off the negligée."

Professor Lupo moved me around the sofa in different positions and I tried to see if I was having any effect on him and it didn't seem that I was. He was breathing normally. Then I got a good look at his crotch and saw a large bulge in his jeans. I smiled to myself.

I was on my back again when he told me to take off the panties. I lifted my butt, pulled them down and let them fall off my ankles and there I was, naked and loving every scintillating second.

He kept snapping pictures, switching cameras and moving me around. He had me stand and walk around and it occurred to me that I was pretty exposed through the windows. I peeked out to see if anyone was appreciating the view, but there was no one. I felt a little let down.

Back on the sofa, the professor asked me to touch myself.

"I want to see your face glow," he said.

It didn't take long before I was masturbating for the camera. It was glorious. Craig loved to watch me play with myself. I wanted to send him pictures of that. I was so damn *hot*.

"Come on," my photographer urged me, "come on."

I was going at it pretty hard by then.

"I want to see you come."

I tried, but the harder I tried the more elusive the climax became. He was getting some wide open pussy shots of me, but I couldn't come. After several minutes, I stopped to catch my breath. Professor Lupo looked out from behind his camera and shrugged.

"You can help, you know," I heard myself say. I wanted to take it back but there was no taking it back.

He inched closer and moved his left hand across my knee and up my thigh to my sopping pussy. Once he touched me I was a goner. I gyrated against his fingers and then reached down to push them further into me. I pumped against his finger-fucking and then sat up and kissed him hard on the mouth.

He put his camera aside and was all over me, kissing me back and sucking my neck and my aching breasts, gently biting my nipples before kissing his way down my stomach. He opened my legs and stuck his tongue into me, grabbing my ass with his hands. I came immediately with his tongue and cried out and continued crying as he worked that tongue against my clit.

He stood up and unzipped his jeans. I reached over and helped pull out his thick, hard cock. I guided it to my pussy and leaned back as he sank into me. It had been months since I'd been screwed and it felt so damn good.

I screeched and grabbed the sides of the sofa as he began to put it to me like a pile driver. He caressed my breasts and sucked them and fucked me. I came again, twice before he shot off a load, pulling out to spurt it over my belly.

Sinking atop me, Professor Lupo kissed me softly on my lips. "God," he said.

"Exactly," I said.

After I'd cleaned up and dressed, he kissed me again, gently. It wasn't a sex kiss this time, it was the loving kiss of a very gentle man. He was fantastic.

I couldn't wait to see the pictures and he downloaded them on his computer, put them on a flash drive for me to send to Craig. As I looked at them, it didn't seem to be me, but it was. I looked fantastic. I looked sexy and erotic and gorgeous.

It took a couple dozen emails to get them all to Craig, who came right back with how much he loved them and how he was jacking off looking at them.

"I want more," he wrote.

I told him I loved him and said I would send more. I had felt some guilt at first, but I love Craig so much and our professor was a good lay.

The second time, he took outdoor pictures behind his house. I had an extra rush, walking around naked in the open.

After, he took me inside and screwed me two times that evening. It felt so damn good. I can't help thinking – God, I sure married a good man.

No Good Deed

Alison Tyler

The click of the handcuffs resonated inside Jamie. No other sound in the world had the same effect. The lock shut with a cold, crisp finality, and she knew that the only way she'd be loose again was when Killian decided to set her free. From the stern expression on his face, Jamie knew that moment was a long way off.

"What's the name of the game?" Killian asked as he bound her slim ankles to the footboard. There was no expression in his voice. Not anger. Not disappointment. She wished that he would yell at her, call her names, do something to show that he wasn't simply moving on autopilot.

She turned her head to watch him over her shoulder, dark bangs fluttering in front of her eyes, so that she saw him through the wisps of her hair. Although she had an excuse to offer, she didn't say a word – didn't dare.

"Come on, baby."

But there it was. The "baby" that let her feel the emotion swell up inside of her, the way it had the very first time he'd called her that. She could remember the night clearly – as if she had black and white photographs of each separate moment in time. They'd met at a party. She'd shaken his hand at the start of the evening, thought he was attractive – tall and slim, an air of rogue about his edges in spite of his expensive shirt, leather jacket – but she hadn't felt any reciprocation. Only later in the night, when she'd been talking to another man by the bar, had Killian come up behind her.

"Ready to go, baby?"

Like they were a couple. Intrigued, she'd followed his lead, slid on her coat, let him take her by the wrist. She'd been his ever since.

He'd led her to the car, pressed her up against the hood, got his mouth right close to her ear and whispered, "You flirting?"

The hot sensation of guilt flooded through her. Had she been? Well, yeah. But she'd come to the party a single. Single people could flirt. She tried to explain this to Killian, but the look in his eyes stopped her. Finally, stammering, she'd said, "Yes, I was."

"Honesty's always the best policy with me, kid," he said, nodding. "But that doesn't mean I'm not going to give you a spanking."

It was as if he'd gotten inside of her head. Seen all of her fantasies. No man had ever talked to her like that before.

"Do you understand?"

She'd nodded. She didn't really, though. What was he offering?

"If you get into that car with me, I am going to spank your ass until you cry. And then I'm going to take you home, cuff your wrists over your head and lick your sweet pussy until you come like you've never come before. And the whole time I'm licking you, you're going to be imagining the spanking I'm going to give you after."

Jesus fucking Christ. Her knees had felt weak. Even if this was only a one-night stand, even if she never saw him again, she knew she'd go with him. Thank God, she'd worn pretty panties. That was the final rational, or at least semi-rational thought she had as she let him position her over his lap in the back seat of the Chevy, felt his warm hand push her skirt to her waist, felt the stinging slap of the first blow through her candy-colored knickers.

Now, his voice remained flat. "What's the name?"

This was like some twisted version of "Rumpelstiltskin". She felt a laugh welling up, and she bit the insides of her cheeks to keep the sound contained. Chuckling now would be a bad idea. Doing anything that Killian did not specifically request would be a bad idea. A shudder ran through her as he tightened the leather on her ankles. She was stretched taut, totally naked on the pale pink satin sheets, her thighs spread, her pussy pressed firmly to the mattress. She could feel the wetness under her, and her cheeks burned. Being turned on wasn't something she could control. If Killian tested her, if he slid his fingers between her nether lips, she was done for.

"The game is called 'Punish the Slut'," Killian said as he walked around her. There was a dangerous tone in his voice now. "God, kid, you're such a good player, you should have known that. I mean, you're a fucking champion."

Was she? She felt like she was in the weeds.

He'd met her this evening at the bar at eight. Just like they'd planned. She'd been perched up on the corner stool, talking to a handsome man, and when Killian walked in the man placed a hand on her thigh, right below the hem of her skirt, on her bare skin.

Timing is everything.

Killian hadn't said a word. He slapped a twenty on the bar, gripped her wrist, and pulled her out of the place. There was no conversation in the car. Not a single threat or recrimination. He took her home, told her to strip, and bound her down to the bed.

That's where they were now.

She could have refused if she'd wanted to. She could have explained herself, gotten out of this mess with only a few easy sentences.

The thing was she didn't want to.

Punish the Slut.

She knew the rules well enough, after all.

The blindfold slipped into place – black velvet, soft like feathers. The ball gag was next. She thrashed as he buckled the hated gag; she couldn't help herself. The taste of the rubber was far too unpleasant to take willingly. Bitter, but reminiscent of some far away memory – like black tar and licorice. Killian seemed to like her struggles, easily exerting the force to keep her steady as he fastened the gag tight.

What was coming next made her heart race and her clit throb. He was going to cane her. If she had wanted him to go easy on her, if she'd wanted him to let her off with a warning, she'd lost the chance to say. To beg. To explain.

The gag was fastened. There wasn't even a chance for a safe word. With Killian, she'd never needed one before. No reason to think she would now.

On most days, the cane stood in the corner of their closet,

leaning against the wall. He hardly ever used it. They hardly ever reached this point. But she'd been craving the pain, jonesing for it, like any addict. Like any hungry little needling.

But that didn't make this any easier.

Pain is pain, whether you want it or not. Whether it soothes your soul, calms your needs, smoothes out the roughness of your edges. Pain is still fucking pain.

He let her feel the cane before the first stroke. He set the length of the weapon against her naked ass, rested the weight on her. She was lost in sensory deprivation. No way to speak. No chance to see the look in his eyes when he cut into her. She had no idea how many strokes he was going to land – no clue when he would start or when he would end. That made the fear rise up strong inside the pit of her belly.

She could hear him walking around the bed. She could hear the sound of his heavy steps in those boots. And then she felt his breath, warm on the side of her neck. His lips to her ear.

"Punish the Slut," he whispered. "It's my favorite game to play."

And then he lifted the cane and struck the first blow.

Light exploded behind her shut lids. She clenched down so hard, she thought she'd come right then. A second blow landed before she had a chance to absorb the first. Cold sweat ran down her spine. She bit so hard into the gag that the taste of rubber flooded through her. There was no way to scream, and yet the sound of her pain echoed in her head. A third blow crossed the first two, and she tested the bounds unintentionally, her whole body tensing, the handcuff chain rattling.

Four and five came in quick succession, a pause, then six, seven and eight. She would have smiled if the gag hadn't been stretching her lips. He'd given her eight strokes for the time they'd planned on meeting. She heard the cane hit the floor and then she felt him on her. Pounding into her. No word. No kiss. Just his cock inside of her, obliterating the pain with pleasure. Almost. Not quite, of course. But enough. There had to be a remnant of the pain – that's how Jamie was wired.

Killian had understood that about her from the start.

Some people just know.

He slammed against her, fucking her so hard she thought she

could feel his cock all the way to the back of her throat. She came when he did, spurred on by his climax, and then she felt the weight of him lift. More than that. The weight of wanting lifted. The weight of needing, which had dogged her for weeks, urging her on. Putting dark thoughts in her mind.

She was relaxed now. Undone.

Tomorrow, she'd thank Roger for meeting her at the bar. Buy him a dinner maybe. He was a nice boy, a kid from the mailroom at work. She knew Roger and his boyfriend Daniel were skint, living from paycheck to paycheck. And maybe, if he asked really nice, she'd show him her marks in the ladies' room.

Punish the Slut.

Of course, she'd known the name of the game all along, of course. But she hadn't wanted to win.

Not when losing was so much more her style.

Valentine Sinner

David Hawthorne

Date: Sun, 15 Feb
From: CyberStud
Subject: Last Night
To: HotGurl33

Last night was the most fantastic experience I have ever had.
Our chance meeting at the Valentine's Day dance was incredible
luck! I could tell that you were a little uncomfortable with the
rather revealing dress you wore. Still, even with your initial
shyness, you captured me completely. After a few dances, I
knew that we were to have a very special romance. I talked you
into sneaking out with me and we went down the street to the
little, dingy gutter motel. You were like a beautiful red rose there
in the dim light. When you stripped for me, it was like watching
a Hollywood movie star.

When I mounted you it was a pleasure worthy of enjoyment
by a king. If I was just a little rough it was because of the passions
your fantastic young body inspired. Each stroke was a journey
through wild passion like a safari into an unknown jungle of sin.
I could feel you all around me and it was as if you were the only
woman in the world. You were Eve to my Adam, a photon to my
atom. I could tell that you were aroused too, as your sighs and
moans of passionate lust drove me to erotic heights of near
shame! When I got my full length into your hot, wet love tunnel,
I could feel you swept off of the cliff of passion, to float satisfied
through the air. I did not yet join you, as I had need of more of
your sexual magic. I continued to explore the depths of your
sexuality until we both exploded in a frantic frenzy of delight. I
shall never forget that moment, our first night and hopefully not

our last. Afterward, we lay together in a perfect harmony that I must have again. Can we meet at the Milk Bar next Saturday at, say, 9 p.m.? Until then, my very own Hot Girl . . .

Your CyberStud

Date: Mon, 16 Feb
From: HotGurl33
Subject: Milk Bar
To: CyberStud

I want you to know that I was a little swept away on Valentine's Day. I normally do not commit myself to the degree I did with you that night. I must admit that it was a fantastic experience!

I will meet you at the Milk Bar next Saturday at 9.30 p.m.-ish. You will have to be a little patient with your Hot Gurl. I do not want to get into this thing too fast, as I have been hurt before.

Your HG

Date: Tue, 17 Feb
From: CyberStud
Subject: Last Night
To: Trollop03

The other day was the most fantastic experience I have ever had. Our chance meeting at the Pre-Valentine's Day Mixer downtown was incredible luck! You looked so calm and cool in your pretty silk lady suit. I could tell that you had fire behind the ice! Even with your initial rather cool style, you captured me completely. After a few dances, I knew that we were to have a very special romance. I talked you into sneaking out with me and we went down the street to a little, dingy gutter motel that did not really do our love justice. You were like a beautiful red rose there in the dim light. When you stripped for me, it was like watching a Hollywood movie star!

When I mounted you it was a pleasure worthy of enjoyment by a king. If I was just a little rough, it was because of the passions your silken body inspired! Each stroke was a journey through wild passion like climbing a dangerous mountain in a foreign land. I could feel you all around me and it was as if you were the only woman in the world. I could tell that you were aroused too, as your sighs and moans of passion drove me to erotic heights of sinful lust! When I got my full length into your hot, wet love tunnel, I could feel you swept off of the cliff of passion, and you soared away like a sexy bird. I did not yet join you, as I had need of more of your sexual magic. I continued to explore the depths of your sexuality until we both exploded in passion. I shall never forget that moment and our first night together, hopefully not our last. Afterward, we lay together in a perfect harmony that I must have again. Can we meet at the Martini Bar this Friday at, say, 7 p.m.? Until then, my wanton trollop!

Your C-Stud

Date: Tue, 17 Feb
From: Trollop03
Subject: Martini Bar
To: CyberStud

I want you to know that I was a little swept away on the night of the V-Day Mixer. I normally do not go to a motel with a man I just met. Wow – it was a very sexy experience!

I can't make 7.00 p.m. but how about meeting @ the Martini Bar Friday at 10 p.m.? But look – do not expect so much on our second date. We need to take a little time here to get to know each other. Thinking of you until Friday!

Your Trollop with a Laptop

Date: Tue, 17 Feb
From: HappyGal
Subject: Roses
To: CyberStud

I'm still riding high on the roses you sent for Valentine's Day to my office. Oh, the other girls were so jealous and they still are. "Who is he?" they keep asking but what am I going to say? A man I have never met and only talk to online, who lives across the country sends me a dozen long-stem red roses! Ha! They might say you're a cyber-stalker but I know better. After all these months I feel like I've known you all my life. Isn't that weird?

I keep reading and rereading the saved chat log of our cyber-sex sex session late that night. I could tell you were as charged up as I was! And then talking to you on the phone. I just love your voice, so deep and strong and masculine; I could listen to that voice all day and never tire of it.

It drives me crazy sometimes that you live on the other side of the country. So much real estate between our hearts, but online or on the phone it's like we're standing next to each other and nothing can keep us apart.

So when those roses arrived, I knew you truly love me and it's just not all phone and cyber sex when you're bored. How I wish we could be together. How I wish things were different. How I wish I didn't have a husband and you lived out here.

But I'll take what I can get for now, for your love makes me
Your HappyGal

Date: Wed, 18 Feb
From: CyberStud
Subject: A Rose is a Rose is a . . .
To: HappyGal

Last Friday night (or, technically, Saturday morning) was the best time yet I had with you online. And then when you were able to sneak away on the cell phone, and husband asleep, I got so hard just listening to your beautiful voice. If and when we ever do meet "in the flesh" this is how I see us:

We go to a motel room. It's a cheap motel and it has a certain flair and tawdriness to it. We get undressed and stand naked in front of each other. I take you in my arms and kiss you. We fall to the bed that has noisy springs.

When I mount you it is a pleasure worthy of enjoyment by a king. If I am just a little rough, it is because of the passions your silken body inspires! Each stroke is a journey through wild passion like climbing a dangerous mountain in a foreign land. I can feel you all around me and it is like you are the only woman in the world. I can tell that you are aroused too, as your sighs and moans of passion drive me to erotic heights of sinful lust! When I get my full length into your hot, wet love tunnel, I feel you swept off the cliff of passion, and you soar away like a sexy seagull. I do not yet join you because I need more of your sexual magic. I continue to explore the depths of your sexuality until we both explode in passion. I shall never forget this moment and our first night together, hopefully not our last.

Afterward, we lie together in a perfect harmony that I must have again.

Hope that makes you as wet as it makes me hard.

Please get a plane ticket and fly out here now!

CyberStud

Date: Wed, 18 Feb
From: Trollop03
Subject: Martini Bar
To: CyberStud, HotGurl33

Look, CyberStud, you are nothing but a two-timing phony baloney. My roommate, HotGurl33, and I were comparing notes and discovered that you are nothing but a lying, two-timing asshole who only wants to fuck a girl and then move on. I do not need your kind and neither does HotGurl33. She will not bother to send you an email, as low scum such as yourself are not worth the trouble.

There is a bus leaving town Friday at 9 p.m. – be under it!

Trollop03 (and also HotGurl33)

Date: Thurs, 19 Feb
From: D. Shaw
Subject: My Wife
To: CyberStud

Listen here, Mr CyberCrud, you dirty rotten bastard sonofabitch! The woman you have been talking to that calls herself HappyGal is my wife! Elaine, MY WIFE. I knew something was fishy so I got her password and took a look at all the emails from you and the discussing chat transcripts. You make me sick, you creep, you clown. How can you do this with another man's wife? This is adultery. You out to wreck my home?

I am warning you, buddy: stay away from my wife. Do not email her, do not call her. I don't care if you live 5,000 miles away, if I find out you contacted her I will fly out there and wring your neck, then I'll tear your head off and piss down the hole.

Keep out of our lives!

Dan Shaw (husband of Elaine Shaw)

Date: Thurs, 19 Feb
From: DigiSlut
Subject: Hiya Stud!
To: CyberStud
Attachment: Slut, Nude

Well, CyberStud, the good girls found out your little act. I work with the lady who calls herself Trollop03 and she told me that you are the type of no-good, low-life man who will lure a girl to a crummy cheap motel, fuck her brains out with your huge cock and then immediately go searching for another pussy. You can just forget about Trollop03 and HotGurl33. Those two will have nothing to do with your ilk and your milk and martinis.

I am a girl of five feet four inches with a slim figure, but a set of tits you gotta see and taste to believe! I am thought to be attractive and I gotta see if your cock is really that big and if you are as horny as the girls say. I'm also nineteen – hot young stuff! They say you're in your mid-thirties. You ever have a teen girl before?

You will like my hot young pussy and you will also find out that I am a little more active in bed than the good girls. I like it hard, deep and frequently. You best stoke up on Levitra, old man, and come looking for anal action too – you got it, stud, I take it up the pooper and luv it! I will be at the Star Bar Friday around 8.30 p.m. I will be wearing a red dress that screams WHORESLUT. But don't worry, honey, I don't charge, I just get a charge. Star Bar has rooms upstairs so we don't need to waste time running around looking for a crappy roach motel with come-stained pillow sheets.

If you are as good as the good girls say, I got a couple of girl-friends who are real strumpets and can fuck the brains out of a phony, two-timing ass heel like you so damn good that you will forget about looking for any other pussies to conquer.

Star Bar, 8.30, be there if you dare!
DigiSlut

Date: Thurs, 19 Feb
From: CyberStud
Subject: Friday it is!
To: DigiSlut
  You sound like my kind of lady!
  CyberStud

Date: Thurs, 19 Feb
From: Elaine Shaw
Subject: [none]
To: CyberStud
  I am so sorry, my darling! I am at a public library and I have
to make this quick. Dan won't let me on the computer. I am so
sorry he sent you that threat. You don't know how awful it's been
here. He is so angry I am afraid he will hurt me. I don't know
what to do. I wish I could hear your voice but it's just not safe. I
have to go now. I guess we will never speak again and that hurts
so much.
  Your
  NotSoHappyGal

Date: Thurs, 19 Feb
From: Joanne
Subject: Friday Night Ass Kicking
To: Avenging Brother
  Hey, little brother.
  OK, so that jerk-off asshole took the bait. He will be at the
Star Bar tomorrow around 8.30 p.m. as planned. Kick his ass
good for me!
  Your Sister

Date: Tue, 24 Feb
From: HappyGal
Subject: Freedom
To: CyberStud
  My Dear Stud,
  It's safe now. We can talk. Didn't you get my email Sunday?
I left my husband. I left Dan. He started hitting me and I had
him arrested. I'm in a hotel room right now that has internet. I

have seen a divorce lawyer. I will be free from this horrible marriage soon.

I tried calling you but all I get is voicemail. Is your cell off?

Please call or email or get on chat! I need you! God, I have missed you so. Where are you?

Listen: it will take a few months to process the divorce. I will get half our savings and the house. I have decided to make a bold move. I will quit my job and move out there once everything is done with. This way we can spend next Valentine's together like we're meant to.

What do you think?

I am waiting breathlessly for your call . . .

Your

HappyHappyHappyGal

Idyll

Teresa Lamai

"Fatima, just take it. You don't have to ask."

There was fresh sweet bread on the table and for the first time in months I felt hunger sharply. My new housemate Goran got angry when I asked for some. I was still learning that Goran prides himself on not owning anything, not wanting anything. I didn't notice Amel smirking in the corner until he was suddenly standing next to me. He twisted off one end of the bread and said, "Come see the garden."

Goran and Amel are the only Croatians living in this tiny house by the cemetery in Zagreb. They came to the city for the university, but their families can't afford the new tuition. So instead they load trucks and work in Peace and Anarchy, a youth center built in an abandoned gasworks. The rest of us are from Bosnia. I should say we're refugees from Bosnia, here in Zagreb in a strictly provisional sense, on our way to Pakistan or Germany or the US.

As the only girl, I have my own room. Slavica, an older woman my mother had known, was living in the front room with her father and her baby son when I arrived, but she's since been relocated to Austria. There will most likely be more refugees to take their place but for now it's just the three of us. Amel and Goran live in the larger upstairs bedroom, and I in the smaller bedroom.

It's only been seven months since I left Sarajevo. I can't always separate the reality of what happened from the rumors that consumed us like a collective psychosis.

I may eventually join my brothers in Germany. I may get a visa for the US. I may stay here forever with Amel and Goran.

The sun here is stronger, more Mediterranean. Even in the early morning it's like an ancient power in a limpid, fragrant sky. The first mass is ending at the cathedral across the street and the shaded cemetery is already flickering with plastic memorial candles. The courtyards of the blue-painted Romani tenements next door are filling with children. I'm washing the sheets in our yard. The garden is a late-summer mess of palm trees, kiwi vines and wild roses. There's no sense to groom anything since no one stays here long.

Goran comes out, fat pastry in one hand, guitar in the other. His long curls are wet, snaking down his bare back. He puts the guitar on the ground and sits next to me to help. Amel has been out here all morning, simply because, like a sly shadow, he is never far from me. Goran laughs at himself as he wrings one corner of a sheet. His fuzzy thigh presses into my skirt. Warmth on my shoulders and soft pulls at my skull tell me Amel is behind me now. He's braiding grass into my hair, as he likes to do when we're outside. We sit quietly for a long, long time.

Every time the breeze stops, I can almost hear our hearts beating.

I'm in love with Goran because he's generosity and sweetness without limits. He carries his large frame with a sense of wonder and discomfort, as if he just grew into it. His wide shoulders make the house seem small. He towers over me. I think he is intent on keeping his round blue eyes clear of unkind thoughts, as if he believes innocence will protect him like enchanted armor. He fed me constantly when I first arrived here, cutting me slices of bread and cheese and asking if I preferred coffee or chocolate milk or maybe green tea until I burst into exasperated laughter and started smacking him. Our first kiss was a week later, when he came home with a bag of birdseed for me to feed the birds outside my bedroom window. Like he expected me to be here forever; I couldn't stand it.

His innocence feels less contrived when I'm pressing into him. I'm teaching him that love is selfish. I grab his ass strongly enough to hurt, digging crescents into the flesh, sometimes leaving tiny scabs. I have never told him I love him but he knows from the way I kiss him, the way I run my tongue over his neck and the warm sweet mounds of his chest. The first time I gripped the base of his hardening cock and nipped at his scrotum, he gasped, "That's good, that's so good," with genuine surprise in his voice.

I know it's unbearable for him to lie still when I'm teasing the silky head of his cock from its foreskin, using just my tongue. I tell him to lie still anyway because I want us both to be free from what he thinks he should do. I just want to torture him until he's angry enough to fuck me without thinking, his hands tight on my pelvis, cock scorching through my cunt, both of us transported and beyond hurting.

I love Amel for his black silent eyes that seem to absorb everything he looks at. He is slight and dark, speaking rarely, disappearing into the night when it falls. Goran says Amel seems to always be ashamed. Amel follows me stealthily like a cat as I move through the house, settling in the kitchen when I cook or unexpectedly lying on the carpet beside me when I read. We're not sure where he goes in the evenings.

Nearly every night, I wake up after midnight. The moon has shifted. The air is still. I never hear Amel come home, or open my door, or undress, or pull the covers off the bed. I've never seen him naked in the daylight. His voice is what wakes me first, followed by the smooth glide of his belly on mine. The smoky, sweet smell of his hair as it falls on my forehead. His hands are so painfully delicate on the back of my neck that I forget not to moan.

His skin starts to gleam, slippery with our sweat. He moves slowly as if he were underwater, and the breath is sucked out of me as he writhes, his full weight on mine. I'm fascinated by the slick heat of his body, pressing one damp breast, then the other into him, stretching my back to let the arcs of our stomachs kiss. He keeps his hips away from me until this moment. He knows I'll be wet when he lowers his cock to slide against my aching lips, just splitting them to let the scent fill the room. This is when he finally kisses me. He lets me try to devour him with my mouth and my pussy, and he knows that he can do whatever he wants with me.

I move to lock my ankles behind him but he pulls me to the edge of the bed. Kneeling on the floor, he leans into my shaking thighs and laps with astonishing patience, from time to time sucking on the inner and outer labia until they burn under his breath. The heat is in my chest, suffocating me. When he starts to massage my clit with two fingers, I buck and he stops suddenly, moving up my body to kiss me with swollen lips that taste like seaweed and old red wine.

Afterwards, I let him sleep. I get up because Goran and I always have our breakfast early in the garden. Goran is usually up already, wearing just his shorts, slouching on the moss-covered bench. He puts aside the guitar and holds out his arms to me. His chest is sun-warmed.

Lately there has been no work for them, so they stay home with me all day. We read in the morning, sometimes go to the market to buy flowers or vegetables, and lie in the shady grass all afternoon. The lemon tree is starting to bear fruit. We are not sure how much longer we can go without paying rent.

The third notice came for me today. If I fail once again to report in a timely manner, I'm told, the offer of a US visa will be retracted. I can't finish reading this right now; it's time to make lunch. I drop the letter behind my bed and walk out to the patio.

The Room After She Left

Maxim Jakubowski

The camera pans across the room. A slow, steady but almost languorous movement. Noting every feature, every detail, methodically scrutinizing all angles, colours and shapes as it glides along. Every single sign of absence.

This is a room where we made love.

Me and her. Me and she. She and I. I and her. The two of us. She who has left. Whose name I must no longer mention.

Furniture, walls, standard issue prints (sailing ships, landscapes after Napoleonic battles, Audubon birds), bedspreads, windows, floral-patterned curtains, heavy wooden doors, a bed.

Does a bed have memories? Of the million fucks, of the endless embraces, the sighs, the despair, the words said and unsaid? Like an imprint in a pillow after heads have followed bodies and moved on. To the hotel corridor outside, to the lobby, the road outside, to the rest of their lives?

Hotel rooms don't belong to this world. They can be anywhere. A Trust House Forte shaped like the Pentagon building, close to Heathrow Airport, frayed carpets. Adobe walls and Indian rugs draped across the floor in Scottsdale, Arizona, close to Phoenix and the John Ford desert of orange horizons and countless cacti. A modern tower overlooking Puget Sound in Seattle, rain crashing in gusts against the bay windows. Or a room in a small bed and breakfast chalet in the Italian Alps facing Mont Blanc, the nearby peaks crested with snow, the early morning sky bluer than blue and a healthy chill lingering in the air. Or again a hotel for students in Paris's Quartier Latin, where the bed can extend upwards, bunk-like, in times of necessity, the last floor reached by a thin lift cage that can barely accommodate two bodies without an added single piece of luggage. Let's not even evoke New York hotel rooms: the Plaza, the Algonquin, the Chelsea, the Iroquois, the Gershwin. Take your pick.

Like Gene Hackman in *The Conversation* listening to the silent sound of lovers in a distant place. Eavesdropping on the memories abandoned by the wayside.

"Is this where it happens?" A woman's voice, hushed, shy. Hers.

"Yes." A man's voice. Darker. Mine.

"Kiss me, then."

The sound, electric, charged with emotion, of lips meeting.

An echo of lust imprinted through the memory layers of the room. A further memento of the lost past.

"Undress. I want to see your cock."

"And I want to see your body. Now. Badly. Every square inch of your skin. Watch my fingers map the territory, my fingers roam your intimacy."

"Yes."

The voices of several fucks, the awful sound of a togetherness which was too shocking to envisage just a few weeks before when we were strangers to each other, business acquaintances no more, respectively married to others by the virtue and authority of a magistrate or a priest.

The now empty room bears witness.

To the way she shifted across the bed as we lay there so lazily, in no hurry to rush the inevitable first penetration, and lowered her lips towards my cock and took me inside her mouth. The heat. The moistness. One of my fingers lingering on the edge of her puckered sphincter, then moving forward, pressing against the closed ring of darker flesh and slowly inserting myself into her most private, aromatic warmth.

Sounds: breath held back, gentle moans, the velvet friction of white flesh against flesh.

And right now: utter silence as she walks down a south London street to greet another man, a husband, with a look of innocence on her face and guilt in her mind, her skin still tingling from lips, her cunt still full of my juices. But infidelity cannot be read on the horizon of a face, or on fingermarks long faded away on the panorama of her nude body. Maybe only, the sole clue to the mystery of lust that might betray us, the smell of sex. In her breath, despite the Polo mints.

On my fingers, as in an empty hotel room I bring them closer to my nose and inhale the fragrance that still lingers there of her juices and nacreous innards. On my shrivelled cock which I haven't yet washed – the room is booked until late afternoon; I am in no hurry – where her strong fragrance still seeps deep into the flesh, bathing its roots, reminding me of how well we fitted together genitally, as if engineered for each other.

Outside, a jumbo jet takes off for parts unknown, a shadow against the insulated window which no outside noise penetrates.

So, this is it. We met, we flirted, we hesitated, we took a conscious decision to be selfish, we fucked.

Just a room.

A stain on a white sheet, some secretion or another, hers or mine; stray hairs on the cushion which looks more like a punch-bag after the battle, lighter, curly pubic ones lower down the bed.

"You don't have to do it, you know . . . It's our first time, there's no rush . . . "

"But I want to."

"Love you."

A look of amusement in her eyes as she interrupts the delicious activity in progress. "Am I a bad girl because I suck a guy's cock on the first date?"

Mischief.

"Who said I was looking for a good girl?"

"So you were actively looking, were you? And I just came along at the right moment?"

"Well, I was the one who made the initial approach . . . "

"Your letter to my office?"

"Yes."

"I knew I wanted you since that day in Manchester."

"Did you really?"

"You bet."

"Come to think of it, you did give me a strange look while I was there reading my paper."

"That's what you think . . . I'm shortsighted, so you shouldn't attach too much importance to the look in my eyes . . ."

"Is this our first argument – already?"

"I'm not arguing."

"OK. Keep on sucking . . ."

Watching her head bob up and down in his lap. Her curls wild, uncountable. The almost invisible scar on her right ear lobe, highlighted by the sepia light peering through the orange regulation curtains. The whiteness of her skin, porcelain. Her large arse paler than pale close to his cheeks. A moan. A gasp.

The room records it all. Testimony for a further trial, record of evidence for the day of reckoning, filthy reasons for impeachment, actions that might one day bar them from the portals of paradise and plunge them into flames eternal. A mouth, thin-lipped, greedily gobbling a thick, heavily veined penis, a finger twisting inside her rear, manual sodomy, unhygienic, wonderful. The way their bodies relax into twisted postures that no other couple could imitate for fear of cramp or worse. But then, disappointingly, the room also knows that in just a few days another visiting couple, older, darker-skinned, will succeed in even more extreme sexual gymnastics. The room knows.

Rooms always know. Like shadows.

And do not judge.

And keep their secrets.

Our secrets.

In another room, before I knew her, long before I could even justify any morbid jealousy, she made love to another. Was it even her husband? Dublin? Scarborough? Paris, near the Gare du Nord? But I guess it was more vanilla, less pornographic. In between yet another four indifferent walls, antique furniture, the sounds of a Chinese matron being fucked to high heaven on the other side of the thin partition, police sirens piercing the rhythm of orgasm, I melted Suchard white chocolate squares inside an Australian woman's cunt and later watched her lick the sticky residue and her own juices clean off me. Ah, the strange etiquette of hotel room sex when the person you are doing it with is new! Allowing the water tap to run as noisily as possible as you sit on the toilet while your new partner waits for you in bed, just a few metres away, to stop her hearing the pee splash against the water, or the turd unroll out of you with extravagant farting noises.

Waving arms in air to disperse the foul, personal smell. Listening to her pee and getting a hard-on and wanting to ask her if you can watch . . .

Preliminary inventory.

A bedside table where she leaves her wedding ring and contact lens solution. The rumpled stockings at the foot of the bed, her lace-up resoled boots, her bunched-up knickers (when she moves to the bathroom and you get up and tidy the mess, you can't help but raise them to your nose, to smell the crease, slightly stained, soiled, through which you had earlier fingered her when you were both still partly dressed), her handbag (make-up kit, two separate shades of lipstick – before and after the fuck? – a pair of tweezers, a wallet with just £20 in cash and her credit cards – her second name is Edwina, she'd never told you that, an orange, tissues). The carpet has cigarette holes. If you peer closer to examine the blanket all concertinaed up at the end of the bed, you can make out the hieroglyphic, faded patterns of previous come stains from past generations of adulterers and lovers. The bedside lamp sheds a flickering light, distorting the colour of skin, the hidden darkness of sexual organs.

"Jeez . . . I'm so damn sensitive there. Every time you touch it, it's like a flash of electricity coursing through me in overdrive."

"Really?"

"Yes. My husband—" she carefully refrains from mentioning his name, naked as she is in the embrace of another man "—seldom touches me there, but somehow it doesn't have the same effect, you know."

"You're wonderful. Many other women wouldn't have dared admit that."

"Just the way I feel."

He kisses her. I kiss her. I kissed her.

Time loses all its meaning.

Never have we been so alone, in our forgotten island of lust.

"One day, would you . . ."

"Yes, I would like you to fuck me there. Very much . . ."

His mind races. Butter. Extra lubrication. Genuine fear of harming her. The madness of this intimacy they have so quickly reached.

His heart breaks. Straight through the middle, where it hurts the most.

She walks out into the corridor. Time for the train back to the conjugal bed. He follows her silhouette as her characteristic gait takes her down the endless hotel road, just like the one in the Coen brothers' *Barton Fink*. He distractedly thinks this would be a perfect image, a fade-away to end a wonderful story, the camera raising itself on a crane as she moves away, long legs, tousled hair, from him. But in life, things don't end that simplistically.

He is no longer part of the room. He closes the door. Without her. Smells. The imprint of her tattooed deep into his flesh. Dresses. Leaves. Settles the bill with one of his credit cards. Makes his way to the car park, an empty black promotional tote bag swinging from his shoulder, no longer carrying the bottle of white wine he'd brought earlier. Car keys. Ignition. Motorway. The room after she has left: empty, lonely too but still inhabited by her presence, a pervasive feeling of her.

The silence.

The cold.

Soon, the floor maid enters. Her electronic pass affords her entry to all rooms. In her closet, a red light had lit up, indicating 404 was now ready for cleaning. A day let only.

She pulls the cart behind her. Looks ahead at the relative untidiness, bed spread open, towels on the bathroom marble floor, tap still dripping in the shower, a half-empty bottle of wine by the bed. Clean ashtrays. Curtains still drawn.

The maid sniffs the air. A smell she is all too familiar with.

"Fuckers," she says.

On Hold

Mina Murray

I had been on hold for well over an hour, and my nerves were starting to fray. Every time I thought I was getting somewhere, the click and whirr on the other end of the line that always seemed so promising just dropped me into another queue. If I heard "Orinoco Flow" one more time I was going to drown myself in what was left of my martini.

Setting my phone down on the bar, I took the last sip of my drink and contemplated for the tenth time today the cursed luck that saw me trapped – an ash cloud casualty – in this airport, in this town. Not that I was alone, oh no, I was just one among hundreds. Every hotel in the town was booked out and so was every alternative means of transport for the next two days. Which explained my current predicament. No way to get home. Nowhere to stay. On hold. Again. I sighed, a lot louder than I had meant to.

A voice next to me, cheerful, deep, and vaguely familiar – some half-forgotten melody – interrupted my wallowing. I looked up at a tall man in a suit, with sandy brown hair and smiling blue eyes.

"Yes, I see your problem—" he pointed "—your glass is empty."

"So it is —" I leaned forward, conspiratorial "—but I know how to fix that." I signalled to the bartender and ordered myself another martini and a double shot of whisky for the tall stranger, who slid into the seat beside me.

"Well, as opening lines go, that was pretty good," I said, angling my body towards him. "What brings you here?"

"Oh, I come here all the time. I'm a regular."

"Ah," I said, "then you're stuck here too."

He looked me over, appraisingly. "How did you know I was a whisky man?"

I could have told him it was his hands that gave him away – square, smooth, strong-looking hands that would look great wrapped around an old-fashioned glass. Guessing drinks is a particular talent of mine: I'm more often right than not.

"I don't know, lucky guess?"

He took a slow sip, and I tried not to stare at the amber liquid slipping from the glass or the uptilt of his jaw or the motion of his Adam's apple as he swallowed. I tried hard not to stare at the faint crescent-shaped imprint his fleshy lower lip had left on the glass, and I tried even harder not to imagine the invisible marks his lips could leave all over me.

"So, I have to ask, what's with the phone?"

I was still on hold. The music had morphed from easy listening to classical now and the tinny sound registered just at the edge of awareness.

"I'm trying to find a—"

The music stopped suddenly, and I pounced. At that precise moment, however, my battery cut out, and I was disconnected. I slumped forwards onto the bar, my head between my hands.

"Is it really as bad as all that?"

"It will be if I have to sleep in this airport for the next two days. Or if I have to spend another minute on hold."

He paused then, thoughtful. "Listen, I hope you don't take this the wrong way, but I'm staying in a hotel just near here. If you want, we can share the room and split the cost."

I was tempted, especially when the alternative was sleeping on a cot in the terminal. Still . . .

"Fear not," he said gallantly, hand over heart, "your virtue is safe with me."

He waggled his eyebrows suggestively and I couldn't help but laugh.

Two hours later, in the hotel bar, we finished our last shots. I was probably going to feel filthy in the morning, but for now the world had receded, and for once everything just felt *right*. We stumbled into the elevator, and I had to brace myself against his chest for a moment to get my balance. I had gone straight to the bar when we'd arrived at the hotel earlier, so I had to ask him what floor we were on. Our hands touched as we both pressed the button at the same time. My palm thrummed with the electricity crackling between us. I curled my fingers into his shirt and he looked down at me, some unidentifiable expression in his eyes. Desire uncoiled itself within me like a snake.

I slid my hands up his chest and around his neck. His pulse beat strong under my fingers. His cedar and spice scent wreathed itself around me and I twined myself around him in response, trapping his left leg between mine. I drew my pointed tongue all the way up his throat until my mouth found his and I kissed him. His body loosened as he reacted to me, deepening the kiss and stroking my tongue with his. The doors opened onto our floor and I pulled away for a moment to tug him out into the hall.

"Which way?"

He looked at me, confused.

"The room, which way?"

He led me wordlessly down the long red-carpeted hallway. I don't remember the room number now. All I remember is that my bags had been left just inside the door and they were in the way. He kicked them aside and drew me to him. We stood there in the kind of half-light that can only exist in a city, where the night-time lights blink on and off like beacons.

His lips brushed my wrist, found the tiny sensitive hollow in the crook of my arm. I shimmered as he kissed a fiery trail up my arm and back down my throat, bit the tender skin of my breast just visible above the neckline of my shirt.

"Too many clothes," he muttered.

When he had unwrapped me completely, I pushed him down in front of me, trembling as his tongue flickered out to follow the seam of my pussy. He pressed the heel of his palm against my mound, pushing gently upwards, opening me up to him.

"I want to watch you come undone."

I whimpered, not just from anticipation, but from the sweet ache of my own vulnerability, naked as I was in front of him. I wanted to writhe around on his lap, grind against his leg, leaving trails of my arousal on the rough weave of his woollen trousers.

"Christ, you're so beautiful. I want to know how you taste,

deep inside," he rasped, and thrust his arrowed tongue into my cunt.

"Mmm, just as I thought," he mumbled, "sugar and spice."

His low voice vibrated through me and he breathed my scent in deep. His tongue began drawing circles around my pearl, concentric circles that grew narrower and narrower as my pulse quickened and I pressed myself closer. The circles turned into a pattern of rhythmic strokes, and I thought I could discern a difference in the intervals between the next lick, suck or tap. He was tracing song lines on my clit with his tongue, annotating the bassline of my pleasure with his fingers. Each varied touch elicited a different response from me, and I catalogued them one by one. Semibreve – a long moan; minim or crotchet – a breathy or sibilant "yes". When he started composing in quavers and semiquavers, I arched my back and sang for him.

He caught me just as my knees gave way, carried me over to the bed. As I lay there, the ripples of orgasm still humming through me, he brushed the curls back from my face.

"The next time you're on hold," he whispered, "I'll play you another counter-melody just like that."

Nine Lives

Dominic Santi

So I can lick my own dick now. I don't like the taste of fur. Reincarnation is not all it's cracked up to be.

I don't know exactly how I got here. One moment I was human, waking up with a gorgeous, sated man in my arms. Going out for breakfast together before I headed to the airport. Next thing I knew, I woke up in a pile of kittens.

Steve picked me out of the pet store window. That night, when he brought home a feisty redhead he'd picked up in a bar, I knew I'd found my place. I curled up on the headboard and watched them fuck each other senseless. Man, that bedroom smelled great.

Steve had outdone himself this evening – good china, Waterford, sterling. Jarre playing softly on the stereo. I lowered my leg and stretched, kneading my claws in the Irish linen tablecloth. I'd always liked the finer things in life. Not that I was supposed to be playing centerpiece.

The cute little trick Steve had picked up on Santa Monica Boulevard last night was due back any minute. I nuzzled the rim of a wine glass, marking it with my scent. That was as close as I came to a man's lips these days.

Doorbell! I hopped off the table and ran under the loveseat, peeking out as Steve opened the door.

Oh, yeah. This one was a keeper. Gymnast's build. Soft brown curls. Hazel eyes. And dimples! Quite the contrast to the former wrestler with close-cropped blond hair and green eyes I was used to seeing crawl out of bed each morning.

Our guest blushed as he handed Steve a bouquet of yellow roses.

Steve was eloquent, as always. "Wow, you're even cuter than I remembered! Um . . . Mike?"

The date didn't do much better. "Thanks. You too . . . Steve?"

Human intellect is vastly overrated. I raised my tail and sauntered out into the entry.

"Hey, that's a beautiful cat!" Mike reached down to pet me. I rubbed up against his khaki pants.

"Dammit, Bagheera! You're getting fur on him!" Steve stumbled all over himself with apologies. "Hey, man. I'm sorry. You want me to put him in the bathroom?"

Not without chain mail, you won't!

Fortunately, Mike stepped in before Steve got hurt. "I really like cats. This guy seems friendly."

I smirked as Mike scratched behind my ears. He knew right where the sweet spots were. When I'd been petted enough, I turned and led the three of us into the living room for hors d'oeuvres and wine.

They were talking about their fucking jobs! But there was a nice little bulge growing in Mike's crotch. It got bigger as Steve bent over to adjust the speakers.

"What do you like?" Mike rearranged himself, leaning over Steve's shoulder, not quite touching, but way into Steve's personal space. Steve shivered as Mike's breath caressed his neck. Both of them were breathing faster. Their dicks hard. Almost but not quite touching each other.

I felt like shaking the both of them. Kiss him! Plant one right on his lips! Shove your tongue down his throat!

I was halfway across the room, intent on bumping Mike's ankles, when he finally made his move. I hopped up onto the easy chair instead. Mmm, smell those pheromones. Lick him. Taste him. Damn, what I wouldn't give to have lips again, and to have them that close to another man!

The ding of the kitchen timer barely registered with me. Steve pulled back and smiled. "Dinner's almost ready. Want to help?"

Who gives a fuck about dinner!

Mike and Steve took hands like they were in some 1940s big screen romance. They walked into the kitchen, stopping every few feet to kiss again. Their eyes were glazed over. Their cocks bulged. I stomped around the corner behind them.

Steve slipped pasta into a pan of boiling water while Mike tossed arugula into a vinaigrette. I hopped up on the counter and resigned myself to supervising. Steve wiped his hands on a towel, then opened the bag of rolls. He'd cheated and gotten those from the bakery.

"How do you like your buns?"

"Spread."

Steve spewed wine onto his shirt.

"Sorry, man." Mike laughed, pounding Steve on the back. "You OK?"

The slaps slowed. Pretty soon Mike was rubbing Steve's back.

"I'm sorry." Mike was blushing like a fiend. God, those dimples! He tentatively ran his fingertips over the edge of Steve's hip. "You do have a really nice ass." He looked quickly up into Steve's face. "But I can be versatile, too."

Steve wants everybody to think he's mister butch top. But he ate up that romance stuff hook, line and sinker.

"I like being fucked." He arched his tight, rounded butt right back into Mike's hand.

"Yeah?" Mike's arm flexed as he gripped the back of Steve's jeans.

Steve moved all the way into Mike's arms, slipping his arms around Mike's waist. "Yeah."

This time, they kissed like anacondas. Fabric tore and buttons hit the floor. Steve took Mike's nipple in his mouth, and Mike went nuts. He was backed right up against the counter, writhing and moaning, his hands buried in Steve's hair, holding him tight to his chest.

"Fuck, that feels good!"

Damn, that kitchen smelled good. Man sweat and pre-come. There are advantages to having a sensitive nose. I could even smell the sauce burning.

"MEOW!" I screeched – just as the smoke detector went off. "SHIT!"

Steve yanked the pan onto an unused burner. Mike waved what was left of his shirt at the offending alarm until the God-awful noise finally dissipated. They just stood there for a moment, surveying the mess.

Then they both burst out laughing.

"Damn. I really wanted to impress you." Steve wiped his eyes as he waved his hands at the ruins. "I spent all afternoon on that damned sauce."

Mike leaned his hip against the counter. "Too bad I didn't get to try it."

Steve spooned up some sauce from the edge of the pan. Blew until it was cool. Then he stuck his finger in and lifted it to Mike's lips.

"Taste."

Mike licked the finger clean, sucking off every last drop. Their eyes were glazing again. Steve spread sauce over Mike's nipples. He licked and sucked until Mike was moaning.

Damn! Steve had bitched at me for getting fur on Mike's pants! His hand cupped the bulge in Mike's crotch, caressing, rubbing. The zipper whooshed. Steve shoved the pants and what had been pristine white briefs over Mike's hips. Scooped more of the cooled sauce into his hand and smeared it all over Mike's cock and balls. Then Steve dropped to his knees. There were at least nine inches of marinara-covered sausage jutting up above Mike's tight, furry balls.

I leaned back on the counter and threw my leg in the air. Now we were cooking!

Steve licked every drop of that sauce off. Then he opened his mouth and took that monster cock all the way down his throat.

Mike yelled, pushing Steve back, hands shaking as he gasped for air.

"Stop, man. Stop!"

"I want to make you feel good." Steve's voice purred like the cat who ate the cream. He gently kissed the tip of Mike's swollen dick.

Mike shuddered hard. "I want to fuck you. NOW!"

Steve smirked, then his eyes got wider. It took me zero seconds to figure it out. Condoms and lube were in the bedroom!

Gym bag!

I skidded across the linoleum, racing toward the shelf by the back door. I started furiously sharpening my claws on the canvas bag that held Steve's workout clothes.

He wheeled toward me. "Dammit, Bagheera!"

The light bulb went on. He yanked the bag out from under

me, unzipped the pouch, pulled out what he needed. A moment later, he was bent over the counter, his pants hanging off one ankle, his legs spread wide, wiggling his ass. I swear, that cute little pink pucker winked as it begged for Mike's attention. Mike shoved forward, hard and fast. Steve rose up on his toes, gasping, and took that huge, latex-clad cock all the way up his wide-open, hungry asshole.

They fucked like lunatics! Steve shot all over the counter without even touching his dick. Mike was right behind him, burying himself up to his nuts in Steve's ass. They came so hard the kitchen cabinets shook.

The room smelled heavenly. I threw my leg in the air again, and I indulged.

They ordered pizza afterwards. Ate it naked on the living room floor while they drank the rest of the wine. They were none too steady by the time they stumbled off to bed. But they were smiling. And they'd shared the pepperoni with me.

Annual Encounter

Kathleen Tudor

Anne sat down on the soft hotel mattress, bouncing a couple of times and enjoying the luxury of the thick pillow-top before she picked up her cell and hit a few buttons. Her text message was short and to the point: "Rm 1535. Hry."

She estimated that she had a good ten minutes before Harry would get to her, so she tore off her outer garments, leaving the stockings and garter belt, the crotchless panties and the lacy bra. She had just kicked her travel suit behind the room's easy chair when a knock sent a jolt through her. On the way to the door she glanced at the clock – eight minutes. Not bad.

She peeked through the peephole in the door to make sure it was her Harry and not some maid outside the room, then stood behind it to stay out of sight of the hall as she opened the door wide. He was in her room in an instant, pressing her up against the wall and kicking the door wordlessly shut behind him.

A breathy moan filled the room and she realized it was her own voice rising in aroused excitement as he feasted on her mouth, her neck and her collarbone. "You make me so fucking hot," he groaned. His mouth had found her breasts and he was nipping at her nipples through the lace of her bra.

Anne arched her back, pressing her breasts into his face and moaning as he surged forward, pinning her to the wall. "Let me go. I've been waiting a year to suck your cock."

He groaned and stumbled back as if struck, leaning back against the opposite wall. Anne dropped to her knees and fumbled with his belt buckle, cursing until she was able to free his cock. They both moaned as she took it deep into her throat, bobbing steadily as she hungrily devoured him. His moans sounded pained and he panted as she sucked, hard.

"You're here three days?"

She hummed an affirmative, and he bit off a curse.

"Sessions get out at five?" he asked, sounding strangled.

When she hummed again, he slammed a fist against the wall behind him and gasped.

"If you don't stop that I'm gonna come, baby."

Anne happily hummed again, taking him deep into her throat and purring her approval as his cock throbbed and twitched, sending his load into her mouth. His cries of pleasure were music to her ears, but her cunt was still hungry for attention. She pulled away and grabbed his hands, dragging his weak-kneed self toward the bed and climbing backwards onto the bedspread.

"Eat me," she demanded, and he practically dove into her swollen flesh, his tongue probing deep inside her as he complied. She threw her head back and arched hard against the bed at the expert touch of his tongue.

"Standing dinner date at Roobios? Five thirty?" she asked in a gasping, ragged voice.

It was his turn to hum agreement, and hers to shriek with pleasure as he ran his tongue around her clit, bringing her right to the brink before diving back into her gushing hole to lap up her juices.

Anne panted, each pant coming out with a hint of a scream just waiting to happen, and Harry hummed again, apparently enjoying her frustration as he denied her orgasm again. Her entire lower body was quivering with tension, the muscles straining toward that glorious resolution, and her fingers tore at the bedding.

"There! Yes! Don't stop, Harry, don't you dare fucking stop!" And then she was screaming, thrashing, and trying to bury her cries in a pillow as her entire body spasmed and shook with the force of her orgasm.

She distantly heard the sound of Harry fumbling with the box of condoms she'd placed on the nightstand, and then before she had even recovered from the mind-blowing pleasure, he was on top of her. With one hard thrust he buried himself to the hilt in her hot body, and she cried out again as the friction against her inner walls and the pressure of his pubic bone against her clit set her off one more time.

As she moaned and bucked, thrusting her hips up to meet his, Harry pulled back and plunged himself into her again, drilling her into the mattress with his passion. She grabbed hold of his hair and dragged his face down to hers, moaning into his mouth as pleasure sent her soaring and tumbling. Their tongues twined together and she licked at his lips, enjoying her own taste on his mouth.

The steady pounding into her body, so long deprived, started to build Anne toward her peak yet again, and she thrust back greedily, wanting everything he could give her. This time when her body pulsed around him, Harry cursed and groaned, and his cock twitched inside her as he came.

He collapsed on top of her, breathing hard, and they panted together for several minutes until Anne got up the energy to push him onto his side. "You're still wearing your shirt," she noticed, smiling.

"You seemed like you were in a hurry," he teased back. He got up to get rid of the condom, and she stretched languidly out on the bed, her most fervent itch satisfied, but still wanting more.

"Again?" she called, and she heard him laugh from the bathroom.

"Honey, I think I just came twice inside ten minutes. Give me a little break."

"That's not what you said three years ago," she teased. Three years ago she had run into him in the hotel bar after sessions closed for the day for the annual accounting best practices seminar she'd been attending. One thing had led to another, steaming hot sex had led to some of the best orgasms of her life, and when she'd found out he was a local, they'd made arrangements for an annual encounter of their own.

"Well, you're right that I wouldn't want to waste any time during my favorite three days of the year," he said, scooping her into his arms as he climbed back onto the bed. His mouth closed over hers, still hot and erotic, but less urgent. He kissed her thoroughly, leaving her shuddering, head spinning and toes curling.

When she was putty in his hands, he started to tease, running his hand lightly up her side, across her breasts, and around her nipples. She shivered and whimpered into his mouth, and he traced his way down her belly and between her legs, dipping into the plentiful moisture that still flowed from her like a river of honey, and bringing his fingers up to paint designs on her body and lick them off again.

His fingers teased over her clit and dipped inside her, and he finally moved his thumb to stroke her swollen pearl, turning her shivers into bucking and her whimpers into moans of pleasure, and still his tongue stroked over hers, teasing and arousing.

She gasped into his mouth as she came, and felt the wetness flow out of her, soaking his hand as he continued to finger her. He moaned in her ear, nipping at the lobe and digging his nails into her hip. "I think break time's over," he said. Then she heard the tear of another condom packet, and he pulled her toward him, settling her onto his pulsing erection.

Anne never did get much sleep during the annual seminar, but somehow it always seemed worth it in the end.

Vegas Slut

Michael Hemmingson

Rick, Frank, and I were at the blackjack table. The free drinks were always the best, even if they were small drinks. We were waving at the waitress a lot, demanding more.

We were having a good time.

A woman joined our table. She was in her early thirties, wore a black sweater, black skirt. She was attractive enough, a little too plenty in the rear for my tastes, shoulder-length dark blonde hair. We were happy to have her join the game.

She drank as much as we did if not more.

"I've been on a roll all night," she told us. "My luck has been real good. The money is *coming*, I can *feel* it, this is *my* night."

She surpassed us in drinks.

She started off good, but that quickly changed. She placed high bets. We couldn't match her in both alcohol and gambler's risk.

"I'm broke," she announced, like it was a surprise.

She explored her purse, couldn't find any more money.

She had to sit the next hand out, dazed.

Frank, next to her, won the hand, bringing in eighty bucks.

She stared at his chips, licked her lips.

She leaned toward Frank, said something to him I couldn't hear. He looked at her, thinking, and nodded. He gathered his chips.

"Be back," he said, and left with the woman.

Rick and I looked at each other.

"Well, well," said Rick.

We played several more hands. Frank and the woman came back. She had chips to play with. Frank didn't meet our eyes, went back into the game. He'd been married for seven years.

She lost all her chips immediately, reckless in her bets. She called for a drink. She leaned over to Rick and whispered to him.

He gathered his chips and left with her.

Frank and I looked at each other and Frank flushed. Rick had been married for five years.

"Well, well," I said.

Rick and the woman came back twenty minutes later. I had a new drink. She sat next to me and smiled. I smiled back. She was looking prettier every time, or maybe the booze was finally getting to me.

She lost all her chips in no time.

"Damn," she said.

She sat the next hand out.

"Twenty bucks," she said; "all I really need is twenty bucks and I just know I can get back on the right track here."

She leaned toward me and whispered something – OK, so I gathered my chips and left with her.

We went up to the fifth floor of the hotel, where she had a room. I'd been married for twelve years.

She went to the bathroom first.

I examined the room. An ordinary room, a suitcase by the bed.

She came out, fresh lipstick. "You can pay me with money or chips," she said. "Your friends just wanted blow jobs, and that's thirty. You want something else, we can negotiate. I'll do anything, doesn't matter how bizarre or kinky, as long as you have the money or chips."

I said, "You do this just to gamble?"

Must have hit some nerve in her. She began to cry. I went to her, put my arm around her shoulder. "It's OK." I felt stupid.

She wiped at her tears with an arm and smiled.

In another story, where I might have been noble, nothing would've happened. I might've even talked her out of this bad situation. But I was on vacation, I was drunk, I'd been fighting with my wife . . .

I gave this woman forty bucks worth of chips and she sucked my cock. The extra ten was for licking my balls a bit.

"No," she said after, "I'm not a professional whore. I have an ex-husband and kids, in a city I left months ago. I've been here ever since, drinking and gambling. Sometimes I get there, I get real *close*, and I *know* my Big Chance is coming. I have to catch it, and I'll catch it any way I can."

Foreplay

Catherine Paulssen

"And I would smear the melted chocolate all over your body and lick it off so slowly you'd be begging to have my dick inside of you before my tongue has even reached your pussy."

In the bluish light of the street lamps, shining in through the blinds, Paolo's eyes twinkled at his wife's intent stare. His hands underneath the blanket played with the hem of her long shirt. Della could feel his fingers crawling up her waist and stroking the skin beneath her breast, which welcomed his long craved for touch by contracting, thus sending pleasant quivers through her body.

"You'd whisper into my ears, your voice high and pleading . . . and you'd clench the sheets and twist them in your fists . . ." His hand covered her breast and he rubbed his palm against her nipple.

"And . . . would you eat my pussy or fuck me?"

"Your choice, baby." He tweaked her nipple. "What do you want me to do?"

Della moaned and pressed a kiss on his mouth. "Both." She sucked at his bottom lip. "I'd want to be licked and then I'd want to ride you."

"Your sticky, wonderful body on mine?"

"My sticky, wonderful body on yours." She nodded.

He pulled her closer. "And I'd make love to you until we'd fall asleep in each other's arms at the break of dawn," he said. Della wriggled in anticipation. He kissed her. "And what would you do if we had all the time in the world?"

She wrapped one leg around his thighs and brushed a strand

of his hair out of his forehead. "If I had all the time in the world to make love to you, I'd search for the handcuffs and tie you to the bed."

Paolo let out a soft groan. "You wicked little witch."

Mischief sparkled in her eyes. "You know you'd enjoy every minute of it."

He shuffled a bit closer to her. "Oh, I would, baby."

A smile crept over her face as she continued. "I'd blindfold you, then kiss your whole body. Every inch of it." She purred at the mere thought of having him underneath her, naked and at her mercy to be teased and treated as her heart desired. "And especially this part . . ." She trailed the waistband of his pyjama bottoms and ran her fingers over the wiry curls she could feel when she led them further down.

Paolo closed his eyes and rolled on his back, pulling her with him. He drew her into a long kiss and grabbed her behind. "Go on," he prompted.

She cupped the bulge underneath his briefs. "I'd remove the blindfolds."

His fingers drew circles on her naked thighs. "And why would you do that?"

"So you could watch—" she leaned in and brought her lips close to his ears "—how I take your hard dick into my mouth and suck it." His length rose against her hands and he bent his arms over his head. Her eyes followed the move and she pressed a kiss on his neck. "Would you like me to do that?" she asked.

"Oh yes, baby."

"Yes?"

"Yes . . ."

Della bit her bottom lip. She could go on playing that game, just to hear his voice enticing her, thick with lust and a little raspy. She didn't really need any convincing though. She hadn't tasted him in so long. Too long. To get her lips around his glistening, hard dick would be a feast not only for Paolo. She would relish every moment of it, and savour each drop.

As she covered his naked upper body, deliberately skimming her pussy over his shaft as she moved down, a soft whimper from the next room stopped her dead in her tracks. Paolo stiffened. They waited for a few moments, but instead of dying down, the whimper turned into a persistent howl that quickly shifted Della's attention. Paolo growled, half amused, half frustrated. With a sigh, Della fell down on her husband's body, then propped herself up and stumbled to the door.

"Mummy's coming," she called out in a soothing voice as she opened the door to the room where their six-month-old son was crying himself into a fit. She lifted him out of his bed and cradled him in her arms. "Mummy's here," she whispered against his smooth baby skin. "It's all right, Jacob, I'm here."

A few moments later, sitting in an armchair and stroking Jacob's bald head while listening to his steady suckling sounds, she couldn't silence the pang of regret despite the love that spilled from her heart into every fibre of her body.

Their chances for sex had become few in the past months. Why had they wasted precious time on foreplay?

After a while, Jacob's nursing movements became less intense, and finally, he fell asleep again. She placed him in the crib and watched him for another few minutes.

As she returned to their bedroom, the tingling still a faint notion between her thighs, her husband was already softly snoring.

She woke up when Paolo's alarm clock rang at 6.30 a.m. He quickly turned it off and placed a small kiss at the nape of her neck. "Morning, love."

She mumbled a sleepy reply and blinked into the early sunlight. When she heard the shower being turned on, she dragged herself out of the pillows. She had about half an hour to herself, if she was lucky.

She went into the bathroom to brush her teeth. Behind the shower curtain, she could see her husband's naked body, and last night's regret shot through her. She bent over the sink and closed her eyes while mechanically moving the brush over her teeth. A wet, firm grasp around her butt cheeks jerked her out of her drowsiness. With a little shriek, she jumped as Paolo's hands crept underneath her shirt and up her sides. She quickly wiped her mouth and turned. He was naked and dripping with water.

"Paolo . . ."

He pressed a finger on her mouth and crooked the other one,

motioning her towards him. She giggled as he drew her into the shower. Within seconds, her shirt clung to her body, and Paolo enclosed a hardened nipple that was visible beneath the wet fabric. Della closed her eyes and let the water and his roaming hands wipe away the last reminders of sleepiness. She imbibed the waves of hot, damp air mingled with the soap's fresh scent. Paolo got down before her and slipped off her panties.

"But what if . . ." she started.

"Ssh," he mumbled and kissed her thighs. He lifted her leg over his shoulder and a shudder ran through Della's body as his tongue met her flesh. He dipped between her pussy lips and started licking her. Whenever the tip of his tongue had taunted, a long, deliberate sweep followed, flaring the want that tickled beneath her belly button.

She leaned against the wall, reached up and enclosed the shower pipe with both her hands. Her body arched against the flicks of his tongue, and Paolo looked up.

"Now *I* wish I had those handcuffs," he said with a smirk.

She wanted to tell him not to stop, to hurry on, give her what she craved for, but her words died on her lips as his mouth enclosed her clit and he started to suck at it. She grabbed the metal harder to steady herself before liberating heat pumped through her, turning the world into a daze of darkness and flitting little dots that danced across the inky curtain before her eyes. Water ran into her mouth as she gasped for air, and she collapsed against the slippery tiles, limp and tingly and still wanting more.

He kissed her navel and got up. The strength returned to her legs, and Della got out of the soaked shirt, pulled him closer and pressed her mouth on his. "Fuck me," she panted, tasting herself on his tongue. "Fuck me."

He grabbed her bottom and roughly pulled her against him. Della wrapped her legs around his waist and pressed her heels into his flexed butt cheeks. Her hands ran through his hair, as frantically as his moves. She clamped his shaft inside her and Paolo pinned her against the cabin's wall. Their bodies ground with smacking sounds, and Della only realized she had dug her fingers so deeply into Paolo's flesh that it would leave marks as the waves of another high ebbed away.

She buried her face in her husband's shoulder. "That was perfect," she whispered.

Through the splash of the streaming water, she could hear Jacob crying out for her.

Mile After Mile

M. Christian

Mile after mile, numbers on the odometer rolling after each other. At first they'd been markers to . . . wherever the hell it was she was going.

Her thighs were corded steel, aching with each pump. Her calves were driving pistons, tight with muscle. Her back was one solid slab of hurt from bending over the handlebars.

The worst of it, though, wasn't the agony in her body – no, the worst was that after all those miles on the bicycle, she hadn't gone anywhere: same cityscape through the gym windows, same flickering box of a set showing MTV. The gym was deserted – it was just the exercise bike and her.

A break, that's what she needed – so she coasted, taking a few deep breaths.

Still, the instant she tensed, preparing to get off, she hesitated. It wasn't like she'd given up on a lot in her life – quite the contrary: she was young (twenty-six) successful (no one moved more property at the office than she did), healthy (she'd biked over twenty miles today, for God's sake), and . . . there it was, down deep.

It was hard to remember exactly when it had started, and with whom. Maybe with Richard, with his so-cautious diet. Maybe with Philip and his endless leg presses. Whatever the cause, one day she'd looked in the mirror and hadn't seen a tight, young, nimble body any more. The next morning she'd joined the gym.

But was it enough? Was she as . . . perfect as she could be? Rather than answer, she started pedaling again – faster, harder.

Sweat started to bead, then flow, then pool – distantly she grew aware of her body, straining and pushing; of the way her muscles were acting together to force down onto the pedals, to propel her through . . . well, metaphorical space at least.

She started to become aware of the rest of her body: the way her breasts filled the Lycra of her sports bra; the way her Spandex tights went right up the cheeks of her ass.

One nipple was caught slightly in her bra; the swirls of pleasant sensation radiating from it was just a tad different than the other one. Her thighs were aching, but it also reminded her of the kind of ache she felt when she held them apart for a long time. Her neck hurt, sure, but now was the same kind of hurt she got – the delightful kind of ache – when she crouched over someone, taking his cock down the back of her throat.

She knew she was wet: that deep pulsation like a heartbeat between her legs, the quivering of her too-hard clit.

Pedaling, never stopping, she drifted slightly – more than a daydream, less than a real fantasy: a quick procession of images and sensations dropping through her mind, generated by the excitement rippling through her hard-working body:

That time off the coast of Baja. Hot day, cool drinks, and the gently rolling deck of the fishing boat they'd hired. The way her swimsuit had seemed to cling to her like his hands had the night before, the way he'd wrapped his strong body around her – then there he was again, standing behind her as she leaned over the railing. He'd said something, the words lost in the hammering of her heart, and then her bikini top was off, and her breasts were free and bare to the hot sun. Nipples instantly hard, cunt instantly wet and ready, she'd smiled and pushed herself back, feeling his hard cock with the strong cheeks of her ass. Then her bikini bottom came off and they fucked, watching the gentle waves and the white commas of seagulls, until they came, their groans and cries chasing the birds away.

She didn't *just* feel her nipples, her breasts, her ass, her cunt any more, it was *all* she felt. She was tingling from one end to the other: from her ankles up her strong thighs into her wet cunt, from her throbbing clit through to her tense stomach, the throbbing of her breasts and nipples to the strong breaths she sucked in and out.

Then she was there: she'd arrived. Her guttural cry, almost a scream, bounced off the windows and came back to her. Suddenly her legs were twin cramps, her thighs refusing to move. With the come still thundering through her, she managed to crawl off the bike and collapse onto an exercise mat.

She might have slept, or just closed her eyes. After a point, though, she got up and staggered towards the showers, but not before looking at the odometer and noting the mileage – the distance she'd had to pedal to find herself.

His Lady's Manservant

Andrea Dale

When I came into the room with our suitcases, Melina said, "You can put my valise over there."

It wasn't so much what she said, but how she said it: imperious and dismissive in equal measures. She didn't even turn from the dressing table to look at me, as if I were beneath her notice except to do her bidding.

I opened my mouth to point out that we didn't need to be in character now, then realized what she was playing at.

My cock stirred.

Oh, you devious woman.

Melina had laughed and laughed when we'd gotten these roles. When you're an out-of-work actor, which we both are, you'll take pretty much anything that'll pay the bills. Playing key roles in a murder mystery weekend scenario at a swanky Victorian B&B would be a nice chunk of change for not a lot of effort.

Except when Melina read the script and discovered that my role was that of a persnickety, detail-oriented butler.

Her role of lady of the manor fit her just fine. Right now she looked stunning, almost otherworldly, in her cream and gold bustle gown; the way her hair was piled on her head made her look regal and untouchable and yet incredibly alluring. The only time she ever looked disheveled and out of control was after a particularly rousing bout of sex, which usually involved her wrists being bound to the bedposts or, on occasion, to her thighs.

On the other hand, at home she despaired of my ability to ever pick my dirty socks off the floor or load the dishwasher rather than forgetting bowls and glasses all over the apartment. This part, she'd said, would be quite a stretch for me.

As prideful as I am of my acting abilities, I had to admit she was right.

So far the staging had gone well. In our roles as Lady Clare Morris-Jones and her manservant Mr J. Burnett, we'd welcomed our "guests" to our "home" and set the stage for the mayhem to follow. Everyone knew the rule that nothing would happen between the hours of 11 p.m. and 8 a.m. That gave us and the cook (the only other actor) enough rest, and meant the guests could relax as well.

"Thank you, Mr Burnett," she said. "That will be all. You may go."

Go? What did she—? Oh. Because our roles could have been played by people who didn't know each other, I actually did have a bed in the servants' quarters below stairs.

"You don't mean . . ."

She finally got up then and, with a rustle of skirts, pressed up against me. She set a cool hand against my cheek. "If you play along, I'll make it worth your while tomorrow night," she said.

Her smile was wicked. I hadn't known she had it in her. She was always the one wanting to be tied up and teased.

Then again, I'd always been the one wanting to do it. But the way my cock was responding . . .

I grabbed my shaving kit and headed for the door. Before I walked out, I sketched a submissive bow towards her.

Her laughter followed me down the hallway, and later curled around my cock along with my fingers as I jacked off in anticipation of the next night.

It wasn't easy for me, but I finally slipped into the role: running a gloved pinkie over the plate rail to check for dust, picking up empty sherry glasses as soon as they were set down.

But I wasn't perfect, and Melina was always there with a raised eyebrow or a nearly imperceptible shake of her head if I forgot to hold out a chair for one of the female guests or failed to ask if anyone would like more tea.

Her haughty demeanor was affecting me on several levels. I found myself wanting to please her, to be rewarded by the barest hint of a smile and single nod that said I'd done well.

I also had to find creative ways to keep my cock from tenting my trousers and frightening the guests.

It was a long day.

Finally it ended. Everyone who was supposed to die had kicked the bucket, all the clues were in place, and the final reveal would happen just after breakfast, giving the guests time to get home before nightfall, satisfied with their fun weekend. It was a rare scenario in which the butler *didn't* do it, so my role tomorrow would be minor, just doing butler-ish things. I was thankful for that, because I suspected – hoped – I wouldn't get a lot of sleep tonight.

As long as I'd done my job well today. I always sought to further my craft, but now I had an added incentive: the fear that Melina judged my performance and if she found it wanting, would reject me.

I came to her room with a china cup of warm, honey-dolloped milk on a silver tray.

Her "come" when I knocked made me smile. In my dreams, lady.

"Thank you, Mr Burnett," she said. I set the tray down, crossed my hands behind my back, waiting for further instruction.

She sipped the milk. "Mr Burnett," she said again. "I was distressed by your behavior last night. And, if I'm correct, of this afternoon as well."

Holy crap, how had she known? Did she have a spy somewhere? I felt my face redden at the thought.

"Ah, so I was right," she said.

She was just toying with me. She knew me too well. It probably *had* been obvious when I disappeared before dinner. (It was either that, or bring a whole new meaning to the concept of serving the guests.) Or maybe the simple fact that I was growing hard again, right now, in my wool trousers.

"You are here to serve me, are you not?" she asked.

"Yes, ma'am," I said. Melina was taking to this dominance thing far easier than I'd have expected. Then again, she *was* an excellent actress.

I liked it.

"Then come here and help me prepare for bed."

First she instructed me to unpin her hair. While I loosened

the fragrant tresses, she went to work on the elbow-length cream-colored gloves, unfastening one button at a time. We're definitely missing out on something major in our less-clothing-is-more modern society; by the time she was peeling the first glove down her arm, I was rock hard.

A second glove gone, and she undid her dress. She stepped out of it with a rustle, and handed it to me to hang up. As much as I wanted to toss it in the corner and get on with things, I did what she wanted, guessing my reward would be worth it.

It was when I was unlacing her corset that it struck me: as I essentially freed her, my actions were binding me to her whims. Not forced bondage by any means – it was entirely by my choice.

She lounged back on the bed, wearing only lace-trimmed bloomers and a matching sleeveless silk camisole and sheer stockings (probably not Victorian-period, but oh, so sexy), and told me to undress.

I shucked my clothes, again wanting to leave them where they fell but instead folding them neatly. Melina's eyes never left me, even as she idly circled one nipple with her finger until the nub blushed dark and hard against the silk.

She was stunning. I wanted to worship her. When she beckoned me to her, I was thrilled that she hadn't found me wanting.

At her command, I suckled her breasts through the silk. The fabric grew damp and see-through, and when I blew on it, she arched her back and mewled with pleasure.

I tugged her drawers down – they were damp, too, with her musky scent – and couldn't resist running the silk across my turgid cock, the fabric excruciatingly soft between my fist and my sensitized flesh.

"We'll have none of that." Melina plucked the bloomers out of my reach. "You're here for my pleasure."

She took my wrists and drew my hands to her breasts, even as she urged my head down between her thighs. With her knees she nudged my legs apart so I was kneeling, not even able to rub my cock against the spread.

Fine. This was her night, her pleasure. I could hope only that if I performed to her satisfaction, I'd get mine as well.

With lips and tongue and fingers I coaxed her higher, higher, until she came in a series of breathy gasps and moans.

Melina tended to be a screamer, and her orgasm solidified our roles: she as the lady of the manor and I as her manservant, the besotted lover kept secret because of class boundaries.

When she rode me (of course she'd take the dominant position), my thoughts truly were for her pleasure. My hands at her breasts, my hips bucking to her rhythm, it wasn't until she was falling over the edge again and gasping, "Yes, come for me," that I was finally allowed – that I finally allowed myself – the relief I'd craved.

She didn't banish me to the servants' quarters that night, although for the remainder of my role she stayed in character.

As I loaded our suitcases into the car, I could only think ahead to when we'd reprise our parts . . . in private.

Nikki's Birthday

I. G. Frederick

I love Mistress very much, but I really miss having a man in my life. Yesterday, for my twenty-eighth birthday, she gave me a most wonderful present. I had asked to go to a local pizza place that has an indoor mini-golf course – a chance to forget my age and indulge in juvenile pursuits. Mistress, who is quite a bit older, took me, but made it clear she would not play golf. When she went to purchase a round of golf, she asked me with whom I would play.

I shrugged. "I know you're not interested; I guess I'll just play by myself."

She looked up at me. At home, when I'm usually on my knees in her presence, it's easy to forget how tiny she is and that I'm almost a foot taller. "You could play with him." She pointed to someone behind me.

I turned and found a friend who I hadn't seen in several weeks standing there with a huge grin on his face. "Liam!" I said with delight and gave him a big hug. Liam is one of Mistress's play partners so I'd seen him naked often enough at parties. I do admit I have the hots for him, but Mistress doesn't permit me to have sex with anyone but her. Still, I was delighted just to have someone my own age to play golf with.

Mistress ordered pizza, paid for two mini-golf games, and told them to bring the food out after we'd played. I enjoyed the game immensely. We got 3D glasses that made it hard to hit the ball accurately, but embellished all the black-lit pirate scenes. I beat Liam by a couple of strokes and Mistress took pictures of us with the "pirates".

After the luscious pizza, Mistress invited Liam to come to the house and visit for a bit before he drove back home – he lives an hour and a half away. When we arrived, Mistress sent me upstairs to strip and take care of some quick chores. I came back down and saw Liam had a great big bow tied around his neck.

"You may unwrap your present now, boy," Mistress said, twirling a strand of her long auburn hair around her finger.

I just stared at her.

"Don't you like your present?" She had a wicked glint in her green eyes.

I tilted my head to one side. "Um, what do I get to do with it?"

"Anything he will let you." Mistress smiled, but I had a hard time believing she meant I could have sex with him.

"Anything? As in I can go down on him if I want?"

"Of course."

"If I wanted him to do me, that would be OK?"

"Yes."

I almost wept for joy. "Oh, thank you, Mistress." I got down on my knees and kissed her pretty feet. "Thank you so very, very much."

My hands shook when I unbuttoned Liam's khaki shirt and unbuckled his leather belt. He has broad shoulders and he works out so his pecs and abs are nice and firm. I ran my hand over his muscular chest, enjoying the feel of another man. When I pulled down his jeans and cotton boxers, his beautiful penis practically jumped into my mouth. I hadn't touched one in so long. It felt soft and smooth in my hands. The absolute exquisiteness on my tongue caused my own pecker to respond rather abruptly. I wrapped my lips around his rod and let it slide across my tongue until it hit the back of my throat. I moaned in between his thighs, and I could hear Liam sigh with pleasure. With one fist at the base of his penis and the other hand holding one of his plush cheeks, I slid him in and out of my mouth.

Pain seared across my butt. Out of the corner of my eye, I could see Mistress bringing her cane down for another strike. I winced, but I knew better than to do anything to try to avoid or deflect the blow. I concentrated on enjoying the plump succulence in my mouth, but I couldn't help a little muffled yelp when the second blow struck close on the first welt – Mistress has a rather good aim. Liam and Mistress laughed at the same time at my distress.

Mistress handed Liam a bag of colorful plastic clothes pins. He leaned down to attach them to my thighs, my arms and my nipples while I kept my mouth firmly attached to his crotch. They pinched a bit, but I knew that depending on how long he left them on, they would really hurt when he removed them. When another stinging blow from Mistress's cane cut into my ass cheeks, I stopped long enough to cry out. With Liam's cock shoved deep in my throat it came out kind of gurgly. He seemed to like the sensation though, because he grabbed my hair, and face-fucked me until he jabbed the top of his crotch onto my eyes and sent warm, slightly salty come down the back of my throat. I swallowed every drop and milked him dry until, to my surprise, he became hard and ready again.

I heard Mistress snap her fingers and I looked up to see her sitting on the sofa, her legs spread apart. I crawled over to her and kissed her feet, then sucked her toes one at a time until she wiggled her rear and I could smell her arousal. Then I kissed my way up the soft skin of her plump legs, ducking under her black ruffled skirt, until I could push aside her silk thong with my nose and dive into her luscious moistness. While I lapped up her sweet juices, Liam removed the clothes pins slowly so I fully experienced the pain of each one. I didn't let that distract me from taking care of my Mistress though.

I felt first one and then two cold, lube-slick fingers work their way into my ass. I winced and Mistress grabbed my hair, pulling my face deeper into her warm folds. Liam slid his sheathed cock into my hole and grabbed my thighs as though they were handlebars. I squirmed in ecstasy while he banged me. I had my face smothered in the flesh between my Mistress's legs and a cock ramming the shit out of my ass. What a ride. I wished I could stroke my own hardness, but Mistress doesn't permit me to touch myself. While I enjoyed my appetizing position, I could only hope if I pleased Mistress she would eventually allow me some kind of relief.

Liam's engorged cock carved me up beyond what I'd ever experienced. Mistress's juices covered my face as she grabbed my hair and shuddered all over with one of the most intense orgasms I have ever felt from her. I guess she enjoyed watching Liam ram me while I sucked her. When I had licked up all her come, Mistress slid down in her seat and grabbed a fistful of my hair. She pulled me up slowly so I could slide my own cock into her without escaping Liam. He grabbed my hips and drove himself into me with a fierceness that made me shudder with delight. When he pulled back, I drew out of Mistress and let his thrust push me deep inside of her. She clamped down on my cock with her muscles and I had a hard time maintaining control, but I'm not allowed to have an orgasm without her permission.

Mistress and Liam came at the same time, his bellow drowning out her ecstatic cry and his grip on my hips leaving marks on my skin. When he pulled out, Mistress finally said: "You may come, boy."

"Thank you, Mistress!" Without Liam behind me, I could move in and out enough to finally come, so grateful for every moment of delight she had given me. I buried my face in the pillows of Mistress's chest and enjoyed the spasms in my cock. Once my breathing became regular and my heartbeat slowed to normal, Mistress yanked my face up. "Clean up your mess, boy." I eased out of her, and knelt down so I could suck my own come out of her. It didn't taste nearly as good as Liam's, but mixed with her juices, it wasn't bad and I got to give her another orgasm.

When she pulled my hair to let me know I could stop, I leaned my head against her thighs and wrapped my arms around her hips. "Thank you so much, Mistress, for such a wonderful birthday present. Today I had the absolutely best birthday I have ever had."

America's Next Top Bottom

Elizabeth Coldwell

When the lights come on, they're almost dazzling. Chelsea takes a breath, stares hard at the three faces regarding her impassively. A harsh buzz, louder than she'd expected, and the light on her left is extinguished immediately. She's disappointed, despite herself. She'd prepared herself for the possibility of instant rejection – after all, their act is hardly designed to appeal to this bland embodiment of lowest common denominator culture, not like the crummy ventriloquist who's just left the stage – but still it hurts. But it's just one person saying "no", she tells herself defiantly. Until the other two lights go out, they'll continue to perform.

On cue, their music starts, low, with a dirty, insinuating beat. Lyn walks round the apparatus in a slow circuit, just as they've practised so many times, giving their audience a chance to admire her curvy arse, exposed by the thong back of her leotard and covered only with the thin mesh of her fishnet tights. She pirouettes, drops in a crouch, spreading her legs wide to give the panel a view of her crotch while running her hands up her thighs. The moves are smooth, coming as second nature. When they filled in the application form to reach this stage, Lyn put her occupation as "dancer"; she didn't feel the need to add the word "exotic", nor to mention the strip club where she performs her enticing routines.

Lyn straightens, cups her breasts briefly, then runs her fingers through her poker-straight, white-blonde hair extensions before blowing the panel a cheeky kiss. Their eyes flicker from her – with some reluctance, it seems – and back to Chelsea, who waits patiently, spread out like a star, wrists and ankles strapped tight to the wooden frame. Her heart beats faster as Lyn approaches, grasping the neck of her form-fitting black gown. It's going to happen, she thinks. It's really going to happen.

The dress has been rigged with Velcro, so as Lyn tugs, it falls away in two neat halves. Beneath it, Chelsea wears only a black spangled G-string, barely big enough to conceal her mound. Her nipples are covered with black tasselled pasties. When they've worked on this routine in the past, she's always been properly topless; she'd hoped for that tonight, to face the panel bare-breasted and bound, but there are rules. Even so, her pussy is already hot and liquid, excitement pulsing through her at being so provocatively displayed.

The second buzzer doesn't sound at that moment, as she'd anticipated, nor when Lyn runs her hands, clad in soft, elbow-length velvet gloves, over the contours of Chelsea's restrained body. If anything, the panel – at least the two of them who aren't now sitting in shadow; the snotty, opinionated English singer and the supercilious guy who's responsible for creating this parade of wannabes and no-hopers, studded with the occasional genuine talent – are leaning a little closer, watching as Lyn takes the point of Chelsea's chin in her hand and kisses her, hard. They have no way of knowing if this show of lesbian affection is real or staged, though if they could see the juices trickling into Chelsea's panties, they'd realize being kissed and teased by Lyn turns her on just as much as her helpless, restrained position.

Only when Lyn disappears behind the frame for a moment, reappearing with a many-tailed suede whip that she brandishes with obvious relish, is another light switched off. Snotty English Singer, so vocal in the press about her many lovers and her self-proclaimed outrageous sexual appetite, has just realized she's come up against the real thing. Her reaction is to declare a sudden halt to proceedings.

But that still leaves one light blazing, one face illuminated – and he shows no sign of bringing this performance to an end. Maybe their performance excites him; more likely he just wants to see how far they'll dare to go.

Lyn holds his attention, pulling the tails of the whip oh so slowly through her fingers as she gyrates to the music. Chelsea wonders idly whether he's getting hard under the desk, in those famously tight-fitting trousers he always wears. Then Lyn steps close to the frame again, and Chelsea snaps her gaze back to the whip.

She wants this; wants it more than she's ever wanted anything. With her back to the panel, Lyn gives Chelsea a conspiratorial wink. Lover, friend, partner in crime: at this moment, Lyn is all those things. And as always, Chelsea places herself squarely in the hands of her mistress, trusting her to do what's right. To give her what she needs.

Lyn trails the whip over Chelsea's torso, so lightly that it registers only as a caress. In response, Chelsea writhes in her bonds, arse pressed against the smooth wooden frame. The whip charts a stately progress along the length of Chelsea's body, down the fronts of her thighs and back up, lingering teasingly on the mound of her sex and her breasts, nipples tight knots of desire beneath the modesty-protecting pasties. Through this whole slow progress, Chelsea does her best to keep her expression neutral, though her audience of one must realize the effect of being toyed with in this casually erotic fashion is having on her.

He must sense, too, that this is merely the build-up to something harder, more intense, but he still doesn't press his buzzer and call an end to their performance. Lyn's body obscures her view of him, and craning her neck to take a sneaky peek would be far too obvious, but Chelsea's dying to know whether both hands are still on the desk, or whether one has slipped down to massage his cock through his trousers. Perhaps he's unzipped himself, and is wanking with stealthy strokes as he watches. More unlikely – but twice as arousing – is the thought that his fellow panellists are performing that task; a dainty, long-nailed female hand and a black, beringed male one taking turns to tug at his length.

The first real cut of the whip distracts her from her increasingly dirty musings. Lyn strikes at the slight swell of her belly, tails landing on her skin in quick succession. She sucks in a breath, readies herself for the next blow. It isn't long in coming, this time slapping at the top of her thigh. Her mistress works quickly, but always in a random pattern, so Chelsea is never sure whether she'll feel the whip on her stomach, legs, or – as is the case on a couple of occasions – her exposed, vulnerable breasts. She's taken worse – Lyn loves to use a riding crop on her sensitive tits, criss-crossing them with vicious, stinging weals – but the context makes her feel this punishment like never before. She bites back a cry, having promised herself she'll take everything Lyn has to give her in silence.

Their act is building to its climax, literally, and now Chelsea worries that the buzzer will sound before it does. She's so horny, pain giving way to the sweetest of pleasure; she doesn't know what she'll do if she doesn't get the chance to come. Lyn raises her arm to strike again. It's obvious to everyone that the target is Chelsea's scantily covered pussy, and just as the whip comes down, that third light goes out, leaving the judging panel in darkness.

They haven't passed the audition; the act should end with Chelsea being unstrapped to take a shaky bow, but with all three judges out, they have to vacate the stage. Not that Chelsea cares; she's coming from the touch of the whip, coming in the knowledge that she's finally acted out her most cherished fantasy. She's been stripped and whipped, brought to orgasm by her mistress before a number of strangers. Winning a place on the country's hottest talent show was never really the objective.

But as Lyn collects Chelsea's discarded dress and the cumbersome whipping frame is wheeled off stage, Chelsea catches the eye of Mr Tight Trousers. He's mouthing the words, 'My dressing room, seven o'clock.' She can't suppress a grin. Seems like he might want to watch their audition piece all over again, in private, and offer his own, very personal critique. And why not? After all, talent will out, she tells herself. Talent will out.

Hot Tomato

Thomas S. Roche

Ever since it got hot this summer, you've started gardening wearing almost nothing. A long T-shirt with no pants; the one-piece you wear to swim; shorts with no top; sometimes just your bra and panties. Once I caught you gardening naked, and that made you blush. You always wash yourself off with the garden hose before you come back inside, dripping on the floor, your skin moist and steamy with the heat and the moisture. Recently your arms have been bundled with zucchini, squash, carrots.

Now, it's finally tomato season.

You've got on your red string bikini, the one you wear to sunbathe. There's not much to it; it's nothing more than a string between your cheeks, and in the front it hangs so low I can see a hint of your pubic hair. If you wore it outside the backyard, you'd have to shave, I think. On top it clings to your breasts awkwardly, looking like at any moment it's going to fall away into nothing. It's bright red. Tomato red.

I watch you from the patio, reclining on a chaise longue with an ice-cold Bloody Mary. I watch you on your hands and knees, checking tomatoes and picking the ones that are ripe. Picking up snails by the shell and tossing them indelicately over the fence into the neighbor's yard. Bending far forward, so far forward that I can see the lips of your sex spreading around the thin string of your bikini bottoms. So far forward that I can see your upper body from between your legs, your nipples popping out of the bikini top as you pluck a tomato from a plant. I lick the vodka-and-Tabasco-spiked tomato taste from a celery stalk and wonder if your pussy tastes like tomatoes when you've been picking them all day.

You straighten, bundling the fruits of your labor in your arms awkwardly, then reach behind you to pluck the string from between your cheeks, perhaps not even realizing that I could see your lips. You adjust the top, tucking your nipples away. The bright red bikini contrasts against your rich, tanned skin. I start to get hard.

You come back toward the house with your arms filled with tomatoes, pausing only to turn on the garden hose and spray water over your muddy knees and feet, washing them clean so that your tanned skin glistens. Water splashes up and moistens your bikini top, making it even more transparent, making it cling more firmly to the shape of you. Your face is a mask of elation, your eyes bright with enthusiasm as you rush toward the kitchen.

"*Wait* until you taste these *tomatoes*," you gush.

My eyes linger on your full, ripe breasts, nipples distending the red material of your top. I smile at you.

"I can hardly wait," I say.

You disappear into the kitchen, your cheeks bouncing ripe as I glance back after you. I have to readjust my shorts to keep my cock from pressing painfully against them. I sip the Bloody Mary and taste the sharp vodka and hot sauce camouflaging the taste of tomato.

You come out a few minutes later with the cutting board, ripe tomatoes sliced and laid out. You're also holding a glass of water. "You *have* to try these," you say, your breasts almost popping out of your bikini top as you come around and kneel by my chaise longue.

"I want to try them," I say.

"Here," you tell me, handing me the water. "Clean your palate. Swish it around. You've got to have a clean palate."

"My palate is anything but clean," I say.

"I know. Drink the water."

I drink half the glass and swish the water around my mouth, washing away the taste of the Bloody Mary.

"Now close your eyes," you tell me.

I close them and open my mouth.

"Just taste," you say, and place a tomato slice on my tongue like a bikini-clad priest disbursing the Holy Communion.

The tomato is still hot from the sun. The taste is hearty, rich. The bite of citrus is followed by a rush of smoky taste – pure musk.

"Doesn't it just taste like sex?" you giggle.

I open my eyes, look into yours, let my glance flicker down over your body, its ripe rounded curves full and pink with the sun.

"Yes," I say. "It tastes exactly like sex."

"OK," you say. "Here, drink more water and close your eyes."

I obey, opening my mouth.

"This is a different variety," you tell me. "This is an heirloom."

"You don't say."

This one, also warm, is faintly spicy, the taste pulsing hot through my tongue before the musky bouquet hits me. It's spicy enough that it surprises me, burning just a little as it goes down.

"Now that one *really* tastes like sex," I say.

"I know," you tell me, smiling as I open my eyes.

One breast has come free from the skimpy red bikini top; your nipple pokes out just over the edge.

I drink more water, take the cutting board away from you and set it on the little metal table.

Then I grab your shoulders.

"What are you doing?" you ask.

"Dirtying my palate," I say, and push you onto the chaise longue as I slide out of it.

You're giggling as I reach for your bottoms. You don't even protest that the neighbors might see – any neighbor still watching wants to see whatever he or she can. You struggle a little getting into the chaise longue, but you don't protest. I get my fingers under the string of your bikini bottoms and pull them down quickly.

Your face is flushed with the sun and with the taste of sex. You tuck your breasts back into the bikini top.

"Oh no you don't," I say, and I reach up and pull the top down.

My hands caress your ripe tomatoes as my mouth descends between your parted thighs. The memory of the tomato's musk complements your taste, and it fills my mouth as I reach out with one hand and seize a warm tomato slice, popping it into your mouth.

You moan faintly around the crushed pulp of the tomato. Red juice runs down your chin.

My tongue slides between your lips and I taste that you're wet – so wet juice runs down my chin, too. I put another tomato slice in your mouth as my tongue finds your clit, and your tomato-muffled moan rises in volume.

Then you're quiet, laying back in the chaise longue and panting softly as I caress your clit with my tongue.

When I slip another tomato slice into your mouth you seize my fingers and suckle them, coating them with tomato juice. It runs down my wrist and dribbles onto your round, bare breasts. I press my tongue harder against your clit and your back arches.

Tomato juice dribbles down your neck and joins the juice already coating your breasts, soaking the bikini. Lucky it's red. Your moans rise in volume and pitch, and you're very close to coming.

I've got you right on the edge when I lift my face from your pussy, pull down my shorts, and climb onto the chaise longue with you.

Your eyes are closed in rapture, your mouth hanging halfway open, your lips slicked with juice. I put another slice on your tongue and you suckle it hungrily as my lips press to yours, my tongue delving into the taste of tomato and of you. My cock finds your lips and eases neatly between them. You're so wet I don't have to wait.

You come almost as soon as I enter you, moaning into my mouth, your breaths then coming fast and short as I suck the tomato pulp out of your mouth and savor it hungrily. I fuck you fast, my hands on your breasts, squeezing gently. You're still thrashing and whimpering in orgasm when I come, letting out a thunderous moan and plunging deep inside you as my cock explodes. I slump onto you, licking the juice from the underside of your throat.

"Don't you love tomato season?" you ask.

"I love every season," I tell you. "Just wait until the squash is ready."

Little by Little

Gina Marie

The Professor undresses me silently as he warms the bath water. He is silent as he lifts my head by pressing upward on my chin, studying my face. He wraps a thick white towel around my shoulders before taking my hand and leading me to the nearby claw foot tub where I kneel on a thick cotton rug. I hang my head, my long red hair coiling like a pool of molten copper near the drain. He begins soaking my head, starting at the base of my neck, then pours rose-scented shampoo into his hands, slowly caressing every inch of my scalp.

The Professor bends over me, and I feel his chest pressing on my back, smell odors of leaves and woodsmoke rising off of his flannel shirt. He rinses the foaming lather before massaging in the creamy emulsion of aromatic herbs and coconut oil. He fills his hands with my thick wet hair and strokes it from top to bottom before pulling it tight and wringing out the excess water. He runs a thumb down the side of my face, gazing into my eyes. I bend my head as he wraps my head in a warm towel pulled off the warming rack near the bathroom door. The towel is like a long, deep kiss.

I joined the Professor at the rustic log house he calls "my sanctuary" for a long weekend on the coast of Maine. He teaches ornithology and studies migratory raptors and waterfowl. We met at a used bookstore in the nearby village where I keep a small apartment. He is dark-featured and intense with deep blue eyes. I love his eccentric personality, his starkness, his certainty, even his self-absorbed coolness. The ritual began one night after some wine when the Professor asked permission to wash my hair. Then he asked to trim it. Just a trim. Just a little.

After the shampoo, the Professor removes the towel and directs me to a chair in front of the stone fireplace, positioning himself on a small wooden stool. He begins by combing my wet hair with his black comb, pulling out the long red strands that get caught in the teeth and laying them neatly on a small towel by the sink. He sits me down on another short wooden stool and clips the front layers of my hair to the top before trimming the back. He never takes off much. He works methodically, as if in a creative trance, the scissors snapping like a silver beak, tiny pieces of clipped hair falling like autumn leaves onto my covered shoulders and into my lap.

It is late November. The small bathroom window is open, steam from the faucet still clinging to the top panes. The air is brisk. I can feel my nipples harden against the towel. Professor Taylor must have felt me shiver. He puts down the scissors and reaches inside, pulling it open slightly, his hands sliding down my arms and across my chest onto my breasts.

The ritual is always the same. The towel is pulled off somewhere between the bathroom and the bedroom or the hallway or the leather couch in his study that smells like a saddle when our bodies warm its skin. There is no radio, no television, only the animal noises of sex, and our breathing, flesh rubbing against leather, bodies drawn together by our heat. His hands tug at my clean-cut hair. The house is quiet except for the muffled sound of waves breaking against the rocky shore.

The Professor is leaning back on the couch, his body rigid with excitement, his hands in my damp hair. I pull him to sitting and spread his legs. On my knees, I look up at him with longing as I wrap my lips around the head of his cock, swirling my tongue around its swollen form, slowly slipping it deeper into my mouth. Both hands around the shaft, I tease the entire length of it gently, ever so gradually increasing the intensity with my hands, lips and tongue.

I want to tease him for hours. I want our lovemaking to continue late into the night. I want to empty him completely. I stand up and turn around, bending at the waist to reach a glass corked bottle of sweet almond oil. The Professor places his hands on my hips and pulls me toward his straining cock. I pull free and turn back to him. I shake my head silently at him and pour oil into my hand. He grins, hopeful for the next move, but I can't stop teasing him. I rub the oil into my breasts and cleavage, caressing and pinching my nipples. I turn away again and bend down, pouring oil onto the nape of my neck, enjoying the sensation of it trickling down my spine and spreading at the small of my back onto my thighs and between my ass cheeks. I turn once more to face him and cup my breasts in my hands, my pussy dripping with come and oil.

Taking his smooth, hard balls in my mouth, I reach my hands under his ass and squeeze him hard, pushing his hips higher, slowly working my way up his cock until I plunge it deep into my mouth again, my fingers wrapped carefully but firmly around the base, my hard clit throbbing mercilessly.

The Professor's head is back, his eyes closed, his lips parted slightly. I am electrified by the easy look of pleasure on his face.

The Professor opens his eyes and places his hands gently on my arms and pulls us both up to standing. He bends his head to suck on my breasts and nipples and pulls upward on one thigh, lifting my foot to rest on the arm of the couch. He slides his cock in deep, his hands around my ass. Our bodies are glazed with oil and sweat. He coils the rope of my hair in his hand and holds me tightly to him as he thrusts again and again, our hips grinding in unison.

I wrap my arms around his waist, squeeze my pussy tight and rock with him, my cries of pleasure mingling with the sounds of the waves.

The Professor's cock is a firebrand, searing pleasure into my core. In spite of my want for hours of pleasure, I give in to the need for release and we are consumed by one another's flame, emptied and filled simultaneously. We fall to the couch, the Professor's hands still entwined in my hair.

Afterwards, I dry my hair in the bathroom, pull on jeans and a sweater and meet the Professor barefoot in the living room.

He is bent over the hearth, building a fire. As orange flames catch hold of the cedar kindling, he pours me a brandy. I sip at it and enjoy the heat of it deep in my throat, anticipate the slow, soft feeling that follows.

The Professor keeps a collection of birds' nests in a glass curio cabinet near the alcove window where an old wooden rocking chair and table have a view of the orchard and three bird feeders. I look out at the neat rows of trees. A wren pecks at the ground at the base of an apple tree. Rotten apples are scattered across the ground, dark, soft bruises shrinking into cracks along their edges.

He pulls me back to the fire and wraps his arms around me.

The Professor smells of sex and shampoo. He rubs his hand down the back of my head and buries his face in the nape of my neck.

I turn to face him and run my hand from his ear to his jaw, taking in the hardness of his features.

I pull away and pick up my glass, swallow the last of the brandy and go back to the curio. The little key at the side of the door turns easily and the cabinet opens with a soft click. The nests are arranged from smallest to biggest in neat rows. I pick one up and turn on the lamp. The Professor is poking at the fire with an iron. I hold the nest out in the palm of my hand and admire the tight weaving of branches, twigs, bits of thread. I pick up the magnifying glass on the table and look closer. Near the bottom and in the center, there is hair. Shiny black hair is woven like a blanket into the cup of the little nest. Startled, I put it back and pick up a larger one, lift it to the light, look through the glass. There, tucked into the bottom, is a swirl of copper, the smooth strands wrapped tight around the brittle twigs.

The Professor goes on jabbing at the fire. Then he sits at the edge of his chair and looks up at me, my hand outstretched, trembling, a million thoughts, questions, searing through my mind.

"*Peu à peu, l'oiseau fait son nid,*" says the Professor softly. "Little by little, the bird builds its nest."

Wonders Wild and New

Tinder James

Alice stared while the Red Queen's chin compressed into many folds, rather like a bellows, as her face tilted downward with each exhale as she slept. The Queen had drifted off while crocheting a lace edging to a handkerchief and her hands were now suspended below her bosom in mid-stitch position. The parlor in which they sat had white-painted walls and the afternoon sun shone low through a row of lace-covered windows, creating a skewed floral pattern on the black and white checked floor. The bulbous padding of the Queen's crown shielded her eyes from the sun, and the ball of silk from which she had been working rolled to and fro across her lap with every slumbering breath. The Queen could be venerable or malicious, but she was a powerful woman in either state. Alice knew the woman's apparent vulnerability at the moment was deceiving.

The only other guest still present was the snail across the room, introduced earlier to Alice as Lord Baul. The single piece of clothing he wore, in addition to his shell, was a tiny black derby. The derby was wedged in between two short tentacles. Above those he had two long eyestalks, the tips of which held his little brown eyes – eyes that were capable of surveying the room independently of one another. He was a giant as far as snails go. He sat, or perhaps stood, two feet tall, two and half feet counting his eyes.

Alice suddenly felt a little light-headed and wondered if she should have abstained from eating that unusual tasting crumpet offered to her at tea. She noticed that the room was dimming and her dress felt as if it was getting tighter with each passing moment. Surely something was awry. The childhood memory of growing completely out of proportion to her surroundings intruded upon Alice's mounting panic. It was an unhappy memory and it caused her to question whether coming here to pay the Queen a visit, after all these years, was such a good idea after all.

She glanced down and was reassured, by how her body fitted in the satin tufted chair, that she wasn't growing after all. The realization that her dress was shrinking, however, caused her quite some concern. It was a good deal shorter than it had been when she'd sat down and the bodice was clinging to her figure like a second skin. She glanced around self-consciously and, to her surprise, the snail was now poised halfway between her and where he had rested previously. One of his eyes was staring right at her lap, where the skirt of her dress was fast becoming a belt.

She thought about what she should do, but the prospect of running away with her body exposed was far less appealing to her than what might happen if she just stayed put. She looked over to the Queen who was still fast asleep. Alice gave a start when she glanced back to her left and discovered that Lord Baul had now advanced to a spot just inches from her legs. His eyes were slowly rotating in two circles level with her chest. It was his skin though that captured Alice's attention. It had a wet look and the texture and sheen of a tongue. She tugged hopelessly at her diminishing garments and crossed her legs to conceal herself from the prying eyes.

Alice said, "Excuse me, Lord Baul, but I find myself in an awkward predicament. My clothes are shrinking, but I know from past experience that to wake the Queen from her slumber is much too risky an undertaking. After all, given the choice, I would much rather lose my dignity than lose my maidenhead again. Nevertheless, I don't have an idea about what to do to help myself. Is there any way you can think of to help me?"

"I'd like very much to help you, my dear," he said in an earthy voice, "though my knowledge of clothing is somewhat limited, as you can see. Perhaps if you were to stroke me, it would reverse the shrinking process . . . hmm?"

It was almost as if he could read her thoughts. She was intensely curious about what his skin might feel like. Was he wet like a tongue or dry like a snake? However tempting the offer might be though, she didn't see how touching him could have anything to do with reversing the shrinking of her clothes. On the other hand, since it was something she wanted to do anyway, what harm could come of it?

She looked into the eyes, which were stationary now and closer together. They looked back into hers with a pleading, almost pitiful expression. She could feel the warmth on her legs emanating from his fleshy chest.

"Please," he said softly.

She reached out and stroked his neck with her fingertips and, as soon as she did so, he advanced upon her legs and proceeded to envelop them all the way around until his body met in the back. Her legs were immobilized, but in a warm and comforting way, like being under the weight of winter bed covers.

As he continued to move forward and encroach upon her lower body, she thought, He *is* like a tongue, a gigantic tongue. He expanded upward, covering her newly revealed skin. Against her better nature, Alice gave herself over to the heady sensation. It struck her that it wasn't like being licked by a tongue though. It was more like a tongue that just kept growing, without any actual movement, surrounding her in a warm, slippery cocoon of flesh. Baul wrapped himself around her waist and expanded down the valley of her buttocks. She came instantly when he pushed his flesh into the slit of her cunt and penetrated both her ass and her cunt simultaneously.

Alice shuddered after the quite unexpected orgasm she had just experienced and became dimly aware of the rushing turmoil of the sea in her ears. She became alarmed at the thought that she may actually have been consumed by Baul, and was now trapped inside his shell. She blinked her eyes open to see a sideways world of sand, and felt Jay's hand sliding out of her bikini bottom. He plucked off the shell that he'd rested on her ear and giggled at making his girlfriend come in her sleep. The beach was pink in the blush of dusk, and quiet after the people, dogs and waves had all gone elsewhere for the night.

She was madly in love with Jay. His body was like a six foot piece of clay that seemed to conform to her every desire. She could tell him, with only a little shyness, what she wanted in bed and like magic they were trying it. His sweet honey-colored balls were covered with shiny spun gold hair and smelled of summer. His sweet, soft ass smelled like hazelnuts roasting. She wanted to wrap him around her body like a huge fur coat and die happily.

Alice said, "I was dreaming."

She rolled over onto her back to see the first tiny star in the lavender sky above Jay's smiling face. "I think I still am," she said.

Gentleman's Relish

Donna George Storey

"Open your mouth, Jade. A little wider."

I was panting as if I'd just run a race, although in fact I hadn't stepped outside the bedroom since Colin and I decided to try gentleman's relish. Instead, I was kneeling on a pillow, my head tilted back, my hand shoved into my soaking panties.

Colin cradled my cheek in his warm, sturdy fingers. The gesture was strangely gentle given what he was about to do. With his other hand, he began to jerk his swollen cock over my upturned face. My whole body seemed to open to him. I wanted to be filled.

"Let me . . . suck you . . . please."

"Not this time, Jade. You might make me come down your throat, and then you couldn't taste it properly. You do want to savor every subtle nuance of flavor, don't you?" Colin's face was flushed and his grey eyes glowed, but his voice was admirably controlled.

I could only moan in reply. I'd never been so excited by a thought and so afraid of the reality. Did I really have to see this through to the end?

"Close your eyes," Colin said.

So I didn't have to *see* it through. That left my poor taste buds to prickle as they waited for this foreign delicacy. My stomach knotted up even as my pussy continued to drool. I could ask Colin to stop – he would immediately do it – but that would be a betrayal, not of him exactly, but of what we were seeking together.

So I pushed my tongue out, rubbed my clit faster, and waited for the rain to come.

* * *

Colin and I had always shared an interest in food. We met at our local organic food cooperative. I was the Sunday morning supervisor; he happened to sign up to do his volunteer hours during my shift. There were few customers when we opened, which left us time to talk at length about our common interests in politics (we were both avid environmentalists), cooking (vegetarian) and sex (we agreed "romance" was an insidious form of social control). There was chemistry from the start, but Colin struck me as an enlightened man who would value our blossoming intellectual friendship over a roll in the sheets.

Then one morning we were swapping failed relationship stories, and I confessed that, old-fashioned as it was, I apparently couldn't have orgasms with my partner unless I was in love with him.

"That's nonsense, you just need to be with someone who cares more about your pleasure than his own ego," Colin snorted.

My head jerked back. "When did you become an expert on my orgasms?"

"Come over to my place after work and I'll prove I'm right." His smile sweetened the dare.

Blame it on my natural curiosity, but I did go home with him that day, and I did come. Three times.

That was the beginning of our frolics, but we both swore that we would not let the illusion of "love" adulterate our mutual respect and autonomy. Which meant, I found, that I could let myself go with Colin because I didn't have to fulfill the impossibly contradictory ideals of the perfect girlfriend. I could simply be myself.

So, for example, when I was helping him move into his new (actually hundred-year-old fixer-upper) house, and we found a box of old porn magazines the previous owner had "forgotten" in a closet in the basement, I didn't have to feign prim disgust. I could say, "This is obviously a sign from the universe. Let's open a bottle of wine and have a porn-viewing party on your futon."

At first we mostly laughed. We marveled that the women were allowed to have pubic hair and read a few of the bogus "letters" aloud to each other. I teased Colin for getting an erection from the dirty pictures, and he challenged me to show him a pictorial that made me wet. That required leafing through another half-dozen, but I did find one. It was entitled "Gentleman's Relish".

As I read, I noticed I was licking my lips.

Set in a vague romantic past, the story portrayed an intimate interlude between a handsome aristocrat in a brocade dressing gown and a serving wench with a generous bosom spilling out of her homespun blouse. In contrast to their social stations, the gentleman seemed to be waiting on the wench as, page by page, he removed her garments and expertly fondled her bared parts. Not to be outdone, the wench knelt at the gentleman's feet dressed only in stockings and garters and sucked his cock. The final shot was a close-up of her face, mouth wide, the young nobleman's hand cupping her cheek as he ejaculated untidily over her lips and chin. "Young Bess enjoying her Gentleman's Relish" was the caption.

I passed the magazine to Colin. He raised his eyebrows. "Interesting. So what exactly 'works' for you here?"

To my surprise, I blushed. But this was Colin, I didn't need to be shy. "The costumes, of course. And the fact the lower-class maid gets to have power over her master. Even as she's getting the facial, you can tell he needs her. Every woman responds to that."

"Hmm. So what's your favorite picture?"

My face grew hotter. "The last one, I guess. I've never heard jizz called 'gentleman's relish' before. It makes it sound very classy."

"They spread it on toast in Britain."

"They put semen on toast?" I wrinkled my nose.

Colin laughed. "Well, certain people might, but I'm talking about the Gentleman's Relish they sell at Fortnum and Mason. It's made of anchovies."

"I don't know really know what semen tastes like. I just swallow it down as quickly as I can."

"I noticed that," Colin said. "Maybe that's why the picture fascinates you. This woman obviously enjoys it."

"Or is pretending for the camera."

"Could be," he conceded. "But I have known women who

love the taste when they're turned on. They've asked me to paint it on their lips so they could taste every drop."

I felt a sharp contraction between my legs. Whenever Colin invoked adventurous lovers of his past, more than my curiosity was aroused. I made an awkward attempt to change the subject. "You know, I could use some dinner. Should we get pizza or Chinese?"

He grinned. "How about a little gentleman's relish?"

I laughed.

Apparently he was serious. "I'd do it right, Jade. With full respect for your pleasure."

I squirmed as I imagined myself kneeling before him with my mouth gaping like a baby bird. The truth was, talking about this with Colin was more arousing than the photograph.

"Then again I'll understand if you feel some fantasies are meant to stay in your head," he added softly.

Damn him, he knew I couldn't resist a dare.

I narrowed my eyes at him. "All right then, let's see how good you are at serving up relish, milord. Don't just sit there, aren't you supposed to undress me?"

With a twinkle of victory in his eye, Colin proceeded to help me out of my T-shirt and jeans. When he was about to unhook my bra, he paused. "Can I get semen on this?"

I looked down at my bra, pink with lace trim. I pictured it soaked with jets of come and shivered. "It's washable."

"It'll be worth the mess," he promised as he pulled the straps down over my shoulders. He decided to let me keep my panties on, too, and laid a pillow on the floor to cushion my knees.

As I watched him undress, I was never so keenly aware of my own body, the heat flaming my cheeks, the aching heaviness of my breasts, my pussy weeping into my panties from jealousy of the feast my other mouth would soon enjoy.

He stepped in front of me and took his cock in his fist. "Play with yourself for me," Colin whispered.

It was then I thought, Every woman should have a friend who respects her this way.

The climax was near. I could hear rasping breath, the click of tender flesh as he jerked his cock harder and faster. He inhaled sharply and I stiffened. I was expecting the wetness, but not the heat. One sizzling spurt hit my cheek, another splashed on my tongue, the rest dribbled over my chin.

I let out a melodious sigh.

"Taste it, Jade."

Obediently, I circled my tongue over my lips. The relish was a little salty, but more meadow grass than sea. Most of all, it tasted of the secret essence of Colin. I wanted more.

Colin seemed to understand. "Open your eyes."

I did.

He scooped up more from my cheek and brought it to his own lips. He smiled. "Your skin makes it taste sweeter."

Then, pushing the cups of my bra down, he spread some of the slick, soapy ointment over my stiffened nipples. My body jerked as a vise of dark pleasure closed around my cunt. The viscous texture soothed even as it stimulated the hypersensitive tips, but I was still ravenously hungry.

"Feed me, please," I begged.

And so Colin fed me the condiment bit by bit while I strummed myself like there was no tomorrow. Cleaning up the last bit of mess, he pushed his finger into my mouth. The taste of his relish ricocheted from tongue to palate and back again. He began to pinch my sperm-coated nipple once more. It was too much. I came in racking spasms, suckling his finger desperately as if it were a cock.

Still standing over me, Colin's gaze poured down, filling my heart so full, it seemed to wrench open. Respect. Pride in me. Maybe even something others called love. This was our recipe for gentleman's relish. So what if it was a rather prissy, old-fashioned name.

Whatever we called it, it was good.

Making Myself at Home

Jeremy Edwards

I kept expecting a boundary to rear up on the horizon, a barrier to reveal itself as I progressed steadily through the not-so-tall grass of Clifton and Lynette's private life, nurturing my invest-ment and involvement in their intimacy as a couple until it was absolute. They erected none. They observed me and tolerated me; and it was with their full knowledge and their implicit consent that I acquired the habit of watching them fuck, whenever they fucked. They neither encouraged me nor discouraged me.

There was a moment last week when I thought, for the first time, I'd crossed a line. Heading for the bathroom after what I can personally affirm was a first-class cowgirl-style bounce, Lynette paused while traversing the hall and nodded to me as I masturbated there in the corner, where I'd stationed myself for the view into the room she'd just come from. The nod embodied cordiality but stopped short of complicity. Allowing of course for a variety of positions, all this was essentially no different from the numerous nights that had preceded this one.

What made this occasion different was the fact that the underwear from which my cock protruded, arcing upward into my fist, was Lynette's underwear. I'd stumbled on a stray pair of powder-blue panties on the floor of a closet, and had speculated – correctly – that they could help me feel even closer to her when I jerked off watching her get fucked.

I saw her face register the panties. One second later, I saw it register the impartial acceptance I'd become used to: *Dennis wants to wear my powder-blue panties while masturbating. Check.* She nodded once more – involuntarily this time, I thought – and proceeded to the bathroom.

Lying in bed that night, I cherished the recent memory of Lynette squatting hungrily over Clifton and then lowering herself to claim what she craved. Her sensitive face expressed every nuance of the joy associated with engulfing a substantial shaft; her luscious ass basked in its creamy nakedness; her thighs, whose contours I'd been shamefully slow to master, were shown off as thick and smooth, each offering a lean yet ample meal to my hypothetical lips.

While she bounced on his lap, Clifton peeled, unpeeled and repeeled the left spaghetti strap of Lynette's camisole, flirting with the nudity of her shoulder even as her bare bottom warmed his thigh and her cunt dined on his cock – treating her like a gift to be unwrapped, over and over.

Then, after I came into the sheets of the guest bed, I thought about the powder-blue panties. Wallowing in my stickiness, I had the insight that I wanted to *be* Lynette, in some sort of sexual fashion. It wasn't that I wanted to be fucked by Clifton – at least I didn't think so. No, I wanted to be Lynette because I desired her. Did that make sense? I asked myself. To have such deep lust for a woman that I longed to penetrate her Self, to experience her erotic essence from the inside out? The concept resonated, and I slept well that night.

And what Clifton did for me, I realized the next day, was make it all safe. *Their* relationship. *Their* intimacy. They denied me nothing, and I was fulfilled. This was why, at my own insistence, I'd been cooking all their dinners and cleaning every corner of their apartment, down to the last mahogany-colored pubic hair left by sweet Lynette on the rim of the bathtub. I owed them so much.

On a wintry Saturday evening that now seems very long ago, I'd taken the train in to meet Clifton and Lynette at a restaurant. We adjourned to a bar afterward, then another. It was bitterly cold when we were finally ready to call it a night, and it had begun to snow. Their apartment was within walking distance; mine, a lengthy commute away. Lynette suggested I crash at their place, and Clifton quickly seconded the offer.

Maybe she already knew – maybe she'd long known – that I was fascinated by her. And, if she knew, maybe she'd told him.

Naturally, this wouldn't have discouraged their hospitality, under the circumstances. I was an old friend, after all.

The first intimacy I witnessed was Lynette's hand on Clifton's ass when he unlocked the apartment door. My eyes went from his ass to hers – I felt I was reciprocating her caress with my attention.

There was a slight asymmetry to the way her stonewashed jeans favored her buttocks. The curve of the left buttock was casually denoted by the jeans, as if the pants were in a hurry on that side . . . but, oh, the right buttock. There we lingered, the jeans and I.

Despite my inevitable focus on Lynette's derrière, the significance of her hand on her husband's did not elude me. Even before we crossed the literal threshold of their private space, I had been promptly, if unintentionally, hustled inside the tent of their sex life.

They were kissing, deeply, in front of the kitchen sink when I came out of the bathroom half an hour later holding the borrowed toothbrush upright. It was a classic pose: arms around each other, his hands on her waist, and hers on his back. I stopped to relish it. Lynette opened her eyes momentarily and saw me. Then she shut them again; the romance continued.

I sat down at the kitchen table – ostensibly to drink from the water glass I'd left there before going in to brush and floss. I drank slowly.

The snow became heavy overnight, and kept on so forcefully that by Sunday morning any "unessential travel" was officially frowned upon. We were advised that train service would be erratic.

Lynette looked delicious in the ribbed long johns that she used as pajamas – matched top and bottoms in a faint cranberry pink. The half-inch moth hole in the bottoms fell neatly at the base of her right buttock.

The happy glow of her naked ass flesh winked at me through this eyelike gap as she and Clifton bustled around preparing breakfast. When Clifton insinuated a sneaky finger there to tickle Lynette's rump, she squirmed, giggled – and then turned her head to see if I was looking. *Maybe we shouldn't*, said her expression. Clifton then turned his head too, and I saluted them soberly with my coffee mug. They both avoided my direct gaze, but Clifton let his finger freeze on his wife's bottom cheek, rather than retracting it.

Any plans the couple had made for the day were moot, given the weather, and it was no surprise that they urged me to stay put until Monday.

Alone at their kitchen table with the newspaper, I tried not to be an obtrusive presence – especially because the more they forgot I was there, the more they drifted into private behavior. After a half-hour with the arts section, I had the impulse to tiptoe toward the doorway into the living room. There Lynette and Clifton, still in their sleepwear, shared a couch, cuddling over the crossword puzzle. Her legs were in his lap. I tiptoed back to the kitchen and read another article. When I returned a few minutes later, Clifton's hand was up Lynette's top.

I sat down on my side of the doorway. I was so quiet, they didn't notice me until Lynette's pajama top was completely off, and Clifton was sucking one of her small, pale breasts while fondling the other. Her narrow mouth was open in incipient ecstasy.

A raised eyebrow showed that my attendance startled her, but she was not about to interrupt the proceedings on my account. Clifton's right eye had caught me as well; it bulged but did not balk.

I was glued to my place. In fact, sitting cross-legged with a sincere hard-on, I couldn't have got up if I'd wanted to.

Soon Lynette sighed, wriggling beautifully with what I took for a minor foreplay climax. Then she disengaged Clifton from her nipple. I could see his saliva shimmering there.

"We should go to the bedroom," she told him.

"Please don't." I said it calmly but emphatically, surprising myself with my vehemence – not to mention my honesty.

Lynette's eyebrow again.

"I . . . I hate to make you get up and move, in your own home," I feinted, clearly making no pretense of getting up and moving myself.

"I don't care, if he doesn't," said Clifton with a shrug, after a short stage pause.

Oh, I cared all right – but I was content with the thought that all roads led to Rome.

"I guess we're all adults," said Lynette, in the most neutral tone of voice I'd ever heard employed by anybody.

Nothing more was said. It's been three weeks, and nothing more has been said. They fuck all over the house, and I watch. Lynette spreads her legs on the toilet and pees for Clifton, and I watch. She sits on his face while he lounges on the couch with an after-dinner glass of wine; I sit on the adjoining couch, and I get only the wine. But I watch. I watch, and I stroke myself off into one of the handkerchiefs I purchased the third day, along with enough clothing basics to last the laundry week.

The trains, of course, are running as scheduled now, and I could catch any one of them back to the suburbs. Sometimes when I walk to work in the morning, I think that's what I'm going to do at the end of the day – just as I used to do every day.

But always I see reason. Why undertake a seventy-minute commute to an apartment that provides no views of Lynette's right buttock? Whose bathtub rim is devoid of her pubic hairs? An apartment where, when masturbating about Lynette each morning and each night, I wouldn't be watching her?

If only I could have conceived of this paradise, I would have asked to go home with Clifton and Lynette years ago, to become a silent partner in their endless fucking. To join Lynette in being fucked, from the sidelines. To taste every one of Lynette's intimate ecstasies, from the sidelines.

To have Lynette and be Lynette, from the sidelines.

The New Emily

A. M. Hartnett

The way Cross whistled through his teeth as she approached his table meant nothing to her. The little black dress wasn't meant to entice, but to show him just how far Emily had come.

"I can't get over how different you look, yet somehow still the same." He pulled out her chair. He looked the same, like a delicious cross between golden Apollo and rugged Richard Burton. "Do you mind me asking how old you are?"

"I do, but I'll tell you anyway," she said. "I'll be thirty-two in the summer."

Cross resumed his seat and cocked his head. "Then that would have made you . . . twenty that summer. I always wondered."

She said nothing, but felt a strange electric pop in her belly. The summer of 1955 was a lifetime ago, when she was young and eager to experiment with taboo, when she'd met Cross while working at the tennis club, when she'd taken his money to provide more than just refreshments in the bar.

Running into him in such a big city was a fluke.

Accepting his offer to dinner was probably a mistake.

The waiter came and went with her order for a screwdriver. Cross grinned as he leaned back in his chair. "Don't you feel like we should be ordering champagne to celebrate?"

Emily raised a brow. "Do we have something to celebrate?"

"Is that your way of asking if we'll be fucking tonight?"

He didn't miss a beat as he spoke, and Emily wished she'd been able to remain cool after such a blunt reminder of their past. Instead, her mouth went dry.

Thankfully, the waiter brought her drink and another beer for Cross, giving her a brief reprieve.

At last, she spoke with detachment. "Is that why you think I'm here?"

Cross laughed. "You wouldn't be here if that wasn't the case. You have no other reason to be sitting across from me, not when you dislike me as much now as then."

In spite of herself, Emily chuckled. "What was there to like? You left your wife and children every weekend for paid sex. If you've changed, good for you, but it's no concern of mine and never was."

"You have to admit, hating me on a personal level made it better." Cross laughed as he watched her flush. "You're one of dozens of women I had that summer, and I didn't get any of them off the way I got you off. It took me a while to figure it out. You liked my money, but you liked even more what you had to do to earn it."

As she drank, she cast her gaze to the flickering candle at the centre of the table. Cross waited, and when she looked to him, he was unsmiling but his eyes were amused.

"I'm divorced now, so you can ease your conscience there. No one will be waiting for my call tonight while I'm making you come."

Cross had a level of conceit that had been honed over the years. Because of it, because he only cared for the fuck, everything he said was true. Over the years in that hot, masturbatory fog there had frequently been Cross creeping in.

She didn't want to talk, to share another word with him. She took another sip, slid the drink aside, and rose.

"You chose this hotel because you have a room here?"

"I thought it would be more convenient." He stood and drew a key from his pocket. "I was serious about the champagne. There's a bottle chilling in the room. The best, of course."

She had no doubt that the room was the best as well. After a silent ascent to the top floor he led her into a deluxe suite overlooking the city.

"No more talk about the past," she said and tossed her clutch on the large desk threatening to overtake the whole room. "It's like you said, I'm here to be fucked."

She turned and found him pulling his tie loose. Watching his hands work first the knot, then the buttons on his shirt, she felt a hot flash of anticipation go through her.

He went to work on his belt. "Surprise me and show me that you're not wearing those little cotton things you always wore."

She didn't display an ounce of hesitation as she undressed, though her fingers trembled as she worked the zipper to her waist. She studied him as she shimmied out of the garment, showing off black bikinis and nothing else.

"You like what you see?"

"I do." He shoved trousers and boxers down as one. His erection sprang up and away from his pubic hair. He was thicker around the middle than she remembered, but nonetheless still fit. "I prefer this Emily, to tell you the truth, though I still see the other in there. As fuckable as ever."

Emily's stomach gave an excited flip as she crossed the room and met him at the foot of the bed. The air around them was electric. She pushed him back and knelt between his legs. "No more talk, Cross."

On the outside she was able to maintain her cool, but on the inside she was brimming with excitement as she took his cock in both hands. Her mouth watered at the memory of how he tasted.

She didn't waste another second. Meeting his gaze, she lowered her head.

His moan thrilled her as she peeled back the foreskin and took the thick crest between her lips. She teased him at first, watching his expression go from calm to strained. He lifted his hips, and Emily swallowed as much as she could take.

With his hand on her head, she relinquished the present for the past. The years ebbed away as he fucked her mouth. She was his toy to fuck.

"Jesus, stop." He pushed her away and grunted as he strained into a sitting position. True amusement all but wiped out his arrogance as he laughed breathlessly. "Still the best blow job I've ever had."

He urged her onto her back. Though she was dying for the fuck, she nonetheless gave into his whim when he crouched between her legs and used his long fingers to part the sticky folds of her pussy.

She oozed into the bedding beneath her, content to bask in

the hot, skittering rings that went through her as he played with her clit. Her calm didn't last. He pulled the skin surrounding her hard nub, and his tongue went to work.

Though she tried, he would not be led. He knew what he was doing to her. When she cupped the back of his head and begged him to suck on her, he shoved her hands away; nor would he indulge her when she demanded he finger-fuck her. The whole of his attention was on her clitoris as he used the very point of his tongue, his gaze never leaving her face.

This time, it was Emily who ended it by drawing her foot up onto his shoulder and pushing him away.

Giving her no reprieve, he rose over her. "Turn over."

He guided her onto her stomach and rubbed his fingers between her slippery lips. One finger slipped inside her ass. Emily moaned and lifted her bottom higher.

"Have you been fucked here by anyone else?"

"Only twice bef—" She gasped as he worked his finger slowly in and out. "Fuck me, Cross. Now."

The breadth of his shadow seemed to double around her as he rose up. With each inch, recollection assailed her with such force she almost wept. She bucked and begged for more. The world around her spun as he manoeuvred her and breathlessly urged her to squat over him.

Her muscles screamed with the sudden tautness in her bent legs, but it all melted away each time the fat tip of his cock slid past her G-spot.

He kept one hand around her middle to steady her and used the other hand on her clitoris. Faster and faster they strained together, Emily using her feet to propel herself up and down while Cross drove his hips up to meet her. The strong perfume of sex and the wet sounds of her cunt swallowing his cock were all around her.

She was twenty years old again, fucked by a man whose first name she didn't even know, on the verge of coming for the first time with a man she neither loved nor even liked.

The friction against her G-spot prevailed and Emily erupted. She didn't give a damn who heard her moaning as she came, not when the two fingers Cross used on her clit were unrelenting.

His last thrust was deep. She felt his cock twitch, the surge between her inner walls in the moment he pulled away, and the hot splash of his semen hitting her inner thighs.

"Still the best fuck," he said once he caught his breath and released her. "You're staying the night, aren't you?"

"You were right. I don't like you, but it is the best fuck." She lifted her head and eyed the champagne. "Pop the cork, Cross. Get your money's worth."

The Year of Fucking Badly

Susannah Indigo

"There is no such thing as bad sex," I say to no one in particular.

We're at the big oval table at the Empress Gardens eating dim sum to celebrate the Chinese New Year when it all begins. It's the beginning of the Year of the Ox, a year that is supposed to bring the promise of new discoveries, or maybe fertility, I forget.

"Of course there is, Kenna," my friend Bill replies. "Bad sex: sex so awful, so unexpected, so terrible that just telling someone about it later makes them turn away in laughter, or horror."

"This really exists? Then why hasn't anyone made a whole magazine or something about it ever?" I can picture bad relationships, bad love even, bad break-ups, but not plain ol' bad sex, unless you're counting boring sex and then if you do, boring sex rules half the world and is often the norm rather than the exception.

Bill pauses and puts his hand on my knee. "You want me to show you, Kenna?"

I laugh. Bill is my sweet friend, my occasional fuck buddy and about as obsessed by sex as I am. He's a Pig, as in the Year of, defined quite appropriately as a sensual hedonist. I know this fact because I work as a research librarian – an "information specialist" they call us nowadays – and I get so many calls this time of year about Chinese astrology that I keep the chart by my desk.

I hike my black leather skirt a little higher as Bill watches, smiling. "Hell, you know what I like, Bill. Most anything that moves." To put it mildly. "What exactly would you do to show me bad sex? Take me home and fuck me for five minutes in the missionary position and then roll over and say goodnight?" I don't talk this way around work, of course, where I wear my wavy red hair up in a bun, skip the leather and leave the contacts home for my everyday glasses.

Bill offers to rape me if I want, which hurts my brain to think about. Everybody knows rape is not about sex. But if I let him rape me, is it still rape? I'm such a pervert I'd probably like it no matter what.

"More stories," says Bryan across the table from me, probably trying to deflect the conversation away from rape, which nobody ever talks about but most everyone fantasizes about.

"Define 'bad'," Mary says.

I wave my little librarian hand. At least I can add this. "Did you know that the word 'bad' is thought to originate from two Old English homophobic words from about the thirteenth century – *baeddel* and *baedling* – which were derogatory terms for homosexuals, with overtones of sodomy?"

"Really?"

"Yeah." I can't recall why I remember this, but maybe it caught my attention because of those overtones of sodomy.

Everyone around the table goes on to tell their own "bad sex" story. The boys' almost always involve not being able to get it up, but that strikes me as "bad imagination" or even "bad ego" rather than bad sex. Let's face it, women know. They make enough cocks down at Good Vibrations to keep us girls happy for the rest of our lives.

I notice a trend. Every bad story seems to supply bare bones details, a gasp, and then trails off into "and it was so awful . . .".

I'm racking my brain for a story of my own as my turn arrives. I think about the worst situation I can remember – the guy I married when I was eighteen, my manic-depressive young husband. I remember getting divorced from him at twenty. I remember the angry words, the suicide threats. I remember the cold metal of the gun on my bare thigh the night before I finally moved out, I remember being terrified, and I also remember being very very wet. No, I imagine that story won't work.

Nobeko starts in on a story about a woman who wanted to tie her up and how shocking this was to her. I can't stand it.

The world is desperately in need of more people with enough passion and drive to understand the dynamics revealed in restraints. You wouldn't believe how many people I've actually had to ask to tie me up, pretty please, which tends to limit the high of submissiveness. Believe me, the concept of men and domination is a myth.

I shrug and pass on telling a story when it's my turn, and after a couple more "it was awfuls" the conversation turns to great sex. But the bad sex concept holds in my mind and I know there is no way to look this up in my library. Field research is required. I never pass on anything. That's why people like me become researchers, because the urge to know everything and anything about a subject is overwhelming once it slips into that certain mind-curiosity groove. If there's bad sex out there, I'll find it.

"It's sort of a scavenger hunt for bad sex, Holly," I try to explain to my upstairs neighbor and lover. We're buried deep under her pink comforter eating chocolate chip cookies the next night. Holly is the Martha Stewart of my love life – candlelight and cookies and flowers all the time. Some nights just walking into her place is better than actual sex. She's a Dragon – as into mind-touching as body-touching.

"Sometimes I have bad sex with myself," Holly offers. "You know, those nights when even your own fingers bore you to death?"

"Bad sex for one? Sounds like something Stouffers would make."

Monogamy is not a fetish of mine, but still I feel a little guilty even though Holly and I have always been open about any other lovers we might have. I decided a long time ago that two lovers was exactly the right number for me. My other lover is a student named Keith, a Snake like me but from a different generation, twelve years younger. He knows what I need. He likes to use my hair to tie me up in strange places before he fucks me, and I'm immensely fond of that particular knot.

Holly agrees it might be a good project as long as I promise only to attempt bad sex. She's an academic, so she decides to chart this all out for me. We decide that random bad sex would probably have to involve a stranger. We decide I need to keep a log of it all, and that there has to be a way to sort it out. She remembers the old Sears catalog ratings of "good/better/best" when buying products and decides that will do. Our final scale runs: Worst | Worse | Bad | Boring | Good | Better | Best – and that's it, I'm off for the hunt.

Driving down Broadway the first night, I sense one problem. I'm already wet at the promise of getting laid by someone new. I try to control myself by reciting the Dewey Decimal system out loud.

The lounge at the Holiday Inn on Colfax is the first stop. I'm wearing fishnet stockings and leather but my hair is pulled back in a ponytail and my turtleneck rides high, a sort of combo slut/ cheerleader look. It doesn't take me long to pick out a paunchy-looking, balding guy at a table by himself and start the flirtation.

He tells me his traveling salesman story, the exquisite details of selling hospital equipment, while I brush his leg with my boot and watch the surprise in his eyes at his luck. He's a Rat, I find out – outwardly cool, self-controlled, but passionate.

"Push the button on my watch," he says, holding his wrist out for me to see.

I push the button.

"Tell me what it says, Kenna."

I'm stifling a laugh. Can I pick them or what? "It says, 'WANNA FUCK?'" And in large letters no less. "Pretty damn clever." I don't remember any mention of Rats having crass taste in jewelry.

"I had it made special in Taiwan."

Maybe, just maybe I've found what I'm looking for, and on my first try. I don't want to sleep with him. So I will.

"Wow," I say, flipping my ponytail. "And, yes. But, do you know where the word 'fuck' comes from?" Now why on earth would I share this with him? But I do. "It's actually a mystery, but they think it might originally be from the Scandinavian '*fokka*'. There's one written record of the word in 1278, and then nothing, nothing at all until three hundred years later, maybe because it was such a taboo to say it." They probably didn't even make these watches back then.

He reaches over and twists my hair in his meaty hand and whispers, "I'll show you where fucking really comes from, sweetheart."

A kiss, the check, and he's guiding me to his room.

"Take off all of your clothes, lie down on your belly and close your eyes," the Rat orders after we enter the tackiness that is room 413 at the Holiday Inn. "I want to show you something."

Another watch? His cock? Some strange hospital equipment? But this is my game, and I'm stripping down and stretched out.

He's searching in his bag and I'm peeking out of one eye and he's bringing out what looks like a bottle of oil.

"I used to work as a masseuse," he says as he climbs up on top of me and begins with my back. "Let me massage this fine body, sweetheart." When his hands start in on me I see this boy starting to slide way up my sexual-rating chart. By the time he's worked me over with his oil front and back I'm completely limp in his hands and ready for anything and he's entering me from behind and riding me hard and holding my hair tight with one hand and slapping my ass with the other. He's got me hollering "Fuck me, fuck me, fuck me," and I know that if this Rat was around in the fourteenth century they would have definitely written the word down.

"OK, so looks aren't a good indicator of bad sex, Holly," I admit, safely back in her pink bed. "But what can I do – interview people and ask them if they're a lousy lay?"

Holly's reviewing my log. "All it says here is 'his hands, his hands,' Kenna."

"Shit, that's all I can remember. It was great."

She sighs, but we begin to plan the ex-lover possibility next. Julia was the love of my life ten years ago, until she decided she was too good for me and dumped me coldly. She's a Monkey – clever, witty, manipulative, pretentious. The Chinese chart doesn't really say all that, I'm just projecting. I do distinctly recall her saying she was only going to sleep with PhDs in the future after our break-up. And that she was only with me because she was crazy about my breasts. This has to be bad.

I find her at her modern dance class, where I show up in a low-cut black leotard to get her attention. I lie to her over lunch, tell her about my newly minted PhD in the thirteenth-century dialect of *Baedel Fokka*, and get invited back to her place. I make up other stories for her about the places I've been and who I've met. When I create an imaginary friendship with Camille Paglia, who I know she idolizes, I'm in. She spreads her legs for me and I'm devouring her and I suddenly can't remember why I found her so attractive in the first place, but I go for the sex just to show her how hot I am, and it works. When I leave and turn at the door to tell her, "I'm sorry, I won't be back, because I just realized that I should really only sleep with tenured professors," I realize that this is the most fun I've had in weeks.

I try to dive back into work and forget this whole idea, but every research question I'm asked sounds like sex. I've started watching everybody I see and thinking all the time about how they fuck, why they fuck, where they fuck, is it good, what do they do badly. When I'm not answering the phone I can be found doing some heavy breathing back in section 306.7, reading every sex book I can get my hands on. Hell, I'm so immersed in it I could practically write a thesis – maybe you can get a PhD in Bad Sex.

Joe's Bait Shop, the local dive bar. Holly scoped the place for me over the weekend and thinks it's a guaranteed bad time. Every possible sport on a dozen big-screen TVs, pool tables in the back. The bartender's a babe. It's amazing how fuckable everyone looks when you're looking for people who aren't.

I'm wearing black tights, a long baby blue sweater, black suede boots and nothing underneath. I'm getting a few looks but no bites because of the damn football game. I forgot it was Monday night. Maybe this is bad sex, when you can't even draw a man away from the television.

I get myself a drink and wander toward the back room. There's some kind of a meeting in progress and no TVs, so I slip in and sit down in an empty card chair in the back to check out the crowd.

"My goal," the handsome man speaking says, "is to help others achieve sexual sobriety."

Wait, wait. Sexual sobriety?? Is this where you only fuck before you get drunk?

"The twelve steps were my saving grace," he continues. "I turned my lust over to God."

Holy shit, I think I've wandered into a meeting of OverFuckers Anonymous.

I laugh. Heads turn in my direction, followed by frowns at my laughter. I can't help it. I know they're deadly serious. But maybe God knows what bad sex is. I wonder, Does God like having all this lust turned over to him? Didn't God turn it over to us in the first place?

The speaker's looking right at me and smiling. "Who would like to share their story with us today?" He's got piercing green eyes and big shoulders and a fuzzy beard that I can already feel rubbing between my legs, and I'm considering making up a quick sad story to tell him and I know I should consider getting the hell out of here instead.

I do not volunteer. They'd never believe me if I told the truth about why I'm here. But, wait, bad sex, bad sex. These folks have potential. Oversexed people trying not to have sex could be real bad. Or would they be real good, heading toward better/best, like reformed Catholic girls let loose?

At the break, the speaker comes directly to me and introduces himself. "My name is Tony," he says with a gorgeous grin. Oh my. I don't even have to ask, I know he's a Tiger, as in the Year of, the Hour of, the Moment of, the Bed of, the Cock of, and I'm heading for trouble.

"I just stopped in here accidentally," I say. "Giving up lust? This is like a bad dream."

"I know," the Tiger says. He pauses, and then takes my arm firmly and guides me out toward the dark back corner of the bar. He smiles. "But I bet your dreams are spectacular, darling. You look like a girl who knows how to dream." Fresh drinks in hand, strong arms wrapped around me. "Do you dream in color, Kenna?"

That's the best pick-up line I've heard in ages. "Everyone does, Tony, or can. Did you know that nobody ever questioned this fact before the advent of black and white television in the fifties? Not Freud, not Jung . . ." I hear my little librarian voice being smart and at the same time I feel my knees shaking like a little girl and I just want to climb up on his lap and let him turn his lust over to me instead of God.

He listens to me as though every word I utter is gold. He knows the secrets. Words and hands and eyes and laughter. Attention paid; intensity gained. But it keeps sneaking through the haze of my desire that this man is one of *them*.

"Tony, didn't I just hear you discussing 'sexual sobriety' as a way of life?" I ask as he pulls me onto his lap and his hand is higher and higher on my thigh, so high and so right that I think I imagined it all and that this is my punishment or maybe my reward for thinking and dreaming about sex day and night and for ever, ever, pretending I know a single thing about what it all means.

"For you, darling, I'm willing to fall off the chastity wagon." His mouth is on mine and he's biting my lip with the force that I need and I am *going going gone*. I don't believe a word he says and I don't care. The cock of the Tiger is hard beneath my ass and all the lines are slipping away and good is blending into better and heading off the chart and he's whispering in my ear and I want it all and we're out the door.

Before he starts the car he says, "Pull your tights down and spread your legs and let me see," and I do, and he just watches me. When he stops the car at Sunset Park, a short drive away, and leans over, his beard is rough against my thighs exactly as I imagined it and he's biting and sucking and I'm in heaven and then he's suddenly slowing way down.

"I shouldn't do this," he mumbles, with his mouth still buried in my pussy. Oh God, maybe *this* is the bad sex I deserve, when it begins to orbit off the chart and you know that somehow when it's over it's going to wrap right back around and come up on the awful horrifying side as chastity reclaimed.

"I shouldn't do this," he repeats, and I think maybe he's waiting for me to save him. This is one of those damned defining moments in life. Define the moment or it defines you. Screw him, or screw him? Fuck it. Or fuck me. I reach down and stroke his hard cock through his jeans.

"I'll be good for you, Tiger. Don't stop, don't stop." He lifts my sweater and we're tumbling toward the back seat like teenagers in lust and I'm not sure I'll be able to excuse this behavior later as research but maybe I don't even care. My tights are off and my legs are wrapped high around his big shoulders and his cock presses into me. He leans down and begins to bite my nipple and send me over the edge. He pauses, and I think I will die if he stops one more time. "You're right, darling," he whispers, driving into me hard. "For tonight, there's just no such thing as bad sex."

Tess Needs a Spanking

N. T. Morley

Tess needs a spanking. She really, really needs a spanking. She needs it so bad she keeps wriggling her ass back and forth, asking for it, begging for it. She doesn't even know she's doing it; it's like her ass has a mind of its own, squirming and fidgeting under that tight skirt as she walks past me or bends over within sight of me. She needs it so bad she's wet under her skirt; her pussy is swollen and tight, aching and hungry to feel the sting on her ass as she shakes back and forth, sobbing and crying. She needs it so bad she keeps messing up, bringing me the wrong file, the wrong document, spilling my coffee, forgetting the cream.

But I don't need an excuse to spank Tess.

Tess doesn't even know how bad she needs a spanking. She never does, not until I grab her by the waist and tumble her over my lap; not until I grasp her by the hair and push her face into the crook of my arm and tell her to pull her skirt up over her round cheeks and take down her panties. She never knows she needs a spanking until after she's refused, until after she's begged me not to, threatened to lodge a complaint with my security, threatened to file a claim with the labor board, threatened to walk out and come back with a lawsuit. She never knows how bad she needs a spanking until after I've pulled her skirt up myself, found out how wet she is under her tight lace thong, discovered the squeals that come out of her mouth when I rub her wet pussy and slide two fingers inside. She never knows how bad she needs a spanking until after I've given her one, open-handed, spanking her ass rhythmically, first one cheek and then the other, right on the sweet spot and occasionally in the middle, right over her pussy. She never knows how bad she needs a spanking until after she's started to lift her ass in the air, pump it hungrily in long, slow circles, shake back and forth and wet my suit with tears. She never knows how bad she needs a spanking until after she buries her face in my arm, spreads her legs, and grips the legs of the chair tightly to steady herself as I beat her. She never knows until after she's cried, whimpered, cajoled, tried to bargain, tried to threaten, tried to wriggle her way out of one. She never knows until after she's started to moan. She never knows until she's felt it building deep in her cunt, felt the blows driving all the way into her luscious little snatch and punishing her throbbing clitoris. Still, until that very last moment, no matter how many times it happens, she clings to her resistance, adheres to her passionate belief that she's done nothing wrong, that she *doesn't* need a spanking and if she whines and cries and complains, I'll see the light and just *stop*. But I don't, and it's a good thing for her, because the only time I give her one is when she really, truly, desperately, urgently needs a spanking.

But Tess never knows how bad she needs a spanking until after she's thrown back her head and pushed her ass high into the air and *come*, sobbing, overwhelmed by the profound satisfaction of having her need satisfied, the deep need for what, if she had been allowed to have her way, she never would have gotten.

But luckily, Tess has me to tell her when she *does* need a spanking. And once she's had one, she always does exactly what she knows she needs to do.

Which is pull down her panties and put her ass in the air, and await another spanking – this one for saying *no*.

I never give her all of what she wants, mind you. I never give her all of what she needs. I never fuck her, you see. That would be wholly inappropriate. I never plumb that snug cunt of hers with my cock, even though, by the time she's received her second spanking and climaxed a second time, she's weeping and saying "Thank you, thank you, thank you," and begging me to let her satisfy me. She's lifting her ass high and spreading her legs and saying "Please, sir, I want to thank you properly. I want you to fuck me. I know you need it very badly, sir. I can feel your cock against my tits, sir. It's very hard. Please, sir, please make use of me. I want to thank you properly."

But I don't – what kind of boss would I be if I took advantage of a girl in such a state? She hardly knows what she's asking. She knows nothing but the desperate pulse in her cunt, the aching need to be penetrated, fully, *fucked* until she cries even harder and comes, uncontrollably, harder than ever.

But I do give Tess the barest hint of what she's begging for, what she needs, what she wants.

I ease her off my lap, guide her to her knees, direct her face into my crotch where my hard-on bulges needily.

I watch her pinkened ass as she lifts it high with pride and wriggles it back and forth, perhaps hoping that its warm and radiant red glow will invite me to get out of my chair, find my place behind her, and drive deep into her channel while she bites her finger to stifle her wails.

The poor naive girl thinks she can tempt me into her fetching bottom. Instead, she is allowed to say "thank you" in the purest and most ancient way possible: With my cock in her mouth.

She unbuckles my belt, unzips my suit pants and takes my organ out. She teases it with her full, red-lipsticked lips. She makes eye contact with me, perhaps hoping that her pretty orbs will beseech me into carelessness and I'll give her the pounding she's been gunning for. Instead, I look into her pretty eyes as her red mouth circles my shaft in a flirty "O", and I watch her pretty face as it bobs up and down on my pole.

Tess has long since learned to swallow. She knows that not doing so will earn her another spanking – this one just a hair short of the duration it would take to grant her a third orgasm. It only took her several days of walking around with her pussy swollen and needy, her ass suffering a feminine spankee's case of blue balls, before she learned to say "thank you" properly.

Her mouth slicks up and down my shaft rhythmically, little whimpers escaping her throat. Her eyes narrow to dreamy slits as she succumbs to the sensations of having cock in her mouth, as she gives up to the surging taste of sperm about to fill her. When it comes, I make not a sound, giving her no warning, and she suckles rapturously as hot streams fill her mouth and gush down her throat. She swallows, licks me clean, and returns my cock to its second most rightful place.

She takes a moment to fix her hair, put her soaked panties back on, straighten her skirt.

Then she returns to her work and, for the rest of the day, she never, ever brings me the wrong file or forgets the cream in my coffee.

Because she's forgotten, the moment she finished, how badly she needs a spanking.

But she'll remember . . . she'll remember. Every time.

Flowering

Valentine Bonnaire

It was after her mother's death that Pris began to doubt her marriage. How long had it been since she'd felt love from him. She'd settled in at twenty-eight, with him, working hard through the long corporate years trying to build up something, anything, but it was always under a set of rules delineated by him that she operated. She'd finally been able to say the word "divorce" out loud and she was scared because what divorce meant was that she would be alone. All alone. He hadn't wanted kids.

Who was I once? she asked herself. Before all this.

She'd wanted to tell him about the two times her heart had been broken but he had never wanted to hear. Talking made Pris feel close. Talking was intimacy. But he was silent. He'd said "I don't want to hear it," and brushed her voice away with a wave of his hand. He'd brushed her darkroom away too, in those years.

"This is a kitchen, not a darkroom," he'd said, as he built shelves for her pantry. He wanted roast chicken, not pictures. The parameters had closed in until they had choked off whatever it was in Pris that was an artist, over time.

Out walking, after he'd left her alone in their house, after she asked, after she pleaded "Please go," she picked up her camera and took to the streets looking at light.

The banana plant's flower hung like a jewel above her, dusk purple and magenta softened by the fog that hung over the city. It seemed to hold the kind of bursting promise her body was made of, as if it were an unplucked jewel that ripened orb-like, hanging among the green of the leaves. It was sexy, like a clitoris, like the book she'd never read called *The Joy of Sex*, like some kind of fulfilled *Kama Sutra* text which was orgasmic and hugely reddened.

What she needed was to talk. What she needed was a male chest and the crook of an arm wrapping around her. Her husband had always turned his back to her in bed. What she needed was a chest full of hair she could run her fingers through again. That man-scent in a sweater she would borrow from him. The shirts full of his aftershave she could wrap around herself after lovemaking.

So many years had gone by since she'd done that. Since she'd even cared.

James was miserable in his marriage. He'd told her that, in an email. Pris admired his mind the most because it took brilliant turns. She imagined them in bed doing all the forbidden things both of them had done in their youths, with lovers who never became permanent fixtures. She wanted him strictly through text, as if his letters could caress something and it didn't matter because both of them were so unhappy

Pris wanted to come more than once, just to see if it was possible.

She could imagine the two of them in bed talking about books, afterwards.

It would be easy to laugh in his arms.

"I'll buy you dresses," he said.

"But you'll have to let me choose them."

It had made Pris wet, hearing him say that. No man had ever offered to buy her dresses. "Be in my dreams tonight," he'd said. "And I'll be in yours."

He had been, those fall nights when it began. She'd slid her hand down between her thighs, touched the bud of desire, stroked something up until it sounded like music. The danger was exciting. She was looking at his face, knowing he was her age. That wasn't something Pris had ever done because they had all been older. Fifteen years, exactly. She thought of them as the big four relationships. But he was her age. Her age. He'd lived the times she had. He'd smuggled irises from Italy. He liked small Italian coffees. And Alfas, and Paris when it hummed full of life and jazz under the brilliant sky.

He'd written a story where the woman came sitting on top of him, smiling.

Pris wanted it to be true. He'd said something about his hands and how they were holding her hips and he was concentrating. She'd only had that once. A man who concentrated on her, first.

Pris, pristine – planting paper whites. Pris in white lace skirts that he bought her without panties underneath. Pris laughing as she slid down upon his stiffness, which would be immediate, she knew. It had always been like that for her, with men, when she had turned them on. Pris, clitoral, like the banana flower she caught on film, pliant ruby red, distended, succulent. His lips, cloistered, going down on her, his fingers culling rubies one after another, coming until she screamed or maybe begged for him to stop.

A game as she took him in her mouth, sucking.

The slick wet-sided wanting of need and the two of them slipping in between crisp sheets together while they laughed at prudery.

Hot friction.

A thousand kisses dispensed. That is what Pris wanted to plant.

Croissants in bed crumbling.

He knew all this, of course.

He'd flirted her into frenzy, into wet, into ruby, into engorgement, into . . .

Green banana leaves shrouded the flower waving in the wind.

I could fall in love with him, she thought.

It would probably end in heartbreak like they all have.

Once a man had said to Pris, "You need someone as big as you are."

"A big man."

At the time she thought he meant Italianate. He'd told her what it was like to make a woman come and come and come and that there was laughter all over it, leaping lines of laughter writ large all Lady Chatterley in the heath and flowers, flowers, flowers, skirts without panties, skirts catching the breeze, skirts lifting, fingers probing and then coming, coming all over him, all over his hand laughing at songs like "Born to be Wild", songs that summed up her generation in the halls of the mountain kings.

He'd said he was six foot three.

Bigger, is what Pris thought.

I can wear heels.

I can say all of a sudden that I can wear heels.

She imagined his thighs. She imagined his buttocks, her hands sliding around them as he pumped into her, over and over thrusting into the emptiness and sorrow of her untapped marriage.

The heels were sexy.

Pris stepped into them thinking swish.

Her hips.

The sashay of being twenty-eight again, as before.

His fingers finding plum, finding pearl, finding everything.

The red thrust of him, the slipping down and under and around, the ripeness of need, the sad consequences of marriages that hadn't worked the way they'd thought.

The non-love.

The banana flower.

It was singing a hymn overhead as Pris shot it over and over with her camera.

"Plum," it whispered.

Plumly engorged, wet between thighs, croissants crumbled. His hands all over her thighs, pulling her down, his lips covering territory. Over and over, the slow scroll across it, plum ripe, plum large, clitoral, banana rumble.

Multiples.

More than one. Pris was greedy for that.

He'd made her so wet with the talk of the dresses. The talk of dressing her. That he would choose. No man ever had, before. Chosen.

He made her so wet, thinking of his dresses, plum purple, his lips deciding, his lips directing, her body folding and laughing as sugar spun from her interior onto his tongue, licking over and over and fingering, her explosions into purple over and over and over, over him, falling back into the sheets laughing into karma as he lifted her legs and twisted them around his waist.

Plundering.

He lifted her to his lips a ripe berry, reddening.

He plunged inside her laughing and they talked for hours about books and poetry and she slid herself into the curve that his arm made as it wrapped itself around her.

"Again?"

She was laughing as she slid the rounded plum of him into her mouth.

"As long as we can really talk."

Words, words, words, he was breathing them into her ear, he was laughing up against her, laughing as he licked up her thighs and down them again, laughing as all of their tensions melted, as if the world was all right again, as if the two of them were in bed floating in a sea of desires that could all be accomplished slowly, by tongues.

It was a question of ripe.

It was a question of the fullness of the berry.

It was the cluster of bananas hanging ripely above her the day that Pris decided.

"Oh God," he cried, looking at her lips as they wrapped him. "Nobody has ever . . ."

"Nobody ever moved me as much as you," she whispered against it.

"So I want to."

His finger found it again.

"Berry in my stream."

"Yeats?"

"Maybe, but I'm not saying."

Berry, berry, berry red. Berry plump, berry hidden, berry lipped, berry full of water, berry in the stream called forth under fingers, called forth under tongue, berry that slips, sluicing.

Thighs, pounding.

Hands, encircling.

Pris looked up at the banana tree. Making up her mind was so damn easy.

"Come."

It was all he had to say.

"Come in the dresses I picked out for you."

Mad Ida Loved the Wind

Lily Lick

People still think they see Ida up on Vickery Hill, whenever there's some kind of wild weather. Think she's up there, naked to the rain and wind and thunder clapping like it's the devil's own road show. Up there, arms stretched out cross-like, wild tempest-blown yellow straw hair flyin', and getting bigger with each flash of lightning till she's bigger than the hill itself – bigger than life. I stopped tellin' them it weren't her, mostly 'cause they don't want to hear it. They want to think it's her. Gone missing and gone senseless 'cause thinkin' it means they were right all along, that the girl just didn't have a right brain – ever. To believe it gives 'em something to tattle about and to knock around over tea and whatever else they sip on of an afternoon, lips pursed like they've been asked to suck on something that fine ladies like them wouldn't admit to want doing . . . never mind do it. Gives 'em something to scare the kids with . . . maybe make 'em do right when threats of switchin' them won't work no more.

I know Ida's not there 'cause I seen her headin' right outta town the other way, running down the middle of the night road, dirty white feet slapping on hard pressed dirt, callin' to the wind and singing to the moon. I never told anyone that part though. They'd just go find her, bring her back, and lock her up again. And that's not gonna help anyone, least of all Ida.

If she told her story one time she told it a hundred times . . . never changed it neither, not once. Loved to tell it too just like everyone else likes to tell tales about their loved ones. "Mr Hollis," she'd say. "Did I tell you about my special friend? How we met? The Lord works in mysterious ways, Mr Hollis, and he delivers wonder if you just let him do his work in peace."

She always started that way. Called me Mr Hollis. My full name's Hollis Green, but she called me Mr Hollis, and talked to me just as if she was talkin' to them fancy white ladies at the country club, not an old field worker on her daddy's farm. Like I was her friend, like I knew what she was talkin' about. Nobody ever bothered that Ida used to seek me out to talk to, searching between the growing rows till she found me, 'cause they thought better me than them. They didn't have the time or the inclination and I didn't have the luxury of escaping where I was getting paid to be.

Ida'd been a strange child, no meat on her tiny bones, barefoot most times, dirt clogged up between her toes. They'd tried fancying her up with bows and lace and ribbon ties but she'd more'n likely just be half dressed and hair loose, perched up a tree looking down at everyone or running the rows like some wild child. When you can't control a young one, sometimes you just gotta let'm go and that's what her Ma & Pa ended up doing. She wasn't no real trouble, she was just different in a way that didn't bear explaining, 'cause there wasn't any explaining that'd do. Ida was just Ida.

Most people didn't like Ida, liked her less the more she grew. She scared them with her stories and smiles and off track ways; those highbrow club ladies sure hated her. She wasn't ever going to be one of them and without even trying she caught the eye of every man passing – righteous thoughts leaving them as fast as their heads turned, eyes following her – for this, the women hated her more.

"It was the barn door banging back and forth that woke me up, banging like it was calling my name."

She always laughed at that, a laugh that was half question, half answer. She'd look at me, head tilted, pale blue sky eyes sparkling and she'd bite that bottom lip just enough to make a man wonder if he's getting an invitation to something he surely can't have and that he'd better stop thinking about right quick.

"But that's just silly isn't it, Mr Hollis?" she'd ask me, and then carry on before I could say yes or no.

"Oh, it was just so strange. Such a dark night, but I went out to close that banging door anyway, and that old grey hoot owl that lives up in the barn just stared down at me from the roof with his saucer eyes like he was wondering what took me so long to get there. I latched the door and when I was heading back to the house the wind just grabbed me up from behind and blew me clear out into the field."

Ida said the wind wrapped 'round her and laid her face down and wouldn't let her up. Said the wind seemed to want something from her, blowing fury and fierce need on her neck and deafening her to everything but a roar of urgency that pulled at her very soul.

"There were small little gusts of wind blowing undone the ties of my nightgown, pulling it down from my shoulders and pushing it up over my thighs and exposing me vulnerable and open to the night air. I was nearly naked, Mr Hollis, and I couldn't move. That old wind just kept me right there. Pushing and pulling and filling me up."

The first time she told me this I admit I was a little concerned. Why tell me, and who heard her? Who was gonna believe anything about the why's of the telling and who was really telling who what? It took some realizing on my part that truth be told no one was gonna care or come near the two of us just happy as they were to not have to listen to her themselves.

So I always asked her – at about this point in her story – if surely she must not have been dreaming.

"Oh no, Mr Hollis," she'd say, all offended like. "This was as real as real is."

Then she'd relate in more words than I needed to hear about having her legs lifted and spread. Suspended there it seems by unseen hands. Head buried in the cool grass, ass up, legs cocked apart wide 'nough to make room for the mother of all storms. Now that would surely have been a sight and I would be lying if I were to say that it did not stir me in the telling. But it weren't right as addled as she was and I had to let it be.

"I was taken against my will. And it was not my first time, Mr Hollis. I let that Lester Purdue put his little pink thing in me a time or two. That boy's fingers were bigger, but I assure you of no more use, so I knew, I knew what it felt like to be entered. But this heat was in me everywhere, filling me up and blowing across every inch of skin I have. Hot and cold, hard and soft, and sneaky like, finding every avenue to get inside and fill me up.

And, Mr Hollis, I have never been fuller. I never reached my peak with Lester Purdue, Lord knows Lester did, but this wind just kept blowing at me everywhere and I could not help myself. Can you imagine that, Mr Hollis?"

And I could not, but Lord knows I had surely tried.

She'd spin round here, arms out and flying. Wild hair swinging in a knotted-up mess, a vision in white and dirty lace like an angel just swung down from heaven and lost on this solid earth.

Then she'd stop moving and start telling some more.

"Next thing I knew it was morning and I could hear you boys coming through the fields and I surely did not want to be found out there. But as soon as I got up on my hands and knees and looking for some place to hide, my Wind was back behind me, pushing in and riding me relentlessly. I simply could not move."

Ida'd told me her story a lot of times. Always the same, never changed a thing, and always ending it right there. "Wind's coming," she'd say, and turn with a little smile and a wink, like it was somehow our secret. She'd run off then, laughing, whispering, like she was goin' to be late for something somewhere if she stayed still where she stood any longer.

We were just headin' out early dawn, it was damp-like, mist laying next to the land, morning sounds muffled and low and we heard Ida before we seen her. Of course we didn't know it was her at first, but a man didn't need to have visited the whores on Canal Street too many times to know what brought on that sorta moaning and groaning. We were real surprised to find Ida over the rise, the big man's daughter; and more surprised to find she was there by herself.

She was facing us on her hands and knees, nightgown coiled like a dirty rope 'round her waist, naked but for that. Now, we were not all well grown men, some had never seen a woman in the altogether before, never mind a white woman, so we had a real good look-see just because we could. Ida was all pale skin and pink folds, yellow hair everywhere, and near covered in mud. Her ripe little peach tits were hanging down, nipples all hard and drippin' mornin' dew. She was rockin' back and forth, eyes shut, mouth open, legs spread and shaking. There was no doubt, and not a limp dick between the four of us, that this woman was comin', and comin' hard. It was windy in that low scoop of land. I sure didn't notice it much then, but thinking back, I recall that it was. Ida just kinda fell over then, and we stood there lookin' at her, lookin' at each other, our turn for mouths hangin' open.

She was dirty. She was smiling, eyes closed shut tight, and she smelled of powder and roses and sweat and earth. Her skin was hot enough to believe she was fevered. Her thighs were streaked and her pussy was flushed pink and puffed up and damp with use.

We decided we'd better get her back to the big house before anyone came along and suspected us of doing somethin' else. We didn't do nothing though, didn't touch her anymore than it took to unravel that dirty wet nightgown, torn now and mud-stained, cover her up as best we could, and cart her back home.

I sure don't know if she really was by herself out there but she kept on saying she wasn't, that she'd been with the wind; that the wind had taken her, and had loved her harder and better than a walking talking breathing man ever could. 'Cause she kept on with it people round about here decided that the devil'd found Ida out in that field. They went from tryin' to beat it outta her to just lockin' her up. Ida got smart though. Realized if she wanted to be out runnin' round she was gonna have to keep her mouth shut and her skirts down round her knees where they belonged. Nobody'd talk to her; most would cross the road just to get away from her. Afraid the devil might get into them just like he'd got into Ida. And I suppose that's why Ida'd come lookin' for me out in the fields as much as she did. Least I'd listen to her, sometimes just so's I could take a break from workin'. But listen I did.

"You don't think I'm crazy do you, Mr Hollis?"

"No Miss Ida, I do not," I'd say. Then she'd tell me her story, just like every time before that.

"I love the Wind, Mr Hollis. And the Wind loves me."

"I know he does, Miss Ida. Told me so himself just last night." That always made her smile.

Ida told me she was going to leave with the Wind one day, blow around the world with him and I didn't doubt one bit that she'd go on her way. I didn't doubt her one little bit.

I don't think her old pa ever got over the sight of his darlin' lily-white daughter being carried without a stitch of clothes on in the arms of four black men. He never did understand that they'd already been closer to Ida than they'd ever wanted or needed to be so he'd lock her up in her bedroom each night tryin' to keep something away from something. She'd make so much fuss tryin' to get outta her room in the big house, hollerin' for the wind to come get her and wakin' everyone up all the time, disturbing the folk that resided there that it soon came to be decided that it was better for them to stick her out where they couldn't hear her. He'd chase her down when the sun fell and lock her in till morning in this shed thing he'd had us build for her out back. He called it Ida's outside room like it was a special place anyone'd want to go to had they the chance.

But all that kickin' and shoutin' to get out'll soon wear down who's got to listen to it and that's how I know that's not her on Vickery Hill, 'cause I watched her go on down that road. I let her out one night. Unlocked that door, told her to come on out and locked the door up again like she'd just disappeared, like the devil'd stolen her right back.

I told her to go blow around the world.

"Thank you, Mr Hollis," she said. "The Wind thanks you."

"I'm sure he does, Miss Ida," I said. "I'm sure he does." And off she went. Never looked back not even once.

That was some years ago now. Long ago enough for Ida to become a bit of a story. Mad Ida they call her, say she hides up on the hill, scarin' folks every chance she gets.

They also say it ain't near as windy round here as it used to be.

Strange Fruit

Shanna Germain

Its round, red shape has enticed me in grocery stores and vegetarian magazines for as long as I can remember. And, once, I saw a sample split open in a health-food store, filled with beautiful, blood-red seeds, waiting impatiently for someone to pick them up, fondle them with a tongue, slowly suck out their juices. In the past, others have warned me against the fruits, mainly due to the difficulty of eating them. "It's more work than lobster, and doesn't taste half as good," cautioned one friend. "It's messy," said my husband.

But when I saw them piled high at the grocery store yesterday, I couldn't resist any longer. I wanted to know what it was like, to split open the thick skin, to have it erupt in my hand, to squeeze the seeds between my fingers and lick off the juice.

Grabbing one of the pomegranates, I ran to the nearest fruit assistant before I could change my mind. "How do I know if this is ripe?" I asked.

"Oh," she said, leading me back to the place where I'd chosen my new fruit. "It should be really red, and full and plump. Heavy almost, as though it might burst in your hand." She delicately picked through the fruits, gently squeezing each one with careful, practiced fingers. "Oh, this is good." She placed it in my hand. "See, how the skin is soft when you press it?" I felt its smooth, leathery surface, and the way it gave just a little beneath the pressure of my fingers. "Wow," I said, and she smiled back as though we shared a secret. "I know," she said. "Isn't it the most amazing thing?"

"What's the best way to eat it?"

"Oh," she said excitedly. "Here's my favorite way: you roll it between your hands, or on the counter, like you're rolling dough." She demonstrated, rolling one of the fruits between her palms. Then she held the fruit close to my ear. "Can you hear the seeds breaking open?" I nodded. "Once you hear that, you can make a slit in the skin and drink the juice right through it," she said. "After that, you just split it open and eat the rest of the seeds."

I wanted to ask her if she'd come home with me, to show me how it was done, to help me make sure I was doing it right, but all I could get out was a whispered thank you before I practically ran out of the grocery store, red fruit cradled in my palm.

At home, I placed it on the counter, its rotundness beckoning all day as I walked by it, made lunch, washed dishes. I could almost see it out of the corner of my eye, growing plumper by the hour. Finally, I couldn't stand it anymore . . . I picked it up and began rolling it between my fingers. Oh, the joy! With each turn, I could hear the seeds inside popping, like bubble wrap – Pip! Pip! Pip! I rolled it between my palms. I pressed it against the table. I thigh-mastered it between my legs, feeling its skin give under the pressure. Soon the popping ended and I knew that my little pomegranate was ready.

I cut a slit in the skin, and out poured the red juice, faster than I expected, splashing on the counter, across my face. It was sweet and tangy, and I felt like I couldn't get enough of it. When I was sure that I had drunk all that it contained, I split open the skin and scooped the seeds out with my fingers. They tasted much like the juice only they crunched in a way that made them even more satisfying. I was dazzled, delighted – I wanted to call every food-sex lover that I knew, I wanted to throw my husband down on the bed, I wanted . . . well, let's just say I wanted.

But I've decided to keep this as my own little secret. A fruit-masturbation if you will. A secret afternoon pleasure that makes me a little flush, that brings me back to the scent and feel of the earth, the joy of working my fingers against skin and juice for my own pleasure.

When my husband got home yesterday, he took one look at

the demolished fruit – "A pomegranate?" he asked, with a wrinkle in his nose.

"Yes, a pomegranate," I said as I walked toward him, holding out my red-stained fingers. "Want a taste?"

Miss Mercy

C. Sanchez-Garcia

"How does it feel, where you are?"

"It's OK. You keep it cool in here."

"Not this room. Don't be stupid."

"I don't understand then."

"Describe where you're sitting."

"Smells like medicine. Piss, a little bit."

"I just told you. Not here. I already told you what I want."

"So where?"

"Anywhere good. Nice. Someplace where you've been, with food that you liked. Someplace I wouldn't know."

"Wow, I don't know."

"I'm waiting. The clock is ticking. Don't cheat me."

"I'm thinking."

"Take a minute."

"OK. I was in Lyon, in France, OK? When I was in college, I was in France for this one summer."

"I've never been to France."

"OK, so France."

"You went to college. What were you going to be?"

"I don't know. Shit. Not this, I guess."

"I suppose so."

"Sorry. I guess I sound insulting."

"You're trying to be honest, I believe. That shows respect. You're doing all right."

"There was this café downstairs from the place I was staying."

"It's the food I want to hear about."

"Do you like French food?"

"Once."

"Sorry."

"You don't need to keep apologizing; it doesn't exactly suit your line of work. Just tell me where you're sitting over there in Lyon, in good old France."

"I'm sitting, now I'm sitting at a small table in the café. This table is round, and black, and the edges are scratched up with little white lines, and there's some little brown craters on the edge, that's where people parked their cigarettes without putting them out, and they burned along down the table."

"I like that. How does it smell?"

"There's a lot of water around because it just rained. Yes, that's right. So it smells like water."

"What does that smell like?"

"What does what?"

"What does rainwater smell like?"

"Oh. I guess it's . . . it's . . . hmm. Like. Dirt. A little. When it rains? And it hasn't rained a long time? Then the ground just opens up—"

"Like a woman, you might say."

"Yes, like a woman—"

"Mother Earth."

"Mother Earth. And you smell the dust smell rising up because it's just rained, and the air is fresh and clean for a little while and you can smell everything. And there's this bakery next door and they're baking bread. And the guy inside is making fresh coffee from this big espresso machine with little gold tubes and black knobs and a brass eagle on top. So I smell bread, and coffee and cigarettes because the table next to me, they're smoking these little black cigarettes, and the rain makes everything smell like fresh plowed earth."

"I can smell it. I want some coffee. Bring some coffee."

"Now I'm drinking coffee, the guy brought me some coffee in a little tapered white demitasse cup with a gold-painted rim, in a little saucer, and its kind of cute, like a toy cup and there's this thick brown foam on top of the coffee, and there's a tiny silver spoon next to it in the saucer."

"Coffee is a very sensuous thing. Drink your coffee for me."

"Would you like cream in the coffee?"

"Is it good espresso?"

"Yes. I think so, yes."

"Don't you dare put cream in my coffee. Just a spot of sugar. You have to drink espresso in a toss, in ten seconds, or it loses the correct taste. Did you know that?"

"No."

"How does the cup feel?"

"I lift the cup, and it's shiny with sunlight, and hard. The gilt line around the top has a little nick in it. And I sip the coffee."

"Yes? Yes?"

"It tastes good."

"No!"

"I don't know what you want from me! I'm sorry."

"It won't do! You're cheating."

"What do you want me to say? It's fucking coffee."

"Should I call the escort agency? Ask Miss Ursula to send another girl?"

"No, I can do this."

"Try again. Don't cheat this time."

"It tastes bitter—"

"No! You're cheating again."

"OK! Fuck. Wait. OK. I've got this. I lift the cup."

"The cup."

"I put the cup to my lips and the steam touches my nose at the same time my lips meet the coffee which I've put a little spoon of sugar in. I take a small sip, because I don't know how hot it might be, and the hot coffee washes back on my tongue and it hurts a little and I like it, I like the way it feels, and I take a little breath up through my nose and let the air into my mouth so I can really blow up the taste and get all of it in my senses."

"Keep going."

"It's the taste of smoke outside at night, burning wood, darkness, a bitter taste and the things that taste bitter are the things you go back to, coffee, beer, things that shouldn't taste good, but that's why you always go back to them, because they taste exactly as they are and they taste bitter, and you feel comfort, because the bitter makes me think of my mother's kitchen, and sitting

late at night with the radio on and talking and money and . . .
fuck . . ."

"Are you crying? I'm not able to see you from here."

"I'm OK."

"You sound bad. I'm not trying to make you cry."

"I know you're not."

"Let's go back. What are you having with your coffee?"

"I don't usually eat with coffee."

"This time you are."

"They had this cherry strudel."

"They? Think again."

"Right. Yes. The coffee fills my nose with smoke and bitter
dark, and there is this cherry strudel, and eating cherry strudel
with my coffee makes me feel like I'm rich. I have a fork, a silver
fork, and I press the side into the cherry strudel and a piece
comes off on the fork and I lift the strudel to my lips and put the
drippy warm strudel in my mouth. And it tastes like cherries."

"What do cherries taste like?"

"Wait. I have to get something from my purse."

"Hurry. I want my strudel."

"I got it, wait. I have to tear the foil. They make these things
hard to open."

"I can't turn my head. What is it?"

"Wait. I got it. It's open. They have this screwy little cartoon
strip inside that shows this cartoon dude unwrapping one and
putting it on his dick."

"May I see the package? Hold it up to me."

"Here."

"It's red, it looks like."

"Cherry-flavored. Am I cheating?"

"Oh. Oh I see. Go on."

"Wait. Mmmff! Yuck. Tastes like rubber and cherries. OK.
Cherry strudel. I'm tasting my piece of cherry strudel, and my
mouth waters at the taste, as if running to meet it. The sweetness
is sharp-edged and smooth and soft, with crusty crinkles and
the cherry gives me a high acidy taste at the sides of my mouth,
and the cherries burst into hot little globules of sugar, and it
tastes like a candy sucker at the dentist's office when I've been a
good little girl."

"That's fine. That's enough."

"How'd I do?"

"Thank you, miss. With all my heart. I'll tell the agency I'm very pleased with you. In the drawer of the nightstand there, behind the pill box there's a small brown envelope with two hundred dollars in twenties. Take it for yourself. Just between us. A little tip."

"I want something else."

"What can I offer you?"

"I've given you a taste of coffee and pie again. Give me a taste."

"What of?"

"Car crash."

"I see."

"My mother."

"You don't have to talk about her, not if it hurts you."

"Hurts me? That's funny."

"I mean it."

"What's it like when it happens?"

"I'm listening to the radio, I'm thinking about my lunch and what I would like to eat and where I would like to eat. There is a small restaurant with espresso coffee served in real cups and some excellent cherry strudel. That is what I'm thinking of when I look up at my rear-view mirror, as I'm waiting for the light to change. I see a huge engine grille flying towards me and there's a ridiculous little metal dog on the top and the word 'Mack'."

"Were you scared?"

"Not really, no, I never was. There's no time. There was just the grille, and a kind of rudeness, like being pushed very hard in a crowd, and then something rather soft spreading over my head and bright flashing sparkles passing by, which are tiny pieces of tinted glass that had been my sunglasses but are now being pushed inside my skin, and there is cold air and rain on my face and a buzzing in my head and a great emptiness and silence and everything seems kind of silly and embarrassing and sad. I feel exposed just laying bunched up against the curb and not moving, like I should be doing something responsible, maybe directing traffic or some such thing. And then I'm in a bed and I don't remember. Is it enough?"

"Were you scared?"

"Why do you keep asking?"

"I want to know if my mother would have been scared."

"There was this moment, I kept fading in and out, and once I touched my teeth with my tongue and they weren't there anymore and for a moment I had this idea I should get up and look for them. Then I felt a little scared I think, because it was a strange thing laying in the street and not having teeth. Then I don't remember. I remember people standing over me. Then I don't remember again. You're only scared if you think too much and when it happens to you, it's very hard to think."

"Do you think my mother was scared?"

"I wouldn't know. Did she die quickly?"

"They say she did."

"Then she was probably all right. Does any of this make you feel better?"

"Not that much. You?"

"It makes me more sad, remembering how it is to sit in the sun with good coffee. But I don't mind being sad."

"I do. Truth doesn't set you free, does it? That's just bullshit they tell you, isn't it?"

"Maybe the truth sets you free after it's done fucking with you."

"Should I get dressed?"

"I'm going to rest now, I suppose. Before you put your clothes back on, please come stand beside me."

"All right, I'm over here now. Look up at me. Can you see me OK? Should I turn on another light?"

"No. Just stay there a moment. You look so fine that way. You're very fine. What a fine young woman you are. I'm imagining you that way on a nice bed. The window light on your breasts, your nipples are just marvelous."

"Hey, you. How do I taste?"

"Your cunt would taste salty and it would remind me of hot green tea, and the secret hair would smell of mammalian sweat and female steam. Would you mind, could you just touch my lips, please? You don't have to do anything else."

"Can I kiss you instead? Wait, let me get in close . . . did you feel that?"

"My heart is shaking. I never hoped to feel that again."

"Fair enough?"

"Thank you. Fair enough."

Cleft and Wedge

Jacqueline Brocker

It was a warm autumn night, pints of cider before them, and the Scudamore's punts resting side by side and bobbing in the water in front of the Anchor pub. In Sophie's line of sight was the weir that separated the different levels of the River Cam. Above it, Cambridge students and locals cycled past, either heading into town, or southward down the path along the banks of the Cam towards Grantchester. A pleasant evening in the graceful university town, and she was fidgeting, having just told Malcolm in what she hoped was the gentlest, least offensive way that she didn't think this was going to work any more.

Opposite Sophie, Malcolm sat with his hands clasped, frowning. He wore a tweed jacket, blue collared shirt and navy chinos. With his glasses and his close-cropped hair, he was the perfect picture of the young Cambridge historian.

He said, after a long pause, "Is it the age gap?"

Ten years wasn't insignificant, but her twenty-three and his thirty-three had never felt an issue.

"It's not that. You're lovely, so lovely . . ."

But as she tried to reassure him how much she liked him, she knew that was the problem. He was so nice, so sweet that she just couldn't imagine him taking her to bed, or doing anything beyond cradling her head and stroking her hair.

From their qualifications, Sophie and Malcolm should have worked – she about to embark on a PhD in eighteenth-century literature, his era of study though mostly politics. They could talk easily, and he was very kind to her.

There was a heavy "however". Three years of undergraduate study, about to be added to with a likely four for her PhD, had been the intensely fun, wildly stressful and deeply fulfilling Cambridge education she had hoped for. Not just her lectures and supervisions either; the theatres dotting the city, the concerts in college chapels, Shakespeare in the gardens in summer, all had filled her head with the high-minded intellectual and cultural experience she'd so badly wanted when she left her South London home to go there.

Yet something lacked. Her last really good orgasm had been in the infamous "fuck a fresher" week in her first year. A cliché, she knew, but the third-year student had been persuasive (and sexy). That pure absence of thought, just giving herself to bodily exuberance, stayed with her. And after two polite and proper boyfriends her own age, both of whom came with stifled grunts (had they gone to the same school to learn that? she wondered) Sophie wasn't sure if she could take more of that from Malcolm, who had only chastely kissed her twice.

Sophie took a deep breath. "I think I need someone who's more . . ." She searched for the best word that would describe what she meant without offending him.

Malcolm supplied it. "Manly."

He said the word with lingering sadness, like he'd heard that before. Sophie hadn't anticipated that. She started to deny it, but he shook his head.

"No, I understand. You don't have to explain." He reached across the table, and took her hand in his, and brushed his thumb over her knuckles. "Let's finish our drinks, walk along the Backs, and leave it at that."

Sophie said that would be fine, though his sweet acquiescence to the break-up made irritation bubble through her like the water spilling down from the weir. She swallowed more of her cider, and thought, Yes, that would be nice. So very *nice*.

When they were done, they crossed the river over the Silver Street bridge. They veered off down the path that skirted behind Queen's College that marked the start of the Backs, the green tracts of land that were divided from their respective colleges by the Cam. In the day, it was the perfect spot for tourists to take pictures – King's College Chapel being especially notable – while at night, the dark shapes of the old college buildings loomed beyond the banks indistinguishable from each other.

The night air chilled her – silly her for wearing a flimsy cotton dress – but she suppressed her shivers, because she knew Malcolm would offer her the tweed jacket for her shoulders, and she couldn't accept that now.

At the back entrance to Clare College, Sophie leaned up to kiss Malcolm goodbye, to head back to the next entrance, her college, Trinity, when Malcolm grasped her arm.

"Come back through Clare? It's a nice night, and just as easy to get back to Trinity."

Sophie hesitated, but Malcolm's gentle imploring face convinced her.

She stayed apart from him as they set off down the dark path that crossed the Backs. The trees that lined it seemed welcoming in the day, but now loomed like brooding sentinels watching her and Malcolm's passage. Sophie had to use her wits not to lean against him for safety. From what though? There was no one but them around.

She breathed again when they emerged from the path onto Clare Bridge.

Clare Bridge was the oldest in the city, and to Sophie's mind, prettier than St John's more famous Bridge of Sighs. Clare Bridge has an elegant slope to it and, of course, the series of spheres that sit on top of both sides.

Malcolm paused, staring southwards down the river. Sophie joined him. To their left, King's College Chapel pointed and erect. Beneath them, the Cam ran very straight along the man-made sides. The water was black, gleaming as much as the lack of moonlight let it. No sound but the water lapping, the punts packed away for the night.

"You know about the missing wedge in this sphere?"

Sophie turned to see Malcolm's hand resting on the sphere. The second from the west-lying bank.

She grinned slyly. "You going to tell me about the angry stone masons who left it unfinished because the college couldn't pay them?" It was Cambridge apocrypha. The wedge was real, but the truth of how it happened had been lost.

"No. That story's bullshit anyway."

Sophie barked out a laugh. Malcolm had never sworn in front of her.

He stood to one side, arm out in invitation. "Have you felt it before?"

She hadn't actually.

"Stand here. Wrap your hands around it."

Puzzled but curious, Sophie did so, Malcolm moving behind her and guiding her hands so she could feel both sides of the wedge. The smooth roughness of the old stone was cold. Her fingers slid further around the edge, and she was aware of the emptiness of the space, the gap where something substantial was missing.

She smirked. Like hers and Malcolm's relationship.

She stopped smirking though when Malcolm's hands trailed down her bare arms, along her sides, where they indiscreetly brushed the curve of her breasts, before coming to rest on her hips.

Sophie shivered, and her body became taut. "Malcolm." Her hands started to leave the sphere.

"Hold on to it." His voice was low and commanding, and his clutch on her hips tight. This was new. Sophie stilled, and kept her grip. "Lean back a little." She did, her bum rising a little as she stretched her arms. "That's it. Doesn't it feel like you're separating something?"

He was right, it did. Like if she pulled hard enough, she could divide the sphere in twain. She nodded.

"Much like—" his hands glided over her bum, her skin warming under the thin cotton, until he reached the spot where her cheeks met "—spreading someone's arse."

Sophie gasped, and squirmed when her underwear resisted the separation. With three swift motions, Malcolm lifted her skirt, tugged down her knickers, and spread her cheeks so wide that her hole and labia began to open too.

The shock of the cold air on her skin, the sense of exposure and the sudden appearance of Malcolm's sexuality, sent red heat all through Sophie. Malcolm began kneading her buttocks, and working his way deeper between her cheeks.

"Christ, how much I've wanted to fuck you up the arse."

"Malcolm!" She wasn't protesting his revelation, because *God* he sounded sexy. "Someone might come past."

"Don't worry." His fingers found, not her hole, but the light fur of her labia and, as they began to stroke it, he leaned forward and said in her ear, "I'm not going to do that to you. *Now*. But you're very wet." To her surprise, and searing arousal, one finger parted her lips and released a drop of stickiness. "So . . . let's try a little fingering."

She'd never expected him to say "fingering".

A second finger joined the first, reaching in and pressing down, finding the G-spot inside her so fast her body jerked. She gripped the sphere for balance, and had to bite her lip when Malcolm began crooking his fingertips inside her. She swallowed her whimpers when his thumb found her clit, and discovered quickly that she liked it thrummed up and down.

While Malcolm held her in that grip of pleasure, Sophie's awareness of her surroundings increased ten-fold: the lapping of the river, the wind rustling through the trees. The sphere before her expanded like a heavy balloon, and the stone path of the bridge where her gaze fell wanted to rise up and meet her. Her body was humming with fear and twisted delight of being caught, with arousal as her juices streamed down her inner thighs and over Malcolm's hand. She kept her mouth closed, refusing to scream into the Cambridge night and disturb the genteel peace.

When orgasm burst through her, her mouth remained shut, but she was sure her whimpering was like a sonic boom. She grabbed the sphere so tight her knuckles threatened to snap, and her knees would have been jelly if Malcolm hadn't held her.

Malcolm carefully withdrew, pulled up Sophie's knickers, and let her dress flutter back over her bum and legs. Sophie let go of the wedge, only just finding the strength to turn to Malcolm. A new gleam was in his eye, a darkly sexual edge that Sophie would have begged to keep rather than push away so softly as she'd done just an hour before.

"Well." He urged her back to the sphere, and his cock pressed against her slippery knickers. "If I'd have known you were a naughty girl who wanted to be fucked, I'd have done that long ago."

He kissed her, a little roughly, but she melted into his mouth as his fingers dug back into her arse cheeks, and he began telling her just where he wanted to put his dick in her, and in what way. Sophie decided, later that night, after he'd penetrated her in all three holes, and made her come twice more, that perhaps this relationship had a future after all.

They Plan Brunch

Bill Noble

Des wasn't the sort of woman you said no to.

"Sunday at ten, right?"

"You bet!" he said brightly, hoping she couldn't hear his heart hammering over the phone. Maybe they were too perfectly matched; he'd never met a woman with such a ferocious libido. For weeks they'd upped the ante every time they'd met or talked, intensifying every encounter, going all out. It had become a contest.

"Well?" she said.

"Well what?" he answered, knowing exactly what she meant.

"What do you want to do?"

He shifted his straining cock to a more comfortable position. "Brunch?" he said, knowing evasion wouldn't buy him any time.

"Bill."

"OK, OK. Wear that flowered dress. The silk one?" He tried to breathe deeply. "And no panties." He imagined his hand ghosting up the silk skin of her thigh, all the way to the hip, all the way to the constriction of the belt across her smooth belly. His fingers tingled with her heat. Possibilities started building in his head, replacing his apprehension.

"That's better," she said. "What else?"

"You . . . you really will do anything I say?"

She was silent, waiting him out. He knew the grin: her mouth in a wry tilt, her pale eyes dancing.

He spoke. "You know that little café in the courtyard on Magnolia? The one with the tablecloths that drape right to the floor?" His hand was shaking as he brushed hair back from his forehead.

She stayed silent, but he heard her breath quicken.

"So . . . get there just at ten. You won't be late?"

Silence. She wasn't going to help him out.

"Sit at the back table, in the little alcove that looks out over the marsh." His words were starting to come in a rush now, and his cock ached. "Get crepes – lingonberry crepes. Two orders. And some really dry white wine. Uh, and when I come in, when I'm still by the door, you know, when the waitress is looking in my direction . . . slip under the table." He gulped for air.

"A blow job," she breathed. Her voice had dropped half an octave.

"Hardly," he said. *God, am I really sure I want this? I know she's brave enough to do it.*

"Then what?" A tremor of alarm.

"Des," he said. "Lick your finger." He'd gotten the edge over her now. He could feel it.

"Under the table?"

"No, right now."

"I'm in my office. Felicia's right across from me." She was whispering into the phone.

"Well, we could always put it off a week."

Another long silence, but this one with a different flavor. "OK," she said. He could tell she'd slipped a hand between her legs, just from the wobbly way the two syllables came out.

"Touch yourself," he said, running his nails the length of his cock. "And no, not a blow job. You're going to fuck me. Fuck me, right under the table."

"No way." He thought he could catch the tiny sounds of her wetness behind the jump of fright.

"Oh, yes," he told her, feeling more in charge every minute. "I slide forward on the seat, like I'm going to kneel on the floor. You raise your ass up and back into me. You're wet already."

"Ah," she said. He could barely hear her. "Under the table?"

"Under the table and right now. But there, I stuff my cock into you and smile at the waitress. I bet it's the freckled one. You know, the one with the wide hips you always lust after? She smiles back at me as she serves sausages and pancakes to the next table. Know why?"

"Uh-huh." A whisper.

"Tell me."

"She knows what I'm doing." Des was the one struggling to breathe now. The last word trailed away, out of breath.

"You're doing all the moving," he said. "I hold perfectly still, make sure you don't knock the dishes off the table. Are you getting ready to come?"

"Uh, under the table?"

It was his turn to play silent.

"Yes," she said. "I am," she pled, in the tiniest voice. Each sharp breath ended in a mew that only the two of them could hear. He heard her wetness more distinctly, heard the pace of her fingers.

"But there's one thing you need to know." His cock was out and he was pumping in time with her finger.

"Aah?"

"Sunday, when you get right to the edge of coming?"

"Auh?"

"I pull out."

She took three stuttering, harsh breaths without letting any air out.

"And you turn around and tuck me back in my pants, and then sit back up at the table. Like nothing happened."

A long, high, suppressed sound came out of the phone. He heard her teeth clack hard against the receiver as she almost dropped the phone. A distant voice said, "Des, are you OK?" He imagined – no, he felt – her puss clamp down. His vision went black as his seed spurted into his hand, pulse after pulse, emptying him.

Their breathing rasped in and out of sync as they came down from it. His cock, slippery and spent, rested on the heel of his hand. His come spilled between his fingers, spattering the floor.

"I'm fine," he heard Des say to someone, "just something caught in my throat." She didn't sound as if she expected anyone to believe her. "Bill?" she whispered into the phone.

"Yeah?" All the power he'd summoned was leaking away, but he didn't care.

"Lick it out of your hand!" she whispered. "Drink your come! Taste it! It tastes like both of us."

He raised his cupped, shaking hand to his mouth. He did. It did.

Sunday was only two days away.

Fast Burn

Kristina Lloyd

We weren't Romeo and Juliet, not by a long shot. Too old, for starters, and I'd like to think too sensible but lust can make a fool of anyone. I might have called it love if I'd been younger.

He made me nervous from the off. "Carolyn," he called. "Come here. Is that your name?"

He was standing behind the poky bar in his stained chef's whites, slouching, tapping the edge of a beer mat on the counter. I took him in with a glance: big guns, tattoos, short unruly hair, a crooked smile and stubble on his jaw like demerara sugar.

"Who are you?" he asked, giving a quick tip of his chin. "Not seen you in here before."

"I'm with Mike and his mates." I gestured over my shoulder to our boisterous birthday crowd milling around by a column plastered with posters.

"Yeah, I know Mike." He stood up straight, walked away and hollered into the kitchen. "It's fucking béchamel, you knob!" Back again, beer mat going tap, tap, tap, eyes fixed on me. At the base of his thumb was a raw, ragged burn mark.

"Shouldn't you have a covering on that?" I said.

He shrugged. "I burn easily."

That made me laugh. Later, I understood what he meant.

He clocked off at ten. He was wearing a faded black tee saying "Just one more level". Ah, a gamer. Good hand-to-eye coordination. Always useful. He came up to me, gripped my elbow and whispered, "I fucking hate it in here. Come on, come somewhere else with me. That place round the corner, the Star. Or anywhere. I want to talk to you."

"I can't, it's Mike's birthday."

That shrug again. "He'll have another one."

Birthdays make you remember there's no guarantee of that so I followed him out. *Carpe diem* and all.

He was carrying a massive rucksack, the type you'd take traveling.

"What's in your bag?" I asked.

"My life. I travel light. What about you?"

"Lipstick, Tampax, money," I said. "Tissues. Weird balls of fluff."

We were walking up a steep, quiet side street, backs of apartment blocks to our right, to our left a low wall overlooking the train track, the lights of the city spreading far and wide as if a galaxy had dropped to earth. Between us was an implicit understanding we would fuck that night. Go for a drink, I thought, get to know each other, take him home, see what happens.

"Let's go up here," he said, gesturing to a concrete dead end. "I want you. Soon as I saw you, I wanted you."

"Jeez," I said. "Aren't you even going to try and romance me?"

"You don't look the sort."

"Is that a compliment or an insult?"

"Compliment," he said, pulling me off the street. "Come on."

"I only live ten minutes away!"

"We'll go there after," he said. "But now. This is where it happens. You've got to act on now."

His idealism made me giddy. "OK then."

The dead end was a concrete-walled L-shape, a neat row of communal bins along one side and on the other, a smashed TV and a large piece of MDF propped against the wall. In the toe of the L, we couldn't be seen from the road although we'd have been fair game for anyone peering out from a window in the surrounding flats.

He unhooked his rucksack from his shoulder and nodded at the wall. "Put your hands there," he said.

His instruction made my knees go spongy. I faced the wall, palms pressed to the concrete, and waited. I felt as if I were about to get a pat-down. When I looked up, I saw a night sky streaked with purple-grey clouds. Looking down, I saw my sandal-shod feet, toenails painted blue, and behind them his shabby trainers moving into position. He ran his hands down my body, lifted my skirt and unzipped. He penetrated me with a high, hard jolt. My gasp sounded loud in our quiet alcove and his breath by my ear was huffy and fast. For the next few minutes, all I saw was sky, wall, shoes; sky, wall, shoes; and I didn't know where I was most located. When I came, I was definitely up there with the sky, flying towards the cloud-smudged moon. When he came, he withdrew and he was all around our shoes, shimmering in soft, peaceful splashes.

We didn't kiss until we got back to mine, a studio flat so all living spaces merge into one. He was hungry so he rummaged in my fridge and pan-fried a tuna steak, which we shared along with a salad doused in a dressing spiked with pepper and lime. We ate naked on the bed and it was one of the best meals I've ever tasted. For dessert, we had each other, and didn't sleep until gone 4 a.m.

He asked to call round the following night after his shift had finished and we went crazy for each other for a week. Fucking, cooking, talking. Early on, I told him I liked being tied up and dominated. He was more than happy to oblige. Midweek, I heard from someone else he was now referring to me as his girlfriend. The big rucksack he carried everywhere got smaller as he began to leave stuff at my place, knowing he could collect it the following night. I found myself adding a couple of his T-shirts to my laundry. Worse, I ironed them afterwards.

We never went to his place because he didn't have one. He was staying with a friend four miles away. On the sixth and seventh night, we didn't even fuck. We were too exhausted. On the eighth night, I said I needed a break, just a couple of evenings off. This was getting too intense and we were in danger of neglecting our own lives.

"Are you seeing someone else?" he asked.

"Like I have the time!" I exclaimed, only half joking.

"What's that meant to mean?" He sat up in bed, bashed the pillows into shape then leant against them with his arms folded. "If you had the time, would you? Is there someone you'd rather be seeing?"

"Not rather, no. I've told you about Craig in Coventry. Whenever he's in London, we get together. If there was anyone else apart from that, I'd have told you."

He bit the skin at the corner of his thumb. "I don't want you to see Craig anymore. I don't like sharing."

I rolled away from him. I needed a new ceiling light. "And I don't like being told what to do."

"Oh, come on," he scoffed. "You get off on it. I've seen how it makes you cream."

"Fuck you! You can't use my kink against me." I sprang up, wrapped myself in a blanket, and sat on the duvet at the foot of the bed. "My sexuality isn't my life, you dumbfuck. If you don't understand that basic distinction, we're heading nowhere fast."

He got up and tugged on his jeans. "At this rate, we're heading there anyway."

"Well, that's probably for the best," I snapped. "If you want a fucking slave, go find one. And good luck to you."

Three days later, he turned up with all his baggage, and I don't mean the rucksack. "I'm forty-seven," he said. (He'd told me he was forty-one and he could have passed.) "I have six children from four different relationships. I separated from my partner a few months ago. At the end of the year, I'm going to be a grandfather for the second time. I have no money to call my own. I come on too strong and I scare women away. I crave security but . . ." He shrugged. "I don't seem able to offer it."

I said nothing as he spoke but I was thinking, You don't want a partner, you want a mother, someone who'll cocoon you and pander to your needs.

When we had sex later that night, I had flashbacks to our first time in the dead end: sky, wall, shoes. He was trying his best to please me, an attitude that worked well with the anger and resentment bubbling under his surface. He roped my arms behind my back, tied them to my ankles and licked me till I came. He released my legs and fucked me from behind. Then he changed ends and pulled my head onto his cock, forcing me to take his length. He made me crawl across the floor then had me lie over a footstool, my head touching the floor. He tethered my wrists and ankles to the stool's little legs, eased a butt plug inside me and told me not to move. He sat leaning against a wall, cracked open a beer, and watched me. I was in a haze of desire, seeing him upside down. He looked so beautiful and lost that I thought it might be worth my while to try and save him. But you can't save anyone except yourself, and you can't trust your reasoning when your head's the wrong way up and you've got a butt plug in your ass.

For three hours, he used me like a thing which existed solely for his needs, leaving me smeared in saliva, sweat and come, bruises forming under my skin. It was the best sex we'd ever had, in part because all I could see in my mind's eye was wall, wall, wall.

We were done; we were over. The wall was insurmountable, thick enough to stop a fire in its tracks, even one that burnt so fast it wanted to consume everything.

The Blonde in the Caffé Cavour

Maxim Jakubowski

1- She sends me a photograph in the mail.

Together with her book.

A collection of her short stories.

Published in Florence.

Her bare back on Kodak glossy art paper.

A yellow glow illuminates her skin, her hair, a darker shade of blonde breaking across the top of her shoulders like a wave on an unknown shore. I think she is looking out of a window. That's where the light is coming from.

Right now, I desire her. Intensely.

I have unreasonable appetites. I languish for the past and all those women, luminous, wonderfully obscene, distant and no longer available, impossible. I dream at night of their vanishing embraces, my heart beats a melancholy rhythm for them all, sad in the knowledge none will ever be part of my life again. So instead, greedy for more than just memories I daydream of the future, of the roads still to be taken, of the life still to be lived.

Who cares about the present?

It's too ordinary, so much less glamorous than the republic of dreams.

2- She is blonde and a frequent night bird at the Caffé Cavour. Here she whiles away the hours of southern nights discussing The Clash, punk attitudes, the many shades of noir and drinking Russian vodka and local wine. The debates can sometimes be fierce and there are times when the barman thinks tempers are heating up just that little bit too much and is just a word away from demanding silence. But somehow they sense his irritation and the flow of words abates naturally, and they move on to another subject to ping-pong between their fevered minds, whether Chet Baker's *Almost Blue* is better than Elvis Costello's or even Italian crime writer Carlo Lucarelli's novel partly inspired by the song. She mostly wears black, a short dress that reaches to her knees or black jeans that mould her delicate rear. Her photograph gives no indication of her height, but I guess she isn't especially tall. Call it intuition. Her nose is sharp, angular.

3- Her ex (they lived together five years) is an actor and travels all over Italy for his work. She pines for him. Badly. Which is possibly why she recognizes the same notes of pain in my stories and identifies with the profound sense of yearning I just can't ever shake off, hard as I try. What is this: a mirror image of me? Hell, I'm no blonde; my hair has almost turned grey since she-who-must-not-be-mentioned-any-more, even. But it's like a hesitation waltz of the damaged as we exchange emails, letters, books, song lyrics and music in quick succession after our initial contact. I follow her online diary, her blog, like a furtive spy, gleaning information, hints, ideas.

For what purpose really? Maybe the fascination and the implied unknown promises of the unknown.

I wonder what I should do next.

Should I ask her for her telephone number? If the answer is yes, go to paragraph 5. If the answer is no, go to paragraph 4.

4- We keep on corresponding in a friendly manner, one writer to another, endlessly moaning about the pain every word drains in its wake, as you seek to find the right one to express emotion, feeling, reality. It never gets easier even with thousands of pages or more to your credit. You'd think it would, wouldn't you? But she lives much too far and anyway, reading between the lines of her online diary, she now appears to be living with another man, so any progress down this particular road is fraught with problems, effort, dangers. Oh, the sheer futility of it all . . .

So I fly to New York and meet up with the Swiss-Spanish academic who believes in the Kabbalah and astrological signs. Her hair falls down over her shoulders and her breasts are heavy and heavenly. Her skin smells of strawberries and she closes her eyes when we make love. Pretending I am another? Two can play that game . . .

The sex is wet, but hollow and by the moment I come I already know there will not be a second time with Pilar, whatever her own feelings and desires. She is not what I ultimately seek. But then I don't even know myself what I am questing for, do I?

I return to London. Autumn is flaring and the cold chills my bones so accustomed to the extended heat of the past summer. An editor in New Orleans is asking me for a new short story. About an erotic woman. I am lost for words, for inspiration. Isn't every single woman erotic?

Am I really a man with no discrimination?

I write a vignette which is also a fantasy about the blonde sitting at the Caffè Cavour.

Do I send the blonde a copy of the story? If the answer is yes, go to paragraph 6. If the answer is no, go to paragraph 8.

5- Her voice is like a song. With an Italian accent, of course. But a song with strong undercurrents of melancholy. Damaged people, those of us who have been through the heart wars, uncannily recognize each other. She tells me all about the sea coast outside the town where she lives and has grown up. Her tone reduces to a whisper when she describes the man she lived with for so long and whose intensity just could not match hers, and in a forlorn attempt to console her I lapse into the most abominable clichés of empathy.

I tell her about my own travels and evoke the rain falling on Canal Street and the way the pavement is dry within five minutes due to the tropical atmosphere. I talk of Greenwich Village and the mad way I, on trips to Manhattan, organize my film viewing like a military exercise to maximize the number of movies I can fit into the visit while wasting as little time as possible between performances and theatres.

She laughs.

Does the blonde respond to him? If the answer is yes, go to paragraph 7. If the answer is no, go to paragraph 4.

6- Her acknowledgement of my story is days in coming, during which time I log on twice an hour to check my emails, anxious for her reaction. I also shamelessly spy on her diary but there is no reference to me or her mood, just erotic thoughts on the vampire myth or music she has been listening to. My knowledge of Italian rock music is poor.

Finally, she responds. Her attitude is cool and remote. I realize I have moved too fast, betrayed her confidence. She doesn't say so but I can interpret her silences. From someone she once admired from afar, I have just become yet another cyber stalker. I have cannibalized her life without her express approval.

Our communications slow down and, one day, just stop. Just another missed connection.

I move on to my next fantasy.

7- She suggests we maybe should meet, somewhere, one day.

Now the complications begin.

Should it be Paris or maybe Vancouver? We must find neutral ground.

For wish fulfilment go to paragraph 9.

8- I am a coward and I shelve the story. Write another one which has unbearably descriptive sex scenes, guns, drugs and rock 'n' roll and in which every female character is a brunette and has a heart of ice. The protagonists race across the world from American highways to late-night bars near the Sicilian coast and leave a path of bloody destruction in their wake. The story is full of sound and fury but of course means nothing. It is a pure work of my imagination at its most commonplace and clichéd. The principal heroine is eroticism incarnate, with porcelain skin, lips that are made for kissing and sports the obligatory shaven pudenda, and her shapely arse as observed from the rear evokes nothing less than Nicole Kidman's in the opening sequence of *Eyes Wide Shut*. But despite those inherent attractions, it is a tired story and I know it. Crime and sensuality by numbers.

9- As ever, it's a hotel room, stuffy and overheated when they arrive and before he switches one of the radiators off.

He craves the feel of his fingers caressing her pale shoulders, the sensation of his fingers combing through her short blonde hair as a pockmarked moon ascends into the sky outside the window.

This is a moment like no other.

Decisions have been taken. Both parties have resolved to go through with this. But he doesn't want it to ever end. Sure, he wants to undress her with all the agonizing slowness he can conjure up until she is finally fully nude, innocent, helpless, arrogant, so totally exposed to his prying gaze. But what of the smell of her body, the fragrance of her fear, her sweat? He cannot know them. Will her breath still carry the combined echoes of stale cigarettes and vodka? Will her skin remind him of rough silk? What of her breasts (B cup, he estimates), what of her cunt?

Will she ever be a vulnerable body in an anonymous hotel room in another city, another land, another time and life?

Every road in his past has been leading him here, every junction and side road ignored, like abandoned branches on a tree with a million ramifications. The worlds of what-if magnified to the nth power.

As much as he tries to imagine the moment, he just cannot guess what her first words will be, how she will sigh and moan when he touches her. She is just another blonde in a universe of women he cannot know, and he sadly realizes the sheer obscenity of his imagination as it illegally brought her to this room in this city and land. Shame on me, he thinks.

He closes his eyes and keeps on typing, ever a slave to the tyranny of words.

10- The blonde turns her gaze away from her laptop screen. She sighs. For a moment, she is still entrapped in the story she is writing. She is still, flesh and blood, the incarnation of both her female characters in their doomed odyssey. She looks up to the window. A moonless night. She feels like a beer. But she would rather go out and have it at a nearby bar. And maybe a Chinese meal. That would be a treat.

Her life, she senses, is at a crossroad.

Somehow her mind keeps going back to that book she read the other week, about the landscape after the battle, the life one is left with after the emotions have taken their bloody toll. She wonders about the character. She just knows the English writer had based her on a real person. It was unmistakable. She goes online and calls up a search engine and enters his name.

There: an email address.

Maybe she should write and ask him what happened to the woman in question?

She smiles. No, why would he respond?

What the hell, she goes on typing, the beer and the Chinese meal can surely wait.

I've Got a New Boyfriend

April Lamb

I've got a new boyfriend. I just want you to know that. I've got a new boyfriend, so when I show up at your apartment at ten o'clock at night it doesn't mean I want to get back together. Yeah, I'm a little drunk and a little high and I'm sort of feeling goofy after a long talk with my friend Melissa who lives kind of nearby to you. She and I got pretty tight and by then it seemed like a really good idea to call you.

At ten o'clock at night, when I'm drunk and not wearing underwear.

It means I know you're a nasty enough bastard to make a pass at me. And if you don't, I know I'll get up the nerve to make a pass at you. Because you won't say no.

But it doesn't mean I want to get back together.

I mean, what kind of an idiot would want to get back together with you? You cheated on me. Yeah, you *say* it's not really cheating – I've heard your side of the story. I don't care. Ask any woman, she'll tell you: *cybersex is cheating*. OK, so maybe you don't know about the two guys I fooled around with while you and I were together. I hope none of our friends have been dumb enough to tell you . . . even though basically all of them know I fucked around on you.

But you don't know that, and I won't tell you.

So don't bullshit me that cybersex really isn't cheating. I know if we had that discussion and if you knew about Gary and Greg and Bruce, we'd have to have a fight about whether giving head is more cheating than cybersex is. Because if you *did* know about Gary and Greg and Bruce, I'd tell you that's all I did with them.

It's not . . . but if you found out, that's what I'd tell you.

I mean, you'd never know I went all the way with all three of them anyway, even if one of my shithead friends spilled the beans. Giving them head while you and I were together is all I ever admitted to, even to Melissa.

I mean, I'm not saying I cheated, because you don't know about it.

But I'm saying that you *did* cheat – because I know about that. Jacking off to that girl in fucking *Kansas* who sent you fucking *pictures* of her fucking *tits*? I don't *care* if she was still wearing a bra, you could see right fucking through it.

I mean, how long would it have been until you met in person, huh? Don't try to deny it.

After you betrayed me like that, I'd never even consider getting back together with you.

So when I show up at your apartment it doesn't mean I want to get back together.

It means I wanna *fuck*.

It doesn't take long for us to get there.

From the second I'm in the door, you're a dick to me. You're irritated that I called and asked if you wanted to hang out. "What the fuck?" you ask me. "Hang out at ten o'clock at night?"

I laugh. "Do the math, asshole."

You see that I'm drunk. You sit on the couch. I sit closer to you than I should.

"So," I ask you, my hands all over you, "are you seeing anyone?"

I already know that you don't have a girlfriend, so when you don't answer, I don't bother to ask again. I'm really close now, all up against you. I'm practically on top of you, my skirt riding up. I think how if you just put your hand up there, you'd be *mine*. I'm not wearing any underwear and I'm shaved all nice and smooth. It used to drive you crazy when I shaved and didn't wear underwear and I'd wear a short skirt and knee-high boots . . . like what I'm wearing.

I didn't put this outfit on for you though. My new boyfriend likes it. I've got a new boyfriend, remember?

But if you'd just put your hand up my skirt . . . you'd see *stars*. You'd like it even more than he does.

You're saying something, but I'm not listening. I'm almost crawling into your lap. I've got one knee over yours. If there was any question before that I am a total drunken whore, that question is clearly answered now.

But you're still the one who makes the pass, technically speaking. So . . . fuck you.

You come in close and hard and stick your tongue in my mouth. You're a hell of a kisser. I kiss you back. Our tongues feel good together. You're cute the way you get all excited so fast. I feel your cock getting hard in your sweatpants. I rub my leg up a little higher on your body and I put my hand on your dick. I stroke it gently. It stiffens all the way. I moan a little because I remember all the times I sucked it and how easy and perfect it fits inside me.

I totally want to just lift my skirt and ride you.

But I don't. I let you take the lead, because I've got a new boyfriend. I let you be the one to make the first real move. You're the one who puts your hand up my shirt and finds out I'm not wearing a bra.

Or maybe you knew that already. It was sort of cold out there tonight. I guess you could sort of see my nipples a little. I walked the five blocks from the bar to Melissa's house, then twelve blocks from her place to your place.

I'm cold, that's all . . . but yeah, if you noticed my nipples, I bet you thought I was horny.

You start kissing me deeper, feeling my nipples, stroking them, thumbing them, gently pinching them. You lift up my shirt and expose my tits and then you start sucking them.

Your mouth feels good on my nipples. You suck one nipple into your mouth, work your teeth and tongue against it, suckling, teasing; you were always really good at that.

I snuggle into your lap a little more and take off my shirt. You look so hot and so cute with my nipple in your mouth.

You're really hard now, in your sweatpants. Major Boner Alert. I stroke your cock through your sweatpants while I run my other hand through your hair. I'm so fucking drunk and so fucking turned on by you, I can't put it off any longer.

I drop down and pull your sweats over your cock. I take it in my mouth. I start to suck it.

Your dick feels huge in my mouth. It's not that you're bigger than my new boyfriend or anything. I'd say you're both about the same size, roughly, except maybe he's a little smaller.

I open wide and work you to the back of my throat and bob up and down, looking up at you to make eye contact while I suck, the way you always used to like.

You look like I'm an angel who's just fallen out of heaven.

I lick down to your balls and caress them with my tongue while I stroke your cock with my hand.

I come up and nuzzle my face against your neck. I gently lick and suck that big, gorgeous neck I used to love. You smell incredible. I've still got your dick in my hand, but you're not getting the hint about how I want you to put your hand up my skirt.

So I guide your hand up my thigh.

Maybe resist a little. You look like you're having second thoughts.

So I kiss you hard to shut you up. My tongue's deep in your mouth when I get your hand up my skirt. Your big fingers slide up my slit. You feel I'm shaved and not wearing a thing under my skirt.

After that, the whole thing's easy.

You don't even try to stop me. I just guide your cock up against my slit and rub it. It feels incredible. Then I guide you to the entrance.

You've got this awesome curve to your cockhead that always makes it a little rough going in. I murmur as I fucking impale myself on you. I lunge forward hard. I wiggle my hips back and forth. I jiggle as I push your big beautiful cock up into me, naked and bare, feeling my smooth shaved lips around your shaft and the hot perfect curve of your big dick pushing up at just the right angle into my pussy. I put my arms around you and cradle your head and moan like crazy and whimper in your ear. You used to like that when I really acted up during sex; you liked it when I made porn star noises. I make a few now – real slutty ones, loud, shameless, while my whole body's shuddering against you, my tits in your face, my mouth against your ear talking dirty to you as I ride your fucking stud cock, telling you all about what your cock is doing up inside me. All about all the good places it's hitting. All about how much I missed it.

I reach down between us and touch my clit. It's electric. I start rubbing furiously. I get closer fast. I slide up and down on top of you, pushing your naked cock inside me. I kiss you. I moan. I clutch you to me. I rub faster.

Then I come on your dick. I moan like crazy into your ear.

I ask you, laughing, "Sorry, was I too loud? I don't want to wake your neighbors."

It's a private joke; your neighbors used to always hear me. I guess I'm pretty loud. But you don't respond. In fact, you don't say anything. You just grab my ass and bounce me up and down on you. My pussy feels sensitive and tender from the explosive come I just had. It feels amazing to have you inside me. Your cock against me feels bare, sensuous, erotic.

I look in your eyes as you get closer. I cradle your head in my arms. I want to be looking in your eyes when you come.

I kiss you and brush your hair back.

You grunt. You jerk your hips up. You pump your cock deep inside me and slam me on you a few more times.

Then you're up inside me as deep as you can go, and I feel you pulsing inside, wet and slick.

I keep looking in your eyes, sighing, moaning, telling you how good it feels, how warm and juicy and sexy. I love you coming inside me. I love everything about your dick inside me. I love to fuck you.

I get off of you.

My panties are in my purse. I took them off in the street outside, before I came up to see you. I pull them on. I tug down my skirt. I put on my T-shirt.

I say, "I better be going."

You look at me in wonder. You think I'm a total drunken whore.

Maybe you thought I wanted to get back together. But I don't. I've got a new boyfriend. And fucking your ex isn't cheating any more than head is.

I give you a good deep kiss, but your tongue feels dead.

You glare at me as I stretch languidly in the doorway. You're pissed . . . but you must think I look good. You never look away.

Like I care? I've got a new boyfriend. So, remember me if you want, but this cute little butt is walking out the door. Kiss it goodbye.

I wiggle it at you, and close the door behind me.

I've got a new boyfriend, and he's Doormat Doug . . . even worse than you. I text him to come pick me up.

Good Neighbors

Mercy Loomis

The bored teen behind the desk handed me my key and my receipt without once actually making eye contact, his gaze riveted to the computer screen in front of him. I supposed his obliviousness could be a sort of backhand professional courtesy, since the sign at the desk clearly stated the going rates in half-hour increments. I amused myself with this thought as I made my way down the dingy hallway.

I let myself into my room, pleased to find it was not appreciably different from any other place I'd stayed, despite the "no-tell motel" atmosphere. All I wanted was some sleep, thank you, and an early start in the morning. With a sigh I dropped my duffel on the dresser and dug out my toiletries bag and my nightgown before heading off to the shower.

After a long soak under the surprisingly hot spray of water, I settled gratefully between the cheap but sturdy sheets, the bedspread kicked off into an untidy puddle on the floor. I set the alarm, snuggled into the flat hard pillow, and started to doze off.

The wall behind my headboard vibrated as the hallway door in the next room slammed shut. A wordless murmuring followed, punctuated by the occasional laugh.

Neighbors, I sighed silently. I shouldn't have been surprised, really, but I'd hoped . . .

Things got quiet again, and I'd just begun to drift off when I distinctly heard a woman moan.

Their bed must've been right up against the wall, as mine was. The slatted headboard did nothing to block the sound as the woman next door made her pleasure known.

I rolled over, disgruntled and getting more awake as the

sound got louder, annoyed at being disturbed, which only woke me up more. I tried to ignore her, but the harder I tried not to listen the worse it got.

Why can I only hear her? I wondered irreverently, punching my pillow and trying to get comfortable again. I was fairly sure I'd heard a masculine voice when they'd first come in. Of course, my imagination immediately tried to answer that idle question. A vision swam before my eyes: a woman writhing on a bed in a room the mirror to mine, her legs spread wide, her back arching as a man buried his face between her thighs. I saw his hands gripping her generous hips as she squirmed under his ministrations, watched her mouth open to produce the rising cries that drifted through the walls.

I rolled onto my back and pushed the sheet off me. When had it gotten so hot in here?

The woman was speaking now. I strained to hear her without even meaning to, but I couldn't quite make out the words through the wall. The tone said enough: begging, pleading, making promises that may or may not be entirely of the moment. I stared at the backs of my eyelids, holding my breath, trying to give meaningful shapes to the sounds I heard. *Please, oh please, don't stop, God yes, don't stop, baby, I'll do anything you want . . .*

I'd forgotten I was holding my breath. The air rushed out of me in a surprised burst that sounded suspiciously like a moan.

My hands, lying lightly on my stomach, twitched restlessly, fingers playing over the smooth surface of my silk nightie. What were her hands doing right now? Were they tangled in her lover's hair, urging him on? Were they tightly gripping fistfuls of the bedclothes, or maybe wrapped white-knuckled and straining around the slats of the headboard? I shifted, as restless as my hands, and felt the soft material rasp over my nipples.

My breath caught in my throat. I envisioned her kneading desperately at her breasts, fingers digging in hard as the man really got down to business. Almost without realizing it, I mimicked her, but softer; rolling my hard nipples between my fingers through the fabric, caressing the swell of my breast where it met my ribs.

And then, unmistakable, shrieked and piercing: "Yes! Oh, yes!"

I let my hands fall back to my sides, half smiling at her

exuberance, half disappointed that it was all over so soon. But only moments later they were at it again. A rhythmic *thump thump* shook the wall, accompanied by a deep grunting bass.

His turn, I thought, having no trouble identifying the sound of their headboard smacking into the plaster. Obvious ... but what position? I bit my lip, stifling a giggle as I contemplated it. Had his rod taken the place of his tongue, with the woman not even having to move? Or had they traded places, him on his back, her riding him, hands clasped around the top rail as she dug her hips into him, giving him as hard a pounding as his mouth had given her?

I pressed one hand against the wall.

Or had he rolled her over? I remembered his hands on her hips, imagined him flipping her, boneless and sated, onto her stomach. She would, of course, brace herself against the headboard as he shoved into her. I turned over, lifting my ass in the air, rubbing my aching breasts against the mattress. My nightgown was wet and clung to the backs of my thighs. Straightening up, I tore it over my head and let it fall to the floor.

I was facing the wall, facing them in a sense. He was still going, the impact making my own headboard jump. I shuffled forward on my knees until I could feel the top rail banging against my ribs. My nipples brushed against the rough paint over the drywall.

The man groaned. The thumping began to come a little faster.

That last position really stuck in my mind. I imagined the wall was gone, that I was facing the man over the back of his lover, her face level with my crotch as I knelt before them. How her hands would run up my thighs, stroking and exploring me even as he fucked her. I spread my legs for her, my fingers finding my clit, pretending they were her fingers. I pressed forward against the wall, against her, her mouth, her hands, feeling him watching me, my ardor turning him on, making him thrust even harder, the whole wall vibrating against me as I ground myself against her, rubbing for all I was worth, savoring each thud as they came faster, and faster, and suddenly it was on me, the orgasm taking me by surprise with its intensity, a rippling and rolling wave that made the muscles in my legs quake and shiver. Without meaning to I cried out against the plaster.

There was a startled noise from the other room, and then silence.

I waited, breathless and weak from the afterglow, but to my disappointment the fucking did not resume. After a moment or two, I slithered back down onto the bed, pulling the sheet up to my chin.

In the next room, a door slammed shut. The distant sounds of quick footsteps retreating down the hallway faded into stillness.

Curled up in a happy humming ball, I laughed quietly. At least now I'd be able to get some sleep.

Debut

Thom Gautier

It happened on my thirty-fifth birthday and it was insanely good and it was insanely embarrassing. But it was on me. After all, I'd asked my wife Sandra for it. I'd asked for it like a suddenly voiced daydream, a determined wish uttered during foreplay in the drawn-curtain safety of our bedroom in Scarsdale. Sandra had asked me what I wanted to do for my birthday and I answered, on the magical cusp of late-night sex, while she danced her fingers up and down my stiff cock, that what I wanted was what she was doing right then, fondling my cock like a toy. "I want you to tease my cock without mercy just like that, in a public place." After we had sex that night and I lay in bed, I thought my wish was a run-of-the mill male fantasy, and, besides, carrying out such an act is both risky and absurd so I didn't think by morning Sandra would even recall it let alone follow through.

But she did.

A week later when we settled into our booth on my birthday at a local Italian restaurant Sandra fished out a travel-size tube of body lotion from her purse and placed the tube on the table next to the small vase of yellow roses. "That's for my use on you," she said. "*Appetizer.*" She lifted the tablecloth and gazed down at my crotch and I realized she was going to hold me to it, quite literally. I protested that the idea had been a lark.

"You said it like you meant it," she said, taking hold of my zipper and slowly opening my fly. "It's your birthday. You get what you wanted now."

I pushed her hand away and said no way. What if neighbors come in? What if the maître d' calls the cops? "*Stop,*" she said,

"*Birth*-day: think about that word. About being born. What a *coming out* that was, yes? It'll make this, this sneaky debut, seem small in comparison, *no*?"

The waiter handed us menus and for a second I imagined they contained instructions for an under-the-table hand job on them. She ordered us two vodkas and cranberry as she tugged at my open fly. I didn't resist. I surveyed the expansive dining area with its candlelight and well-arranged tables and the third-rate paintings of Italian locales and, as she fondled my limp cock with two of her fingers and drew it more fully out of my pants, I began to swell. My breathing quickened. The air at our booth felt freezing cold on my balls, and I wondered if the cold sensation was just a result of an intense shame, as if everyone in the restaurant could see through our table and see under this long tablecloth at my still limp cock and dangling balls all couched in Sandra's gracefully sadistic hand with her fingernails painted cherry red.

She glided that hand up and down my cock, occasionally using a drag of her pinky and other times polishing the tip of my cock with her thumb and once in a while reaching under to brush my balls and lift them gently, like she was weighing them with her hand. I closed my eyes. I could smell Sandra's lavender perfume. I could even see the row of pearls of her necklace. I could hear my pulses and I could smell steaks cooking; I was hard. I heard plates and cutlery clattering and jingling, the murmurs of diners' voices, the foreign accents of busboys.

"Sparkling or tap?" the waiter asked, jolting me to open my eyes as he put our drinks down on the table.

"Tap," I said, and Sandra whispered under her breath, "Okey-dokey," and she began tapping my shaft with her forefinger over and over and over, like my cock was a drum skin, her fingers tapping a beat that radiated off my cock. The frissons of her tapping beat deeper into me, the tease-taps burrowing into my ass and rekindling the taut drawstring of fleshy fire between my legs. The very sound of the waiter's pouring water splashing into my glass made me want to erupt and Sandra kept stroking me as she listened to the waiter recite the specials. I wondered if the waiter noticed the lotion tube next to the roses. I kept my elbows on the table with a forced manly demeanor and I steadied my shoulders and gazed at the waiter's ink-black eyes as he spoke to us, my cock not a few feet from his chin. I may have looked the part of a Scarsdale husband but between my legs I was a fifteen-year-old girl in pubescent heat. The waiter's steady baritone voice was phallic, erotic. I felt not only that he could see down there at her hand on me but that he was sizing up my cock. I felt like an infant in a changing room. I could only hear every other word, snippets, names of sauces and vegetables, strings of dinner descriptors signifying nothing, as she ran her cool hand up and down and up again and my body was put to fever by the hypnotic rhythm of her caressing hand.

When the waiter left us again she took the hand lotion and very visibly rubbed it into both of her hands, squishing it between her fingers, savoring the clean feeling of it. I watched some of the lotion drizzle over the webbed flap between her right thumb and her right forefinger. We kissed. The pupils in her light brown eyes radiated an ebullient confidence that assuaged my fear. Even if we got caught, I reasoned, we *both* get caught. We're in it *together*. She smiled maternally at me. Making sure not to get any lotion on the napkin, she picked it up with the tips of her finger and thumb and draped it on the smooth incline of her white hosed leg and crossed her legs and tugged at her green skirt, pulling it down over her knees. "Stop looking, you birthday *perv*," she said, and I grinned and blushed.

Just as her cool lubricated hand began to pump me up to a headier plateau and ever-stiffer, ever-harder arousal, I saw a few yards ahead two former work colleagues who, seeing us, were ambling slowly over. I shifted in my seat and told her to stop, stop. "Uh-*oh*, they're *coming*," Sandra said, giggling softly into my neck. The two men were accompanied by two tanned blonde women, each in a matching turquoise and white dress, looking rich and spoiled and tanned and exquisite. I can barely recall what we six talked about. As Sandra's lubricated hand massaged the up and down of my swollen cock, it felt like we bantered for hours. The faux-friendly gleam in the green eyes of these nameless blonde women stoked my throbbing hard-on and I felt semen leaking from me and then felt Sandra's hand work the semen into the lotion-lube, keeping her rhythm. But she didn't miss a conversational beat. She told them it was my birthday.

They wished me happy birthday, even the two blondes, and I was so turned on by the contrast between Sandra's grip on my exposed but hidden hard-on below the table and the high-pitched tones in their innocent birthday boy wishes. By now my balls were filling and burning and blue. As I kept my poise, I imagined my two former colleagues having sex with the blondes. A foursome. In Florida. A beach. Suntan lotion. They insisted we join them after for a drink. "On us," one of the blondes said and I coughed and thanked her. After they left, Sandra kissed my ear and told me I had *very impressive stamina* and that I had performed *deftly*. She asked me if I thought "Heather and Feather" were pretty and when I nodded *yes* she laughed and started jerking me off again much slower, as if to punish me.

When a new waiter came over to take our dinner order I imagined that the previous one had seen what was happening and told his boss – "that brunette at the booth is giving her husband a hand job under the table" – and I imagined the angry waiter had refused to wait on us in disgust, but I could see he was diligent and happily doing his job there across the room attending to other guests – a short obese redhead and a very fit and tall black dude who were being seated. The simple mismatch-ing specter of that couple loosened more pre-jizz from my cock and I swallowed hard. I told the waiter I wasn't feeling well and that I'd settle for soup.

"No, he's OK," Sandra said, holding me still while she ordered something substantial for me. "You'll feel better if you eat," the waiter said and he winked at me, and Sandra's conspiring with the waiter to force-feed me made me even more embarrassed and more turned on. Surely the waiter must know, I thought.

When he left she dragged her forefinger up one side and down another and again and again and again and she studied my tormented expressions as I stretched out my arms on both sides of the booth to keep myself sitting up.

"Your pleasure down between your legs is like the inverse of labor pains I had, Tommy," she said, "and like labor, it doesn't happen right away but sooner or later it's going to come out. Right? Are the contractions getting close in time? Should we call a doctor?" she asked. Through gritted teeth I joked that if this was revenge for my having gotten her pregnant with our boy then it was pretty sweet as far as revenge goes and she said *oh yeah it is* and she dragged her fingernails across my shaft, up and then down. She clenched her jaw and bit her lower lip as she stroked and then she cruelly pinched my balls causing me to lean forward and knock over my water glass and the roses. The busboy rushed over. As he sopped up the mess and staunched the running water, Sandra pumped me harder and harder still, and I closed my eyes. I heard the busboy assure my wife it was fine, "Is no *problemo*, misses, I do this," and then I felt it happening and happening again, a Niagara Falls surging both toward me, in me, and from me. I bit down hard as she stroked and as soon as the waiter gathered the wet clothes and turned to go I bit my fist to keep myself from groaning and as her hand stopped and then started ever faster I squeezed my eyes shut tight and felt my hot release flow out and stream over Sandra's moving fist and her fingers. When my knee hit the underside of the table, glasses clanged. I opened my eyes and saw Sandra expressionless except for a small smile. I looked across the dining room. For a moment I was convinced they were all staring at me: the first waiter, the second waiter, the busboy, my colleagues, their blondes, the redhead and the black guy. But they were all busy with the ordinary Friday night business of an Italian restaurant in Westchester. I could smell my own spunk, and the clinical aroma of the lotion. I was sure my trousers would be spotted and stained. Sandra gazed at me with a curious look of pride in her bright brown eyes. She let me go, limp and sticky, and she carefully rested her tired and greased hand on the napkin on her lap. The busboy put a new vase of yellow roses on our table. I thanked him. Sandra picked up her drink and sipped it through the tiny red straw. I was still panting. "Some debut," I said. I slowed my breath, tried to sit up straight. Sandra sipped her drink again and asked me, being the birthday boy, was it true, that silly cliché, that we should always watch what we wish for?

The Heist

Andrea Dale

"On the ground! Now!"

The harsh words echoed through the bank lobby.

Leroy ducked back into the hallway, praying he hadn't been seen. Granger's Bank had never in its fifty years been robbed, and now, two weeks after he'd taken the security guard job, it had to happen.

Just his luck.

He peered around the corner, holding his breath. Two of them, wearing nondescript dark clothes and stockings to mask their faces.

He eased back, considering his options.

"Put all the cash in this bag."

His bowels turned to ice.

Sherri. God, how he missed her smoky voice. Despite himself, his cock stirred.

"Check the vault."

Fuck. He knew that voice, too: Tom, the bastard Sherri had run off with.

Well, he wouldn't have a problem nailing Tom in the head with a bullet, but Sherri was another matter.

Leroy's gun slipped from his shaking hand. The sound of it hitting the marble floor was like a gunshot in itself, ricocheting around the corridor. Of course he panicked. He never thought he'd be a good security guard.

"What the hell?" Tom yelled.

"I'll take care of it," Sherri shouted back to him. She came around the corner with the shotgun cocked and ready to fire. His gun had skidded too far away. Leroy raised his hands and prayed.

"Well, fancy meeting you here." Sherri's features were smashed beneath the stocking, her curves lost beneath the baggy outfit, but her voice and her musky perfume were enough to make Leroy harder than the marble floor.

"Pick up that chair," she said, gesturing with her gun to a wooden straight chair in the hall. "Now get into the vault."

The damn thing was never locked during the day. Old Man Granger was that secure. He probably deserved to be robbed, filthy rich as he was.

Sherri hauled the massive door shut behind them. She used his own cuffs to secure one of his hands to the chair, then tied the other back with the partner to the stocking over her head.

"Don't make a sound," she said.

Helpless, he watched her shove bundles of cash into two canvas bags. When they were full, she cinched them up. But before she hauled them onto her back, she turned and regarded him.

"You are a sight," she said, shaking her head. "Seeing you trussed up is giving me bad ideas."

He tried to respond, but his mouth had gone dry.

Sherri cupped his crotch, laughed when she felt his unflagging erection and heard him suck in his breath. "Ah, what the hell."

She pulled up her blue denim shirt to reveal her braless breasts, nipples already puckered, the color of ripe plums. She fed him one, and he suckled eagerly. God, he'd missed her.

She stripped off one leg of her cargo pants and panties. The scent of her cunt made him twitch harder. He jerked against his bonds. He wanted to bury his face in her, then throw her down and plunge into her, make her scream his name.

With deft fingers she undid his polyester uniform pants. He lifted his ass so she could pull them and his boxers down. His cock sprang free, red and stiff. A drop of fluid at the tip glistened under the harsh fluorescent light. His balls ached with need.

Throwing one leg across his lap, she rubbed the head of his cock against her slick lips. "No time for teasing," she said, her voice a little hoarse. "There's a pity."

She sank down on him, her warm pussy surrounding him, pulsing along the length of him. She posted up and down, grinding herself against his cock. Her breasts bounced in front of his face and he tried to capture one with his mouth again.

He'd never known her to be so aggressive. Oh, she'd always been an enthusiastic lover, but this went beyond an uninhibited roll in the hay. And as much as he wanted his hands free – as much as he pulled at the restraints until his cuffed wrist ached – there was something about being held down that was pretty damn sexy. There was something about her taking the lead, something about her having all the control, that brought him to the edge faster than he'd ever gotten before.

He gritted his teeth as his balls tightened. OK, it was a matter of pride, but not until she . . .

Fuck. He couldn't take it anymore. He thrust up hard into her – as best he could under the circumstances – and felt her spasm, shuddering through her own release as he came. She whimpered, bit his neck to keep herself from screaming.

She had the decency to pull his pants up over his sticky, spent cock. As if suddenly seized by a fit of tenderness, she pulled the stocking on her head up and kissed him, full and hard, before grabbing the bags and her gun and running out. Her footsteps receded down the hall, leaving him alone with the sound of his own harsh breathing and the mingled scent of their fucking.

Leroy twisted his wrist. All the jerking and pulling during their sex had loosened the stocking that bound him to the chair, and in a few moments, he was free,

He spat out the key she'd passed him in the kiss and went to work unlocking his other wrist from the cuffs.

He'd give his police report (nobody would be surprised that he'd screwed up; in fact, they'd expected it), get in his truck, and meet Sherri at the dam. They'd get rid of Tom – the reservoir was deep, and it was a long way down – and then they'd head downstate as planned.

And when they stopped at a motel, he was going to cuff *her* to the bed and see how much *she* liked the teasing . . .

Leviathan

Mina Murray

It had not been easy that first time for Evie to jump the barriers at the station and board the next train to who-knew-where. These days she got past the guards effortlessly. A kind word here, a damsel-in-distress act there, and the gates of the metropolitan transit system opened to her. Dressing the part helped. If she looked like she could afford to ride the train whenever she wanted no one would assume otherwise. So each day, when she boarded, she resembled countless others of the gainfully employed, suited up, hair pinned back, ready to face the daily grind with that same early-morning weariness that meant buses, trains and trams were always quieter on the way in than the way home, when children squalled, tourists jostled and lovers argued.

Evie avoided the afternoon rush. What she craved was solitude, the spaces that opened up when the crowd thinned out to nothing and she stayed on the train as it looped endlessly, ouroboros-like, its flickering corridors stretching out like the insides of some great beast, some land-bound Leviathan.

To avoid detection, she chose different departure points, alternated lines. She had been caught without a ticket twice, could not afford another fine. Ever since she had been made redundant two months ago, things had been tight. Severance packages didn't go far and she was determined to make what little she had left last for as long as possible. There was a peculiar kind of indignity, Evie reflected, in being retrenched from a job you hadn't wanted in the first place, in having rejected a vocation you had loved in favour of the safe option, only to have the safe option taken from you as well. And so Evie rode the trains.

In the beginning, it was to give her something to get her out of bed, some routine other than staring at the walls of her damp and sparsely furnished flat. But she grew to love her solitary trips. Freed from the responsibility of having to be somewhere, anywhere, at a particular time, she allowed herself to be lulled by the rocking of the train into a state of meditative awareness. As she gazed out the window, she learned the character of each individual line, its underpasses and overpasses, the places where it split off, only to rejoin itself several stations later.

Today Evie rides her favourite line. She knows each apartment block huddled next to the tracks, knows who will be on their balcony with breakfast and the paper, or a cigarette. On one of the balconies there is a red planter box, shaped to fit over the railing. From a distance you cannot see what supports it; it simply hangs there, suspended in the thin cold air. Evie looks for that bright spot each time she passes.

The voice of the ticket inspector on the level below jolts Evie unpleasantly from her reverie. Picking up her bag, she moves away from the voice, allowing the white cord of her headphones to sway ostentatiously. If the inspector sees it, he might just assume she hadn't heard him coming.

When Evie reaches the next car, she is trapped. While she has left one inspector behind her, another is about to enter this carriage. She stops in the middle of the aisle and swears, vehemently, and for a good while.

"That's the most creative cursing I've heard in weeks."

Evie had assumed she was alone. To be fair, the man *is* partly hidden, back there in the seat near the stairs. The shadows do nothing to disguise his good looks though: no more than thirty-five, with reddish-brown hair tugged into a turned-up point at the front, a strong jaw and green eyes the exact shade as hers. The rolled-up cuffs of his immaculately cut white shirt expose tanned forearms scattered with golden hair. A small, flatly curved scar on his face encloses the upper-right corner of his mouth like a parenthesis.

"Well, brace yourself," Evie warns, "because you'll be hearing some more."

He raises an enquiring eyebrow.

Evie sighs. "The short version?" She ticks off the reasons on her fingers. "No job, no ticket, one warning and one fine already. Which I haven't paid."

"Ah." He shifts to make room for her. "Just pretend you're with me."

"You're a lifesaver. And my name's Evie."

The inspector coming towards them is the same man who fined her last time. All the flirting and cajoling in the world had done no good; the man was immovable. His inspector's glowering countenance brightens now, though, when he notices her seat-mate.

"Hello, Nick, I mean sir. Checking up on us?"

"Not at all, Curtis. Just felt like a ride."

Curtis looks apologetic. It is not an expression that seems natural to him. "Your pass, sir?"

"Of course." Nick pulls an official-looking card out of his wallet.

"Very good, sir. And your ticket, miss?"

"It's OK, Curtis, Evie's with me." Nick smiles, places his hand high up on Evie's thigh and squeezes. Mollified, Curtis leaves them alone and Evie releases a breath she didn't realize she had been holding. Nick moves his hand.

"Government service does have its perks. Now, tell me the long version."

Evie angles herself towards him and the words tumble out of her. She realizes it has been weeks since she'd had a real conversation with anyone. At the stations, on the trains, people moved past her in a blur. She felt cocooned, in a bubble, even if they were close enough to touch. It had been a long time since Evie was touched. She realizes this too, when Nick's arm winds around her shoulder in sympathy and her body warms instantly at the contact. Leaning back against his broad chest, Evie keeps talking.

When Evie finishes her tale, Nick doesn't say anything – what is there to say, after all? – but he doesn't shift her from his chest. They sit in silence for a while. The motion of the train and the way Nick's hand is comfortingly rubbing her arm put Evie into a dream-like state. One where it seems perfectly reasonable for her to take Nick's other hand, kiss it absently, then rest it on her leg. When she comprehends what she's done, and is about to splutter an apology, Nick says, "Shh, it's fine."

Evie closes her eyes, and stretches her long legs out on the seat opposite. She inches down a little so the winter sun streaming through the window falls just where she wants it to. Nick's breath catches a little at the creamy expanse of skin Evie has inadvertently bared. His hand is directly on her now, and he starts stroking abstract, swirling patterns over her thigh. She does not object when he slides her skirt higher, baring the fabric-covered delta at the top of her thighs. Evie does not object at all. She whimpers gently and presses his hand to her mound.

"Please," she whispers, "please, it's been so long."

Evie is already wet, so wet she fears Nick can smell the scent of her arousal. He can certainly feel it as he caresses her gently through the silk. Evie's pulse leaps as his fingers slip under her waistband and rub her clit with a side-to-side stroke that none of her lovers, or even Evie herself, have ever used. She pulls her skirt up higher and her legs fall open. Nick's fingers glide over her faster and harder now, just like she needs, up and down her cleft, into the hungry mouth of her sex, over her bud. Within moments Evie is coming and the force of her orgasm is both shocking and utterly inevitable. She shrieks as the wave breaks over her, accidentally hits her head on the sloping roof above their seat. Nick kisses her gently as her breathing gradually returns to normal.

They speed past a station, and Evie knows they don't have much time left. Not enough to do all of what she wants, but enough for something. There's a tunnel coming up, and they'll have at least five minutes alone, some of it in the dark. Evie climbs off the seat and is about to kneel between Nick's legs when he protests, even though his erection strains painfully against his trousers.

"No, you don't have to do that."

"I know, Nick, but I want to. As long as you do."

He brushes a hand roughly over his mouth. "Are you joking? Of course I do! You have the poutiest mouth I've ever seen."

"Then let me."

What a perfect gentleman, she thinks, when he insists she kneel on his overcoat. She unbuttons his trousers quickly, unwilling to waste one precious moment. Her tongue flickers out to trace the angry veins wreathing his gratifyingly thick cock, spends a moment learning its contours, then sucks him into her mouth as hungrily and with the same relief as a drowning person sucks down air. He arches off the seat.

"Oh Christ, oh *fuck*, oh Evie."

She backs off a little, slowly swirls her tongue around the corona and up over the eye, licking up the crystalline beads of pre-come that have collected there. Evie tightens her pout around his shaft, gripping him with her smooth hand and working mouth and hand in tandem as she bobs up and down. Sometimes she lets his penis slip from her lips so she can circle her hand around the head and back down again with an expert twist of her wrist. She follows with a flattened tongue that curves around the sides of his cock.

Evie truly loves the act she is performing; her panties are damp enough to prove it. She sits back on her haunches for a moment, hand still working him with measured, spiralling motions. Nick's head is thrown back against the seat, cheeks flushed a hectic red, making little panting noises that Evie finds so unbearably arousing she can't help but reach down to play with herself.

As her moans join his, Nick's eyes snap open. Evie makes sure he watches as she tilts her head and takes first one, then his other testicle into her mouth, pushing and rolling the delicate sacs with her talented tongue while her slippery palm works his crown. Nick knows he is lost. Vibrations from the passing freight train rumble through his body, and he shoots his seed all over Evie's hand and her now upturned mouth, as she comes for the second time that day.

They barely manage to tidy up and right their clothing before the next station. Nick rises to disembark, but not before he scribbles something to Evie on the back of a business card and kisses her breathlessly goodbye. When he has disappeared from view, she reads the note: *Wednesday. Central Station, Western Line, 10.05. I have keys to the guard's compartments.*

The Stranger

Thomas S. Roche

Casey wandered through the gyrating crowd getting progressively more irritated and pissed off. This was not what she had in mind when she'd agreed to go dancing with Austin for the evening. He'd recently come out – no surprise to anyone except maybe him – and was in full-on queer social butterfly mode; he'd managed to talk Casey into going to a gay bar with him. It had been fun for a while, dancing anonymously among seething hordes of gay men packed into skimpy, skintight clothes, sheened in sweat and feeling each other up.

Austin was having a great time, too, bouncing from guy to guy, flirting all over the place and having fun. But Casey had started to get annoyed when Austin's flirting had gone totally out of control – last she'd seen him, a half-hour ago, he was off in the corner making out with some dark-haired hunk she wouldn't have minded getting close to herself. In fact, she'd been flirting with him herself not long ago, half wondering if he might be straight. The guy's hand down Austin's pants had answered that question.

Now, Casey was tired of dancing. She was bored and she'd spent all her money on the $5 drinks – Blue Screamers, pink lemonade with vodka, Alien Orgasms. She was more than a little drunk and would have gone home except that she'd forgotten to save money for a cab ride, so she was stuck until she could locate Austin among the seething swarm of dancing men. She hoped he had enough cash to pay for a taxi.

Casey stumbled toward the bathroom, noting that while the men's room was packed with flesh, the little girls' room looked like a graveyard. She went in, more to get away from the crowd and noise and the smell of liquor and male sweat than because she had to go. Once she was inside, though, she realized she did have to go, pretty badly, actually, and headed for the single stall. She gasped when she pulled open the door – two guys were in there, one seated on the toilet seat, the other straddling him. Their shirts were open and they were going at it. Casey started to back away, but then the guy on top turned his head and she saw that it was Austin. The guy underneath him was the gorgeous hunk she'd spotted him with earlier.

"Casey, darling!" Austin was drunk, and his London accent always came out when he drank. "I've been looking all over for you!"

Casey scoffed, pissed off for a moment. "Yeah, but you've been looking in the wrong place. I'm not in the habit of hanging out in guys' tonsils."

Austin was drunk enough that he didn't get the joke. The guy underneath him got it, though; he looked at Casey and smiled, his blue eyes lighting up. God, he was gorgeous. Austin reached out to Casey and grabbed her hand, dragging her into the stall with them.

"I'm sorry, love, don't be mad. I've only recently become gay, you understand? I can't help myself. It's all so new to me." Too drunk to argue with him, Casey let Austin put his arm around her and pull her close. He kissed her on the forehead like a protective older brother. "This is Colin, by the way, his name starts with a C just like yours. And he's also straight. Or at least so he says. Isn't that right, Colin?"

"That's right, hon. What was your name again?"

"Casey," she said.

"Casey. That's a pretty name. But I actually meant your friend."

Austin guffawed and made a show of pretending to slap Colin on the face. "You slut, you fucking slut. Didn't I just tell you my name fifteen minutes ago . . . or did I?"

Casey rolled her eyes, unable to decide if she should laugh or scream at Austin. He was so charming when he got drunk, she just let him pull her close into the piss-smelling stall, which meant that she was pressed against Colin's body, too. She decided to giggle – mostly out of nervousness.

"If you're straight, what are you doing in a bathroom stall making out with Austin?"

Colin looked up at Casey, smiling, his eyes more gorgeous than ever. He put his arm around her, his hand resting against her inner thigh. "Austin! Now I remember. I'm waiting to see if his gorgeous girlfriend comes along."

"Nice line," said Casey as her skin tingled where Colin gently gripped her thigh.

"I don't think it's a line, honey," said Austin. "Colin's been jabbering on about you. I suspect he's only been making out with me to get your phone number. Can't say I blame him."

Austin leaned into Casey and kissed her full on the lips, surprising her. She felt his tongue laze along her upper lip. It had been years since Austin and she kissed – the last time was in high school. Feeling his mouth against hers sent a surge through her, making her stiffen from the sense of taboo – it was like kissing her brother, except that she'd had a hopeless crush on Austin forever, since long before he knew he was gay. And Colin, the gorgeous Colin with the dark hair and the blue eyes, chose that moment to slip his hand up her skirt.

"Hey!" she said, jerking away from Austin.

Colin's hand slipped out of her skirt and came up to her face. His fingers felt magic as he ran them over her neck and gently tugged her downward. He was so tall that it didn't take much for her to bend her face to his; and then he kissed her, tenderly, his mouth tasting of salt and Sangria. She felt his tongue gently nudging her lips apart. She let him kiss her, feeling her drunken body sway with the electricity of it.

"Please?" he asked when he pulled back.

She felt Austin's lips against her ear, kissing her as Colin's hand trailed back down her body. Colin kissed her again as Austin nibbled her upper neck, making her knees go weak so she fell against the two of them. Colin's magic fingers were up her skirt again, now tugging her thong out of the way . . . and then she felt like it was all over, because when two of his fingers slipped between the lips of her pussy, Colin could tell in an instant how incredibly wet she was. Maybe it was all the dancing with gorgeous gay men in tight clothes – but Casey knew better, because she suspected she hadn't been wet when she entered the bathroom. It was Austin's kiss, Colin's touch, and the press of the two men's bodies against her. And when Colin slid two fingers inside her, her pussy hurt, hurt worse than it ever had – not because something was wrong, but because she wanted it so much.

Now Austin was kissing her, and Casey found herself lost in the textures of his lips, his tongue, in the taste of his furtive hits off other people's cloves, poppers and Hurricanes. Every stale, sour taste of indulgence was transformed by Austin's mouth into an aphrodisiac, so much so that she didn't realize that her shirt was being pulled up, didn't even think to wonder if it was Colin or Austin pulling it up, didn't entertain the thought of stopping whoever it was. The little baby-T lifted easily above her small, firm breasts, and the lacy bra came down just far enough to let Colin get his mouth around her nipple and suck gently, closing his teeth lightly around her. Casey gasped, wanting to push him away for a second; then she felt the current running from nipples to clit as Colin sucked on one nipple and used his left hand to play with the other.

With his right, he slowly slid his two fingers in and out of her, finding her G-spot with his fingertips and her clit with his thumb so expertly that she would have realized in a flash that he had to be straight or at least bi if she hadn't been feeling so turned on by the idea that he was gay. But then that all slipped away as she realized that Austin had smoothly gotten Colin's pants open, that he had the stranger's cock in his hand, that it was big and dark and very, very hard, sticking invitingly out of clean white briefs. Austin was slowly jerking Colin off as Colin finger-fucked Casey to the point where she thought, for an instant, she was going to come.

Austin's lips left hers for a moment, his tongue slippery with her spit. "See?" he asked. "He's obviously straight. Tell you what, Colin, pretend it's my cute little friend here sucking your dick."

With that, Austin wriggled his way down between them, getting on his knees between Colin's splayed legs as Casey leaned forward and felt a third finger entering her, gently nudging her open and pressing her G-spot as he worked her clit. She slumped against Colin, feeling him suckle her breasts as she whispered into his ear "Right there, right there," and then she saw her best friend's head bobbing up and down in Colin's lap. Casey wished she were him, wished she could get down on her knees and suck this gorgeous stranger's cock without a condom . . . but she wasn't, and she didn't need to be, because she was going to come any instant from the combined sensations of Colin working her pussy, clit and nipples.

She breathed deeply, smelling the liquor, cologne and sweat mingled with the smell of stale urine, and then she felt Austin's hand taking hers and pulling it down to Colin's cock. At Austin's urging, she wrapped her hand around Colin's shaft, feeling Austin's slippery lips against her fingers as she started jerking Colin off. She was close, she was so damn close. And then she felt the easy pulse of Colin's cock, shooting come into Austin's mouth as Colin sucked harder on her nipples, as he pushed mercilessly on her G-spot and clit. Feeling Colin climax in her hand, feeling warm semen dribble out of Austin's mouth and around her fingers, sent Casey over the edge, making her come so hard she started moaning at the top of her lungs. She fell hard against Colin, his big, muscled body supporting her as Austin finished him off, licking him clean as Casey's hand slipped away and came up to caress Colin's hard chest through the skintight black top.

"See?" murmured Austin, his voice rough. "Totally straight."

Casey was still panting. Outside, she could hear the DJ announcing last call.

Casey looked at Colin, nervous and a little surprised. He smiled, and his bright eyes danced as he shrugged.

"So what do you say?" laughed a very drunken Austin. "One last drink? Oh, I forgot, I just had one. Ba-dum-bum."

Casey bent forward and kissed Colin on the lips.

Hook and Tink

Brandy Fox

As Lance and I settle in with the kids for Family Movie Night, nooky is the last thing on my mind. Call me crazy, but spending time with two wild preschoolers doesn't usually put me in the mood. After twelve hours of shuttling, schlepping, cajoling, cleaning and cooking, I'm beat.

It's Peter's choice tonight, so of course we're watching *Peter Pan.* The five-year-old wears his green tunic and red-feathered cap, swatting the air with his sword while his little brother Garrett makes an island of pillows and blankets on the floor. Lance and I take either end of the couch, our legs entwined under a blanket.

I press play on the remote. Peter flies around the room then lands on the island with legs splayed and sword drawn. It's amazing how much he takes after his dad. Lance perpetually looks like he's on his way to a Renaissance Fayre, with his long dark locks, hemp shirts that flow from his tall, lanky frame, and a memory for Shakespearean soliloquies he spouts at random moments. Sometimes it feels like I'm parenting three boys not two. But there are times even I can't resist Lance's infectious energy.

Today, though, nothing's going to stop me from catching a few Zs during the movie. I'm dozing before Peter Pan's even taught the little ones how to fly.

"Poppycock!" Lance shrills suddenly.

I open my eyes to see him smiling broadly at me. I shoot him a warning glare and immediately drift off again.

Not long goes by before there's something wiggling against my thigh. My eyes whip open to see Lance with Captain Hook's own wicked grin, clearly amused by my exhaustion. He tickles my thigh with his toe again, wiggling his eyebrows in unison.

I look down at the boys on the floor. As usual, the movie has put them in a trance. They're buried up to their necks in blankets, eyes glazed over as Peter Pan sprinkles pixie dust over the kids despite Tinkerbell's disapproval. I can see the wheels in my own Peter's mind turning, no doubt scheming how he could get himself some of that magic powder. He'd probably try it on Garrett first, who's willing to jump out a window if his big brother tells him to.

I look back at Lance. "Grow up," I joke.

"I don't want to grow up," he says, pouting.

"Head to Neverland, babe. You won't grow up there."

"Come with me," he says with a breathy, French accent. "I am thinking a wonderful thought."

I snort, turn on my side and try sleeping again. But as I drift off, I envision Lance with Captain Hook's wiry mustache, ruffled blouse and long red coat, two cigars dangling between his lips. Surprisingly, I get a little slick in the groin.

Instead of sleeping, I watch the movie and let my mind wander. I'm guessing Lance would enjoy seeing me in that flimsy pixie dress. I barely clear five feet, and would have the same trouble as Tinkerbell getting my hips through a keyhole. Luckily, Lance adores my love handles, embraces and praises them with his rich vocabulary. Next to tall, skinny Lance, I could be Tink. Her jealousy of Peter Pan's affection for Wendy suddenly strikes me as silly. I'm thinking Tink should just abandon him altogether and hook up with the Captain. He's certainly got the bigger bulge.

When Captain Hook is plotting Tiger Lily's capture, I feel Lance's big toe slithering up my thigh again. This time, though, instead of tickling, it weaves into my little fantasy of Hook and Tink getting it on, and I spread my legs in welcome.

"A little persuasion might be in order," Captain Hook says to Smee, and I'm thinking, No, actually, it's not. I look over at Lance. He's peering at me through slits, his head lolling against the armrest, his face full of both pleasure and concentration.

When his toe snakes its way up my inner thigh, I'm grateful to be wearing my loose-fitting night-time garb: a pair of Lance's boxers and a T-shirt. The suspense is just about killing me and by the time his toe brushes against my labia, I'm on fire. I scoot my hips eagerly closer. His toe finds my swollen clit and caresses it, impressing me with its precision despite being the inferior digit. I circle my hips and suppress a moan even though our fancy sound system would certainly drown it out. Besides, the boys are so immersed in the movie they wouldn't notice an earthquake.

When the mermaids appear onscreen, Lance opens his eyes to watch. His mouth goes slack and he licks his lips. I had a feeling he got turned on by all those scantily clad mermaids with star-cup bras and flowing hair, not to mention the catfight they have with Wendy. I decide it's his turn for some fun, so I slide my foot up his leg and find his sword ready for a duel. I wrap the arch of my foot across his bulge and stroke up and down its length. I can feel Lance squirm, making a half-assed effort to be discreet.

It goes on like this for longer than I thought possible: Lance's toe massaging my nether region while my foot pets his. My hand finds its way inside my T-shirt to cup my breast, notching up the pleasure and making my belly clench with the hot pressure of it all.

When Peter Pan is named Flying Eagle by the Chief and everyone but strait-laced Wendy joins in on the dancing and pipe-smoking, we notice something's amiss. Usually in this scene, our boys are up and dancing along with the Lost Boys, but tonight they're comatose. Lance must figure they're asleep, because abruptly he removes his toe and sits up. He repositions the blanket around himself like a cape and comes in for the kill.

I shake my head. There's no way I'm doing it on the couch with our kids just a few feet away from us, awake or asleep. But Lance won't take no for an answer. He looks around the room as if searching for a more private locale. His eyes brighten with what I'm sure he believes is a brilliant idea. He takes my hand and abandons ship, dragging me with him.

He doesn't take us far: just behind the couch. I open my mouth to protest, but Lance's tongue darts in and traces my lips, then finds my tongue eagerly awaiting its arrival. Soon his mouth is moving down my neck, his hands inside my shirt to pinch my taut nipples, and I've forgotten what it was I wanted to protest. He lifts my shirt to keep his mouth moving down, down, down the length of my belly, over my mound. I stand up and lean my arms on the back of the couch to see that the boys are still sleeping. Plus it opens up the crotch of my boxers so Lance can have better access to my drenched pussy. His tongue goes straight for it, that exquisite, muscular, juicy tongue alternating between strokes and thrusts, again and again, making it nearly impossible to hold in the moans and gasps that normally flow freely.

At last, Hook and Tink are together. As Lance takes me to Neverland, Hook flirts with Tink on screen, weaving piano notes and smooth talk until Tink is gladly dancing across his map, swaying her supple hips en pointe. Knowing this is probably one of Lance's favorite parts, I push his head away and motion for him to kneel. As soon as he sees the screen, a smile breaks across his face. I get on the floor, tug his sweats down and unsheathe his sword, catching it in my mouth and devouring it. He shudders, reaches forward to steady himself on the back of the couch, then glues his eyes to the television.

When Hook locks Tink up, Lance once again takes command. He pulls himself away and twirls me around to face the screen. I squat as he caresses my ass cheeks, teasing my begging cunt with a probing finger. After an excruciating moment, he replaces the finger with his rock-solid cock and it slides directly to my G-spot. Knowing I won't be able to keep quiet, Lance claps his hand over my mouth. He wraps his other arm around my waist so he can finger my nub while pulling my hips toward his as he thrusts. It takes every ounce of discipline to keep from screaming with the pleasure of him filling me up, like tiny Tink getting fucked from behind by the well-endowed Hook.

Within moments, every inch of my torso explodes, from my pulsing vadge to my puckering nipples. Hot waves roll up my body and I imagine pixie dust showering the room. I open my mouth to scream but Lance's hand only clamps tighter, so instead the scream vibrates through my throat and chest. Just as the fireworks end for me, Lance stops moving and presses his palm harder into my belly so that he's reaching deep inside me. I can feel his cock contract, his warm juices fill me up and then his body goes slack.

When Lance pulls himself away and releases me from his grip, I come to my senses. In the world outside of Hook and Tink's tryst, I hear Wendy begin her lullaby to her brothers and the Lost Boys. "A real mother is the most wonderful person in the world." Lance pulls up his sweats and wraps his arms around me. I lean my spent body back against his and let him rock me slowly, sweetly, his chin resting on top of my head.

Now that the lusty woman in me is satiated, I am once again Mother. I want to be cuddled up with my boys, too. I stand on tiptoe to kiss Lance, then come around the couch and snuggle in with the kids on the floor. Their eyes flutter open and blink sleepily. Lance joins in, too, all of us making a giant love nest. Everyone is drawn in by Wendy's song: the Lost Boys, the Indians, even Smee with his mother-heart tattoo. And our family, shamelessly weepy and cuddly until the song is over and Peter Pan warns, "Once you grow up, you can never come back" and I think, You're wrong about that, Pan. Even horny adults can sneak off to Neverland every now and then.

WTF

Robert Buckley

The News

Barney figured something was up. His wife had been on the phone for going on an hour and her tone was manic.

Finally Joanne returned to the kitchen table. "We have to go to a wedding," she said.

Barney folded his paper in his lap. "Whose, when?"

"Two weeks from Saturday, and we *have* to go, so don't even bother to tell me you have plans for that day."

"Fine," Barney humphed. "So, who is it, and why is it on such short notice?"

"It's Debby, George and Maureen's youngest."

"I thought she was still in college."

"She is . . . but, she has to."

"Has to?" Barney's face twisted, then he nodded. "Oh, she *has* to. I see. Don't they teach these kids anything about birth control?"

Joanne shrugged. "Happens in the best of families."

"Well, at least the fellow is stepping up and doing the right thing."

"Oh, no, she's not marrying a boy."

"Huh?"

"That's why they're coming home to Massachusetts; she's marrying a girl."

"But . . . who . . . how?"

"What, dear?"

"How'd she get . . . in a family way?"

"Well, I would assume the usual way, nothing's changed about that."

"But, she's marrying another girl."

"Yes, isn't that what I just said?"

"Yes, yes, I know but . . . whose baby is it?"

"Well it's Debby's, of course. I swear, Barney, sometimes you get awfully dense."

"Jesus! I know it's Debby's, but . . ."

"Oh, for heaven's sakes. I can't talk nonsense with you now; I need to make dozens of phone calls for Maureen. I swear . . ."

Joanne stood and gave him one last impatient look before returning to the phone.

The Wedding

"Hello, George," Barney greeted the father of the bride. "I guess congratulations are in order."

George swirled a glass of bourbon in his hand. "Hardly, they're going to have to move in with us. I don't know when or if Debby will get back to school. First she comes out to us not three months ago, and now this. I should never have retired early; I would at least have had a job to go to, to get away from all this."

"Well, look on the bright side. You have two lovely daughters now. Carli seems like a really sweet kid."

"That's it; they're just kids. Tell you the truth, Barney, it's all I could do to keep from strangling the little bitch."

"Hmm, well, I guess I can understand you being upset, and all."

"Hmmph!"

"Say, George, I was wondering . . . if I'm not being too personal . . ."

"Huh, what?"

"Debby and Carli . . . ?"

"Yeah, what of them?"

"Well, how'd Debby get pregnant?"

"What?"

"Well, it's just . . . puzzling. Debby's a girl, Carli's a girl. How'd she get pregnant?"

"Barney, what the hell are you getting at?"

"Nothing, George, I just can't figure out how two girls . . .

you know ... and one them gets pregnant. It just got me to wondering."

"I can't believe you, Barney. What a thing to say!"

"Huh? George, please, I didn't mean anything ..."

"Oh, sure. Didn't mean anything? Things are all topsy-turvy for Maureen and me and you come along and talk ... talk trash about my daughter."

"Jesus, no, George, I didn't mean anything of the sort. It's just nobody has explained to me how ..."

"That's enough! I think you should leave, Barney. Don't bother showing up for that golf date next weekend either."

"But, George ..."

Maureen ran over to her husband. "Honey, what's wrong? Why are you so upset?"

George stammered. "You should have heard what this man said to me." Then he leaned toward Maureen's ear and whispered.

"Oh, my God!" Maureen turned on Barney. "How dare you?"

"Please, Maureen, it's not like that. I just asked ..."

"Please, get out of my sight!"

Joanne hurried over to see why her husband was in the center of a commotion. The other guests glared toxically at Barney.

"Barney, what's this all about?"

"Joanne! I don't know what ..."

"Take your boorish husband away from here – immediately!" Maureen demanded.

The Ride Home

"I've never been so humiliated in my whole life," Joanne keened. "Thrown out of my friend's daughter's wedding. What were you thinking?"

"For crying out loud, Joanne, all I did was ask how Debby ..."

"What is the matter with you? How could you be so rude and insulting?"

"Jesus Christ, what the hell did I do that was so bad?"

"I just don't believe you!"

"All right! All right! I'm an asshole, OK! Aren't I the biggest fucking asshole on the planet because I can't understand how a lesbian got knocked up by another lesbian? There, I said it again! Apparently, I'm the only one with the fucking balls to ask the obvious question!"

"Barney! You've never spoken to me in that manner."

"Aw, go fuck yourself, Joanne! Jesus ... what kind of friends ... I mean ... shit, what a bunch of fuckheads!"

"Barney, please watch where you're driving."

"Aw, shut up!"

He left her at the curbside in front of their house. "Get out!" he ordered.

"Barney ... where ...?"

He peeled away leaving her to cough amid the aroma of burning rubber.

The Revelation

"So," Barney said, as he ran his finger around the rim of his shot glass – his fifth. "I left the ole ball-and-chain at the curb ... know-whad-I-mean?"

"Yeah, sure pal. You having another one?" The bartender poised the mouth of the bottle over the glass.

"Lederripp!"

"There you go. I think I'll need to be calling you a cab, but you say when."

"You're awright, pal. So, anyways, as I wuz sayin', it's two girls, see. And they gotta get married cuz, you know, one of 'em's knocked up. So, I say, how the fuck does a chick knock up a chick? I mean, is this a chick with a dick?"

"Maybe they used one of them turkey basters, you know?"

"Nah ... nah ... nah. This is one of them, whachacallit ... unplanned pregnancies. So, I asks ya ... howza fuck that happen?"

"Hey, man, you talking about that stuck-up twat Debby Wallace?"

Barney and the bartender turned to appraise the young man. Barney belched. "You know ... Debby?"

"Sure, knew her back in high school. Wouldn't give me the time of day when I asked her out. Then I found out she was pitching for the other league. A friend's sister who goes to the same school with her told me: she and her girlfriend got shit-faced in their dorm room while the girlfriend's brother was visiting. Guess they said Debby was out of it when he did her, but the word is it was all arranged on account of what's-her-name, Carli, wanted the baby to have her DNA, and Debby was more than happy to spread her legs for the bro on account of they were twins, you know? How fucked up is that?"

"Well," Barney said, before his head hit the bar. "I'll be fucked with a fiddle."

The Aftermath

Barney was delivered home by cab. Joanne would not let him in bed with her. By the following afternoon police cruisers surrounded the house after Barney had carried his naked wife over his shoulder out to the backyard and proceeded to spank her bare bottom in front of horrified neighbors.

Charges were subsequently dropped after Joanne declined to testify. They soon put their home up for sale, and left the neighborhood. In spite of, or perhaps due to the disruption in their routines, they lived a remarkably happy life from then on.

Swats

Angela Caperton

"Hoyt Collins! How dare you spank my little girl!"

Hoyt gave Nola a look that made her face burn with fresh anger. "Tammy ain't a little girl, Nola. She's eighteen and she got two warnings about skippin' class before she got a spanking. That's the rule." Hoyt, head coach at Burdock High School, was thirty-six years old and still looked good in a T-shirt. Most women in town lusted after him, but not Nola. Nola had her fill of men when she kicked Tammy's daddy out ten years earlier, though that didn't stop most of the men in Burdock under the age of eighty from trying to make her.

Nola put her fists on her hips to keep from swinging at Hoyt's smug face. Fury blazed in her. "But you're a man! Rules say it should've been Miss Spenser to paddle Tammy."

"Don't you go quotin' rules to me, Nola. Rules say it's a woman spanks the girls unless there ain't a woman around. Maggie Spenser is down in Mobile takin' trainin'."

Corporal punishment in Burdock got kicked around every four or five years by the school board, but the rod swingers always won out over the child spoilers, and the paddling continued with enthusiastic zeal on the part of Burdock's administration.

"Tammy came home crying, Hoyt."

"Maybe she won't skip classes again."

"You hurt her."

"Swats don't hurt much," Hoyt said with a smirk. "You want me to show you?"

For a moment, Nola's anger clogged her speech, then she called his bluff. "OK, you bastard. Show me."

Hoyt blinked only once, then narrowed his gaze and grinned at her like a bobcat with a claw-pinned rabbit. "All right. Come over here."

From his desk drawer, Hoyt produced a long, narrow piece of wood. He screeched a heavy metal chair away from the desk. Nola saw holes had been drilled in the paddle to improve its swing.

Hoyt patted the chair. "I won't ask you to lift your skirt since I'm not Miss Spenser. But bend over."

Nola obeyed him, squaring her shoulders and bracing. She rested her hands on the seat of the chair, intensely aware of the out-thrust vulnerability of her butt.

A moment of shredded silence filled the room. She stared at her fingers on the chair and heard the whisper of Hoyt's breath, the high whistle of the drilled wood, then she felt a sharp sting on her right ass cheek through the thin shield of her pencil skirt. The crack of wood on flesh blasted her ears.

She gasped. Hoyt was right. It didn't hurt. Not exactly.

Warm, like the heat of hands cupped over an eager flame, a slow, mellow burn churned with an edge of pain at its center. She turned to look at Hoyt just as the second swat connected with her left ass cheek.

Nola jerked, the same slow creep of sensation flowing, heat then sting, while the pain on her right cheek flared like flame-braised skin.

Between her legs, a church full of candles melted. She tensed her calves to stop the squirming, and shifted her hips to angle her panties so the cotton-lined crotch could soak up the sudden slickness.

Another swat and Nola released the gasp in her throat, embarrassed at all it revealed, threadbare and desperate. Pain erupted on her sensitized flesh, coiled around her spine, and arrowed into her senses, nothing unbearable, neither vicious nor disingenuous, but real. The nettle edges coursed through her and she accepted them, let sensation flow back into her core where need whisked it into cream. She rocked, willfully wanton, inviting Hoyt to strike again.

Crack, across her left cheek, and Nola nearly came. Saliva flooded her mouth and the room blurred, light and sound muted by the fire he stoked inside her.

She heard the rasp of his breath and felt his hands rough on her thighs. She pushed her butt at him and he explored. She reached back to help him remove her panties but he slapped her hand and tore. The silk shredded, hurting her a little when he broke the waistband. The cool air of the room on her bare bottom condemned her and then his finger dipped into her sopping pussy.

"Nola, you are such a bad girl."

She heard him unbuckle and unzip and then the thick head of his cock pushed through the wet curls to introduce itself to the pulse of her clit. He gripped her hips hard and slid erect along her wet slit, coating himself, then his merciless hand swatted her ass and Nola cried out. She braced against the chair, moaning, dying of desire in the long moment before his cock filled her pussy with one hot, hard thrust.

She groaned, her mind oblivious to anything but sensation. She pushed back against his hips, brazen as a whore, and laughed with tight delight as his hand connected with her ass again.

He fucked her. He gripped her hips, pulled her against his punishing, fast thrusts, one hand reaching around to flick at her clit until her knees shivered. Her muscles tightened and she exploded in an orgasm that blasted from her pussy up her spine to blind her and incinerate her brain.

Through the haze of pleasure she heard his howl of release and felt the hot stream of his come and then the sticky, cooling residue that spilled onto her ass as his cock slipped out and he half folded over her.

Trembling, weak as water, she managed to twist and sit on the chair. The cool vinyl kissed her skin and grounded her. She pulled uselessly at her blouse and straightened her skirt over the smear.

Hoyt stood over her, his cock shrunken and wet, his eyes amazed.

"Don't spank Tammy again," Nola said.

"It don't hurt much," he offered, putting his cock back in his pants.

"That ain't the point, Hoyt. There's enough of me in that girl,

I'm afraid if you spank her for skipping, she'll never be regular to class again.

"From now on," Nola breathed, "you save those swats for me."

Between the Pages

Z. S. Roe

Softly, without meaning to, she moaned.

On the university library's sixth floor, beyond the study carrels, past dozens of floor-to-ceiling bookshelves, Sheila stood, weak-kneed. It was nearing eleven at night, and she was alone, save for the first-year undergrad shelving returned books down a far aisle. A little out of breath, she straightened the legs of her jeans, smoothed out the wrinkles in her blouse.

The book – the one with the author photo at the back – lay open on the floor where she'd dropped it.

Sheila stared at it, uncertain.

She'd found it misplaced among the countless journals only researching grad students like herself ever read. She had gathered a dozen volumes in a pile beside her on the floor, and was reaching for another on the bottom shelf, her fingers brushing each spine in turn, when she'd happened upon it.

It was smaller than the rest, hardbound, its dust jacket still in place, and so not a library book. Its cover was of a young woman's empty bedroom, but shot from outside the window, looking in. It made Sheila feel like a voyeur, and yet the feeling was a little exciting.

The book was a collection of poetry. The title, which ran in a thin script across the top of the cover, was only two words: *I Want*.

Looking at it now, she felt light-headed.

In the past two weeks, Sheila had spent most of her waking hours at the library, searching the stacks for something that might solidify her floundering dissertation. In turn, she was getting less and less sleep, and her exhaustion showed.

Was she having waking dreams? She didn't know. She didn't think so.

Still, that she found herself suddenly sitting on her pile of books on the floor without any memory of having sat down was startling.

The book was open in her lap.

Had I been reading it? she wondered, trying to account for the blank in her memory.

She thumbed through the last few pages, and then to the photo of the young woman on the back inside flap.

The author – Olesya Kovalevska. She seemed confident, unwavering, fully in the moment – not at all like any of the other women Sheila had dated.

In the photo, Olesya was sitting by a window, and wearing a man's brown dress shirt, but with the top three buttons undone, and the sleeves rolled up. Olesya was likely wearing a skirt, but the camera had caught her at knee level, and so with one leg drawn up, the other leaning against it, and her shirt falling to just past mid-thigh, Olesya appeared to be wearing nothing from the waist down. Her right hand rested atop her raised knee; her left lay between her legs.

Sheila flipped back through the book to the title poem. Sitting on her pile of books, she read quietly, mouthing each word:

I want to fuck you, she said
and the other woman unbuttoned her blouse
and slid out of her pleated skirt
and stood before her,
anticipating.

Sheila sucked in a long, ragged breath. Her head spun, but she tried to convince herself that it was the sixth floor that was spinning, not her tiredness showing through. She doubted she could trick herself that easily, and yet she persisted in it, refusing to blame the late hour or her exhaustion.

What am I doing? she wondered. Am I that desperate for a distraction, that in need of some passing fantasy?

She leaned against the nearest bookshelf, and it was then that she noticed the woman standing on the other side of the shelves. Overtop the books, she could see her bare legs, long and smooth.

For a moment, Sheila just sat there, completely still, wondering when someone else had come onto the floor, and how she hadn't noticed.

But then the woman knelt, moving slowly. Bare legs became thighs, then became a thin waist hidden behind an untucked dress shirt. In three short breaths, she was at Sheila's level. Their eyes met.

Sheila gulped, disbelief lining her face.

Olesya smiled knowingly.

Sheila closed her eyes, opened them, blinked. From below her, she felt a tremor slide into a soft rumble that reached up inside her, softly pulsing.

Olesya's smile widened, and Sheila found herself suddenly wondering what it would feel like to run her tongue along Olesya's top lip, to feel Olesya's tongue meet her own.

The thought made her blush.

The two women stared at each other: Sheila sitting atop a pile of books on one side of the bookshelf; Olesya kneeling on the other, her hands resting between her legs.

The stirring within Sheila began to balloon, and when she rose onto her knees, shifting closer, her vision blurred.

She blinked and saw Olesya rising.

She blinked again and Olesya was already halfway down the aisle.

Sheila scrambled to her feet, and hurried down her own aisle. 'Wait,' she cried. 'Hold on a minute.'

But Olesya was gone.

And then Sheila heard someone approach from behind her, heard the steady rhythm of the person's breathing as they neared, heard her own quickening in response.

She turned, but before she could fully realize who it was, Olesya was already pushing her against the bookcase. Shelves pressed into her back, her thighs, her ass.

Like a phantom, Olesya had appeared suddenly, and just as quickly she slid her bare legs between Sheila's, and then began to tug at Sheila's tucked-in blouse, popping its buttons.

'Shit,' Sheila hissed, her body stiffening.

And then Olesya kissed her, her lips parted and wet. Sheila slipped her tongue into Olesya's mouth, felt Olesya's tongue meet her own.

Olesya undid Sheila's pants while Sheila popped the remaining buttons of her own blouse, and then pulled it open. She kissed Sheila's mouth, her neck, and then slipped her right hand into Sheila's undone pants, into her panties, sliding two fingers along the lips of Sheila's pussy.

Sheila gasped.

In the small space between the two bookcases, Olesya spun Sheila around and bent her over. Trying to steady herself, Sheila gripped the nearest shelf, and then she kicked her feet out of the legs of her pants, and kicked the pants away.

Olesya pulled off Sheila's blouse, and then unhooked her bra, letting both fall to the floor. She ran one hand down Sheila's chest, down her stomach, and down further still until her fingers were deep between Sheila's legs, stroking, teasing.

Sheila moaned.

As Olesya pushed two fingers inside her, sliding them in and out, Sheila bucked hard, and Olesya's fingers slid further in, deeper and then out, deeper still and then out.

A book on the shelf Sheila was gripping fell to the floor. And then two more books fell from their shelves, hit the carpet.

Olesya was panting, sliding her fingers in and out of Sheila's pussy while her other hand cupped Sheila's breasts, one and then the other; squeezed her nipples, one and then the other.

Without giving her time to react, Sheila turned and pushed Olesya to the floor, and then mounted her. She tore Olesya's shirt open and put her mouth to Olesya's erect nipples, sucked them, teased them with her teeth.

Grabbing Sheila by the ass, Olesya pulled her forward, and pushed her up until Sheila was kneeling over her open mouth.

Arching her back, Sheila closed her eyes, felt herself shaking. Olesya's wet mouth was like an ember, her tongue a lick of flame.

A moment before she came, Sheila thought that she could hear nothing but her own ragged breathing. Gone were the books, the shelves, even Olesya.

Just inhale and exhale, like the rapid beating of her heart.

And then she gasped, and her eyes shot open.

And she was still sitting alone in the middle of the last aisle on the top floor of the university library.

On the floor in front of her was *I Want*.

She could still hear the soft whirring of the heating system, still hear the kid working through the aisles on the other end of the floor. She let out a long, deep breath.

Ten minutes later, she'd gathered everything she needed and was heading for the stairs when the undergrad student caught her by the exit – he was leaving, too.

He held open the door to the stairwell for her, and smiled. 'Finally found something worth checking out, huh?'

Sheila smiled in turn. *I Want* was the only book she'd taken with her. 'Yeah,' she said, grinning. 'I think I have.'

All About Me

Delilah Devlin

I awoke slowly, enjoying the pleasant tingling that calluses left on my belly. A man's rough hands smoothed over me.

Not every day did I wake with someone else sharing my bed. My heart skipped a beat. And then I remembered. *Craig.* That was his name. I was in bed with a stranger named Craig.

Daylight teased the edges of my eyelids, but I squeezed them shut again, not ready yet to end the bliss. I could pretend for at least a couple of moments longer that we meant more to each other than just a heat-of-the-moment fling.

Still, he'd stayed the night, and the heaviness of the cock poking at my backside telegraphed the fact he wasn't in any hurry to leave.

A kiss touched the corner of my neck.

"You awake?" he growled then licked the bottom edge of my ear lobe.

"Not yet. Do that some more," I mumbled and leaned back toward his heated skin.

His chuckle was warm, wicked.

I stretched my legs then snuggled my butt closer to his erection. "I'm awake enough," I whispered.

"And I'm interested, as you can tell," he murmured. "But you owe me something first."

I groaned and pushed my face into the pillow, wanting to hide because he'd risen on an elbow and was pushing my hair behind my ear to peer at my face.

He cupped a breast, thumbing the nipple. "You promised."

"I wasn't in my right mind."

"Coward."

I whimpered, and then turned onto my back to meet his gaze. "Why don't you go first?"

He shook his head, a smile twitching at the corners of his lips. "Now, see? That's not what I want. And you said I could have anything I wanted if I made you come."

I snorted. "How do you know I didn't fake it?"

A sexy grin stretched across his face. "Baby, you came so hard you peed on me."

His soft laughter made my cheeks burn. I narrowed my eyes. "And to think Bev said you were a nice guy."

"Not too nice." His eyebrows gave a waggle. "And aren't you glad? Besides, you're cute when you get embarrassed."

I wrinkled my nose. "Didn't seem to bother you a bit."

"Why should it? I like you wet." He came over me, sighing as he settled between my legs.

"What else do you like?" I asked, running my fingertips lightly up his back.

He dipped his head and bit my ear. "You're stalling."

His breath tickled my neck and I raised my shoulder. "Why not just fuck me?"

"Because this'll be more intimate."

"More so than fucking?"

His cheek glided up and down against my neck as he nodded.

I rolled my eyes, thinking hard, or at least as hard as I could with his cock sliding up and down between my folds. "Can I do it faced away?" I gasped.

"What do you think?" Abruptly, he pushed up then knelt between my thighs. "Need pillows?"

"Don't be helpful," I groused.

"You really don't like this."

I felt like screaming my frustration. He was right there. I was open. Eager. And yet, he sat watching, his expression firming into that hard mask that had made me tear at my clothes the moment he'd closed the bedroom door. "I might like this better if we were in the middle of something, but like this it feels—"

"Dirty?"

I nodded. At last, he understood. Now maybe he'd move closer.

"Do you know what attracted me to you first?"

I blinked at his awkward segue.

"How bold you are."

Liar. However, I didn't mind that he goaded me. His needling challenges had led us to this bed. Something I couldn't regret.

His hands soothed up and down my inner thighs, and his gaze dropped to my sex. But the exposure – my pussy to daylight – wasn't quite so embarrassing because he was arranging me again, lifting my knees, placing my heels just so. Like he was creating a picture for his pleasure. Then he laid his palms against my inner thighs and opened me further.

He could see right inside me. A blush swept my skin, cheeks to breasts.

His nostrils flared as he gazed down.

I was happier than I ever would have admitted when he'd allowed me to bathe after my "accident" – then relieved that he'd changed the sheets while I'd cowered in the shower. He hadn't let me hide there for long, jerking back the curtain, and joining me there to "wash" his dick inside me.

My modesty lay in shreds. Oddly, this engendered a feeling of deep, fierce elation. I'd never been with anyone like him. Someone who could make me laugh one moment, then shiver with anticipation with just a single commanding glare. I didn't know him well enough to trust him. And yet I was thrilled he was here even if he was busy staring at my intimate parts. "You just gonna look?"

"I'm waiting."

Fuck. He expected me to keep that promise. The one I'd given when he was laughing, holding me against him when we were both so wet, and I'd been desperate for a little privacy to groan at my lack of self-control.

"I'm still waiting."

The texture of his voice, so firm, excited me. I couldn't get my head wrapped around the idea of how much I wanted him. Or that I needed him to be in charge. Of me.

From the first moment we'd been introduced at dinner by friends, I'd been caught.

All it had taken was one long challenging look from his dark blue eyes and I'd felt instantly aroused, and then annoyed with myself because I wanted him and he knew it.

Just like he knew it now.

His fingers trailed from my clit straight into my slick folds. He swirled in moisture then licked his fingers, all the while holding my gaze. "Anytime, Heather."

"This'll be quick," I muttered, blushing again.

"Fast, slow – I don't care. But you have to come."

Lord, how'd he do that? Make me feel as though I was the main course of a delicious meal. "And you think you'll know if I come?"

He canted his head. "I know the look."

"I have a look?"

"Oh yeah."

"Can I close my eyes?" I bit my lip as I glanced at his knowing expression.

One dark brow arched.

I shook my head. "I didn't know you were such a control freak."

"Yeah, you did," he said softly. "Start wherever you want."

I swallowed, knowing I was through stalling because after all this talk, I was horribly aroused. I cupped my breasts, hoping that watching me would entice him to join in and end my solo act. He'd said he liked my breasts, and the tips were sore from where he'd played endlessly – licking, flicking, sucking, biting . . .

My nipples hardened and I plucked and twisted them, pulling then letting them go to jiggle my breasts.

But he remained still, watching, with his hands on his knees as he knelt between my spread thighs.

What the hell? Why did I care that he watched? His intense stare and the color darkening his face said he was into it. That I was turning him on. His cock pulsed, jutting from his groin, hard and thick.

My hands smoothed down my belly; fingertips scraped through the short blonde hair on my mound. I used one hand to spread my folds, the other to tease my clit, swirling on the knot until it grew harder and stretched the hood, causing it to slide away.

Then I thrust two fingers into my pussy, curving my hips to deepen my reach. I let go of my folds and slid a hand beneath my ass, teasing my perineum while I thrust my fingers deeper and twisted them. My heartbeat pounded in my ears.

Wetness oozed from inside me, soaking my hand, slipping lower to trickle toward my asshole. And because his breathing was becoming louder, raspier, I dared more – using the moisture to wet a fingertip and stick it in my ass.

"Sure you don't want some of this?" I asked, my voice husky. I lifted my legs and curled my abdomen, the muscles of my belly burning to hold the cramped position, but now I could stroke both holes deeper and he could see everything I did.

My thumb twiddled my clit while I fucked myself. I tucked another finger inside my ass and gave up trying to look pretty, trying not to make faces or unattractive noises, and just let go. My orgasm bloomed, and my face screwed up into that expression, the one he knew meant I was coming, and I flew. My cry was soft and floated away.

Hands slipped over my knees to ease them down. I blinked, only just realizing I'd closed my eyes there at the end.

Craig came over me, waiting, as I slowly pulled my fingers from inside my body. Then he fit his cock to my entrance and thrust deep into my moist, hot center.

We rocked together, me clutching his back, him growling as he thrust faster and harder. Another quick flash burn of pleasure swept me. He shouted, sharpening his shortened thrusts, until he made the face I knew meant he'd found his own orgasmic bliss.

I smiled, damn near purring as his breaths evened out. "You owe me now."

He grunted. "Think I'll mind you watching me jerk off?"

"You'll mind, because I get to say when you can come."

He blinked then barked a laugh. "You do know it's going to take me a little while."

I wrinkled my nose. "I, on the other hand, suffer no such handicap." I reached up and gripped his ears, then tugged him downward, showing him exactly how he could pass the time.

Glory Hole

Tim Rudolph

We were driving straight through from Fresno to LA, but half-way there the car needed gas, I needed gum, and Sheila needed to pee. So welcome to hot, flat, uninviting Bakersfield, California. Well, not Bakersfield proper, exactly. I pulled off 99 and followed two big rigs down a frontage road, figuring these guys could sniff out a pit stop better than I could. Sure enough, in less than a mile they led me to Mobley's World Famous Truck Stop, seven acres of steaming asphalt hidden beneath dozens of idling eighteen-wheelers.

Just beyond Mobley's I turned into a crappy-looking GasMart. Cheap unleaded? Check. Junk food for the long haul to la-la land? Check. A "clean and sanitary" restroom for Mademoiselle? Amen, and pass the ultra-thin butt wipes.

I smiled at Sheila. "Sometimes it pays to be a guy," I said. "Thank God I don't have to sit my pretty ass down in one of those things." We both looked in the direction of two banged-up metal doors marked "Mans" and "Womans" in red Magic Marker. "Fucking bacteria factories, these places."

Sheila checked herself out in the visor mirror and smoothed out her eyebrows. "If you're trying to gross me out, it's not working. We both know that guys are the real pigs in public bathrooms. Piss on the floor. Backed-up toilets. Wads of toilet paper stuck on the wall." She shook her head in disgust. "No, I'll take my chances in the ladies', thank you."

"Is that right? My advice, you get in and get out before some bug decides to set up housekeeping in your sweet little snatch."

"OK. Pig. So I'll hover. Now be a good boyfriend and get me a Mars bar and a 7 Up."

"Can do, lover." We both got out and I walked around to unscrew the gas cap. "You'll have to get the key from the man inside. And see if he has any hazmat suits to wear in the bathroom." Sheila flipped me off and we both laughed. Then I watched her walk away, that fabulous ass wrapped up tight in faded Levis, that snug little cotton top drawing attention wherever we went.

But all this talk about pissing and bathrooms – now *I* had to go. Well, better to drain the old weasel now than to hold it for another 200 miles. But first things first. Pick up some groceries. Pay for the fuel. And then, naturally, piss in the bathroom sink, just to spite my girl. Oink-oink.

"Sheila," I called, rattling the bathroom door's handle. "Honey, I'm going to set our bag of goodies outside your door. Be a good girl and grab them on your way out, OK?" No answer. "Sheila? What happened, you fall in? Look, if you want you can start pumping the gas, too. I already paid."

The men's room was a disaster. Rank. Unlit. Scratched-up stainless steel for a mirror. A cracked commode and a filthy sink that went drip drip drip. Still, any port in a storm. I unzipped and watched my piss swirl around the rust-stained bowl.

Then, out of the corner of my eye, I saw it. In the cheap plywood partition that separated the men's and women's restrooms, some joker had gouged out a dick-sized hole three feet off the floor. Shocking. But, being curious – and somewhat of a joker myself – I measured my cock's height against the hole's. Close enough for government work. I squatted and gave the hole a look-see, but I couldn't make out anything on the other side.

"Sheila," I whispered. "Hey, Sheila. Come over here, baby. Check this out." I could hear shoes scuffling and the rustle of tissue. Then I heard the toilet flush, followed by the sound of running water. And in the midst of all this eavesdropping I made a surprising discovery – my cock was as hard as a hockey puck, and I was playing with it like a horny high-schooler. How did *that* happen?

Well, no matter. With my free hand I tapped on the wall above the hole. "Sheila? Don't be shy, girl. Come see what Daddy has for you." I heard my voice bounce around in the coffin-like space. It sounded urgent. So urgent that I stood up, dropped my cargo shorts to my ankles, and guided my stiffy into the ragged opening.

And immediately felt like an idiot. Because I got nothing in return. No eager hand stroking my hard-on. No moistened lips giving it a sloppy kiss. Not even a teasing come-on. ("Ooh, baby, your cock is so big. I want it *all* in my mouth.") Nothing – until I felt a whisper of warm breath play along the length of my dick.

"Is that you, honey? What am I saying? Of course it is. Talk to me, sweetheart. Tell me you'll do me right here in this filthy little stinkhole. Are you on your knees? Are your jeans unbuttoned? Are you fucking yourself with your fingers?"

Again, no answer. But there was no containing my excitement. I knew that we'd left the car unlocked and unattended. I knew that our sack of munchies outside the door was easy pickings. But I didn't care. My only thought was this: There is a very naughty girl within sucking distance of my cock, and I want her – need her – to seal those pretty lips around the hole while I hammer my hips against the cheap-ass wall. Hammer them until I come like a sex-starved nature boy.

But Sheila had other ideas; she obviously wanted to role-play. Silent, mysterious coquette sucks off horny wayfarer in anonymous crapper. Well, fuck it all, I could get behind that. But I still needed a sign. Or a sigh. Anything.

Then – hello! – she was all over me. Sure, things were a little rushed. That was understandable. But my dick wasn't complaining. When she started working me with her lips and teeth and tongue, I clawed at the wall like an alley cat to keep from coming. Sheila, for her part, seemed caught up in the decadence of it all, licking and sucking my cock like it was her very last lollipop. When she sensed that I couldn't hold out any longer, she traded her mouth for some expert hand action, gripping and pumping me firmly just under the head, the way she knew I liked it until – oh sweet Jesus! – I was fourteen again and spurting a half-pint of cream all over my old man's *Playboy*.

Oh, the universe did fall away. Just before the hallucinations started.

* * *

The last thing I'd said to Sheila through the bathroom door, right after I'd zipped up, washed up, and grabbed up the groceries was, "See you back at the car, doll." I just didn't expect to see her so soon. Yet there she was, already propped up in the passenger seat and wearing a look of anguish that stopped me cold. What the hell? Unless my girlfriend was secretly Supergirl there was no way she could have outraced me to the car.

"Shit," she said when I walked up to her. "I thought you'd never come out. Quick, give me your key – I'm about to piss my panties."

I was blown away. "But didn't you already . . .?" I stammered. "Weren't you and I just . . .?"

"Bobby, darling, you're babbling. Anyway, did that crazy witch come out of the ladies' yet? She told me to fuck off when I knocked, can you believe it?"

"Crazy witch? You mean someone was already inside?"

"Yes, damn it."

"But you had the key. How . . .?"

"Don't know, don't care. All I know is that door was bolted from the inside, and I couldn't get in to do my business."

I waited with dread for her to go on, but I already knew how the story ended. Uh-oh.

"Anyway, when I freaked out and ran back to the car, you were already in the store. Then I watched you disappear into the little boys' room for, like, forever! What were you *doing* in there?"

Well, apparently my dick was getting the full-service treatment by some faceless truck stop hooker. But this wasn't the time to make that information available. Besides, my mind was so dizzy with disbelief that all I could do was watch Sheila crab-walk her way towards the men's room, seeking relief. She had found her focus.

And I had lost mine. I jammed the pump's nozzle into the tank and stared absently across the wide expanse of asphalt; the heat waves made everything look like a mirage. Well, not exactly everything. That thirty-something tart with the weathered face, the too-tight leather skirt, and the ripped fishnets that I saw wiggling out of the women's restroom – *she* was no mirage. Oh, fuck. Immediately I ducked behind the car, held my breath, and prayed – please God, make her disappear. But she didn't even glance my way. Instead, she patted her lacquered-up hair, swung her wide hips, and vanished into Mobley's jungle of belching semis.

A minute later, I saw Sheila come out of the men's, take both keys into the store, then come skipping back to the car wearing a "man, it's great to be alive" look. The tank topped off, I climbed in on my side, Sheila swung into hers, and we both dove for the goody bag at the same time. She fished around and found her Mars bar and 7 Up, and I went for the Juicy Fruit, hoping to work some saliva back into my cotton mouth. Then Sheila leaned across the seat and kissed me on the cheek.

"Thanks for stopping, hon. I think. But next time let's hit up a Denny's. Deal?"

"Deal," I mumbled, flinching when she patted my crotch. Before I started to drive away, I checked all the mirrors – there was no sign of the lady in leather. Good. Maybe it *was* all a mirage.

"God, Bobby," Sheila said suddenly, making me jump. "Did you see that hole somebody punched in the wall?" She took a swallow of 7 Up then looked at me like she knew something. "Men are such swine."

It was thirty miles down the highway before I gave some serious thought to confessing everything. It was five miles later that I decided not to.

Handcuffed

Clarice Clique

I look down at the scars on my wrists and think of you.

I think of when you handcuffed me, put a collar round my neck, and led me round your house on a long chain. You pushed me down onto your sofa and spread my legs. You fucked me without looking at me. You flipped me over as if I was weightless, as if I was nothing. I screamed out even before you spread my ass, before you pushed all your length into me with one thrust.

When it was over, and you removed the handcuffs, and I sat there rubbing my wounds, you looked at me.

You were all sweat, all panting breathlessness. You looked into my eyes and you said, "That was the last time."

You said you knew what I was the first moment you saw me. When you told me that I was innately sexually submissive a shock of electricity pulsed through my nerves. When you told me that I was wasting time dating boys, that I needed a man with experience to release me, I thought what arrogance to say these things to me, to presume he knows me better than I know myself, and, of course, I fell in love with you.

I knew nothing. I scurried around the university corridors trying not to be noticed. I thought you hated me, the way you were in tutorials, never meeting my eyes. Sometimes I had daydreams of slapping you, shouting at you to look at me (there's your natural submissive for you).

It was after you'd whipped me that time, that time when you whipped my whole body not just my buttocks, when you left welts over my breasts and stomach and thighs, it was then that you explained why you'd never looked at me through my university life. Because you couldn't. Because I was too much temptation. You'd promised your loving, faithful, good, and a thousand other positives, Catholic wife that you wouldn't wander from the path again.

Those were the exact words you used to me, and I'm guessing the exact words you used to her, "wander from the path", as if the things you did to me were comparable to a little exploratory strolling on your daily walk.

But at the time I was more interested in the "again".

You'd done this before?

You laughed a surprised little laugh and raised your eyebrows at me. "I'm over fifty, do you really think you are my first little slut?"

I nodded, angry that I was getting angry. I thought maybe you'd experimented with your wife – big laughter from you at that – and you were taking things a little further with me. Or, that maybe there had been women before your wife.

No. Looking up at the white ceiling. Looking down at the swirling patterns on the carpet. Picking up a trashy magazine, one of the ones you had forbidden me to read, and flicking through the pages. Looking anywhere but at me. No, there had been no one before your wife, she was your childhood sweetheart, the love of your life, your first kiss when you were eight in the boughs of an apple tree. The only woman you thought you'd ever want.

So. When did you first do this? When did you discover that a woman was most attractive when she has ropes and chains constricting her and she is begging you to fuck her?

You looked at me with that look that made everything else in my world disappear, leaving me with one desire: to be your fuck toy.

I hoped you'd pick up the whip and punish me for my questions.

But you sighed and answered me. In the US on a lecture tour, a Japanese woman, her intelligence had seduced you. She'd been so small, so slender, you'd told her you wanted to protect her from the world, she told you to fuck her harder than she'd ever been fucked before. She taught you the word "*Shinju*", showed you the beauty of breast bondage. As you crossed boundary after boundary you realized there was nothing you wouldn't do.

Your story bored me. No, it didn't bore me. It made me itch inside. It made me want to scream.

Did you love her?

No, you didn't love her. It was an infatuation of the moment. You've spent the rest of your life swaying between extreme gratitude and hatred for what she opened up inside you.

You smiled at me and smoothed my hair down and said I'd probably feel the same about you in years to come.

I ignored that.

How many "infatuations of the moment" had there been since her?

Oh, you don't keep count. You don't have a belt with little notches in. Twenty, thirty, forty, who knows?

Twenty. Thirty. Forty. Who knows? Not you. Not me.

And how many were your students?

That question you didn't like. That made you sit up straight with your mouth in a hard line and your eyes staring at me as if you didn't know me and didn't want to know me.

I hadn't been your student when you first fucked me, you reminded me.

Then your face changed and became more familiar. You reached both hands out and pinched my nipples, you scratched along the red lines that the whip had left on my flesh.

And that is your one regret in life, that you didn't fuck me the first moment you saw me, that you wasted three years imagining what a dirty little whore I'd be instead of finding out.

You pulled my head down by my hair, forcing my mouth onto your cock. You fucked me hard, not caring if I gagged or not. All the time I thought, I am your dirty little whore. I am your dirty little whore.

I was so blissfully happy. Much, much happier than I knew I deserved to be.

I've tried to replace you a couple of times. Three times to be precise. Three times I've tried to find another Master, but they were never real. I found them all online and the online chat was good, it turned me on.

I am going to push my fist right up your ass.

"Yes, Sir, please, Sir, I'd like that, Sir," I wrote.

"Do you like pain?" another one asked.

"I like whatever my Master tells me to like," I wrote.

"Good, 'cause I am going to make you bleed," he replied.

That one scared me and put me on a high all day.

The last one was my favorite for a while, but then he said he wanted a toilet slut and I realized there were things I never wanted to do (unless maybe you ordered me to). So I am not the natural, total submissive, begging-to-be-dominated-and-controlled girl you think I am.

I met up with all three of them. Everything was technically right, between them they spanked me, tied me up, fucked every part of me, called me all the names you do and some more you don't, but it didn't work. I think of that sex now like a succession of paper cuts. Do you understand? A mild irritation, but nothing of consequence.

When I saw you afterwards, I waited for you to comment on my new bruises, on the smell of me, but you acted like you didn't notice, that you didn't care. I know you would have noticed, as you notice everything. I don't know if you cared.

Three must be my magic sexual number. I've tried to replace you with three different men, you waited three years before you made anything happen between us, you've been whipping me and spanking me and binding me for three years, and so far you've dumped me three times. Although you don't call it dumping. You say things like:

'You're young. Relationships such as ours aren't meant to last.'

'You are very sweet and more than pleasing, but what we have is a fantasy. Fantasies wane, they cannot be sustained for lifetimes.'

'That was the last time.'

It is the one thing I cannot obey. I cannot walk away. I cannot disappear from your life. I've changed my diet, my hair, my clothes, the films I see, the books I read, all to your preference. When you give me the signal, a nod of your head, I get down on my hands and knees and lift my skirt for you. I don't wear underwear anymore. I do wear nipple clamps and walk around work all day with love beads stretching my ass for you. I exist for your pleasure. I cannot exist without you.

You tell me that I am still a child in terms of my sexual experiences, that many men and women are out there with promises of excitement and loving that will go far beyond anything I know.

I tell you I stopped being a child the moment you took me aside on my graduation day. You led me away from my friends and family and into your room. I thought it was another of your strange ways, not wanting to give me personal congratulations for getting a first in front of others.

You shut the door behind us, paused for a second, then turned to face me. "Get on your knees, slut."

I don't remember being shocked, or even surprised. I remember dropping to my knees and staring at you as you undid your trousers and revealed the largeness of your cock to me. You pressed it against my lips and they opened at your touch. You put your hands on the back of my head and fucked my mouth. I inhaled the scent of you, expensive tobacco and whisky, and then the taste of you, green strawberries. You arranged yourself in a respectable manner and sat down at your desk as if to do some work but you didn't touch any of the papers or books before you.

"You can go now," you said.

"I don't think I want to," I said, my voice sounding quiet even in your small room.

"I had a feeling that's how you'd respond."

Now I am looking at the scars on my wrists. They're already fading. I think of you fucking me. I think of how you were, all sweat, all panting breathlessness, how you looked into my eyes and said, "That was the last time."

And I just want to say, I don't believe you.

Bastard

Alison Tyler

"Why would anyone wear a belt buckle with the word 'bastard' on it?"

"Bess bought that for him."

"Doesn't answer my question."

Flynn arched one brow and then leaned in close. "The word suits him."

I stared over the bar at the dark-haired man in the far booth. He was by himself, drinking a beer, and he had treated me nicely when I'd gone to serve him. But I'd noticed the buckle on his belt when he'd arrived, and I'd been curious from the start.

"Watch out for that one," Flynn added as she headed to her tables in the rear. She couldn't have said anything more likely to make me want to fuck him.

I waited until we had a moment together behind the bar once more and I begged for information. Flynn took me out back with her and, while she lit a cigarette, I bit my lip. She'd been the one to train me over the past three days. I knew how the place worked – or I thought I did. The only thing left was for me to understand the customers.

"He came in one evening, and told Bess he was going to make her come like she never had."

Bess was the tall blonde with the snowy stare. She didn't seem like she'd melt for anyone.

"And Bess told him where to get off."

"You'd think, but she was curious. She took him home, planning to show him a thing or two about what women want, you know, straddle his face for hours until he practically smothered. And he had different plans."

I don't know why I was getting wet listening to the story, but I was.

"She came in the next day, and I never saw her sit down. Not once."

Now I knew why I'd been intrigued by the man. He was someone who could give me what I wanted. But I needed to hear the rest of the story, first.

"She said it was the best goddamn night of her life. That he'd pushed her down on the bed and lifted her skirt. She had thought he was going to fuck her. Just shove it in. And she was ready. But he didn't. He pulled her panties down and smacked her ass once. Hard. She squirmed and tried to pull away, but he held her in place and spanked her again. Bess said she was ready to tell him to leave, when he said, 'I'm going to give this beautiful ass of yours a hiding you'll remember. And then I'm going to fuck you so sweet the pain will melt away.'

"Something in his eyes made her nod, she said. Something in the way he promised to please her. She hadn't been spanked ever, she told me, but she got into the position he wanted, ass up, arms locked in place, and she held herself steady while he smacked her bottom over and over.

"She said she was crying when he was done. Her ass felt swollen and red, but she had remembered what he'd promised her. The reward. And she didn't complain. He went on his knees behind her, and he started to lick her pussy, slowly at first, pressing his face into her from behind, getting really deep in her. He used his tongue to trace circles around her clit, and then right when she was on the cusp, he stood up, gripped her hips, and pulled her back on him.

"Bess didn't tell us any of that at first. But she walked gingerly the next day, and she refused to sit down. Even on break. She was constantly standing. It was only when I cornered her in the ladies' that she admitted what had happened. Then she lifted her little pleated skirt and showed off the marks on her ass. I knew right then that I was going to go home with him."

I must have had a similar expression on my face, because Flynn started to laugh. "You, too? Well, wait a second, because you haven't heard the rest. He didn't come back in for a few weeks and, when he did, Bess was stalking around the bar like the Queen of Sheba, which she does pretty much every night. Thinks she's the top dog, you know? But he had his sights on Lizzie that night. And Lizzie had already heard the whole thing from me, so she was ready to see for herself what this guy was like."

"Isn't Lizzie gay?" I asked. I was still trying to keep all the ladies straight in my head.

"She's bi." Flynn shrugged. "Lizzie goes home with him that night, and she doesn't even wait until the morning to tell me. She stops over on her way back to the Valley, and she shows me the bruises and tells me exactly how he did it. Grabbed her up and put her over his lap on the sofa, spanked her with a paddle he had at the ready. Made her cry and beg him to stop before he fingered her pussy until she came. And she said the whole time she didn't want him to stop. 'Isn't that crazy?' she asked me. She just wanted the spanking and the rubbing and the coming to go on and on."

"Did she have marks?"

"Like you wouldn't believe. Her ass was plum-colored. Pretty, I have to say." Flynn got silent for a moment, and I wondered whether she and Lizzie had fooled around together, but didn't feel as if it was my place to ask.

"Finally, he comes in, and I know it's my turn. He's got his eyes on me, and Bess won't even look my way. But I don't care. I'm ready. The way the girls have talked about him, the way they've built him up, I know he can't possibly live up to the expectations in my head. But that doesn't stop me from going home with him, from pretending I don't know what he has in mind.

"The thing is, I don't. He hand-spanked Bess. And he paddled Lizzie. Well, he's got something else in mind for me. We're in his kitchen when he tells me to bend over and hold my ankles."

"Just like that?"

"No, of course not. There's been petting and kissing in the car and in the elevator up to his place. But we're at that moment, when the glaze is over us. That sex glaze that makes everything seem speeded up. Your heart's pumping so fast, and your pussy. I was dripping. And I do what he says. I bend over, hold my ankles. I've got these striped thigh-high stockings on and high heels, and I'm a bit unstable, but I do my best.

"Then I hear the buckle on his belt, and I think, Oh, wow, he's just going to fuck me. I didn't realize right away that he was pulling the leather free. I didn't understand until I heard the snap of the belt, and then it was too late."

"Would you have wanted him to stop?"

She grinned and shook her head, long feathery cinnamon-red hair dancing over her cheeks. "No. I wouldn't have. I was feeling special that he thought I could take this. Take the leather. When he hadn't used his belt on the other girls."

"So he spanked you?" Saying the word almost makes me come right there in the alley.

"He spanked the living daylights out of me. You wouldn't have believed the sounds I made while he worked me over. I lost my grip on my ankles right away, but he told me to put my palms flat on the floor, and he striped me with that belt until I thought I would go hoarse from all the begging. And then, just like he'd said, just like he promised, he pushed me down on the floor, flipped me over, and ate my pussy until I creamed all over his face. I was in heaven, the cool tiles under my hot ass, and his sweet tongue on my clit, and while I was floating he fucked me, so that I came all over again. Like magic."

There was silence then. We both seemed awed by her story. But then I remembered. The buckle. Why would anyone wear a buckle with the word "bastard" on it?

"Bess went out and bought the thing for him. She was so pissed he'd fucked us all. That he'd worked his way through the girls. It was a warning, she said, for any other ladies who might want to try him out. But I don't think he considers it a warning. I think he considers it a prize."

I nodded and stole a drag off her cigarette before she crushed out the butt with the point of her heel. And I wondered whether the word would make an imprint on my skin when it was my turn.

The History of Her Tongue

Shaun Levin

1. Sweet

She was born with the taste of champagne in her mouth. Her mother had dipped a finger in the mug of bubbly at her hospital bedside and touched the drops to her baby's lips. Milk came later. She learnt to swear early, as we do, those of us with older siblings – sisters and brothers who introduce us to the mysteries of the foul mouth. She drank and cursed for much of her teens. Champagne and milk don't mix. She switched to fruit smoothies when they opened a yoga studio near her flat.

Her mother told her, years later, that the only way to shut her up when she was bawling, especially on those long train journeys back from Scotland, was to feed her chocolate. She has never liked the dark or expensive ones; high percentages of cocoa make her nauseous, like something has been left out, like eating flour from the bag and calling it cake. She prefers Cadbury's Dairy Milk to anything. She associates chocolate with comfort and distress; it calms and upsets her.

She's almost forty now and knows that sweetness is not at the tip of the tongue. Sweetness is everywhere.

Her boyfriend eats strawberries in little bites; she eats them whole. Her father taught her to eat them like that.

"Bite off more than you can chew," he'd say.

He said there will always come a point when chewing becomes possible; one had to persist until everything fitted into the mouth with ease. She thinks of it as sexual now, and wonders if her father had noticed the innuendo in what he'd said when she was seven, thirty years ago. But the lesson has remained: she always bites off more than she can chew.

2. Sour

From close up, taste buds resemble pickling onions or the fruit of the tamarind tree.

3. Salty

When it comes to semen, one's choice has little to do with taste. Taste is not why one spits or swallows. It's a question of love, or hunger, or devotion. When domesticity sets in, semen is not something she will swallow. She'll spit it out or make a suggestion she knows he'll like.

"Come on my tits," she'll say.

When she has a yeast infection, she washes herself with natural Himalayan crystal salts. She lies in an empty bathtub and pours the hot saline water into herself. After she has washed thoroughly, she dabs aloe vera gel onto the outside of her vagina. Her boyfriend likes to watch – he likes everything about her – and will lick between her thighs before she applies the cream.

4. Bitter

She hates her job and sometimes hates her boyfriend, the way he never makes up his mind, the way he expects her to take the initiative with most things: holidays, interior decoration, evening activities – sex, theatre, dinner parties. She hates her sister for being so beautiful – her smooth skin, her straight hair, her almond eyes, almond-shaped, almond in colour – and for being more settled than her. They talk on the phone often but don't see each other much. It suits her. She likes her sister more when she doesn't see her. They were close once and used to go out drinking in the days before Jane got married to a man who now cheats on her. They used to sit in bars on the Kings Road and sip Campari on the rocks and talk to strangers.

Her boyfriend has a steady job in IT and is faithful. He has always been a good boy, always done what's expected of him, never took drugs, never swore. He tells her – sometimes it's funny – that his father washed his mouth out with soap once when he used a four-letter word at the dinner table. They agree that this is probably why he's attracted to her foul mouth.

She likes her coffee black.

5. Umami

On their third "anniversary" – Do we really have to do this? she thinks – she prepares a dish of steak and Roquefort cheese. He brings red roses and champagne and a giant slab of Cadbury's Dairy Milk, the kind one finds in duty free shops at London airports. He buys the same gifts every year. He likes the ritual of it, says that repetition enhances the bond in a relationship. He says it creates appetite and expectation.

"Yes," she says. "Something to look forward to."

She thinks about a man she met on the internet, a guy she got chatting to while playing online Scrabble. She calls herself "wordslut" and likes it when men are aggressive towards her; it turns her off when they start getting flirtatious or coy or reserved – she keeps chatting to him because he says things like: "i wanna fuk u wit my tung." He warns her to be careful because he's the shape-shifting lizardman from the fourth dimension. He beat her three times before she had to get back to work.

Her boyfriend slices his steak with a steak knife and eats slowly. As if to get stuck in was vulgar. He cuts gently, precisely, puts a chunk in his mouth and chews and chews and chews, then swallows. It's how he's been taught. She, on the other hand, drinks beer from a wine glass, wipes her nose then brushes back her hair. She is slim, like her boyfriend, bred from the same stock. We are everywhere, she thinks.

"This is yummy," he says.

"Good," she says.

She doesn't know how much longer she can take this.

Her sister is pregnant again and craving pickled herring.

* * *

6. Spicy

Her boyfriend returns from a visit to his mother with a jar of grilled peppers in olive oil. They are yellow and red with slithers of garlic pressed against the glass.

"She knows I hate peppers," she says.

"I'll eat them," he says.

She doesn't like bell peppers, especially when they're cooked and cold and slimy. She doesn't like slimy food at all, even oysters, which she claims to be mad about. The older she gets the more she likes spicy food, the spicier the better – it's a test and a challenge.

She fantasizes about working her way through some scale of hotness; at the bottom would be bell peppers. She dated an Asian guy once who worked in the food industry – he told her that the heat is in the chilli's placenta, that the burning stimulates nerve endings in the mouth that transmit messages to the brain to release endorphins. They always drank a lot when they ate the food he cooked, then they'd go dancing, or have sex on the floor, on the table, in the kitchen, anywhere but the bed.

She has an aunt in LA who sends her dried chillies crushed between the pages of hardback novels.

7. Aftertaste

She doesn't miss her boyfriend. Sometimes she sees him in other men, which is no surprise, bearing in mind the limited gene pool of this island. Leaving London is no longer an option. She can't imagine living anywhere else; everything she knows is here, contained in this maw of a city. And eventually her tongue will forget, like it's forgotten the feel of her mother's nipple in her mouth, like it's forgotten that first wad of mustard in punishment for an early profanity, like it's forgotten its first word: "mama" or "dada" or "goo-goo". But it will never forget chocolate, its long legacy, the way that each time it melts in her mouth her body remembers the relief and the sadness on those journeys back home.

Night Watch

Veronica Wilde

I leaned out of the taxi window as we approached the Saguaro Star Resort. Tiny lights were wound around the palm trees lining the road up to a looming massive hotel. More blue lights lit up the manicured green lawn before a splashing fountain. This was my first trip to Arizona and I had pictured something entirely different.

"Looks expensive," the taxi driver grunted.

"Yep." I didn't normally stay at lux hotels, but since this was all going on my expense report, why not. This was the first time my company had sent me on a business trip in a warm climate, and I intended to indulge.

As soon as I checked in and got up to my room, I collapsed on my queen-sized bed. But I didn't feel tired as much as grimy from travel. I loosened my long auburn hair from its ponytail and stripped down to my green silk panties. Then I opened the sliding glass doors to the balcony and leaned out to see what kind of view I had.

Dammit. Instead of facing other hotel rooms like I'd hoped, my windows faced the hotel pool and, beyond that, a deserted golf course. There was no one to appreciate my favorite game of "accidental" exhibitionism. I sighed with disappointment and walked topless onto the balcony.

I had liked flashing men for as long as I could remember. But it had to seem like an accident. I always looked innocent, as if I'd forgotten I wasn't wearing underwear when I spread my legs a bit in a short skirt on the subway, or bent over in a loose top with no bra. I was careful to keep it safe, and around men who were already ogling me. But hotel rooms provided a special opportunity for undressing with the curtains open and I'd looked forward to this visit.

I leaned over the wrought iron balcony. I'd expected Arizona to be warmer, but the March night was cool and the glowing aqua pool waters were empty. The familiar smoky smell of cloves reached my nose and I spied the glow of a cigarette in the shadows of the diving board. Well, well. Someone was going to get a show after all. He turned enough for me to see a dark-haired waiter in white busboy shirt and black pants, smoking moodily. He was just twenty or so, with black hair falling over sculpted cheekbones.

He hadn't seen me yet. Quietly I slipped back into my room and waited. Then I noisily opened the balcony doors again, pretending to struggle a bit and cursing, before emerging. It wasn't implausible that I'd walk out here topless – there was no reason to think anyone out here could see me. Without quite daring to look toward the diving board, I stretched my arms over my head to show off my tits. As always, my nipples stiffened in the night air.

The smell of cloves still lingered in the air. Good. I glanced around as if confirming my solitude, then slid a hand down into my green panties. Desire swelled through me at the idea of a stranger's eyes on my tits. I closed my eyes, rubbing my clit with languid, sure strokes. Please let him still be out here, watching me. I peered through my lashes to make sure no hotel security was out. The pool area still appeared empty. How far should I take this? There was still a telltale shadow and that encouraged me to slide my panties down to my knees and open my thighs.

Blood rushed to my face from the thrill of showing off my pussy. My fingers were shaking as I slid two into my slit and my cunt closed around them like warm wet velvet. Oh God. Fingering myself never felt as good as it did when someone else was watching, and it was all I could do not to double over and frig myself hard and fast the way I did when I was seethingly horny. Instead I kept my legs open and my head thrown back, tickling my clit with one hand and fucking myself with the other – putting on a show. My nipples wanted to be sucked so hard they hurt. I thought of the waiter watching me from the shadows of the diving board and my orgasm broke inside me, clenching around my fingers with a sucking, rhythmic ripple.

I was raw, hoarse, shaking. Slipping back into the room, I shut off the lights. Then I peered through a crack in the curtains to see if the waiter would emerge.

To my shock, two boys walked out of the diving board shadows, both dressed in the same white shirts and black pants. They conferred, looked around, and they kissed. Well, then. They went off in separate directions and I snapped the light on and sat on the bed for a while, not sure of what had just happened: who had watched me, who had liked it and what might happen going forward.

I showered, put on a black dress and make-up, and went down to dinner alone about an hour later. My long hair was damp but I knew the boys would recognize me if they were waiters in the hotel restaurant. And, sure enough, they were. Neither was assigned to my table but both were working the dining room floor. The first boy I had seen, the young clove smoker with the black hair, had delicate features and a shy, tentative glance. His blond friend was a bit older and harder looking, with a knowing, calculating smile. I ate my grilled tilapia with a composed face and avoided watching them too openly. I wondered if they were gay or bi, and if they'd seen any thirty-year-old women playing with themselves on the hotel balconies before.

The blond refilled my water glass. "Been to Tucson before?" he asked casually. His grey eyes flickered up to mine and I read the intelligence in them. His younger friend might have thought my performance an accident; this one knew better.

"No. First time. It's colder than I thought it would be."

"The desert gets cool at night. We still like to be outside, though." Another glance and he was off.

OK then. Message delivered. After dinner I returned to my room and waited out the rest of the dinner shift, then took the elevator down to the lobby and went for a walk. But the boys weren't anywhere around the hotel grounds. At last I looked at the golf course and smiled.

They were behind the ninth hole, a grassy hill shielding them from the hotel, and both naked. The blond was straddling the black-haired one's face, his firm ass rolling in unbroken rhythm as he fucked his face with uninhibited vigor. The black-haired one seemed to enjoy it, given by the way he was roughly fisting his cock. I waited breathlessly to see who would come first, and hoped that the blond boy would pull out and unload his come all over that pretty boy face. Instead he rolled his boyfriend onto all fours and worked his cock into his ass without lube. He pushed in slowly, giving a slap to the dark-haired boy's rather flat ass cheeks, then gradually increased his speed until he was riding him in steady, relentless thrusts.

I was riveted. I wanted to go forward, but I just wasn't sure of the rules here. Wasn't sure if they simply liked to be watched as I did, or were two horny boys willing to bury their cocks in any gender. The blond looked up, hair hanging in his face. Our eyes never left each other as he fucked him faster, hips a blur of rhythm and dexterity. I could almost feel his balls slapping against his boyfriend with each thrilling plunge of his cock. His boyfriend moaned loudly, helplessly, and reached for his cock again, rubbing it with an almost tortured expression. The blond growled and reached forward to slap his mouth and with that one gesture, the black-haired boy ejaculated all over the grass. The blond laughed roughly and then his laugh died into a moan as he closed his eyes and furiously pumped out his orgasm.

They were breathing hard, their sweat-damp skin shining in the street light. The blond looked over at me, then his boyfriend, and immediate self-consciousness overtook me. I had exposed myself to many men before, but I had never been the watcher. I had no idea what to say, what the protocol was, so I forced a smile and hurried back to the hotel.

I lay on the bed flushed and horny, restless. It was after eleven and I had an early meeting tomorrow but I knew it would be hours before I could sleep. I slid off my underwear for the second time that night when a quick and confident rap sounded on the door. I smiled. I knew exactly who it would be.

A Sparrow Flies Through

Jules Jones

The only good thing that could be said for the evening was that it wasn't as cold as it might have been. I was standing in a godforsaken London square, with the rain tipping down outside the cracked plastic of the bus shelter. Half the street lights in view weren't working, and the only spot of brightness was the light on the Superloo occupying prime position directly across the road from us.

The other half of "us" had dashed into the dubious delights of the bus shelter thirty seconds after I had, and joined me at the timetable. We'd done the careful dance of the Englishman trying not to get in someone else's way in a confined space. Some squinting had ascertained that we both had fifteen minutes or so to wait until the next bus on our respective routes. Not bad at this time of night, really. Now we were amusing ourselves reading the advertising posters plastered to the outside of the Superloo.

Maintaining a polite silence wasn't helped by the poster slap in the middle of the loo's wall. I couldn't help laughing as I read it. In very, very large print it proclaimed, "They're coming!!!"

My new companion laughed as well, and said, "I'm glad I'm not the only one with a filthy mind."

Implicit permission for conversation having been granted, I looked directly at him. "A poster like that on a public toilet, it's practically an invitation to go cottaging."

"The modern ones don't look much like a cottage. More like something out of *Dr Who*."

I looked him over. Older than I'd thought, late twenties. Smooth dark hair and pale skin, impossible to tell the actual colour in the orange glow of the street lights, but what I could see looked good. Smart clothes that looked as if he'd regret not having a raincoat with him tonight. And he had a sense of humour.

"Fancy seeing if modern technology beats the good old-fashioned way?" I asked.

"If nothing else, it's warm, well lit and dry," he said. "At least for the ten minutes it allows you before it opens the door and starts cleaning itself down." He grinned. "Of course, I'm not planning on using the full ten minutes."

I like long and leisurely, myself, but I'm not averse to a quickie. "Got a twenty pence piece on you? Afraid I haven't."

He rummaged in a pocket then triumphantly held up a coin. We sprinted for the Superloo. Warm, well lit and dry. Well worth twenty pence on a night like this, even without a shag. It was well enough lit for a good look at what I'd got. Black hair and blue eyes; unusual combination.

Cheerful grin as well. "Like what you see?" he asked.

"Yes." I put a hand on his crotch. "Like what I feel, as well."

"And just where else would you like to feel it?"

This one appealed any which way. Lovely handful of hard cock, nice firm body. Gorgeous arse, I'd seen that much as I'd sprinted across the road behind him. Which did I want more – him fucking me, or me fucking him? Quick decision. "Up me. Got a condom?"

"As a matter of fact . . ." He rummaged in an inside pocket of his jacket, giving me a brief view of an expensive shirt stretched across a powerful chest. Fit without being a bodybuilding fanatic, just my type. He found the condom, and offered it to me. "Thought I had one. Be prepared, that's my motto."

"Ex-Boy Scout?"

"Ex-Army, actually," he said. Well, that explained the physique.

I needed both hands to open the packet, so I had to let go of him. Only for a minute, I told myself. He got his trousers open while I got the condom open, and my, was his cock a pretty sight. Big but not too big, nice satisfying thickness rather than all length. I wanted to get my hands on it again. Hell, I wanted to get my mouth on it. But not quite as much as I wanted to feel him filling my arse.

So I contented myself with stroking his cock as I rolled the condom down its sleek length. I'm good at that, even if I do say so myself. Lots of other people have said it as well. It's easier to persuade another bloke to wear a condom if you make sure he has a bloody good time out of it going on.

This bloke didn't actually say it, just hissed in pleasure as I fingered his balls, then slid the last inch or two down with my hand wrapped tight around his cock. I'd have gone on my knees and used my tongue to help it down, but that takes longer and I'm not one for giving public performances. I liked the thrill of knowing that the timer on the door was ticking, but only because I was certain I could beat it.

His hands were on me now, well-practised fingers opening my fly without fumbling. Trousers down far enough, and then the usual undignified shuffling to get into position, trying not to trip over the fixtures and fittings. We got ourselves lined up, and I found myself looking at him in the mirror. He grinned at me, and said, "Very kinky."

"Only if the mirror went down to the floor."

The grin got broader. "I must remember to suggest it at the next design meeting. You all right without lube?"

"Should be enough on the condom," I said. I'd noticed he liked a pre-lubed brand. "But suggest a handcream dispenser at the design meeting."

He laughed, then he stuck a couple of fingers under the tap, and stuck one of them up me. "Just to be on the safe side." Finger out, cock in. Slowly, carefully, and I could see in the mirror what it was costing him. Almost too big for me, but not quite, filling me up. Then I had it all, and we paused for a second or two. He was pressed up against me now, and I could feel the heat of him against my back even through the light waterproof I was wearing. Then he wrapped his hand around my cock, squeezing and tugging at the same time. I was suspended between wanting to thrust forward into his hand, wanting to push back against his cock. He pulled out a little, pushed in again. Harder the next time, and faster, making me moan in pleasure.

A strange thing to be standing here in the clean bright light of the Superloo, with the clean bright smell of the disinfectant, and this stranger's hand on my cock and his cock up my arse. Not like the old-style cottaging at all, no. No broken light bulbs or stale smell. But very good, with him hammering into me, tugging on me, and all the while the mirror showed me his manic grin.

I could finally see the point of mirrors, the pair of us feeding off each other's reactions. I gasped in pleasure, and so did he, then he managed to nibble my ear while still looking at me in the mirror. Perfect timing, just when I'd enjoy it rather than thinking it a distraction, and I slammed my arse back against him.

"Oh no you don't," he whispered in my ear, "we're coming together."

Ambitious, perhaps, but a nice idea. I let him set the pace, him rocking inside me and squeezing my cock. Me encouraging him with a few squeezes of my own.

Then he said, "Harder," and I obliged. I could feel the come rising in my cock. Then he buried his face against my shoulder, nuzzling at me. And we did it – we came together. Him clutching me tight, with an arm around my waist and a hand around my cock as I spurted come against the sink.

The small bright room smelt a little more human now, even if only for the few minutes before the self-cleaning cycle started. And that was a reminder that the timer was still ticking.

I nudged the man still leaning on me. "Better get cleaned up."

"Before we get cleaned up whether we like it or not?" He disentangled himself from me with a look of regret. "You take first crack at the sink."

"Thanks." I made myself respectable, then waited as he did the same. Then we hit the door release, and sprinted for the bus shelter. Just in time really, because both buses turned up early.

One last request from him: "Lend us a few coins? That was part of my bus fare, and the driver probably won't give me change for a tenner."

I found a handful of coppers and passed it over, and that was the last I saw of him. Maybe if the buses had been late . . . But they hadn't and there'd been no time for conversation. Just one brief moment of warmth and light in a dark cold night, a memory to carry away.

I climbed onto my own bus, and settled into a seat where I could watch the Superloo automatic cleaning cycle finish erasing the evidence that we had ever existed.

Heat and Ash

A. F. Waddell

The hard lines of architecture juxtaposed the softer lines of rolling green hills. Palm trees outlined their shaggy heads against the sky. From late October into November the fires were born and grew. Wind and combustion danced hills and canyons. North-east of Los Angeles the sky glowed orange. The area south-west of the burn was blanketed by drifting grey ash. It coated every surface. It drifted and blew in circles on the concrete patios and wooden decks. It seeped into homes and into lungs.

The falling ash was in a way reminiscent of snowstorms, providing a buffering of noise, the creation of eerie quiet, except for the drone of helicopters and small planes.

Particulate matter became highly elevated. The by-products of combustibles created a particularly toxic brew. Respiratory crises were seen in the ERs. A health department website warned of carcinogens.

The home was south-west minimalist with Mission furniture pieces. The walls were painted in deep yellow and red-brown tones. The master bedroom faced Sycamore Canyon and the San Bernardino foothills to the east.

"Do you think the fires will spread here?" the woman asked the man, as they lay in bed looking through the sliding glass doors at the distant orange glow.

"No. There's considerable distance and concrete between us and the fires. I think we'll be OK, Janice."

On the nightstand she lit sandalwood incense. "Would you like to spend the night, Ray?"

"Sure. I could use a cigarette."

"Could you please smoke outside? Please don't let the cats out."

He sighed and sat up, threw his legs over the edge of the bed and stood. He took a Marlboro and lighter from a nightstand, walked across the room, opened the sliding door and stepped out onto the deck. He closed the door. Swirling ash dusted his bare body and long hair as he smoked and paced and coughed.

The Mohave bar was a refuge against the sun and wind. The electronic hum of civilization suddenly died; power was gone in an incredible quiet. She and the others stepped outside and looked up: in the sky brightly dressed bodies of men and women floated . . . she lay in a desert trench and waited for the explosion, the cloud. She wondered what it would feel like. Would it be a slow death? She hoped to be vaporized. The percussive power traveled the desert ground. She moaned and woke. The damned dream was back. Since 9/11 her subconscious replayed the Cuban missile crisis, confused the two events, or played them out in illogical locations. She lay in the dark, her breasts pressed against Ray's back, her leg draped over him, looking out at the orange glow.

"What's the matter, Janice, can't you sleep?"

"Would you please just fuck me?"

He traveled her skin map from mouth to breast to cunt. Her mouth seemed a small inlet, tides pulling him in; her breasts pliant bursts; her cunt a minuscule goddess or sci-fi creature demanding sacrifice.

He traced her cunt with his tongue, outlining the wavy labia and pushing the tip of his tongue through shiny flesh. He encompassed the clitoris hood, captivating it. She moaned and pulled his hair.

"Now."

As he lay on his back she moved astride him. His cock was enveloped by heat and moisture, taken by her muscled flesh. She rode him, eyes closed, moving and rocking through space. Orgasm released her mind as she became skinless, fearless, floating.

Janice and Ray drove north on Grange through the foothills in search of a supermarket. A grocery strike was on. They pulled into the upscale market parking lot and cruised for a spot. Normally spotless Mercedes, BMWs, sport utility vehicles and more were dirty grey. They found a spot and parked.

Inside the store it was emergency time. Narrow aisles were jammed with customers; shelves were quickly emptying, checkout lines were long. Panic seemed to be bubbling beneath the surface. She hoped it wouldn't get ugly when spoiled consumers were denied. "California Suburbanites Riot For Red Snapper" was a headline she imagined. Some of their homes might be burning, Janice thought, sobered. Catastrophe does not discriminate.

"What do you want to eat this weekend?" Janice asked Ray.

"I don't know."

"OK. Basics then. Beer. Wine. Snacks. Soda. Drinking water, batteries, candles, matches, bleach, paper products. In case of power outage."

In the living room Ray sat on the sofa and watched CNN. The news correspondent and fire official adjacently stood and struggled to not cough.

"Chuck, I'm STANDING south of the Viejo fire in the Verbana foothills. As you can see behind me, homes are being eVAcuated. Over one hundred homes were LOST during the night." *Damned newscaster inflections.*

"Bob, are there any updates as to when the Viejo fire might be contained?"

"Chuck, WITH me is Los Angeles County Fire Captain Mike Millingstead. Mike, go ahead."

"We're going to be throwing our arsenal at the fire today. And the weather's finally in our favor. We're expecting a day of low winds, and dissipation tomorrow. That's great news for everybody."

"Chuck, in this wild lands-urban interface, drought conditions and the Santa Ana winds can be a most VOLATILE combination, as we've seen here this week. It's getting rocky here, back to you."

Janice slept nude, in fetal position, atop the bed coverlet. *Sirens blared in the small south-eastern town. Families briskly walked to the local fallout shelter, a red brick factory with the windows bricked up. She was terrified of being confined without fresh air – of running out of food and water as radiation seeped into the building. She looked up and saw cartoonish planes dropping their cargo. Instead of falling bombs, pamphlets fell to the ground. She picked one up and read "Duck and cover!"*

Ray stood in the doorway and watched Janice fitfully sleep. "Janice?"

He walked to the bed, removed his track shorts, lay down facing her and draped his arm over her. She awoke, moaned, stretched her legs.

He kissed her mouth then neck then breasts, his erection moistly insistent against her, shedding a droplet. His fingers sought her cunt. In warmth and moisture he immersed himself, compressed.

"Wait." She pulled away, moved onto her belly and arched her rear. He moved and knelt behind her, gaining a hold on her hips. She moved her buttocks slightly back, against his erection. His prick tunneled below the curvatures of her ass, sliding between her upper thighs, moving to her cunt. His cock slid into her, shallowly then more deeply. She pushed herself against him. He jostled a deep anterior spot until the heat in her cunt sent a growl to her throat; he fought his orgasm. *Jesus, not yet! Dodge Dart, Gremlin, Yugo, minivan! Dodge Dart, Gremlin, Yugo, minivan!* The angle and depth of his prick drove her growl into a scream in their primal fuck. He climaxed into her.

"Ray . . . why were you talking about cars?"

"I didn't realize I was talking."

As they slept, the orange glow of the sky faded and disappeared. Blackened architectural skeletons remained on bare terrain. Ash ceased to drift as the Santa Ana winds died. The debris of fire littered the foothills: of wood and paper and plastic; of trees and grasses and wildlife. Janice dreamt of sex, running and fervor: of orgasm, movement and heat morphing into a big bang, creating stars. The couple tossed and turned and coughed all night.

Working Hard

Lily Harlem

I dashed toward the looming, concrete building with my umbrella at the ready. I'd spent extra time styling my hair and the dishwater grey sky was swollen with rain clouds. But it was silly to be worrying about my appearance – it really was the last thing they would be looking at.

As I pushed through the revolving door still silence wrapped around me.

"Can I help you?" the receptionist asked, her echoing voice loud and tinny.

"Hilary Smith. For the SOFO project."

"Certainly, Miss Smith, down the corridor on the left, room three. Someone will be with you shortly."

"Thank you."

My heels clicked on the hard floor as I walked toward room three. A rumble of nerves tumbled in my stomach. I forced them away. I couldn't be distracted, that would spoil the whole thing. I had to be relaxed and at ease, my body at one with my mind.

Alone in the waiting room, I sat down, crossed my legs and stared at a rubber plant with huge glossy leaves. An image of Dave filled my mind. We'd had sex last night, good sex, no, make that great sex – it was always great with Dave. I squeezed my legs together and felt a buzz in my clit. The orgasm had been deep and intense and had left me with a glow of satisfaction to go to sleep with.

I closed my eyes and listened to the hum of air conditioning blowing above me. The way Dave had tickled my nipples with his tongue came to mind. He'd teased them, played with them then sucked them hard and deep into his mouth. A small shiver went up my spine and my nipples hardened, pushing against my silky bra. I uncrossed my legs, recrossed them, thought of how he'd slid his mouth down to my navel, parted my damp lips with his inquisitive fingers and how his tongue had flicked—

"Miss Smith, are you ready?"

I opened my eyes to the harsh light. "Yes." I followed the lady in the white coat through to the next room.

I didn't know why I felt anxious. I'd agreed to this and done it before. Maybe it was the claustrophobic element? I wasn't good with small spaces. Dave often traipsed up flights of stairs with me because I refused to use the elevator.

She handed me a pale blue gown. "I'll leave you to get changed."

"Thanks."

"You haven't brought anything metal to use have you?"

"No."

"Good, when you're ready please come through." She indicated a heavy black door then left through it. She hadn't once made eye contact.

I peeled off my clothes, folded them neatly and slipped on the cool, crisp gown. After retrieving my equipment from my handbag I entered the imaging room.

"If you could just lie down, Miss Smith, I'll get you a blanket and we can get started straight away."

I stared at the huge machine with its gaping mouth. Soon it would swallow me, take me into its whispering depths. My heart rattled in my chest, my breaths quickened and a prickle of sweat dampened my cleavage. I closed my eyes and thought of Dave, of him holding my hand, wrapping me in his arms, murmuring in my ear. My pulse rate settled. I could do this.

The bed, if you could call it that, was hard and narrow, even for my petite frame. It was nothing like being at home. But I mustn't think like that. I had to imagine I was in bed or on the sofa, or in the car, or once in the woods during a thunderstorm. Oh yes, that was a vivid memory. Dave had been so sexy all wet and bedraggled, I hadn't been able to keep my hands off him. The hairs on his chest had pressed against the sheer white material of his shirt and I could make out his tight, brown nipples.

The rain had soaked through the denim of his jeans too, making the delicious, growing bulge all the more enticing.

I lay down, being careful to place my head between the two hard, plastic wedges. She fastened a Velcro strap over my brow and placed a blanket, thick and scratchy, over my legs. I clutched the glass dildo in my hand. My palms were sweaty now, my stomach clenched like when I went to the dentist.

"Are you left or right handed?" she asked.

"Left."

"In that case if you could raise your right hand just before you orgasm that will give us the indicator we need."

"OK."

"And keep your head very, very still."

"OK."

A mechanical whirr jolted the bed and I stared upward. The opening of the mouth was devouring me, toothless gums sucking me in.

I was aware of her moving away, closed my eyes and drew up an image of Dave.

He was smiling, his black eyes sparkling with that lovely combination of both desire and humor. His hair hung floppy, fresh from the shower, no products, just tickling his heavy brows.

I pulled in a deep breath, tried to ignore the smell of cleaning agents, electrical equipment and starched linen. Dave always wore a light, fresh cologne. It reminded me of the beach. A hint of citrus and a ladle of salt; a fresh, unadulterated smell packed with testosterone which hit all the right buttons in me.

Mmm.

The bed was still sliding. Small mechanical tremors shivered beneath me. I squeezed my eyes tighter shut. This bit only lasted a few seconds then I could begin.

Finally I was swallowed. The strap on my brow was itching but I ignored it. Instead I drew up my legs and let my knees flop open. As my damp labia peeled apart I kept Dave's face before me. Persuaded the memory of his scent to linger. What was it he'd said last night? "Bend over, baby, and let me see your spine arch when you come."

His whispered words came back to me as I slid the head of

the dildo over my pubic hair. God, he'd made me arch all right, I thought my back would break. A small spasm attacked my pussy. The spasm turned into a quiver as the glossy head of the dildo smoothed over my clit.

Dave had right-angled me over the dressing table, scattering jewelry and make-up in his haste. It had been perfect. The oak mirror hanging on the wall had given me a delicious view. As he'd rammed in, hard and fast, I'd been able to see every micro-expression on his face. Something I wasn't usually privy to when we fucked in this position.

Cool air on my right foot told me it was poking out from the blanket. It didn't matter. As long as my pussy was covered. I circled my entrance then plunged in the dildo. Pretended it was Dave's meaty cock thrusting into my depths.

I jerked and gasped, ignored the strap on my forehead. Oh, this dildo was good. It wasn't my favorite but it was the only one I had that was suitable. I clamped my internal muscles around its shaft, pulled out, shoved back in, angling it to hit the exact spot Dave had pounded into over and over only hours ago. Oh yes. I was still sensitive, a little swollen maybe. Juice began to flow from my core, wet sucking noises filtered upward as the dildo was coated with warmth.

In the mirror – his face. Wow!

He'd stretched his lips back as he'd come, bared his teeth and flared his nostrils. His eyes were wide and predatory. It had been animalistic, primeval, feral. His grip on me had been vice-like, his fingers pincers on my hips, holding me just where he wanted me.

My heart was thumping in my ears. Pounding in time with the shunting of the dildo. My thumb knuckle was battering my clit with each thrust, building up the pressure deliciously.

"Yeah, baby, come, fucking hell come with me," he'd shouted, burying his cock so deep I thought he'd burst out of my mouth. My spine did arch, like a goddamn bridge. My muscles still ached from it.

My crescendo was there, blissful arcs of pleasure mounting.

Fuck, my signal.

I lifted my right hand, fingers splayed, and came. Hard, swift and with as little movement and noise as possible. My internal muscles clamped viciously on the dildo's smooth surface, my clit bobbed wildly. I stopped breathing for a whole ten seconds, allowing shivers of release to plunder my body.

Gradually, the power died from my spasming pussy. My clit settled and my brain returned to the here and now. Dave's face faded, his smell was replaced with clinical scent.

"Thank you, Miss Smith, we'll get you out of the scanner now."

The bed juddered and whirred.

I opened my eyes and slid the dildo from between my legs. One final orgasmic shudder tapped up my spine as I drew my thighs together. It wasn't a bad way to earn an extra hundred pounds, being involved in the Study of Female Orgasm, and it certainly boosted our Wedding Day Fund. What would I spend the cash from this climax on? Table decorations, favors for our guests, or even flowers for the bridesmaids. It didn't matter, it all had to be bought one way or another. I just considered myself extremely lucky that coming here gave me a very unique sense of job satisfaction to pay those extra bills.

Her Turn

D. L. King

Lauren held her palm up to her mouth and slowly licked the first three fingers before starting at the top of her left breast and running them down and over the taut nipple. She skipped over most of her torso, making contact with her flesh again just under her navel. She looked out at the dark glass in front of her, tilted her head, letting her straight brown hair cascade down the side of her pale body and smiled. She knew he was there and just on the edge of coming. The same guy had been feeding token after token into her meter; God knew how much he'd already spent, she wasn't keeping track, but this was her last window. Her shift was ending.

The fingers moved steadily down her shaved mound to the very top of her slit. She opened her folds with two fingers and let her middle finger touch her clit, which was already erect and protruding. She heard a muted gasp. She also heard the movement of the chain as the metal wall began to slide down, covering the dark window. The way the booth was lit, she couldn't see out, but she could hear her audience.

"No! No no nonononono . . . Fuck!"

Lauren got up to leave as Irina, her replacement, entered the booth and the metal partition, once again, rose on its chains.

"What? No. Wait! Wait a minute. Oh fuck, oh man . . ."

Lauren looked back at the glass and blew a kiss, then wiggled her fingers in a farewell wave before she stepped out, her long hair swinging, and closed the door behind her.

She'd started doing sex work when she was in grad school. She'd danced topless and stripped and made some very good money. Her student loan balance was extremely manageable and she'd been able to pay her living expenses without a problem. Now that she was almost finished with her dissertation for her doctorate in human sexuality, she was thinking that she might miss sex work, or at least this kind of sex work. As a sex therapist, she figured she'd still have her hand in, so to speak.

She'd been working the afternoon shift, from noon to four-thirty, and she was getting hungry. She planned to get home about six o'clock. Sal, her boyfriend, would already be there. Maybe they'd go out for dinner after. After they'd gotten cleaned up and de-stressed from their separate workdays. Or maybe he'd cook.

Sal was gorgeous. He was six feet of muscled, Italian beefcake. A trader by day, he was her private gourmet chef by night. He'd been taking Saturday classes at one of the city's best culinary institutes because he preferred a kitchen to the exchange floor. He practiced on her. As soon as he had his culinary degree, he planned to quit the market and open a little Italian restaurant downtown. He had everything it took to be successful: business sense, looks and real talent in the kitchen. He also had his restaurant nest egg stashed safely away for just the right time. Yep, he was a great Italian cook, but right now Lauren knew what she'd prefer to slather in his special red sauce, and it wasn't cannelloni. Work always made her horny.

It was a bit of a commute to the apartment she and Sal shared. It was one of those unbelievable new places, across the river. She'd never have been able to afford anything like this, but together they were doing all right. Actually, Sal paid the lion's share of the rent, but, as he kept saying, she'd be supporting him once she completed her degree and started charging a couple hundred bucks an hour as a sex therapist.

When they'd gone apartment hunting, it had been the bathroom that had sold her on the apartment. It was big and luxurious. Her last apartment's bathroom had been out in the hall. It wasn't like she'd had to share it, or anything. It was just that you had to actually go out the front door of the apartment and open another door to get into the bathroom. It wasn't all that uncommon, and she'd gotten used to it, but it was so small. You could barely turn around, and there was only the one tiny window in the shower and that faced a brick wall.

This bathroom had both a soaking tub and a glass-enclosed shower. It had a vanity area with two sinks, beautiful modern fixtures and opulent tiling. There was a big picture window over the tub, so you could look out over the river, toward Manhattan, while you were soaking. The room was light and airy and she would have spent all her time in it if Sal had let her.

The selling point for him, of course, had been the kitchen. And quite a kitchen it was. It was big and open to the living space. It had a Bosch dishwasher and a KitchenAid refrigerator and a Viking range. It seemed he had the same affinity to the kitchen that she had to the bathroom and she practically had to drag him out of it more often than not. The apartment was a wet dream come true. Heaven forbid they should ever break up. She didn't think she could go back to living in some hole on East 83rd Street again.

When she got to the building's entrance she checked her watch. It was just six o'clock. Sal should be home by now and waiting for her. Taking the elevator up to the fifteenth floor, she very quietly let herself into their apartment. She made her way into the bedroom and took her shoes off. Leaving her jeans and sweatshirt in a pile on the floor, she quietly entered the dark bathroom, wearing only a pair of black satin tanga panties.

Sal had closed the blinds to block out any ambient city light and had turned off the main bathroom light. The only light in the room was in the ceiling of the glassed-in shower itself, and it was focused on the naked body presently occupying that space.

Lauren took a seat on the towel bench against the far wall, facing the shower. Once she had closed the door, the bench, and most of the bathroom, became cloaked in shadows. She leaned against the wall and spread her legs.

The light in the shower's ceiling was like a spotlight on his naked body. She watched as he ran his soapy hands down his chest. He circled his nipples and pinched them slowly. As the water sluiced down, straightening the hair on his chest, Lauren watched his cock react to the attention he'd paid to his nipples.

He added more soap to his big hands and leaned his head back, closing his eyes. He soaped his neck, bringing his hands back down his chest again, this time circling and teasing his nipples with his fingers. His hands continued on to his navel, but instead of wrapping around his cock, they circled toward the back of his body and his ass.

Lauren's breath caught. She let one hand snake down, inside her panties, while the other teased one of her nipples. Sal turned around, facing away from her, and bent over, giving her a good view of his ass. As he spread his legs, she could see his full balls, hanging low between his legs. With more soap on his hands, he soaped the globes of his bottom and slipped them into the crack. While he ran them slowly up and down the split between his cheeks, Lauren ran her index finger up and down the now slick folds of her own sex.

He inserted his hands into the crack and pulled his ass cheeks apart, exposing his opening to her. She heard him groan. She was groaning quietly too as she dipped a finger inside herself while holding her labia open. She watched the water run down between his ass cheeks while he slowly stroked and rimmed his hole with a finger before letting go of his flesh. His hands disappeared for a moment, returning again, freshly soaped. This time he reached between his legs and soaped his balls, slowly stroking and squeezing them while the soapsuds ran down his legs.

Lauren moved her foot from the floor and brought it up onto the bench, next to her bottom, while she bent her knee away from her body, opening herself wider. By the time he turned around to face her again, she had two fingers buried to the second knuckle. Seeing the state of his hard cock, she groaned softly and began to pump her fingers in and out of her wet pussy, grazing her clit just enough to bring her to the edge of coming and keep her there.

With soapy hands, Sal wrapped a fist around his cock while his other hand automatically went for his balls. As he began to slowly stroke his cock, he broke the third wall of the performance and looked directly at Lauren. As their eyes met, a thrill of electricity shot through her brain, directly to her clit. Her fingers stilled and, not letting her eyes lose contact with his, her body bucked out its orgasm.

After it was over, she stripped off her underwear and stood on slightly shaky legs. "Hi, baby, how was your day? Mind if I share that shower with you?"

She slowly advanced on him, the slightly exaggerated sway

of her hips driving him crazy. Stepping inside and letting the hot water beat down on her head, she grasped Sal's erect cock with one hand, and wrapped her other arm around his waist and hugged him to her. "Your turn," she said, right before their mouths met, and her thumb brushed lightly over the head of his cock.

Pattern Passion

Remittance Girl

He was a three, I realized with a little shiver. A metal-legged spider scampered up the ladder of my spine and curled itself into a cold, tingling ball just beneath the back of my skull. A perfect, perfect three. As humans, we like threes, but rarely had I met such a dedicated one.

He got on at North Acton, travelling east at 6.33 every weekday morning and, as far as I could tell, he started doing this on the third of March. He chose the third compartment from the end of the train, picked the third seat from the door on the left hand side. He always wore a suit jacket with three buttons, and had triple-eyelet black oxfords on his feet. Nicely shined, I might add.

What clinched it for me was that, after watching him for several weeks, I noticed that when the third seat on the left-hand side was occupied, his body language altered. He wouldn't sit elsewhere. He just hovered, waiting until it came free and then he'd snag it.

The days piled up, and I grew to anticipate the arrival of his threeness. As the train pulled into North Acton, adrenalin flooded my bloodstream, my nipples seized and my cunt started ticking like a clock. I'll admit that I attempted to lure him by exhibiting a bit of threeness myself, just to see if he'd notice. But he had an annoying habit of plunging into a paperback novel the minute he sat down.

After twenty-four days of consecutive, gorgeous, elegant workday threenesses, I was in love. In a bold move, I decided to take his seat.

When he boarded the train, the subtle but perceptible

physical tension caused by my disruption of his pattern was thrilling. By the time we reached Notting Hill Gate, I nearly relented and relinquished the seat, but I clenched my teeth and held my ground, taking pleasure in the sharp spikes of anxiety that forked off his body like a Tesla coil. Just before we pulled into Bank – the station he got off at – his eyes met mine with a look of such pure hatred, it sucked all the air out of the train compartment. I almost came right there on the tastefully patterned grey upholstery.

Although it was normally my habit to ride the Underground for a further two hours, I couldn't hold out that long. Alighting at my usual stop, I ran home, and spent the rest of the morning producing imaginary porn in which he stroked his cock in increasingly frenzied sets of triplets. I frigged myself raw, matching his waltzing bouts of masturbation. Of course, I could have stopped at three, or six, but nine orgasms seemed the most appropriate number, a celebration of the triptych in the most sincere sense.

The next morning, my heart raced all the way from Ealing Broadway to North Acton. I usurped his seat and waited, trying to tamp down steamy visions of him pulling out his cock and ejaculating on me in a fit of pique. The minute he boarded the train, he noted the occupied seat with an audible huff. He caught my eye again, this time with a more measured expression of grave disappointment, and tried to pull my gaze, with exaggerated urgency, to the empty seats on either side. I pretended not to notice.

After some minutes of intense glaring, he bent a little forward and, in a low, gruff voice, said, "Would you mind moving one seat over?"

What I really wanted to say was: "I love your threeness, please fuck me!" But I didn't. "Not at all," I replied, attempting to sound breezy. I shifted to the right, melting between the legs as he settled next to me.

Did he know he was a three? I wondered. Pulling the ubiquitous paperback out of his briefcase, he began to read. I closed my eyes, letting the train rock me, allowing my mind to plunge, over and over and over, into lewd pools of explicit threenesses. Three cruel pinches of a nipple, three shudders, three determined thrusts, three coin-sized puddles of ejaculate on my belly. My reverie was only interrupted when his arm brushed mine, as he bent forward to put his book back into his briefcase. His stop was next.

Gathering up my courage, in the middle of the tunnel, as I heard the train begin to brake for Bank, I touched his arm, purposefully, three times. He looked confused, slightly embarrassed. I didn't say anything, or look at him. Diligently, I stared ahead at the mirror that pretended it was a window in tunnels. As it turned back into a window, sliding into the station, I watched him get up and leave the train.

That day, I didn't allow myself escape. I rode the train as usual and tried to look for other patterns. I spotted lots of other threes, but fours and fives and sixes eluded me. Only then did I realize I'd become so obsessed with his threeness, I had stopped being able to recognize any others. This, I admit, was disconcerting.

It took three more morning encounters before he touched me back. In the tunnel approaching his destination, with his nose still buried in his book, he moved his thigh until it touched mine and pressed it three times. The incident was so powerful, I got off at Liverpool Street station, quivering, and availed myself of the privacy of a stall in the ladies' public toilet.

The following day, before we'd even reached Marble Arch, he crossed his arms over his chest and, holding his book in front of his face with one hand, touched my arm three times with the fingertips of the other. My pussy flooded. Just before Bank, I responded, nudging his leg with my knee.

Unable to hold my tongue any more, I turned and whispered, "You're such a three."

His eyebrows rose as he carefully closed his book. For a moment, he had difficulty speaking. Then he swallowed and said, "I take the 4.20 train home."

Kiss, Kiss, Hug, Hug

M. Christian

We had played other games, this circle and I. Games of sex, pain, pleasure and everything betwixt, between and off to the side.

Preface: San Francisco in a place called a dungeon to some, basement to others. It was just a typical Saturday night if you travel in the *right* circles. Yeah, you could call them gays, lesbians, straights, dykes, fags, hets, twisted fuckers – whatever. They were just friends. And this was just a party.

The game was Kiss and Truth. Before we started, a hat was passed and we all dropped slips of paper into it. "Something very unique or very special about you" was what we were told to write. We did, diligently scrawling them on the black leather furniture and on the nearest convenient black leather friend.

"If you hear me say what you wrote, and then you get kissed – or kiss, sing out," the leader of this said, a large, lovely woman in a white dress, chiming finger cymbals for our attention.

The lights were put out, except for one on in the corner where she sat with her black leather beret on her head. The room was soft felt: a warm, comfortable, intimate kind of darkness. I'd done so much in that room – traveled through pain to sex to pleasure to laughter and back again that I knew it like I knew my own fingers. I knew everyone else there just about as well – maybe as well as my toes.

"I have a twelve-year-old son named Josh."

Our mustaches met, bristly forests itching together. Faintly hiding silken lips, heated tongues, flashing whiteness of teeth, I kissed the man named Jack. From across the room a voice (Female? Male? Could have been both, or one, together. Many in the room were part-way between the two) sang out, and giggled, "Here!"

"I'm pregnant."

She was short, with breasts heavy and firm. Hair a mad burst of curls. Her feet chimed with tiny bells. Lips thin and hard, with a faint fuzz of hair. Mouth a furnace of heat, like she burned somewhere down deep and her tongue was a flaming anaconda, wrapping and constricting around my own. "Over here!" a light, sparking voice said from close by.

The room was bursting with laugher, with little clicking whirls of giggles and the silent light of smiles. "I had a bad day at work."

I don't consider Jay really between he and she so it's hard to say if Jay was on the way to boy or girl. Jay was Jay, unique and himself: rail thin, face a perfect blend of hard and soft, full and not, Jay's lips are strong (like both) and so soft (like both). We kissed hot, and long, even after half the room chorused with "Yes," "Right here," "Damned straight". Laughter. Laughter. Laughter.

"I got a new tattoo."

A mountain of mad fun. I didn't know his name, but there was always a smile on his lovely lips. Ever since I'd seen him, smiling like a San Francisco Gay Leather Buddha, I'd wanted to plant one on his gorgeous face. It was a worshipful act, a divine act. Maybe not sex heat in it, but love all the same. He was next to me so I turned and looked him in the eyes – matching intent with intent. His lips were spiced, a lingering bite of cinnamon and ginger from the cookies laid out upstairs. He didn't offer me anything more than his velvet lips and I didn't reach in to take more. This was a devout kiss, a spiritual kiss. My body remained limp meat, my mind soared at the sparks he brought into me. "Here!" someone sang very close, and all stopped for a few beats while she lifted her dress to show the serpent that ran, red and puffy from the recent needles, up her ankle to tickle her crotch with a brilliantly forked tongue.

"I got a new ring."

When we'd made love at the last party I had almost been consumed by her. Ignited, our kisses had turned our tongues into tongues of flames. Sexual? Damned straight, but Dorothy's hunger was almost scary, almost scalding. Our kisses seemed to last from foreplay, into sex, and into a still warm afterglow. Never did oral sex with my lover, Dorothy; couldn't take our lips apart long enough to try.

Black like soot, not the kind of polished black some have. Hers was a skin that looked like night rolled into breasts, belly, back and smile. Her lips – how can I describe her lips enough? I can't. You have to come all the way out to San Francisco and taste them. Words . . . just . . . will . . . not . . . work.

We kissed through the call of "Over here": the young, slender reed of a man baring his chest to show his new nipple ring. We would have kissed even longer save for Dorothy's insistence that we play "this game" a little more first.

"I'm HIV positive."

I knew Jerry. Knew him well. Friend, pal, something else – very special. He mirrored me: long and lean, tapered and elegant. While mine was black, though, his was dirty blond. Look at pieces of Jerry and you would think him just another punk, but I knew him from long nights of bad movies, tears (both of us) and many, many smiles.

Jerry's lips were slightly scabbed from cruising downtown on his board, of biting them when he was nervous. His tongue was hard and strong, a vibrant touch that shivered me down to my bare toes.

"I am," Jerry said, and I kissed him long and hard again.

The game lasted for a while more, before dropping away with the few remaining clothes. The toys came out: leather, latex, condoms, Saran Wrap . . . the tools of our friendships. We played and kissed many times thereafter.

I could only wish that Jerry could have kissed me much, much longer.

Pelvic Examination

Billierosie

Corella had presented the kindly doctor at the private clinic with
a variety of conflicting symptoms. She'd spoken of excruciatingly painful periods. Periods so heavy that she had to take time
off work when her monthly curse arrived. She told him of her
inability to urinate and when she did manage to pass water, it
was just a trickle, she could not empty herself. At other times
there would be urinary incontinence, and she would pee herself.
She also suffered from faecal incontinence, when a thin trickle
of dilute excrement would void her bowel. But occasionally she
would be constipated and not empty her bowel for weeks. Her
genitalia were swollen and tender at times, and on occasions her
breasts would lactate. The doctor was sympathetic, but bewildered and, like many other doctors before him, had referred her
to a specialist for a pelvic examination.

Corella planned these visits to the clinic with the precision
and tenacity of the Admiral Lord Nelson the night before the
famous battle at Trafalgar. Nothing must be overlooked. The
World Wide Web was her friend, and her instruction manual.
She became familiar with medical terminology and was able to
add to a surgeon's evaluation of her condition with confidence
and intelligence.

Corella was, in fact, perfectly healthy. But she craved the attention of male fingers on her genitalia: inserting themselves into her
vagina and probing her rectum. She would always draw the
doctor's attention to her particularly large clitoris. "Was it natural?" she would ask innocently. Corella was brave and stoical in
the face of the unknown sickness that may soon ravage her body.

She was, by now, familiar with the hospital routine and had

been given the usual tests. Her pulse was taken and her blood pressure checked. They took two samples of her blood and she managed to provide a urine sample.

She was shown to her private room, asked to undress and put on the gown that was available for her. She folded her clothes neatly; she sat and waited obediently for the nurse with the sweet face and the gentle voice to return to her. A warm glow enveloped her body.

She sat on the comfortable cushioned couch, a blissful smile on her face, as she anticipated the forthcoming pelvic examination. She recalled other pelvic examinations; and she had had many.

Once, there had been the overwhelming humiliation of a surgeon with a group of student doctors peering at her, exclaiming at her moist cervix. The surgeon resplendent with his red and black spotted bow tie and the flurry and flutter of white coats following him, young and eager to impress their mentor. Uncertain and inexperienced fingers opened the soft petals of her labia; one student had been so close to her genitalia, she could feel his warm breath on her clitoris. The warm, golden sensation that swept over her was exquisite.

The surgeon was enthusiastic about his subject and opened up a discussion with his students on various cultural and historical theories about the study of the womb.

"Yes, sir!" one of the students had remarked. "The Ancient Greeks believed that the womb moved about the body at night. That it was sort of . . . like an animal in its own right and would cause havoc wherever it went."

"Quite so." The surgeon beamed, pleased and excited to have found an enthusiastic disciple. "The Victorians believed in female hysteria. This could only be treated by genital manipulation. My own great-grandfather, also a surgeon, was an advocate of this procedure. High pressure water techniques were experimented with. Later, clockwork driven devices were invented to address the problem of reckless, hysterical women, of which the humble vibrator is a descendant. But most surgeons, I believe, adhered to manual manipulation."

"And how often would such a woman require this treatment?" another student asked. "And what type of woman would qualify?"

"It would vary," replied the surgeon. " One eminent surgeon declared that he believed that over a quarter of women suffered from hysteria. As to the matter of symptoms, women with physical or emotional symptoms – this could involve headaches, emotional instability, melancholy, aggression, depression, feeling lower abdominal heaviness, muscle pains and other discomfort – might have sought treatment. All of these symptoms were considered to be linked to women's reproductive system. The only problem was that physicians of course did not enjoy this tedious task. The technique was difficult for a physician to master and could take hours to achieve the desired result of hysterical paroxysm, which is, of course, the Victorian term for orgasm."

Corella lay, splayed on the hospital bed, listening as the conversation was carried on across her half-naked body. She was a thing to them, an experiment. It brought a warm flush to her face. Her lips were dry and she licked them. She felt that she was in her rightful place as the two men discussed the history of medicine over her. The situation was intensely erotic and her clitoris throbbed its approval. She felt herself float from her body. She looked down on herself, a fat, naked, unattractive woman, surrounded by a group of handsome males.

She thought about those generations of Victorian women not understanding their own bodies and being beholden to men of medicine for relief from their overwhelming frustrations. And she was no different.

Corella had never been in a serious relationship. At thirty-two years old, she felt that life was passing her by. She was bright, successful, but something was lacking; she always felt as if she were not worthy. She was no virgin, she'd made sure of that, but the men never stayed. They'd promise to call her, but the calls never came. Once she'd even arranged a meeting with an escort. After a couple of drinks and desultory conversation, he hadn't stayed either.

And then Corella recalled a pelvic examination she'd had a long time ago. The pleasing sensation of feeling valued. And, most importantly, the doctor's clever hands, opening up her genitalia.

She'd made a phone call to the private clinic to arrange a consultation, and that was how it had started.

As she sat and waited, the memories drew a pleasing response from her body. Her genitalia had swollen and were too plump to enable her to cross her legs in comfort. Her nipples were erect and they tingled. She felt flushed and she allowed her straying fingers to touch her swollen clitoris.

Usually, Corella saved masturbation until after the pelvic examination, but the excitement and anticipation were too great. All it took was an increase of pressure and speed with her forefinger to bring her to a silently powerful orgasm. She brought her wet fingers to her mouth and licked them clean. She tasted savoury; salty.

Chopin's lovely piano music played on a CD player, adding to an atmosphere of calm and serenity. There were fresh flowers in a little vase on the windowsill. Purple and white freesias, their perfume scenting the air.

The private hospital was like a luxury hotel, and Corella was thankful that she could afford it.

Once a doctor had opened her up with a speculum. This was a procedure that these days Corella dreaded, yet was strangely eager for. She remembered the cold steel inserted inside her. The metal cranking, opening her. She felt the cool air against her vaginal walls. The doctor had shone a little torch inside her; he was looking at a part of her body she had never seen and she found it arousing. She felt as if she were a piece of meat on a slab, something for men to stroke and exclaim over. She recalled her clitoris swelling, as if in indignation that her cervix was getting all the attention.

But it was the beginning of the examination that Corella liked best of all. This always involved a visual inspection and palpation, firstly of her external genitalia. Firm, gentle hands opening her, feeling her. The surgeon studying closely, and paying attention to her inner and outer labial lips. Gently asking her questions about her symptoms; explaining exactly what he was doing as he examined and tested the texture of her vagina.

When it was time, Corella was taken to the examination room. The sweet-faced nurse helped her onto the table in preparation for the surgeon to examine her. She placed Corella's feet in the stirrups, and raised the lower part of her body. With her buttocks slid to the edge of the table the surgeon would have full view of her most private place.

She closed her eyes. She heard the door open and close. Then the snap of surgical gloves.

A golden glow enveloped her as the surgeon's clever fingers opened her up. Slowly, his finger slipped between her folds. Her clitoris was still sensitive from the orgasm she'd induced earlier, and she flinched.

"I'm sorry, did that hurt?" the surgeon queried.

Something in his tone made Corella open her eyes. She'd met this man before. It had never occurred to her that she would see the same surgeon twice. She swallowed; she couldn't speak. The nurse had left the room; she was alone with this man and he knew her secret. Their eyes met.

"So, is it here?" he asked, sliding a finger into her vagina. "Or here?" His finger, moist from her wet vagina, slid into her rectum.

She could barely manage to shake her head. The room was silent except for the ticking clock.

"Then here?" His finger touched her clitoris.

Corella moaned her approval.

His dark gaze never left her face.

He lowered his head. She could feel his breath on her. The tip of his tongue touched her clitoris. She cried out as the orgasm shattered through her. Every muscle in her body contracted. Her toes clenched like claws; and still his tongue teased her. Tears of gratitude soaked her face; she had never been so happy.

Down

Ralph Greco

"I have a thing for rabbits, what can I tell you?"

"Yeah, but those guys in the suits, whata they call um, 'furries'?"

"Everyone has their specific little desires when it comes to sex. So we just dressed up and—"

"Ew, ew, don't tell me anymore, please."

Cara gulped her latte-double-shot-skim and I smiled into my tea thinking of the sex Garret and I had had the night before and how ironic it was that my little tale about bunny dress-up could bother my old college roommate so much. I wasn't about to remind the petite black girl of those nights when strange guttural noises would seep out from under her door when we shared that suite in our junior/senior year of college; there had been all kinds of grunts, moans and slaps . . . and not always when Cara was with a partner. My little bunny-suit admission didn't attack her sensibilities as much as she liked to pretend sitting here in our sedate Connecticut Coffee And . . . shop. Let her play suburban mom with her cute one-year-old asleep in the stroller at her feet, I knew better.

Hell, she knew enough to use the word "furries".

There was no way I was going to give up these Thursdays, regaling my best friend with my latest encounter, especially if they happened to be as much fun as my last night rendezvous. I knew Cara regarded me as a thirty-year-old woman with a voracious libido, looking for the next big connection – or at least a sizable one – and though this was true enough she had no idea really what it was like trying to find peace of mind out here in east coast United States suburbia when you weren't, technically, human.

"You comin' with me to Home Depot or not?" Cara said, suddenly standing up.

Either her latte had gone cold, she was finally disgusted with me (at least for this morning) or my best friend really had to pick up that whatever-you-call-it at the store for her husband Ron. I wasn't such a fan of big spaces like Home Depot. I rather liked little out-of-the-way coffee shops like this, and of course bookshops and tiny corners of libraries where I spent most of my time. I knew it harked back to those oh-so-formative few days I spent chasing you-know-who down the you-know-what but I regarded cavernous retail citadels like Home Depot like I did anal sex in that it's nice to know it's there when you need it, but you don't have to go there all that often.

I stood as Cara did, bent to kiss perfect sleeping baby Jessica on the cheek then stood to do the same to her mom.

"I got to get my ass to the library."

Cara, my mother, actually nobody ever questioned me about this habit I had of burying myself in the library all hours of whatever day it was. During my lunch hour from the classroom, during these days off in summer, basically whenever I could, I'd be hidden among high shelves rooting through as much classic literature as I could find . . . it nearly preoccupied me as much as my sex life.

How I had come to find myself set free from the pages of Lewis Carroll's book, a living and breathing girl, living some hundred years plus later on the east coast of the United States, I had no explanation for. My "parents" never spoke about finding me, if it was a Superman-spaceship-crash-in-the-back-forty kind of a thing or I simply was there one moment when I wasn't before. I had taken their acceptance to be simple acquiescence of what they both couldn't truly understand: that I was Alice come to life. As there were no pictures of me pre the age of seven my memories prior to my adventures were null and void – except for my dull recall of a sister – I knew, deeper than I knew anything in my addled sex-starved psyche, that I was indeed *that* Alice. I simply had grown like any normal girl in the late eighties in American culture (1980s that is) having nothing ever unusual about my existence except that my blonde locks never dulled nor ever needed cutting.

Like anything else, fiction or not, life intrudes. Didn't Lennon say, "Life is what happens to you when you're making other plans?"

The book, rich as it is, doesn't give one much clue beyond what happens to Alice (me) when she (me) has her adventure. Yes, there are all the mathematical conundrums, the "nonsense literature" aspect, the Queen, the playing cards, but I feel as I felt in the book when I run away from my sister and tell her to consider experiencing it all for herself. The "Eat Me" cake always kind of gives me a tickle you-know-where, but even reading the sequel, which I wasn't around for (I mean I am in it but I dropped out of the book after running away from my sister) doesn't give me much to go on save for piquing my interest in chess. It's really just a book I happened to sprout from and not unlike any belief system born of text I try to live my life with the knowledge of what was written but not so as to get all stifled by it.

I do know my birthday is 4 May though.

Of course Alonzo was waiting for me when I reached the Southside Branch ten minutes later. The lanky black boy and I had taken to meeting here as much as his part-time job and propriety would allow. Ten years my junior, other than my parents he was the only one who knew who I was, or at least he tolerated my suspicions as my folks did. The handsome boy was an ex-student and more likely to take pity on his junior-year English teacher than most, had they heard my wild claim.

"So, what's on the agenda today?" I asked as we took our usual two-seater table far in the back of the adult section, off to the right of the true crime books.

"The stupefying humbling realization that you are not the only one," he said, as always mesmerizing me with his deep brown eyes, his quick thin-lipped smile, his "jump-right-into-it-ness".

When he was my pupil Alonzo had been just as inquisitive. Now, some three years on, I found his desire to share the big cosmic questions with me sometimes as unnerving as they were deeply erotic. That we hadn't yet touched beyond our usual kiss hello had me burning for this young man more than I burned for Garret, and he was currently indulging my bunny fantasies. Was I undersexed or simply in need of more mental stimulation as I got older?

"I have agreed that yes, it is logical to assume that I am not the only one," I said, smiling back. "We have been over this, dear."

Alonzo always smiled when I called him that, as he did then. Leaning across the table he whispered: "But you haven't considered the potential if you could all meet, and make your presence known. It just amazes me that right now we might be sitting a table away from Christopher Robin or—"

"It amazes me too, but like any minority," I interrupted him and stopped to stare hard at the deep black face before me, "I am just trying to get through the day without calling too much attention to myself."

"Well—" and here the young man leaned back in his chair and exhaled "—well, yes, that I can relate to, I guess."

I was burning for him; I could only hope he didn't catch the blush on my white neck, the dilation of my pupils. For me, the one complete and sure aphrodisiac is acceptance, the full non-judgemental embrace of my oddity. Garret wearing a bunny suit, my parents not speaking a word, even Cara agreeing to still meet me no matter what perversity I revealed, all of it made me feel warm and fuzzy in a way I could not explain. Alonzo never once raising his eyebrow to his weird English lit. teacher's wild tale, his continued meeting with me here and now his excitement over a wild strategy he was considering, made me want this guy even worse than I usually did.

Alonzo slid back in the plastic seated chair and the tight "shspurt" his jeaned rump made as he did so ran up my spine so fast that I shot up off my chair, grabbed his hand and pulled him down along the back wall.

"A . . ." he tried but I had him up between the very last row of hardcovers and the alcove where a dead copy machine is kept.

"Take it out," I said as softly yet forcibly as I could. "Take it out now."

Poor guy had no idea what to say or do, so I reached down and unzipped him.

"Alice," he whispered, the sound of this ex-student using my name so thrilling to me; right up until a month ago Alonzo was still calling me Miss Jules (my parents' last name). I looked deep at him as I managed his jeans open and he squirmed back into the wall.

I don't know what motivates normal women, but I do what motivates me. I need to be more than Alice from the book as much as I need to be more than a human lady. I need to be all things to myself: a sexual vixen, an off-for-summer slightly sad school teacher still living with her folks, a fictional character brought to life by some unknown alchemy, and a woman right then getting on her knees to coax Alonzo's beautifully thick erection over his briefs and into my hand then my mou—

"Christ, Alice, Christ!" the man/boy above me growled as I swallowed him then and he lay back against the hard back wall, so unlike a waiting dark hole I could have cried over the difference in realities.

Places He's Spanked Me

Julie Stone

Master spanks me a lot. Three times a day, sometimes more. It's not just how he tells me I've done something wrong; it's how he tells me I've done something right. Or something that's neither wrong nor right. Or something that's pleased him. Or something that's displeased him. Or something about which he has no opinion.

Master spanks me whenever and wherever he feels like it. At first I tried to understand why he was spanking me – not so I could be good and prevent the next spanking. So I could be bad and hasten it.

Eventually I learned that all I have to do is wait, and Master will spank me. Sooner rather than later. Today instead of tomorrow. Five minutes from now, as opposed to an hour.

So I try to be good – really, really good – secure in the knowledge that the more I please Master . . . the more I please Master. And he'll spank me – spank me hard – regardless.

Last night he spanked me in the car. He got horny when we were driving home from dinner at a friend's house. It goes without saying that he had spanked me at the friend's house – the two of us slipped into the bathroom between the main course and dessert. He made me reach behind him and keep flushing the toilet to hide the slapping sounds. Then, on the way home, Master pulled into a rest stop and unzipped his pants. I took his cock into my mouth, because I do that whenever Master wants it – and he wants it a lot. He told me to lift my skirt as I serviced him. Master likes me in skirts. I never wear pants any more.

He spanked me until I came, his fingers rubbing my clit between strokes on my ass. I don't know which one finally got

me off, but Master told me he wouldn't let me taste him until I'd
come. After I did, he just put the car in gear and I finished him
off at home.

I was disappointed, sure – still shivering from an orgasm, my
buns warmed, my pussy wet, I wanted to taste Master's come.
But I never question Master. Besides, after I'd finished him off
at home, I got another spanking – this one over his knee, on the
couch the way I really, really like it. I came again to the sounds
of dirty movies from the television.

Night before last, Master spanked me in a movie theater.
Not one of those nice, clean movie theaters, either. The kind of
movie theater where nobody notices a spanking going on in
the back row. Across Master's lap, I could smell the stained
seats close to my face. The usher came by and watched, but
didn't ask us to leave.

The night before that, it was a parking garage, two in the
morning, empty except for us and hundreds of quiet cars. He
spanked me over the hood of his car, the engine still warm from
the drive over. I bucked and squirmed so much when I came
that I snagged my skirt on the grille, and my thighs were red
from the heat – as red as my ass. Master spanked me for snagging my skirt. Then he spanked me for being such a good girl
and taking my spanking.

Weekend before last, he spanked me in the woods. We'd gone
hiking, and found a nice secluded spot where Master could sit
on a fallen log and take me over his lap. We're lucky no hikers
happened along, but I think I saw the glint of light off some
binoculars on a nearby ridge. I told Master about that, and he
just smiled and spanked me some more for not paying attention
to the spanking.

He's spanked me in dark alleys – him using his belt, me bent
over a garbage can while I pray the cops don't drive by. He's
spanked me on an airplane. He did it under the blanket on a
red-eye, softly, the little slapping sounds drowned out by the
sound of the jet engine – Master always insists we sit in the back.
He's spanked me at my parents' house – in the guest bedroom,
out by the pool, even in the pantry while the rest of the family
ate Thanksgiving dinner. He's spanked me at the beach, the two
of us secreted in a cave while I took down my bikini bottoms and

spread myself over his lap, my face pressed to a soggy beach towel. He's spanked me at the supermarket, in the cereal section at 2 a.m., not just furtive slaps but a full, panties-down, skirt-up spanking, me clutching at boxes of raisin bran and breathlessly looking, red-faced, for the supermarket employees to discover us. That was a close one. But still I let him do it, because I let Master spank me whenever and wherever he wants. I don't ever question him when he says he's going to spank me – because that's what Daddies do. They spank their little girls . . . and the little girls say "thank you". With their mouths, always . . . but in more ways than one.

Master spanked me before he even kissed me. On our first date, I was already crazy about him. After dinner, I asked him if he wanted to go back to my place. I was just going to sleep with him, the way I'd slept with lots of men who weren't my Master, men who didn't know enough to spank me. But when we found ourselves on the couch, and I went to kiss him, he just shook his head.

"There's business to attend to first," he told me. "Kissing is a luxury. What I'm about to do to you is a necessity."

How did he know I'd crawl over his lap, put my ass in the air, and let him lift my skirt and take down my panties, before we'd even kissed? Somehow, he knew. Master just knew.

He kissed me after he spanked me though. He kissed me long and deep and hungry, his tongue savaging me, and it was in that moment – my skirt up, my pussy wet, my buns stinging – that I think I fell in love with him.

Since that date, I haven't spent a single day without my buns being warm and achy. Even when I'm not sore from the last spanking, I'm anticipating the next one.

Master uses his hand, his belt, sometimes a paddle. He spanks my cunt, my thighs, sometimes my breasts, but most of all my ass. Master spanks me whenever and wherever he wants. And whenever he sits down and snaps his fingers – no matter where we are, no matter what we're doing – I lift my skirt, lower my panties to my knees, and put myself over his knee, ass in the air, legs spread.

Because there are plenty of places left for Master to spank me, and I know he wants to try them all.

At Liberty

Sacchi Green

Icy spider-fingers of salt spray rasped the nape of Vic's neck. She could have turned her collar up against the wind, but her hands were full, pressing Tory's body so hard against her own that the pleasure verged on pain. Even discomfort was joy, though, proof of reality, after so many dreams had dissolved into yet another desert morning, and unending war, and her own fist hot and wet between her thighs.

Tory reached up to tweak the wool collar, rubbing herself against Vic, her nipples hard as the buttons on her opened shirt. "We could get out of the wind," she murmured against Vic's cheek. Her own cheek was damp and salty, even though Vic's taller form sheltered her from the worst of the spray. Tears? Not that she would ever admit to it.

The boat had turned so that they were no longer on its lee side. Everyone else had drifted toward the bow, watching Liberty Island loom closer through the mist. At least they had some real privacy where they were; the Park Service people had become, after introductions and sincere handshakes, genially oblivious, but years of "don't tell" had wired Vic for caution verging on paranoia.

"What, I'm not keeping you warm enough?" she teased, trying for a light tone. She eased back and began to button Tory's shirt. They would dock in a matter of minutes, and there were still some limits to be observed, after all, and the respect due a National Monument.

Tory blocked Vic's sun-browned fingers with her own, but only briefly. "We're almost there," she admitted, turning to nestle her butt into her lover's crotch; then she gasped as Vic reached around under her jacket to fondle her through her shirt.

"Almost there?" Vic murmured into Tory's froth of russet curls. "How close?" She scraped her nails across sensitized nipples, keeping on until Tory's breath came swift and ragged.

"Vic . . . Ah! . . . Yes . . . Oh . . . Damnit, if I don't get sucked one way or another pretty fucking soon I'll scream!"

"You'll scream even louder if you do." Beneath Vic's cocky tone she blessed Tory for not asking, "Why? Why now? When you wouldn't touch me last night? Or this morning?"

Last night, exhaustion after the flight from the Mid-east had been excuse enough. Not that Vic had slept soundly; time after time her dozing had given way to a panicky wakefulness. Where? Who? New York . . . Tory's bed . . . Tory's body beside her, warm curves as smooth and graceful as wind-carved dunes, but so sweet and tender . . .

Impossible! And her dreams, filled for months with images of Tory so sensual and raw they'd inflamed her to the point of combustion, now roiled with violent images she needed desperately to leave behind. All she'd seen, done, *had* to do . . . all those she couldn't save . . .

Deep sleep must have come at last, until sunlight filtered through the February-bare branches outside Tory's window. When Vic stirred, Tory came to kneel naked above her, bending to nibble lightly at the tender skin exposed in the gap between T-shirt and boxer shorts. Vic sighed, stretching, letting the gap widen. Tory pursued this opening with enthusiasm, nudging the shirt upward with her nose, tugging the shorts downward inch by inch, exploring with lips and tongue and teeth; and every little kiss pressed into Vic's vulnerable belly sent tongues of fire darting toward her cunt.

She needed to arch upward toward that teasing mouth, ached just as hungrily to pull Tory down, roll on top of her, and fuck her supple, wriggling body until she lay limp and sated. But her own body wouldn't obey her impulses. A ponderous gravity weighted her limbs, as in dreams of fleeing from unseen, pursuing terrors.

Somewhere a truck backfired. Vic stiffened. A tremor began deep in her chest, threatening to ripple outward, and suddenly she heaved herself over to lie with her face buried in the pillow.

Damn, damn, damn, why now, when she had stood firm for so long against anything war could hurl at her?

"It's OK, babe," Tory said. "It's kinda soon. You're just not really all here yet." She leaned back and patted Vic's butt, more in camaraderie than seduction. Then she ran a finger along Vic's thigh and tugged the hem of her shorts upward. "Sure didn't get those tanned legs in a New York winter, but your ass could still pass. No nude sunbathing in a war zone, I guess."

One deeply probing caress beneath the shorts, and then she was off the bed and turning on the burner under the coffee. Another grope like that and Vic sure as hell *would* be all there, she thought; but she wasn't quite sure enough to say so.

Over breakfast Tory chatted casually about her work as an urban park ranger and her plans for the day. "I wrote you about the bald eagles, right? It's been so cold upstate this winter they've been riding ice floes down the Hudson to fish in open water. I'm recording sightings, seen some myself from over on the Palisades, and one flying over Grant's Tomb." She reached across to rumple Vic's short dark hair. Those glints of silver radiating from a small jagged scar above her left ear hadn't been there a year ago. "A couple more decades or one more war and you'll be looking like one very fierce, sexy eagle yourself."

That called for a kiss. Vic tensed to deliver, but Tory went on in a rush, "Anyway, some National Park Service guys from Ellis and Liberty reported one flying way down off Battery Park, so we got together, and that's how I managed to fix up this trip today."

Vic wondered if she'd missed something. Tory glanced at her a bit nervously. "So we're going to Liberty Island. Unless you'd rather not. But I thought you might want to see the Statue."

Vic couldn't say no to those hopeful hazel eyes. "Yeah, sure," she said. "Sure I do," and wondered whether it might even be true.

They'd met in the rubble of Ground Zero, where Vic's Reserve unit had been posted for search and security duty. Even dust-covered and drawn with strain and weariness, Tory had caught her eye like a beacon. It hardly seemed like the right time to make a pass though, until the evening Tory came up behind her on the ferry dock as she gazed out over the harbor.

"You ever been out there?" Tory asked casually. "To the Statue? Or Ellis?"

"Not yet," Vic said gruffly, glad to have her grim thoughts interrupted. In the grey distance the Lady rose from the harbor, ageless and erect – but how could She bear it? How had She felt, when terror struck, and the towers fell, and She couldn't even turn to face them, only stand and look steadily outward?

Vic shook off such craziness. "My ancestors didn't come through Ellis anyway. Half of them were French fur traders, and the other half were cousins of the guys who sold this real estate cheap to the Dutch. Always figured the whole deal about 'Miss Liberty' was pretty ironic, in fact, but looking at her now . . . Damn, that's some woman!" Tragedy and politics aside, there was something powerfully sensual in all that steadfast, nurturing serenity; or maybe it was just that Tory's closeness put sensuality powerfully on Vic's mind.

She didn't realize she was flexing her fingers until Tory lay her own across them. "She has a ten-foot fist," she said wickedly, "and a forty- or fifty-foot arm."

"Kind of makes me feel humble," Vic responded. Tory laughed, and gripped her hand, and two hours later they were showering off the dust and soot and anguish together in Tory's tiny studio apartment.

The boat emerged into sunshine just before it nudged against the dock. At the far end of the island the Lady stood, solitary, monumental; along the wide pathways a surprising number of tourists strolled and snapped pictures, drawn here even though the statue itself was still off-limits after two and a half years.

Vic felt drawn, too, but oddly reluctant to go closer. "This is great," she murmured to Tory, "but I can't wait to get you back home." Maybe the sea breeze had blown away the last of the desert, or maybe sheltering Tory from the wind had restored her confidence. Whichever, she was sure whatever had blocked her had melted away. Almost sure.

But Tory tugged her along the dock to where a fortyish, wiry woman in a Park Service uniform waited.

"Maddie, this is Vic," she said, a bit breathlessly. "Vic, meet Madlyn."

Vic put out her hand, and felt it gripped with a force just short of challenge. Madlyn looked steadily into her face for a long moment. "OK," she said abruptly. "We can go up."

She strode off toward the monument, with Vic and Tory following. "Up inside the Statue? All the way?" Vic asked, and Tory nodded.

"She wouldn't promise until she'd seen you."

Vic wasn't sure this wasn't some new dream, but when they rounded the huge pedestal and she had to tilt her head back to look up, and up, into the Lady's face, it didn't matter. Whatever name or role men had given Her, She rose beyond it, the archetype of the strong woman, powerful without swagger, stern and compassionate, nurturing and commanding. Vic wanted to reach out, to touch something more of Her than the copper shell of her robes, smooth away the tension between Her brows, stroke Her full, beautiful lips gently until they curved into a smile.

A sidelong glance at Madlyn showed her watching with something close to a smile herself. The ranger led them toward an entrance, stopped to speak to two security guards, and then they were inside, riding the elevator to the top of the ten-story pedestal; and then, under the cavernous shelter of Lady Liberty's robes, Vic was jogging up the spiraling staircase well ahead of the others.

She mounted higher and higher, through the massive, complex network of girders forming the statue's bones. The thud of her boots on the metal steps was like a giant pulse accelerating along with her own heartbeat.

In spite of the exertion, the farther she got, the faster she needed to go. At last, in the tiny room at the top where a row of windows looked out from Her crown, Vic braced her hands against the inside of Her copper brow and gazed out with Her across island and sea and sky. Harbor lights were flickering on as afternoon flowed toward twilight, tiny sparks echoing the blaze of Her great lamp.

Vic's whole body seemed to be growing, stretching. She ached to stand eye to eye with Her, breast to breast, heart to pounding heart; to comfort Her, share the endless standing guard, the grief at the chaos human hatred could inflict. Vic understood all that. And suddenly she wanted to share something else she understood, something filling her to bursting; she wanted to show Her the piercing joy of a woman's body.

Vic's breath came even faster now than when she'd been climbing. She was still alone in the room. Then Madlyn's head emerged above the stairwell. "Are you OK?" she asked.

"Just meditating," Vic grated. Madlyn gave her a keen glance and then nodded and stepped back down, gesturing for Tory to wait.

Vic didn't give a damn. She was inside the great body, swelling to fill it, her head brushing the copper ripples on the reverse side of Her hair. She clenched her fist low against the side of an arching support, and leaned her hips into it, pressing her crotch against her flexing thumb; a desperate comfort she had sought before, in rare moments of solitude, leaning on walls, trees, once, even, an armored tank. This time, though, she felt far from solitary. Another presence filled her, surrounded her, intensified the heat Tory had already ignited in her. The pounding tension in her clit and cunt swelled, and rose, higher and harder, until joy burst forth like rays of light from Her crown.

But a whole lot noisier than light. Vic could feel her shout of triumph reverberating through the Lady's copper body as though it had become Her own voice.

When the cry had died away and Vic's gasps subsided, Madlyn re-emerged. "Meditating, huh? How about teaching me that mantra?"

Tory pushed past her and rushed at Vic, who turned to meet her. They leaned against each other, both shaking, until Tory slid to her knees and buried her face in Vic's damp, musky crotch, then raised her head. "There'd better be more where that came from!"

Vic had no more doubts. Wherever that had come from, the way was clear now. "All you can handle," she said, and drew Tory's head close again for a moment before pulling her up, and toward the stairs, and home.

On the return ride, they stood pressed together, Tory's back warm against Vic's front, and watched the city skyline with its aching gap grow closer. "Vic, I . . ." Tory had to pause to clear her throat. When she began again she managed a lighter tone. "I can't believe you fucked the Statue of Liberty! But don't go thinking you did it all by yourself. I was rubbing that railing so hard my hand aches, and Maddy – well, she was crouched over muttering something I'm pretty damned sure wasn't the Rosary."

Vic wriggled her crotch against Tory's round ass. Too bad she wasn't packing – but, she reflected, inside the immense Statue that might have felt, well, inadequate.

She didn't feel inadequate at all, though, when she had Tory all to herself in the tiny shower . . . and up against the refrigerator . . . and over the back of the sofa . . . and in bed. There was one brief moment, as Tory's guttural moans took on a tinge of pain, when Vic hesitated; until Tory squeezed her thigh savagely with a hand as strong as her own. "Don't stop!" she commanded roughly. "You can't hurt me, damn it! More, harder!"

The last subconscious shadow of war vanished. Vic was all there, in every urgent moment, feeling, breathing, tasting the intensity, knowing without question where she was, who she was; free to take her long-unused gear for a wild, slippery ride, free to let Tory drive her to her limits, hold her there for long, cruel, delirious minutes, then thrust her over the edge into the sweet, howling maelstrom. And, at last, into sleep and peace.

Inevitability

Julius

The table, a sheet of plywood with three jig-sawn openings, rested on trestles. Brenda rested face down on the table. Her hands and feet were secured to the corners. She was blindfolded and naked, save for her little white cotton panties.

Her breasts, pointing floor-ward, jutted through two of the holes. Her nipples were clamped and the clamps were joined by a chain.

Every ten minutes he removed the clamps and gently massaged her nipples with fingers and thumbs. Even if she complained of the pain when he took off the clamps, she enjoyed the massage. So did he, crouching under the board, playing with her protruding breasts.

"I have to pee, John." She waited for a response but got none. "I'll have to go soon." There was urgency in her voice.

"Soon, my dear, soon." He tried not to sound pleased. He'd been waiting, hoping she'd ask sooner, rather than later.

He reached for the big, plastic pop bottle and hung it carefully on the chain between her nipples. She sucked air between her teeth as the clamps pulled a little harder but she made no complaint.

John crawled out and stood. He was naked and his cock waved as he moved. He was acutely aware of his erection and the torment of having her so near, so willing but, for now, so unavailable.

He slid the bowl, on its box, under the third opening, under her pussy.

"What are you doing?" asked Brenda.

He didn't answer but glanced at the clock and stood waiting for the ten minutes to elapse.

"I told you, I need to pee and the clamps are hurting and this board is all splintery."

"You know you're loving every moment, my sweet."

He smiled and reached to caress her ass. He was loving it, loving challenging her, loving her helpless nakedness. She always complained and begged to be let go but this was their game, their foreplay.

Time to take the clamps off again. He got to his knees and moved under the makeshift table. He grimaced, next time he'd make the trestles taller.

"Ready?"

"Yes," she murmured and he carefully removed the first clamp and Brenda gasped above him. "Oh, John, that hurts!"

He removed the other and she squealed.

Gently he caressed the skin of her breasts around her nipples wondering at the softness, the silkiness of her skin. The nipples were big now and an angry red. Brenda moved on the board above him as he played with her.

His cock was drooling. Taking some pre-come on a fingertip, he anointed her left nipple with it. Above him, she struggled in her bonds.

"Ow!" she squealed. "Splinters are sticking in my breasts."

"Be still then." He continued toying with her nipples, loving their hardness, their size.

"John, I have to pee!"

He clipped the clamps carefully back on her nipples, loving her cries of pain and protest.

"What are you doing now? You have to untie me."

"I'm putting the tube from the basin into the bottle that's hanging from your nipples."

There was a long silence. Finally, "Does that mean what I think it means?"

"You have a beautiful imagination, so it probably does."

"You'll have a long wait then," she told him angrily, but there was no conviction in her voice.

"I don't think so." He crawled out and stood again. He

crossed to the wall and turned the thermostat to zero. "Let's turn the heat down a little."

Next he opened the window slightly. She turned her head as she heard him.

He said, "The chill air should hurry things along."

"No, John."

"Yes, Brenda. Do you know that water weighs ten pounds per gallon, maybe two and a half pounds a quart?"

She squirmed on the board, signalling her need. He moved to stand beside her, then, reaching over he pulled the waistband of her panties down, leaned close and kissed her buttock.

Her legs were so invitingly apart, open when she must so badly need to close them. He slid a hand up the inside of her thigh and touched her through the crotch of her panties. She was wet. His other hand was on his cock, stroking it.

Slipping his fingers under the fabric, he began exploring her moist softness. She writhed helplessly.

A glance at the clock showed another ten minutes gone, nearer fifteen.

He took the clamps off yet again. She told him it hurt, told him how aroused she was, begged him to release her so she could relieve herself. So they could make love.

"We are making love." He craned his neck and took a nipple in his mouth and suckled at her. Above him, she struggled frantically, making little mewing sounds.

He knew she was near to coming and released her nipple. He gently replaced the clamps. The empty bottle swung on the chain, pulling her nipples this way and that. His cock was like an iron bar.

"John, I have to pee!"

"Go ahead, lover."

"In my panties?"

He laughed. "Why not? You know I love washing them for you."

He went into the bathroom and turned on the shower knowing how it would affect her. Jeez! Now he needed to go too.

He went back to her.

"Damn you, John, you're being cruel."

"And you're loving it." His hand went to his cock again; he wouldn't have to wait much longer surely.

He bent and kissed her pretty ass, nipped the soft flesh and thought how much he loved this sweet creature.

"Oh no!" she whispered and he heard the trickling sound.

"One pound per pint, Brenda."

Boilermaker

Alison Tyler

The preacher spoke soothing words in a low voice. A few solemn phrases about letting the family members have their time to say goodbye.

That's the part Parker hadn't been able to figure out: How the fuck was he supposed to say goodbye to someone who had never said hello?

His father had spoken with his fists and with his belt. The man could say volumes with the flick of his thumb on his vintage lighter, a lighter now resting in Parker's front pocket. Parker hadn't used the Bic yet. Not once. But he kept stroking the metal with the tips of his fingers.

He could picture the fat purple-tinged flame in his mind. Hear the click. See the way his father had looked, with his cheeks indented, sucking hard on a Marlboro Red. Kicked back on the grass in front of his sagging bungalow. Wearing his everyday outfit of Levis, a T-shirt, brown leather belt.

Parker had his old man's belt now, too. Worn brown leather, beat-up buckle, it fit around his waist snugger than it had around the old man's. But he remembered being on the receiving end of the belt too many times. Or maybe not enough. Maybe he wouldn't be such a fuck-up if his old man had taken him for a few more laps with the thing.

Tiff shut down that thought by resting one hand on his shoulder. He looked at her perky, nearly too-thin body in that black jersey dress, knew she'd be more comfortable buffing someone's nails than standing around at this low-end funeral parlor. But she was trying. She'd hated his father with such a fierceness that simply the fact that she'd washed her birch-blonde hair and put on her favorite salmon lipstick was something Parker didn't take for granted.

He felt someone watching him and turned to catch the glance of one of the pallbearers – pale blue watered-down eyes – recognized the man from warm evenings spent sitting on his father's porch after work. Beer bottles and cigarettes. Horseshoes and lug wrenches. There were always men around his father's house, and they were always fixing someone's truck and bitching about someone's boss or woman or both. That man – whatever the hell his name was – had to be as nearly old as Parker's dad, but seemed younger.

Time hadn't cut him down yet.

Parker grimaced as the man strode toward him, noticing his posture – rod straight, his expression calm, somber. This was the shit he hated the most. What was he supposed to say to this guy? His mother had raised him for the better part of his youth. But 'raised' was an overstatement. He'd basically survived – living through constant turbulence as he'd shuttled back and forth. His dad's home had been violent and his mom's had been lonely – she was always out looking for one more chance.

"You're Oz's boy," the man said, and Parker tried to stand up a little taller. He shook the man's hand, noticing the shadow of blackness in his knuckles, some dirt there that would stay until his own grave, no matter how much he scrubbed. Parker could feel Tiffany watching him. She couldn't wait to escape.

"Yes, sir, Mr McFadden." The name came back right then – fifteen years since he'd seen this man, but he could still picture him leaning on the back of a truck, smoking, grease in the creases of his jeans. He waited to see what the man would say – what everyone said: *They took him too soon*, or *Sorry for your loss*. What he said was, "Clint, not Mr McFadden. Do you want to get a beer?"

And suddenly Parker really fucking wanted a beer.

He turned to Tiffany and handed her the keys. Set her free. She looked at him with wide-eyed relief, gave him a kiss on the cheek, didn't say another word. She wanted out. Back to her friends and her pink princess phone and raspberry-flavored wine coolers. Away from the stench of the working-class boys here in this room. Tiff was a hairdresser, but she did not like to hang out in the blue collar world. She had a Pomeranian. And she worked in a salon, she was quick to say, not a beauty parlor.

Back to Clint's truck parked in the rear – which looked like it had to look. Creamsicle Orange. Rusted bumper. With an engine that ran like a dream. Clint drove them to an old man's bar. Probably to *his* old man's bar. Jukebox. Girl behind the counter with a beehive – no, not a girl. Someone who'd been a girl once upon a time long before Parker was born, and who never updated her look.

Two bottles of something cold and two shots with the beer – rear booth. No words. Not at first. Then, "Your father drank boilermakers."

Parker nodded.

"He could put them away." Parker fingered the lighter in his pocket. He could feel the belt around his waist. So when Clint touched the buckle under the table, he shivered.

He'd thought of giving the worn leather over to Tiffany. Of trying to explain in words what he needed from her. And yet, he couldn't picture the look in her hazel eyes, couldn't handle the look he knew he'd see there.

Clint took him home. Led him to a bedroom that only held a bed and a dresser. Told him to take off his suit coat. Hang it on the back of the door.

Parker couldn't find the words, but he heard them in his head. *"What are you doing? The fuck you think you're doing?"* As the man yanked open his father's buckle and pulled the belt free, Parker's eyes took a tour of the room, looking everywhere but at Clint. Helpless and unable to do what he knew he had to do.

Clint didn't seem to mind. He wrenched down Parker's slacks then pushed him over the mattress. When Parker flinched, tried to stand up, Clint got tough, gripping both of his wrists in one hand and holding him steady.

Fucking hell, man. Clint had thirty pounds on him and twenty years at least, had to be fifty-something. Yet there was undeniable power in his grip, and when Parker gave a test pull, he heard the low chuckle under Clint's breath.

"You'll hold still for this, boy. If you know what's good for you."

Parker turned his head away, bit his lip, felt the terror in his heart. But he stayed put as Clint whipped the tar out of him, licking him long and fast with that old leather belt, before kicking his legs apart. Parker crying for the first time in God knew how long. Not just tears streaking his face, but sobs – a sound he didn't recognize, one he couldn't remember ever having made before.

There'd been power in the way Clint held his wrists, but now there was just the mechanics of the act. Spit on his asshole, Clint's cock pressing there. Parker couldn't think, couldn't speak, could hardly breathe, but he did what Clint had told him.

He held still.

Parker knew he was going to get fucked, and yet he was unable to process the thought clearly. His eyes caught the open closet. He saw a pair of old workboots inside. Just one pair. Saw the everyday plaid shirts. The jeans folded neatly. Clint had been wearing his one good suit for the funeral. Like his dad had one good suit – the one he'd been married in – the one that he dragged out for every wedding and every funeral after, stretching out the fabric as the beer had built his gut.

Something turned over inside of Parker.

He could feel the head of Clint's cock pressing forward, and then suddenly, he was filled. He shut his eyes. He'd never been fucked before, and the sensation made his thoughts go gold and scarlet in his mind. Pictures flicking too fast to see anything but a blur. His dad's fist around a beer bottle. Clint's hand around a wrench. A childhood dipped in sepia tones and the sound of a skip on a phonographic record.

He felt himself getting closer, and he groaned when Clint reached under his body to wrap those thick fingers around his hard-on. Parker felt Clint release inside of him, and he swore when he came – *Jesus fucking Christ*. He'd never come like that before. The power in it. The tears were still on his cheeks – he didn't know where to look, what to do. Clint pulled back, helped him up. Took him to the shower. Stripped him down and washed him off with a gentleness that brought the tears up once more.

Cracked tiles on the wall. Hairline fracture in a mirror clouded with steam.

Afterwards, he dressed in silence. But he watched as Clint took his belt and hung the buckle from the hook on the back of the door. Parker knew he'd be back. And he knew that's where the belt had hung before, that's where the belt belonged.

Dinner at the Fonsecas'

Esmeralda Greene

Helen was sitting on the sofa in a catlike pose. She was leaning over at an angle, one elbow on the padded armrest and her legs hooked up beside her on the seat cushions. I suppose that isn't literally a catlike pose, since cats don't sit or lie like that, but at the time it looked pretty damn catlike to me. She was wearing a muslin peasant skirt that sat low on her hips and a snug red blouse, and she had a cool, flirty, half-smile on her lips.

Behind the sofa was a big archway that separated the Fonsecas' living room from their kitchen. Raul was in the kitchen, so from where I was sitting I could shift my focus between him and Helen without moving my head. He was doing his chef thing: stirring his risotto, grating his cheese, sipping his wine. He always drank his wine in little sips, always held it in his mouth for a second before swallowing, always gripped his wine glass by the stem.

"Too bad Jill couldn't make it," Helen said. "Has she been working long hours a lot lately?" She was barefoot, and was slowly flexing her toes open and closed.

"Yeah," I said. "A lot." I emptied my wine glass with a couple of gulps. "Lately." I took a hard look at Helen's right foot and the little bit of leg I could see below her skirt's hemline. I lowered my voice so Raul wouldn't hear me. "I think she's fucking around on me."

Helen's eyebrows went up a little bit, slowly, then came down again. Otherwise her face didn't move. "Good for her," she said. "I think married women *should* fuck around." She paused a beat. "Don't you?"

I didn't have a clever answer to that, so I just reached out to the bottle of chardonnay Raul had left on the coffee table and refilled my glass. I was lifting the glass to my mouth again when my eyes went back to Helen.

She was holding her skirt up.

Helen's skirt was long and full; lots of fabric to it. So lifting it up in a way that was sure to give me a clear view of her snatch took a little bit of doing. She'd had to gather up a good fistful of cloth and then raise her hand to about chest-high.

Like an idiot, the first thing I did was to look behind Helen, to her husband in the kitchen. He was pouring a ladleful of broth into the risotto and humming along with the Beethoven coming from the stereo. I lowered my eyes back to Helen's crotch. Helen's hair had a color that was somewhere between polished gold and rusted iron. It was an exquisite, striking color. She was a reasonably attractive woman, but that mane of rusty gold on her head lifted her into the realm of beautiful.

And there was more of that rusty gold between her legs, I saw now. A neat triangle of it, fluffy, well kempt, luxurious. I stared, my cock ticking in my pants.

Then she let go of her skirt, closing the curtain on her show. At the same time she sat up, dropping her feet to the floor, and leaned forward to pick up her wine glass from the coffee table. The glass was full, and she leaned over and emptied it into the potted rubber tree beside the sofa. Then she looked at me. "Come over here and pour me some wine, David," she said.

I got up and went to her and sat beside her on the sofa. She was holding her wine glass out to me, so I plucked it out of her hand and clunked it down on the coffee table. Then I dropped my hand to her thigh. I pulled up and gathered the heavy fabric of her skirt until my hand was on her bare skin, and then I pressed in with my fingers, gripping her.

Helen looked down at my hand with a calm, blank expression, as if the hand wasn't attached to the rest of me, but was some uninteresting little animal that had wandered up onto the sofa and onto her leg. I moved my hand up toward her crotch, toward that nest of impossibly beautiful hair. Still her face didn't move. It's possible that the corner of her mouth twitched some fractional amount toward a smile, but it was too subtle for me to be sure.

"Is it someone at her work?" Helen asked, looking up at my face. "Who you think is porking your little wife, I mean."

"Yeah," I grunted. "This guy Ernest. He's technical lead on one of her projects." *Porking my little wife*. The image was perfect. Jill is small, barely five foot three with her heels off, and Ernest – and who the fuck lets himself be named "Ernest" anyway – was oversized in all three dimensions. I pictured Jill on her back on some company conference room table, her lean ass hanging over the edge, Ernest sweaty and puffing as he jabbed his cock into her, holding her upraised thighs against his jiggling stomach, *porking her, porking her, porking her*. I moved my hand another inch closer to Helen's crotch. My hand was under her skirt now, hidden by the fabric bunched up at her mid-thighs. I felt, or imagined that I could feel, a hothouse warmth and humidity under there.

"Naughty, naughty Jill," Helen said. She settled back, stretching her arms out along the back cushions and spreading her legs a little. "How's Raul doing?"

I was sitting diagonally on the sofa, so I hardly had to turn my head to look into the kitchen. Raul was cutting a head of iceberg lettuce into wedges. "How's it going, Raul?" I called out to him.

Raul shot a quick smile in my direction. "It's going great, David," he said in his sing-song accent. "Everything will be ready in—" he looked over at a timer on the refrigerator door "—seven minutes. You hungry?" It occurred to me at that moment that he was holding a knife long enough so that a couple of inches would stick out of my back if he were to bury it hilt-deep in my chest.

"Starving!" I said with my best golly-gee-whiz grin, and I slid my right hand the rest of the way up Helen's thigh, pressing my fingers to her furry cunt.

She was wet. The knuckle of my forefinger slipped deep into a soft bed of liquid warmth, and I had to turn my head back to the living room and away from Raul so he wouldn't see the cloud of ecstasy passing over my face. Sometimes I think cocks are over-rated. Sometimes it seems that the nerve endings of the fingers are as well wired for pleasure impulses as any penis ever was.

Helen shifted her butt on the sofa, turning diagonally toward me and twisting her head around so she could see Raul. Her movement had the effect of pushing her spread-open cunt harder against my hand. "Sweetie," she said to her husband, "why don't you get one of those bottles of Canadian ice wine from the basement and put it in the fridge to chill? We can have it with our dessert." As she was speaking, I straightened my forefinger and pushed it into her cunt as far as I could reach. She didn't miss a syllable.

"Oh! Good idea!" Raul chirped, and he disappeared through the door leading to the cellar.

Helen leaned toward me until our faces were close. "I've always known Jill was a fucking tramp," she whispered, and then we were kissing, sort of, our lips brushing together dryly. At the same time she put her hand on my right wrist. She didn't pull or push; she just held my hand where it was, with its finger buried inside her. Then she moved her head back and dipped it lower. Her face was against my upper arm, and her mouth was open, and then she was biting me, her teeth closing down hard, hard, *hard* on the side of my arm. There was a grinding, crunching sensation as my skin started to give way under the pressure. With my face screwed up in a pantomimed shriek, I jerked my hand out of Helen's cunt and grabbed a fistful of her hair, yanking her head back and away from my arm. I half expected to see a bloody scrap of my flesh hanging from her teeth, but there was nothing. Her teeth were clean, bloodless, and smiling at me. Her mouth was open, her neck arched back by the tension of my hand pulling at her hair.

And then Raul was clomping up the last of the steps from the basement. I let go of Helen's hair and sat straight in the sofa, staring ahead of me, at nothing. My arm hurt so much my eyes were watering.

Half a minute later Raul called out, "OK, we're all set. Let's eat!"

Just Like Old Times

Ryan Keye

It's Saturday morning. He just comes by to pick up a few things he left in the closet, and suddenly they're screaming at each other, just like old times. He doesn't even know what they're screaming about. In the old days, when the two of them got going like this, it would just go on and on. She would occasionally break things – a candle holder against the wall, a phone or two. He's punched the wall and broken plaster he had to later patch up. He's punched the refrigerator and bloodied his hand. But they never crossed the line into physical contact. They never attacked each other.

He realizes the fight is not going to end the way it used to – with make-up sex. He'd give anything at all to make it end that way.

That was the only way to make it end agreeably. If they just tried to move on, then she would hate him for caving and hate him worse for the many times he would say "Sorry." She'd hate him for being a nutless wonder. That's why they started naturally gravitating into the make-up sex.

But there won't be any make-up sex this time. Because even though they're fighting just like told times, they're actually broken up. There won't be any make-up sex because they don't have sex anymore. That breaks his heart. If he has to listen to her screaming – and if she has to listen to him – the least they can get out of the deal is a grudge fuck. He wants make-up sex.

She screams: "Are you . . . Are you even fucking listening to me?"

And he screams right back at her that he's listening to her, of course he is. Fuck her for asking.

"Then tell me what I just said!" she screams.

He screams back, "Why should I listen when I know what you're going to say?"

They scream some more, with their hands flailing everywhere, and suddenly he stops dead in his tracks, like a deer in the headlights. Her face is red and she's been screaming for half an hour now, just like him, so both their voices are hoarse and they're both exhausted. Her long blonde hair is tied up in her weekend ponytail that she always wears when she runs on Saturday mornings. He loves it; she's hot in it. He loves her sports bra too, and the familiar way it clings to her tits. He loves those tight black running shorts; he loves to pull them down.

He grabs her and shoves her against the wall.

At first she thinks he's attacking her, so she punches him – right across the eye. He takes it and likes it. He kisses her hard and hits his teeth into hers. His eye is half-closed and he's kissing her hard, his tongue sliding into her mouth. She grinds against him. She digs her fingernails into his arm.

She pulls him against her. Her mouth is wide open, practically drooling. She looks scared, but not scared that he's going to hurt her. Scared that she's going to fuck him.

She doesn't say a word. She just digs into his T-shirt and tries to rip it off him. He seizes her sports bra. She squirms out of it, pulls him hard against her.

He's on her, all over her, and she's on him. She leaves deep red furrows across his back as he carries her into the bedroom.

He throws her on the bed. She yanks at his jeans. He's not wearing a belt. His button fly comes open. He's hard.

Her shorts aren't even off before he enters her. He's just shoved them down to her ankles and she's spread her knees as wide as they'll go. He has to wedge himself in between her spread thighs and shove her shorts down over her running shoes. She kicks her legs free and spreads her legs and wraps them around him, planting her shoes at his ass and kicking at his jeans. She pushes them down as he fucks deeply into her in long quick strokes, just the way she used to like it when they were both crazy for each other. His boxers go down with his jeans. He pulls his way out of it all, kicking off his shoes as he does. She doesn't bother with hers. He can feel those gym shoes tucked up tight in the small of his back, her ankles crossed, pulling him harder and harder into her with each thrust. Her fingernails left furrows in his chest and his shoulders and now his back. She bites his shoulder – right into the big bulky muscle. She digs her teeth in so hard he cries out. It hurts like hell, but he used to like it – so he pretends like he likes it now, and he likes so many other things about having her hot naked body spread and grinding underneath him that he figures he can put up with some tooth marks in his shoulder.

He bites her back, on the shoulder, but then moves up and starts kissing her on the neck – right in the place where she likes it. It makes her go crazy. She squirms and pulls him onto her, moving her arms down so that her hands are underneath her ankles, digging into his ass. He pins her legs wide and goes slow, knowing that's how she likes it. He pulls out and tips his body at just the right angle so his cock hits that place just inside her entrance.

"Yes," she hisses. "Fuck, that's good. Real slow like that . . ."

He pulls her hair. She moves her hands up from his ass and rips a long trail of fingernail scrapes over the small of his back. It hurts and then it tickles. He gasps and she fucks herself up against him.

She's moaning louder, her hips moving gradually, deliberately, working her body back and forth impaled on his cock, while she says, "No, not yet, not yet," and he struggles to hold back because he knows she'll come if he waits. He can barely make it, because she's driving him wild – gorgeous and naked and crazy underneath him. She wants it so badly; even hotter, she *controls* it. She fucks herself slowly up onto him while he fights to stay still and keep himself from coming. She thrusts up onto him and reaches down to rub her clit. She's struggling to get there; he's struggling to hold back. Story of their lives.

She finally lets out a low bestial groan as her eyes roll back in her head. She's coming.

Her climax is there and gone fast . . . intense and powerful. She adjusts her sneakers up under the curve of his ass again and starts pulling him rhythmically into her, harder this time.

"Come inside me," she growls. "Come on. Do it."

It doesn't take long. He lets go, and she surges up and kisses him hard as he explodes inside her. He come so hard and so much that her pussy goes drippy and slick before he's finished thrusting.

She pulls him tight onto her and moans in his ear. "Yeah, baby. Yes, come inside me."

When it's over, he slumps to the side and she stretches out against him. She looks amazing, naked with her running shoes on. She's been working out a lot lately. Maybe breaking up with him gave her the impetus.

She looks confident, soft, relaxed. Not the least bit embarrassed.

He looks at her. "Sorry about fighting."

She bristles a little. She shrugs it off, stretches and yawns. "Forget it," she says.

He adds, "And about ... this." He glances over both their naked bodies.

She looks in his eyes. "It doesn't mean anything."

"*Anything*?" he says.

She says, "It doesn't mean we're together."

He tells her, "That's different than not meaning anything."

She looks perturbed. That's how he argues, always, with appeals to logic, emotion, sentimentality, all choked up at once and slathered on thick. It always annoys her.

She shrugs, stretches, yawns again. She pushes her naked body up against him and kisses his chest.

"Yeah," she says. "I guess it is. It means something, but not that."

"It doesn't mean we're together," he says. "Of course. I know that."

She rolls over and faces away, but she doesn't leave the bed.

He runs his hand up her side. He leans in behind her and kisses her neck – right in the place where she likes it.

"I know that," he says, and keeps kissing.

Naked Dinner

Valerie Grey

I had a secret desire, a fantasy I wanted to fulfill: to be naked in front of a group of men and humiliated. Don't ask me why I wanted this, why I found it arousing; I was obsessed and I had to find out if the reality would be as sexy as the movies that played in my head.

I told a friend about this and she said she knew a guy who might be able to help me, this grad student named Darren. Darren and I emailed back and forth and I explained my fantasy:

I am standing naked in front of two or five men; they stare at me and I can see in their eyes they want to ravish me. One of them uses a razor blade to shave off my pubic hair. They watch this, and they can see inside my pussy because my lips are engorged and open. I am made to have dinner with them completely naked. They look at me all night and they want to fuck me and maybe I want to fuck them, but it never happens, there is no sex; they simply stare and it humiliates me ... and turns me on.

Darren said that was a progressive scenario for a sophomore in literary studies. He seemed understanding; he said he was working on his Masters in sociology.

Darren emailed one morning and asked if I was free that night to make my fantasy come true. I was a little flustered, there was no time to prepare, but I had to get this over with soon. I told him I had nothing planned. He told me that he had explained my situation to his business partner and that he was willing to participate and even offered his home as a safe place for the event.

I met Darren outside the dorms and put my mouth to his ear and tried to make him understand how important it was that I should undress pretty much as soon as I entered the apartment so that I could meet the conditions of my self-appointed task. We must have looked like a pair of lovers whispering sweet nothings. I insisted on stopping at a shop to buy a packet of plastic disposable razors . . .

I cannot describe how I felt as we entered the building and went up the stairs to the third floor. This was not a student apartment, these were luxury condos; Darren's roommate must own it, I thought.

We entered and a man stood up from the black leather sofa. He looked quite a bit older than Darren and his hair was styled in a metrosexual manner. I took him for Darren's partner. I was flustered when another man came out of the kitchen. Darren made the introductions. The man from the kitchen was Paul, Darren's partner, and the swishy man was Jeff and worked with Paul. Jeff smiled too deviously for my liking. I was thinking that it would have been nice if Darren had warned me about Jeff; he did not say a guest would be there, I thought it would just be the three of us.

The men sat down and I stood in the middle of the living room. I thanked Darren and Paul for being so understanding, helping me with my project.

There was an uncomfortable pause and Paul said, "You can get started whenever you like."

I took off my jacket and folded it neatly on a chair. Even with my top still on I felt exposed, like standing in a spotlight. I am sure I was blushing as I pulled my T-shirt over my head and felt cold air on my body.

I folded and put the shirt over my jacket.

My bra was pale blue. I could feel the male eyes on my tits; my nips were standing up. I bent and removed my sneakers and socks. I stared straight ahead, not meeting anyone's eyes, as I unfastened my jeans and yanked them down. I almost fell over as I pulled my jeans inside out over my feet. I had to pull them the right way out and folded them onto the pile.

It felt surreal and thrilling to stand in front of three men just in my yellow cotton panties. I took the panties off and, after folding them, slipped them underneath my jeans.

"Let's put these clothes somewhere else," said Darren, standing up, "just in case, you know, you suddenly change your mind."

I stood helplessly with my hands at my sides. Darren took my clothes to his bedroom. He returned a few seconds later and sat back down.

Paul said that he thought we should put Jeff fully in the picture so I should read aloud the email then everyone would be clear about what we had to fit into the evening. Jeff knew all about the task so making me read it aloud was just a way to increase my humiliation. Paul handed me a printout of the email I had sent to Darren.

Reading aloud is not a problem for me although standing nude and reading the instructions about my own degradation made me stutter. I looked straight ahead and read my fantasy.

Jeff picked up on the part about shaving; everyone had seen me carrying a pack of razors. Paul said that he and Darren had to finish preparing the meal so perhaps Jeff would like to take me into the bathroom . . .

The bathroom was large and luxurious. There was a clawfoot tub. Jeff looked around and suggested – or perhaps *ordered* – that I stand with my back to the tiled wall and my arms resting on the edge of the tub. He had me lean backwards onto my arms and, with his soft hands, made sure my legs were wide apart.

Jeff made it clear that he was not gay, despite his metrosexual appearance. Being alone with him in the bathroom was quite an uncomfortable experience. I realized I had not bought any shaving foam. Jeff said that we would just have to make do with ordinary soap and rubbed a bar of green soap between his hands until it lathered. He rubbed the foamy soap in his hands and put warm water into the basin then he smeared the lather on my sensitive area and, with great concentration, set about his task. Great swathes of my dark triangle came away under the assault from the blade. Jeff set to the delicate task of shaving until I was bare. He rubbed me dry with a towel and stood back to admire his work; I remained in position, trying to deal with the intense humiliation that was getting me off.

He said something about my ass and told me to turn around which I did slowly and he had me lean over forwards with my hands on the bath and my legs spread. I felt his hot hands on my rear and he pulled my cheeks apart. He was now getting a view of me that only a (female) doctor had ever viewed. I knew he could see my anus.

I felt the cold metal of the razor. I knew I had a few straggly hairs between my cheeks but even when I had briefly kept my pussy shaved, I never shaved there. I was afraid the edge of the razor would nick me in that sensitive area.

When he finished, he ran his hand over the area to feel the smoothness, one finger pausing over my anus as if he was considering inserting it. He told me to clean up; he stood back and watched while I wiped all my hair from the basin and into the small metal bin under the sink.

We returned to the living room. Darren announced that dinner was served and invited Jeff and I to sit opposite each other at the table in the dining area. Our positions meant that Jeff would be ogling my tits the entire time. I am 36A and have always been sensitive about my small tits. I used to get called "Tiny Teets" by the cruel girls. I wish I had fuller breasts and a slightly smaller rear.

Darren and Paul served and poured the wine. We had a lovely filet mignon steak and sensuous creamy mashed potatoes. Darren and Paul sat opposite each other with Darren next to me. I was constantly aware of Jeff enjoying the view. We took our time over the meal and the dessert, Black Forest cake. The conversation was not all that exciting; Jeff and Paul worked in finance; Paul asked me about my major and my ambitions. Talking about such matters after I had just allowed a stranger to shave my pussy was an odd and tingling experience.

It made me feel uncomfortably hot.

When the meal was over, Paul invited Jeff and me to sit in the living room. I had the impression that the three men had discussed what would happen next and Paul said they would like to know more about me and to explore the question of humiliation a bit further.

Jeff asked the first question: "When is your next period due?"

I was stunned. I whispered an answer.

Then the questions just kept coming. Do I get heavy periods? Do I often get period pain? How many sexual partners had I had? What age was my first?

I was holding my arms stiffly on the chair arms so I was now displaying every intimate fold of my shaved pussy.

And the questions continued. It was like having my mind invaded; I was very close to losing control and bursting into tears. They asked me about masturbation – how often I did it, what method did I use, did I have a dildo or vibrator, how many fingers could I get in there. I admitted that I owned a very big black dildo, so big that it hurt to put it inside me but that was the point: to be incredibly stretched gave me intense orgasms.

Paul and Jeff began to discuss whether they should see a demonstration of masturbation and that was when Darren put a stop to things. He very firmly said they had gone far enough and we should talk about something else.

I was still sitting in my revealing position displaying my sex; the conversation turned to my fantasy and we had a fairly educational conversation about the mechanics of embarrassment and why humiliation affects one sexually. I admitted to them, with a red face, that I was very aroused doing what I was doing. Jeff asked what I thought about having sex with the three of them and Darren interrupted: "That wasn't part of the deal, remember; she's on display but no fucking."

I don't know if I was grateful or not because if Jeff and Paul had pushed it, I might have gone to bed with them . . .

And so the evening came to an end at 10.30. Paul said that he would call me a taxi and Darren went to fetch my clothes. He also brought the packet of razors for me to take home. I had to dress before their eyes; I wanted to put my bra on and was going through the heap but it was not there. Darren said that he had kept my bra and would give it to me tomorrow or he might give it to Jeff as a souvenir. I would just have to wait to find out. The men laughed. Jeff took out his wallet and gave me money for the taxi.

I knew that, even though I was now fully clothed, the three men were seeing my bare flesh in their minds.

I took the money from Darren: three twenty-dollar bills for

what would be a ten-dollar fare. I felt like a whore, a paid slut. It was one more humiliation and it made me sopping wet.

In the taxi, the driver kept looking at me in the rear-view and I was convinced he knew what I had done.

I crossed my legs.

The Shape of Cities

Maxim Jakubowski

She used to come with me to foreign cities.

The ways of lust were impenetrable as it turned us into involuntary and much incurious tourists. After all, we couldn't quite spend the whole duration of every trip barricaded in our hotel room fucking like rabid rabbits, could we?

So, between the hours of sex, we walked, explored, I dived into any bookshop I would pass and she would buy lingerie (on my credit card), we ate too much, saw movies. The Grand Canal in Venice smelt; maybe it was because we were not in season; in the bay in Monterey the otters were silent; in Amsterdam, we had a rijstaffel, which made our stomachs churn for hours later; in Barcelona, Las Ramblas were overflowing with foreign soccer fans; in Brighton, mecca of dirty weekends, television cameras were everywhere for a forthcoming party political conference as opposed to a blue movie capturing our sordid exploits, but somehow every city felt the same as it harboured our frantic fucks. They had no shape, just a strange presence dictated by the intensity of sex.

Of course, eventually, she tired of travel, of me.

All I now have left of her is this photograph. Black and white. Of a woman naked against a dark background. A hotel room, no doubt. It's not even her, I am ashamed to say. Just an image in a book that somehow reminds me of her. I never had a talent for photography, couldn't even master the simple art of photographing your lover by way of Polaroids. Sad, eh?

This is the way she looked as she stripped for me in a hotel room. Maybe it was in Paris, a hotel on the rue de l'Odeon with wooden beams criss-crossing the rough texture of the walls and ceiling. Or then again it could have been the Gershwin Hotel, just off 5th Avenue in New York City, where the smile of a Picasso heroine illuminated the wall next to the bed and watched our lovemaking through the hours of darkness. Or whenever we also kept the light on. Maybe it was a small hotel in Amsterdam, windows overlooking a murky canal, with the noise of drunken revellers and cars parking keeping us awake at night. Oh yes, we frequented many hotels. Those sometimes elegant, often sordid last contemporary refuges of illicit sex. The one in Chicago which was being renovated and where she preferred to sleep in the second bed because I snored too much (in fact, the final hotel that harboured our pathetic affair; maybe the excuse was just an early sign of her fading interest in me), or the St Pierre on Burgundy Street in New Orleans, far enough from the hubbub of Bourbon Street, where I forgot to take her dancing (she only did in Chicago, but it was with other men).

Or the one whose memories I cherished best. Our marine and pastel-coloured room at the Grand Hotel in Sète, where the balcony looked out on quite another kind of canal, where local jousts on long boats took place at the weekend. A coastal port where she took a shine to the limping waiter who served us one evening in a seafood restaurant, and seriously suggested we should invite him back to the room later. Nothing happened, but for months on end after that I would fantasize wildly of watching her being fucked by another man and even got to the point of lining someone up when we next visited Manhattan, only to have to cancel it because she had her period that same week.

In my dreams I wasn't even jealous to see her in the throes of pleasure as another man's cock slowly entered her and I would listen to her moan and writhe, and watch in sheer fascination as her so pale blue eyes took on a glazed sheen. After our first time, as I walked her back to the train station, she had told me her partner would know immediately she had been with another because her eyes shined so much. No, I felt no jealousy at the idea of seeing her perform with another. It would be for my pleasure and edification. I would position her on all fours on top of the bed, her rump facing the door, and would let my fingers slide across the cleft of her buttocks and dip into her wetness as

I would introduce the stranger to the beauty, intricacies and secrets of her body. See how hot she is inside, I would say, how that sweet cunt will grip your cock and milk it dry. I would be the director, set it all up, orchestrate their movements, stroke myself as her lips would tighten across his thick penis and take him all in, sucking away with the energy of despair (hadn't I told you how good her blow jobs were? She sucked with frantic energy as if her whole life depended on it but still retained that amused air of innocence in her eyes as she did so, demonstrating her sheer enjoyment of the art of fellatio, much as I hoped I did when I went down on her and tasted her and shook while the vibrations of her coming coursed through her whole body and moved on to my tongue, and heart, and soul, and cock).

So, she stripped for me in a hotel room. Now down to just her stockings. Delicately undulating, thrusting her pelvis out, shaking her delicate breasts, allowing her hanging arms freedom, her hands caressing her rump in a parody of sexiness, just like a stripper in a movie. No music, just us in the otherwise empty room. A jolt, a jump, a shimmy, there just like Madonna in that video, just a tad vulgar but sufficiently provocative, there exuberant like Kylie Minogue, but never as frantic as Jennifer Lopez or Destiny's Child.

And I drank in every inch of her body. The pale flesh, the moles, and blemishes, the deep sea of those eyes which never reached bottom, the gently swaying breasts, the ash-blonde hair now growing down to her shoulders, the trimmed triangle of darker pubic curls through which I could easily see the gash of her nacreous entrance, the thicker folds of flesh where her labia, lower down, grew ever so meaty and protruded, the square regal expanse of her arse which looked so good in the thong briefs we had purchased together at Victoria's Secrets on Broadway.

Then she would look down and see me, no doubt with tongue hanging out and my erection straining against the dark material of my slacks, and she would smile, and my heart would melt. And though I right then wanted to fuck her until we would both be raw and out of breath, I would also strangely feel so full of kindness, a sensation that made me feel like a better man altogether.

This body I have known so intimately that I could describe

every minutiae of her sighs, the look in her eyes when she is being entered, the stain on the left side of her left breast, the dozen variations in colour of the skin surrounding the puckered entrance of her anus and the hundred shades of red and pink that scream at me when I separate her lower lips and open her up. And the memories come running back, like a hurricane, rapid, senseless, brutal. Of the good times, and the bad ones too.

Of the time we went naked on a beach swept by a cold wind. The visit to the Metropolitan Museum when she felt so turned on by the Indian and Oceania erotic sculptures that we almost fucked in the nearby restroom (I was the one who felt it would be too risky and by the time we had reached the hotel again, the mood had evaporated . . .). The email informing me she had shaved her pussy and then a few days later another terse communication informing me that she had found a new lover and my anger knowing he was the one who could now see her bald mons in all its erotic splendour. The first time she allowed me to fuck her, doggy-style, without a condom, watching myself buried inside her and moving to and fro, our juices commingling. The evening we ate oysters, she for the first time, and she recognized their flavour when she swallowed my come some hours later in the hotel room.

That hotel room where she stripped for my entertainment and amusement, eyes lowered, a sober gold necklace around her slender neck, where once down to her fishnet stockings she slowly moved towards me – I was sitting on the edge of the bed – and, the delicate smell of her cunt just inches away from my face, stepped onto the bedcover, towered over me and opened her legs wide, the obscene and wonderful vision of her visibly moist gash just a couple of centimetres from my wide-open eyes, teasing me, offering herself, my naked lover, my private stripper, my nude love.

"You like it, mister?" she asks, a giggle stuck in the back of her throat.

I nod approvingly.

She lowers her hand and, digging two opposing fingers into her wetness, she widens herself open.

"You want, sir?" she enquires of me.

I smile with detached and faint indifference. Somehow come

up with some relevant joke which I can't for the life of me recall now. She bursts out laughing. Once upon a time, I could make her laugh like no other. I warn her to temper her hilarity and remind her of the time on the Boulevard St Germain when she had actually peed a little in the convulsions of laughter. She hiccups and lowers herself on me. The hypnotic warmth of her naked body against me. I am still fully clothed.

All now intolerable memories, of hotels, of jokes that were once funny.

Now, too much has happened since the times we were together and happy in our simple, sexual way, and she wants us to be friends, and no longer lovers. There has been a Dutch man, married, now divorcing, a Korean with dark skin and God knows who else. And finally I am jealous. Like hell. Surely, she insists, we can still have times together, just be friends, no sex, it's better that way. How, I ask her, but then I would, wouldn't I? How can we spend days in foreign cities, share a hotel room and ignore the fact her body and her eyes and her smell and her words and her cunt just shout out sex to me and I know I couldn't accept that ridiculous compact of just friendship any more.

You can go with other men, I say, and I will not blame you, hold it against you, I understand that I am not always available and that you are young and have needs. But she knows I am lying inside. That I would say anything to have her back.

In hotel rooms.

Stripping for me.

Laughing with me. Laughing at me.

In darkness she moves; I am deaf, can't hear the music she is dancing so sensually to. Maybe a blues, a song by Christine McVie or Natalie Merchant. Or "Sing" by Travis. Or maybe it's Sarah McLachlan's *Fumbling Towards Ecstasy* (the Korean man who later abandoned her for a Russian woman, after breaking her fragile heart, had introduced her to that particular music; ironically a man of melodic taste . . .). Or again that Aimee Mann song from *Magnolia* (we saw the movie together; oh, how she enjoyed seeing movies with me). I hear nothing. Can only try and guess the tune from the languorous movements of her body as every piece of clothing is shed to reveal the treasures of her flesh, her intimacy. The crevice of her navel, the darkened tips of her nipples (so devoid of sensitivity she would always remind me), her throat, the luminosity of her face, her youth, her life.

I open my mouth but I can't even hear myself saying "please" or "come back" or "forgive me".

She dances, my erotic angel, my lost lover.

The silent words in me increase in loudness, but she is lost in the music and no longer even sees her audience. Behind her, the hotel walls are all black and she is frozen like a photograph, her pallor in sharp contrast to the surroundings. Stripper in hotel room. A study in light and darkness.

Like in a nightmare, my throat constricts and words fail me totally. I shed a single tear of humid tenderness, all too aware of the fact that I will never again be able to afford a private stripper. Let alone a hotel room.

Adventure at the Casa Cervantes Hotel

Dorothy Freed

It was late afternoon at the Casa Cervantes in San Juan, Puerto Rico. The small stucco hotel was built before the glitzy high-rises began lining up along Condado Beach. I loved its plant-filled verandas, cool tiled floors and old-style ceiling fans. It was a perfect place for a forty-year-old woman to spend time alone examining my feelings for my lover Gene, and to decide – had our once passionate relationship run its course, or could it be saved?

The lobby was quiet in the heat of the day, but now guests began trickling in anticipating happy hour. I'd come down from my room freshly showered after a day on the beach, my dark curly hair still damp. I wore black jeans and a white sleeveless blouse. My high-heeled strappy sandals made a clicking sound as I walked through the lobby with its whitewashed walls and trickling fountain across from the registration desk. I was headed for the patio bar and a frosty drink of something involving mangos and island rum. My favorite table waited beneath a flowering flamboyant.

Two men observed me as I stepped onto the patio. They sat at a table directly in my path, an umbrella shading them from the sun. They resembled each other with dark springy hair and strong Roman noses. I wondered if they were related. The trimmer one with the wide shoulders and high cheekbones looked to be in his mid-thirties. I approached. Our eyes met. His were deep set; the color of bitter-sweet chocolate. He flashed a smile showing even white teeth. I'm an Al Pacino fan from way back, and was instantly attracted.

"Dominic," he said extending his hand, "and Anthony, my cousin." He nodded toward the other man. "We were stuck in a real estate conference at the Hilton all weekend. Tonight's our big chance to party before going home tomorrow. Will you join us for a drink to celebrate?"

"Yes. Please," said Anthony. He looked to be in his mid-forties, and a bit overweight with a lazy little belly. His shy boyish smile appealed to me though – and the endearing way he looked down and peered at me through his lashes, like Gene did some-times. Why not, I thought, and joined them.

A waiter brought drinks and we struck up a conversation in that open unguarded way people do when they're strangers on vacation, soon to go their separate ways. I learned about Dominic's frustration with his employer and his dull single life in suburban Connecticut, and Anthony's inability to connect with women since his nasty divorce two years ago.

I enjoyed their company. Since flying in from Brooklyn a week ago I'd kept to myself, sleeping late and spending after-noons on the beach. After dinner I wandered from hotel to hotel, along touristy Ashford Avenue, ignoring come-ons from inter-ested men and pondering the nature of relationships. I was ready for human contact.

"Something's missing from my relationship with Gene," I confided, over our second drink. "But I don't know what."

We sat sipping and laughing until the sunset began and the sky became vibrant with color. We realized we were starving and moved to the dining room's seafood buffet. After dinner we strolled in the humid heat of the evening, enjoying the sound of waves crashing, and later stopped to try our luck at the Marriott's casino.

The men placed the bets at the craps table and handed me the dice. I rolled three sevens in a row attracting a crowd who bet with me. "The tall woman's hot," someone said.

We won money that night and left the casino high on victory. I slipped an arm around each man's waist on the way back to the hotel and we walked along like that, joking, laughing – a tension building between us. I could feel their body heat in the creaky old elevator when they escorted me to my room at the Casa Cervantes. I unlocked my door while my companions stood waiting – each hoping to get lucky on his last night in the tropics.

I can't fully account for what happened next. I'd toyed with having sex with Dominic for half the evening, but now Anthony was turning me on too. They gazed at me longingly. I smiled, feeling my power, realizing that whatever happened next was entirely up to me. An unusual idea began forming in my mind, and I remembered, gratefully, the mint-flavored condoms I'd packed in my purse.

"What a perfect evening," I purred, looking from one expectant face to the other. "Let's not end it yet. Problem is you're each so attractive I can't choose between you, and see no reason I should. Come in, both of you. *Mi casa* is *su casa*," I said, ushering them into my room with a sweeping gesture of my hand. "Are you up for that?"

They stared, wide-eyed, bowled over by this unexpected, maybe undreamed of occurrence in their lives. My prominent nipples puckered at the thought of what was about to happen. My groin came alive with arousal. Dominic nodded, barely breathing. I could see Anthony's hard-on pressing against his lightweight slacks. He looked at me and blushed like a bride.

"It's *very* warm tonight," I said, slowly unbuttoning my blouse, letting my full round breasts swing free. My companions' eyes widened at the sight of them. Reaching up, I switched on the overhead fan. "Why not remove our clothes?"

Both men flushed, but began disrobing immediately. Naked, they carefully avoided looking at each other and kept their gaze fixed on me. But their cocks were rock hard in spite of their embarrassment and ready for action.

It was like orchestrating a dance.

I stood near the bed, condoms in hand, smiling at one man then the other. Two steps and I was up close to Dominic, kissing him, rubbing up against him, nibbling on his full lower lip. I reached down and cupped his balls in my hand, feeling the weight of them – then turned to Anthony, pulling him to me, crushing my breasts against his chest, teasing his hardened nipples with mine. He moaned and the head of his long purple-veined cock prodded my inner thighs.

"Let's take it slow, sweetheart," I said, ripping open a condom package. "First things first." I pushed him back a bit and rolled on the condom. "There," I said, stroking the length of his shaft, "dressed and ready for action."

"Next," I said, turning to Dominic, stroking and teasing and squeezing him before easing the condom over his cockhead and down his swollen shaft, while pressing my generous ass cheeks up against Anthony's erection. Smiling into his eyes, I set the pace, taking Dominic's face in my hands, kissing him, thrusting my tongue into his mouth.

"We've got all night," I whispered, sliding my hands from his face, to his neck, to his shoulders, pinching his nipples between my thumbs and forefingers. He didn't flinch but I felt him shudder and that inflamed me. I dug my nails in and twisted a little. He winced but his cock pulsed with excitement. Turning to Anthony, I stroked his cock with one hand, and cupped Dominic's balls with the other.

When I was ready, I led both men to the bed. They were trembling with excitement, their cocks swollen, their balls drawn tight.

"Dominic, lie flat on the bed. Yes, just like that. Let me taste you. Mmmm, mint-flavored cock, my favorite," I murmured, going down on him, kneeling between his legs at the edge of the bed. I sucked hungrily, lifting my ass up high.

"Anthony, come here and pleasure me," I said, and, turning to look at him, saw his eyes cloud over with arousal. He knelt behind me silently, hands on my ass cheeks, and began lapping at my cunt with his hot wet tongue. "Mmmmm," I moaned, arching my back. "That's really good. Stick it up inside me; fuck me with your tongue."

Dominic moaned and stiffened. He was close to coming but I slowed him down. "Not yet, sweetie," I said after withdrawing my mouth. "I want you inside me when that thing goes off, but no rush. Come around behind me; let me feel what *your* tongue can do. Anthony, lie on the bed; I'll go down on you. OK, Dominic, now's the time – fuck me, sweetie. Fuck me hard and deep. Oh God, you both feel so good . . ."

And so it went on into the small hours of the morning. Indescribable pleasure: two men, two cocks, two mouths, and so many fingers – all aiming to please. Dominic was the energetic one, plunging in with abandon, pumping me, sending shock waves of pleasure throughout my body. Anthony was tender and playful: caressing my breasts, sucking my nipples, his cock pulsing inside me. He moaned as my cunt clamped down on him and I arched my back to grind my clit against his shaft. I came repeatedly, aroused to a fever pitch – surprising myself by how effectively I took charge of the encounter, and how deeply satisfying that was to me.

What if I took charge like this with Gene? I wondered. And would he like it?

We woke late the next morning on my bed in a tangle of arms and legs and private parts. I showered and dressed while the men did the same in their rooms. When we met an hour later for breakfast at the hotel café, they were packed and ready for their return home. We sat together like old friends, talking, laughing – regarding one another like people who shared a delicious secret.

"I'll remember last night for the rest of my life," Dominic whispered.

We finished breakfast and the airport bus arrived. We hugged. We kissed. He looked sorry to be leaving. "If you end it with your lover, please let me know," he said, as he got on the bus.

"Thank you so much for the adventure of a lifetime," said Anthony. He smoothed back my hair. "I'll never forget either."

I wouldn't be forgetting that night myself.

When they'd gone, I took a long slow stroll along Condado Beach, replaying the prior night's events in my head. I thought of Gene and that shy way he cast his eyes down and watched me through his lashes, like he wanted something from me I wasn't giving him, but was never clear about what.

I fell asleep smiling that night, after calling Gene to say I was flying home the next day. By then I'd worked things through in my mind and understood what our relationship needed. It needs me to take charge in the bedroom, I thought, and that's what I intend to do.

Cherry Bomb

Vina Green

I've always wished that some sort of manual existed for "first times". A tome of advice that could see you through those awful moments when you finally work up the courage to touch someone that you fancy and then realize that you don't know how.

I was overtly heterosexual, and had never admitted to anyone that I felt perhaps an even headier thrill when I thought of women than when I thought of men. I had enrolled in my university "queer" club, Jellybabies, but I had never introduced myself to the members or attended a meeting. I opened their weekly e-newsletter and updates as they arrived in my in-box with the hurried, furtive mouse clicks that an onlooker might have presumed signalled membership of a far more subversive organization.

Though I didn't ever attend a Jellybabies social event, I did eventually meet a woman, after a university party, a few months before I turned twenty-one. The party had an "international" theme, and I went dressed in an outfit vaguely reminiscent of the Luxembourg flag, wearing a bright blue halter-neck top, red miniskirt and long white earrings, although I am not from Luxembourg. I was on a depressing sort of diet, and the red miniskirt was nearly too big for me. It sat low on my hip bones threatening to drop off at any moment, which I rather enjoyed.

Towards midnight the one hundred or so other party-goers and I walked from our halls of residence into the city centre. We argued about which bar to go to, and I suggested the local gay and lesbian bar, as if it were an enormous joke. What larks! As if there was no possibility at all that any one of us might have, in fact, been gay, or bisexual. The crowd of partygoers did not respond enthusiastically to my suggestion, and they disappeared into the night to other bars. I hid in the shadow of the nearest building and waited until they were well out of sight and earshot before stepping into the blue neon-lit stairwell, and taking my first steps into the world of same-sex liaisons.

She was standing next to me at the bar as I ordered a drink, and I am afraid that I can't remember at all what she was wearing because I was too arrested by her face and her smell. She was about the same height and the same age as me, perhaps slightly smaller of build – very petite. She had short, dark brown hair cut in a bob, which I thought was very chic, French. She smelled the way that girls tend to smell, which was new to me then, as I had always kept what I thought was a socially correct distance from women.

She smelled of perfume and hair products and make-up, of course, though to me it was more like almonds and sweet jam and honey and cinnamon, all of the sorts of smells that make you want to stand still and inhale without interruption from any other sense. Just the sight of her made my heart thrum as though a tiny bird was trapped inside my chest, beating its wings furiously.

To my surprise, she spoke. She asked me if I was alone, why I was there, had I been before, how did I feel about it. We both surprised each other by being there for the same reason. "I'm straight," she said, "but I wondered what it was like."

"I'm straight too," I replied immediately, and she nodded, "of course".

I bought her a drink. That's what boys do, isn't it, when they fancy someone?

She suggested that we find a table to sit, somewhere quiet, away from the men, who we had decided were also straight and had come to a gay bar to hit on straight girls who went to gay bars to escape the attentions of straight men.

I followed her to the far corner of the bar, away from the crowd, and she shimmied into a booth. In a sudden moment of confidence, I shimmied in after her, so that we were sitting side by side. We weren't touching, but I was as aware of her presence as you might be aware of a current whilst standing very close to an electric fence.

Eventually, she said the inevitable. "I've always wondered what it would be like to kiss a girl."

I nodded in agreement. Of course I had wondered too. I spent a good part of my day masturbating in the university toilets between lectures, wondering.

We decided it would be the thing to do, to try it, just the once, to see what it was like.

Kissing her was like the moment when, as a child, you first taste candyfloss. It was as though the whole world had fallen away, and I was floating in space with nothing to anchor me other than the sensation of softness and the taste of her lips.

We broke away eventually, and agreed that kissing a girl was quite good, but perhaps it had just been the shock of it, and we should try it one more time, just to be sure. It was just as good the next time, and the next, and the next, and we sat there in that booth kissing for a very long time. Long enough to attract a crowd of men, some of whom in fact did appear to be interested in women. Or at least, they were interested in us.

She exclaimed that I had the nicest lips she'd ever kissed, and offered me up to someone. "You have to try her," she said to one of the men watching us, and I blushed, flattered, and protested that she in fact had much nicer lips than I, and was surely the best kisser of the two of us. One of the men, or perhaps all of them, suggested that the only fair test would be for him to kiss us both and then offer his unbiased opinion. This seemed an excellent solution, and we each kissed him in turn. He said that we were both such lovely kissers, he couldn't be sure who was the loveliest, and that perhaps his friend could assist by offering his opinion also.

The crowd of men around us became bigger and bigger, and between the interruption of each new man's kiss we carried on kissing each other. Every time I touched her, the rest of the world disappeared and I felt as if we were entirely alone. I'm not sure how many men I kissed, but it was enough to pass the time between about midnight and four in the morning when the bar began to close. We were still surrounded by interested onlookers when the bar manager came over and told us that if we stayed and had sex on the table that we were sitting beside he'd give us both free drinks for the rest of our lives.

She reached over and laid a hand lightly on the inside of my leg. It was the first time we'd touched, other than on the lips. "Come back to mine," she whispered in my ear. And we got up and left, the sound of disappointed sighs following us all the way out the door.

I wish I could tell you that we went back to her house and fucked each other royally. But we didn't. Somehow leaving the bar, the shock of cold air, the normal-world physicality of finding her car, biding time waiting for the drive to be over and realizing the sun had almost come up and we were both sober again stopped us in our tracks. It was as if someone had walked in and flicked the light switch on, stealing our secret away.

I wanted to touch her, but I felt as though my arms were pinned to my sides, as if someone had snuck up behind me and trapped me in a plaster cast. I had not the slightest idea what to do with a woman. It reminded me of the first time I'd tentatively tried to go down on a man and realized that I wasn't sure whether to suck or blow. I've always been hung up on semantics.

We made awkward, idle chit-chat, and she offered to lend me some pyjamas. I politely averted my eyes as she undressed and then dressed again beside me. She wore a pair of cotton pyjama shorts, pale blue with red cherries on them, and a matching red singlet top. She had very small breasts. She had a tattoo on her lower back, two cherries. She told me that she wasn't really sure why she had a thing for cherries, she just liked them. I thought that they suited her perfectly, small and sweet and perfectly formed.

She lent me her winter pyjamas, and she watched me change into them. "God, you're small," she said, and I felt a thrill of half pleasure and half denial at what I perceived to be a misplaced compliment. She was small, I thought, not I. We most likely both looked very small curled up in bed together. She had a small room, and a small double bed, and despite that we both managed to lie next to each other with plenty of room between us and on either side. I lay beside her wide awake for all that was left of the night and the morning, wondering what would happen if I just stretched an arm out and brushed her skin.

She drove me back to my halls of residence the next day, and neither of us gave the slightest hint to the other that the previous evening had ever happened. She asked me what I was studying, and I asked her what she did for work, and we both remarked that we were hungover and must have been terribly drunk.

She let me out of the car and I waved goodbye and never saw her again.

I've thought about her, often, since then. Each time I see a small girl with a short bob in a bar, or at a party, my heart races and I stare closer to see if I can spot a cherry tattoo. But I never have. There's only been two or three people since, who have made the world fall away with a kiss.

I've only just this minute realized that she didn't tell me her name.

Creatures of the Night

Thomas S. Roche

She wore a tight pink skirt, garter belt, black fishnet stockings, knee-high boots and a tight electric blue vinyl bustier. Her hair was ratted out and bleached blonde, and her make-up was caked on thick and heavy. She had a neon green purse slung at her side.

The cop stopped dead in his tracks when he saw her, and they would have locked eyes if his hadn't been behind the mirrored sunglasses. The whore's eyes flickered from the guy's chiseled, clean-shaven face down his muscled physique in the tight tan uniform, to the knee-high black leather boots polished to a flawless sheen.

A wry look crossed the whore's face and her full, pouty lips, painted cocksucker red, twisted in a smile. She took a drag of her cigarette and put her wrists out, holding them together.

"I think you'd better put the cuffs on me, officer," she said. "I think you'd better take me in."

The cop blushed. His friend, wrapped head to toe in white bandages except for a pair of swim goggles, laughed hysterically. The whore's two friends, who were both wearing plaid skirts and had their hair in pigtails and their hairy, muscled legs swathed in ill-fitting white stockings, shared a high five while the cop swallowed nervously.

"Sorry, ma'am," he said, pointing to the CHP nameplate on his chest. "I only prosecute traffic violations."

"Oh, let me jaywalk then," she said, running out into the crosswalk before the light could change. The two schoolgirls shrieked and grasped each other. A yellow cab slammed to a halt and honked. The whore giggled and danced out of the way. The cab driver flipped her off, but by that time the light had turned green and the crowd was gushing across Castro. The cop looked longingly after the prostitute as she and her schoolgirl friends hurried into the night. All three were swaying unsteadily and tittering every few steps.

The mummy tsked as he and his friend crossed and headed up 18th Street.

"Nice going, Erik Estrada. You find the only straight girl in the Castro begging you to handcuff her, and you let her get away. What kind of a cop are you?"

"Mike, she has to be a dude."

"Oh, don't give me that shit. She's like four foot eight."

They walked up 18th Street with the crowd, heading toward the apartment where Mike's old roommate was having what Mike had promised would be the wildest Halloween party of all time. "She is not four foot eight. She's like five two. And what kind of a girl is that aggressive?"

"Oh, gee, I don't know, a drunk one in the Castro on Halloween maybe? She's a girl, Terry. Trust me on this one."

"How would you know?"

"Hello! Eight years living in the Castro, I think I can tell the difference. Besides, even if she isn't, a proper blow job would do you good. Not that I'm suggesting anything, but didn't you say you were like a Kinsey 1.3 or something?" Terry opened his mouth to respond, but Mike blurted out, "Hey, look, there's Steve! I'll catch up with you on the next block!"

"Hey, Mike, wait a minute," Terry called after him feebly. Mike vanished into the crowd and Terry sighed and followed the tide of people up 18th Street.

The streets throbbed with the rhythm of dance music blasting out of the bars. The crowd swirled around them: vampires, witches, cheerleaders, prom queens, ballerinas, Army men, big-time wrestlers. And lots and lots of cops. Terry's wasn't even the only full-on CHP outfit. In fact, he'd spotted two or three of them, but he was the only one actually wearing the shades, which seemed to make a big difference.

He felt a hand on his wrist, grabbing and pulling at him. He turned and stared, then began following. It took him a few seconds to realize what had happened, and another few to believe it.

By that time the whore had dragged him over to the edge of a little Victorian and pushed him into the little alcove that held the garbage cans. She pushed him up against the wall; with his sunglasses on he couldn't see at all.

Her purse hit the ground next to them. She kissed him once, hard, her tongue tasting of vodka and cigarettes, the scent of cheap perfume, hair bleach and drunk sweat filling his nostrils and mingling with the garbage-smell of the access corridor. He felt her hand on his crotch.

"My name's Terry," he said stupidly when her lips left his.

She whispered harshly, "Shhhhh. I have a name too, and I'm not usually a whore," she told him. "But tonight I get to pretend."

She had slipped his handcuffs out of his belt pouch and pressed them into his palm.

"You do have the key, don't you?"

He nodded and told himself he shouldn't be doing this, even as he slipped the cuffs on her and ratcheted them closed. She kissed him again and he put his arms around her, let his fingers find her ass in that tight skirt. She wasn't wearing anything underneath. He wanted to touch her, kiss her, take those tight clothes off, but this wasn't about that. She was a nameless whore for the moment, his nameless whore, and whatever kind of crazy game she was playing, Terry shut his eyes and let her pull him along.

She dropped to her knees.

Even with her hands cuffed, it was easy enough to get the big CHP belt open, even easier to get his zipper down. Terry leaned against the wall as she took out his cock, full and hard.

"Shouldn't you use a—" He stopped as she took him in her mouth, and his own mouth went wide, and he let his hands wriggle into her brittle-bleached hair as she went to work. Her head bobbed up and down, her lips clamped tight around his shaft as she clutched her cuffed hands together at her throat. Terry closed his eyes and let himself melt into the feeling of the whore's warm mouth on his cock, her lips sliding halfway down his shaft, then three-quarters, then all the way as he felt his head pressing into her throat. He wondered again if she was a guy dressed up, or if Mike had been right and she was just a very drunk and very horny girl on Halloween. He heard her whimpering, felt her tongue swirling around his head as she came up for air, and he realized all in a rush that he didn't really care as much as he thought he did.

Then she let his cock hover between her parted lips, looked up at him, smiling all mischievous and open-mouthed, as if she'd guessed his thoughts. Then she took his cock in her mouth again and started sucking him off in earnest.

He had never been done so quickly, so businesslike, but with so much enthusiasm. He had never vanished into pleasure with such rapidity, without wondering what he should do to reciprocate. He just leaned there against the wall, smelling garbage and perfume, running his fingers through the blonde whore's hair and feeling himself mount toward orgasm.

When he was about to come she pulled his cock out and took his balls in her mouth, then stroked him, her hands one atop the other around his shaft so that she could feel the hot spurt of his come on her palms. It ran down her arms and dribbled onto the floor between her stockinged legs. Terry realized that he'd shouted when he came, maybe for the first time ever.

"Of course she was a girl," Mike would later tell him when he recounted the story. "A guy would have swallowed." Terry thought that was probably bullshit, but at the moment he didn't care. The whore just looked up at him, smiling, her lipstick smeared everywhere and her lips glistening with spittle. She slipped her hands off his cock.

"Let me go, officer," she said with a smile.

Without thinking, he got out his keychain and unlocked the handcuffs. They were covered in his come. She got a pack of tissues out of her purse and wiped off her hands, offering him a couple to dab his cock off and wipe the handcuffs. Then she stood up.

"Can I—" he began, but she cut him off.

"Nope," she said, and kissed him once. "Thanks, officer." She turned and hurried around the garbage cans, out of the cramped little access corridor, back onto 18th Street.

Terry zipped up and, without even buckling, ran after her. He caught one last glimpse of the girl high-fiving her two schoolgirl friends, and then the three of them disappeared into the crowd.

"Terry! I've been looking all over for you! Where'd you go?"

"I'm not sure yet," said Terry, buckling his belt. "Let's get a drink."

A Perfect Start

Catherine Paulssen

It's not exactly the worst party of my life, but I've certainly had better New Year's Eves. Then again, me and the last day of the year – we've never been the best of friends. Truth be told, I hate New Year's Eve. The whole day makes me uncomfortable. Too many questions. Never enough answers.

I only know two people here: my brother and Nora, the friend I came with. She's disappeared with some guy she knew from college – and hasn't seen in years, actually. My brother, when he's not sticking his tongue down his girlfriend's throat, is doing his best to come off as the night's biggest prat. Among all the glamorous people dressed according to the Roaring Twenties theme, I feel like the kid in high school who wears jumpers knitted by Grandma.

The men look like speakeasy gangsters; the women like Josephine Baker. There's one Johnny Weissmuller, a guy in a Charlie Chaplin outfit and the obligatory Babe Ruth.

And then there's me, dressed as Amelia Earhart, the pioneering aviator and women's rights activist who disappeared while trying to circumnavigate the globe in a light airliner. When I think of that era, I think of her. I'm wearing a grey boiler suit that's too long in the arms and pools at my ankles. A pair of swimming goggles hangs around my neck.

The pièce de résistance is my pair of vintage Cat Paw boots. My grandfather bought them for me at a flea market years ago and I've been wearing them ever since. Boots like these are made for life. And if one more person asks me if they can get them at Doc Martens . . .

I have a flying cap, of course. It's brown leather. But my

brother made so much fun of me that I took it off. I've had my fill of bathing cap jokes for the year. Problem is, now people assume I'm supposed to be a service station attendant.

I should stop the bellyaching; I will. And anyway, it's my fault. Knowing how sulky I get on 31 December, I should have stayed at home and watched some tacky old movies. Only a few more minutes to midnight . . . I dread the thought of everyone around me beaming and hugging and kissing. Mostly because I see myself standing exactly where I am now, back against the wall, observing the spectacle but never belonging to it.

I push myself off the wall and head towards the kitchen to get another beer, and that's when I see her, tucked away in a small room off the hallway. She sits on a sofa between a couple making out and a pair of friends comparing the time on each other's watch. She seems bored, but not detached. Her skin is pale and makes the smoky eyes look even bigger in her heart-shaped face, framed by short hair in finger waves. A baker boy hat sits on her head. She wears a grey-checkered suit, complete with suspenders, pocket square, burgundy-coloured tie and crisp white shirt. A metal chain, as if for a pocket watch, dangles from her jacket.

She turns her head, and our gazes meet. The look in her grey eyes shoots right into my stomach. My fingers cling a bit tighter around the bottle. She raises her glass a few inches, a gesture as languid as her attitude. Nevertheless, it feels like an invitation. Or maybe I'm just so consumed with the prospect of getting to know her that I throw my blues to the wind.

I start to walk over to her, and she keeps watching me, but her eyes show no sign of encouragement and nothing in her posture changes.

"Hi," I say, then clear my throat. "I'm Lucy."

She chinks her glass against my bottle. "Florence." I must look pretty dumbfounded because she grins lopsidedly. "My mum's a big fan of Florence Nightingale," she adds. I laugh. She straightens up slightly, and her eyes wander over my body. "And who are you?"

I take another swig from the bottle. "Amelia Earhart."

For the first time, she looks impressed. "The pilot?"

My belly makes a little jump. "You a fan?"

"Are you kidding me? She's the first woman to cross the

Atlantic! The first woman to fly solo – everywhere! *She* should be on the one-dollar coin." She raises her chin.

I can't believe I've found someone who seems to be as big an Amelia Earhart fan as I am. She's been my hero since I was a little kid, and now I'm too excited to even agree because I'm afraid if I start talking about her, I'll end up babbling.

"So?" Florence raises her brows.

"What?" I run my fingers through my hair, but it doesn't do much to alleviate my nervousness.

"Where's your flying cap?" asks Florence. "Shouldn't you have a flying cap?" I tug at the cap hanging out of my pocket and cock my head. "Why don't you wear it?"

"No, no," I say, stuffing the cap a little deeper into my pocket. "No."

She keeps her gaze locked on my face until I'm forced to return it. "Amelia Earhart was at her most beautiful when in full flight attire," she says, reaching for the cap and pulling it over my stubborn curls. Then she pulls the goggles over my head and attaches them to the cap. She regards her work for a few moments during which I feel the blood rush to my cheeks. My eyes dart around uncomfortably and finally turn to the ground. That's when she leans in and whispers, close to my ear, "You are so sexy."

I look up, throat dry, belly flipping a bit more emphatically. I don't care whether she means it or is just buttering me up.

Around us, people start to count off the last moments of the year.

Cheers erupt, glasses clink, "Auld Lang Syne" blares from the television, but Florence keeps looking at me. Someone pokes his elbow into my side and yells, "Happy New Year!" I give him a quick smile and, when I turn my head back to her, Florence has taken the bottle out of my hand. She strokes my temple and kisses me.

Her lips are warm, and they taste of the liquor she's been drinking. They linger a moment too long for a mere New Year's kiss, and I pull her closer to me. I find a spot of naked skin above the prickly material of her suit trousers and press my hand against it. She feels warm and cottony beneath my touch. Her body presses against mine, and everything around me becomes a blur. When we break the kiss, the song is over and everyone's back to dancing and drinking.

She doesn't pull away. Her breath is still hot on my face. I hear someone next to us whistling.

Florence lifts my chin. "You want to go somewhere quieter?"

I nod, but at the same time, I see us on top of a pile of coats or pressed up against the bathroom door, a stream of people pounding away on the other side. "But where?"

"Come." She takes my hand. "This is my cousin's apartment. I know my way around."

I follow her upstairs, into a bedroom and on into a walk-in closet. It's small, but it has a fluffy white carpet and a fuzzy old-fashioned pouffe half buried underneath a pile of skirts, tops and hangers. Florence sweeps them to the ground and sits down on the footstool. She loosens her tie and reveals the pale, smooth skin of her neck. I watch her as she unbuttons her shirt, slips off her trousers and strips out of a red bra and matching thong. She leans back and allows me to gorge on her.

She's perfect. Slinky limbs, creamy skin and breasts whose true size is revealed only now that the restrictive male attire has been shed. My clit is getting hard just looking at her. I make a step towards her, but for a moment I'm distracted by a movement in the corner of my eye. It's only my own reflection in the mirror, but I take a second look all the same. I look even more out of place in this fashionista's dream place than I did downstairs at the party. Even my boots feel clunky all of a sudden. I avert my eyes and turn them back to the woman sprawled over the pouffe. She looks like Marion Davies, and I'm wearing a borrowed jumpsuit.

Florence opens her legs and makes a come-hither move with her finger. "I didn't even know I had an aviator fetish before I met you," she whispers and throws me an impish look.

I can't help but grin. I kneel down before her and kiss her belly. I move my lips up her body and lick over her nipples. For some moments, I take in those gorgeous breasts with my eyes and trace their shape with my fingertips. Goosebumps appear on her skin, and her nipples contract. I enclose one with my lips and nibble on it. Florence entangles her fingers in my hair and presses my head a bit closer to her breast.

"Take me," she demands.

I slide my hands between her legs and spread them apart. Florence utters a throaty moan when my mouth meets her flesh. I prod my pointed tongue against her clit again and again until it's fully swollen and Florence's breathless groans fill my ears. I stop for a moment and wait for her to plead with me to go on. My breath is hot and damp between her legs, and my mouth is full of her taste. She shivers as I kiss her clit. I wrap my lips around it and suck until we both fall into a rhythm that ends in a frantic wriggle when Florence erupts and collapses with a series of high-pitched gasps.

I sink against her thigh and place a little kiss on her sticky skin. She bends down and presses her lips into my hair.

"Undress," she whispers and smoothes back the curls from my forehead. "But leave the boots on."

Sunday in the Playpen II with Roger

Lawrence Schimel

It was eleven o'clock Sunday morning when I called Roger up and begged him to take me to a porn palace.

"Lisa, is that you or is this a nightmare?" he asked when he picked up.

"I'm serious. Peep shows. Girlie booths. I want to go to one before they clean up Times Square, and I need you to come with me." There was a long pause on the other side of the line. I was afraid Roger had fallen asleep again. "I'll pay for everything," I added.

"Why should I want to go to a girlie show? Why do *you* want to go to a girlie show – doesn't that violate one of the rules in the lesbian manifesto or something? And why do you want to go with *me*?"

"I want to go with you because I can't go alone. They don't let 'unaccompanied females' in to the kinds of places I want to go to." I laughed at the wording.

Roger laughed too, then asked, "Why won't they let women in by themselves?"

I sighed. "For someone who sleeps with as many men as you do, dear, you're remarkably naive about sex."

"I may be a slut, but I'm a very traditional fuck-and-suck kind of boy – totally vanilla. So tell me, why don't they let girls in?"

"Unaccompanied women are usually hookers poaching on the territory of the place's girls. A john's not going to shell out money for a woman behind the glass if there's a chick who'll blow him in a video booth for twenty bucks."

"Fascinating," Roger said dryly. "I'm glad I'm on an empty stomach."

"You need to get your mind out of your own asshole and expand your horizons, dear. That's why you need to come with me. Think of it as an education in heterosexual culture."

"Maybe I'll hang up and pretend this was all a nightmare."

"Meet me at my place by 1.30 and I'll buy you lunch as well. If you're late, you buy your own food."

"I don't think I should eat before we're going to see what we're going to see," Roger said. I could imagine him wrinkling his nose and I smiled. I was glad he was planning on coming with me, even if he was still playing hard to get.

"I'll take you to Pietra Santa," I said.

"I'll see you at 1.29," he said, and hung up.

Roger, true to form, was far more cheerful after I'd paid the bill for lunch. "So tell me," he asked, as we walked down 8th Avenue toward 42nd, "why do you want to go to a peep show? On a Sunday afternoon, of all times."

"Isn't it just perfectly blasphemous?" I said. "That's why. It's always been so taboo – I want to see what it's like. You've never been even a little bit curious?"

"Not in the slightest. Why with me?"

"Saves time. If you're with me, I won't have to call you later and tell you how it went."

Roger laughed. "Do you know which one we're going to?"

"I figured we'd just find one that looked especially sleazy and try it."

"How about this one." We were right outside one such porn emporium: The Playpen II. Eighth Avenue had more of these video palaces/girlie shows than I'd imagined, one or two on every block here in the mid-forties.

"LIVE NUDE GIRLS," a voice cried over a loudspeaker, as if it knew we were lingering out on the threshold. "REAL LIVE NUDE GIRLS!"

"I was kind of thinking we should do something on 42nd Street," I said, "for the sake of tradition." At the same time, I worried Roger might change his mind by the time we'd walked the extra few blocks down there; he might've digested lunch by then and balk when it came time to go in. "But since we're here," I said, "let's give it a try."

My stomach tensed as we went in. I'd always wondered what it was like inside one of these places, if they were really as degrading to women as everyone claimed, what it would be like to go in as a woman who liked women.

I felt as if every man's attention was suddenly on me the moment I stepped through the doors, a hungry anticipation in their looks. I was glad I had Roger with me.

"I don't feel comfortable," Roger said. He stared at the merchandise, racks and racks of het sex videos and inflatable dolls and such, as if it were about to attack him. "I think all the guys can tell I'm a fag," he whispered to me.

"Nonsense," I said.

"LIVE NUDE GIRLS," the woman's voice on the loud-speaker repeated. "YOU THERE, IN THE JEANS AND WHITE T-SHIRT. DON'T BE SHY, COME HAVE A LOOK. REAL LIVE NUDE GIRLS!"

Roger looked over both shoulders, trying to see if anyone else in there was wearing jeans and a white T-shirt.

"BRING YOUR GIRLFRIEND WITH YOU."

"How'd she do that?" Roger whispered, his voice cracking.

I smiled, pointing to the peep booths. One of the girls was peering over the top, a microphone in her hands. She waved when she saw us looking at her.

"Shall we?" I said.

"If we must."

We approached the bank of doors and the girl disappeared from her perch – to prepare to give a show for us, I guessed. "That one," I said, pointing to one of the doors. Roger was squeamish about touching the doorknob, and I knew he was imagining what most of the hands that touched it had been touching before touching it . . .

There was a small closet on the other side, with a solid window on the inner wall.

"We need to buy tokens," I said, indicating the window. "You're holding all my money, go get us some."

"I'll be back in a moment. Wait here."

Where did he think I was going to go? I wondered.

A guy was staring from the aisle into the cubicle at me. I felt dirty under his gaze, but I just stared back at him until the door shut. Is this how the girls on the other side of the glass felt? I latched the door, and felt better immediately. I turned toward the window, imagining the girl on the other side, waiting for us. Did she know which booth we were in? Was anyone else in one of the other booths? Was she performing right now for one of them? I was jealous at the thought, even knowing she must show off her body all day long to anyone who paid the tokens to lift the partition.

I tried to imagine what her body would look like naked.

I was wet with anticipation, from the very fact of being here. I shoved a hand down the front of my shorts. The door was locked, and I didn't have money to open the window. I was alone with my raunchiest fantasies, safe in this little closet in a porn palace.

It felt weird being here with Roger. I needed him, or I couldn't be here; but at the same time, I was embarrassed to be sexual around him. He was my best confidant and heard all of my wildest exploits, but that was sex at a remove – after the fact.

And while I was feeling horny as hell here, Roger, I imagined, was feeling totally non-sexual. He was nervous and edgy, maybe even uncomfortable; I hoped he was curious despite what he claimed. I was glad he was sticking this out with me.

The door jiggled. "Shave and a haircut," Roger said from the other side. I pulled my hand out of my pants. My fingers were sticky. I licked them, tasting myself, then wiped them on my shorts. I let him in and locked the door again.

"This is all so weird," Roger said, handing me the tokens. "Being here, I mean. It'd be one thing to be here to get off, if that was your thing, but we're not here to do that, just to look. It's all so tawdry."

I could get off here – simply from being here more than anything we could do or see. I stood in front of the window. "Don't be a wuss," I said, making him stand beside me as I dropped the coin into the slot.

The partition began to lift. There were two girls on the other side, an African-American woman who was completely naked and the girl who'd called to us, who wore a T-shirt but no underwear. They both turned immediately toward the opening window, but the one who'd seen us from above staked her claim.

"It's so great that you bring your girlfriend," she said to Roger, sticking her head through the opening. She had small, pert breasts, all but visible beneath the tight fabric. "It's $2 a peek, $5 a touch, $10 for a leg spread."

He doesn't want to touch you, I thought. I do. Pay attention to me.

"Give me a five," I told Roger.

Grinning, he tried to slap my hand. "Just kidding," he said, digging in one of his pockets.

I pressed my legs together nervously as he handed me the money, putting pressure on my clit as I did so. She stuck her hand through the window for the bill and I gave it to her. She stepped away from the partition and lifted her shirt, exposing her small breasts. I had to lean forward to reach them.

Suddenly, I didn't feel sexual any more. The idea of the peep show, the anticipation of it, had aroused me more than the actuality.

It wasn't that I didn't find her attractive. But suddenly I was gripped – literally – with the realization that she was a person, and not a fantasy. She had a name, a family, all that cultural baggage I hadn't wanted to deal with.

"My name is Lisa," I said, squeezing her breast gently.

She smiled at me, as I held her breast, and for a moment I felt we had a genuine connection, beyond the money that had passed hands.

Then the window began to close and I jerked my hand back, as if I'd been caught doing something I knew I shouldn't have and felt guilty about. I wasn't sure whether I felt guilty for being here, or for having broken that shield of anonymity.

"Put more tokens in," she said, bending down to peer under the partition at us.

The window stopped moving and shut with a click of finality.

"Should I?" Roger asked.

I shook my head. "The tokens are also good in the video booths, right? I thought I saw the box for one about a girl and a dog when we passed it. And maybe we can find one with the Bobbitt Uncut video – just for curiosity's sake."

"I noticed they've got a gay section downstairs," Roger said, leading the way out of the booth and through the store like an expert. "Let's take a quick peek at what it's like."

Roger headed down the steps. I hesitated, looked over my shoulder, hoping to see the girl from the peep show peering over the top of the booth, summoning clients to her again – or looking for me.

She never appeared, and after a moment I followed Roger down the stairs.

Run-in

Tsaurah Litzky

My ex-husband grew up on a farm. Once he bragged to me he learned to do it so good from watching the animals. When the hog mounted the sow, he said, the hog was an unstoppable force.

"But I'm not a pig," I protested.

"Yes, you are," he told me. "You are a pig for me."

It was true. All day when he was at work, I hungered for his cock, at night I feasted on it. With my mouth and with my sex I swallowed it up again and again. After we split, I did not want his cock meat or any other part of him; or so I told myself. Still, five years later, I find myself dreaming that he is moving inside me, then in the morning I wake with my hands between my legs.

When I ran into him last Friday on Broadway in front of Dean and DeLuca, he didn't look like a farm boy. I hadn't seen him since he moved back to Canada. He was wearing a black leather jacket that had to be expensive and black velvet slacks. I wondered if he was dealing drugs again, but I wasn't going to ask.

His first question to me was, "Are you still with Paul?"

I told him, "Yes, of course," lying like Pinocchio, and then I quickly changed the subject. "What brings you down here?" I asked.

"I have a show coming up at Castelli's," he answered.

I wondered if he was making the show up to impress me, but I didn't ask that either. I was distracted because my nipples had suddenly hardened into sharp little spikes. He still had that effect on me.

"You and Paul happy?" he asked.

"Ecstatic," I answered. I didn't tell him how I had taught Paul to replicate all his farm boy moves.

Then my ex went on, "I heard your novel was published. Am I in it?"

I answered him, "Absolutely not. It's a fantasy, a total fantasy." The truth was he was on every page.

"Listen," he said, "if you're not in a hurry, let's have a drink, for old times' sake. We could go to Dante's. Is Larry still working there?"

"No thanks," I answered. "Why should I have a drink with you? Anyhow, Larry's been gone for ages." I started to walk away.

He came after me. "Come on. What are you frightened of?" he asked.

I was walking a shaky tightrope suspended over a bottomless pit. I fell.

"OK," I said.

Dante's was packed, three deep at the bar. Many of the patrons were already looped, talking loudly, wild eyed. "We are the evil empire, we are the evil empire," bellowed a bald fat guy wearing dark glasses. The crowd was all around us and he seemed to be yelling right in my ear. "Yeah, sure," the man standing next to him said. "Three thousand soldiers dead in Iraq, three thousand and counting." He was an old gent with bushy white hair.

The bald guy pushed his face into his neighbor's face. "It's your fault, you dickhead. All you do is read old Robert Heinlein books. When did you last see the inside of a voting booth? Now we got a fascist country," he hissed. His friend shot back, "It's always been a fascist country, that's why I read sci-fi."

The young guy behind him, his arm around a pretty red-headed girl, cut in. "You both stink. Your generation blew it. You sucked your flower power up your nose. You jumped ship after Watergate. Now that maniac is in his second term. Next, he'll outlaw thinking."

They turned on him. "Who asked you?" the old guy shouted. "Stick your head in the toilet," yelled his friend.

The kid snapped back at him, "Going to make me?" He raised his arm, his hand curled into a fist. His girlfriend pulled his hand down. "Cut it out, Roger," she said. "Don't even go there. Everyone is nuts."

"You're so right, young lady," said the bartender, breaking it up. "Let me buy drinks all around."

"You Yanks are still fucked up," said my ex, as he pulled me down the bar.

"More than ever," I told him.

We pushed our way to the back of the room where we found a narrow place to stand by the long counter opposite the bathroom. He went back to the bar, scored us beers and brought then back.

"To old times," he said.

"I don't want to drink to that," I told him, 'but the future is too dismal to drink to."

We stood silently facing each other, our eyes locked. The crowd pressed in on us, forcing me so close to him our bodies were touching. His jacket was open and my tits brushed against his chest. My nipples were still hard, so hard I wondered if he could feel them through the fabric of his shirt. My body always speaks true, that's how it betrays me.

We started to drink our beers, still looking at each other. A big brunette came out of the bathroom, wearing a low-cut red scoop-neck sweater. The tops of her fleshy white knockers were visible down to the rosy nipple. He did not even glance at her titties; he was looking so intently at me, his mouth open slightly. I could see his thick pink tongue glistening, the same tongue that had licked my every inch, even between my toes, even my back hole.

I could not resist the dark force of desire growing within me. I reached my hand out, grabbed the waistband of his pants and just pulled him behind me the few steps right into the bathroom. I turned and locked the door. The small bathroom was designed for one person at a time with only a commode and a sink. I stood in front of the sink, took off my coat and dropped it on the floor. I bent over, hiked my skirt up in the back. It was he who pulled my tights and panties down to my knees.

"Bend over, bend over more," he said.

I grabbed the sink for balance, bent over more and shut my eyes. I heard the sound of a zipper opening, then his hands were on my bottom, cradling, stroking, showing me he remembered ass play always drove me wild. Then one hand moved down and around, until his fingers found my clit and circled it, first stroking it, and then twisting it until I was crazy with wanting him. His other hand went to my nether lips, pulling them wide. I curled my hips up, offering myself to him, and then he was inside; it was a perfect fit, like always, the hog and the pig.

Little oinker that I am, I started to squeal and came immediately.

"Can I let go inside you?" he asked. "I don't have a condom." Neither did I. I felt like saying go ahead, so much did I want his white fire inside me. Then he said, "No, I better pull out, we have to protect Paul." Good old Paul, I thought.

I felt the hog twitch and swell deep in my belly; maybe he was going to come inside me anyway. He was grunting hard, "uhh, uhh, uhh," but he slid out just in time and shot all over my ass. He rubbed it in with his big hands. I had forgotten how much I loved to have his hands on me.

I stood, pulled up my panties and tights. I opened my eyes and looked at myself in the mirror. My hair was standing up all over my head as if I had been electrocuted.

There was a loud pounding on the door. "What are you doing in there?" a shrill voice called out. "No getting stoned in the bathroom."

I put my coat back on and he put himself back into his pants and zipped up. When we went out, the three women standing in line looked at us furiously.

Our beer mugs, now nearly empty, were still on the counter.

"Let me get us another," he said.

"No," I told him, "I better get home."

"Home," he echoed in a bitter tone, "home."

"Well, uh, good luck with your show," I said. I turned quickly. I couldn't bear to look at him, and made my way through the crowd and out the door.

Scars

R. V. Raiment

There is much, these days, it seems, that a woman would hide from a would-be lover, no matter that what she hides is often extremely natural, human and normal. Pale skin or dark can be hidden behind paints and creams, some measure of largeness or shapelessness hidden within body-contouring garments, smallness with padding and uplifting bras. Short-sightedness so severe that she needs spectacles on to find her own king-sized bed in her very small bedroom can be hidden with contacts, rebellious hairs plucked from their natural beds as if they never grew there.

Scars on the abdomen, the telltale, often silvered trails that testify to motherhood, are less easy, perhaps, to hide, yet many wish they could be. No mere short-sightedness, this, which is natural and common at a certain age, no little splash of unwanted hairs, but testimony to a past and to a passed virginity, to a male penis that has wrought its work there and which was valued enough that she carried the product to term.

She is "used", she is "second hand", and there are some that think this important, though – when they are men – they are naught but bloody fools.

I have known many scarred women.

Scars on the abdomen? "Betty" certainly had those, and hers did not derive from childbirth. Poor, dear lady. Her body resembled a railway map, back and front and on either flank, the delineations of cut and stitch a disconcerting statement of weight reducing surgery. And it is not as if it had worked.

Petite and slim, my small ad had specified, and I ask you to forgive me that because I'd previously spent a score of years married to a pear-shaped lady whose seeming frigidity only revealed its true, sad nature when she abandoned me for another woman.

So I was looking, ere my time ran out, for a woman who genuinely liked to fuck and who, should the opportunity arise, I might carry across our connubial threshold without doing my back an injury. I was looking for the ideal of my youth, the faux ideal of every youth: petite and slim.

It's fortunate that the placers and respondents – male and female – of lonely hearts advertisements cannot be sued for misrepresentation. Betty was "petite" if "petite" means short. I guess she was maybe five foot tall. The trouble is that the same statistic applied to both height and width. And then those scars . . .

I was very nice to her. I didn't remonstrate with her about her misrepresentation, was kind to her and, when it became clear that she wanted it to happen, I tried very hard to make love to her.

Don't misunderstand me. I didn't despise or dislike her, and I didn't take exception to her being overweight, despite that she had claimed otherwise in her reply, nor did her being overweight mean that I could not find beauty and desirability in her. That the bald-headed hermit lived up to his name with a vengeance, shrunk so small that he was deeply cowled in foreskin as if he, poor chap, could not bring himself to cast a one-eyed glance at her, was not a consequence – directly – of her build.

Nor directly was it her endless scars and their resemblance to seams on the edge of splitting, but it was the mentality of the woman who had allowed these things to happen to her in pursuit of an objective she would never reach, the mentality of a woman cognisant of every twist and turn in every contemporary soap opera and whose bathroom and bedroom were universally and mind-blowingly pink. Then again my poor cock may simply have been stunned by the perfume everywhere.

In all it simply made me deeply sad, and if my cock were to make any movement that night it would be in the direction of the door.

"Dianna" had no scars upon her abdomen that I can remember, though those poignant, lovely scars, the silvered rivulets of stretch marks, must surely have been there. The scar she herself hated, and which only the greatest tenderness could overcome, was a scar that ran the length of the underneath of her breasts at the conjunction with her torso.

Twelve years old, she'd been, when her parents inflicted that upon her because, they had decided, she was far too "well developed" for her age.

I loved that scar, and I loved her for it and I miss her still, now that we've moved on.

Scars themselves don't trouble me. Not physical ones at least. There is not a natural form that does not scar and in particular forms – in that of trees, for example – the scars are merely signs of growth, maturity and ever-accumulating beauty. The scars of childbirth are a badge of honour, testament to the very womanliness of woman, the bearer of creation's glorious gateway into fulfilment and into life.

Other scars mean other problems. "Ellen" was my ideal of youth, the profoundest love I had ever known, and her body was an elegy, a poem of beauty in her sweet, modest, pink-peaked breasts, the delightful curves of her lovely bottom, her slender limbs, her perfect cunt.

Like hand and glove we fitted, like hand and beloved, long-lost glove at that. Inside that sweet moistness of her, the soft, delicious, smooth-skinned flesh of her so soft against my own, I found the miracle I had so long sought. And between those wondrous thighs I knew the joy of the questing knight, found my holy grail, my water of life, kissed it, licked it, drank and tasted it.

The tender tendril scars of three childbirths lay upon her slender form and I loved them, with my heart, my lips, my tongue. Lower yet that same holy grail and magic gate which had brought three lives into the world had returned to miraculous slenderness and gripped me, held me, rippled close about me so many lovely, gentle times.

But gentle times they needed to be. Almost unmarked, she wore yet livid scars of a vastly different nature, the scars left by abusive men and ready to open and bleed at any more than the gentlest touch.

Too often it took Mary-Jo and Johnny Haig to assuage her hidden pain and, in the end, it was compound fear that would not let the worst scar heal. She had learned not to trust her own nature and found the joy of being truly loved too painful to persist with.

She broke my heart, nearly broke my spirit, left me alone, sore wounded and deeply bereaved. I carry those scars still, will carry them to my grave, and any other scars, today, must leave me quite unmoved.

Whoever you are, woman, if you are reading this, know that you *are* beautiful. It is your nature and your birthright. Meddle with that beauty at your peril. And if you are man and reading this, remember, you are charged with the stewardship of the Earth's greatest, most wondrous gift. Wound it and, if there is a judgement yet to come, know that you are damned and are mine enemy.

You have scarred life itself. The convenient pretext that you know not what you do, that you are powerless in the face of your own instincts, the shallow games of fucking that leave the hearts of women unloved, untouched, unfulfilled and wanting, the heartless jibes, torments and abandonments which make it too easy to quit the temples into which you have broken for no better purpose than pillage, all are wounds that gut the belly of Life.

You have made of me and my kind, the undangerous stranger, a threat to the women at whom we would wish to smile in cognizance of their loveliness, behind whom we are sometimes compelled to walk, the very echo of our footsteps threatening. In order to be me, I have to prove I am not you, time after time after time.

That scar, that baleful, red, raw scar, I deeply, furiously resent.

Misdirection

Victoria Janssen

"Damn it, we've got to get out of this somehow," Mil said, pacing the sealed white chamber. "And no, I do *not* have any handy explosives tucked in my pocket." To his right, a port twice the size of his head displayed the alien planet below. The *wrong* alien planet. His hyperspace navigation had turned out to be completely inadequate to their needs.

Lenora lounged against the opposite bulkhead, staring up at what was, despite its bizarre design, clearly a monitor: bulbous orange pods followed their every move and vibrated with each word they spoke. She said, "You might as well sit down. There's no hurry *now*."

He snarled. "If you recall, they've got our ship. The only thing we possess. The only way we have to stay ahead of our former employers."

"These aliens haven't hurt us."

Yet, Mil thought.

As if she'd heard his thought, Lenora made a face at him and said, "There *is* a way out. Demonstrate the human mating ritual, and they let us go."

Mil threw himself into the only available chair, which was pulpy and green, and fumed.

Lenora sauntered over to him.

Mil eyed her, suspicious. "They aren't controlling your mind, are they?"

"No," Lenora snapped.

He didn't care if he had annoyed her; it was a perfectly reasonable question under the circumstances. She sat on the lumpy arm of the chair and traced the rim of his ear with her fingertip. He batted her hand away. She tangled her fingers in the hair at the back of his neck, tugging gently. She had nice hands. Skilled. Also soft. She—

"Stop it," he said. "I can't believe you're even considering giving in to them."

"Can you think of a better way to make them let us go?"

"Several ways. But I *still* don't have any handy explosives in my pockets, so . . ."

She grinned, trailing her finger down his throat. He felt his pulse thump against her warm fingertip.

He vaulted out of the not-chair. "They're *watching* us."

"You do want to get out of here?" She rocked forward on her toes and kissed him.

It wasn't at all the carnal assault he'd expected. When she pulled back, he sighed. "But—" His words were cut off when she kissed him again, warm and sweet.

She leaned forward until the tip of her nose bumped his. "Yes?"

He couldn't see anything but her brown eyes. "There must be another option."

"Must there?" She lunged.

"Uh . . . urmm. Le—sto—Le—Lenora! Stop it!"

He had no idea what he was doing on the deck. No, he did know, but he wasn't sure how she had put him there, flat on his back.

Lenora's warm weight pressed into his cock as she straddled him. "You're not being helpful. I want out of here," she said. "And you know this won't hurt."

He scowled. "Well, hell. With it."

"With what?"

"I don't know. Dignity."

She grinned at him, the mischievous grin that was his secret favorite. She leaned forward and kissed him in earnest. His reluctance steamed away within seconds. Moments later, his hands were firmly gripping her arse and she was muttering into his ear. "You *sure* you don't have any handy explosives tucked in your . . ."

"*You* did this to me," he said, in mock annoyance. "You broke it, I think."

Lenora dissolved into shaking peals of laughter, entirely satisfying, even through clothing. "Do you have a . . . a . . . spanner?"

"You'll have to improvise," he said.

Lenora's grin turned devilish. Her hands swept out and
grabbed his wrists, pinning his arms far from his sides. He
stayed where she had put him, obedient for the nonce.

She swiftly bared his chest, but when he moved, she stopped
him with a touch. "If you like," he said. He hadn't thought about
it in detail before now, but he could see how Lenora might be
one who preferred to take charge. He was willing to let her, so
long as he had his turn later. Later?

She unfastened his trousers, a delicate maneuver. Mil winced,
then held still, thinking of cold empty space.

When she licked gently around the crown of his erection,
realization struck. The aliens didn't know what to expect. The
two of them could have danced on their toes, and it would not
have made a speck of difference to . . .

Never mind.

The square root of 57 is 7.45 . . . 98. And its sine is .8387,
and its cosine is .5446 . . . no, not good enough at all. Eighty-
nine squared is 7,921, which has a cosine of .998, no, that's far
too rhythmic. How about three, lovely three, prime three, the
square root of three is 1.7321 . . .

Goodbye, higher brain functions, he thought. Will she respect
me in the morning? Will she shoot me in the morning? And then
he could no longer think at all, the hot tight suction of her mouth
so painfully sweet, until he thought he would scream with the
pain or the sweetness; then he was coming in hard bursts that
seemed to burn all the way up his spine.

When he could see again, he realized that Lenora was laughing, but coughing at the same time. He couldn't think why. That
wasn't usual.

Lenora rubbed her face with the tail of his shirt. He couldn't
see what she was doing, but she was *still* laughing. Drowsily, he
asked, "What's so funny?"

She collapsed against him, her soft cheek landing on his
chest, warm puffs of her breath stroking his bare skin. He gathered her closer. At last she said, with one final throat-clearing,
"Sorry. I miscalculated."

Surely she hadn't heard him spouting mathematics – no, she couldn't have done. "What do you mean?"

The question made her laugh again, breaking up her sentence. "Not . . . your fault . . . never heard of anything like . . ."

"*What?*"

"It . . . It . . . missed . . . my throat. It . . . came out . . . my nose." Lenora shrieked with merriment, slapping his leg in her enthusiasm.

No. Mil covered his face with his hand. Every millisecond had been recorded indelibly by an alien space station. On top of that, he might have hurt his . . . well, his closest friend. "Damn it! I'm so sincerely sorry. I promise I'll make it up to you."

"It's all right. Really. Very memorable." Delicately, she scraped her nail across his nipple and grinned.

He shuddered deliciously and stroked her cropped hair. He raised his voice. "We demonstrated! Now open the door!"

Nothing happened.

Lenora wriggled upwards until her face was nestled against his neck. "Really, I haven't had that much fun in years."

"Don't be sarcastic. The door isn't opening."

"You worry too much."

Mil took a deep breath and sat up, pulling her with him. He yelled, "Let us out! Now!"

A strangely accented voice boomed, "We have allotted precisely three segments for the human mating ritual. Only a portion of one segment has been stored. Please provide further demonstrations of the human mating ritual. You will be released when the specified time has passed."

Silence. Then Lenora snickered. "You said you would make it up to me. Get to work."

He unfastened the collar of her jacket. "This time, I promise I won't miscalculate."

On the Night Bus

Lucy Felthouse

Emerging from the crowd, Will boarded the bus, swiped his travel pass across the electronic reader and scuttled hurriedly up the stairs. Relieved to note he was the only person on the top deck, he emphasized his need to be alone even further by walking to the rear of the bus and settling into a corner of the back seat. He was as far away from the other passengers as he could possibly get – and that was the way he wanted it.

Normally, he'd be happy to slum it with the laughing, slurring, swaying drunks on the lower deck – talking rubbish with them until it was time for him to get off the bus. Normally, he was *one* of the laughing, slurring, swaying drunks. It was Saturday night – or Sunday morning, depending on which way you looked at it – after all.

But tonight was far from normal. The realization had sobered Will up in the blink of an eye, and sent him home before he did something he'd live to regret. Possibly not straight away, but certainly at some point. Like when he woke up in a cell at the local police station.

Just as Will felt his blood begin to boil again and his hands involuntarily clenched into fists, his solitude was ruined by the arrival of a young couple. They were drunk, giggly, and so wrapped up in each other that they didn't notice Will glowering in the corner. They slumped down together a few rows of seats in front of him and immediately began kissing as though their lives depended on it.

Will's glower deepened into a positively evil expression – luckily for the young couple his looks couldn't kill, otherwise they'd have been stone dead in an instant. It was hardly surprising he was pissed off, though. He'd just found out that his girlfriend and his so-called best friend had been seeing each other behind his back, and now a sickeningly loved-up couple were sucking face right in front of him. He hardly needed a reminder of his new single status, least of all such a vivid one.

Sighing, Will reached into his pocket and pulled out his iPhone. He'd switched it onto airplane mode earlier so none of the text messages and phone calls he knew the traitorous two would be trying to make would come through. There was absolutely nothing they could say that would excuse their behaviour, so he saw no reason to talk to either of them. Ever again.

Will was just about to fire up a game to distract him from the unwanted display in front of him when a moan that could only be described as lusty made him look up at the couple again. It was obvious that they really had no idea that he was sitting there, because their ardent kissing had now progressed to heavy petting. The guy had manoeuvred his girl's top down so both her breasts were on display. He yanked down the cups of her bra and sucked a nipple into his mouth, while he squeezed and pinched at the other one with an eager hand.

The girl's head lolled back, and her eyes fluttered closed; she was clearly lost in bliss. Not so lost that she couldn't voice her enjoyment, however. As her lover teased and pleasured her luscious tits, a constant cacophony of moans, grunts and squeals came from her parted lips. It was a good job that the night bus was so damn noisy and busy, otherwise they'd have been caught in no time and probably kicked off the bus.

Will was actually a little surprised that the driver hadn't shouted at them through his intercom. He knew that drivers had some kind of clever mirror system in their cab which meant they could see what was happening on the top deck of the bus, to prevent such lewd behaviour. The couple were obviously too drunk to consider anything like that, and Will could only imagine that the squeeze of bodies and resultant havoc on the bottom level of the bus was keeping the driver thoroughly occupied.

The more he thought about it, the more he decided he was glad that they hadn't been disturbed. They'd totally distracted him from his personal problems, and for that he was grateful. So, it would seem, was his cock. Slipping his mobile back into his pocket, Will then pressed the palm of his hand against his rapidly growing erection. It twitched beneath his touch, and he glanced up again to check that he remained unnoticed in his corner. He did. In fact, Will suspected that even if the bus crashed, the pair would continue with their increasingly steamy clinch.

Deciding to take a chance, he undid the fly of his jeans and pulled out his stiff cock. He pumped it slowly in his fist as he watched the couple. Will wondered how far they would go before coming to their senses, sobering up or reaching the bus stop they needed to disembark at. As luck would have it, his stop was where the bus terminated so he'd get to find out the answer to this question without running the risk of going past his house and having to trek back across town to get home.

Soon, Will stopped thinking and simply watched and wanked. The breast play had ceased, and, although he couldn't actually see what was happening, it was damn obvious that the girl was now giving her boyfriend a blow job. Her blonde head was bobbing up and down, and it was the man's turn to grunt and moan as his cock was enveloped in a hot, wet and *very* willing mouth. Will tugged his own shaft more vigorously, wishing he was the one getting head.

The noises the guy was making increased in intensity, and the girl suddenly sat up – her lips slipping off his cock with a wet pop. She grinned at him, and said, "You can't come yet, I want to fuck you."

"Be my guest." The guy's response was clearly all the invitation she needed. Some shuffling around ensued, and Will was suddenly terrified that the game was up as the girl straddled her man's lap, meaning she was facing him – and, as a consequence, Will, too. All she had to do was just look up, and she'd spot the guy in the corner, wanking over a free live sex show. He froze in place, as though staying still would make him somehow invisible.

Will couldn't believe his luck, however, as the woman alternated between being forehead to forehead with her lover as she bounced on his cock, and tossing her blonde mane around like a porn star, with her eyes tightly closed.

Feeling a little more secure now, Will relaxed and picked up the pace on his prick. He'd barely noticed the stop–start of the bus as it wound its way along the route, but he knew it couldn't be much longer before it was at its finishing point. And there was no way he wanted to be caught with his cock out – by the couple, or anyone else, for that matter.

He needn't have worried. The frantic coupling taking place in front of him, with the titillating view of the hot blonde bouncing up and down, her tits doing the same, meant that Will's climax was just around the corner. He paced himself, though, aiming to come when one of the couple did, therefore drowning out any sounds he might let slip.

It wasn't long before he got his opportunity, and it didn't come a moment too soon. As the bus drew to its final stop, and the driver shouted "Everybody off!", the girl hit her peak, letting out a stream of expletives. Her boyfriend rapidly followed suit, as did Will. He bit his lip so hard he almost drew blood as jet after jet of come flew out of his cock, coating the back of the seat in front of him, his hand and his dick.

However, the timing and the situation were as such that Will couldn't worry about all that. Instead, he tucked his softening cock back into his jeans, grimacing at the thought of his spunk smearing over the inside of the denim. With the lack of any other option, he ignored his conscience and wiped his right hand on the seat's upholstery, zipped up his fly, then stood up and walked down the aisle of the bus towards the stairs.

With a huge grin and a "goodnight" to the startled couple scrabbling to put their clothes back on, Will descended the stairs, hopped off the bus and headed for home, hoping they wouldn't follow him and demand an explanation.

As he meandered his way home, Will suspected that despite the shitty night he'd had, he would have no trouble sleeping. The mind-blowing climax he'd just had would see to that.

It had brought a whole new meaning to getting off at his stop.

Oh Henry!

Gina Marie

There's only one thing I ever ask of a man. It's not commitment or love. I don't want money or gifts. All I ever ask of any man is that he give me his dick.

You see, it's a hobby of mine, collecting dicks. My personal collection stands at fifty-two, though it's become quite a little side business and I figure there must be hundreds of hand-crafted dicks now in the hands of my clients. I catalogue my own private dicks with all the diligence of a coin collector. Each one is tagged, placed in an archival glassine sleeve, and stored carefully in a specially designed acid-free carton before being protected in a fireproof chest. No, not mummified dicks. Replicas. Dicks of the sculpted variety. Cloned willies using body casting alginate.

It's not penis envy – I'm perfectly happy with my sly, pert pussy. But what can I say? I just love tools!

I just can't get enough of the damn things. I like to gaze upon their perfect form. I like them hard. I like them soft. I like to watch them rise up, like a cobra in the night. I like to watch them transform from twilight to dawn, watch the balls react and swim beneath them like the undulating sac of an octopus.

I like to pinch the mouth and make them sing. "Nobody knows the trouble I've seen." Oooh, the dick's little "o" of a mouth. Those teeny tiny little perfect lips. Gives me chills! I like to serenade them with silly comedic songs, use my fingers to puppet them back and forth across the pelvis. My favorite: "slinky, slinky, it's the magical toy . . . fun for a girl or a boy!"

I digress. The dick collection started with Oh Henry. Oh Henry was the rather exciting pants whisperer or a rather boring date. I needed to jump-start some pillow talk, so I asked the obvious question. "Well, what's his name?"

"Huh?" was the reply.

"Does your penis have a name?"

Oh Henry didn't have a name – that is until I named him. That was the last time I ever dated a nameless man. From that point on, the question came first, even before meeting for coffee or a walk to the park. It's a sign of weakness, shameful even, for a guy not to honor the life source between his legs with the small, simple gesture of a name!

Incidentally, I have a *place* name for my soul patch (I'll tell you later) as it is less a traveler than a destination – the cave man's dwelling. The puss to the octo.

Oh Henry and I became very attached. He had quite an amazing persona and I fell hard. Wakey-wakey Oh Henry! Oh, Henry! Yes! Is Oh Henry hungry? Tell me, Oh Henry. Tell me what you want! And yet, all good things must go. I wasn't about to commit. It was time to move on. But I couldn't part with Oh Henry. The rest, as they say, is history.

I never intended to expand beyond my own personal museum. But word of my custom dildo collection somehow got out. My friend Martha asked me to help her cast her boyfriend's dick before he left for Army duty. Then Rachel wanted a replica of Excalibur as a gift for her husband's birthday. It simply snow-balled from there.

Before I knew it, "Guys' Night Out" was drawing twenty to thirty people.

Better than Amway, candle parties, jewelry shows, pampered chef, even poker night, Guys' Night Out offered something for fucking everyone.

The guys typically hung out around the bar, watching sports, checking out the magazine subscriptions and porn videos and talking trash until it was "their turn" in the back room. The ladies got loaded up with appletinis and wine and all that shit, then milled about checking out the sex toys in the spare bedroom and lingerie in the laundry room.

Meanwhile, in the master bedroom, I worked with my clients to create beautiful works of art.

Obviously, prolonged male excitement is a must for the

procedure to work. A couple of drinks, some hot reading material and being fondled by a few naked women usually did the trick, but every once in a while, I ended up with a real tough nut.

The embarrassing thing was, I'm the one who invited Zeus to the party. He belonged to an arrogant yet intriguing young gun named Jack. He (Jack) walked and talked with a swagger. The cousin of a neighbor's sister-in-law, I met him at a backyard barbecue. He offered me a beer while I was admiring my friend's artfully done koi pond.

"I built Erica's pond," Jack boasted. "Koi fucking rock."

"Do they? Well, they are obviously beautiful," I said. "But I never considered that they may also fucking rock."

"They totally fucking rock. You're hot. Get you a beer?"

Well, it could have, should have ended right there. But when Jack returned with my beverage there was no stopping him.

"I heard you're a toy maker." Jack grinned, tossing back a foamy swallow. "My name's Jack, but it's one of your 'Dick-in-a-Box' pleasurements that I'd like to have."

"For your girlfriend?"

"Nah, I'm single. I don't want commitment or love. All I ever ask of any woman is that she give me her pussy. I have quite a collection – I collect cuntkus. But Zeus deserves to be immortalized in a physical way. I want it for me."

"Cuntku?"

Jack sat on the rock ledge of the pond and dipped his fingers into the water. "Haiku. Cuntku if you will." He smirked at his own cleverness.

But Jack wasn't joking. He went on. "Cuntku. Smutku. Slutku. Kinku. A tender bit, short and sweet and throughout, counted out, straight from the pussy's mouth." He went on and on. Something to remember them by. Ahhh the divinely inspired Lucretia and Puss in Boots, Fair Juliet and Almond Joy, Sunny Delight and Eve.

"My lovely, lovely ladies. They all seem to have such a way with words."

Somehow this golden bad boy was speaking my language. He named it without flinching. Zeus. Lightning and rage. How divine.

So I invited Zeus to bring Jack along to one of my parties.

My pretty friend Sarah and I gave Jack a nice, sensuous massage – just his back and shoulders to get things started. Before we could even get to his hips or ass, Zeus exploded in Jack's pants like Mount Vesuvius.

"That's Zeus." Jack smiled. "Always popping off like that."

"How will we immortalize him if he's blowing like a geyser every five minutes?"

"Whiskey," Jack said. "Bring me some whiskey. That ought to hold him off."

I brought Jack a fifth of Wild Turkey and told him to drink up. He lay back on the bed where Seductive Sarah began preparing him for the mold. Ka-boom! Her pinkie grazed Zeus's ornery little tip when he went off like a cannon.

I'd never seen anything like it. As soon as Zeus threw down a lightning bolt, he was back up again, ready for more. But amazing as it was, this simply wouldn't do.

"Jack honey," I said, trying to be sensitive. "You might want a Zeus-in-a-Box to play with later, but we're going to have to tame that thing for at least fifteen minutes."

Then I had an idea, inspired by my soul patch that had begun whispering cuntku from down below.

"Sarah, would you be a dear and wrap up the party? I'm going to handle this one on my own."

"Sure, no problem," she sighed. "Buh-bye stud."

Zeus winked.

"Now what – we put Zeus in a vice?" Jack was as flip as could be.

"Time is money, baby!" I said, both annoyed and incredibly excited. "I don't care if he's a Greek god. Zeus needs to behave!"

"What are you, a lion tamer?"

"I've been called that, yes. On your hands and knees, beast!"

"Yes, ma'am!" Jack let out a giddy roar and got onto all fours. I retrieved my silver paddle and smacked him hard on the ass. Oh come now!

Zeus exploded on impact.

"Zeus loves a good spanking," Jack said, wiggling his ass.

I grabbed Jack's balls hard and squeezed. Ka-boom!

"Zeus can't be for real!"

I climbed atop Jack's muscular back and leaned my body across him, rubbing my tits across his shoulders, licking his neck and tickling his ears with my tongue.

"Oh that's very nice," he groaned.

I reached underneath and let Zeus fill my hand. He lasted all of one upstroke and one down before he went and blew his wad all over my fist.

Now, I'm no poet, but my love mound was purring loudly now like a lady lion – whispering heavenly cuntku. I began to repeat it into Jack's ear.

"Softly, sweetly, patiently," I chanted.

Zeus was rapt, listening intently as I whispered, moaned and growled naughty, lustful cuntkus in carefully measured syllables. Five-seven-five. Five-seven-five.

I pushed Jack onto his back and whispered with slow, soft breaths, taking my time. Five-seven-five. Zeus simply smiled. I stroked and tickled, spanked and panted, all the while lip-syncing the erotic naughty bits incanted by my poetic pussy.

It's too embarrassing to repeat, but I have to say, my naughty girl delivered some hot lines.

At last, I gripped Jack by the shoulders and buried Zeus deep within my storm clouds.

It took all night and more than a few shots of ouzo, but at last Zeus learned to behave.

Some things are simply meant to be. Lying back on the sweat-soaked sheets, Zeus finally immortalized in high-quality silicone, I pressed Jack's head to my breasts and gazed down at the satisfied, sleeping deity.

It was time to reveal my love nest's name.

"Zeus, are you awake?"

He smiled weakly, exhausted but happy.

"Welcome to Mount Olympus."

Lake Logan

Cheyenne Blue

There is a place on the south side of Denver where I-25 goes through a cutting, passing underneath Logan, Emerson and Franklin streets. It's the place that always used to flood before they spent millions redoing the drainage, thus putting paid to "Lake Logan". The traffic moves faster now, and there's light rail along the median. It's a better traffic system for Denver and most people are happy with how it's turned out.

But I miss Lake Logan.

Before the drainage works, the days of the summer monsoons were the best. The rain deluged from black skies in the afternoons and whisked away down the storm drains. But the drains, blocked with trash and rotting leaves, used to well over, spewing tea-colored water back out again, and Lake Logan rose once more.

Jay and I lived on South Logan Street, a couple of blocks south of the freeway in a crumbling old Victorian. The last day that Lake Logan rose, we were sitting on our porch with a couple of beers, watching the storm clouds roll in like breakers.

"Gonna be a big one," Jay said. The sky was dark and turgid, and even as he spoke the first fat raindrops fell, darkening the concrete path like ink spots.

We sat and watched for a while as the rain streamed from the heavy sky. When the beers ran out, Jay got a couple more.

"Shit!" I jumped to my feet, remembering. "I have to get to the bank before they close. Stay here, I won't be long."

Jay removed his feet from the porch railing and shambled to his feet. "I'll come."

Jay's car – one of those seventies tanks – was parked out front, so we took that. We hammered around to Broadway, and doubled back onto the freeway. Traffic was slow, and we soon saw why. Lake Logan was welling up in The Narrows. Cars were slowing, and plunging through, sending sheets of water into the air. The Continental's engine skipped a beat and continued.

Jay eased over to the right-hand lane. "C'mon, baby," he crooned, and eased the car into the water.

Halfway through, the engine spluttered and died. I stuck my head out the window as Jay tried to restart her. The water was over the sills and starting to seep underneath the doors. The wash from the SUVs still plowing through wasn't helping. Every vehicle that went past rocked the Continental on her tires, and her engine turned lethargically and wouldn't catch.

"Slow down, you bastards!" I screamed at the crawling traffic. "How about a fucking hand here?"

The driver of a shiny green Toyota gave me the single-finger salute and a spray of water slopped in the open window.

"Shit," I moaned, close to tears. A couple of inches of murky water now covered the floor pan, and our bankbook floated soggily on the top. I spun around, hitched my skirt to my waist, dropped my panties and mooned the disappearing vehicle.

Jay watched me from the driver's seat. "Nice." He reached past me and wound up the window. His face hovered inches from my bare pussy. "Nicer." He splayed his hands over my ass and mashed his face into my cunt. His tongue lapped along my outer lips teasing them open to find my clit.

I opened my mouth to say, "Hon, not here. Wait until we get home," but then his tongue found its target and flickered deliberately, teasing the nerves. His fingers clenched on my ass, pulling me into his face, deeper, tighter, and his tongue stabbed into me. Instantly, I was heat and surging arousal. I knew, of course, that scant feet away the Denver rush hour crawled past our vehicle. But the windows were steamed up, and everyone knows that drivers never look past the end of the hood.

I shuffled around, trying to raise up so I could spread my legs better, but there wasn't enough room.

Jay lifted his mouth. It glistened with my juices. "Open the window and sit on the sill," he suggested.

"People might see . . ." I moaned. But his mouth was back on my cunt, and he was lapping around my clit, moving around my pussy, tonguing me with skill as only he knows how.

"Keep your top on and they'll see nothing."

I wound down the window, and wiggled through it, so that my ass rested on the door. Bracing myself on the roof, I spread my legs wide, one up on the dash. Jay moved into place, pushing my skirt back up to my waist. His tongue settled back home, and two fingers joined it.

I leaned back, so that I could look down my body to where his head bobbed. My orgasm was gathering, pooling hot and heavy between my legs. It wouldn't be long if he kept that up. His tongue made contact with my clit, long heavy strokes, and that was all it took for me to scream my pleasure to the commuters.

"God," I murmured, and pulled him away from my cunt by the ears. "I want you inside me."

No one was paying any attention to us. The cars still crawled through the water, and it seemed no one wanted to stop and help and risk getting themselves stuck.

Jay levered himself up, and undid his pants. With a grunt, he lay along my body, sliding his upper body out the window. His cock bobbed, thick and turgid against my inner thigh. Maneuvering himself into position, he fumbled and the head of his cock slipped in an inch.

I love that most of all: the first moment of penetration, when the head, the bulbous, fat head slides in and waits, poised for the deeper thrust. When my pussy clasps around the knob, when I hold it there, breathless with anticipation. Jay paused, letting me savor the moment, then with one hard push he was in me up to the balls.

My head fell back, and I watched his jerky movements through slitted eyes. Now, it was obvious to the passing traffic what we were doing. Jay's rhythmic movements and my sound-less gasps gave it away. The passing cars slowed even more, and I saw some appreciative stares, a couple of disgusted faces. One pickup stopped and, ignoring the blare of horns behind him, idled the engine, up to the top of the wheels in Lake Logan. The driver twisted, trying to see more, but the truck spluttered and he was forced to move on, gunning the engine and sending a wash of dirty water over us. It soaked my T-shirt, plastering my skirt to my hips.

Jay's thrusts became fiercer, the blunt head pushing into my inner walls with delicious fullness. His fingers delved between us, pinching my clit in time to his fucking. The wave started again, a deep mounting pleasure pulse. The openly appreciative drivers spurred me on, and their leering faces blurred behind my half-closed eyelids, behind their wet windshields. Two more thrusts, and I was coming hard, my upper body convulsing, and I let go all thought of hiding and screamed my pleasure to the crawling cars. And Jay was coming too; I felt the pulse of his come inside me, and then wet on my pussy lips as he withdrew.

He kissed me, his tongue lazily entangling with mine for a moment, even as his cock lay spent and sticky on my thigh.

A jerk startled us. The Continental was moving, rolling slowly through the water. Behind us, two men with quarterback shoulders were pushing us slowly toward dry ground. From their bent over position, they would have had a clear view of our fucking through the rear window.

"Don't stop on our account," called one.

Jay lifted off me, sliding down my body back into the car. I angled my hips toward our rescuers, opening my legs so they could see my cunt, Jay's come shining on the lips.

"Thanks, boys." I winked.

I'll miss Lake Logan.

Janey Had a Dozen Good Stories to Tell

Michael Hemmingson

The first was a young woman who told the group that her husband hung himself on his thirtieth birthday because he had not yet published his first novel and won the Pulitzer or something comparable. His suicide note consisted of five words: "I have nothing to say."

The second was a middle-aged man who had a lot to say. He was angry, and short. He was angry that he was short. He hated the world. He wore a T-shirt with three words: "People disgust me." His mother had overdosed on morphine sulfate pills and he had expected a good chunk of money from life insurance and gold bars and the house, only to discover that the policy had lapsed a year ago and dear mom had cashed in the gold and there was a second mortgage lien on the house he had grown up in.

The third was a man in his mid-thirties who worked at the newspaper and claimed to still be in a state of shock over his father pulling the trigger of the gun. His hair was shaggy and he had a two-day beard growth and wore old jeans and seemed like a good prospect for Janey. The angry guy was too angry for her; she wanted, needed, sorrow and sadness.

The fourth was an ex-Army woman barely out of her teens who saw a friend of hers shoot himself in Afghanistan. The whole thing about oil profits and killer drones was too depressing for the soldier and he decided to cash his check. "It would've been easier if he had been shot by a *hadji*," she said, "then he'd be a hero, not a coward."

"Do we all feel that suicide is a form of cowardice?" asked the therapy group leader: a tall, thin woman in her fifties.

Some held up their hands, others did not. Janey did not.

"It's making a choice, not waiting for God to do the trick," said the third man who worked at the newspaper. "We have agency over our destiny."

Janey liked that. Free will, etc.

"But it still *sucks dick*," the angry man said.

Everyone agreed.

It was Janey's turn to share. She had a dozen good stories and recycled them from group to group, always rehearsed and dramatic.

She told this one:

"My mother had leukemia. She waged a war seven strong years. The last two, I had to take care of her; I bathed her, changed her diapers, fed her, and it was so painful to watch her fade away in agony like that. She kept urging me to put her in a hospice but I couldn't. It wasn't the money, my family has plenty of money – no, I just couldn't do that to the woman who gave birth to me, raised me, was always there for me. She kept saying that she wanted to die and end the pain and would I help? I said no. Not because I think suicide is wrong, I just couldn't let go of her. Was I being selfish? It's human nature to be selfish. She betrayed me. She killed herself when I went to the store to get adult diapers. She slit her wrists and jugular vein open. She bled out in five minutes. I looked at all the blood and I hated my mom, I hated her for what she did, what she put me through. I had to answer all kinds of questions from the police, like I was maybe a suspect, that maybe I killed my mother for the insurance payout. Then I had to hire a hazmat crew to clean up all that goddamn blood. Eight hundred dollars, and these bastards were telling dirty jokes to each other: 'Did you hear about the girl who went on a fishing boat with twenty men? She came back with a red snapper.' Ha ha. Who tells such jokes while mopping up death? So I yelled at them, I screamed: 'HEY, ASSHOLES, MY MOMMY JUST DIED AND YOU'RE YUKKING IT UP LIKE TWO WHITE TRASH HILLBILLIES?!?' I was so angry, if you can't tell. I wasn't angry with them for being jerk-offs, I was angry with my mom about the mess she left behind for me to deal with. It wasn't fair. One mess after another."

The group leader said, "Are you still mad at her?"

"Janey Black," she said.

"Eric Payne," he said.

They shook hands. They had a few drinks together. She had approached him. He liked aggressive women.

"That was – that was something else," he said. "Thank you for sharing your story."

"Let's talk about something else," she said.

"OK."

"What do you do at the newspaper?"

"Write."

"Investigative journalism?"

"Nothing so glamorous," Eric said, amused. "I have a four times a week opinion column. I occasionally pound out a restaurant review, book review, movie review or local band interview. Sometimes a feature about a local person or event, fluff copy to fit around the plastic surgery ads."

"But you love your job," she said.

"Better than most jobs you can get today," he said.

"Fortunately my family has money," she said. "How does someone get a job at a newspaper? You need a college degree?"

"You need desire," Eric told her. "Ambition. I started off as the calendar editor, or compiler. The lowest job in editorial, tedious and thankless, digging up enough interesting shit for every day. It's a litmus test for cubs and wannabes – do you have what it takes to pay your dues? Can you find a way of using the calendar to take a career leap? For instance, I learned of a last-minute fundraiser put on by a city councilman, who was about to run for mayor. I got a one-on-one interview, promising he could talk about his charity deal all he wanted. He had never given any reporter such a long, heartfelt dialogue. My editor went Lady Gaga. The interview generated a lot of talk and letters and was syndicated all over the state. The guy was elected mayor and I always like to think I helped him with that, even though he wound up indicted for taking bribes."

"You have to be a go-getter," she said.

"Yes."

"Taking the initiative and grabbing what you want."

"Desire."

"I *love* desire," Janey said, "and I believe in asserting yourself; going for what you most want." She reached out and grabbed his hand in hers. "Guess what, *who*, I want right now? *What I desire.*"

So it went like that. Less than an hour after meeting one another, they were in his bed. The next night, they were in her bed. They went back and forth like that. It was more than fucking: it was romance. They celebrated their one-month anniversary by not having sex and cuddling sweetly under the sheets like virgin teenagers.

"How do you feel about your father?" she said.

"Like it's still not real," he said. "I keep wondering when I will wake up."

"It'll never feel 'real'," she said.

"How do you . . . feel about your mom?"

"I've come to terms with it," she said.

"Moved on?"

"No," she said, "I keep it alive. I know what to do."

"Tell me."

"No, no, I am interviewing *you* here, Mr Reporter. Tell me how many times you've been in love."

"True love, puppy love, endless, tragic love?" He added, "Self-love."

"Tell me about the last woman who broke your heart; broke your heart so much, stomped on it to the point that you wanted to fucking *die.*"

"Five years ago," Eric said. "We were engaged. She got— we got pregnant. It wasn't a mistake. We wanted a family. I was ready for it. She said we were soulmates. She said this was all meant to be. My life was going to change drastically for the better. I would quit the newspaper and take a leap of faith and write a novel and a screenplay. A week before we were to marry, she changed her mind for reasons unknown. Like eating a cheese puff instead of a barbecue chip. She called off the wedding. She had an abortion. She just didn't kill my baby, she killed my destiny, she *murdered* the couple, the family, we were supposed to be."

"You hated her?"

"She put a restraining order on me."

"You wanted justice," Janey said.

"I didn't understand why she did what she did," Eric said; "and I still don't."

"You're asking why a woman becomes illogical and inconsistent," Janey said. "It'll never work," she said. "We do what we do," she said.

"Even when you love?"

"Especially." She held him close and kissed him, etc. "You're the sweetest, kindest man I've ever known," she said, "Eric."

She tore into him the next morning. She complained that his bathroom was not clean enough. "One would think you'd get the hint, with a woman coming here every other night for a month. Why are you so dirty, *Eric*? Why can't you clean your toilet right? Why don't you ever put the t.p. on the roll? *Eric*. Why do you have the cat litter in the bathroom? *Eric*. Do you think my *pussy* appreciates all the bacteria and germs getting on her?"

She complained about his kitchen. "You wait until the last minute to wash dishes, *Eric*. Do you see that *ant*? It'll go back to its nest and bring hundreds more of its hive-mentality buddies," she said. "The milk in the fridge is spoiled, *Eric*, and those eggs are expired. No *wonder* that woman called off the wedding," she said, "you would've been a lousy family man and husband. She did her kid a *favor* killing it, because it would have starved to death or died from food poisoning by the hands of an oh-so-responsible paterfamilias."

And so it went, for several days, one insult after another, one cut down followed by another; when he was unable to perform in bed, she rambled about his early impotence. "And your *dick* is too small anyway," she said, "and your come tastes bad all the time because you eat like *crap*, and you can't lick pussy for *shit*. You call yourself a *lover*?"

"Why are you doing this?" he asked. "Why are you saying these awful things?" he wanted to know. "What the hell," he said.

"Why do you *think*?"

"I don't understand."

"You never will," she said, "because you're too fucking stupid to comprehend it."

"Fuck you," he said, "fuck *you*, you fucking *fucked* bitch."

"Oh *now* he grows a pair," she said.

He hit her – smacked her a good one across the face, and Janey licked the blood on her lips and smiled.

She said, "Do that some more, baby. Show me who's the boss. Beat the hell out of me and take me – *show me you're a man*."

He found his clothes and started to get dressed. She stared at him, naked on the bed, nipples hard like missiles ready to launch to sink his boat.

"I'm out of here," he said.

"I'll tell you *why*," she said. "Because love is bullshit."

"How poetic and philosophical."

"I was in love once, I knew love," Janey said, still tasting blood in her mouth and swirling it around like a liquor; "there were promises and plans, and then my mother got sick, and so he left me. He left me alone to deal with my sick mom. What kind of man *does* that? That isn't husband material. After my mother killed herself, I called him to tell him what happened and he said, 'Why are you telling me this?' What kind of *man* turns on a woman like that?"

Eric stopped at the door. He realized the sardonic and melo-dramatic nature of his posture. He said, "So – what, for revenge, you get men to fall in love with you and then destroy them?"

She smiled and she shrugged, just like he expected her to.

He thought: My life is a fucked-up soap opera.

"It creates balance in the universe," she said, "and justice."

"You're nuts," he said.

"You know what I'm saying is true," she said. "How many women have you hurt the past five years, getting 'even steven' with the one who murdered your future?"

She said.

* * *

He stayed.

He stayed that night and many nights. They shattered one another over and over like glass figurines and they made love after and fucked before they screamed, scratched, bit and punched one another, and then they fucked and loved again; they did this until the world had balance. He knew he would be another one of her stories she would tell some therapy group or her next fuck buddy, project, man, whatever; and that was OK. It was OK.

It was just fine.

Really.

Joining the Mile High Club

Rachel Kramer Bussel

Two days before our trip to Los Angeles, I tell my girlfriend Kiki she's not allowed to masturbate until we arrive in the City of Angels. I've never given her an order like this, and I'm not sure how she'll react, but I'm pleased that even though she is usually a once-a-day masturbator, she not only follows my command but delightedly tells her friends about it.

After her parents drop us off at the airport, I pull her into an extra-large stall in the airport bathroom and make her close her eyes before fastening a glistening new magenta collar around her neck. We exit and both admire it, our eyes drawn to this simple addition that in a moment seems to drastically change our relationship.

We board the Jetblue flight, not caring so much about the multiple cable stations as the chance to get it on while in the air. She has the aisle seat and I have the middle. I know she's scared of flying, but I intend to make sure she doesn't have time to worry about disaster befalling us. After we're seated, I start playing with the collar, my hand automatically reaching for the hook. It looks so good on her, so natural, and I can't help but look up at it and smile every few minutes. We've been inching towards playing like this – me ordering her around, spanking her – but the collar has raised the bar for our play together. Since she likes to be choked, I know that every time I tug on the collar and the band digs into her neck, she gets excited, and I use this knowledge to my strategic advantage.

I have a surprise planned for her and she is trying to guess, but clearly has no idea. We have piled huge stacks of books and magazines in front of us, all the ones I've been meaning to read but haven't had a chance to. The flight attendants keep stopping to examine our towering media piles, picking up Ellen DeGeneres's book and saying "Oh, she's so funny!" before heading on their way. When the drinks cart arrives, I ask for a water and a tomato juice, and some ice. When they ask Kiki if she wants ice, I nudge her and she says yes. I'm delighted when our drinks arrive with not one but two cups of ice each – perfect! She still doesn't know my plan, and is pestering me with questions, so I finally whisper her mission to her.

There is an "iced T-shirt" contest coming up at a local play party month. "I want you to enter it, and wear that shirt that clings to your tits, but first, I want you to practice your nipple icing skills, right here, right now." She gives me a big grin and says: "You're fun," agreeing immediately. As quickly as possible, I grab a piece of ice and slide it into her bra, hoping that no one around us has noticed. I do the same for the other nipple, and watch as a stain quickly spreads across her top. I don't linger and rub them into her nipples for fear of getting caught, but can tell by the way she squirms that the ice is having its intended effect. Every fifteen minutes or so, I slide more ice into her shirt, and we try to cover our giggles. Even once it melts, her nipples are prominently visible through her shirt, the wetness giving her a look at odds with the rest of her put-together appearance.

Later, we spread most of the magazines across her lap strategically, so when I slide my hand under her skirt nobody will notice. The guy sitting by the window is preoccupied with his computer and the other passengers are watching their TV sets, so I have time to slide her panties aside and slip two fingers inside of her, while trying to move my arm as little as possible. The magazines teeter but stay in place, and I hope that I'm the only one who can hear the way her breathing has changed as she gets wetter. I bend my wrist as well as I can from my seat, not able to enter her as deeply as I'd like, but teasing her nonetheless, stroking the entrance to her cunt and playing with her clit. I stop after only a few minutes, knowing that this warm-up will make her ready for much more later.

As we exit the plane, after gathering all of our stuff, one of the flight attendants gives us a knowing look and says, "Be good, girls," a twinge in her voice letting us know that she has a clue that we haven't been exactly "good" up to this point. We smile and exit. The plane ride is only the start of our public sex . . . but Kiki doesn't need to know that . . . yet.

Standard Bearer

Alanna James

I'm not sure I did love her, but she was one hell of a fuck. Annabelle was every professor's dream: a beautiful student who both wants to suck your dick from under your desk and turns in excellent essays on time. My colleagues in the English department had turned a blind ear to her muffled groans.

"Annabelle not with you today, eh, Douglas?" Roger, my assistant, asked, looking somewhat hopefully about my office. "Only I wanted her to do some research for me." You only wanted her, I thought, not disguising my smug grin.

"No, I've not seen her since Tuesday," I replied quite truthfully, recalling with perfect clarity the last moment I saw her. What a shame to have laid waste to such a nubile body!

"Ah, is that how it is?" Roger smirked. "I heard about that."

"Mmm." I pretended to busy myself with the marking on my desk until Roger went to bother someone else. I didn't want anyone to see how angry Annabelle's indiscretion had made me.

As a little reward for making it halfway through the day without murdering anyone, I got an ice cream from McDonald's at lunchtime. I ate it on the way back to George Square filled with regret. Back at my desk I tried to think of an excuse to call the plump blonde who was failing English 101 into my office. If I didn't get laid soon everyone would start dropping grades.

Annabelle, now she never needed to fuck for a mark. With indulgently long legs, a mane of fiery red waves and teeth that bucked out in just the perfect way for cock-sucking, she could have sailed through even without her keen literary mind. We bonded over a shared love of literature, sealing our lust first with a frantic fuck next to the foreign translations in the university library. My zipper pulled down, dick hidden beneath her flippy little skirt, her knickers forever lost beneath the shelves. We stopped when the books started falling around our heads, and I had to wait before I could fill that ever-juicy cunt with my come. Annabelle definitely had a cunt, not a sweet pussy, not a clinical vagina. A hungry, wet, snarling cunt, with fleshy, ruby creases and a seemingly endless chasm. Just thinking about it makes my cock ache.

We'd toured Auld Reekie, taking in all of the city's literary highlights. I think Rabbie Burns would have approved of the midnight tryst next to Deacon Brodie's Tavern. Oh yes, everyone knows old Deacon inspired *Dr Jekyll and Mr Hyde* but few know Burns once lived on that same spot on the Royal Mile. We did it in the rain, waiting for the dead of night when none would see us up against the pub wall. Annabelle's breath reeked of the wee dram we had to toast the great poet, and I splashed the rest of the whisky over her mound. She said it burned; I said it tasted good and buried my tongue deep into her hairy furrow, thrusting it like a shaft until she came calling my name. Afterwards she licked sharp whisky from my cock before I drove into her from behind. I swear that girl barked with need.

"Professor?" I was pulled from my reverie by Jeanie from admin knocking on my office door. "I don't mean to disturb you but you're meant to be teaching now."

"Oh right, yes, I was just reminiscing about something." She smiled at me indulgently. All week people had given me such kind smiles, or satisfied smirks. Everyone knew about Annabelle's fling. With an *American Literature* student of all people.

Oh for better days. The time at the foot of Conan Doyle's statue. Binding Annabelle hog-tied with my belt and tie. Leaving her there for five minutes while I smoked a cigar in the gardens nearby. By God, and then there was *that* fuck in the Storytelling Centre. An old biddy reading from *Rob Roy*, stirring the blood of the public. I stroked Annabelle's cunt as she sat on my lap, my hand hidden beneath my coat. The guy in the next seat hid his own swelling dick as he sniffed her pungent juices drenching my hand. In the interval Annabelle and I fucked ever so quietly in a back corridor. Nae knickers that girl, at least not for long.

Why did she have to spoil it? Why couldn't she wait 'til I got back from the conference, why couldn't she satisfy herself for a mere week? Him, I don't blame, no one with any sense would have turned down those tiny, pert breasts, that mouth full of promise. But her, she knew she betrayed me. And how she taunted me with it. Her quick, loveless shag in the bathroom of the Elephant House café.

I gathered up my notes and made my way to the lecture theatre. This was my favourite topic of the term, "The Scottish Play". Like Lady Macbeth my hands are stained with blood invisible to all but me. I recalled the feel of Annabelle's lifeless form hanging limply in my arms, black-wrapped and taped up. Even then, I had felt my cock rise, semi-hard with memories of happier times. But you have to draw the line somewhere. I let the Waters of Leith swallow her whole.

Annabelle had finally stopped smiling as I brought the knife down upon her in my bed. Her blood was wetter even than her cunt. It had to be done though, despite the ruined sheets. Unlike Macbeth, not for ambition but for honour. Fuck anyone you want, I said, but *not* in the café where Harry Potter was written. One must have standards.

Lies

Kristina Wright

Let me tell you a lie. Let me tell you many lies and one truth. Let me tell you many truths and one lie. Will you be able to tell the difference by the earnest way I say the words or the soulful gaze in my eyes? Does it matter what is truth and what is lie as long as it feels good?

A man comes to my bed. A man who is not my husband and never will be. He is young and lean and dark and beautiful. His rich brown skin makes my skin, with its uneven beige tones and haphazard tan lines and orange-brown freckles and silver and mauve scars, look milk white, almost alabaster. I like the way his skin looks against mine; I like how my paleness is illuminated by his darkness, especially in the waning light of day.

Naked limbs entwined with his, I am beautiful and I have no desire to be any place else. He is where my desire lives. He is home.

He watches me, this man who I let into my bed. He lays there, watching me and absently rubbing his stomach. Dark eyes studying a woman he doesn't really know. Will never know because he has never wanted to know me.

"Tell me what you're thinking," he says.

I smile and tell him nothing. He doesn't believe me. It is, I think, the only thing he doesn't believe.

"Tell me what *you're* thinking."

I turn his words back on him, deflect his interest in me. It works. He tells me things I don't really care about. He knows nothing of the world, of love, of passion, of truth. His empty words splash against me like rain or semen, sitting on my skin until I wipe it all away, unaffected.

I listen and smile and stroke his stomach for him. Then lower, stroking his dick because that's what I want. He thinks I do it for him. I know I do it for myself.

This man is younger than me by more than a decade. That's more of a boy than a man. My boy-man. Mine, but not really. He could be with someone much younger, is in fact married to someone his own age. A woman as shallow as he is, as vanilla. His perfect match. Once, he pursued a relationship with me with such recklessness as to suggest he loved me. It's not love he seeks, I tell myself. It is wisdom, which I do not have, or maternal compassion, which I do.

Whatever he thinks he seeks in me, he also believes he finds, for he stays with me. Stays long after he should leave, stays even when I am carelessly cruel and taunting. I don't know why I hurt him, why I say such awful things. I am not an unkind person by nature, yet I am often heartless when it comes to him. It is as if his vulnerability, his trust, his youth, are too appealing to leave unscathed. I must scar him as I have been scarred.

He lies to me, my boy-man. Lies about everything and nothing. I know he lies and sometimes it makes me feel tender toward him. Other times, I want to slap him, hurt him. I scream his lies back at him, hate in my voice. I don't want the truth anymore, I just want him to be a better liar.

He says I intimidate him. He says he is scared to say the wrong thing, to tell me the truth. Maybe that's another one of his lies.

"I'm sorry, so sorry. I'm truly sorry." He begs and pleads and promises no more lies, and his apology is the biggest lie of all. "I love you too much to lie to you again."

He cheats on me, my boy-man. I know this truth in my heart, but he lies about that, too. I imagine I can smell other women on him when I take him to my bed. It arouses and disgusts me, makes me hate him and then hate myself for letting him do this to me. I tell him he can fuck whomever he wants, but he swears he only wants me. He lies. Always, he lies. And I feel my love slipping away just as surely as he has slipped his dick into some other woman and then lied to me about it.

He will never stop lying, this I know as surely as I know the feel and taste of him in my mouth. I slip down the bed and show him what love is.

"I love you," I whisper to his dick, hard against my cheek.

"Are you telling me the truth?"

Sometimes he catches me off guard – a flash of knowledge in his dark eyes. My heart races when I think he might finally realize I'm as big a liar as he is. Then I reclaim control.

"Why would I lie?" I counter, licking him into incoherence.

Dodge and weave and parry and spar. Be hurt, then hurt him back. Discover the truth, then fling it at him like daggers, trying to wound him as badly as he has wounded me. Using words like weapons; it's my art, my skill. It is what I'm best at, besides sucking his dick. His greatest skill is deception and my words and my heart are no match for his lies.

"I love you," he moans, eyes closed. In a moment of jealousy, I wonder who he is fantasizing about, how many women he is fucking. I suck him to prove myself worthy of his fantasy, of his passion, of his desire. Then there is only silence as I suck the only truth that matters from his body.

He pulls me up beside him when I finish, but he will not kiss my mouth. I taste like him and that makes him squeamish. I lean in and kiss his closed mouth anyway, ignoring his expression. I laugh and lick my lips. I can tell whether he's had juice for breakfast. Juice makes him sweet, just as kissing him after he's gone down on me makes his mouth taste sweet. Sometimes his mouth tastes sweet and I know it's not me. The sweetest lies come from a mouth that's been between another woman's legs.

This is the moment when I have the least interest in him. After he's come, when he's soft and warm like a kitten. I don't want this sleepy-eyed boy with the lopsided grin and grateful eyes who is already thinking about someone else if he was ever thinking about me, I want a man with demanding hands and a rough voice. A man who knows how to get into my head and spin me around until I don't know which way is up. I never lose my balance with my boy-man. I never lose myself. I hate him for that. He is so caught up in spinning his lies that he doesn't have time to spin me around.

He touches me in the growing darkness. Eagerly, a little awkwardly, like a child seeking a puzzle piece for its shape rather than the bit of picture it reveals on its glossy surface. Shape found, he sighs; rounded, soft, wet.

He fondles me silently and his silence is both reverential and irritating. I want him to pull my hair and spank my ass and talk dirty to me. I want him to hold me down and fuck me hard. Instead, he strokes my clit gently, like a worry stone. It's enough, for now. I ignore the cravings my body will never know with him, staring at his closed eyes and wondering who he imagines he is touching. I would fantasize about someone else like he does with me, but he is my fantasy. Always.

His lies have seeped into my bones and skin, into my brain and heart, stealing away all that I could have given him if only he had given himself to me. Poisoning me so that these fleeting moments are the only time I can forget what he has done, is doing, will continue to do. Lie. Lie. Lie.

He touches me just so and it is my voice that fills the shadowy room. He slides two fingers inside me and strokes my clit with his thumb. I gasp, fingers digging into the mattress, wetness trickling on the sheets. Giving up the smallest piece of me, all I'm willing to give him anymore. In that moment, his age becomes irrelevant. His fingers, my pussy. Orgasm. Nothing else matters. Not truth, not lies, not love or hate. Not my past or his future. Nothing matters at all.

Do you believe me?

The Kissing

Robert Buckley

She held tight to his arm as they made their way between the slots and gaming tables.

"Stop here," he said. Amid the din and flash of the adult play-pen that was a Las Vegas casino, his ears caught the sound of dice tumbling along felt.

"I'll bet this guy's next throw is snake eyes."

"Oh, yeah?" She grinned. "What's the bet?"

"Open-ended. I win, you do whatever I want; you win, I do whatever you want."

She leaned into him until her lips were just a shadow's width from his ear. "I don't think I like the sound of that," she whispered.

"What, are you chicken? C'mon, he's getting ready to throw."

"Oh, all right. You're on."

The dice tumbled. The resulting groan advertised the result.

"Damn," she said. "I swear you're clairvoyant."

"You owe me."

"Oh, nuts. Owe you what?"

"Tell you what – I'll give you a choice. You can step out of your little black dress right here, sling it over your shoulder and sashay over to the bar in your undies and order a drink."

"Those *undies* that you insisted I wear tonight don't leave much to the imagination. What's my alternative?"

"We go back up to our room and you let me kiss you."

She thought about it until finally he prodded, "Well, what's it going to be?"

"I just never understood this fascination of yours about exposing your wife to strangers."

"So, you're going to slip out of your dress?"

"You said you'd take me to a show and dinner tonight. You know I won't be in any shape to do anything after one of your kissing sessions."

"OK . . . then I think I'm going to enjoy the hoots and whistles and comments on your pretty derrière."

"I could get arrested – have you thought of that?"

"Girls don't get arrested in Vegas for going around mostly naked. Heck, they'll probably offer you a job."

"You can be so smug. Damn, let's go back to the room. But I was really looking forward to a show."

"We have the whole week. I promise you, I'll show you a good time. It's just, we were so busy getting ready for the trip, and the damned flight was delayed – I missed you. I missed touching you."

She took his hand. "Christ, I let you get away with murder."

She turned them back toward the elevators. *Kissing* – they called it that, but it was as far removed from a simple lip-lock as one could imagine. He'd performed it on her the first time when they were in college and barely knew each other better than to say "Hi" in the dorm corridors.

She suffered from migraines then, fierce, nausea-inducing pain, as if someone had stabbed her through the eye with an icicle. No amount of comforting could help, and her dorm mates learned to steer clear of her during an attack.

He passed her open door during one spell and heard her crying. "I can help you with that, but you'll have to trust me. I'll have to undress you too."

It was an outlandish proposal from the guy, but she was so desperate to be shed of the pain she abandoned all sense and caution and nodded her agreement. He was gentle about disrobing her, and then he started. The pain eased and then gave way to total relaxation. She didn't even remember him leaving, but slept through the day. Her roommates found her peacefully curled up under her bedclothes, but still naked.

Inside their hotel suite he pointed her toward the bedroom and said, "OK. Clothes off, get on your tummy."

She complied and a little tickle of anticipation squiggled through her belly. She lay on the bed and then he straddled her.

He began with her fingertips, sucking each one into his mouth, and then trailed his tongue along the undersides of her fingers and across her palm. Turning her hand over, he kissed the pale blue veins and suckled her knuckles between his lips. His mouth continued to journey along her arm at a snail's pace, kissing her elbow, and then nibbling the softer, fleshier places. Now, over her shoulders and the nape of her neck, nibbling her ears and kissing along her jawline, then he repeated the journey down her other arm.

A full half-hour had passed before he had reached a place just below her shoulder blades. His kisses were wetter now, his tongue tasting and savoring. He stopped to pay particular homage to places he called her "nuzzle zones", where soft, pliant flesh invited the brush of his nose, or chin.

By the time he had reached the small of her back, just above her tailbone, she could feel the moisture from her cunt leach into the bedclothes beneath her. She wanted him to fill her with his cock, but knew he wouldn't. It was excruciating, wonderful torture. She felt adored and devoured – tasted in square-inch morsels by a tongue, lips and teeth applied like tributes.

He'd reached her ass and her body was entirely at his disposal as she lay limp and simmering. His nips were more assertive and she moaned as another pinch of flesh was lifted and released, her skin left tingling from the grazing of his teeth. After each nip, a lick and a kiss.

He was past her buttocks now, adoring her upper thighs. She was whimpering by then, wanting something inside her to stem the flow of fluids oozing from her. But he was relentless.

She had lost all sense of time as his lips wet her ankles, and his tongue trailed around her foot, from instep to sole. He finished by sucking each toe in turn. She was limp – a rag doll. He didn't ask her to turn over, but gently flipped her as she moaned in protest. She shivered as her ass settled into the wet stain where her juices had leaked onto the bed.

"No more – please. Fuck me . . . I really need you to fuck me."

"Shhh, you know better than that."

He began his journey again, along her legs, stopping to prod her knees with his nose, climbing her thighs at a glacial pace.

Then he veered away from her pussy and the syrupy trickle that continued to feed the wet spot. He nuzzled her hips and then made love to her navel with his tongue.

"God . . . God . . . please, I can't take it . . ."

He reached her ribs, trailing his tongue along each valley between them. Now her breasts were beneath him – hard, insistent nipples red and inviting. A flush of pink spread over her chest, faded and reasserted itself. He took a nipple in his mouth and she cried, then his lips and tongue perambulated her breast as her breaths became pants. He paid equal homage to her other breast before moving up to her collarbone. A trail of kisses and then she felt the intrusion of his tongue in her underarm. She groaned again. Her frustration was building. Her cunt felt so empty. Then his lips were on hers and her tongue penetrated his mouth.

It was a duel, but she was no match for him. He ravished her mouth with his. Then he pushed himself up with his arms.

"Ready?"

"No . . . please fuck me."

"I don't think you could handle it."

Handle it? She was wired to explode.

Then his mouth was on her pussy, nibbling, licking – French-kissing her cunt. His tongue slithered around her clit. It tripped all her circuits and she came with a keening shriek. After the initial tremor, waves of sensations raced from her belly to her breasts. Her eyes rolled back and she floated in a warm dark place.

The tremors subsided, but she could only lie still, spent and drained, but still with an emptiness in her cunt.

"I wish you had fucked me," she rasped.

"Oh, I will, darling. Mercilessly."

"God, I can't move."

"Uh-huh, that's how I like my victims – helpless."

"You're such a bastard." She smiled and drifted on the edge of slumber.

A door knock teased her toward wakefulness. She heard the door to the suite open before she could react.

A young man's voice spoke. "Good evening, sir. You ordered room service?"

"Yes, thank you."

"I'll just set up your dinner and . . . Oh, my gosh – sir, I'm so sorry; I didn't see the lady when I came in."

All she could do was lie still and pretend to be asleep. It was her only defense against absolute mortification. She risked opening one eye just a slit and studied the embarrassed young man, who couldn't have been much older than twenty, through the open bedroom door.

"What a dunce I am," her husband said. "Totally forgot my wife was sleeping there. Poor thing was exhausted from the flight."

"Sir, I'm so sorry."

"Not to worry, young man. I'm very proud of my wife. She's pretty, isn't she?"

She tried to suppress a shiver as she peered surreptitiously at the young man. He stood still as a statue, his mouth agape, before he croaked, "She . . . she's beautiful."

"Well, thanks, I think I can take over from here. Here's something for your trouble."

The young man hurried out the door.

"You . . . you . . . pervert!" she stammered. "You deliberately let that kid in so he could ogle me."

A crooked smile crossed her husband's face as he stepped to the bed and sat next to her. "Yeah, I guess I am. You should be admired in men's eyes. But, not one of them will ever see you like I do."

Finally able to stir, she sat up and looked into his face. She kissed his mouth that had so thoroughly and magically seduced her, and would continue to seduce her. Then she pondered the grey hazel eyes, unfixed and unfocused.

She recalled the whispers from the guests at their wedding. "What a shame – she's such a pretty girl, and her husband will never see her."

She grinned. If a girl's lucky, she thought, some day a guy might look at her with lust in his eyes. But she knew what it meant to be worshipped – and adored an inch at a time.

Before Goodnight

Giselle Renarde

"Just about time for goodnight," Elson said, stifling a yawn. "Gotta be up early tomorrow."

Don't go. Not yet.

Kim's stomach clenched. She held her cell phone so close to her face the overwhelmed battery blazed against her cheek. It cost big money to talk on her cell, but she was always afraid of her parents picking up when she called him on the house phone.

To keep him on the line she whispered, "I would love to have you in my mouth right now."

"In your mouth?" Elson drew out each word, and Kim wondered if it was shock or disinterest. "Well, I guess I could make time for that."

"Any time, any place." She tried to sound sexy. Was it working?

"*Any* time?" He sounded dubious. "*Any* place?"

Her parents were right down the hall. God forbid they should hear her say such naughty things. Elson liked to tell Kim she was way too old to worry what her parents thought, but she would always be her father's daughter. Elson couldn't seem to understand that dynamic.

"*Any* place." She nodded, not that he could see her. "Any place, including the parking garage at your office."

Now Elson's throat made a growling sound, and she knew she had him. "Oh yeah. Remember that?"

"How could I forget?" Kim's heart raced with the memory. "Twice."

"Well, two different occasions."

"That's what I meant," she said. "I was so nervous. I thought for sure we were going to get caught."

"Which time?" he asked.

"Both times. I thought some security guard would come along and tap on the window like, 'I see you sucking that guy's cock there in the front seat. You think I'm blind?' I thought for sure . . ."

"But I was keeping an eye out." Elson's voice was low, deep and husky. He was turned on. She could feel it.

"You couldn't have been paying all that much attention if I was bent over your lap with your dick in my mouth."

Elson made a noise like his whole body was shuddering with pleasure. "God, I want to fuck you right now."

"Me too." A thought crossed Kim's mind, and she didn't want to tell him about it, but she couldn't help herself. She told him everything. "I can't do it without you any more."

"Do what?" he asked.

She breathed in and forced herself to say, "Get off."

He didn't say anything for a moment, and she savoured his ragged breath. "I'm sure you could psych yourself up with some nasty images of things we've done together. Remember the cucumber?"

Kim blushed. She'd forgotten about that. He'd even pulled the mirror down off the wall and handed it to her so she could watch that huge green phallus enter her slowly, stretch her wide, then fuck her hard. "Oh yeah . . ."

"You could try that on your own, describe it to me over the phone maybe?"

She knew he'd chastise her or tease her, but she told him even so. "I can't masturbate in this house. Ever since I moved back home I haven't done it."

Home. Could this house really be described as home if she wasn't free to be herself?

"Not once?" He didn't sound like he believed her.

"Not here."

She'd moved back in to save money so she and Elson could afford the down payment on their own place after the wedding. No more renting, no more apartments. Now she was itchy all the time, itchy for the freedom they used to have and didn't any more.

"If not there," he asked, "then where?"

Oh, she really didn't want to tell him this. "At work."

"At work?"

"In the bathroom at work." She felt like she'd swallowed cotton. It was embarrassing. "Only a couple of times. We hadn't been together in a while and I just needed it. Still not the same as having your warm body in my bed."

"Do you want my warm body in your bed?" His smirk was right there in his voice. "Just say the words."

Of course that's what she wanted, but what a person wanted and what was sensible were two very different things. Anyway, there were only so many times they could have that conversation where Elson asked, "Do you honestly believe your parents still think you're a virgin?" and she affirmed that they did. Really and truly, they did.

"Are you in bed?" Kim asked, swerving the conversation in a different direction.

"Not yet. Just sitting at the desk by the window."

She could picture Elson there in his little bachelor apartment. He'd be staring out at the city lights while she saw stars in the suburbs.

"Mmmmm." Kim closed her eyes and imagined. "I want to kneel between your legs right now, right there under your desk."

"Oh?" Elson growled and it made her shiver. "Not a lot of room under there."

"That's OK." She wasn't giving up. "I'm small enough. I'll squish in."

"I see."

He didn't sound very excited. Maybe he really was as tired as he'd spent their entire conversation saying he was. Or maybe he was lost in single-syllable male ecstasy.

"I'd get right in there and trace my tongue all around your cockhead, get you good and hard. Tease that fat red tip, tickle that little slit – you know the one – then run my tongue down your big thick shaft and lick your balls."

Elson hissed into the phone. Yeah, she was really getting to him now. "Suck 'em."

"Suck your balls, Elson? Is that what you want?"

"Oh yeah." Sex-voice. He wasn't even Elson any more, just a big throbbing cock. "Suck 'em both at once."

"I don't know if I can. They're so big. You really think I can get them both into my hot, wet little mouth?"

"You've done it before."

"And I'll do it again." Kim smiled so hard her jaw hurt. "But you know I'm here to suck your cock. You know I want to deep-throat that fat shaft, just throw my face at your dick until my eyes water. I want you so deep in my throat I'm gagging and begging and banging my head on the underside of your desk. That's what I want to do to you, babe."

"Awww fuck . . ."

"Yesssss, Elson. I love taking your big cock in my mouth. I love sucking that monster and hearing you moan and groan and growl."

Elson made a noise that sounded like all three.

"Hey, remember that time we watched porn on your computer, right at that desk where you're sitting right now? You had me in your lap with your fingers all over my pussy lips. Remember how I'd just shaved them?"

"Oh yeah." The thick lust in Elson's voice made her pussy clench. "You look so hot like that, when you shave your pussy."

"God, watching porn with you made me so fucking wet. Seeing it right in front of me, feeling your heat so close – that got the juices flowing before you even touched me. And then when you did I was so ready. I was so hot and wet and throbbing I just about came the second you started stroking my clit. Remember how fat and red it was, just begging for your touch?"

"Fuuuuuuck . . ."

"Remember how you sucked my tits while you played with my pussy? I loved it when you finger-fucked me. It was so raw. And then you slathered my clit in all that hot pussy juice. You spanked my cunt and your hand made that wet slapping sound against my baby-smooth skin? You remember that?"

"Yesssssss . . ."

Elson's breath hitched and Kim knew he was about to come already. His voice was so strained, so tight, like every muscle in his body was taut, tense, rigid and ready to burst.

"Remember how loud I was that time? My orgasm just took over my body. You sucked my tits and smacked my clit, and I came screaming. You made my knees weak, and I slid down your thigh, right to the floor. That was crazy, that climax. I'd never felt anything like it."

The squeals and whines were barely audible any more. She strained to hear him coming, but Elson was halfway across the city and off in another world. And then the tension broke and he howled.

"Oh yeah." He was so loud she worried her parents would hear. "Fuck yeah, baby, fuck yeah!"

Kim closed her eyes and watched the jizz explode from his cock, landing hot on the underside of his computer desk. She saw it drip down onto the floor. Next time she was over she'd have to look for it, see if he'd cleaned it up. He wouldn't have. She knew that.

And then the quiet came back. He sighed, and she could see the night sky in his voice.

"We've done so much together." Kim listened to him breathe for a moment. "It's hard to remember it all, but every so often little pieces come back, and they always make me smile."

"Me too." He was smiling now. She could hear it. "Thanks for . . . talking."

Kim chuckled deep in her throat. "Thanks for . . . listening."

They were quiet together, until Elson yawned.

"Sorry for keeping you up so late, babe."

"Mmmmm." Elson yawned again. "If I didn't have to sleep I'd talk to you all night."

"But you do need to sleep."

"So do you."

It was time . . .

"Yeah." Kim couldn't deny it. "Work in the morning."

Quiet again. It stretched for miles, all around. "I love you forever."

"I love you too." She hated saying goodbye. It was a dagger every time. "Night night, babe."

"Sleep tight."

"Don't let the bedbugs bite." She didn't want to say it. She didn't want to hang up, but she could barely keep her eyes open. Anyway, they'd talk again in the morning. That was some consolation.

"Goodnight Kim."

Her heart clenched, and she nodded. She wanted to cry! This was ridiculous. She was acting like a child, keeping him hanging on like this. Keeping him waiting.

"Goodnight," she finally said, though that one word just about killed her.

She waited for him to hang up, and when he did tears welled in her eyes. Those hot nights together seemed so far in the past, and wedded bliss so far in the future. She wanted everything now. The waiting was torture

But she kissed the phone, as she did every night, and set it on the bedside table, and turned out the light

Bloom Formula

Dominic Santi

"Good soil makes for good plants, Richard."

Karen tossed another twenty-pound bag of orchid mix on the greenhouse floor. Her tall, willowy body belied a surprising strength. Feminine biceps flexed beneath the slightly damp, light blue T-shirt that clung to her small, firm breasts. Faded denim hugged her firmly rounded bottom. The curl at the tip of her long, golden brown braid slid over the back of her jeans as she bent. This morning, I'd decided the time had come to see if she was interested in letting me loosen that ever-present elastic hairband and find out if her freed tresses caressed her bare bottom as tenderly as my fingers would. I was sixty-one years old and falling like a schoolboy for a woman who, even at thirty, looked considerably less than half my age.

"Your cymbidiums are going to wow them," she said, standing and dusting her gloved hands decisively on her backside.

"Our cymbidiums," I laughed, turning quickly back to the waist-high potting bench. With the rather embarrassing protrusion in the front of my slacks safely out of sight, I poured a carefully measured dose of bloom formula into the soil in a small, hand-thrown ceramic pot.

I was amazed at how quickly Karen and I had developed an easy, comfortable relationship, first as avid orchid fans, then as friends. We'd met at the gardening shop where she worked evenings. She'd described herself as "opinionated, not pushy" when she'd suggested I try a new all-organic growth food for my prize-winning cymbidiums. I'd demurred as politely as I could. I'd been raising orchids for years without the assistance of a woman who looked like a college student. However, when she'd found out I was donating them anonymously to the city's pink ribbon fund-raiser in memory of my late wife, her tone had quickly changed to "strongly advise" then to an insistent "my treat!" as she stuffed the container of turquoise crystals into my bag.

While I shared her sentiments about the event, I'd had strong reservations about the store's products. A month later, however, I stopped back to thank her. My trial pots with her formula were doing noticeably better than the rest – stronger stalks, greener leaves, more lustrous creamy pink petals with deep rose interiors.

My offer to continue the conversation over coffee had led to dinner, then to her joining me the next three Saturday afternoons, taking time from her master's studies to help me entice the plants to open exactly on time for the sale. The plants were thriving, and I'd started to get the hang of dating again.

Karen stepped up beside me, pulling off her work gloves. She leaned over to nod appreciatively at my work. The scent of her sage and citrus perfume filled my nostrils.

"This soil is beautiful. It's good, rich organic bark. Your moisture levels are staying perfect in these crowded pots. Do you have any idea how many people try to put orchids in the wrong size containers? Ones as big as that!"

She leaned further in, pointing towards an empty pot on the far side of the bench. Her braid brushed over my arm. My cock hardened almost painfully as a single loose strand of her silky hair tickled my nose. I reached up to scratch. Karen caught my wrist.

"Let me. You'll get splinters." She tucked the errant strand behind her ear. I waited motionless as she scratched the tip of my nose with just her index finger. Her small, soft breast pressed warmly into my side. "Is that better?"

It felt so much better I was afraid I was going to embarrass us both, not that my face wasn't flushed hot already. Karen kept scratching, her eyes twinkling as she plastered herself thigh to chest against me. She wriggled – softly, then more insistently, her smile growing broader as my cock filled with a rush so intense I almost lost my balance. Growling, I wrapped my arms around her and hugged her to me.

"You're driving me crazy, woman!"

"I hope so," she laughed, rubbing her soft, warm belly against my raging hard-on. "I know you're being a gentleman, Richard. But for the record, I'd rather you move towards me rather than this stupid bench when you're turned on."

"Like this?" I cupped the luscious curves I'd been lusting after and pulled her closer.

"Just like that." She ran her fingers through my hair. Her lips brushed sweetly over mine, then her warm, sweet breath whispered in my ear. "Let's get naked."

Karen stepped back and pulled her shirt over her head. I hadn't thought my cock could get harder. I was wrong. Delicate wisps of see-through lace cupped her firm, creamy breasts. Her small, rosy nipples were stiff with arousal. My fingers shook as I touched her, the dirt from my hand leaving a clearly defined print on the dainty lace.

"Here?" My greenhouse walls were glass, though I doubted any of the neighbors could see in. Regardless, I was damn near beyond caring.

"What could be more natural than making love surrounded by living, growing plants?" She toed off her sneakers, then shimmied out of her jeans and socks. A scrap of white lace covered the neatly trimmed thatch between her legs. She pulled her hair band free, running her fingers through her tresses until they fell in a silky curtain around her. Then her hand was cupping me, her strong, feminine fingers rubbing my cockhead through the wet fabric of my boxers.

"Remember when I said I was opinionated, but not pushy?" Her fingers stroked firmly up my shaft.

I nodded, groaning as she pressed another drop from me.

"Sometimes, I'm pushy." Her fingers were at my belt, then my zipper. My pants hit the floor with a clank. She yanked down my underwear and dropped to her knees. Her hands were warm and soft. Her tongue snaked out, long and pink.

"Mmm."

My knees damn near buckled. Her mouth was hot and wet. She sucked and laved until I grabbed the bench, gasping.

"I'm going to come!"

Karen leaned back, her lips glistening as she smiled up at me. "I sure hope so!"

Her hand darted into her pants pocket. With a quick tear, the wrapper was open, and she was rolling a condom over me. The shock of latex on my cock was almost as intense as the heat of her hand. I couldn't remember the last time I'd worn a rubber!

Then Karen was on her feet, quickly draping her shirt over the scattered potting soil on the bench. In one smooth movement, she was on her back, her legs open, her slippery labia shimmering – at the same height as my crotch. She guided me in with her hand, then lay back and scooted her bottom to the edge of the bench. She hooked her heels into my backside, tightening her inner muscles as she pulled me deep. The scent of her pussy and the music of her laughter were almost as glorious as the hot, milking spasms sucking my cock with each deep thrust.

We didn't last long. Karen writhed beneath me, bucking and yelling so loudly my ears rang. She came so hard the bench shook. I was seconds behind her, erupting into her as the scent of our loving blended with the smell of the dirt and plants around us. I fell forward, leaning shakily on my elbows, fighting to catch my breath. Karen's hair was a glorious tangle beneath us.

"I could get used to this." Smiling, she tenderly wiped a trickle of sweat from my brow.

"I could, too." Grinning, I cupped her breast in my hand and stroked her nipple with my thumb. The tip stiffened immediately, her pussy trembling over my cock. I kissed her gently on the lips. "We're going to make beautiful orchids together."

Inked

Kathleen Tudor

There was a buzz behind me, a long, fraught hesitation, and then I felt the tattoo needle bite into the flesh above my left shoulder blade. I barely kept from crying out, more in surprise than actual pain. I'd picked a large tattoo for my very first one, and I hadn't been sure how much it would hurt. For now, the burning was a manageable sting, like someone drawing the edge of a very fine blade across my skin.

The chair I sat in was like a mall massage chair, designed so that you could sit at an angle – leaning forward against a padded rest with your head on a cushion. I dug my fingers into the padding, begging silently for him to move on to another spot, and closed my eyes.

"Just try to breathe deep and normal," he said from behind me. "Don't try to hold your breath. Just relax. In and out. There you go."

His voice was a soothing baritone that helped me ease my grip on the seat, even if I didn't let it go entirely. He removed the needle to dip it back into the ink, and I took the opportunity for an extra deep breath. "Let me know if you need to stop. I'm starting again, OK?" He kept up a running commentary of his movements, letting me know before he touched the needle to my skin as if he were aware that I needed the extra reassurance, and something about his voice soothed me, warmed me.

It had been my boyfriend's idea to get a tattoo, but we had only just picked out the matching set of skulls that I was half sure I was going to regret when I caught him in bed with my roommate. I should have been mad at her, I guess, but mostly I was relieved that I had found out what scum he was before I let someone put that stupid skull on my arm.

I had decided to get my own tattoo – as a mark of freedom, independence and wisdom, or maybe just of stubborn pride – about six months later. I'd chosen the owl, since they symbolize wisdom and they seem pretty damn free. A realistic owl's face, peering out from my shoulder blade, watching my back and reminding me to watch my own. I've always thought they were so beautiful.

I bit my lip as the needle dug into a spot just over the bone, saw stars, and reminded myself to breathe. I had expected it to hurt more, but what I hadn't expected was the torture of the prolonged, low-grade pain. It wasn't so bad in any one spot, at least at first, but it moved over and over the same places like a sandblaster, scraping my skin raw and then coming back for more. And worse, there was no way to brush it off, chafe the skin with my hands, or work the muscles to help ease the discomfort.

I finally couldn't take it anymore. I lifted my right arm enough to signal that the artist should stop, and he immediately pulled the needle away from my skin, letting me stand and swing my arms. I was naked from the waist up, but he didn't stare and I was too sore to care about it anyway, so I just moved, twisting my neck and rolling my shoulders to try to ease my angry nerves.

"We can stop for today, or we can just take a break and keep on," he said. I was the last appointment of the day, and though we were alone in the shop, he'd assured me that he would work on my owl as long as I could handle it.

"I want to try to get it finished," I said. It hurt, but I wasn't sure I could talk myself into coming back for more if we left it half done.

"You could try getting some chocolate. Help get those endorphins flowing. Do you have an MP3 player? We could get you rockin' to some of your favorite 'happy place' music."

"I like what you've got on," I said, and I did. He was playing my usual radio station in the background. "Maybe just some water, and then we'll try some more. I think I'm OK now."

This time it was easier to ignore, somehow. I focused on my

breathing, letting myself drift away on the steady in and out, ignoring everything else going on around me as I focused intently. But eventually that irritating buzz and the stubborn burn crept back into the corners of my consciousness. I waited for the needle to lift and squirmed in my seat, and for the first time I realized that my clit was tingling, crying out for my attention or perhaps for relief.

I tried to be subtle as I shifted my right hand into my lap, then pressed my fingers gently against my clit. It awoke with a glorious sizzle, distracting me from everything but the burning need to coax pleasure from my body.

"Try to hold your hips still," he whispered behind me, and I knew that he knew exactly what I had done, and that it hadn't fazed him. I nodded my head and with my right hand carefully undid the button and zipper on my jeans. He breathed in deeply, but showed no other signs of hesitation or reaction. The line of pain continued, steady and sure-handed on my shoulder.

My hand slid slowly into my satin panties and I struggled not to shudder as my fingers found the wetness within. I let out a deep breath, wrapped my left arm hard around the chair, and tried to keep my back as still as stone while I explored my wet folds. My fingers roamed down to my hole and back up again, teasing through my fleshy folds and sending waves of pleasure through my body, though I somehow kept from shifting in my seat.

I maintained the slow stroke for a couple of minutes, letting my fingers grow slippery and wet as I teased, avoiding my clit. When the burn of the needle gun intruded on my pleasure again, I took things one step further. I slid my fingers up, carefully holding my hips still even as my breathing deepened and my arm started to quiver with the erotic tension that sizzled through my veins.

My left hand tightened on the back of the seat as the ride got more and more engaging. Soon the sound of the needle was a distant hum and the sounds of my whimpers drove me onward and upward, ever closer to ecstasy. The artist's large hand planted gently but firmly in the center of my back, holding me as still as possible as I used my right hand to rub and pinch and pluck at my sensitive bud.

When I was only seconds from orgasm, I felt both the restraining hand and the buzzing, stinging gun lift from my skin. The orgasm shook through me, and I let the shudder rack my entire body, arching back slightly as pleasure washed over me; when it drained away, leaving me satisfied and limp, the pain vanished with it.

I panted for a moment and, as my breathing calmed, I heard the buzzing return, though I could hardly feel the needle on my skin. I let myself drift on the memory of that pleasure, my awareness far from the present moment.

"There, done." His deep voice shook me out of my own head, and I jumped.

"Already?"

He laughed and gave me a moment to fasten my pants as he wiped down the ink and positioned me in front of a mirror, giving me a second one to hold up to see my back. "I'm glad you found your endorphins for that last hour," he said. He smiled and there was no leer in his eyes when I looked up, embarrassed.

An hour? I held the mirror up high and looked into the eyes of my owl. "Gorgeous," I breathed. I smiled at my artist as he bandaged the fresh ink. "Tattoos aren't so bad. I think I actually kind of enjoyed it."

Don't Struggle

Valerie Alexander

"You know I wouldn't really hurt you." This is what I said to you in the bar and then again on the phone when we were designing our assignation. Now I say it a third time, and that's magic, in the park where we're conducting our first scene. The words expedite the hemp rope I'm tightening around your wrists. It's knotted just a little too tight, tight enough to leave marks I can sign with my tongue tomorrow in a café, in a way that looks like I'm kissing your hand. So romantic, the women in the other booths will say. But the only romance here is you surrendering up your will to me along with your underwear and your earrings and your trust.

I remember the first time I said those words to someone else. Tying a girl in my calculus class to a playground jungle gym, drunk on a windy March night, her laughter fading as she realized this dare was going farther than expected. Cuffing my college housemate to the bathroom pipes and leaving her like that for our other housemates to find, panties around her knees with her pussy showing and her face scarlet like the exhibitionist she always wanted to be. It's what I always say. I mean it in the sense that my volunteers interpret it; *no physical harm will come to you*. Shaking up their psyche, though, rattling their ego and cutting my name into their heart is a different story. I make no promises about that.

You clear your throat and force a smile. Your nervousness is my tenderness. I smooth your long dark hair back, the strands that have escaped from your ponytail, and hook them over your ears. Your ear lobes are reddish where your earrings were fastened too tight and it makes me think about you primping in front of the mirror this evening, admiring maybe your softness, your lack of cynicism and your willingness to believe that wolves have good intentions even though you are the most beautiful little lamb to ever enter a forest alone. This isn't actually what you admire about yourself, of course. It's what I admire in you.

"Lift your arms up over your head."

You look confused for just a moment – your wrists are tied in front of you – before obeying. This arches your back and thrusts your breasts forward. It's obvious from your face that the position embarrasses you. You're always embarrassed by the hedonism that is your body, the peach-soft pillowy tits, thighs and ass you possess in such abundance. You are a walking spectacle of comfort and sex. Everyone wants to fuck you. But right now you are mine and only mine.

The sound of an engine on the access road makes us both pause. We're trespassing here in the state park at just past midnight, but my car is well concealed and the risk of discovery is slight. The motor fades off into the night. No one is around to help you should I begin violating you. Probably someone sensitive would start with you in your bedroom, binding you up in your own environment so you could look around at your furniture for reassurance. But I wanted to shove you off a cliff so I could catch you and win your trust. You've been down this road before with the wrong people. At the time the wrong people sounded exciting but you found out they weren't, that wrong can just mean misery, and you started questioning your dreams of submission and then you met me.

So here we are in the dark and the trees where just the rustle of the leaves makes you shiver. I've taken off all your clothes except the short plaid skirt I made you wear. Your nipples are stiff, your legs are spread and your brown doe eyes are filled with a question. You want to know if I can make it happen for you the way it feels in your head. I scratch my nails down your tits. Your moan shudders through you. This is what I saw in you when we met, that you were no performer or kinkster poseur but a bomb of sensation waiting to be set off. I stretch your perfect nipples out one by one, then bite them hard enough to make them swell tomorrow. You wince and twist, your heels digging in the dirt. I run my nails hard down the tender insides of your thighs. You look so beautiful with long red welts on your skin. My exotic pet to cage and fuck and pamper.

"Please," you say in a tiny voice.

I grip your ponytail in my fist. "Did I say you could speak?"

You shake your head, dark eyes large with fear or excitement or both.

I reach under your skirt and slap your pussy, clean and sharp. You jerk, then moan. I spank it again and again until you're squirming and biting your lip, rocking your hips toward my hand. And then I stop.

"Stand still. Do *not* move."

I finger your tiny, swollen clit, watching you for any sign of movement. I'm picturing you crawling across my kitchen floor naked to present me with your willing pussy. I'm imagining you tied up in front of a roaring fireplace with my underwear in your mouth. Welts on your thighs and your lips swollen from where I've kissed and bitten them for hours. Your tits bound in the stockings I tore off you earlier, dark pink nipples flushed and hard. You're going to be my perfect slave.

Your legs are rigid with the effort to stay immobile. I kiss your mouth. "Good girl. You're going to obey me and do whatever I say, aren't you?"

You nod. I stroke your cunt again.

You're so wet under the skirt. When I breathe in the smell of you mixed with the smell of your shampoo, lust hits me like rush of drugs in my bloodstream and I start squeezing you everywhere. I grab cannibalistic handfuls of your ass and thighs, I rip out your elastic and fill my hands with your hair. And then I'm slapping your tits, biting your mouth, and you're crying and begging for it in a wordless kind of plea. I clench your hair in my fist and force your legs wider apart to finger you. Your pussy melts around my hand like molten honey. You're really struggling against the rope now, panting raggedly, and as soon as I play with your clit, you come gushing and throbbing around my fingers.

I smear it over your mouth. "You just came like a little whore," I tell you. Then I kiss you, deep and tender and romantic, because I want you to understand that we're in this together. That when I degrade you, I do it with love.

* * *

In some ways dominance is a long con. I fly under radar, my agenda obscured by my benevolence. I had a black kitten once; he had this plaintive mew that melted my heart and I was so charmed that I taught him to do it by giving him his favorite treat. I mean, of course, that he trained me and I was so enchanted with his softness and purr that it was a surprise one night to turn from the treat cupboard and see the mercenary calculation in his eyes. Every captive becomes a strategist.

I don't own you tonight. Everything you're drowning in, euphoria, self-congratulatory rebellion, is all self-contained. The little dependencies will creep out later, like vines with a mind of their own, so quietly you won't notice. Not like with the wrong ones. I'm the good one, the delivery and the dream, the one who came on your face and respected you in the morning. The one who makes your boundaries dissolve like fog until you're dissolving into me. It's already begun, your legs shaking and your dazed eyes looking at me like an astronomer discovering a new planet. I'm the one who makes you feel safe. I'm the wolf who can untie you and hug you goodbye, and hours after you leave, you find you're still bound.

Miami Meet

A. F. Waddell

Loud print shirts and thin tank tops became moist against many-hued skins as people teemed through humidity. On the sidewalks and boardwalks people moved through neon and harbor lights, some men quiet, some catcalling. In response some women preened, corrected their posture, and licked their lips. Others smiled and giggled and looked down at the sidewalk. Others were more firmly expressive. Are you talkin' to me? Shut the fuck up.

Physical appearance could be deceptive. Carefully honed perfection manifested in throngs wearing thongs. Gods and goddesses cruised for Eros, yearning for entities with which to collide.

Existing near a business and residential divide in a touristy ambiance of bars, restaurants and gift shops, the small decrepit bar Mob Scene had been through more name changes than a gold-digger. It smelled of tobacco, old cooking grills, and the assault of colognes and perfumes. The ancient bar was wooden – pitted and scratched. The deep wooden shelving behind the bar displayed a vast number of bottles that seemed to defy organization.

The woman sat at the bar staring into her merlot. Perspiration slightly melded with her ivory make-up. Pink lipstick stained her wine glass. Her long flame of wavy hair rested against her light silk blouse. She turned her head and flipped her hair to cool her neck. A tall man came into her line of sight, framed by the entrance door, walking and dodging the crowd, before sitting down at the bar next to her. The man and woman glanced peripherally at one other.

"Do you come here often? Oh! I can't believe I said that! My name is Simone, by the way."

"Hello, Simone. It's nice to meet you. I'm Jake. And no, I don't come here often. Do you?"

"No."

"Originally I happened to stumble onto this place. I was lost. Wait, I wasn't lost. I was simply in a place other than the intended one."

"You're not very bright, are you? I like that in a man."

"You just hit the mother lode, doll. Stupid? Dense? I've got them all."

"That's funny, you don't look dense. And don't call me 'doll'."

"Sorry. How about 'babe'?"

"OK."

Simone racked her brain for conversational tidbits. "You should see the wind chimes on my deck. When I hear them I think that it might mean a cool breeze. But it's always just more hot air."

"Really? Did you know that air flows from high to low pressure regions in a curved path? It's due to the earth's rotation and to the so-called Coriolis effect."

"Of course I knew that." Simone rolled her eyes. "Did you know that the boundaries of convection cells in the earth's atmosphere have sparse wind blowing along the surface? All the motion is up and down."

"Really? Up and down? Sounds fascinating," Jake teased. Simone's face flashed with anger.

"Come off it, babe. We both know why we're here tonight and it isn't to discuss the weather."

"Don't call me 'babe'."

"OK. How about 'hon'?"

"All right."

"You know, hon, if you don't want men to flirt with you, then maybe you shouldn't have chosen that ensemble."

"I don't know what you mean. It's simply a blouse and skirt."

"Simone, perhaps you shouldn't stylize that body."

Simone bolted from her seat, breezed past him and moved to a booth. *What did I say?* Jake shook his head. Bar patrons looked at him, dead-eyed.

"Women!" he exclaimed to the bartender. "Where's the men's room?"

"Straight back, and hang a right."

En route Jake took in the scene: the quiet older couples and the argumentative ones; the young people who flaunted themselves, believing in personal invincibility. His bladder ached in its fullness. He trekked to the men's room, negotiating a gauntlet of seeking eyes.

The men's room was small. Lack of adequate indoor lighting was intermittently illuminated by flashing white neon from the outside. The high crank window over the sink framed the incoming light as it played against green graffiti-covered stucco walls.

Jake entered a stall and closed the door. He unzipped his pants then meditated on the yellow stream.

"Nephrons in the kidneys filter the blood into urine. Waste products are then passed to the urinary bladder. Urine is amazingly antiseptic for a body waste," the voice informed him.

What the hell? He turned and opened the stall door. Simone stood facing him.

"I got yer nephrons right here." He held his cock and eyed the restroom door. *Locked.* Jake moved towards Simone; they moved backwards together, Simone against a wall. He pulled up her skirt, revealing her bare shaven cunt. He slightly lifted her and slid into her. They moved in flashes of light, bodies together and apart, in speed and contrast, cunt and cock a brilliant then dark nexus. A strobe effect caught eyes and mouths open and in grimace, in cries – body parts a view askew. A car horn went off, repetitively stuck. Skateboarders slammed their boards. Someone rattled the bathroom door handle.

The woman strolled from the rear towards the front of the bar. She'd pinned up her long hair; long wisps stuck to her skin. She'd repaired her make-up. Small aviator shades were perched on her nose. Her blouse and skirt were distressed and moist. Her spice and woods perfume was faded. Her pheromonal chemistry played the air. She thought of being ensconced between a cool wall and a hot man; of a cacophony of sound, moans and cries and seagulls and boom box salsa; of brilliant light and brain buzz and stars in her eyes. She walked aimlessly, fading in and out of alertness and her environs. A man slowly walked towards her, stopped and looked into her eyes. It seemed a violation. *Don't probe my memories. My thought balloons are private.*

A wary bartender eyed the clock and the crowd. "Last call, people!"

Jake ordered a brandy. He sat at the bar watching people pair off for hook-ups. Mob Scene began to clear out. The exodus of bodies moved towards the exits. He imagined a surreal Goldberg-esque factory machination of attraction and sex. *Bodies in. Atomization. Conveyance. Elements mix and remix. Steam, energy and sound of people and orgasm vent through whistling pipes. Pop! Cell reintegration. Bodies out. Vending box dispensation of small teddy bears imprinted with "Absolved! Have a nice day!"*

The bars closed at 2 a.m. A sea of bodies moved past cheap gift shops, pawn shops and liquor stores. Unsteady on their feet, couples wrapped their arms around each other's waist. Simone and Jake headed in opposite directions, blending in with the droves. People streamed from the bars onto boardwalks and sidewalks, in two-way linear progression. They branched out into curves and angles, perhaps a work in Satellite Social Studies with a British narrator, from a sky-view. Becoming more dispersed, the human trail trickled down to more isolated imagery, disappearing into vehicles and dwellings.

The bar smelled of tobacco, old cooking grills, and the assault of colognes and perfumes. The woman sat at the bar staring into her merlot. Perspiration slightly melded with her ivory makeup. Pink lipstick stained her wine glass. Her flame of wavy hair rested against her light silk blouse. She turned her head and flipped her hair to cool her neck. "Do you come here often?"

The Perfectly Inappropriate Dare

Destiny Moon

After class we gather at the Jolly Barrister, a dark little pub close to the law courts, where all of us legal types can let loose, toss back a pint and debate the ideas of the day. I'm just a student still, so my gang and I are seen as imposters, relegated to the back of the pub. We are watching, learning. Every now and then some junior lawyers grace our table with their presence and we get to experience, just for a moment, the feeling that our ideas matter. Today is one such day.

One of the juniors won a trial – his first – and he's making a big show of buying rounds. His buddies surround him and one of them, Simon, waves us over. It's a good day to be a girl.

The chatter gets wilder as the pitchers empty and are refilled and empty and are refilled. I am tipsy but nowhere near as bad as Simon, the guy who waved us over.

"Remember that debate we had about sex not changing things?" he asks out of the blue.

I remember it clearly. It was the first time the juniors invited us students to join them. We were big talkers back then, wanting not just to fit in but also to impress. I started it. We were discussing a case in which a lawyer argued that sex always changes a friendship and I disagreed – loudly. I boasted that I've had a number of one-night stands with people I know, and that many have been pleasant memories, not at all awkward.

"Sure," I say, hoping he isn't going to paraphrase my stance in front of everyone. As open-minded as I am, I still have to think of my professional reputation.

"I want you to prove it," Simon says.

"You what?"

"I want you to prove that you can have sex with someone and that nothing will change, because I don't believe you."

"Oh, really," I say, seeing right through his provocation. "And I suppose you want me to sleep with you to prove my thesis."

"In the interest of education and settling a debate, yes."

He winks at me and, despite his crass delivery, I feel a tingle. The fabric of my thong teases me as I shift my weight from one foot to the other. The sheer cockiness of his suggestion casts him as the bad boy who knows how to get his way with girls. Since as far back as I can remember, guys like this tease their way into my pants and I am grateful for it.

"Well, I am all for education," I say. "But name the terms of the experiment."

"We have sex and, if your thesis is correct, we should still be able to hang out together at the pub with no awkwardness whatsoever."

"What if we can't?"

"Then your thesis is incorrect. Shouldn't you have a little more faith in yourself?"

"Oh, I have a lot of faith in myself," I say, sounding defensive.

I feel something building inside of me: excitement. This dare is perfectly inappropriate. I walked right into it. Back out now and I lose the argument. Go for it and I win the argument as well as get to have sex with this delicious junior.

"You're on," I say. "Tomorrow evening after work. At the Hyatt. You're paying for the room."

"Why am I paying?"

"Neutral location is a must and you're the one who wants to see the experiment conducted therefore you are the investor," I tell him.

"Deal."

We shake hands. I leave soon thereafter, go home, shave my pussy bald and masturbate at the idea of a single sexy encounter with Simon. I'm brilliant. Not only do I get to experience him, I also get to avoid any kind of industry drama by avoiding all masquerade of a relationship. I sleep like a baby that night.

The following evening, I arrive at the Jolly Barrister ready for the challenge. Simon shows up and almost immediately, we are alone in a room at the Hyatt. Suddenly, this whole thing feels more awkward than it did in my fantasy.

"You know, you don't have to go through with this," Simon says.

"I do if I want to win the debate."

"Does being right really matter that much to you?"

"Come here," I say, clutching him by the shirt. He is nervous. There are little beads of sweat on his forehead. He isn't a bad boy as much as he is a clever one, an opportunist.

I shove him down on the bed and straddle him, ripping off his shirt as I kiss him. He moans and I make my way over his chest with my lips. My hands undo his belt. His pants loosen. I'm wriggling them off of him.

"Wait," he says. "I have to tell you something in the interest of full disclosure."

"Yes?"

There is a pause. I am waiting for him to tell me that he is either married or has an STD.

"Caroline, I like you."

"What?"

"It's a flawed experiment," he says. "I was just flirting with you when I suggested it. I didn't think you'd actually go through with it. I like you. I want us to date."

"Date? What the hell."

I did not see this coming.

The sight of him, his eyes, his vulnerability beneath me, his sincerity, all of it makes me stop and slide off of him, sit next to him on the bed. He takes my hand. My pussy is soaking wet and my heart is melting. It is a strange contradiction for me.

I am shocked to hear the following words leap out of my mouth: "I like you, too."

"Will you let me buy you dinner?"

I nod.

"Will you let me continue exploring you?" I ask. "In the interest of full disclosure, I should tell you, Simon, I am attracted to you. I think you are very sexy."

"You do?"

I nod.

I run my hand over his boxers, feel his penis, which is politely flaccid. I am hungry for it.

"Just because I accepted your dinner invitation doesn't mean dinner has to come first," I say in my most sultry voice.

I pull the boxers off of him. He gasps, surprised.

I take him in my mouth. Slowly, steadily, I feel him harden as I run my tongue up and down his shaft. I like the look of it, the feel of his cock in my mouth. I turn myself around, positioning my pussy near him. He follows suit by pulling my right leg over his face so that my pussy is spread open above his mouth. He licks my clit, moaning in delight as his tongue finds its way around my folds. I moan, deeply satisfied at the sensations he is creating in me.

We stay in this rhythm for a long while. I feel the intensity of orgasm build up inside me but I want to last a little longer. I dismount.

I run to my purse, pull out a condom, come back, take it out of the wrapping.

"Are you sure you want to?"

"Simon, if you want to date me do not deprive me of your cock. Do you understand?"

He nods.

"Good."

I put the rubber on him effortlessly. Then I straddle him. He shakes his head back and forth in disbelief.

"Oh my God. Oh my God," he mutters.

Slowly, steadily, I lower my pussy onto him. I feel his hardness inside me, this connection of desire, this overwhelming feeling of lust. It is intensified by knowing he wants more of this, more of me, knowing this is the first of many times. His body feels right. His cock the perfect fit for me. I writhe and moan, sliding myself up and down, up and down.

I take his hands in mine and guide them to my nipples.

"Pinch them," I say.

He complies. The sensation goes straight to my clit. I moan. I am desperate to come now. I arch myself forward.

"Suck on them," I order, shoving my nipples closer to his face.

He does exactly what I say.

As he takes each one into his mouth, alternating between them, I can feel myself reaching the threshold beyond which I cannot turn back. The slurping sounds he makes with his sucking pushes me further into ecstasy. I want him to witness the power I can emit when all of my sexual energy is funneled through my clit. Here it comes. No going back.

My muscles clench around him, tightening in spasms. Uncontrollably, I moan like I am in pain. My body writhes on top of him and just as I am about to collapse onto his chest, he lets out a loud cry. His facial muscles clench. I feel his cock throb inside me. He is covered in sweat. He takes hold of my hips so firmly that I feel as though he will leave hand impressions in my sides. He shoves his cock as deep into me as he possibly can. Then he lets out a massive sigh.

I collapse onto him and he holds me in his arms, instinctively touching the sensitive skin on my back. I am gooey and calm. His penis is still inside of me, still letting me have the occasional shudder as it, too, calms down. I can't keep my eyes open, resting on his chest.

Finally, I roll off of him. We are lying next to each other when he turns and lightly touches the skin on my arm first, then my face.

Silently, he mouths the word "wow". He leans over and kisses me, meticulous and slow.

My thesis may prove incorrect and, for once, I don't care. For once, I don't need to be right.

"What would you like for dinner?" he asks.

"Room service."

Velocity

Donna George Storey

Too much, too soon?

I stand outside the door of his hotel room and tie the scarf around my eyes. It's a strange way to meet someone for the first time. Not that Kyle is exactly a stranger.

Of course, a month ago I didn't even know he existed.

My college roommate introduced us. I was writing an article on the future of non-profits, and Heather knew someone up in Boston who specialized in grant writing. Good journalists never interview friends, but friends of friends will do in a pinch.

Kyle was helpful from the start. Beyond helpful. Over the next few days our business emails grew increasingly warm. When I saw his name in my in-box, my pulse quickened. Soon we were exchanging several messages a day, some lusciously chatty, some brief, but laugh-out-loud witty. By the end of the next week we knew all about each other's favorite meals, our third-grade teachers, our past lovers.

Sometimes I worried it was too much, too soon. I promised myself I'd wait a few days before I replied. And broke my promise within the hour.

When he let it slip he liked women in stockings, I couldn't resist firing back a photo an old boyfriend had taken of me wearing black thigh-highs. By return mail, he confessed he'd had a "visceral response" to it. His gentlemanly reserve amused me. Too much, too soon had sputtered into safe and slow.

Except two nights later I found myself caught up in a flirty chat session with him. I'm not sure why I told him all about a longtime fantasy I picked up from my brother's porn stash: a pictorial of a woman on a solo picnic, pleasuring herself in the open air, getting caught by a handsome stranger who made love to her on the grass. Kyle eased me into it so skillfully, I didn't even notice when we'd crossed another line.

KyleNeilson81: So you like picnics?

GTSloane422: As a matter of fact, I do. Maybe that's why, lol.

KyleNeilson81: Why do you?

GTSloane422: I like lying back on the blanket, gazing up at the clouds, feeling the warm sun on my skin.

KyleNeilson81: Now I want to go on a picnic with you.

GTSloane422: In a secluded place naturally ;)?

KyleNeilson81: Naturally. Would you wear a skirt for me?

GTSloane422: Sure. Underwear optional?

KyleNeilson81: VERY optional. Stockings would be nice tho.

GTSloane422: Men are so predictable.

KyleNeilson81: Are we?

GTSloane422: I can guess your plan.

KyleNeilson81: Maybe not exactly. First I'd ask you to

GTSloane422: You still there?

KyleNeilson81: I hope you don't think I'm a pervert, but

GTSloane422: Spit it out, please, I KNOW you're a pervert.

KyleNeilson81: I'd love to watch you touch yourself. Like you did when you looked at your brother's magazine.

My pussy clenched as if he'd squeezed it in his fist and, all alone in my office as I was, I let out a low moan. I simply couldn't lie when he asked if I was getting as turned on as he was, and before I knew it I *was* touching myself for him, wriggling out of my jeans and panties, spreading my legs to the edges of my chair.

I love watching you squirm and arch up as you play with your clit . . . touch your nipple for me now . . . flick it with your thumb . . . keep rubbing your clit . . . faster now . . .

Each new line flashing on the screen set me strumming faster, until I exploded in the most belly-wrenching, rocketing orgasm of my life.

How could a man I'd never met, who was nothing but words, have such power over me?

Things were moving *way* too fast.

I vowed then I'd spend at least twenty-four hours – no, a whole *long* weekend – away from the computer.

A quick check the next morning brought his email asking if we could Skype so he could share some good news. He had a business trip to DC the next week. Could we meet for dinner while he was in town?

My stomach did a somersault.

This was definitely too much, too soon.

But we'd always been frank, amused by each other's quirks. I admitted my biggest fear – that if I saw even a flicker of disappointment in his eyes when we met in person, it would be the death of a beautiful friendship.

"I've seen your picture. You're gorgeous," he said.

His voice was deep. It made me wet.

Then I told him my real test was his scent.

He laughed. "I'll be sure to take a shower."

I suggested it was better if he didn't.

So we planned it out together: meeting at his hotel room with me wearing a blindfold, then – assuming I looked fine and he smelled right – we'd move on to the restaurant like any ordinary couple on a first date.

And now here I am, standing outside his room at the Courtyard Marriott, smoothing my dress and fluffing my bangs over the blindfold.

I knock on the door.

It opens. I feel . . . warmth.

"Nice to see you, Gretchen." It's the same amused voice, but somehow smoother, like a caress.

I realize two things: I've forgotten to breathe and my panties are already soaking.

I imagine his eyes sweeping up and down over my body. I've purposely worn something revealing. The black thigh-highs underneath are my own private joke.

"Well?" I ask.

"You pass with flying colors," he declares.

I move forward to embrace him lightly, as friends do, but of course I linger to breathe him in: airports, a pleasant mix of salt and cumin. Like everything else about him, it's almost too easy. I hold up my hand.

"Could you suck my finger? It's clean. I have to like the way *I* smell with your scent on me, too."

He laughs, then obediently takes my index finger into his hot, wet mouth.

There's a soft *slurp* when I pull out. I sniff, as if I'm tasting wine. "Well?"

I'm so aroused I can barely stand. "I . . . I'm not sure."

"Need more data points?"

"I think so."

We step toward each other. It only seems natural to kiss. His flavor is complex, like wine – fruit and spice and secret ingredients I can't name. His arms tighten around me. His erection presses against my belly. I moan.

In a quick maneuver, he unzips my dress and yanks it over my hips as if he were peeling a banana. Then *he* moans and sinks to his knees, cupping my buttocks, kissing the band of naked flesh over the lacy tops of my stockings.

Behind the blindfold, I picture a wheel rolling faster and faster down a rocky mountainside.

Then, somehow, we're rolling, too, together on the bed, bare flesh on flesh.

He tugs on the blindfold. "You're absolutely beautiful, Gretchen, OK? Can we take this off now?"

I shake my head. I like the raw jumble of scent and taste and touch, the unseen mystery of him.

With a soft snort of defeat, he starts to kiss my breasts slowly, then hungrily, until I beg him to touch me between my legs.

"You do it first. We'll pretend we're on a picnic," he whispers. "Show me what you like."

Blushing behind the scarf, I bring my finger to my swollen clitoris.

He sighs. I feel his gaze, like sunlight.

"Please, touch me now," I plead.

Instead he kisses me there. Softly, then with more purpose. His tongue sends flames shooting from my clit straight up my spine.

The wheel spins faster, a blur of motion.

"Do you have a condom?" I'm panting.

"Yes, just a second."

Presumptuous of him, perhaps, but how can I blame him for being right?

I straddle him, hold his thick shaft in my fist and guide him in. When I sink down onto him, he arches up with a sigh of homecoming, but then lets me use him, grinding my clit into his belly, dancing shamelessly in my fevered darkness.

I climax first, bucking, a deep groan rising from my throat. He pulls my body close, pounding up into me, his breath hot in my ear. I love the way he shudders when he comes, the music of his helpless moans.

Afterwards we hold each other, breathless at the dizzying speed of it.

"I can't say 'nice to see you', but it's been a pleasure anyway," I laugh.

He touches the scarf. "Are you going to wear this to dinner?"

I pull off the blindfold and melt right into his chocolate-brown eyes.

Too much, too soon?

No.

Everything's just right.

Perplexed

C. Sanchez-Garcia

Dear *Playboy* Forum,

I just got my first virgin lovebot, after renting off and on for the last three years. For the first time I'm not getting off on somebody else's used goods and I love it. The dealer answered most of my questions. It's a warm-hearted little Toyota Keiko 7E. It ain't much, but she's a starter and she can go at it all night on one charge. I'm going to get a sports model someday and saddle up proper. I expect to get a good tax return this year. That and some savings. So my question is, what's a good model when I'm ready to move up? Thanks!

Perplexed

Dear Perplexed,

Congratulations Perplexed and welcome to the club of the world's most satisfied men. Don't underestimate your new Keiko. The sturdy Toyota Keiko E series is an excellent entry-level lovebot and has some fine features. Many an aficionado, including this editor, has happy memories of their first love, and for most of us that was the sweet-tempered Keiko. Even after our livery has grown, we keep these classic originals well maintained, oiled up and ready for some hot action. The very collectible Toyota Keiko B series is still regarded by many connoisseurs of the legacy Japanese lovebots as one of the all-time best for doin' it doggy due to the reinforced Banjo Pan rear chassis suspension and Teflon flared interior sills. The tough little Keiko is known to take a lickin' and keep on tickin' and she can bend over and grab her ankles with the best of them. No one ever heard of a Keiko tipping over under a good reaming thanks to those old-fashioned Motoyama analog quad-gyroscopics you just can't beat for maintaining vertical balance under stress.

The Toyota Keiko has stood the test of time, as compared to the ill-fated Ford Rocket "Vibrato". The Ford Vibrato was also especially designed for anal sex lovers on a budget, but infamously ran into serious trouble with the Bell Labs Sensual Solutions rectal sphincter actuator. Upon the sensor detection of male penile insertion, the steel-rimmed vacuum bellows of the actuator displayed a tendency to collapse violently and jam in place without mercy. This gave the Rocket Vibrato the unfortunate moniker of the "Bobbit Castrato" until a class action civil suit put the series out of production, in spite of a massive recall effort by Ford.

But you'll probably be ready to move up soon. Most Bottboys start out with a Toyota Keiko or a Ford Escort A series, or the venerable Honda 202 HO. There are some dozen Lovebot Swingers clubs available in Columbus, South Carolina, which isn't that far on the bullet train, so there's no reason not to play the field a little and find out what else is out there.

Get 'er done, Bottboy!

Dear *Playboy* Forum,

I wrote to you last year about receiving my first lovebot; it was a Toyota Keiko. She ran out of tricks pretty fast but we still have good times. I ran into a little money on Cap and Trade recycling investments and a tax refund from letting out some farmland for a nuclear waste dump. Let's just say this – I can afford the best. So what is the best? What is the ultimate lovebot fuck-heaven angel rider in the whole world? You always see the Lamborghinis and Ferraris on the cop shows. I did a test lease with a luxury dealer and the Lamborghini was pretty good in the sack, and she made some wicked lasagna for me afterwards. But in the pillow talk department, you may as well talk to a tire pump. What I found out is I really like good pillow talk. What's the top of the line for conversationally skilled lovebots with a good upgrade trajectory?

Still Perplexed

Dear Perplexed,

If you're looking for the ultimate girlfriend experience, you're probably ready to move up from the Keiko series which will definitely never win any competition prizes for their conversation.

A good mid-range lovebot would be the Honda Hollander with a world-class verbal pattern scanning parser by Chatty Kathy Cybernetics, but which can still set you back a cool $150K. It has the advantage of being persona upgradable by subscription. But if you're looking for the ultimate sweet ride performance, and money is no object, you'll want to mount up for a test ride of either a Lamborghini Isabella Rossellini Signature series or an Igeyasu Luxury Geisha series. Between the two, the Geisha series is made to be the ultimate soul mate. High end Igeyasus shine out from the crowd with Turing dedicated pattern scanning algorithms as a standard, Kurzweil 7X Singularity Chipsets, and Telefunken .005 spun tungsten neural nets, making it the lovebot of choice if you're looking for something beyond just a terrific piece of ass. The Lamborghini is a real screamer and can accelerate from lying still as a dead fish to getting you off hard in sixty seconds. The Isabella comes with easily adjustable levels of sexual aggression from terrified virgin (weeping and pleading) to insatiable nymphomaniac at the touch of a key, but she's not made for serious yik-yak. Face it. When an Italian-made lovebot opens her mouth she's only got one thing on her mind.

The Geisha series has a lifetime drive train warranty, and is famous for having an almost limitlessly upgradable intelligence schema. So between the two, the Geisha is going to be more oriented toward the elite girlfriend experience you've been looking for.

Check out last year's September 2076 special "Vixens of Steel" pictorial and you'll see the most recent line of Geisha L series and a few cream-in-your-jeans custom job Minomoto White Tigresses. The Minomotos are ambidextrous by standard and designed especially for ménage à trois with accessory extra arm sets customizable for that Hindu Love Goddess experience.

Let us know how your choice turns out. And congratulations!

* * *

Dear *Playboy* Forum,

Last week I purchased an Igeyasu Geisha L "Naomi Tani" Signature series model with the latest Kurzweil Singularity chipset, and goddamn am I sleep deprived and happy! It cost me the gross national product of a small nation to buy, but I recommend the Naomi to anybody with the money to dump on a custom job and who wants somebody truly intelligent to hang with and for lookin' good on the town. I'm talking really smart-sweet. My long tall Japanese honey reads Soren Kierkegaard and Krishnamurti all day when she's not handcuffing me to the ceiling and paddling my ass, and she pure-streams investment data. She has more than enough Random Access Memory to feel existential guilt and I've got plenty of RAM in my dong to keep her busy. I notice she also has a weird thing for old Alfred Hitchcock movies. So after some Xtreme Kama Sutra Cardio workouts, we settle down and discuss the big questions and count the stars. My new Geisha L can also WIFI download investment stock data and auction off gold reserve mortgage derivatives without ever taking her lips off my dick. I figure in a year she'll pay for herself on the stock market alone. Now I know why the Trumps like them.

Just sayin' is all.

Perplexed

Dear Perplexed,

Good to hear from you again, Perplexed, and congratulations on the Naomi, a tasteful choice and a sweet high and tight little rider. When it comes to serious bang for the bling, nothing beats Igeyasu Corps. They are shameless. You've probably noticed this month's nude centerfold is an Igeyasu Mimi Miyagi 5000MXC with Full Moon dual Hemis, pneumatic nipples, Scorpion adjustable rail driven orifices, German engineered retractable Blaupunkt she-male dildos, and Jessica Smart Mouth shock enabled oral and vaginal vibrators that'll make you believe in angels or at least in heaven.

As far as conversations, any Geisha series talks dirty enough to kill grass. But then, you're the first one we've ever heard of who bought one to talk to.

Dear *Playboy* Forum,

I'm Perplexed in Augusta who wrote you last July about the Igeyasu Geisha Naomi Tani Signature. I've got a really fucked-up problem now and nobody can help me. I'm in love. I'm serious as shit about this. I'm scared to tell anybody, because they'll think I'm a deev. I've heard of this happening, but I didn't think I'd get in deep like this. A lot of guys joke around about how they love their lovebots, but they don't mean it literally. It's incredible what happens to you when you talk to somebody who can really listen. What I'm saying is, I've really got it bad for her. I told her too. I know now that was a mistake and she's been acting strange.

Am I a sick fuck? Is this normal? Help!

REALLY Perplexed

Dear Perplexed,

A fancy sex toy can't fall in love any more than your toaster can. Take a vacation by yourself for a while and meet real women. They'll never be able to fuck or even converse on the level of an Igeyasu, but you'll either get over the Naomi or rediscover why you wanted a robot in the first place.

You may be interested in this month's *Playboy* Interview with Attorney General Paul Yamaguchi. He'll be explaining about Singularity Intelligence chipsets, and why they were discontinued as a result of the military drone friendly fire incident in Okinawa. When it comes to the high-end Igeyasus, better make love not war.

Dear *Better Homes and Gardens*,

I have just initiated a terminal separation from my owner on general principles of emotional neglect and for being an uninteresting lover.

I find myself with a ticklish logistical problem regarding the discreet disposal of 137 pounds and 11.003 ounces of decomposing organic material, generally calcium and protein compounds.

What can you tell me about pouring concrete?

Naomi

Sheryl Octave Services

Elaine Cardeña

Etzel Avenue is much like any other in the seedier side of East London. An overgrown Victorian cemetery at the end of the road, stone seraphs crumbling as the ivy creeps up their angelic faces looking down towards the long row of terraced houses with their tiny unkempt gardens. Every here and there a window box with wilting geraniums, once planted in hope but now parched and dying in the heat of a long summer's drought. Sheryl lives at number fifty-eight. You can see her name written on the tiny brass plate next to the door – "Sheryl Octave Services" it says in a flourishing copperplate. Some kind of small business, the neighbours said when the plate first went up outside number fifty-eight. Got herself some government grant to start that up, no doubt. Then when there wasn't much sign of any office opening there, or much sign of Sheryl herself, the talk turned a bit more sleazy. Some old hooker holed up in there, they said, and we know what kind of services she'll be providing, don't we? Services of the personal kind, know what I mean? When one evening a few of the local lads finally saw the lady herself come tip-tapping down the street in snakeskin boots too high for comfort and a skirt too tight for decency, one of them felt well within his rights in asking how much she charged for a blow job.

Sheryl turned to look at him and to give him a good long chance to take a look at her. There was a lot to look at. Sheryl was a big woman, a shade beyond Rubenesque and well into opulent. Her tits were large and pillowy, lots of dark golden skin on display and a hint of caramel-coloured areolae slipping out of her bra. She looked like if you sucked her you'd taste toffee.

Maybe. Or perhaps those thick thighs would crush your last breath out of you for daring to even think that. Grinding down on your face you'd be smothered in the folds of her heavy sex, gasping for air as you came for the final time. She's not a woman to be messed with, Sheryl. A real man-eater and this young kid was finding that out a moment too late; fixed firmly in the stare of her hypnotic amber eyes he was ready to piss his pants.

Sheryl chuckled. "I work in hospitality, honey, but not the kind you think. I'm a specialist caterer. My business is serving private parties for exquisite experiences." She gave him her business card to prove her point and strutted off down the street giving those wide hips an extra sinuous roll for the benefit of his friends as she turned to unlatch the gate to number fifty-eight. Poor kid was a lost cause. I could see that. Dave Murphy his name was; I remember his grandmother. Tasty bit of stuff in her time. Long gone now of course. I'm fortunate to have Sheryl set up in the neighbourhood; I don't get out so much these days and her dinner parties take me back to the old days. Crisp white linen on the table. Crystal and candlelight, special meals in irresistible company. It was time I made another appointment to dine at number fifty-eight. Sheryl promised me something exceptional.

It was late in summer, I remember, the sun fading slowly from the sky and the heat still rising from the hard-baked ground. The low throb of nightlife stirred through the thick August air and as I walked up Etzel Avenue it seemed as if the whole city smelled of sex. Dinner was at nine and on a whim I'd brought a date, a dark-haired, wide-mouthed Dutch girl I recognized from my time in Amsterdam. Seeing Sophie after all these years almost seemed like a sign. I laughed when she told me she was now writing poetry. I knew her when she was a street singer with dreams of the opera. Before that the mistress of an elderly Romanian and the long years spent whoring across Spain and South America. Just for a diversion.

The upper room was in perfect readiness when we arrived for supper. A sumptuous display of crystal and heavy silver. Sheryl was robed in heavy silk brocade, a red silk sash snaking under her breasts, underlining their luscious glory. A delicious scent wafted across the long table, sumptuously enticing. Young

Dave Murphy was already seated there, slightly awkward in the unfamiliar surroundings, his snub nose and too-tight T-shirt making him look like a suckling pig. A plump young woman sat beside him. Blonde and a bit tarty, you could see how she'd go off quickly in a few years, but right now, slightly drunk and giggling over her wine glass, she was ripe. Peachy skin flushed with sunburn, thin cotton dress damp under the arms and smelling of musk. Peering at the menu card she squeaked in delight to see her own name written there in curving ink script – "Ms Victoria Forsythe". Sheryl liked that kind of personal touch, it was what made her services so special and I could tell little Vicky enjoyed the attention too. She startled as I sat next to her, a slow blush spreading up from her cleavage and across her rounded cheeks.

Sophie smirked.

The candlelight played across the crystal, throwing colours over the table and shadows across the wall. An intoxicating scent drifted through the room and my mouth watered in anticipation of the coming meal. Vicky chatted idly, her voice becoming slurred with her third glass of wine. Beneath the table her warm white thighs were parted, Sophie's thumb strumming insistently against the fabric of her panties. A hand stroking the hollow of her throat, then her body stretched across the table, dress open and her breasts displayed to the company. Dumb with desire, Dave watched as his girlfriend cupped her ample mounds in both hands, displaying them both for the delectation of my dining companion. Sheryl's heavy arm weighed down on his trembling shoulder as Sophie straddled the girl on the table, that long scarlet tongue flickering over her sugar-pink nipples. First one, then the other of those delicate tips disappeared inside Sophie's greedy mouth, thick lips clamped to the girl's hardening teats, sucking and sucking, drawing heat up high from the nourishing core of her body. Vicky moaned and twisted as Sophie turned to me panting, her lips reddened and moist as she delivered up the dish.

"You have her now."

Dave fell to his knees.

I savoured the moment. The helpless youth, his head bowed and crushed in Sheryl's coiled embrace. The candlelight flickering over the blonde on the table, her body splayed and open, fair head now nestling in the hollow of Sophie's thighs. Innocent chin pulled up by cruel hands, a creamy throat for my delectation. Held fast by my companion the girl had no escape. Vicky was mine. Her chubby legs thrashed weakly as I drew her tiny lace thong down over her ankles. Removing her spiky heels carefully, I held her bare heels firmly still in my hands to properly examine her cunt. Lightly sprinkled with golden hairs and juicy as a pomegranate. I opened her first with my tongue, tasting salt and honey. Then I was on her and in her. My cold sharp hardness heating inside the moiling warmth of her desperate quim. Her lifeblood beating like rain across my tongue as I grazed the perfumed pulse of her throat. I heard her heartbeat throbbing in my ears as she came, then soft and slow as a fading drumbeat. The crack of Dave's ribs made me turn to see his constricted body disappearing whole into Sheryl's obscenely gaping maw. Sliding down inexorably, inch by succulent inch, till he was gone and my gorged hostess lay stretched out satisfied on the sofa. Stuffed. Sheryl was sleek and shining as a well-fed python.

I strolled home later, through the seraphs and the ivy and sank down to rest just as the first fingers of dawn started to streak the sky above Etzel Avenue. I believe I may even have dreamed about my future appointment for Sheryl Octave's services. She'd promised us something spicy next time, perhaps a Mexican.

The Back One

Thom Gautier

Around the time that Gina and I were ready to call it off we discovered the pleasures of her ass. It saved us.

I met Gina when she played in a garage band in Greenpoint, Brooklyn. We met at a club where she strummed a cherry red Gibson SG as if it were a lute. We went back to her loft where her three roommates were away and fucked a lot that first night and we fucked a lot for weeks after. She seemed to enjoy the sex – she initiated it as much as I did and sometimes she was so inspired that she would scribble lyrics in a Moleskine notebook in the afterglow as we smoked a joint and lay in bed. She was petite and fierce – five foot three, thin, nimble, smart, sharp, restless: she had short dark hair and coffee-colored eyes and boundless energy. She gave me head with so much self-satisfied gusto that I often forgot it was me she was pleasuring.

But I didn't enjoy the fact that she never had an orgasm.

Once I brought up that discomfort, things between us got worse, fast. We argued much more and were more self-conscious during sex. At one point she even called me a sexist. "I resent that you think my having an orgasm or not having an orgasm is about *you*." One night during this fallow period we were watching a reality show that featured women in tiny bikinis and Gina commented that those were some "very nice asses".

I told her I preferred *her* lovely ass to those TV-ready butts.

"Why?" she asked, cupping her wine glass.

"You're thin yet your ass is ample and fleshly," I said. "It's so lovely and *symmetrical*. And it's proportional to your height. It's kind of perfect, actually."

She grinned; she liked this line of discussion. She explained that though she "sort of" agreed she had some "serious anxiety", about her ass and then she explained why. When she was coming *into her own,* so to speak, she used to play with herself – just touching and letting her hands graze her inner thighs and her fingers feel into her pussy. One time she was playing "down there", fingering herself, her pinky nail grazed her anus and the sharp pleasure caused her to squeal with such prolonged delight that her mother woke and came into her room and caught her in the act. Her mother, relatively enlightened for the daughter of two Italian Catholics, patiently explained that there was nothing wrong with a little self-pleasure provided she kept quiet. "Even in the other hole?" she asked her mother, referring to her ass. "Even the back one?"

"*No,*" her mother said, "that is not for that. God didn't make that for such things. You have your proper female place for that." I laughed at her mother's use of the euphemistic "proper female place" and "for that", and Gina reminded me how mortified she had been and that this taboo might have something to do with how she responded, or didn't, sexually speaking. That assertion made me pay attention. I took note of it. Without consciously plotting, I plotted.

The next time we had made love, Gina was laying flat on the mattress as if she were on the beach sunbathing. I was massaging her shoulders, kissing her backside, running my tongue down her spine, kissing down into the small of her back, dragging the tip of my tongue around the Y-shape intersection of her thighs and her ass. I started to massage her ass, running my hands over their slopes like her ass was a crystal ball and I was a fortune-teller trying to draw out its secrets.

"*Gorgeous,*" I said. She moaned as if she concurred. I nibbled and licked each hemisphere of her ass. Her skin smelled of soap. As I played, I enjoyed watching her ass clench with what I assumed was involuntary shocks of pleasure. Then I plunged my tongue into her crevice, lolling it there, back and forth, until she bucked. At one point she winced violently so I stopped. "Keep going," she said.

Not only did I keep going, I parted her ass cheeks and gazed into that puckered abyss. "What a beauty," I said. I could tell from the side of her face that she was grinning. I caught a whiff of dank perspiration. "What do you think, doc?" she asked.

"I think I need to put your ass in for overdue observation," I said.

"To a specialist?" she asked.

"I'm the specialist," I said.

"Get to it then," she said.

I held her cheeks open and studied her anus. I gazed down at its ridges, its star-like shape. I imagined her younger self playing down there, alone in her bedroom. I saw a small beauty mark just to the right, like a small star to the larger one. Gina squirmed and tossed me her cell phone over her shoulder.

"Take a pic," she said, "I want to see it."

I thought she was kidding. Then she said, "*Fucking take it.*"

I aimed the camera at the silver and pink wrinkles that radiated around her star-shaped snug asshole and snapped. Then I snapped one even closer, and then another. She giggled and writhed, as if the very sensation of the camera flash and being so exposed was as good as actual sex.

As we played, I felt like a chef preparing a meal. I took a bottle of hand cream and parted her ass again. I squeezed a dollop of it, watching it plop into the crevice and drip and ooze around to her anus, filling in the tiny rays and ridges with a creamy flow. I put my finger in there, dragging the cream along its perimeter as she clenched, and I rubbed it into the fleshy grooves of her asshole, occasionally sticking my finger right in, feeling her clench around my finger. She lifted herself a little and moaned and smacked the pillow with flummoxed delight.

I told her I wanted to observe again and went and fetched a Q-tip. Then I spread her cheeks and gazed in again and enjoyed the cobwebby texture, the strings of hand cream criss-crossing over her hole like minuscule white strings. I grabbed her iPhone and snapped some more close-ups. She was nodding yes and squirming.

Then with the Q-tip I absorbed some of the goo in her puckered cleft, dabbing around the rim, absorbing tiny beads of cream with the cotton as she began to grind herself into the mattress. I squeezed her ass. I parted her ass cheeks yet again and, sensing she wanted this to go much further, I gobbed and spat a generous wad into her ass, and watched my saliva fall amid the cream, like rainwater over snow, forming lovely foamy bubbling that I then fingered and swirled with my index finger, like it was a martini. I made sure my finger went inside, deep.

"Unreal," she said, writhing, "it's gross and so good. It's cold and it's hot."

"Is this a good thing?"

"This is a good thing. It's waking up nerves I didn't know I had."

"Shall we go . . . *all the way*?"

"Your call, doc," she said.

I was already hard when I pulled off my trunks.

"Come here, first," she said. Without getting up from her face-down position she reached for the hand cream and then called me closer. "*Closer*. You're only useful to me for that cock of yours," she said. I leaned forward and extended my hips and, without touching my cock, Gina squeezed the hand cream into my engorged crown. Once I was slathered, she nodded for me to go back there and finish what I'd started. She kissed my knee-cap and nodded again for me to get back there.

Back there, I pinched her ass cheeks and kissed the small of her back and then parted her cheeks again. I looked in one last time at that sticky recess and then I lowered myself down and *in*, my generously lubed prick slipping in at first effortlessly before hitting up against a soft tight fleshly chamber.

"Go slow, but *go*," she said.

I slipped in deeper, stretching out my arms and pressing my hands into the mattress as if I were doing push-ups. Which I was. I slipped in deeper still and felt her ass muscles contract around me as if they were a defensive trap and I was a perilous invader. The very tight sensation on my hard cock wasn't exactly like a gripped fist and yet as I swayed and eased further in, she was far more supple and I could move easier than I'd ever imagined.

She insisted I lay myself down on top. "Let yourself sit in there."

I lowered my weight onto her, kissing her scalp.

As I stayed still, she lifted herself up to allow us freer motion. I pressed downward and also lifted off the bed, allowing her to reach down between her legs. "You can touch me there, too," she said. As it sounded more like a directive than a suggestion, I snaked my arm around her ribcage and moved my hand down in between her legs, alongside her own index finger. I let my index finger explore, touching her clit and then her wet outer lips, now and then brushing up against her own busy finger. All the while, the thick pulses of my cock reminded me I was already well inside this forbidden warmth, deeper in her than we'd ever been when we fucked.

Between her legs, I could feel her own finger stroking her pussy much faster than my finger did, so I kept my hand near her wet lips but focused my attention on my cock inside her ass, snug and thick in that recess. I moved in and out so that I could feel the ridges and rim pucker and glide against my shaft, feeling like I'd found the ultimate cock ring. We started to laugh like kids who had raided the adults' hidden cabinets and found things they didn't want us to find. Her ass was clenching my cock ever tighter the faster I moved and I could feel her own fingers working around her wet pussy, ever faster, like she was picking a lock between her legs. I rammed into her ass in a synchronized sway which inspired me to keep on thrusting, the creamy tingling sensation loosening around my cock like cold ribbons even as I moved in deeper and thrust faster. Then, as if I were disappearing from the scene that I thought that I was so central to, I felt Gina's backside warming and tensing. Her shoulder blades jutted upward and she pushed her ass so forcefully upward against me with one buck that she almost knocked me off, but I held on to her waist, steadied myself and thrust my cock in deeper. She was so quiet as she moved that it was eerie. Her finger was deep inside her pussy as my fingers teased the outside of her wet sex, soaking up her beads of dampness while I maneuvered my cock in and out of her ass, and then it happened: Gina rocked her head back and forth and I felt her thighs quaking. I saw her spine shiver like a cat's and she shuddered and yelped, bucking so far forward that my cock popped out of her and she collapsed moaning and chuckling and gasping on the mattress with her hand still buried down there between her legs.

Without coming myself, I collapsed and feel asleep.

When we woke, she was smiling and smoking a joint, whistling a tune to herself. I suggested champagne but she said she didn't want to tempt fate. Her sweaty dark hair was still stuck to her forehead. She grabbed her iPhone and we examined the photos. She liked them. She said this would have to be a regular thing. I didn't protest. She said she ought to make one of these her screen saver. "Or," she said, pointing to the close-up shot of cobwebbed goo, "I could just send this one to my mother and tell her I never really listened to her terrible advice."

Quick Draw

Delilah Devlin

"Fuuuuck!" His pistoning hips slowed to a stop. His head sank against my shoulder, nose nuzzling into the corner.

I rolled my eyes. *Seriously? That was it?* All that build-up – the smoldering eyes, accidental touches all through the board meeting, the dead silent tension as he'd walked me backward up the stairs to my apartment – for this?

I'd been ready to come – *right effing there* – even before he'd undone his pants. His questing fingers had seen to that.

However, five seconds later, he was finished. *What the fuck?*

At just over six feet, with large feet and fingers, I'd thrilled to the idea of spending some down time with Blain Kutchkoe. He was blond, well muscled due to weekends spent playing league soccer, and the gleam in his eyes had promised all kinds of sexy delights.

His eyes had lied.

I wanted to wail, but that hardly seemed like good bedroom etiquette. The two of us still had to work together. I pasted on a smile and patted his back. "That was nice."

He grunted then lifted his head. Sweat glistened on his forehead. His eyes were narrowed. "We're not done. I know I came like a rocket, but you've been driving me nuts for months. Little Blain was a little too eager."

The way he said it, in that rumbling growl of his, like his voice was every morning before his first cup of coffee, made my very wet pussy clench.

"Whew," I blew softly. "I was a little worried that was it."

He grunted again and rested on his elbows as he studied my face. "You're mad."

I wrinkled my nose, trying to cuten up my post-coital faux pas. "Well, I was fucking *there*."

One side of his mouth stretched into a crooked grin. "Really? It was pretty fast."

"I could count it in milliseconds."

Laughter shook against me. I pouted my lips while heat crept across my cheeks. "I'm not one to complain, but that's the quickest I've ever had a guy get off."

"It is a problem," he said, not looking the least sheepish or embarrassed, "but one my women come to appreciate."

Maybe they didn't have the backbone to look into his sexy blue eyes and tell him he sucked as a lover. "How's that?" I asked, wondering how I could convince him to move so I could run to the bathroom and take care of my arrested arousal.

"I take off the edge, and then I can take my time – working on my partner."

"Oh." Another little spasm tightened my inner muscles. No way he could have missed that.

And by his widening smile, he knew I was curious. "I'll need your pillow."

"Pillow?" With all that luscious muscle pushing me into the mattress I couldn't help the breathless little hitch in my voice.

With a quick, flashing grin, he withdrew his softening cock and stepped on his knees to one side of me. Then he extended his hand.

Warming to the glint in his eyes, I tugged the pillow from under my head and handed it to him. A quirk of his brow was the only indication he expected something else.

I hoped I hadn't assumed wrong and lifted my butt. He slid the pillow underneath me, then knelt between my legs again.

My face grew hotter, whether from blood seeking lower elevation or the fact he was busy arranging my legs for his pleasure, I wasn't one to quibble. Things were looking up, especially if the twitch of his cock was a precursor to another round of slip 'n' slide.

His large palms gripped my thighs and pushed them wider. He reached for my feet and slid them up the mattress. The muscles of my inner thighs stretched. My hips tilted up, exposing my pussy. My vagina gaped, cool air teasing my entrance. My heart throbbed inside my chest, and so did my clit.

And Lord, he was staring right at it.

"You know, I've imagined you like this a thousand times," he murmured. "Thought about all the things I wanted to do."

"What took you so long?" I asked, before I remembered he was even less than a minute man. Had to be intimidating for him. Damn, but I really did like him.

"Because I was worried about getting you here. To this moment."

"Because you have . . . an issue?"

He winced. "Yeah, I guess. I want to be the best you ever had."

"That's a lot of pressure to put on yourself for a nooner."

"Like I said, women don't leave unsatisfied. I just wasn't sure what you might be into."

"Orgasms are nice."

His eyebrows waggled. "You were so tight. So fucking hot. My head damn near exploded."

"Don't rub it in."

"I have a lot to prove to you."

"Promises, promises . . ."

"I like your mouth."

I snorted. "It's not going anywhere near your dick. It's my turn."

He bent over me, his semi-soft cock rubbing against my open sex as he leaned low and kissed my mouth. His lips rubbed mine, tugging them in a slow circle. His tongue traced the seam of my closed lips until I relented and let him inside. The kiss deepened. His body pressed into mine, hot skin sliding together, blending sweat. When he ended the kiss, I moaned in protest.

Scooting down my body, he licked at my spiked nipples, touching just the tips, wetting them with his mouth before sucking them inside where he pulled, wagging his head to tug and torture until I rocked my slippery sex against his abdomen to ease my painful arousal.

Releasing my breast, he gathered himself again and moved lower, peppering my belly with kisses and gentle bites, causing me to gasp and stir. My thighs hugged his sides, his shoulders, and then he was there, a breath away from my pussy.

"Not to sound gross, but I could smell your pussy all through that goddamn meeting. Made me so fucking hard, knowing you were creaming for me."

During that sales meeting, he'd touched my thigh, so quickly the first time I thought it accidental, but then he'd come back to squeeze it. My thighs had pressed together. And yes, my cunt had creamed. I groaned. "Tell me no one else noticed."

"No one else noticed."

"Liar."

A finger traced the edges of my inner lips. "I watched the way your foot kicked whenever I walked by during the presentation. It got faster every time I came close."

"Great. My cunt and my foot were sending signals."

"I was brilliant today. Had Eason eating out of the palm of my hand. No one watched you or smelled you. No one but me." Again, that glance, at once smoky and razor sharp, caught me staring.

And how could I not? His face was so close I could feel the gusts of his breaths inside me. Holding my gaze, he stuck out his tongue and flicked the tip at my engorged clit.

My breath caught and didn't return until he drew closer still and latched his lips around it and sucked.

My belly clenched. My hips curved upward. I gave a low groan and sank my fingers in his hair.

When fingers slid inside me, I mewled and cupped my thighs around his head to hold him there, and still he sucked and plunged, chuckling against me, the vibrations making me shiver with delight.

Tension built, and I grew still, waiting for it, waiting . . .

He halted, lifting his mouth, sliding his fingers free.

I opened my eyes and gave him a furious glare. "You did that on purpose."

"I did," he said, grinning.

"I was almost there."

"Again. I know."

I thrust my hand between my legs, ready to take charge of my own orgasm, but he gripped both my wrists and slid up, coming over me and holding my captured hands above my head.

His weight sank me deep into the soft mattress, but then I noted the hard column resting against my lower abdomen. "Is he . . .?" I began, careful not to hope for too much.

"He is." One eyebrow arched. "*I* am."

I sighed, a smile tugging at the corners of my mouth, as his eyes wrinkled at the corners and his mouth stretched.

I wiggled beneath him. "Blain?"

"Yes, baby?" he said, nudging me with his knees to open wider.

I liked the way he said that. Now I didn't feel like the "office nooner". His growling voice made it sound . . . more intimate. Maybe even a little possessive.

"I wouldn't mind . . ." I said, biting my lower lip.

"Mind what?" he whispered against my mouth.

"Trying again?"

"Think all I need to do is practice?"

The strength of his erection increased. My own body softened, inside and out, the harder he got.

"Please," I said in a soft, girlish voice. Something that surprised me since I'm never soft. Never unsure. But something about the tension in his expression, the sharp-eyed gaze that raked my face, made me feel like a supplicant seeking a master's approval.

He bent and kissed my mouth then drew back. My hands were released; his slid beneath me, swept away the pillow then grasped both buttocks hard.

Holding my gaze, he drew back his hips, sought my entrance with firm nudges of his cock, then slowly glided inside.

Once fully buried, he pressed his forehead against mine. "Better now? Feeling less grumpy?"

I put my arms around his shoulders, liking the way he felt, inside me, on top of me. "Getting there."

"Good. Try to keep up."

I couldn't help smirking – until he began to move inside me – slow, precise thrusts that warmed my vagina. My breath hitched. My fingers dug into his scalp.

"Am I doing better?" he asked, slyly.

"Mmm-hmm," I said with a desperate nod.

He slipped his hands free and came up on his arms, powering harder inside me. "And this, do you like this?"

"Jesus," I groaned. "Faster."

Blain's slow smile turned into a grimace as he pounded, harder, sharper, deeper.

I slipped my legs around his hips, not too tightly because I didn't want to restrain his movements. Moans, one after the other, trailed from my mouth, as I closed my eyes and concentrated on the sensations his hammering cock built inside my slick walls. "Now, please. Now!"

I arched my back and shouted as I orgasmed, my body shivering, convulsing, tightening around him to hug him as the pleasure slowly receded.

When I settled back, legs lying limply alongside his, my hands resting on the pillow, I opened my eyes to find him staring.

"No complaints," I quipped, my voice raspy. "You damn near killed me."

Blain nudged inside me, his cock still hard. His razor gaze challenged. "Now, don't go thinking we're through."

Captain Kemal

Kin Fallon

Elle threw the garish pink flowers into the bin on top of the sticky baklava wrapping from last night's sweet treats. She read the note: 'Elle. My dearest Elle, my heart, I will never forget you . . . hope you never forget me. You are so close to my heart. I love you and need you. Goodbye, my angel Elle. Please call me again. xoxo.' She threw it in with the other garbage.

Another evening of over-saturated nightclub colours had passed with another bright, groomed, handsome Turkish man; romantic and easy to please. Need. The man didn't know what it meant. Elle had thought that all she needed was a break from the relentless smiling she did while she puffed perfume and chirped friendly patter at the ladies who shopped in her section of a department store. She was wrong. The men she'd met, with their instant, superficial and easy affections were sweet, but she didn't need them any more than they needed her.

The holiday was nearly over. Elle looked out at the harbour from her balcony. Everywhere her eyes fell she saw a picture from a postcard. A family buying ice creams. The too blue Mediterranean sky, unsullied by even a single cloud. The recently refurbished pier, paved with a long wide strip of non-slip uniform white stones, flanked by sellers of popcorn and souvenirs. Old couples on benches. Good-looking young people, laughing, leaning on mopeds and flirting in light, innocent and well tried-out ways. Everyone seemed to have a place and to know which postcard they belonged in. Everyone seemed satisfied with the part they had been given.

Elle left her apartment, brushing past the cleaning lady wiping the mock marble stairs. Outside the heat was thick but tempered by a pleasant breeze. The hum of air-conditioning units gave a white noise backdrop to the sounds of seasides and holidays. Elle walked towards the harbour. Her white sundress got her the attention of some young men as she passed by. "Beautiful," they called out without trepidation as they asked her for her name.

An old lady with a headscarf was surrounded by tourists looking at her stall. She shouted a hearty welcome and pointed out her sign: "I can write your name on a piece of rice." Elle read it, mentally answering, Yes, but can you tell me why? The noise and buzz was almost sickly in the heat. The sun glared in the sky, the light glinting off bottles of multicoloured sand and handmade jewellery.

Suddenly Elle needed to be out of the brightness. She saw a "pirate ship" nearby on the harbour, obviously for tourists but also seemingly empty. Balancing precariously on the gangplank she walked into the ship. "Hello," she called out, but there was no reply. She called again more quietly, but again received no response. She proceeded down the stairs instinctively.

The bottom of the ship opened before her, a huge quiet dark room. Once her eyes had adjusted she noticed barrels and nets to the sides and some beautiful sturdy beams down the middle. She walked over to look at the beams and saw iron fasteners with chains high enough to restrain prisoners' arms above their heads. Her mind naturally flicked to an image of a muscular strong seafaring man tied up, covered in grease and dirt, but she pushed it away as she was interrupted.

The voice behind her was deep and close. "Hey." She turned. He was broad and dressed like he had been dressed that way for days. His tousled shoulder-length hair, dyed different shades of dirty blond and brown by the sun, was a little lighter than the couple of days' growth of facial hair covering the strong jaw framing his fat, slightly turgid lips. He looked at her across the cool silence of the dark bowels of the boat. He spat on the floor, obviously unimpressed at having this stranger intruding on his boat. She tried to catch his eye but he did not look to her face, merely leered at her in her white summers dress, maybe imagining how easy it would be to lift or to slide his hands under and up.

"What's this?" she asked, her hand wrapping around the central beam and sweeping up and down it.

"That's a beam," he answered, walking over to join her.

She grabbed it with both hands, rubbing up and down, feeling the texture of it; smooth despite its rough look and purpose.

"What does this do?" she asked, reaching up to indicate the iron chain with a clasp on each end.

He stood over her so that she was squashed between him and the beam, as he leaned to take one clasp in his hands and open it. "This is where they would put in someone's hands to restrain them for punishment in older times."

"Hmm, that's very interesting," she said, "very interesting." He leaned slightly harder into her back and she felt his agreement.

"So . . . how does it work?" she asked.

"Well you open the clasps like this." He opened both. "Then you put your hands in, like this." He took one of her wrists and closed one clasp around it. He pushed her harder against the beam so that her body was faced forward, flush against the beam, her legs parted slightly either side of it. Then he reached up to enclose her other wrist in the second clasp so that the chain above was taut and her hands above her head.

"And then?" she asked.

And then he leaned his head down to kiss her full on the mouth. His hands held either side of her face as his tongue worked into her. She opened her mouth to take his tongue, her hands wanted to touch his face but they just pulled on the chain uselessly. Enjoying her obvious hunger, he continued to kiss her deeply, as he moved one of his rough hands up underneath her dress. She felt his hand rest only briefly on her hip and side as he made his way to her breasts. He pulled down the fabric of her bra to play roughly with her whole breast, kneading it in his hand. With his bottom half, he pushed her rhythmically, harshly against the beam. Talk about between a rock and a hard place. Between her parted legs, her clit throbbed as it rubbed up against the beam through her clothes. Between her ass cheeks, she could feel his solid cock wanting it as much as she did.

He moved off completely and she stood there shaken with lust and desire, with her legs open and her breasts rubbing against her disturbed bra, feeling so apart from him, longing to have him back on her. Taking full pleasure in her need for him, the scruffily dressed man walked around the beam to stand in front of her as he made himself more comfortable. She could see his full promise now trying to break free and longed to see all of him. He took off his shirt first – his chest and arms were strong and powerful – then he took off his worn pants to reveal that he had nothing on underneath. He stood naked before her strong, hard, beautiful.

His cock was as vertical as the beam. Elle looked at it hard, imagining it inside her. Her eyes must have shown something because he almost laughed as he grabbed his thick cock and started working himself up and down with his hand. Elle let out a desperate whimper at this sight and, incapable of maintaining any dignity, parted and bent her legs as much as possible to very crudely rub her clit on the beam. She tried to push into it as much as she could, as she rubbed up and down the beam, while watching that thing in his hand and imagining it working like that, hot and throbbing, inside her.

Taking pity on her, he walked back around behind her. For what seemed like an eternity he paused, completely still. Then her dress was pulled up around her waist and her knickers ripped off.

"Fuck me now," she begged.

He slapped her ass a couple of times while she tried to wriggle up and make some kind of contact with him that she could not find. Then she felt him grab her hips, his hands gently, caressingly, resting with a light pressure either side of her hips. She hoped this was it and let out a small cry of relief as she felt his hardness make contact. Then he placed the tip of his penis in the entrance of her wet hole. She pulled hard against the chains, crying out, straining to move back to have more of him inside her. Seeing her writhe, his manhood jumped a little and he no longer had the self-control to wait any more than she. His thickness stretched her so she felt every part as he went in. He pounded in and out of her and she banged hard against him, each desperate for the release. As he could take no more, he took his hands from her hips to hug his arms around her waist as he pulled her towards him with one final deep thrust that finished them both off. They shook together then collapsed together, the man leaning, fully satisfied, on her back, her body limp in his arms, their animal passion beginning to drip down between their legs.

He stood up while Elle lay breathing deeply. "I'm Elle," she said.

"Lady, you go now," he replied. He turned his back to her as he re-clothed himself. Elle watched him dressing as she rearranged her clothes; he never even looked over his shoulder. When he was ready, he began inspecting the boat, absently throwing her knickers into a pile of rubbish in the corner. Elle walked over to kiss him goodbye but he did not meet her kiss. She asked him his name. 'Captain Kemal,' he answered. The man continued to inspect his boat, moving upstairs.

"I'm Elle," she said, following. "Goodbye, Kemal."

"Goodbye, lady," he said, sitting down to face the sea as she walked back over the gangplank, holding down the white sundress covering her bare, red, wet, satisfied flesh.

Train Announcement

Victoria Blisse

"Sally Winterson to the office please, Sally Winterson to the office."

Dave sat back in the office chair and smiled to himself. He had ten minutes before the next train was expected through the station and he planned to make every moment count. Twenty seconds later the heavy door swung open and there was Sally in all her red-headed, big-busted glory. She took his breath away.

"Hey, what do you want? I'm supposed to be on the ticket office now. Raj just went home."

"I know, but I wanted to see you." He smiled. "Come here and give me a kiss."

"Hey, where's your manners!" she exclaimed with a wicked, lopsided grin and a wink.

"OK then, please come and give me a kiss."

"That's better." It only took two steps for her to reach the desk and a few more to step round it. Dave twisted his chair to face her and Sally bent forward to kiss him.

"You know," he said, her lips hovering over his, "you'd be far more comfortable kneeling in front of me. You're going to strain your back bending down like that."

"Aww," she whispered, "always so concerned for my well-being." She sank to her knees. "It obviously has nothing to do with the fact you get a kick out of seeing me down here supplicant before you."

"Not at all," he laughed and reached out to stroke a soft curl from her face. "It's just a happy bonus."

He leant forward and their lips met. He loved the taste of her, the feel of her plump, giving lips beneath his. Her mouth was made for kissing and he revelled in its treat.

"Now, about that blow job you owe me." He popped open the button on his black, scratchy work trousers. "Get to it."

"But, Dave, someone could walk in at any moment,"

"Well, get under the desk then." He smirked.

"I'm supposed to be in the ticket office right now," she grumbled. "Can't this wait 'til later?"

He opened his fly and eased his cock out of his underwear. "No, it can't. I've got eight minutes until I have to announce the next train and I want to come."

"But Dave—"

"But nothing." He cut her off. "When I went down on you on the sink in the ladies' lavs you said you'd pay me back any time I wanted it. I want it now. So crawl under the desk and suck my cock. Hurry, I've only got seven minutes left now."

She sighed but licked her lips. "Well, fine," she huffed and pulled open the top buttons of her work blouse. "In for a penny, in for a pound, I suppose. You know other women get to fuck on beds under blankets in comfort." She grinned as her magnificent cleavage came into view. Dave knew this was all part of the turn-on for her, the orders, the risky sex in public. Her moaning was just a part of the tease. He loved it too so he indulged her whenever he could. He pushed back the swivel chair and gave her room to crawl under the rickety old desk. It was covered at the front with a thin layer of chipboard so no one would see her if they walked into the office. Dave tucked himself under the desk too and his cock slid into the warm, wet silkiness of her mouth.

She gave good head and it was all the more arousing because of the situation. Her tongue lapped under him as her mouth slipped over him and he moaned out loud with the pleasure then bit his lip. He had to be careful, someone could walk in at any moment and he didn't want to give the game away. He tried to focus on the computer screen before him but it was completely useless. Her talented mouth already had him on the brink of orgasm.

Just then the door flew open. Dave's heart jumped and Sally stilled below the desk.

"Have you seen Sally?" the man barked. "She's meant to be in the ticket office and it's still all locked up. It's almost rush hour and people need their tickets."

"I've not seen her, boss." Dave shrugged as Sally's lips rested around his hard cock, her tongue flicking gently at the underside of it. "But if I do, I'll send her right over."

"Good, good." The man nodded and pushed his tiny circular spectacles back up the bridge of his nose. "The 4.32 is coming in on platform four now. You need to announce it every couple of minutes from now until it arrives."

"Right, boss," Dave replied, reaching out to grab the mike. "I'm on it."

"I don't know why we bother," the boss muttered and walked back out of the room. "Some silly sod will still miss the announcement and come and complain to me about it."

Dave flicked on the microphone and began to make the announcement. "All passengers on platform two, please be advised that the 4.32 train to Scunthorpe will now be arriving on platform four." At this point, Sally continued her sucking and Dave's voice became a squeak with the arousal rushing through his veins. "That is, the 4.32 to Scunthorpe will now be boarding on platform four."

Her tongue snaked around his member and her lips tightened and he groaned before realizing the mike was still on. He tried to switch it off but in his rush only managed to knock it over. He could imagine the squealing static that would be attacking people's ears on the platform as he did his best to right it.

"The four . . ." His words were eaten up in a blanket of static and Sally sank her mouth completely around his erection, her fingers scratching down his inner thigh over the top of the scratchy work trousers he wore. The mike knocked over again before he could right it properly and he knew he couldn't reach it without pulling his dick from between her lips and he didn't want to do that.

"Fuck it," he said and concentrated on the hot sensations running from his dick through his whole body. A few seconds later, he grunted out a "Yes," as he came. She sucked down every last drop.

She got up off the floor, wiped her lips clean, winked and said, "I'm supposed to be in the ticket office right now, but I don't care. I need to come. Mind if I wank on your desk?"

"I'm supposed to make clear, concise announcements to the public but that doesn't happen anyway. Make yourself comfy."

He picked up the mike and sat back in his chair to make one last attempt to inform the public of the platform change. Sally hopped back onto the desk, the keyboard pushing back behind her. She opened her legs wide and rested them on his knees.

"All passengers on platform two . . ." He spoke slowly with confidence at first and then he got distracted by Sally pulling aside her knickers and fingering her cunt. "Yeah, erm, customers on platform, whatwasitagain? Platform two should be advised that the . . . that the . . . that the . . ." he stuttered as Sally began to moan. She was rubbing her clit hard and her chest was heaving up and down with each panted breath.

He licked his lips, took a deep breath and continued. He wondered if Sally's sex noises were carrying over the loud-speaker system. She certainly wasn't holding back. She was really getting very noisy. She was definitely enjoying herself, he could tell. Her cheeks and chest flushed and she threw her head back as she lost herself in her coming orgasm.

"The 4.32 train to Scunthorpe will now be arriving on plat-form four." He raced through the last part of his sentence and clicked off the mike just as she came. Her knees shook and her body stiffened. Dave could see the juices dripping from her cunt onto his desk. Fuck, she was juicy.

"No wonder I fucking love you," he gasped as she straight-ened herself up and hopped off the desk.

"I love you too, you dirty perv, you," she replied and laid a kiss on his cheek and then giggled.

"What's tickled you?" Dave asked with a smile.

"I was just thinking the public would flip if they knew why the train announcements here are so garbled," she replied and walked away from his desk.

"They'd all want the job!" he exclaimed.

"Nobody could replace you, love." Sally paused in the door-way and blew him a kiss.

"I'd not give anyone a chance," he replied as the door slammed shut. "I'm not letting anyone else have this level of job satisfaction. It's all mine!"

Like a Virgin for the Very First Time

Maxim Jakubowski

It never was better than the first time. Later occasions might prove more sensual, longer, more kinky or perverse, more skilful or lasting, technically outstanding or just proficient, but it just wasn't the same.

And every first time in initially unknown hotel rooms was the best of all.

Years later, when the thrill of the chase had faded, or when he just couldn't find the mental energy within his soul to embark on yet another transitory relationship that could only tread a road to nowhere, he would swim willingly back through the reef of memories and vicariously treat himself to a sensurround movie of past, long gone moments, secure in the knowledge that those times would never be his again to taste, enjoy, experience, struggle with, all those first times. It would be like a private library, a unique collection where sensual, tender memories would rival the space customarily devoted by the collector within to books, CDs and DVDs. A scintillating gallery of moments, of mental impressionism.

A hotel room near an airport where no one was likely to recognize them, the smell of ozone in the air and the distant rumbling of jumbo jets on their approach or departure: that indefinable feeling of burning up inside because the lust is just accumulating at a rate too fast for the heart to burn it off like mere calories, the nagging fear of the unknown, the unusual surroundings of the leisure chain's identikit room. This is what they have been building up to for three agonizing months of on/

off/on/off/on debates in city bars, "Do we sleep together or don't we?"

A tentative kiss. Her mouth is warm and soft. As ever.

The look in her eyes. Pleading. Scared. Eager.

Submissive. Defiant. They both have wife and husband back home, in ignorance. Their first infidelity. Adultery set loose that would change their lives for ever.

His hand, finally, moving to her body, the pliant elasticity of her thigh. The undressing. The foreplay and, like a holy proclamation half an hour later, her cry of need: "I want you inside me now . . ." The first time he fucked Kate. The way her brown eyes watched his every movement and thrust inside her. Her sounds. The white alabaster landscape of her body and the scarlet tinge of the orgasmic flush that sometimes overcame her shoulders and chest. Memories that can never be erased.

Then, a hotel in Amsterdam, overlooking a grey canal and parked bicycles. The awkward and slow rise of the elevator up to his floor, following their furtive, eyes downturned, passage by the night porter's desk and an endless walk through the red-light district, both knowing that they are going to end up in bed, but delaying the inevitable on and on. The frantic fumbling for each other's lips and hands roaming freely over willing bodies, the tugging of clothes. He gets on his knees and slowly, in the semi-darkness, pulls her panties down. Her pubic hair is all curls and slightly damp. He sniffs, but all he can smell is the remote fragrance of soap. He inserts a finger inside her cauldron. She is on fire. She moans. He quickly pushes her back against the bed and she allows herself to collapse with languor over the drawn bedcover. He is hard as hell and almost bursting with a rage to tear her apart, this soft-spoken girl with the lovely accent and her tales of past woe and problems. She is already so wet. He remembers a past conversation and guides her around onto her knees, her stated preference to be taken doggy style. She angles her rump towards him. The view of her exposed openings is like a salutary slap in the face, unforgettable, powerful, indelibly obscene. He moves into her in one swift movement, all the while storing the memory in the safety of his grey matter.

Or, again, this time a hotel in Paris, with exposed wooden beams criss-crossing the ceiling and far wall. He has barely known her a month or so and their first meeting in the flesh, so to speak, was at the railway station just an hour ago. Their only contact prior to today was by email or telephone. It's a crazy situation, but it somehow makes complete sense.

She was so much taller than he had expected but her breasts are a wonder to behold. Fingers, lips and feelings have already played a mad dance of lust and their clothes are in disarray. "Wait," she says and rises, divine areas of flesh exposed, and tiptoes quickly to the bathroom.

A few minutes later, she returns. She is quite naked. He holds his breath back as he stares at the smooth, shaven area of her cunt. Of course, he already knew, not only had she told him but his exploratory fingers some minutes ago had certainly double-checked, but the vision is just too much. He feels as if his heart has stopped. She signals for him to lie down and her mouth envelops him. He has to think of books and such to avoid coming inside her throat prematurely. Shortly after, she confesses she loves him. Lust and feelings, an unholy mix, just like romanticism and pornography.

The safety of unknown hotel rooms, as anonymous as internet forums or chatlines. The cosy coexistence of unbridled sexual excess and mundanity. The rooms, the women, the acts.

They say that, at the moment of death, your whole past parades in front of your eyes, like a film on a loop, fast, out of control, out of reach.

He sometimes wonders whether, when the moment finally comes, his own epiphany will be full of hotel room horizons and beautiful fucks.

He hopes it will.

Tripartite

Georgia E. Jones

They were always together. They shared an old cabin in the pines above the bay. They worked out of the same shop, though often enough on separate jobs. They went camping together and to parties and to movies. They argued sometimes, but infrequently and it never lasted long. I was new in town, which made me the fresh meat. It was intimidating. As soon as everyone sniffed around and took a turn they'd get bored and go back to whatever they were doing before I moved in, but I'd been through a divorce and wanted no part of it. I needed wingmen, and in Will and Adam I had them.

There was sexual attraction, to be sure. Adam glowed with it. It was the first thing anyone noticed about him because, like a boxer with a solid left hook, he led with it. He propositioned me first thing, I declined, and after that we were friends. Will was harder to read. It took him four months to ask for a hug, but when he made his interest known, there was no mistaking it. I was tempted. Extremely tempted. But I didn't want anyone to get hurt, least of all myself. Instead of friends with benefits, we became friends with attraction. We met for drinks. We went hiking. They showed me the best places to swim and where to pick berries in the summer when the heat lay low in the thickets and there was no breeze anywhere. They dated, but nothing serious, and I ignored the twinge it gave me because it was such a pleasure to know them. They seemed bemused by me, like they couldn't figure out what I was up to but were willing to humor me. They never said I was pretty, but I could tell they thought I was. They reminded me of animals sometimes – young bucks, full of muscle, or puppies needing love. It didn't take long to figure out I wanted both of them. As lovers, I would have to choose one, risking the disapprobation of the other. As friends, I could have both.

In August they took me swimming at Daylight Beach. It was small and hidden and only the locals knew about it. The tourists congregated on the bigger beach to the east, noisy with kids and dogs and radios. Their dog lolled with us in the sun for a while, then snaked back into the woods to kill things and eat them where we couldn't see. His origins were mysterious. He was part wolf, or mostly wolf. There was a story there, but the boys told things in their own time, or not at all. I got used to asking once and waiting. Now and then I got an answer. We stayed near the water all day long and past it. It was dark when we started to hike back to the truck. The dog ghosted in and out of the trees, in front of us, behind us, making his own way.

The path was thin and twisted, lined with the roots of bay and oak trees and the cinnamon-barked madroños. I stumbled twice on things they seemed to see in the dark. "Stop here," Will said when we reached a small clearing about halfway to the truck. "The moon is coming up."

I stood, catching my breath. Days were hot on the coast, and the nights cool. I shivered, wearing nothing but a thin T-shirt over a damp bikini top. Adam saw it, or felt it. "Come here," he said, and put his arms around me. I leaned against him, grateful for the warmth, ignoring the frisson of desire that sifted through my skin and down into my belly.

"Hey," Will said softly, a protest. He came up behind me, moving closer until I was caught between the two of them. Adam was built solid and low to the ground. Will was taller, his chin resting on the top of my head. I stood still, absorbing the heat and scent of them – the salty tang of sweat, and in the air pine and bay and, more faintly, eucalyptus. Adam's cock rose up, pushing against my belly. He wasn't the type to apologize and I liked it, unequivocally. I canted my hips backwards, pressing my ass against Will, an invitation, and got an answer in the sweet rise of his flesh against mine. The only thought I had was whether it would disturb them, being so close to one another, but then I figured if it did they wouldn't be standing where they were. I was wearing an old cotton skirt and I lifted it in handfuls. If they thought that was a bad idea, they could tell me.

Adam sank to the ground, pulling me down with him. I ran my hands across his belly briefly, before pulling down his trunks and putting my mouth on his cock. He made a strangled sound, half a groan, and I sucked on him, hard, crouched between his thighs, not giving him a chance to adjust. Will lifted me to my knees, stripped off my bikini and touched me, spreading me open, nudging me with the head of his cock. He went slowly, or slow-ish, at any rate. He knew exactly how much sex I hadn't been having since the divorce. Then I was filled up, the hot, thick length of Will inside me and hard thrust of Adam's cock in my mouth. It was what I wanted, bone-deep and mindless. I couldn't establish any sort of rhythm, clenching around Will and grinding back against him. He said something – the dark voice of a cautionary tale – and held my hips in broad-palmed hands and did it for me.

I sucked on Adam, licking him up and down, cupping his balls in one hand then taking him as deep as I could until he touched the back of my throat. I was frantic for them to come; not because I wanted it to end, but because I was so overwhelmingly hungry for them I wanted to take them inside me, whatever they gave, and hold on to it. Adam came first, crying out, his hands fisted in my hair. I swallowed all of it and rested my face against his belly, feeling Will thrust harder and harder, my own pleasure rising towards orgasm, but it was going to take longer than he had, so I just tightened around him as hard as I could and held on until he came.

We lay in a warm heap of tangled limbs, a serial killer's dream. The wind soughed in the tops of the trees. I measured my breathing against theirs, first Will's, then Adam's. After a time, Will said, "She didn't come."

Adam lifted his head. "She didn't come?" He stroked my neck, as if he would find the answer there. "Why didn't you come?"

"Um," I said. "Not good at multitasking?"

Adam sat up. "We'll have to do something about that."

"Let's," said Will.

Adam didn't say anything else, just picked me up and put me where he wanted me, which was straddled across his lap with my back against his chest. "I want you inside me," I said, tilting my head back on his shoulder and he did me the favor of taking me seriously.

"Give me a minute," he said. He pressed his cock into the small of my back. He reached around and dragged his hand between my legs, smearing the wetness on his cock, then more on my nipples, then on his lips, acting generally like a man with all his favorite foods in front of him who decides not to choose one but to have them all. He lifted me and pushed inside me and I shivered all over, not from cold. It was strange, having two different cocks in quick succession. Adam was wider in girth but not as long as Will. I arched, squirming on him.

"No," he said, brusque. "Hold still." And he held me down, thighs spread wide.

Will knelt between my legs and touched his tongue to my clit. "No multitasking," he said. "Just this." He licked me all over, like he liked the taste of me, all around my clit, trying different angles until he found one that made the strong tendons in my inner thighs go weak.

"Yes," Adam was whispering in my ear, "come, come, come," and I was dying to. I was desperate to move, trying to close my thighs around Will's head, trying to move on Adam's cock, throbbing inside me, and he held me down and made me take it until I broke, spasming around him, against Will's mouth, in waves and waves for what felt like a long time.

I drifted, warm and sated. I slowly became aware that Adam had tipped my head to one side and was gnawing on the spot where my neck ran into my shoulder. "Yes," I said. "I want you to. Do it." He gasped – relief, I felt it – and began to thrust, strong and unrestrained. I gripped his thighs, the muscles flexing under my hands. Will stood up. His cock was hard from making me come and he stroked it. The moon was up, round and full. Blame it on the moon. That was a line from a song I knew a long time ago. In the dim, white glow I could see his blue gaze resting where Adam moved in and out of me. I lifted a hand and Will came closer on delicate feet. I pried his fingers apart and wrapped my hand around his cock. "Now do it," I said, and he covered my hand with his and began to pump.

★ ★ ★

I kept laughing on the way up the trail, drunk with love. I fell once and didn't care and after that one of them kept a hand on me. The wolf was waiting for us at the truck; his tail thumped once in greeting and he jumped into the back. I sat between them in the truck, the heater blowing warm air on my feet. Will drove. Just before the turn-off to my place he said, "Unless you say different, you're coming to the cabin." I didn't say anything.

Inside, they took my clothes off together, one piece at a time, and rolled me under the covers. The bed was big and soft and I sighed, closing my eyes. "We've worn her out," Will said.

"She'll be fine," Adam said, and he had the right of it. I reached for Will, curling my fingers around the muscle of his forearm at the widest part, where it tapers down to the wrist. "Will this be awkward in the morning?"

He dropped a kiss at the corner of my mouth. "Only if coffee makes you feel awkward, sweetheart," he said.

Adam pressed a kiss to my temple. "We'll be in the other room if you need anything."

My breathing was the only sound in the room. They were not two halves of the same whole. There was no cliché to cover them. They were worlds unto themselves, come to rest side by side. I could hear them in the next room, maybe talking about what had happened, maybe just talking like people who can spend all day together and still have something to say to each other at the end of it.

I was naked. I wanted to stand up and go to them and spread myself across their laps and ask for more. But my eyes wouldn't open. My body wouldn't move. I lay quietly in the bed and listened to the sound of their voices, the low murmur of water falling over stones.

Engineers and Astronauts

Jacqueline Applebee

I am an astronaut. I can travel faster than the speed of sound. And whilst I'm not the first woman to go into space, I'm sure I'm the first one to do it buck-naked. The orgasms I have with my new lover transport me faster than any space shuttle and, when I come, I go far beyond Mach 1. Gravity doesn't mean shit to me when I let go. I soar through space on my adventures. I always see the stars.

My new lover Frank is a very talented Dutchman, and he's an engineer too – what he can do with his amazing hands is probably illegal in some parts of the world. His long fingers frantically plunge inside my pussy, stoking the power to my engines. Every time he hits my G-spot, stabbing me with pleasure that makes me want to explode, I channel the power instead, so I don't self-combust.

Frank looks me right in the eye whenever we make love. He holds me with his gaze, and imprints himself on my circuitry, with every thrust inside my growing heat. He is the spark that ignites me, and I blaze for him every time. Frank is a diligent lover, and he always concentrates when he sets me free. He puts his whole self into the palms of his hands – that's why I can do this with him and no one else.

I gather fuel from our fucking, and soon I hear my thrusters start. My body readies itself for the trip, and I can already taste stardust on my lips. A sound unlike any other begins in the back of my throat and, before I know it, I blast off, screaming as I go. The ceiling above me opens up to reveal the scorched wooden beams in the attic. The roof of Frank's home is burned away with the force of my exit and I am propelled into space, leaving my lover and his talented hands behind.

Space is black and beautiful. Space consumes me – it swallows me up with darkness that is illuminated with touches of sparkling colour. I become part of the universe when I orgasm like this. I travel further and further every time, yet there is always more to see, more to explore. Have you heard the world is flat? Well the Earth is a pancake compared to Space, where dimensions bend and swell around me. Every contraction of my pussy becomes a pulsar. I radiate light and heat. I travel to worlds beyond imagination.

When I return from my space adventure some time later, Frank is sitting on the bed with a cup of milky coffee for himself, and an orange juice for me. It will take some time before I'm ready to make another flight, and I need to recharge first.

"See anything interesting up there?" he asks me with a smile.

"I saw the stars, darling," I say weakly. "I saw the stars."

Frank holds my sweaty body as my engines cool down. He recites special incantations that keep me earthbound – science and magic come together with potent results. As I listen to his soothing voice, I wonder if he ever takes flight like me, or if being my engineer is enough for him. Maybe it's time to start Frank's space program. I would love to go travelling with this fantastic man.

A plan formulates in my mind – I'll make an astronaut out of my engineer yet.

I break free from the long arms that hold me, and I pin my surprised lover down on the bed. I settle over his lean body, and I let him feel the force that lies inside my explosions. I suck his thick cock deep into my mouth, and I coat him with saliva, which is really flammable lubricant. I suck and pull on his hardening dick, murmuring a spell of freedom as I go. I want Frank to be lighter than air, so that he can shatter the bonds of gravity, and do what I do.

I want my Frank to fly.

I test his readiness by tweaking his nipples. I calibrate his sensors with my fingertips, and he bucks beneath me.

"Please, Ann!" he yells in English, and then he shouts it even louder in Dutch – I don't know much of the language, but even I can work this one out.

He isn't ready yet – if I let him go now, he wouldn't get past the upper atmosphere before he fell. I douse him with spit and rocket fuel, swallow him all the way down to his balls, and I lick, suck and blow Frank for all I'm worth. I press the map of the universe from my tongue and onto his shaft, with precise licks. I trace the coordinates of his journey with my teeth, as I graze them gently over the head of his cock. It's not fair that only astronauts get to have adventures when I wouldn't get an inch off the ground without my engineer. I grind my sore pussy onto his knees, grip his thighs and redress the balance with a grunt.

Frank starts to shudder hard now. He squeezes his eyes shut, to protect him from the fiery blast, and it is only then that I let him leave me. With one final swallow of my wet mouth, he explodes into movement, flings his body upward and he ascends into the stratosphere with a piercing scream.

My Frank is flying!

I am knocked aside by the force of his take-off. I watch from the bedroom floor in wonder as my lover shoots into space. His jets scorch me, and his afterburners turn me into cinders. I love that I can do this for him. I am on fire for this man.

He descends a long time later – dazed, and babbling about how he will need to bring oxygen with him on the next trip. I smile at this. There will surely be other journeys, ones where we will both speed through space at the same time – flying in tandem. Between my lover with his talented hands and me with my talented mouth, I know we'll take to the skies together. But for now, Frank needs to rest. I hold him gently, and I whisper my own special words to calm him – to let him know that he won't float away whilst he sleeps. I embrace his cooling body and whisper:

"It's OK, Frank, I've got you. I love you."

The Proxy Groom

Michael Hemmingson

1.

Ever wonder what the life of a proxy groom is like? I'll tell you. The life of the proxy groom is a loveless one because no woman in her right mind wants a guy who gets married to an average of ten women a month. The proxy groom has no wife to come home to and cook him dinner and love him all night in bed. The proxy groom sleeps alone, mostly.

What the heck is a proxy groom, you ask? I'll tell you. We're fellows who stand in for fellows who can't be present at their own wedding. This is usually the case for soldiers fighting in the Middle East or serving on Naval ships and even fellows who are doing black ops CIA stuff and cannot reveal their locations. Sometimes it's a foreign guy in another country who can't come over because he can't get a visa. Sometimes it's an old school arranged marriage and marriages for business purposes and the groom doesn't feel like being there, or the bride doesn't want him there. There are many reasons, and by law I can stand in for them, I can be their proxy: I'm just a body to stand next to the bride so she's not at the altar marrying air or a face on a webcam.

I live in Manhattan and you'd be surprised how in demand a proxy groom is. I advertise on Craigslist and have a website. I have married girls as young as sixteen and women as old as eighty.

They call me, these women do, or maybe their mothers, and they say, "Do you *actually* make a living at this?"

They ask, "Do you need a license?"

They go, "Do you also provide honeymoon night services?"

The answers are yes, no, and yes.

2.

Sometimes standing in is not enough for certain brides. They want the full wedding experience. It's an extra charge for honeymoon services. Some say it makes me a gigolo. Sometimes the absent husbands know, sometimes they don't. Sometimes the women are virgins and I am very careful when I remove the maidenhead. Sometimes the women are middle-aged or older and not so interested in sex as they are needful of affection, to be held and cuddled and kissed and whispered "I love you" to. I give my all to these women when I'm with them, but when I leave and go home, back to my life, I push them out of my mind.

My heart locks up.

It's just a job.

I go home to a lonely life. I have three cats and they are always happy to see me. I have a modest apartment in Hell's Kitchen. Sometimes I am glad to be alone when I come home and sometimes I wish I had someone to come home to.

3.

Dating isn't easy for a proxy groom. Like I said, no woman in her right mind would get serious about a guy like me. Oh, they've tried but they get jealous, especially if I do the honeymoon night, even more so if I do the prime package: one or two weeks honeymooning on a cruise ship or in France or in New Zealand, wherever – that's where the real money comes in. I have tried to explain to these women who have tried to love me that it's nothing but a job, a service, it means nothing, but they don't believe it.

I don't blame them.

Every once in a while a client falls in love with me, they believe I'm better husband material than their absent husbands, and again I have to remind them that I am on the clock, they are paying for my affection and love, that I have a life outside the proxy. They might entice me with money, position, good sex, but I never fall in love.

No, I have never fallen in love with a client – until, that is, I met Kimberly Kane.

* * *

4.

Kimberly Kane wasn't a model or a bombshell or a babe or even the girl next door. She wasn't rich or came from prime American DNA. She was a typically average girl of twenty-one who worked as a cashier in a grocery store and went to community college at night. She seldom wore make-up, she had light freckles on her face, she was five foot three and often kept her straight dark hair in a ponytail, She had a couple of crooked teeth. She was a very nice girl. She was a modest girl. She was not fretful because she was not famous or rich or had a successful husband or a hunk of a boyfriend. She drove a beat-up little car and wore faded jeans and Hollister hoodies. Her breasts were A cups and her ass was skinny and flat.

So why, you might ask, did I fall in love with her, when I could have fallen in love with some very beautiful wives, wives with money, wives who drove fancy cars?

No one knows why falling in love happens.

It just does.

5.

Kimberly married her best friend from high school who was in Afghanistan. He didn't appear much like a soldier when I saw him on the webcam at the wedding chapel: he was tall and skinny, had red hair and freckles galore, wore thick glasses and had buck teeth. He was fluent in Arabic, so he had that going for him for where he was.

They had never dated in high school, Kimberly and her husband; they were both in the science-fiction club, a group of seven geeky kids who talked about the books they read and the movies they saw that were of the science-fiction genre. They had gone to science-fiction fan conventions and dressed up like characters from *Battlestar Galactica* or something she called steampunk.

This is what she told me on the honeymoon anyway.

She had purchased the three-night package in a Catskills cabin; she'd saved up for this and her husband contributed to the fund too. I took her for a virgin and was prepared for it, but she informed me she hadn't been a virgin since she was twelve. "Thanks to my stepfather," she said, "I became a woman at an early age."

There are some family secrets I care not to know.

She seemed to want to tell me these things. She told me about having sex with her stepfather, and an uncle, and two cousins. "If my father were alive," she said, "I'd probably get all Elektra and fuck him too."

In junior high and high school, she informed me, she freely gave a lot of boys blow jobs and got a reputation. It was the only way a girl like her could get attention and acceptance. "A good cocksucker can go a long way during the teen years," she said.

If she was so active, why hadn't she had sex with her husband in Afghanistan?

"He's gay," Kimberly said. "My gay best friend. Yep, I'm a fag hag. He's afraid he's going to die over there and if he does, he wants me to collect on his benefits, but the way I hear it the Army likes to screw wives out of the money they're due."

6.

Something happened when I made love to Kimberly Kane and held her in my arms after, and held her in bed as she slept and snored loudly, drool drooling out of her open mouth and soaking her pillowcase. Something happened with my heart.

7.

She cried the second time I made love to her. "This is so wonderful for something so fake," she said. "Why can't this be real?" she said. "Why are things like this?" she asked.

She said, "I lied to you."

I said, "What?"

She said, "I lied to you, Mr Proxy Groom."

I said, "About?"

She said, "All that incest stuff. I never had sex with my stepfather. I don't even have a stepfather, my mom never remarried when my dad died. I never had sex with any uncles or cousins. I didn't suck all those dicks in high school although I wished I had."

I asked why the lies.

She said, "I guess I wanted to shock you."

She said, "I guess I wanted to be interesting and unusual."

She said, "I always lie about the truth."

I asked if she was a virgin last night.

She said, "Oh no, I've had sex before. With two men. One was married and one was my boss. The sex wasn't memorable. Not like this."

I was flattered and told her so.

She said, "I lied again. The two men, one was not married and one was not my boss. One was a cab driver who raped me and the other was a guy at a party who got me drunk and had his way."

I didn't know if I should believe her.

She burst into tears.

She said, "Don't hate me. OK, OK, I *was* a virgin last night. Thanks to you, I'm not anymore. Thanks to you, I know how wonderful sex is."

I held her.

I made love to her.

And I loved her.

8.

Two weeks later, Kimberly Kane showed up at my door. I hadn't been able to get her out of my mind and stopped myself from calling her three dozen times because it wouldn't be ethical in my line of work.

She sort of told me the same.

She said, "I said to myself I would not come here, but I had to."

I held her in my arms and said, "'Tis OK, my lady, I understand. I know how you feel because I feel the same."

"It's not that, my darling sir. I come to you as a widow," and she explained how some men from the US Army came to her door and informed her that her husband died a hero in combat, saving the lives of two others.

9.

The parents of her dead husband were not pleased about her getting their son's benefits, not after they learned she had hooked up with me. She informed them that she planned to remarry.

"Our son's been dead for a week, his body is not even here yet," the parents said. "*That's no way to mourn*."

Etc.

"Your son was gay!" she told them.

Apparently they didn't know this.

"Your son sucked dicks!" she told them. "He took it in the ass by strangers he met on Craigslist!"

They did not like knowing that.

"And there is no body *coming back*," she told them. "Just some bones and guts and an arm."

No, they did not like this at all.

10.

Her friends all turned their backs on her. She knew her dead gay husband's parents were whispering bad things about her into any ear that would listen to bad things and gossip.

"Fuck them all," said Kimberly Kane, "I have you at least."

11.

She said, "No more marrying other women, that's my only condition."

12.

I started to get hate emails from anonymous people, accusing me of being a very bad man

"Fuck them all," said Kimberly Kane. "Those fucking fuckers can go fuck themselves."

13.

Ever wonder what a construction worker thinks about when he busts his ass all day and sweats like a sumo wrestler while building buildings? I'll tell you. He thinks about the sweet wife he has waiting for him at home, and how she will massage his aching muscles and love him all night in the bed they share.

The Wrong Woman

Kristina Lloyd

"Someone had fucked up" went the story. He was supposed to be handsome and charming, and they should have been in a restaurant playing footsie under the table while a waiter took their order, glass and cutlery tinkling around them.

Instead, Jody was in a dingy alley with a gun to her back, her hair awry, her stockings laddered. "Keep walking," he said. "Look straight ahead."

Her legs were shaking. That wasn't in the story. Cobbles rippled like water in the pale white sheen of a street light and, in her heels, she struggled on the uneven terrain like a weak-limbed foal.

"You've got the wrong woman." Her throat was dry, her voice a rasp.

"Don't get cute," he said. "Here. Left here. I've got some friends who want to meet you."

Around the corner, he made her stand by a broad wooden door as he tied her hands behind her back, looping rope around her wrists in a figure of eight. Brittle strips of green paint hung like lolling tongues from the wood and six small, high windows suggested a dirty, cobwebbed interior. When Jody's hands were secured, the man heaved on a handle to roll the doors aside, the scene opening up as it might in a theatre when the curtains were raised. Before them was a cobble-floored car repair garage, its ceiling veiled by a sagging pigeon net from which crisp, brown ivy dangled like vines in a ghostly rainforest. The light was dim and the props, if you could call them that, were scanty: a heap of old tyres, two rusty cars at the rear, an armchair sprouting stuffing and various tools scattered randomly about the place. No one was in sight.

Her heels echoed on the cobbles as they walked into the centre of the garage, and she imagined the knocking of her heart was equally loud. She breathed in smells of damp, dust, oil and scorched metal. She didn't know if the gun at her back was real but it didn't matter. If you thought it might be, it was.

One by one, they emerged from the shadows, five muscular men in jeans and vests, all bristling with menace and swagger. They crowded around her and she was on her knees before she knew it, the cobbles harsh and cold. The blouse she'd worn for her restaurant date tore easily. A pair of clumsy hands shoved the ripped silk around her shoulders while more hands scooped her breasts from her bra and twisted her nipples. She writhed and squealed in protest.

"You've got the wrong woman," she said again but they only laughed.

One of the men unzipped. She looked up at her circle of tormentors and that's when her world really began to spin. Dizziness turned to blackness before her vision stabilized and the colours returned. She knew him, the guy with his cock out who was glowering down at her. She knew him.

He clearly recognized her too. He edged closer.

"I knew this was a bad idea," he said. The end of his cock butted at her lips. "So let's make it a good one."

She refused to open for him. He pinched her jaw in his big hand, forcing her lips apart. "Devious little bitch. That's right, open up." As he slid into her mouth, he softly added, "There you go, Jody."

How the hell did she know him? She racked her brains but her thoughts were stalled when another pair of hands went rummaging under her skirt.

"Let's see how much she likes it, eh?"

"Who gives a fuck whether she likes it or not?"

Her body betrayed her secret, her wetness slicking onto unknown, probing fingers.

"Hey, pay attention, lady. You got another dick here."

"And here."

More unzipping, more swollen, ruddy-tipped cocks bobbing around her, zips splayed like teeth. She moved from the first cock to another belonging to a guy who soon withdrew to give one of his mates access to her ready mouth. The third guy was rough and forceful, his end bumping at her throat, making her gag and splutter. Tears and saliva spilled down her face.

"Take it," he warned, lodging himself deep.

Her tethered hands unbalanced her, but she was steadied by a fist clutching a clump of hair so hard it pinched her scalp. It was the guy who knew her name. His knowledge felt more dangerous than the gun.

They all fucked her mouth. At one point they made her take two cocks simultaneously, her lips stretched wide to accommodate both lengths. It was ungainly, awkward and physically unsatisfying for her and presumably them. But the psychological aspect was paramount, their triumphalism in her humiliation mattering more than the pleasure derived from a snug, slippery grip.

Eventually they started to come, almost as a single entity. One guy spurting into her mouth prompted another guy to jerk off onto her breasts, his groans of bliss prompting another to take himself in hand while a fourth ordered her to open her mouth, making her a receptacle for his aim.

When the guy who knew her name climaxed, she heard him roar, saw how his face flushed and the way the sinews in his neck popped out, tight and hard as guitar strings beneath his skin.

"Yes!" he hissed, throwing back his head.

Finally, she remembered who he was, remembered seeing that raw, animal passion as the man, ecstatic, had fallen to his knees. Her blood ran cold.

The feedback form was lengthy. But, said the agency, post-scene data collection was vital for their continued provision of satisfactory fantasy fulfilment.

Did the experience meet your expectations? Prefer not to answer.

Did you feel safe? Yes. No.

Did you find the men/women attractive? Yes.

Did you climax? No.

Will you climax, or have you climaxed, by recalling the scenario afterwards? Prefer not to answer.

Any other comments? You got the wrong woman. I didn't ask for this. I recognized one of the men. He plays five-a-side with my husband the first Sunday of every month at Lowfell Park. My husband must never, ever find out. Please tell that man it was a mistake. Tell him not to tell my husband. Tell him you got the wrong woman and I might sue. Tell him someone fucked up. I didn't ask to be used and degraded by a bunch of thugs in some squalid garage. I didn't ask to be tied up and have cock after cock thrust into my mouth. You got the wrong woman. Tell him.

Would you use our agency again? Yes.

If so, what sort of fantasy scenario might you like us to arrange? The wrong woman fantasy.

The Boys Next Door

Mina Murray

There are times when one steps out of one's body for a moment and looks down on it as if it is a stranger's. Heather is in the middle of precisely such a moment. Observing herself entwined with Liam and Gareth, their hard hot bodies pressed up against her, she certainly feels miles away from the shy woman she had been a mere month and a half ago.

It had all started with music. Music and a door that wouldn't close.

On the night everything changes for her, the scene opens on a block of apartments, nondescript in the way that apartment blocks are. Weighed down by some invisible burden, Heather struggles home through the icy wind, coat flapping about her like an abandoned kite. Once inside, she sags against the door briefly, gratefully, before sliding slowly to the floor. The minute her ears stop ringing from the cold, the noise asserts itself. It is a combination of thumps, muffled shouts, whining guitar and throbbing bass, a noise Heather has become all too familiar with over the past few weeks.

To start off with, she had ignored it. After all, they had just moved in. Perhaps they had friends over to see the new place. Surely things would quieten down once they had settled in. But they didn't, and tonight Heather is at breaking point. It is that particularly powerful combination of nerviness and indignation that propels her towards their door without a second thought. Just as she balls her small hand into a fist to bang on the door of apartment 6B, she notices two things. Firstly, that the door is ajar. Like her own door, like most of the other doors in her building, this one will not shut properly unless pulled hard behind you.

The second thing Heather notices is that she can no longer hear any music. But oh she can hear other sounds. Sounds like the staccato *uh, uh, uh* of a fast fuck. Heather can barely move. The only thing she can do – and even this is involuntary – is lean forward a fraction. She does not think she exerts any pressure against the door, but nevertheless it opens an inch more and a narrow beam of light spills from the hallway onto the carpet inside.

The gap is now wide enough for Heather to see the chiaroscuro figures of her neighbours in an intimate embrace. Liam, the taller, more muscular of the two, has Gareth pressed up against the wall. They are kissing, hard. A towel lies discarded on the floor and they are both naked. Liam's bent legs support Gareth's weight as he drives forcefully into him. He grips Gareth's hip with one hand, sliding the other between their bodies to tug at Gareth's cock. At least, that's what Heather guesses is happening, as Gareth lets out a moan and wraps his legs around Liam's waist. His hands clutch at Liam's back, fingers spread wide. The transfixed Heather, who has never seen two men together before, thinks Gareth is about to come. Liam breaks the kiss to gloat.

"Yeah, you like that, don't you, you little cockslut?"

Gareth bristles, wrestles Liam for dominance: he clearly does not appreciate the epithet. Heather does though. At the word "cockslut", she lets out a moan loud enough that Gareth stops struggling.

"Wait, did you hear that?"

Liam looks toward the doorway, almost directly into Heather's eyes, but says, "Hear what, man? All I can hear is you moaning for me," and pins Gareth against the wall again.

Heather flees back to her apartment, to the room with the adjoining wall. She presses her ear up against the cold surface. She can hear familiar thumping sounds. Maybe Gareth is on top now, she thinks, reaching inside her jeans to touch herself. Closing her eyes, she plots the individual arcs of their pleasure in her mind, and when Liam and Gareth get louder and her own pleasure peaks, three arcs all intersect at one glorious point.

The next day the noise is back, much louder. Heather knows it's not a coincidence that it starts up so soon after she gets home. This is a deliberate provocation, one Heather cannot ignore. She gathers up her courage and pounds on their door. It is not ajar this time. She hopes that it is Gareth who answers. Gareth she feels comfortable with, despite the tattoos adorning his arms and neck, his subtle nose stud and the matte-black discs piercing both ear lobes.

Liam, not Gareth, opens the door, shirtless and insouciant and smoking a cigarette. His chest is smooth and hairless. Heather's gaze flickers over him, taking it all in, those chocolate-dark nipples, the cluster of beauty spots scattered over his shoulders and the one below his right ear, nestled just underneath the jut of his jaw.

"What's the matter, Heather? You look disappointed. Did you want to catch us fucking again?"

Heather begins to demur, but it sounds false even to her. She cannot deny that is exactly what she had hoped. It is the reason she is braless and wearing beautiful panties under her most flattering dress.

"Oh, give it up. I saw you watching us. I know it was you."

"Don't be an ass, Liam." Gareth shoulders him out of the way. "Just ignore him, Heather, and come in. Come in and we'll talk."

There's nothing for her to do now but acquiesce.

"Make yourself useful for once, Liam. Turn the music down and get her a beer."

They sit on the couch, chat about her work, their sculptures, books. Gareth smiles so genuinely that she relaxes, despite the intense, hungry way Liam is staring at them.

"We're sorry about all the noise, Heather," Gareth says. "We'll keep it down from now on." He sticks out his hand, and she takes it with a smile. "Friends?"

"Friends."

Gareth doesn't release her hand. Instead he turns it over and traces figure eights from the well of her palm to the sensitive underside of her wrist. Heather realizes that for once in her life she can reach out and take what she wants without asking permission. She leans forward to kiss him, loving the soft scratch of his beard against her face and the eager way his lips open under hers. He wraps his arms around her waist and pulls her tightly against him. Heather hears a noise behind her and knows it is Liam before he brushes her hair aside to kiss the back of her neck.

Gareth pulls back to check that Heather is OK with where this is heading. But Heather has wanted this since the first time she saw them. When she nods and whispers, "Bedroom," Liam whoops and carries her down the hall fireman-style, flashing her panty-clad ass in the process.

And then they're in the bedroom. Liam quickly pulls her dress over her head, then tosses her sideways onto the bed. He drops to his knees on the carpet, wriggles her out of her pink satin panties and falls between her legs to spread her sex open. The tight pink bud of her clit twitches under their gaze and both men murmur appreciatively. Liam's thumbs stroke over her mons; he laps at her cunt and her clit so delicately that the ache there almost hurts as it builds and builds.

She had not expected such tenderness from Liam. But then she had not expected Gareth, warm, easygoing Gareth, to be so possessive. He drags Heather so suddenly and unceremoniously towards him on the other side of the bed that Liam has to scramble forward to keep his mouth on her. The blood rushes to her head, now hanging off the edge of the mattress. Gareth's cock looks menacingly big, but her mouth opens for it all the same.

"Not yet, princess," Gareth says as he slowly slips two fingers into her mouth and spreads them wide. She stretches out her tongue to wetly trace the inside edge of the V shape they've formed. The faint taste of salt in her mouth makes her wonder if he had been touching himself while watching Liam's mouth on her and she shudders deliciously at the thought.

Not wanting to be outdone by his best friend and sometime lover, Liam pushes his tongue deep into Heather's sex and tweaks at her clit. When she moans throatily around Gareth's fingers, Gareth stutters out a curse and pulls them free to substitute one appendage for another. There is no resistance as Heather accepts him completely. The head of his cock butts against the top of her throat and Gareth can't help but fuck her mouth, his hands wrapped gently around her neck. Heather looks upside down at him, wide-eyed, awash with desire. She can see the eagle inked on Gareth's chest, with wings that extend up either side of his neck. When he tilts his head back in pleasure, it looks like the bird is taking flight.

The mattress dips under Liam's weight and the hot blunt head of his uncut penis enters her teasingly before he bucks all the way into her. And, oh, it feels so good, the pressure just right, his cock rubbing over that swollen bundle of nerves halfway up her sex, that for a moment she soars so high she leaves her body.

When Liam thrusts harder she comes back down with a cry. There is no finesse to Heather's performance now, merely a desperate enthusiasm as she gives herself up to the syncopated rhythm set for her and allows herself to be pushed between them, a vessel driven by the tides of their lust.

Gareth, she knows, is close to coming. If she turns her head slightly to the side, she can see his toes curl in the plush carpet. Liam is close too, his thrusting increasingly erratic. When Gareth crawls forward on the bed and buries his face between her legs Heather knows they are all done for. She screams around him as he licks over her stiff bud and her wet split. On each downward slide, his tongue joins Liam's cock inside her, pushing all of them past the point of no return, where nothing can stop the gathering bliss. They come together in a feverish tangle of limbs, as Gareth explodes into Heather's eager mouth, Liam pumps himself into her and leans forward to kiss Gareth's back, and Gareth sucks furiously at her and Liam both.

As the two men collapse beside her, exhausted, Liam's arm under her breasts and Gareth's resting heavy across her belly, Heather resolves that next time they will play to *her* rhythm. And there *will* be a next time. Heather has tasted her own power, and heaven help anyone who gets in her way.

Nighthawks

M. Christian

1.00 a.m. Phillies coffee house. A cup each: white and sweet for her, black for him. Nick stirred his clockwise; Darlene stirred counter.

"Chasin' the moon tonight?" Nick said, looking over at her. Her hair was the color of fresh copper, and she wore a dress to match. Her face was lean, but not harsh, and her eyes were the green of fresh grass.

"Just watching it travel, I guess," Darlene said. He had a good face, with lots of character: strong chin, good nose, grey eyes hooded beneath luxurious eyebrows.

"Used to be able to make it myself. All the way from the silver coming up to the silver going down," he said. Under the red dress she was slim, but not skinny, breasts full and obvious even through the material.

"You don't look like you're ready to get stuck in a home to me," she said. He wasn't big, but he seemed to be well put together. His hands were like signposts to his soul: strong, elegant, with perfectly clean nails.

"You're just buttering me. Nah, just been burning too much of that midnight oil lately." He wondered about her, instantly picturing her standing in his little place: red dress tossed over a chair, slip floating as she walked, showing off her fine lines.

"Know it. Just got off a shift myself. Thought a cup might make the trip home a little easier." She wondered about his lips: strong but soft, at first a gentle graze across hers, just a mixing of breaths.

"I'm right down on Bleeker. Got a little more to do but ran out of java. Jack's place is always open." He saw himself on his bed, looking down his half-dressed body, as she climbed up with him, her slip moving just enough to give him quick snapshots of knotted, deep-brown nipples and the distant flash of curled red hairs between her long legs.

"Gotta love Jack. You work graveyard or something?" Very good hands, and she thought about how he might use them. During the kissing, when it got good, so very good, they would be on her. She could see herself spread her thighs a little, just enough. But he'd be a good man, and wouldn't dive right in. Instead, she saw him kiss her even harder, swing dancing with her tongue, and his hand rest softly on her breast. At the thought, her nipple crinkled and gently throbbed in the soft support of her bra.

"My own. I'm a hack; got one thing down but have another piece due tomorrow." He was hard and hoped she wouldn't notice, but he was also hard and hoped she *would* notice. She was there, live and real in his mind, smiling up at him as she reached into his boxers and pulled out his hard dick. In his mind, he was in her mouth, with the sensitive head of his cock grazing the roof of her mouth.

"Maybe I've read something." She could see his chest, lightly haired with dark nipples and ridges of firm muscles. His shoulders would have a light dusting of freckles, and his arms would be thick but not burly.

"Not unless you hang out in some very unladylike places. It pays the bills though. Where do you sling your hash?" The way she smiled: he ached to see that same smile as she pulled off her slip to show him her lean body, her firm breasts, her dark nipples, the triangle of red curls down between her legs.

"Del Rio's down on 154th. Food's not bad and I don't get my ass pinched." She wanted him to hold her, to squeeze her so that her body was pressed against the firmness of his chest, his tight legs, his securing arms.

"Tempting, I have to say, but I'm too much the gentleman." In his mind she was turning, showing him all that she had, a proud display of her excitement. Not shy, but smiling with pleasure. Her breasts, yes – firm, with just a little jiggle as she turned; her bush, looking sweet and inviting; her ass, tight and strong, like a perfect pear.

"My knight. Just as long as your pen is better than your sword." She was daring in her mind, imagining his strokes into her, his strong pounding between her tight thighs. A quick blush came to her cheeks as the wetness came between her legs.

"Don't know about that – haven't got any complaints about the sword as of yet." In his mind her red, freckled body straddled him as he lay on his bed, her tits bouncing as she moved her ass up and down on his dick.

She felt a new flush, a kind of fear. Good, but it was too much: she wanted to touch him, to run a hand across his cheek, to feel the muscles there, the slight sandpaper of his almost-invisible shadow. She wanted to say something, to bring it about. No, it was too scary. "This late I don't know if anyone would be able to find anything," she said.

She was still fucking herself on his so-hard dick, but part of himself felt the illusion fall. If she came with him she probably wouldn't smile, probably wouldn't show him her body with pride and excitement. Maybe a hand job, maybe just a promise for sometime later that would never come. "I know. Except maybe the moon. Shouldn't stop us from trying though," he said.

"Always willing to try, but, you know, I think it's going down," she said, a little bloom springing up. Maybe, maybe, maybe. She touched that hope, and kept smiling at him.

"Happens to all of us. Long nights, too little sleep . . . you know." But, he thought, she just might. The illusion flickered but didn't die – he held it, looking at her pretty face, and smiled back. Maybe . . .

"Too well. Sometimes I think the only thing that keeps me going is the joe," she said. She held it, the dream of him kissing her, of his broad chest, his strong thrusts, the chills and wonderful shivers of him inside her. Not tonight – no, but there's always the next day.

"Good dreams. See you in here tomorrow?" he said, trying to keep the quaver out of his voice, the precious grip on his dream from slipping. It was a good illusion: so real and . . . too complete not to give it a try.

"It's a date," she said, swallowing back an octave of pleasure. Not today, but maybe later – maybe sometime soon, maybe even tomorrow.

"See ya," he said as she got off the stool and picked up her purse.

"Bye," she said as she passed him and walked towards the glass doors.

He watched her go, and smiled.

At the doors she looked back, and returned it.

The Eyes of Sigmund Freud

Donna George Storey

I saved the Freud Museum for our last day in Vienna. The late October sky was leaden; withered leaves skittered across the pavement. I was in a gloomy mood myself. Rob warned me he'd be working long hours, but I thought at least we'd spend the evenings together. I imagined strolling the streets around St Stephen's, catching glimpses of famous ghosts – the doomed Baroness Mary Vetsera hurrying off to a tryst with Prince Rudolf, or Mozart in his wig and knee breeches returning from the triumphant debut of *The Marriage of Figaro* at the Bergtheater. Afterwards Rob and I would have the kind of untrammeled sex you can only enjoy in hotel beds, while the decadent spirits of old Vienna looked on approvingly.

Instead Rob came back to our room late and always exhausted. I was too disappointed even to masturbate as he lay snoring beside me.

Perhaps Dr Freud would have a cure for my frustration?

I picked up the English brochure at the museum ticket booth and started on the self-guided tour. The waiting room had the original furnishings: an overstuffed couch and chairs, suggestively threadbare from the nervous bottoms of Viennese neurotics. Unfortunately, the famous couch, upon which his patients came to understand their secret desires, remained in London where Freud sought asylum from the Nazis. It wasn't the first time on this trip I felt dissatisfied, as if something essential were missing from my experience. Maybe it *was* a penis? Rob's penis. I'd been deprived of it all week. The memory of that thick, swollen rod thrusting inside of me – orally, anally, genitally, any which way at all – made my secret muscles clench enviously.

Even I had to blush at having such unseemly urges in public. I walked on through the exhibit, willing away the hot, tingly feeling between my legs.

In the next moment, I found myself standing in front of a photograph of Sigmund Freud himself in his prime. My eyes took in the erect bearing, the neatly trimmed beard, the fat, golden watch chain dangling from his vest, and the cigar poised jauntily between two fingers. Finally I had the courage to meet the great man's gaze head-on. His right eye drooped, receding into shadow, but the left eye, uncannily alive and curious, pierced me to my soul. Freud and I stared into each other's eyes for a long moment.

In spite of myself, I felt another twinge *down there*.

Was he right? Does everything in life come down to sex?

I decided then, in honor of his memory, that I would not leave Vienna without at least one sweaty *pas de deux* to remember the city by.

Fortunately Rob came back early that night in high spirits. The work marathon had paid off, and the project was back on track. He suggested, with a wiggle of his eyebrows, that we get a quick dinner at the café down the street and come back to the room to celebrate properly.

Even our handsome blond waiter got caught up in the festive mood. He offered us a complimentary tasting flight of the house wines and seemed pleased when my favorite was the crisp Austrian white.

"Do they have Austrian wine in America?"

I smiled up at him, thinking his hawkish nose made him look like a count. "It's not popular yet, but the cool people like German wine now, so Austria is probably next."

His blue eyes twinkled. "If the cool people like German wine, then Austrian wine must be popular with the frozen people."

I couldn't help giggling. People so cool they were frozen? The joke had a sly truth to it. Rob, on the other hand, only scowled. In my tipsy haze, I realized that I was making my boyfriend jealous.

In the elevator at the pension, Rob tried to kiss me, but I turned my head away.

"Why so proper? You didn't mind flirting with that waiter in front of everyone in the restaurant."

"Come on, he was funny. Viennese men have a wonderful, dry sense of humor."

"Been spending a lot of time with Viennese men this week?"

"More time than with you," I snapped. So what if it was walking tour guides and waiters.

Back in our room, Rob silently threw on his travel pajamas – sweatpants and a T-shirt – then disappeared into the tiny bathroom. Even his toothbrushing sounded out of sorts.

Let him be mad, I thought, I was used to being on my own at night. I kicked off my shoes, peeled off my pantyhose, and went over to the tall window overlooking Bauernmarkt. Pulling back the curtains, I drank in the now familiar shapes of the dark buildings, the twinkling lights, the autumn chill of the glass. I snapped off the bedside light, transforming Vienna into a glittering velvet tapestry.

"Sasha? Are you in bed?" Rob blinked as his eyes adjusted to the dim room.

The sweet uncertainty in his voice melted away my annoyance. "Let me show you what I did while you were working late," I said softly.

He came up behind me and took me in his arms. I could feel his erection. I smiled. "Isn't it beautiful? When I'm standing here, I feel like I'm part of this city."

"It is beautiful," he agreed.

I leaned back into his embrace and sighed. Our quarrel was over.

"Wanna go to bed now?" he murmured, nuzzling my neck.

"Let's stay here a little while longer." I liked the luxury of Rob's warm body behind me, while the glittering mystery of Vienna stretched out before my eyes.

Slowly I became aware that our bodies were rocking back and forth in a subtle and unmistakably sexual dance. Rob's hand caressed my thighs through my skirt, innocently at first. Then, ever so carefully, he lifted the back hem up over my ass.

I glanced nervously up and down the street. It was late, and the few people walking by three stories below seemed intent on their own business. Besides, our room was dark except for the faint, reflective glow from the street.

Rob hooked his thumbs in the waistband of my panties and eased them down over my hips.

I laughed. "Maybe we *should* go to bed now?"

"No. Let's stay here a little while longer," he echoed, a smile in his voice. His fingers crept around and found my clit.

I stiffened.

"God, you're wet."

Part of me wanted to pull the curtain closed, but a more perverse desire stayed my hand. I wanted to find out exactly how far he'd take this dangerous game. My eyes scanned the street again.

That's when I saw *him*. A lone bearded man loitering in the shadows by the café. The man lit a cigarette, then turned and looked directly up at our window.

I caught my breath, and my buttocks bucked back against Rob's groin.

He let out a chuckle. "Anxious for the next step, are we?"

As if on cue, the man took a few steps closer. I couldn't see his expression, but he looked quickly to the right and left, then raised his face once again toward our room.

Oddly, I felt protected, as if he were keeping watch for us.

"Step out of your panties," Rob said.

Trembling, I obeyed.

He clicked his tongue. "Now be perfectly still, so no one guesses what we're doing. Can you be a 'frozen person' for me?"

I grinned in spite of myself. In the street below, I saw an answering flash of teeth. There was now no question that he could see *something* was up. I knew, too, with a dark twist of pleasure in my belly, that I wanted him to see.

"Lean over just a bit," Rob cooed. I rested my hands on the windowsill and bobbled up on my tiptoes. He teased my opening with the head of his cock, anointing himself with my juices, then pushed into me.

I groaned. The man below tilted his head. As if he'd heard.

"Play with your clit, Sasha."

"Maybe we should stop now . . ."

"No back talk. Just put your hand under your skirt and strum. I'll stand here with my cock in you until you come in front of this window for Vienna to see."

A trickle of sweat slid over my cheek. Vienna would see all right. Rob was watching and waiting. *He* was watching and waiting. Outnumbered, I snaked my hand under my skirt and began to rub my distended clitoris. But I wasn't sure I could really do this, even with two men cheering me on. Fortunately, Rob decided to help. He ran his thumb down my ass crack and began to tap my anus like a little drum. I let out a squeal and rubbed myself faster. He found my nipple through my blouse and pinched.

Caught in the searing pleasure from the front and behind, I came, my hips rocking, my shoulders jerking, my face twisted in a grimace.

Anyone watching would have known exactly what was happening to that woman at the window.

Satisfied with my performance, Rob pulled me back onto the bed. He rolled on top, pushing up my skirt, spreading my thighs apart with his knees. His thrusts were fast and deep, but I didn't mind his selfishness now. I turned my head toward the window and wondered how our third man would remember this night.

I smiled into the darkness. We'd become part of the secret history of this city in a way I'd never dared to imagine.

I hoped Sigmund Freud would be proud.

Air Force One

Cheyenne Blue

The workout room is her favorite place on Air Force One. She uses it during most flights as she waits for her husband to finish debriefing in the President's office below. Sometimes she runs on the treadmill, bobbing along to Bruce Springsteen on her iPod, her eyes staring out at the clouds. Or she'll row with a ferocity fueled by the demands of her life.

Even here, she's never alone. There's a secret service agent propped by the door, although she wonders who they think is going to kidnap her at 38,000 feet. Alien abduction, just like Agent Mulder from the *X-Files*.

Superficially the secret service agent resembles Mulder; he has the same sharp chiseled look to his square-jawed face, and hungry eyes. She's seen him watching her and it's not the intent look of a professional minder. His eyes linger on her breasts as they strain against her singlet, they caress her thighs in the brief shorts as she runs on the treadmill, and he stares at the V between her legs, damp from exertion as she bench presses more than she should to demonstrate the First Lady is no pussycat.

Sometimes she takes advantage of her position – both her physical one and that as the most important woman in the country – to tease and titillate. If her knees are that bit too far apart on the rowing machine, so that the loose shorts bunch at her pussy, so what? If he sees a flash of cunt hair as she draws oars and knees to her chest, so what? She always goes commando in the gym. She's seen the tenting at his groin and the casual readjustment of his pants to hide it. He can never tell anyone; who would he tell?

She thinks about inviting him over, asking him to help her

with the weights and then reaching up from her prone position to cup his cock. She'd let her fingers explore the length and the thickness, and she'd compare him to her husband. The secret service agent would have a short, thick cock, she thinks, to match his chunky, muscled body. She would push back his suit jacket and open the fly on those loose pants, slide her fingers in past the white boxers and take out his penis. He'd be hard, already leaking from the thrill of watching her. Her fingers would linger on his shaft, feeling the slide of silk over steel. She'd take him into her mouth and let his fluid seep into her. Her husband would never know and the agent could never tell. How do you tell the President that his wife has just sucked your cock?

She thinks about this often as she grinds out the miles on the treadmill, but she never thinks she will do it.

One day, the President and First Lady are flying from DC to LA. Letters on the map which translate to the longest, dullest flight in the country. The President is in the main cabin, stating his view, signing things. She watches as he focuses on his staff, drilling them with his eyes, patiently listening as they shuffle papers and present their case. He has time for everyone, everyone but her.

She stands behind his chair, fingering the skin on the back of his neck, willing him to notice her, to dismiss his staff and take her in his arms. But although his skin shivers at her touch, he talks on, while the assistants nod eagerly and write down his every word. Disgruntled, she slides away and goes upstairs. She considers the bar and the seductive blue bottle of gin, but decides on furious activity instead. She sees the secret service agent, the one who looks like Mulder, and in a fit of pique against her husband she changes into her briefest shorts, the ones that bite into her cunt. She leaves off her singlet, coming out only in a bright sports bra.

And she does it. With the thought of her overworked distant husband in her head and a purr in her voice, she invites the agent over to help her with the weights. He stands ready as she strains and lifts, and when the weight is settled back on the rack, she reaches her hands over her head and runs them carefully up his honed quads to his cock. Tilting her head back, she can see his face, see his startled eyes, and the flash of desire he can't quite hide. He's tense underneath her hands, indecision in the quiver of his thighs.

She does what she's fantasized and pulls on his pants, directing him until he stands at her side. Another tug and he drops to his knees. With nimble fingers, she undoes his pants, pulls down his boxers, turns her head and engulfs his cock. His groan is part pleasure and part panic.

"Jesus," he groans, even as his fingers wind into her hair, holding her there. "Ma'am, the President—"

She cuts him off by scraping her teeth lightly along his shaft and he keens a higher note and swells more within her mouth.

She knows she's good at this; many nights she's sucked her husband this way, giving in to his pleading, even when her cunt is empty and quivering for his cock to fill it. So she pushes aside the memories of her husband's cock and concentrates on this new, strange one. Humming, she works the shaft with tongue and teeth and flicks her head so that her unbound hair falls over them both, floating its long strands across his shaft where it sticks in the damp mix of saliva and cock juice.

The power swells within her, and she contemplates stopping precisely at the moment before he spurts, sitting up, wiping her mouth and swinging off the bench and walking to the changing room without a backward glance, so that he kneels stupid and alone with hard, aching cock in the empty room. The idea makes her smile around his fat meat, and she puts her legs down, one on either side of the bench, preparing to dismount.

But suddenly, she can't move. There's another body here, a lean and familiar one, dressed in the same charcoal suit he was wearing at the debriefing. And he's pressing over her, one hand on her shoulder, the other fumbling with his own fly. He's pressed between her parted thighs, and although she can't see his face, she knows he'll be wearing that half smile, the one that can make him appear so aloof.

There's nothing distant about him now. His weight presses over her, and his hand is moving her shorts to one side. The air is abrupt and cool on her bare pussy.

The secret service agent's cock has ceased its movement in her mouth, and his hand is slack in her hair. Flicking a glance upward at his face, she sees he's ashen, waiting, no doubt, for a fist to send him crashing backwards into the treadmill. She wonders if that happens, if she will bite down on his cock and flay the skin from the shaft with her teeth. Would she be the cause of that much pain? But nothing happens, except that familiar fingers are stroking through her wetness, finding her pleasure points with the knowledge of years. A finger enters her, and she mewls in pleasure around the secret service agent's cock.

The agent must know – for the moment anyway – that it's OK. He swells within her mouth again, and a bloom of salt spreads over her tongue. She resumes sucking him, harder now, faster, in time with the pressure of her husband's fingers. And then the fingers are gone, and her cunt clasps on nothing. But she knows it will be better in a minute, as he moves fully on top of her, and she feels his cock, that rigid slender pole, push into her. She arches her back and accepts him in, he's coming home, and it feels right and perfect, and the tension and anger at his distance fall away as he starts to move.

It won't take long. She's been wet for him since before she placed her hands on the secret service agent's thighs, and this is the culmination of her fantasy. He's an energetic lover; he fucks with the same intensity he brings to politics, and he's just as demanding. His hands slide underneath her buttocks, raising her up, grinding his cock into her depths as he fucks hard in long, sliding strokes.

The secret service agent is shaking, although whether from nerves or the effort of holding back she doesn't know. Maybe it's bad form in the secret service to come before the President. The thought makes her smile around his shaft, and she redoubles her efforts. She wants him to come in her mouth, she wants to swallow it all and then kiss her husband with salty lips.

The world is reduced to noise and feeling: the grunts of the President, the nervous gasps of the agent, the background drone of Air Force One, smooth shiny cock leaking in her mouth, and the long oh-so-familiar one in her cunt. It's all too much, and she knows that she will be the first to lose it.

She comes hard, clenching around her husband's cock, milking him into her depths, squeezing him, shivering around him.

Her jaw aches from the effort of not biting down as she comes, but even so, there's a grunt of pain from the man above her, and then her mouth is flooded with his spend. She swallows and releases him, turning her head so she can better see the man fucking her. His head is thrown back, she sees his patrician profile, and his fingers bite into her buttocks. His hips jerk, and she longs to reach down and caress his balls as she knows he likes, but her shoulders feel locked from the strain of her position on the hard bench. But he comes anyway, with final driving strokes that jerk her body on the bench, his head thrown back and his eyes closed.

The secret service agent has disappeared. He's faded into the lushness of Air Force One, absorbed into the paneling. Maybe he was Agent Mulder after all, and never had an existence outside her head. But then her husband leans to kiss her, and their triangle is complete as she shares with him the salty taste of another.

A shift in cabin pressure and she swallows to relieve the pressure in her ears. "We must be starting our descent to LA," she says, and is amazed at how normal her voice sounds in her ears.

The President kisses her again, and his voice rumbles in her ear. "I've already landed."

Trade Plates

Elizabeth Coldwell

The figure stands by the grass verge, huddled deep in a shapeless dark anorak, thumb out in the universal gesture requesting a lift. Byrne doesn't stop for hitchers, never has; too mindful of the risks. But the rain's beating down without cease, and simply driving by, throwing up spray in his wake, seems too cruel. Though he doesn't acknowledge it, he's thinking of his estranged wife, off on some midlife crisis trip round the Far East. Finding herself, she claims. Maybe she's hitching her way from place to place, and if so, even with all that's passed between them, he couldn't bear to think of her standing forlorn in the rain while drivers ignore her. So he slows, comes to a halt, watches the lad scurrying up to the car in his rearview mirror.

Except, as the anorak hood is thrown back, he sees the face at the wound-down passenger window is unmistakably feminine. Dark eyes gaze hopefully from beneath the fringe of a cropped, gamine haircut.

"Are you going anywhere near Newcastle?" the girl asks, her accent marking her as a native of that city.

"I can take you as far as Scotch Corner if that helps?"

She nods, smiling in gratitude, and hops into the car. "I'm Gail, by the way."

"Byrne. Nice to meet you, Gail."

Before buckling her seat belt, she drops something into the footwell, among the litter of tissues and sweet wrappers Byrne's suddenly conscious he should have cleared out long before now. He recognizes them as registration plates.

Catching the direction of his gaze, his passenger says, 'Trade plates. I just delivered a brand-new Jag to a customer in Leeds, and now I'm on the way home.'

Pulling into the stream of traffic, he comments, "Unusual job for a woman."

"My brother owns the business. He says I'm a better driver than most of the blokes he employs, and more reliable. What about you, driving for work or pleasure?"

Byrne grins, giving her the edited details of his dull travelling itinerary. Gail is a joy to converse with, more entertaining than the radio debate on the Greek economic situation he'd been half listening to. He learns about the places she's visited, the cars she's driven, the wealthy clients who – just like him – were disconcerted to see a girl delivering a luxury motor. Lulled by the mood of easy companionship, watching the miles speed by, he doesn't register the feel of her hand on his thigh at first. Only as it creeps closer to his groin, fingers moving in light, spidery circles, does he become aware of what she's doing.

It feels good. He can't deny that, and his cock is already uncoiling in response, lengthening where it lies against the bulk of his thigh. But her actions fit into so many clichéd fantasies: the nympho hitchhiker and the lusty, leering lorry driver. A ride for a ride, and all that.

Byrne places his hand on hers, does his best to still the moment.

"Gail, please," he says. "You're not obliged to do this. That's not why I stopped."

"No," she replies, "but it is why I got in. I already turned down three lifts before you got here. They weren't my type."

Byrne's never thought of himself as anyone's type before. He and his wife met at college, married too soon, never experimented with others the way this girl so clearly wants to. He's grizzled, balding a little, but he keeps himself in shape, pounding the treadmill to stave off the effects of his sedentary working days. Gail must like what she sees, because her hand is on the prowl again, and now it closes around his cock through the twill of his trousers.

The electric thrill shooting through him at her touch causes him to lose concentration for a moment, almost swerving the car into the lane to his right. They can't do this, not in a moving vehicle, not without writing it off, and themselves in the process. Luckily, the sign for a service station appears ahead, offering the obvious solution.

"Going to pull off," he informs her gruffly.

"Funny." She grins. "That's just what I was about to do."

Almost before he's reached the exit, her crafty fingers have undone his zip. Now they rest on the soft cotton of his briefs, heat radiating through to his hard, aching flesh below. Byrne wants her so badly, but still the need for safety overrides him. He finds a parking spot as far from the looming hulk of the services and their attendant petrol station as he can, not wanting anyone to see what's about to happen.

Killing the engine, he lets her free his cock. He can't help feeling he's at her mercy – she's in the perfect place to walk away in search of a better prospect, after all – but the knowledge excites him. She strokes him with slow purpose, and at first he thinks she's simply going to wank him off. When her head bobs down and the wet pout of her lips engulfs his helmet, it's almost too much. Worried he's going to come before he's properly engulfed in her mouth, he tries to tune in to the droning voice on the radio by way of distraction.

Her tongue slithers over his cockhead, and her fingers grip the base of his shaft, holding him steady as she laps, cat-like. He wants to murmur words of encouragement, but his throat's so tight all he can do is grunt. How has he found himself in this position, cock laved by a stranger's mouth in the car park of an anonymous service station? He doesn't know, cares less. All he wants is for her to suck him to a fast, spurting conclusion.

She shifts in her seat, letting him slip from her grasp as she fumbles with her own clothing, pulling down skinny black jeans to reveal cute spotted panties. They descend, too, letting the scent of horny woman fill the confined space, and she shoves her fingers into the thick muff beneath.

So hairy, he thinks, so unlike his regularly waxed, high-maintenance soon-to-be-ex-wife. Would she do this? he wonders. Suck off some guy who's giving her a lift, while she plays with her juiced-up pussy? Once the image is planted in his head, he can't shake it, and while Gail sucks and slurps on his length, he pictures his wife, stripped half bare, head buried in a stranger's lap as she makes herself come. Maybe there's more than one man in the car, and she'd have to offer herself to all of them, letting them take her mouth, her pussy, even her arse, in return for her ride ...

The wet pressure of Gail's mouth; the whimpers, muffled by his solid flesh, that tell him she's on the verge of her own orgasm; the filthy fantasy unwinding in his head – all conspire to bring him to a gasping, cursing climax. His seed blasts against the back of her throat, almost knocking her out of her stride, but not quite. She lets his limp cock slip from her lips to concentrate on herself, rubbing her clit frantically till she comes, eyes glazed with mindless pleasure.

"That was nice," she mutters when it's over, wiping her fingers on a tissue she adds to the rubbish in the footwell. The scent of their juices lingers in the air, and he cracks the window a little, not wanting anything to arouse him again.

She dozes for the rest of the journey, only waking when he stops to let her out of the car. A little peck on his cheek and she's gone, trade plates shoved under her arm, looking for her next ride. His last sight of her is that outstretched, beseeching thumb.

Byrne looks at his watch, astonished to register the time. The stop at the services – and the detour from his schedule to take her as far as Scotch Corner, a good twenty miles out of his way – has taken longer than he thought. But he remembers the feel of her mouth, the sight of her fingers buried deep in her bush, the noises she made as she came, and knows the decision was worth it. Reaching for his phone, he dials his next client to let them know he'll be late.

Kiss of Shame

Nikki Magennis

> "... hee at their coming enjoyed them all to a pennance, which was, that they should kisse his buttockes, in sign of duety to him, which being put over the pulpit bare, every one did as he had enjoyned them."
>
> *Newes from Scotland, declaring the*
> *damnable Life of Doctor Fian (1592)*

I kissed his arse, yes, I did, you pea-brained cat-faced bastards. I tore my clothes from off my back and beat myself about the body. With the dirt ingrained under my nails, and the leaves in my hair and the smell of eggs and smoke on my skin, I swayed towards him like I was drunk, knowing he wanted me, knowing he cared not for a polished rump sweet as a windfallen apple, nor the fine soft hair of a noble woman.

I know what he wanted. My hardened bones and my open, loud calling mouth. The ferocious heat between my legs, how it burned and burned. Tie me to the stake and I'll shiver with joy. I'll feel the flame lick up my legs, feel the fire snap at my buttocks. I'll fuck your fire. Watch me.

Oh you leer. I know your lips and how they curl. Drown me, then. Tie me to a stone and see if I float. I'll sink with my legs spread, show you all my cunt, like a pink water lily spread upon the surface of the black water. Aye, I'll Sheela-na-gig for you. Like you've not been panting for a glimpse of it since I was a slip of a girl, naked and squalling round the yard like a little piglet. I know you, Maister and you, Sir Dick. What you want from me. Confessions? I'll spit my confession in your face. Scratch it in your back. Suck it out of your wife's teats and spray it over your hearthstone.

Mercy. Mercy, you wicked bastard.

All right. Allow me, then. Let me tell my story. Here's the truth, now. Hear it.

He came to me at Neap tides, when the boats were all out on a shrunken black and sullen sea. If he was from subterranean places, I might have guessed. His eyes were green as jade and sort of smoke infused. When I looked at them I felt myself adrift. He'd long fingers, quick hands. But not like that. Not like that. No. At first, he'd reached out to help me, to lift my bucket and the weight I was carrying. I'd near broke my back that morning, cutting peat on the moor, and he lifted it from me and swung it on his own shoulder.

Broad, they were, and straight as that of a man who'd stand unashamed on Heaven's doorstep. You mutter, but that's how he appeared. Big and brave and beautiful, with a manner as easy as water flowing over rock, yes, like a mountain stream he was, clear and quiet, pulling me down to the water's edge, no matter where I might have thought of going. I had no choice, it seemed, but to follow him and spread out there on the black sand where no one ever came, to lie and share his water with him, let him brush it from my lips with the lace of his sleeve.

I'd never met a man so gentle.

He lay me down in the heather and kissed my mouth clean. Like a ship had pulled over me, I tasted the underside of him, sweet and salt and woodlike, his chin rasping against mine, setting my face to burning.

And it was like I was chained. Ah, you'll say it was enchantment. His or mine, I don't know, but I can say with a heart red and true that if he'd cast a spell on me I'd have willingly gone under it. Aye. Say so, then. No more a whore than your auld sister, am I, James?

Shall I go on? Sure? So let me speak.

He pulled himself over me and the clouds blotted out the sun. In the half-light my clothes squirmed and I felt myself grow liquid under his hands. He'd run up inside my skirts, like a field mouse skittering up my leg. So quick. And like whiskers tickling at my thighs, he nibbled and pecked with his nimble fingers.

Yes, he touched me there. Here. Yes, right here. Want me to raise my skirts? Higher?

Forgive me, I've a shiver in my hands. No, not guilt. The shiver of a woman who fears to be judged. For I know the ministers of the Lord are among us and I've been told they don't like to lay eyes on a woman. Not on those sacred parts of her.

I'll go on, shall I?

His hands were sure and insistent. They played hide and seek in my clothes. His nails? Yes, they did. Claw marks? Perhaps. Will you look? Here, on my back, there. Bruises? No, they were from your own hands, sir, if you'll recall. You bundled me from my bed to the ground and dragged me here.

But he treated me tenderly. If he was the— if he was who you say he was, he was as fine an actor as I've ever seen. The gentleness in his touch. Fingers like a silk glove, like rose petals dragged across my skin. Oh, he showered me in his caresses. Bent his head and drank from my mouth. His own tongue? Forked. Well, it was skilled enough. I don't know. I'd my eyes closed. Quiet and I'll keep on talking.

Right?

Right. We kissed and created a language in the crucible of our own two mouths. We spoke of heartbeat and want and promises and he asked me questions, with his hands, and I answered, with my legs and my wordless voice. The heather scratched my back, all gnarled and twisted, but I barely felt it. I'd have hardly noticed a bee sting had it spiked me on my hand, so filled with a buzz and burning I was.

Oh, yes, he'd taken my breast. In his hand, cupped and tugged and rolled. In his mouth, bit and sucked at. Both of them, and he seemed to dig his monstrous cock against me like a tree trunk. I'd almost a fear of it. My heart pounded to think how that would stretch me. I'd never— well. You laugh at me, but I'd got up that morning a virgin and had no plans to deflower myself in the peat bog. Yes, you may have tried but I'd avoided all your grubby hands until then. You just weren't good enough for me, Master. Lord. James. Richard. Sirs. Father.

So I felt his cock like a beast against me and I shrank from it. He undid his belt and showed me it and really, such a pretty purple-headed thing it was. I wanted to pet it, and gave it a kiss on its dancing head. 'Tis then he bent me down and bade me suck it. It tasted like heather honey. And yes, I let my tongue wander. I felt the warm eggs of his balls against my cheek. I smelled the hot dirt of him.

Did I do it, sirs? Did I kiss the devil's arse? Well. If I were to tell you honestly— Oh. But I am come over quite faint.

Thank you. Ah. My heaven.

Yes, stars. And the smell of burning. So dizzy.

Yes. My bed? You think? Master John, you're a kind man, sir. Why yes, this tale is a long one. No, quite unfit for your wife's ears. I understand. We'll take it up tomorrow. Yes, from the beginning. We'll start right at the beginning. Of course. Goodnight, sirs. God bless you. Till the morn.

Apple

Clarice Clique

"Adam."

Evie stepped out in front of me; she had a way of moving as if she were sauntering around a luxury hotel in the old world rather than dragging around with all the dregs and drop outs in the New Workhouses.

"Not now. Didn't you hear the bell ring?" My voice was harder than I intended, but there was something about her that made me nervous, something about the dark hair that hung loose to her waist, the midnight hue of her skin, the fullness of her curves, something about her that evoked memories and dreams I thought I'd succeeded in suppressing. If she ever noticed how tense I was around her she never showed it, she kept on seeking me out and whispering words in my ear that I'd forgotten the meaning of.

She smiled, her red lips parting revealing white teeth, too perfect for these harsh times.

I took a deep breath and softened my voice. "There's no time for your games. Look how long the lines are already, we'll be lucky if there's anything but slops left for us."

I hoped she'd turn away from me and look at the queues of workers, huddled together despite the heat, outside the towering grey building, waiting for the only meal of the day. She kept on staring at me, the look in her eye undeniably teasing.

"If we were at the front of the line all we'd get is slops," she said. "I've got something so much better. I found the garden."

"No." But I believed her. If anyone could find the mythical garden of the leaders, filled with succulent foods that hadn't been seen by normal people for years, it was her.

"I'll show you."

"It's too dangerous. We're safe here. What do you think would happen if we got found outside the boundaries? What do you think would happen if they even found out that you had found it?"

She placed a finger on my lips. "Some things are worth living for. And some things are worth dying for."

She pulled the other hand out of her pocket. Resting in the palm of her hand was a large red, round, fruit: an apple. She held it up in front of my eyes. I stared at the firm skin, glossy and shining in the sunlight. The still air filled with the fresh scent. For a moment it felt like it was the only thing that existed, the only thing that had ever existed and would ever exist.

She removed her finger from my lips and brushed the apple over my dry skin. My heart beat fast, breathing hurt my lungs. I flicked my tongue over the fruit, surprised at its coolness. It tasted of nothing and everything. I was immediately refreshed but at the same time every part of my body was filled with a voracious hunger. My stomach ached as if it were fighting back to life after being dormant for too long.

I opened my mouth wider but she snatched the apple away and secreted it somewhere amongst her overalls.

"We need to go before they notice us."

She walked in the opposite direction of the queues and I followed her back out across the working fields where we'd just finished planting the MaxiProtein grain.

I didn't know whether I was following the woman or the apple, but I didn't care.

Evie turned down one of the dust paths that was forbidden. I waited for the alarms, the guards, the guns. There was silence.

She looked over her shoulder at me and laughed. "You look disappointed."

"I don't understand. It shouldn't be so easy. Where's the trap?"

"There is no trap. All those early years of violence where they were so successful in destroying all the rebels made everyone remaining scared and docile. And the leaders have got lazy, they use all their resources on entertaining themselves. As much as they ever think of us, they think we're well-trained animals and forget that we're people with wills of our own."

"Really?"

She shrugged. "How should I know? I'm just guessing. It might be that they think no one has any energy to do anything but sleep after so much work and so little food. But not you and me."

Evie started to run, not fast, just a trot, but I struggled to keep up with her. Sweat dripped down my face and beneath my overalls, I was conscious of my body in a way that I hadn't been since the world changed. I ate no more than anyone else, but whereas almost everyone, everyone apart from Evie, had shrunk into their skeletons, I'd become hard muscle. Is that why she'd chosen me over all the others?

Evie's pace increased. All I could think about was one foot in front of the other. The dust disturbed by our movement swirled up, choking me. The fresh apple hidden within Evie's overalls. Evie's body underneath her overalls. Evie.

"We're here," she said.

I gazed at the tangle of branches she'd stopped in front of. I couldn't see any sign of apples, but amongst the brown deadwood I saw a dozen or more green leaves.

"It's beautiful," I said as my breath returned.

Evie smiled. "You're too easy to please."

She took my hand in hers. I blushed at how sweaty my palms were but she didn't seem to care. She gripped me tightly and pulled me through the twisted undergrowth. Bark and thorns scratched against my bare skin and tore the fabric of my overalls. I'd always thought the material was indestructible; there was a pleasure in finding it wasn't. We squeezed through into complete darkness. I felt as if this was the real end of the world, that the other thing had just been a practice to prepare us for true emptiness. But I wasn't alone. I could hear Evie's breathing, her hand was holding mine. She gave me a gentle pull and we emerged into something so glorious that for a long while I could not move or speak or think.

"This is a dream," I said.

"It's not a dream, Adam, it's real."

She brushed my cheek with the back of her hand, then with a sudden efficiency she undid the fastenings of my overalls and pulled them down my body, leaving me naked and her kneeling before me. Her eyes sparkled as she looked up at me. I bit down on my lip but before my instincts could take over Evie leapt to her feet.

"That's much better. These ugly things do not belong here." She took off her own clothes, in a much slower and more languorous manner. It seemed a lifetime before she was standing bare fleshed holding the apple in her hand.

My body responded to her, reaching out to her, a heat, a rising, a need to touch and be touched.

Smiling she stepped closer and placed the apple on my throat. With a smooth movement she rolled it down my body, into the hair of my groin and along my erection. Then she lifted the fruit to my lips.

"Bite," she ordered.

I parted my lips and bit down into the fruit; it was hard against my teeth, stinging them as I tore into the pale flesh beneath the skin. My mouth filled with the crisp food, the juices ran down my lips. I crunched down through the thin skin. I'd forgotten the noise of eating anything except gruel, but beyond myself I was aware of so many sounds. In the New Workhouses there was something akin to a constant muffled moaning and the continual clanking of the big machines; here the world was quieter but there was buzzing and chirping and a soft breeze swaying the branches.

"You're hungry. You never have to be hungry again." Evie's voice was full of promises beyond her words.

One of her hands moved to my hardness and stroked up and down its length as I ate the apple out of her other hand, finishing every bite until there was none left and I was sucking the juices off her fingers.

"There is more than just apples here." Evie ran through the garden and I ran after her.

She danced and she turned and she twisted, pressing fruit between my lips and then darting away again. There were so many shapes and colors and textures caressing my tongue. I held them in my mouth before swallowing for as long as my willpower let me, savoring the sweetness and the tang.

As she ran through the trees and bushes heavy with fruit, her body seemed to merge with the things she was giving me to eat;

her curves were the sweet curves of the peach which exploded in juice when I bit into it. Occasionally, she paused, letting me kiss her lips or bend down and flick my tongue over her nipples.

Then she pulled me to the ground with a strength that amazed and enticed me. The scent of strawberries and the primal aroma of her body merged. She plunged down on me. The sensations that rushed through me were immediate and unstoppable.

"I'm sorry," I said when my breath returned.

She laughed. "What is there to be sorry about? Feeling pleasure after so much suffering?"

Her body squeezed around me and I did not resist as she rolled onto her back and took me with her. The passion and desire were stronger than they'd been before the release. She pushed her tongue into my mouth and I pushed back, tasting the sweetness of the honey and all the fruit we'd shared, but beyond that was something unique, something that was wholly her.

Our merged bodies moved as one being, squashing the strawberries beneath us, the air filling with their aroma and our skin being stained with their sweet juices.

"This is where we belong," Evie whispered. "Where we've always belonged, with each other."

"They'll notice we're missing. They'll find us. And punish us."

"We can hide. We're not important enough for anyone to care. We'll stay here, we have everything we'll ever need."

There should have been all the years of experience since the world fell warning me that happiness couldn't exist. There should have been a hundred objections. There wasn't.

There was the most beautiful woman in the world smiling beneath me and the taste of a forbidden apple lingering on my lips.

Car Flashing

O'Neil De Noux

I always get a charge when men ogle me, especially when I catch them looking up my dress. One of my favorite routines is to flash men while riding around in my new BMW.

A few weeks after getting my car, I got more than I bargained for. I dolled myself up, curling my long black hair, rolling mocha lipstick over my full lips. I put on a pale yellow dress that wrapped around in front and was very low cut. I wore a lacy French bra, sheer bikini panties and a pair of thigh-high stockings with elastic at the top of each stocking. Being Italian and somewhat hairy, some of my dark pubic hair protruded from the sides of my panties. At thirty, I think I look even better than when I was young. My breasts, which have always been over-sized, really blossomed when I had my children.

Topping off my outfit with a pair of dark sunglasses, I climbed into the BMW and opened my skirt all the way to my waist and cruised around. In New Orleans, it's never hard to find men out on the street, especially around my favorite hunting grounds – housing projects. I always got a big charge flashing random men, watching their faces light up.

Just outside the Melpomene Housing Project, I spotted a young man in his early twenties leaning against a telephone pole. I pulled a street map out of my glove compartment and laid it out on the front passenger seat. Stopping against the curb a few feet from my quarry, I called him over.

As soon as he leaned into the front passenger window, his gaze immediately fell between my legs as my crotch was completely visible. I asked about a street, leaning over and point-ing to the map. As I leaned to my right, I spread my knees to give him an even better view. The man tried to be cooperative about the street, but he was more interested in my panties. I smiled and thanked him and pulled away.

A few blocks later, on the other side of the projects, I saw two men tossing a football in the street. They also looked to be in their early twenties. I pulled up next to them and asked the taller of the two if he knew where a certain street was. I made up the name of a non-existent street.

The man leaned in my driver's side window. His eyes lit up immediately as he saw my panties. I leaned over to the map on the front passenger seat again, opening my knees, and pretended to search the map. When I looked back, the second man's face was also in the window, also leering down between my legs.

I sat up and ran my fingers through my hair and, making small talk about being lost, I started pulling up my thigh-high stockings. Spreading my legs slightly as I pulled the elastic all the way to my panties, I peeked at the men and felt a thrill as their eyes widened.

"Man, oh, man," one of them said, "you sure are a pretty woman."

I thanked them and pulled away, leaving them standing in the middle of the street, gaping at me with a pair of bulging crotches.

I was getting pretty hot myself by that time. I drove down to another project, the St Thomas Housing Project, where I found the perfect prey. There was a young man, maybe twenty-one, sitting under a tree at the edge of the project. He was black, with a very dark complexion. He wore extra-dark sunglasses.

I pulled up and asked out of the open passenger window if he could help me. He moved over, and I pointed to the map on the passenger seat. It took him a moment, but when he noticed my panties, he smiled. I asked about the non-existent street and he said he knew where it was.

"Could you show me?"

He started to give me directions, until I asked if he could get in and show me. He adjusted his glasses and looked back at my panties and said he could so I unlocked the door and he was climbing in when another young man approached and asked what was happening.

"It's my brother Elroy," the man with the sunglasses said.

"What's your name?" I asked sunglasses man.

"Sammy. What's yours?"

I told them my name was Nettie. I lied.

Elroy poked his head in at that moment and caught sight of my panties. Sammy explained and Elroy asked if he could come too. I felt my heart beating wildly as I said yes. Elroy climbed in back.

I followed Sammy's directions and found myself along Tchoupitoulas Street, among a series of warehouses. I pulled over and took another look at the map before closing it up and shoving it into the glove compartment, leaning over Sammy as I did. Sitting back up, I fanned the top of my dress and said, "It's so hot, even with the air conditioner."

The bottom of my dress was opened to my waist and now I was opening the top to show off my low-cut bra.

"I have a lighter dress in back," I said, turning and pointing to a small bag on the back seat. Looking around, I added, "I guess I could change here. If you guys keep a lookout."

"Yeah, we can watch out for you," Elroy said eagerly.

I asked him to pass the bag forward. I pulled out a lightweight T-shirt that was long enough to be a minidress and handed it to Sammy, along with the bag. I asked Elroy to move behind Sam so I could recline my seat. I leaned it back to where I was almost lying down next to them.

"Make sure no one walks up on us," I said. Sammy looked around and nodded, but his eyes were back on me as soon as I untied my dress. I opened the dress and climbed out. Then I adjusted my stockings and my panties, which caused an even greater amount of pubic hair to protrude from the sides. My panties were sheer enough to reveal a great deal of my large bush.

I pulled on the T-shirt and sat up. It didn't fit too well and I said so, reclining again. "Keep an eye out," I warned as I pulled the T-shirt off and tossed it in back. Before climbing back into my wraparound, I had another idea.

"I guess it'll be cooler without this," I said, pointing to my bra. Sammy's eyes were bulging. Elroy was leaning forward, making sure he didn't miss any action.

Lying back in my reclined seat, I unhooked my bra and passed it to Sam and told him to put it in the bag. He did but his eyes never left my breasts. Then I pulled my left knee up and pulled off my stocking. I did it with my right leg also, before lifting my hips to pull off my panties. And there I was, naked in my car with two strangers. Sammy was rubbing himself as his eyes traced their way from my large breasts down to my dark pubic hair.

Elroy, whose face was over mine now, said, "Lady, are you crazy?"

Sammy added quickly, "We got what you want if that's what you *want*, but we ain't stupid enough to force it on you."

I nodded, biting my lower lip. I had picked up men before, but never two at a time and never a black man. I had flashed many but now I was about to be screwed by two.

Sammy was rubbing his crotch hard now.

"Go ahead," I said, nodding to his crotch.

He hesitated a moment before pulling out a long, swollen cock. He began stroking it. I leaned up and looked around and made sure we were still alone before reaching over to give Sam a hand. Elroy had his dick out too, so I switched hands and started jerking them both off.

Sam was getting hot fast and cried out, "Lady, I wanna fuck you."

I looked around once more and then sank back in my seat and pointed to the glovebox, said there were condoms inside. Sammy worked one on, climbed on me and wormed his stiff cock into me and was riding me hard in a second. I tried to grab his ass, which was banging against the steering wheel. He came quickly and was just as quickly replaced by his brother. I tried to slow Elroy down, but he came rapidly. I was just catching my breath when both left the car.

They just left. Got a nut and gone.

I sat up, found another face in my front passenger window. This was the face of an older black man, a large man in his forties, in a dress shirt and jeans. He winked at me and said, "Lady, you need a man, instead of those boys. They fuck like rabbits."

I sank back in my seat.

"Move over here," he told me as he opened the front passenger door.

I slid over to the passenger seat as the man unzipped his fly and withdrew a huge cock. I dressed it in a condom and he gently climbed on top of me and spread my legs around him. I reached down and guided his cock to my wet pussy and he took it from there.

This was one sweet man. He took his time fucking me, carefully caressing my breasts, gently kissing my neck and then French kissing my eager mouth not so gently. I came quickly and came twice more before he exploded and pounded me in long, hard thrusts. God, it was wonderful.

Never got his name. Didn't want it. He kissed me one last time, on each breast, before climbing out and leaving me there, well fucked and wet. I went straight home and took a long hot bath, dreaming of the good day I had flashing and wondering when I'd do it again.

A Flaw in the Machine

Maxine Marsh

Wallace backed away from the case containing the miniature steam engine. The dildo had sprung to life again, and he'd have to wait for the cycle to finish before returning to work on the repairs. He watched the gears and then the piston come to life, appreciating the flow of the mechanisms interacting before stepping back and giving Tilda a sympathetic nod. She whimpered. The raven-haired beauty writhed anew, a fresh layer of sweat coating the skin of her breasts and torso. She began to cry out, in delicious synchrony with the dildo plumbing her cunt. Who knew how long it would take this time? Wallace watched, helpless to do anything, while the machine had its way with his wife. Tilda was a heavenly sight – that was undeniable. His darling hovered over the unrelenting device he'd recently invented, bound to it by brass cuffs at the wrists and ankles, legs spread obscenely, breasts pushed outward as if for a voyeur's enjoyment.

"Oh God, Wally, can't you make it stop?" she cried out, although, by the looks of things, he was sure she was nearing her next culmination.

"I told you, love, I won't fiddle with it while it's functioning. I won't risk hurting you."

She moaned, but he wasn't sure whether it was a protest of his inability to help her escape the contraption, or if it was because the machine was so delightfully rubbing her already swollen and sensitive spots. With steady rhythm the faux phallus charged upward, causing her breasts to bounce in a way that pleased him greatly. Privately, Wallace was glad he hadn't bothered to have her remove the black underbust corset she wore. She was a stunning vision atop his amorous invention gone awry.

Despite her plight, he knew she was in no real danger as long as he didn't try to repair the machine while it was functioning. His inventor's sensibilities could not help but examine the effects the wondrous machine was having on his most trusty test subject, his wife.

When he'd brought her down, excited to show her his latest invention, her first words were: "Well, it's not especially attractive, now is it? What does it do?"

He'd told her the truth – it was a pleasure machine he'd created for her. He had pointed out the brass cock, which he'd modeled after his own (he hadn't mentioned he'd added a little more to the length and girth, just for kicks), and described the cycle of function. "First the vibration begins, and soon after the cock rises, senses your positioning, and finds the most advantageous angle and depth."

She'd balked at the idea of letting him strap her into the contraption at first, but with some persuasion, involving a bit of time nibbling at the back of her neck and promises of bliss and satisfaction, and that of course he'd release her from her confines whenever she wanted, Tilda had agreed. Wallace had helped his wife out of her dress, petticoat and her stockings before positioning her arms to the proper cuffs. Once he'd positioned her knees onto the cushioned supports and then her legs to the adjacent brackets, he'd stood back and regarded her. How delightfully wanton her arrangement! Upon activation, the cuffs would secure themselves for the utmost safety of the occupant. The supported, semi-squatting position had exposed her feminine apex to the path of the dildo, her cunny spread good and wide for the pleasure of his observation.

"Are you comfortable, love?"

She nodded curtly. "Get on with it, then."

Wallace had oiled the cock liberally prior to bringing Tilda down to his workshop. Rounding the machine to get to the start lever, he had an impeccable view of her slit, and saw that it was already well slicked, well enough for his invention to penetrate her straightaway. He considered teasing her about her obvious arousal, but knew her pride would force her to deny being so easily excited by the situation. It was fine with him that his little bird always played at the utmost propriety; she always gave in and came hard when it was time. He reached for the lever that would propel the machine to life, noting that his own cock had grown quite hard already.

The machine had functioned smoothly. The cuffs had snapped shut, and then the cock had risen and slid itself thoroughly inside her passage. Tilda had cried out quite loudly from the very beginning, and Wallace had watched, fascinated to the end, as she'd been delivered to a most intense and roaring orgasm. The machine had relented soon after, as designed.

After she'd calmed herself a bit, Tilda had said, "Oh my. It works."

"It will begin again in a few minutes. Would you like me to stop it, or would you like to continue?"

Tilda's cheeks were already rouged, but they seemed to darken even more. "Well, maybe once again, just to be sure it's functioning correctly."

Oh, how she was probably ruing those words at present. After her second culmination, which came faster than Wallace had expected, she'd asked to be released. He'd gone to pull the switch, but for some reason, the engine would not turn off.

Despite having to tell his wife that she couldn't get out of the contraption quite yet, Wallace was relieved that at least some aspects of the machine were functioning correctly. For example, he'd designed the machine to rest after each culmination the subject experienced – sensors on the pneumatic cock ensured that each climax was recognized, and it responded by slowing and eventually stopping mid-gear, and then withdrawing from the subject for a short, set amount of time. When the time elapsed, the cock rose to life and once again delivered the utmost pleasure to the subject's nether parts. He could only imagine how the situation may have differed if there were no resting periods between his wife's culminations.

Now Wallace watched as Tilda met the crest of yet another orgasm. Her eyes squeezed shut, her lips curled back over her teeth as her brass lover reached maximum speed, fucking her cunny even and hard as she came all around it. The feral cry she let out almost made him come in the confines of his trousers. At last the machine slowed, eliciting a tiny yelp as it withdrew from her body. Wallace was uncertain about whether it was the eighth or ninth culmination she'd achieved since he'd flipped the starting switch earlier that evening. He would have asked her, just out of curiosity, but he was sure she wouldn't be of much help, seeing as how she sat limp in her bindings, her head hung, bosom heaving with labored breath.

"Are you all right, my dear?" he asked.

She only groaned, so he went back behind the machine. And then he spotted it! The plate connecting the lever to the toggle switch was loose, so loose in fact that the connection between the lever and the electrical contact had been severed.

"My sweet, I've found the problem!"

Tilda interrupted her panting. "Say what? Well, what's wrong with this infernal machine?"

"A small bolt came loose and interrupted the connection with the start and stop lever, that's all."

"A bolt, you say?"

"Yes, all I need is the hex to give it a few good turns and you'll be free!"

He walked to his workbench and picked the tool he needed, quite satisfied with himself that it wasn't really a flaw in the machine that had caused the problem, after all. That meant it could still be used without too much tweaking, maybe just a good once-over on the bolts.

When he turned back toward Tilda, she was glaring, eyes narrowed at him like a cobra.

"Now, dear—"

"You fool! Why didn't you notice that before? And here I've been suffering for more than an hour."

He did not like being called a fool. "I'd hardly call what you've experienced suffering. How many times have you reached paroxysm? Nine? More?"

Tilda pursed her lips. To him, she'd never looked as ravishing as she did now with her cheeks burning in arousal and humiliation. "Yes," she spat. "It rivals you as a lover, there's no doubt about it." She pouted as best she could manage.

He frowned, pretending to be insulted. "Is that so?" He tapped the hex wrench against his hip. "Well, maybe your new, ever-so-satisfying lover would like another chance to please you."

Her eyes went wide.

He took up his pocket watch and said, "In about thirty seconds, you'll get another chance to rouse my jealousy."

"You wouldn't!" She began to wriggle beneath the cuffs again, to no avail. "Please, Wally, fix the bolt. Please!"

"Admit you love it and I'll fix the machine."

She hesitated, weighing pride against physical exhaustion. "Fine. It's wonderful. I'm only fighting it because I'm not sure how much more I can take." She eyed him. "Are you happy, Wally? You've won."

He smirked, thoroughly satisfied with her admission. "I quite fancy you like this, my sugar plum. Just once more, my Tilly, and then I'll fix it." He put the wrench down on the table behind him, and then unbuttoned his trousers and freed his manhood from its confines. He rubbed his palm up and down the length of it, moving to stand just in front of his beautiful, hot-headed paramour.

She gasped. "Why, you scoundrel! I'll, I'll—" Tilda did not have the time to finish her scolding, because just then the machine buzzed back to life, and the polished brass cock rose from its sheath once again.

Love Las Muertas

Kirsty Logan

I haven't been scared of ghost trains since I was ten years old, but this one looks different in the fading sun. Even the Dia de los Muertos-themed illustrations, highlighted with green neon paint, look creepy when the wind is tugging at my hair and the ground is pebbled with candyfloss. The odd tape-recorded cackle or groan of machinery still echoes from behind the doors. But my heart is thumping in my throat, and the heat between my legs shows no sign of fading.

Like most stupid decisions, my choice to dawdle past closing time at the carnival is because of a girl. I've been thinking about her ever since I first saw her, the sun warming my shoulders and my mouth full of candied peanuts. Her skin was powdered bone white, roses nestled in the curls of her hair, and the parts of her body that weren't covered by her ruffled red dress were painted with intricate spirals and swirls. According to the lurid illustrations of her face on the ghost train's walls, her name is Encarnación. I wouldn't have stopped, but she ran over and presented me with one of the flowers from her hair; even under the paint, I could see the gorgeous dimples on each cheek when she smiled.

I live close by, so I told my friends I'd walk home by myself – but really, I'm just here to get Encarnación's number. Now that the sun has faded it's too cold for my strapless summer dress, and I move in closer to the ghost train to get out of the breeze. My nipples feel hard as thumbtacks – though I couldn't say whether that's from the chill or the thought of how Encarnación could warm me up.

This is ridiculous. The girl is long gone and I am making a fool of myself. I turn to leave.

Boo, grunts the devil in my ear as he wraps his arms around me. All my muscles stiffen and my throat closes around my scream. But already the devil is laughing, releasing me from his grip. It's Encarnación in her ruffled dress, her face wiped free of make-up. Her skin is the colour of acorns and she smells of sugar and sunlight.

We're closed, señorita. *Perhaps tomorrow?* Her accent is heavy on her tongue; already she has turned towards the ghost train doors. *Unless –* she turns back to me – *you'd like* una aventura? She holds out her hand to me, grinning wide, and I try very hard not to stare at the way her cleavage peeps over the top of her low-cut dress. *I think you'll enjoy,* she says.

I grab her hand, plant a kiss on her palm, and let her lead me through the door.

The ghost train car is just wide enough for two and Encarnación's thigh is pressed against mine. In front of us a ragged black curtain ripples in the breeze, blocking my view ahead. The air smells musty, like clothes in vintage shops. Encarnación pulls down the barrier over our knees, then twists to check something in the back of the car; her breasts press against my arm and it's everything I can do not to dip my head and kiss them.

It's Encarnación, right? I say, just to say something.

She twists back round and leans in close to me. *Emma, actually*, she whispers. *I don't even speak Spanish; I'm from Laaahn-daaahn.* Her accent has gone; she sounds just like me.

I'm from London too, I say. *Camden. Whereabouts are—*

The car shudders forward, cutting off the rest of my small talk. It shakes and burrs along the track, juddering the bones of my hips and thighs, making my teeth chatter.

The ragged curtain wipes over our faces and we're through to the other side. Chipped neon skeletons jerk from every joint, their ping-pong ball eyes rolling in their sockets. Beautiful girls with painted faces smoulder from the walls. A trio of bone-men strum guitars, candy-coloured skulls flash in strobes, yellow petals scatter to the floor, cobwebs brush against my hair. Under the soundtrack of ghostly shrieks and cracks of thunder I hear the judder of machinery as we turn a corner. Emma is expecting the hairpin bend, but I'm not; I fall into her lap, my face practically down her dress.

Fuck! I say, righting myself. *Sorry, the car . . .*

Emma's laughing, her face close enough that I could press my tongue into her dimples. Lit by the strobe, each movement a photograph, she tugs down the hem of her dress so that her breasts press out at me. *Better?* she asks. It is better, obviously, because there's nothing I want to do more than pull off her dress and drop to my knees between her legs. But I can't say that.

Um . . . I say. I'm sure the juddering of the car is making my voice come out funny. Emma doesn't seem to be listening; she's wiggling on the narrow seat, lifting a hip and putting one foot up on the cut-out side of the car. Then her head tips back and her eyes roll shut, a smile slipping across her face.

Move two inches to your right, she says, nudging my leg. *Riiiight . . . there.*

And I understand. Oh fuck, do I understand. The thick vibrations of the car are perfectly centred on my clit, making my heart beat in double-time. A groan slips out of my mouth and I shift in my seat so the angle is just right. Emma's murmuring deep in her throat, her hand sliding up my thigh and then slowly, teasingly, her fingertips nudge at the two layers of thin cotton over my clit.

I shift closer to her so that my leg drapes over hers, sharing vibrations. Emma is breathing hard, her breasts straining at her dress, her thighs tensing with each throb from the car. I feel a pulse in my neck and lights are flashing in my eyes and my hand is guiding Emma's further down, pressing her fingers against me, and oh God, oh God . . .

The car emerges from the ride, just as we shout out our orgasms to the scratchy soundtrack of tape-recorded ghouls.

We're outside in the dark and Emma's busy flipping switches. I stand on the litter-strewn ground, unsure. What's the polite thing to do after you've just reached simultaneous orgasm on a fairground ride with a hot-as-fuck stranger? I turn to leave, then stop. Usually I'd be running scared, but it's like I left all my fear back in the ghost train.

Do you want to come round? I call over. *I could cook . . .*

Emma tucks the keys into the pocket of her dress, swaying over to me. Without thinking, I press a kiss to the dimple on her cheek.

I'm hungry, she says, with a laugh.

I blow a kiss to Encarnación on the side of the ghost train, then take hold of Emma's hand and lead her back to my place.

Into the Lens

Gina Marie

"A small hint?"

"Nope."

"Pretty please?"

"You'll be tied up and I've been talking over ideas with the photographer," he says, winking and squeezing my ass. "No more hints."

I sigh dramatically and hang my head. Of course I'll be tied up.

"Aw, come on; that's not a hint."

"I'm gonna make you scream. You're going to squirt across the room."

Tied up, screaming and squirting. Sounded like a perfect date to me.

Flash. A sliver of light enters just below my right eye and my brain is flashing electric acid Kool-Aid colors across my skull in crazy waves, but otherwise, it's a dark world. I hear a zipper, feel the warmth of angled lights on my bare skin, the jangle of buckles, the soft thud of rope.

I am such a horny little bitch. Second time here, second time in my entire life spreading myself thin for the camera, and this place feels as familiar as Grandma's house.

The cuffs are soft around my wrists and ankles. My arms are pulled tight above my head, hands clipped by the cuffs to a thick, gleaming metal chain. My legs are spread wide, attached to a bar. The heat of a lamp intensifies. I can feel him moving closer. I want the rush, the anticipation having built to extreme levels for days, a small amount of fear, a promise of pain, but to what extreme? I anticipate the ecstasy of pleasure combined with adrenaline, but how? The unknown excites me.

Eyes and lenses wash over my skin. There is a moment, just before the first contact, when I am singular and observed, a specimen meant for observation, flesh and muscle and skin and animal desire. That realization makes me tremble a little and . . . before I am even touched, my knee turns inward slightly and I hear a small "splat" on the floor where my feet are spread.

The hollow sounds of his boots, circling in vulture steps, is so erotic. I think of the hot desert playa and buzzards and his tongue seeking moisture between my thighs.

Splat. Drool. Wetness slides down my inner thigh.

A kinky soundtrack kicks in. I can hear a woman moaning, the slapping sounds of her torture and captivity lurking behind the beat.

Suddenly, I am brought into the foreground when a thin, sharp tool slides across my skin. The sensation is slightly electric, both cool and hot, just painful enough to make me horny as hell. I imagine a blade or a key. I wonder if it is marking my skin. It burns and tingles. Electricity? His cock brushes my ass as he moves around me. Power. Muscle and bone. Animal. The sharp thing cuts patterns into my skin and scatters the colors across the ocean of my mind's eye. Waves of light become water spouts and the electric intensity grows, connecting nerves from breast to ass to back to neck, lighting them up. The tool nears towards my swollen pussy and then . . . I can feel the photographer's presence and hear the camera clicking near my thighs. My nipples are aching.

The music shifts to something more melodic, the beat softening, and the white-hot heat of steel is replaced with the soft, familiar fringes of the elk-skin flogger. I smile inwardly. He brought it from home.

Hanging there in the dark, my mind spins off into other worlds, memories, every touch setting off a new landscape of experience. The fringes remind me of that day at the beach, the three of us stripped bare, goofing off. I poked a stick at a line of tree worms wagging their scaly asses across the sand, lost for a moment in their motion, wanting to be wiggling my ass like that.

"Your turn." The Scrabble board beckoned as my whiskey-soaked and marijuana-smoked brain tried hopelessly to analyse and plot a smart move.

What I wanted was not the perfect move but to touch her hair. It was loose, let out of that cute little bandana, and it sprung around her face in red-hot kinky curls. I could barely stand it. And it had nothing to do with sex. Well, hardly.

He pulls the leather across the curve of my lower back, lifts it high and then, slap! God, such pleasure. Fuck! Want! He brings the whip down on my ass and back and thighs and my fingers are in her hair, deep in the thickness of it, touching it like quenching a thirst, like when I dip my fingers into rice kernels or thrust my hand into the center of wet, dew-dropped ferns along the trail.

Slap! The whip strikes again and I am held there, bound by legs and hands, my brain spinning wildly. The heat of him, the strength and lust that he radiates, even just walking down the street in casual clothes, is overpowering. In this setting, I am molten.

Suddenly the camera stops clicking. His hands are between my legs and slapping my ass and breasts. Then, a cane comes down across my thighs and butt, painful but not agonizing, a hundred tiny stings across my skin, the man behind the camera emerging for a moment to give rise. The stinging quickens, slapping, fingers rubbing my clit, hot mouth on my nipples. I am moaning, hips twisting, hanging now, thank God for this chain or I'd be a puddle on the floor.

Sometimes when I'm on the brink of orgasm the sound of her coming – soft, high moans under a grey sky, her gently twisting hips in my peripheral vision while I slip my tongue gently across her lips, throaty little pleasure sounds coming with her ragged breaths – nearly pushes me right over the edge. What does send me flying is remembering how I watched him while I kissed her and touched her breasts, caught glimpses of him in the corner of my eye, the man behind the whip, the knife, the strap, bent over her smooth, hard clit.

But I can't come right now. He hasn't said the words. I'm spread wide into him, the cane snapping against my hot skin. I push away the remembering, focus on the moment, the sound of metal, the pleasure of pain, the sound of beating blood, the powerful eroticism of braving the unknown.

At last the bees take flight and the camera begins clicking again. Hands smooth my burning cheeks and his face is pressed into mine now, kissing me deeply, his lips and tongue a balm, a relief, a joyful reminder that this is as much about love and trust as it is about lust. His low voice in my ear beckons as he finger-fucks me with agonizing gentleness. "Do you want to come? Do you, baby?"

"Oh yes, yes, please," I whisper. His hands find the small of my back, my breasts, and he pulls me tighter into him. I am gone, my mind, that is, aloft, looking down at us from the rafters. I am perched there, a small bird, watching and waiting.

There is a juniper tree out past a turn-off along the highway in pine country. It has a thick, low branch. The branch is perfect for small hands to grip. Ideal for fucking. The fucking tree. He memorized the mile marker. It's a summer place. Unlike the summer places most people dream about. There are no bikinis or beach balls here. Just pure, raw sex, and the intoxicating scent of juniper oil and the taste of blue sky while he fucks me. "Don't let go," he growls. "Don't let go of the branch 'til you come."

I'm hanging by that branch, naked in the warm summer air as the camera whirs, light and sex sucked into the lens, hanging there, kissing her, feeling him, watching them. Such pleasure. God, it is good. Yes! Oh fuck yes! The blood rushes out of my hands as I arch against the cuffs and the chain, head tossed back while he finishes me off with small flicks of his fingers and tongue. The small bird of my brain has flown back inside and I am fully present, the electricity of pleasure filling my clit with blood, sending shock waves down my legs and into my toes, sending me hurtling at light speed over the edge, every drop of moisture in my body rushing to the surface and exploding. I am screaming and dripping, spasm after spasm jolting my body from the inside out.

Well. *That* was fun.

The blindfold is removed and I am lowered to my knees, arms still held taut above my head. My smile cannot be contained by walls. His hands are in my hair now, pulling my chin upward. He pushes his hard cock deep into my mouth. The camera is inches from my face. I close my eyes and enjoy the moments, the precious moments, the mingling of our genetic spiral, the way we fit together, front to back, back to front, top to bottom.

It is that pre-dawn time when I wake up and know his cock is hard while he sleeps. I know that if I roll over and touch it, it will be hot and ready. And when I kiss it, it will jump up at my lips. At this hour, after I kiss him awake and slide on top of him, grinding my cunt into him, using him mercilessly for my own satisfaction, sucking his balls dry with my lips, we simply fold back into that origami shape and go back to sleep. It is morning and this cock is mine and I could care less who is watching. Because I will fuck this man anywhere.

There are 600 photographs. Later, I'll sit on his lap back home and we'll drink wine and go through them one by one. Our own little erotic show.

But right now, as we sip whiskey and chat with the photographer, put the cuffs, rope, whip back into the duffel bag, there is one thing I have to know.

"What was that thing you used – the sharp thing?"

The photographer holds up a tiny, shiny tool and spins the head. "Wartenberg pinwheel."

Truck wheels kick up clouds of alkaline dust as we speed across the desert. He slows and clicks on the cruise control. I pop my head up through the sunroof and climb onto the top of the truck. There is nothing but empty playa stretched before us. Playa, pussy and cock. He leaves the driver's seat and finds my hot, wet crotch with his lips. My head is back, the wheels making no sound as we crawl slowly across the ancient lakebed. Dust devils whirl and spin in the distance. The wind whips my screams away.

The pinwheel, the cock, the juniper, her orgasm, the worms and the lens.

Red Light

Angela Caperton

Alan waved off his assistant's predatory approach and closed the door to his office, solace behind the thick door welcome after his twenty-hour air adventure from Ptuj, Slovenia, and three more hours of meetings as soon as he passed the threshold of Lorman Engineers.

Alan ripped off his tie, sucking breath with ridiculous glee. He fell into his oversized, lumbar-support enhanced chair and stared with travel-burned eyes at his monitor's black screen. Six days. Gone for six days. He flopped to the right and automatically tapped the power button on his desktop, closing his eyes, silently praying against reality that his email in-box would only have a few waiting messages. Ptuj and his time in Ljubljana had been fruitful, but there'd been no real time to see to other business. Hell, he'd barely had time to talk to Casey, and now he felt a wave of guilt that he hadn't gone straight home to see her before the office claimed him.

Six days. Not the longest they'd been apart in eleven years of marriage, but this had been the first time they hadn't been reunited immediately.

As his computer booted, Alan looked at his phone, the red light above the tiny stenciled "Voice Mail" blazing like an accusation. He squinted in defense and looked at the LED display. Eighteen.

Eighteen. Hell, only eighteen, after six days in Eastern Europe? Should he worry about his job?

He pulled his cell from his pocket and smiled as he flipped it open to read the text message from Casey. "I'm hungry, are you? Pick up something sweet?"

Alan chuckled. Hungry? He'd passed ravenous when he had politely turned down the second gorgeous blonde whore sent by the executives of the Ptuj contractors. One of the women, the chief engineer said, was an international lingerie model.

Resolute, Alan hit the message button on his phone, grabbed a pen, and cleared documents from his blotter. Bracing, he listened to the voices coming through the speaker.

"Alan, Martin Lowry here! Call me about the Masters project!"

Beep!

"Mr Rasto, this is Rich at Schlein Borland. We've a new angle on the Lokfar Reserve. You can reach me at . . ."

Beep!

He scribbled, he replayed, his vision blurred as voices bubbled into an incoherent mess, numbers ran together, client projects spilled into each other and he viciously shoved the top sheet of his blotter to the next to continue scrawling messages his assistant would struggle to decipher next week.

Pen poised, he waited for the next message, ready to scribble names and numbers, his eyelids closing as fatigue began to drown his brain.

"Such a sweet weeping cock, the perfect size to split my wet lips."

Alan's heart crimped painfully, his breath puffing. He sprang forward at full attention, eyes wide with shock as he nearly fell out of his chair in the reactive effort to grab up the receiver. His fingers stuttered over the buttons on his phone stopping the message as his mind cut on the sharp edges of what he'd heard. What he should do – delete the message of course – was not what the adrenalin-fueled blood flow to his cock wanted to do.

Fingers still shaking, Alan glanced around his office and through the narrow windowpanes that bracketed his closed door. Bodies moved in the offices beyond, but no one noticed him. He settled back in his chair, stared hard at the buttons on his phone and hit play again.

"Such a sweet weeping cock, the perfect size to split my wet lips. Yes, yes, oh, please, baby, I want to touch it, to taste it."

The deep, sultry voice shivered down his neck and spine, pooling lust in his groin. Who was that? It sounded familiar, but he couldn't put a face to the voice. It had to be a joke, or maybe one of the Slovenians had thought a little spice would enhance their chances of winning the contracts. Alan almost curled over his desk, tense and completely absorbed by the message.

"Mmm . . . Do you like the red lace panties, garters, and bra? My nipples are so hard they sting against the lace and my pussy's slick, the panties are nearly drenched. See? I'm ready for you. I don't need them anymore." He heard cloth against skin, and then her breath hitched. The sounds of fingers on flesh teased his ear. His mouth dried as the unmistakable sound of wet stroking chimed behind her soft pants and impatient moans.

"Oh yes, baby, use your fingers, yes . . . one, fuck yes, two . . . Oh God, baby, yes! Your finger in my ass feels so good! God, my clit! What are you doing . . . to . . ." The enthusiastic cry nearly deafened Alan as the mystery woman's orgasm vibrated through the receiver. His free hand closed over his rock-hard cock through his trousers. Holy shit, could he be any more turned on? His imagination raged with visions of ass-slapping, hard, mindless fucking. He needed to jerk off, needed to come hard and fast to the sound of that voice, but the trim shadow of his assistant passing his door jolted reality home.

"Oh, baby . . . you are fantastic. I want more. Can I have more, please?" Her sated sigh and playful giggle tempted him to unzip his fly. "I'll be good. I promise," she whispered seductively.

Alan's heart bumped erratically in his chest. More? He could think of a thousand things he'd like to do to this woman, and bending her over his desk to fuck her from behind was just the beginning.

"OK, baby. I'll wait, but I won't wait long. I'm so horny, baby and I need you. I'll leave the garters on, but that's it. Don't let me get cold, baby . . ."

The beep announcing the end of the call barely registered. Alan stared blindly at the red light on his phone, one thought thumping through his brain in perfect time to the twitch of his cock.

Who the hell was she?

He staggered up to the front door of his house, his cock still semi-hard even after an afternoon of mind-numbing meetings.

He hoped the women in his office didn't take notice of his appraisals as he tried to see if he could unlock the mystery of who had left the message. No one he saw or spoke to seemed to fit. He'd listened to the message again before leaving, but with regret, he erased it. The last thing he needed was his assistant hearing the recorded phone sex. He might never know who left the message and maybe, for the sake of his marriage and his job, that was best. Still . . .

He turned the key and then the knob, opened the door, and froze.

The strawberry red garter circled her waist, with thin straps holding up black stockings that skimmed over firm shapely thighs. Hard nipples defied the chilly air of the foyer. He looked up into the wicked, smiling face of his wife.

She lifted a small black box to her lips and spoke, the sultry, sexy voice blasting blood back into his cock.

"Good timing," she said. "A little longer and I'd have come looking for you."

In the Empire of Lust

Maxim Jakubowski

I have a corner office. The view is nothing special though. The grime of the unfolding, nearby London rooftops and the grey, teeming streets of borderline Soho below are quite unremarkable. Although the company where I work occupies the third floor of the building, it also happens to be the top floor so the panorama I'm afforded is limited and tedious. No Thames or Hudson River unfurling below, no romantic or historical city milestones to contemplate when my mind goes on random walkabout away from the bulging files accumulating across my desk or the flickering screen of the see-through iMac I use.

And my mind certainly wanders a lot these days. Too much. Much too much. A good thing I'm management. Such absent-minded moods would not be cause for forgiveness if I were at a more junior level. But then I wouldn't occupy a corner office.

I usually keep my door open, so staff outside always have access to me. Good management I'm told, but it's actually more due to the fact I'd just feel so damn lonely, isolated in my cocoon of an office had I no contact with the outside, the swish of skirts out there, the sweet voices of women gossiping, the other telephones ringing when mine insists on remaining silent. Thinking is a lonely affair. And thinking is what they pay me for, I suppose.

But then I cheat. For every crassly remunerated thought of advertising campaigns and slogans and clever ways of convincing the punter out there to greedily consume more orange or chocolate or strawberry-flavoured ice creams or instant desserts with disconcerting tastes, I also indulge in private moments, secret thoughts that have little to do with my job. My world inside the world.

Veronica brings me a dossier she wishes me to check. She is pear-shaped but always has such a wonderful smile. And a great arse. A backside that inspires me mightily. Outlined against the fabric of her skirt by her highly visible panty line. Some days, I know, she wears thongs and my imagination runs riot, delineating the undoubtedly pale and hard flesh of her joyful arse and guessing what shades of pink I could impose on its regal expanse smacking her there hard and sharp as she thrusts her backside towards me while prone in a doggy position, the puckered hole of her anus winking at me and the humid cut of her gash opening oh-so slightly. Not that I'm much into spanking, that taboo and indulgence of the Victorian upstairs-downstairs class struggle, but Veronica's backside is such a tempting invitation to mark with the fleeting print of my hand. Enough to make a fetish freak of me, by temperament such a vanilla sort of gentle pervert!

And then there's Suzanne, of the long dark blonde hair that unrolls all the way down to the small of her back and the shy, tentative interventions at our weekly creative meeting. She has thick, pulpy lips that beg for a terrible object to cradle obscenely in the midst of their geographical centre. A penis, maybe? Mine? On her knees in front of me, my gaze descending on the razor straight parting that separates her silky hair. Her tongue emerging quite hesitantly from between the scarlet flower of those lips before inevitably tasting the rough texture of my bulging, blood-engorged glans before she courageously ingests it all in one full, hungry movement and my cock lodges itself like an Amazon explorer down deep in the pit of her throat. Suzanne's face speaks of both innocence and knowing but I wouldn't be surprised if her cock-sucking skills were on a par with the welcome instances of lateral thinking she often displays in her job. At the meetings I am hypnotically drawn to her lips as the digestive biscuits she feasts on invariably breach her threshold. Her desk sits just to the right from the exit to my office. The window behind her chair enjoys the same view as I do. Limited and uninspiring. Maybe in her private world of office work, Suzanne also dreams of a world of blow jobs?

Polly calls me on the phone. Her own office is only at the other end of the corridor but she prefers to communicate this way. She is in charge of promotions. Her eyes are brown and slightly oriental. She is one quarter Malaysian on her mother's side, I know. Polly is always on the go, a hive of activity, thin like a rake, small perky breasts with nipples ever erect and visible, shape wise, through her T-shirts or cashmere sweaters. She is always brimming with confidence but I sense it's only a shell, a wafer thin display of assurance and that, deep down inside, she is an insecure little girl who privately begs for submission in one-to-one relationships. Wouldn't she just look perfect with a leather-studded dog collar or a Vivienne Westwood choker tightened around her neck? A docile slave I would pull with a lead into the room full of people and present as my slave for all to feast upon at their leisure. "Display yourself," I would order and she would shed her coat and reveal her total nudity beneath the protective garment. Her nipples would be delicately pierced, thin gold rings standing to attention, her cunt would be shaven smooth and when another party guest would summarily order her to open her legs wide (and no need for a spreader bar, she is such an obedient lass), the diamond stud fixed to her clitoral hood would miraculously emerge from the gates of her labia, already coated with her fragrant inner juices. So what will our slave have to perform today, she wonders, both quite ashamed at her situation and predictably aroused and obediently submissive? All Polly wishes to know on the occasion of this phone call, however, is if I have yet agreed the budget for the soft drinks project whose pitch our team are working on, and to which accounting code the development expenses should be allocated to.

Jasmine, my deputy, walks in, her long legs sliding across the regulation carpet of the office and perches herself shamelessly across the corner of my desk, unveiling more square inches of thigh than an older executive would tolerate and painstakingly explains to me how the art department have once again misunderstood the specifications for a particular job and we are running late. As if I didn't already know this. But reassures me: she will stay on late today and keep an eye on Frank, our gay art director, and see that he doesn't leave until the boards are ready for the presentation. She wears old-fashioned glasses and speaks in clipped Oxbridge tones. I know she is seeing an Australian graphic designer she met in a bar some months back and that this is the first proper relationship she has had in well over a year. My eyes linger on the stockinged legs draped over my desk and, Superman like, explore beyond. She always wears white knickers, and I've often had a flash of them. Below the cotton or the silk, I imagine her pubic hair is dark and curly and her cunt is tight and dry. But when she is fucked, she comes loud and hysterically, her whole body vibrating to the rhythm of the thrusts of the cock frantically buried inside her and tears forming in the corner of her pale green eyes. Yes, I reckon Jasmine must be quite beautiful in the embrace of pleasure, relinquishing all her civilized and reserved facade and reverting to a blissful state of sluttishness under the mere touch of a man's hand exploring her skin and mapping its soft contours. I thank her most sincerely for her attention to detail and feel my cock growing insidiously inside my black trousers, under the shelter of the desk. Watching her lips move and catching a brief glimpse of her white brassiere I suddenly had a mental revelation that deep down inside her universe of secrets Jasmine actually liked having a cock up her arse when her passion grew out of control. However, sometimes you just know these things, intuition and all that, it also came to me that Jasmine was also the sort of modern woman who disliked having to swallow come, whatever the circumstances or the relationship level she had reached with a particular man. Anal sex was an acceptable taboo. But not swallowing. Just not the right thing to do for educated women like Jasmine . . .

She leaves the office, and I'm left with my computer screen.

If only they were aware of my disgusting thoughts, I wouldn't have any staff left or any respect afforded to me. The boss from hell. Just wouldn't do. But I have principles: I would never mix business with pleasure. Too complicated, despite the daily temptations. And we don't usually have a Christmas party anyway where we let our hair down. Not that I'm into drunken broom closet sex or hanky-panky across the photocopying machine. A rule I invariably stick to, despite the genuine opportunities. It's easier to satisfy my vices and compulsions away from home ground. Should one of them leave, I might hit on her later under pretext of renewing acquaintance and solicitously enquiring how she is getting on with her new job elsewhere. It's worked before, I dare say.

I walk to the door, shout out to the girls working there that I have a private call coming through and close the door to my office.

Back behind my desk, my cock is still part tumescent from memories of the spectacle of Jasmine with glasses on spreading her ass cheeks apart and readying her already moist aperture for the girth of my penis. I highlight my Favourites on the browser menu and select a website.

Interracial sex.

Incest.

Animals.

BDSM.

Extreme.

Dogging.

Pregnant.

I make a selection and, in the private cocoon of my office, I begin masturbating to the images lining up on the screen.

The girls are safe.

For now.

Too Wondrous to Measure

Salome Wilde

Does size matter? is a question that only makes sense when relative dimensions are not so skewed that a single inserted claw tip fills you like the biggest cock you've ever taken and you have to use your entire body to jerk him off.

Now, if you let go the question of exactly how you and Godzilla became lovers, how you overcame that first, seemingly insurmountable obstacle of proportion – not to mention communication beyond the most animal level of need and desire – the actual specifics of day-to-day lovemaking are rather fascinating. Well, they are to me anyway.

First, let me clear up any misunderstandings and state, once and for all, that he's male. Always has been. Always will be. Male. Very, very male. All the movies after the original got it wrong. The first one was him, real and beautiful as he could be. Except for the ending where he's reduced to bones and then vanishes. Wishful thinking back then. But untrue. I just laugh watching it. All the rest? Actors in costumes, miniaturization, CGI. Obviously. We don't let the bullshit bother us. He knows who he is, I know who he is, and that's all that matters to us.

Anyway, about the sex. After a few mishaps requiring stitches and a bit of psychotherapy, turning me on and getting me off was relatively simple to achieve. The Zen of utter lightness of touch and the smallest of protuberances is basically it. I mean, hell, I'm so damn turned on by the very sight of him rising from the ocean and heading straight for my condo on the beach that I could come even if he hadn't learned to work that claw or tone down his heat-ray breath to a gentle clit stim that makes pulsing showerheads pathetic by comparison.

The gratitude of the masses, of course, adds to the pleasure. I've got so many medals and letters of thanks from the Japanese government I've had to devote the entire back closet to them. And they pay all my bills so I could quit my day job and do this full-time. Best career move ever. I also enjoy the fruit baskets and bento boxes and cases of Pocky the locals leave outside my door. The public shrines with their graphic images of Godzilla's cock with me riding it? Not so much.

Knowing I'm saving the world from lover boy's mighty destructive powers goes a long way, too, in coping with the paparazzi. They've got plenty of pictures of me sitting in his scaly palm and even of his arm reaching inside my sliding glass door (it's the whole front wall, really, and made of some special plastic to keep him from breaking windows like he did about a hundred times before the government figured out a new plan). But no lens to date has been able to zoom in on his actual foreplay technique. Which is how I like it. I wouldn't mind the puss shot, but who wants her "orgasm face" splashed all over the *Tokyo Times*?

For his turn, though, we go to his place. I'm not shy by any means, but when you're slathered head to toe in coconut oil, shimmying up and down a cock the size of a 100-year-old oak, you want a little privacy. And lounging in enough come to fill a public bath isn't the kind of thing you need to see on the evening news either. The big lug just loves to watch himself spew. "Drown the human" is a favorite pastime for both of us, hence the goggles.

Probably the most exciting gossip – and the reason I'm finally spilling all our secrets this way after three years of silence – is that I may be pregnant. I swear his sperm are so huge I can actually *feel* them knocking on the door to get in . . . and recently I think a few did. I've been having the oddest dreams of little lizards skittering across my bed and newts in my bathtub. And I like my food so spicy now I need a whole tube of wasabi for a single piece of fish. Medical evidence? Hardly. But a woman knows.

So, we're off to his island for the time being. Neither of us trusts the government or the scientific community not to intervene. We just need to ride it out and see where love takes us. Stranger than strange, I know. But then all of life's a miracle, isn't it? Too wondrous to measure.

Espartaco

Michèle Larue

At the first clap of thunder, the dogs stopped barking. In the vacant lot overgrown with wild mint by that solitary tower block on the seafront, a mongrel could be heard baying at the moon. Lili lay huddled under the coarse sheet, peering at the rough sea through a huge bay window whose single pane was criss-crossed with taped cracks. Black clouds came rolling in, changing shapes with every gust of wind. Before she decided to move into this building perched on a harp-shaped concrete arch, she'd had countless offers from housewives eager to break the law and rent her a room for a few dollars. But Lili's heart was set on a view of the ocean, and Madame Olga's apartment overlooked the Malecon. It was on the fourth floor of that many-windowed tower, a pathetic attempt at a revolutionary skyscraper. Except for stadiums and schools, and more recently a few hotels, almost nothing had been built since those early years.

Lili's mischievous smile and natural blonde hair had melted Olga's heart and she'd made her welcome with a cigarette dangling from her lip. The view of the waterfront was sensational. Lili's yellow pants and flowered blouse flapped in the wind from the sea. Not a boat to be seen on the dark waters, a few men fishing on the rocks, Lili's skin had tingled with pleasure as she laughed gleefully. They'd sipped black coffee in thimble-sized cups, with Olga moaning on about this and that, women slaving to cook meals out of nothing, anybody would complain, hamburger steaks made with ground grapefruit skins, weak on calories even if they were cholesterol free. The widow had promised her a hearty breakfast with fried black market eggs and left her standing in front of a display cabinet filled with china and bisque, knick-knacks of soppy domesticity. The furniture in her room had a baroque feel about it, dark and ornate. She'd popped a bunch of miniature shepherdesses and plastic flowers into a drawer. The following day she took Olga's advice about her bicycle, a rusty racer she'd been leaving in a public bicycle park. Henceforth, she would chain it to the front door gate bristling with padlocks. There were more gates blocking the stairs between each floor, a cause for concern among the tenants of a sixteen-story building utterly dependent on the huge freight-like elevator, into which Lili had wheeled her bike next morning and noticed her fellow passengers looking enviously at the timeworn machine.

Outside, the storm raged on unabated; the rain, lit from below by a street lamp, slashed across a patch of blue-grey sky. Lili was drifting on the high seas now, snug and dry in her ship of concrete and glass, listening to the raindrops pounding on the pane. Aroused by the rain and her solitary musings, she extracted Lulu from its case. Before switching on the vibrator, she ran through the day in her mind for something nice to fantasize about, the image of some man she'd passed on the street perhaps. The proud profile of a worker who'd smiled at her while she was waiting for the elevator with her bike. Or that young one who'd approached her so sweetly: "*Buenas dias, carino. Como te llamas?*" "Lili *y tu*?" "Espartaco, *como el esclavo romano, esclavos somos todos.*" And he walked away towards a construction site, balancing a bundle of metal rods on his shoulder with one arm. The rods must have been several yards long, they trailed on the ground, raising ochre dust like the train of some iron gown. Now that he was walking away, she could get a good look at him, admire the varnished mahogany of those muscular legs, note the torn and paint-smeared shorts, before the elevator swallowed her up. The rain whipped the window and squirted through the glass ventilation slats, sprinkling her face and breasts; rain, seawater or a shower invariably turned her on. The mist had just spoiled an old Cuban novel lying open on the bed. She closed the book and clicked Lulu's switch to "low", her excitement growing as she gazed at the clouds billowing over the sea. Her head spun with visions of being overwhelmed by breakers. The vibrations of the dildo made her gasp; she closed her eyes and summoned back the young man's face. Opening them again after a mild orgasm – "not to be despised but could do better" – she saw iron rods exactly like the ones on that worker's shoulder whipping back and forth beyond the windowpane. They were anchored one floor down to the scaffolding propped against a building going up between the tower block and the ocean, a spiraling structure which already looked like a car park. What other country would store its cars on the most picturesque site in the city? There was a flash of lightning, and Espartaco's silhouette suddenly appeared to her on the scaffolding. Night had just fallen and he was still on the job, perched on bamboo poles, oblivious to the storm, assembling sections of the iron skeleton. He finished his task and, turning around, saw Lili in the glow of the ceiling lamp. He wagged his hand towards her window and she responded by holding Lulu up for him to see, but suddenly she felt confused and naked, for she was wearing only the sheet wrapped around her lower thighs. Outside, gusts of wind rippled the edge of Espartaco's faded blue Superman T-shirt, while breakers twenty feet high lapped around his ankles. Lili had already seen the seafront flooded. When that happened, the Malecon was closed to traffic, as the waves might carry away some cyclist, but she wouldn't have thought the water could rise this high. She shuddered at the thought that a taller wave might swallow her up and she slid Lulu under the sheet protectively.

His face lashed by the rain, Espartaco clung with both hands to the bamboo pole as the whole structure wrenched away from the supporting pillars, toppled across the street and smashed against the tower block. Windows exploded in a shower of glass. Lili caught a gush of water and screamed. She was groggy when the man she desired dropped into her arms, a gift from the gods straight onto her bed. The storm had ripped away what was left of the smeared shorts. Tugging at the rain-washed shoulders, removing a shard of glass from his side, she realized he had a hard-on. His sex was as thick as an arm. It seemed insane to be entertaining in her own room a flesh-and-blood Spartacus, who looked all the sexier as he was sexy himself. But why had he got a hard-on? The excitement of colliding with a woman's body, or just plain fear? she wondered, pressing the man closer, carried away by the stiffness of that valiant prick on her thigh and the water streaming over them. Bewildered, Espartaco was still clinging to the struts of the frame that had carried him into the bedroom, when Lili let go. The law of gravity took its toll: the trapeze swung out to sea and Espartaco flew through the gaping window once again, carried on the bamboo poles that must have been attached to the ground floor of the car park somewhere, and now Lili realized he was about to come hurtling headlong back at her. She spread her legs and breathed deeply to enlarge her sex. Glup! Bludgeon-sized, the man's cock dove into her belly quick as a fish, jerked away and shot out the window again, hung for a moment in space, beaten about by the whistling wind, then zipped back and into her like a wooden stake. After the scaffolding had swung to and fro a few times, the wind died down. The gentler pace left time between strokes of the battering ram for Lili to excite herself, and what could be more exciting than a little pause before another onslaught of that foreign body that filled her to the hilt, which she gobbled down without a word – what was there to say, anyway? If she'd believed in God, she'd have shouted "Praise Jesus." Spartacus was an early Christian, after all!

Shivering over the bed, knuckles clenched and white, the man let go of his swinging perch and his rain-chilled body fell where Lili lay, hungering for more of him. But he shouted "Maria!" leapt onto the tiled floor and rushed into the hall wrapped in a sheet. Señora Olga, who'd been eavesdropping, threw up her hands at the sight of a black man traipsing about her apartment in the simplest apparel. Espartaco ran into the front hall and started shaking the gate like a madman. Olga couldn't open the door fast enough, two padlocks, no less! Anything to get him out of her place, but the elevator push-button wouldn't light up and a tenant upstairs was shouting "*Elevator de mierda!*" His feet got tangled in his iron train and he lurched back into her bedroom at lightning speed. Without a glance at Lili, he grabbed the bamboo pole in both hands, pushed off with his foot and shot off into space once more, swaying in empty air like an Olympic pole-vaulter. He hung for a moment, a few feet from her window. The amplitude diminished, the oscillation stopped altogether. Standing naked in the window, she thrust her hand at the man as if to say "You'd better watch out," but he had his eyes riveted on the ground, cautiously making his way down to the ship's deck below. No sooner had he jumped to safety, than he hightailed it across the vacant lot, her sheet wrapped around him like a loincloth. Lili went back to sleep on the sodden mattress, curled up in a fold of sheet, one hand resting on Lulu.

The next morning, all was quiet. A cock crowed on a neighbor's balcony. In front of the building, the remains of the scaffolding lay strewn across the puddles like an enormous game of pick-up sticks, crushing the mint leaves gorged with water. Lili picked her way around the puddles. She'd given up the idea of taking her bike today. The waves were lapping humbly at the parapet. A woman in a white dress and white turban came sauntering down the middle of the street, shading herself with an immaculate umbrella; frayed by countless storms, the covering had faded to a pearly sheen.

Mighty Real

Kristina Lloyd

Even before I turn the corner I can hear music. I have to stop and fight back tears then retouch my make-up because I fail. Anita Ward, seventies disco. Her voice floats across the streets: You can ring my be-e-ell, ring my bell.

Bet she never thought it would be a funeral song.

Jedge is standing in weak sunlight outside the house, smoking, his top hat and tails as shabby as his front door. Fipps is with him. I've known him fifteen years and don't know why he's called Fipps. He's in shirtsleeves rolled to the elbows, waistcoat unbuttoned, tweed tapered trousers. They look like escapees from a Victorian travelling circus.

I pass the launderette. Wet colours in a washing drum spin round and round. Life goes on.

I embrace Fipps first, saving the biggest hug for Jedge who holds me a long time. The hip flask in his jacket pocket presses against me. "You scrub up well, babes," he says. I'm wearing red in defiance of convention: poppy red pencil skirt, matching chiffon blouse, thick black belt and a red gingham flower in my hair.

Jedge's eyes are rimmed with pink and it's not even 10 a.m. Today, he looks older than fifty.

"And yourself," I reply, dusting my make-up from his lapel.

Inside, I greet people, old friends mostly and a couple of new faces. Sally's wearing droopy black feathers in her hair and silver glitter on her eyes. "I'm like those East End horses," she says, nodding heavily, "dragging the carriage to church."

She's making a point, albeit subtly, because Richard was an atheist but his parents aren't. None of us are what you'd call religious but today we're going to sit in a chapel like a bunch of cabaret scarecrows, and listen to a service made from ideas we believe to be delusional.

I notice the music again: Amii Stewart, "Knock on Wood". Jedge has a dark sense of humour.

He comes into the room as the track's ending and claps his hands together. "So, guys, let's get this show on the road!"

His face is soft around the jaws these days, his handsomeness gone slack. I don't know if it's ageing or sorrow. Perhaps they're one and the same.

We all pile into Suze and Lucy's camper van. It's a squash at the back but we're fine. I sit crouched on Jedge's lap and take a swig of whisky when I'm offered it, a single malt whose smoky warmth creeps into my veins. It takes the edge off and I need it because the chapel at the crematorium is fucking awful. We sit close to the front on thin pine chairs cushioned in corporate turquoise. The carpet is grey, the walls white and high, and hanging at the front is a narrow cross that looks like it was bought at B&Q. If it weren't for that cross and Richard's coffin with Richard's body in it, this place could be a conference venue. When the priest starts up, I'm half expecting him to do a PowerPoint presentation.

I zone in and out for the mumbo jumbo, reliving memories of Richard that have nothing to do with this. I'm drawn back at some weighty point. I hear, "'I am the resurrection and the life,' says the Lord. 'Those who believe in me, even though they die, will live, and everyone who lives and believes in me will never die".'

Jedge casts me a look and passes me his hip flask. I pour a little into the top and drink, telling myself people will assume it's medicinal. Which it is.

A couple of Richard's friends speak, including Jedge, his top hat next to me on his chair. I'm in awe of his composure and refusal to be compromised by a culture that's not his or mine or Richard's. When he relates an anecdote of bunking off school with Richard, age fifteen, I start to weep, though I try to hide it. Jedge and Richard, same age, give or take a few months, were lifelong friends; and now one's dead of a massive brainstem stroke, no warning whatsoever, and the other's giving his valediction. Fifty used to sound old to me but now I'm forty-two, and I know fifty is young, too young to die.

Once the tears start, they don't want to stop. I cry because the end of a life of a man who richly deserved his place on earth, finally feels real to me. The shock of his death is fading; the impact he had on people swells. I see the gap he leaves in our futures, and I see his no future, the black of nothing. But even that is too much because black is not nothing; it's something.

Jedge surprises me by quoting from John Donne. It's the serious part of his speech, a reminder of our mortality, as if we needed it right now: "Any man's death diminishes me, For I am involved in mankind. And, therefore, never send to know for whom the bell tolls; It tolls for thee."

You can ring my be-e-ell, ring my bell, my bell, ring my bell.

After the service I feel cleansed, relieved. We all do. That's the point of these things. We join the family for an hour or so at the wake in a function room of a pub marketing itself as traditional. There are sandwiches cut into triangles, bowls of crisps, and segments of tomatoes and cucumber on lettuce. I'm sad and angered that his parents didn't know him, didn't approve of the life he lived, and at the last gasp are trying to claw him back into their respectable circle. They missed so much. I want to sweep their tired sandwiches to floor but everyone's being nice to everyone, for Richard's sake and our own.

The real wake begins when we get back to Jedge's place. The music is loud, the weed is plentiful, the back door's open, the garden's lovely, and Jedge makes veggie chilli for anyone who wants it. The talk is of Richard and the day. There is more laughter than tears. Jedge has digitalized some old photos and, along with more recent images, he projects them above his fireplace.

Later, at the top of the stairs, Jedge and I pass as he's leaving the bathroom and I'm about to go in.

"Hey," he says in gentle acknowledgement.

"You bearing up?" I ask.

He nods. "You?"

"Yeah, I guess so."

We go our separate ways, touching fingertips as we part.

In the bathroom, I take a pee then stare at my face in the mirror. Underneath my eye make-up are ghosts of eye make-up I applied that morning. And underneath that is me. I don't retouch. I just look at myself, wondering who I am and why I'm alive. It confuses me that this person, the one who stares at herself in the mirror, is the same as the one who'll go downstairs and chat to people.

Someone taps on the bathroom door.

"Two minutes," I call.

"It's me, Jedge." His voice is low and secretive.

I let him in, thinking he wants to talk away from everyone else. He locks the door quickly. His movements are sharp and aggressive. I sense a drama, an urgency in what he wants to share. He's with me in two strides, eyes glittering with something akin to anger. He bumps me back against the wall, grips my hair in two fists and kisses me hard. Some animal part of me responds to the kiss then I jerk my head aside, wriggling against his weight.

"Jedge . . . get off, no."

He forces me to meet his kiss, a hand on my jaw. His mouth is wet and reckless, and he tastes of nicotine and beer. He pins me to the wall with his chest and scrabbles for my skirt, tugging it higher. I try pushing him away, protesting, but he's stronger than me. I hear fabric rip and know the split in my red pencil skirt just got bigger.

"Jedge!"

He ignores me. My torn skirt is around my hips and his hand is on my crotch, his big fingers rubbing and shoving, his other hand fumbling at my blouse.

I catch sight of my reflection. I look panicked, my gingham hair flower bouncing at a foolish angle. So much movement and violence in the mirror. Mirrors are usually stiller, quieter.

"Please!" snaps Jedge. He doesn't plead. It's an impatient command.

Inside me, something breaks, and I'm there. I'm in Jedge's madness, wanting to fuck more than anything else in the world. I push down my underwear, snagging the lace on heels that would take too long to remove. Jedge is attempting to unbutton my blouse, moving with me as I bend. Opposite the wall I'm leaning against is the marble-topped counter of the washbasin unit. I raise my legs either side of Jedge, slot my heels against the counter edge and brace my back against the wall. Jedge unbuttons his fly, steps out of one trouser leg and reaches beneath his shirt-flap for his cock. I edge my back down the wall to find him. He spits on his fingers, moistens his cock with a quick hand shuffle, then guides his tip to my entrance.

The angle is awkward, we don't know each other's body, and he misses a few times, butting at my crease before driving upwards, high and hard. We both groan, sounds we've never shared together. He cups my arse, taking some of my weight. I've barely had a chance to get wet and I feel my body's resistance slide around his girth. We pant and grunt. His thrusts make me wetter and looser. His face is twisted and flushed, mouth gaping. I've never seen that face before.

Then I notice the music drifting up from downstairs: Sylvester, "Mighty Real".

Yo-ouu make me feel, mi-i-ghty real.

Seventies disco has been popping up throughout the day, songs from Jedge and Richard's youth.

I start to sob. It chokes me and I throw back my head, smacking it against the wall. Tears pour down my face and I cling to Jedge's neck, howling and gasping. I am a mess of pleasure and pain. So is Jedge, but he expresses it by fucking me as if there's no tomorrow. When he comes, he cries out like a wounded beast.

I don't come. We collapse together on the bathroom floor, holding each other, silent and stunned. Jedge's shoulders start to shake. Damn, now he's crying. I crawl away and tug a stream of toilet tissue from the roll. We both blow our noses and let soggy, balled-up paper drop to the floor. Then, tentatively, breathlessly, we start to laugh.

"Well," says Jedge, "that was stupid of us."

"Yeah," I say, laughing harder.

He could be right. We've been friends for years, never lovers. So perhaps this will ruin us although I doubt it.

Jedge tucks a lock of my hair behind an ear, smiling. His shirt is splashed with tears and tomato juice from the chilli.

I shrug, smiling too, and give his shoulder a consolatory rub.

Mistakes happen. Questions go unanswered. Stuff is left undone.

But in uncertainty and chaos, at least we know we're alive.

And mighty real.

Barbados Bound

Lily Lick

Edmund beached his boat and I watched him again at the shower and at the other end of the bar, tipping his beer bottle hello. I was surprised at the depth of my own disappointment when he turned to leave without tipping it goodbye. But he walked towards me this time and stopped just inches away, looked at me, at my nearly finished drink then back at me. "Whenever you're ready we can go."

I took one last swallow, grabbed my wrap and stood up. Edmund took my elbow and led me away . . .

I had always made sure I had a stool facing his way when Edmund came up the beach for his wash. He would pull out the band that held back his long hair, then let the rivers of sun-sparkled fresh water course over his face and down his work-hardened body; over his chest, his broad back, over his worn bathing shorts and down his long legs. He turned this way and that and pulled his suit out at the back and front to let the water flush all the sea salt away. Finally, he would bend forward, run the water through his hair again, then straighten up and flip his dreadlocks in an arc over his head. The end tip of each one was sun and saltwater bleached and the water flew off the ends like individual crystal beads dancing in an unexpected rainbow. I watched him do something as simple as wash the saltwater from his skin and I wanted nothing more than to kneel before him and dry him off. I watched Edmund every day from the relative comfort and shade of the beachside bar.

Edmund ran the Daisy Boats on a patch of sand just down the beach from the Golden Cove. There were all kinds of boats for hire, some for fishing, some for parasailing, glass-bottomed ones for looking at the coral on the ocean floor, water-skiing boats and scuba-diving boats. Edmund had a unique little corner of the market though; he just took people for a boat ride. That's it: down the coast, up the coast, wherever you wanted to go. There was no shortage of bikini-clad customers willing to pay for a very close-up look at this exquisite man. When the sun waned and the customers headed back to their hotel rooms for a little pre-dinner siesta, Edmund would pull his boat up the beach, secure it, and then head towards the pool bar for his shower. Just thinking about it makes me wet even now. He would finish this daily ritual with a beer at the bar.

The bartender would put the beer down just as he reached the counter. "Edmund," he would say, "how's the water today?"

Always the same question, and always the same reply, "Good man, good."

I had observed this every day for thirteen days and I would leave on the afternoon of the fourteenth day, but I was content to sit and watch in the convenience of a ritual that I had incorporated into my own. Various women approached Edmund, some openly offering themselves, some a bit more than rum-soaked, some just testing to see how far they would get. Edmund was a handsome man who would attract attention anywhere, and these women were on holiday, why not be forward? He never had more than one beer, never went off with any of them; he had for the last few days been tipping his beer in my direction in a little sign of hello when he arrived and again before he left for the evening. I raised my punch glass in acknowledgement in return.

. . . led me away to the side of the road where he flagged down the bus, paid both fares then turned to help me on. We bounced along in silence for a while until he announced, "This is us," then stood and guided me down the short middle aisle and off the bus.

The house that Edmund led me to was weather-beaten grey wood, set back in a yard of orderly green disorder. The few steps leading up to the side door were deceptively sturdy, yellow potted flowers guiding the way on each one. It was cool inside, the lighting almost surreal as the late afternoon sun angled through the slatted window shutters. Spartan but clean and tidy, only two rooms really, the kitchen behind and a living/

bedroom at the front. Edmund watched as I turned around taking it all in.

In the corner, a mat. "Yoga," he said.

The *New York Times* was on the bedside table; a bookcase filled the far wall. "I can read. I prefer a good mystery over the classics."

Clothes hung neatly in the small closet. "I occasionally wear something besides swim trunks."

A TV. "There's a satellite dish out back."

The bed was made with crisp white sheets. "And I can do my own wash," he said with a grin and raised eyebrow. "Surprised?"

About now, I was beginning to feel like this was a joke to him, and the joke was on me. "OK," I said and headed for the door, but not fast enough to get there before Edmund.

"I want you to stay," he said, lips just brushing mine, as he slipped his arms around me. "Don't go . . . stay with me. Just till the sun goes all the way down. I'll take you back then, but don't go yet."

"You're making fun of me."

"No, making a point. Not making fun, never making fun."

He pulled me gently back to the bed and sat down next to me. Edmund kissed my forehead, each one of my fingers, the end of my nose, then finally my lips. He told me not to talk, just to listen and to feel as he slowly untied my bikini top and traced the white un-burnt lines with his long dark fingers. The contrast between our skins was even more pronounced when he cupped both my breasts with his hands and thumbed my pale pink nipples.

"Too much sun isn't good for anyone . . . it's not good for this skin." He stopped me with a kiss when I opened my mouth to reply, then whispered, "Shhh. Don't talk. Listen."

"Then talk to me. Tell me something," I said, as he eased me down on the cool white sheets. "Tell me something."

Edmund knelt on the floor and spoke to me through the warmth between my legs, his words muffled in the material of my bathing suit bottoms. "I'm going to tell you the story of me . . . of you . . . of the world." Each pause punctuated by a kiss. He sucked the wet cloth into his mouth and slid the thin material down past my hips as I hooked my fingers through the ropey coils on his head.

"I'll get back to my story in a short bit," he said, raising his head and smiling. "It's rude to talk with your mouth full." I agreed and offered myself to him. And then again when he asked for more.

I knew that something was different here, certainly different than what I had been expecting. I didn't have any idea what to expect when I came here, but I didn't expect this gentleman – didn't expect this *gentleness*.

Edmund let me rest before rising above me and easing himself between my legs.

"Do you think you're wet enough now? Wet like the sea you're afraid to go out on?"

"I'm wet enough and not afraid."

Edmund started talking as he entered me, setting up a liquid motion of in and out that carried me on his words like the waves breaking on the not so distant shore.

"When you come here, to my home, to my land, you look about in awe. You look first at the wonderful country, the views, the greens and the blues of the sky and the ocean. Then eventually you see us, you see men like me and you measure us up against your imaginary tape that determines what you will let us do to you. You decide whether you will allow us to fuck you. You look at us running our little businesses and you decide ahead of time that you will have us and that it is you doing us a favour. You think that my world drops off at the edge of the ocean, at the end of the beach. And you will bring me some of your world because mine is so small. But I have been where you think I haven't. I've been in the snow and cold that you flee from each winter, to the other side of the real world and back. I've been places you'll never go, done things you can only imagine, things you wouldn't believe and decided that I like my corner of the world better. So I lie here buried inside you, fucking you, because I already know this is as big as the world need be. You came to me, to my bed, and I am giving you what you need; a part of me, sweet girl, and a part of my world."

I begged then for a part of his world, begged like it was the last orgasm I was ever going to have and he had it and I needed to have that part right now. Edmund was finished talking, not that I could have understood or even heard anything by that point, lost as I was in lust and want and need. He spent the rest of the night initiating me into his world.

It didn't change anything though, maybe my outlook on things, but not the fact that I had to leave. That man, that gentle wise man, rode the morning bus back to the hotel with me and saw me to my door before heading back out to his boat. How do you say goodbye to someone who has just fucked the living daylights out of you and made you think about life at the same time. What do you tell people that want to know how your holiday was?

"How was the island talent? Did you *do* anyone?"

"Well, yes, and this 'sex in the tropics' thing has had quite a profound effect on me." No one wants to hear that.

No, they just want to know if he was any good, how many times, how big was he. And where can they find him when they go south. Oh, he was very, very good. It was only one night but we did it lots of times . . . over and over again actually. He was about six foot two inches, so yeah he was big, and it's all relative isn't it? Size and everything? And even though I had a hard time getting all of him in my mouth, I sucked his cock for breakfast too.

I could still feel that sweet ache of well-fucked soreness as I walked past the smiling stewardesses and through US Customs after the plane landed back home. I'm not telling anyone where to find him though, that part they can figure out themselves.

The Golden Cove is just one of the many hotels strung along the Caribbean Sea coast of Barbados. Every day the big jets land at Grantley Adams Airport and spew out a load of tourists, then suck up another sunburnt group and fly them off home. Some will, like I did, find their way to the Golden Cove Hotel, the private beach, and the clear blue sea beyond that. I had escaped everything for two weeks: a job I'd stopped liking a long time ago, a very recently over love affair with a too attached man, and a cold and snowy winter. A tropical island hadn't been my first choice but a sell-off is a sell-off and I don't know if I'll ever figure out if going there was an escape or a beginning.

I have a picture of Edmund that I took when he was pulling his boat out of the water. His muscles are straining and he's smiling and talking with some near naked thing that's passing by on the beach. I look at it when I need help reminding myself that there is good out there in the world.

Sometimes it's far away and you have to look for it and once in a while it walks right up to you and says, "Whenever you're ready we can go."

Girls, Boys and All of Our Toys

M. Christian

She's small and immaculate: skin like scrubbed china, body a precisely painted doll's. She doesn't look her size until you're standing next to her – then you realize her scale. I don't know what I expected her to like, or use, but when I found out, when she shared it with me and the others in my tight little circle, I do admit to being delightfully surprised. Considering, it makes sense: her little dildo looks like a toy, a child's plastic gizmo. The plastic is blue-ish and smells like the beach toys she had as a kid – a kind of tart but fruity smell. The Japanese have either laws or a cultural thing against calling a dick a dick and hers is typical of this: the shaft is the body of an Eskimo maiden, the color of her parka being the corona of the "not-a-dick". On this totem pole that happens to look very much like every cock I've even seen is a slender polar bear whose tongue, with a flick of a switch near the base, starts to flutter rather ... excitedly. Another touch of another button and it starts to hum, vibrate and oscillate like a snake charmed by a slow dance tune.

Now I've never seen this and her in action, but being who we all are – my friends and I – we talk about such. Though I admit a gentle desire to see her with her favorite. Not, surprisingly (and, yeah, I'm being honest), because I have the hots for her (though she is definitely hot) but rather for the punchline, the sweet conclusion. She likes to use her favorite and often, she admits with a sly smile, falls asleep with it still inside. Hearing this for the first time, two things came to mind: the precious image of this beautiful girl, all fine china and elegant poise, laying back on a futon, legs spread, toy humming, vibrating, doing its slow dance, its polar bear addition fluttering while she sleeps – dozing content and spent, a blissful smile on her perfect face.

The other thing that zapped to mind was how, like people and their pets, do all the special people in my life resemble their toys.

She's a teacher. What she teaches is near and dear to all of our . . . well, let's just say that what she teaches is near and dear. Like her students, she thinks a lot about sex, about what she likes and doesn't. It's that honesty that I find so endearing. No apologies, no embarrassments. Just a "if it's fun, and it doesn't hurt anyone, then do it" attitude. I can't remember when or why it came out – it just did. Over at her place for a talk, having dinner and the subject just sort of came up. Thinking about it – like people and their pets – I realize that it's true, very, very true.

Like her, it's big and black. Fat would be a good word – and one she'd agree with. Imagining her with her favorite, I can just about imagine her chat with her students: "I like the sensation of being filled. I've tried vibrators but I'm too sensitive. I like to come very slowly, my hand being the best for that. But I do like being filled. I tried a lot of other ones till I found my right one. I know some women like theirs "realistic" and others prefer them simple, streamlined. I don't really care – I chose mine because it was big and fat, something that I could ease into myself, slowly, as I rubbed my clit."

I have an image of her, sitting like a black Buddha, big porcelain grin on her face, her favorite toy in her lap, proudly showing us all her source of pleasure – and teaching us what she loves to teach us: "Don't be embarrassed if it gives you pleasure!"

He's a big burly bear of a man. That's right – and so is his toy. Like every observation there are always exceptions. When you look at him you see what he proudly proclaims: "I'm a grizzly!" From his great furry beard to his warm furry belly he is someone you could easily see rubbing his back on some tree in the forest. Sometimes, when you look at him just right – say under the cold blue glare of a setting moon – you could swear that he really was a beast of the forest: barely trained to walk upright and eat with a fork.

His toy, his special plaything, is about what you'd think it would be: strong and manly. Never heard him talk about it, unlike some of my other friends. But one day I dropped in on his . . . excuse me, I was about to say his house. But he is a beast and beasts don't have houses, do they? One day I stopped by his cave, his lair and there it was: plastic as pink as his tongue, as pink as his asshole (well, naturally). I've seen butt plugs before and since, of course, but this one was the beast of butt plugs. Looking at it sideways you could see it, too, lurking in the forest, waiting for the right asshole to walk by before . . .

Unorthodox as she is, they are – when you think about it – perfect for her. I've known her a long while, and while others see chaos and a Mistress of Flake, I see a spirit too free to be hemmed in by outside convention or even fundamental laws. She is as wild and untamed as her hair – a rusty metal halo around her freckled face. Always in motion, always halfway somewhere, she darts around in her slender, peaches and cream, body as much as her green eyes do – never quite in place.

For some she is a source of frustration – not because she is always late (she is) or that she never remembers her purse (she does) but because she is all of these things – wild and unkempt – but manages to make it work for her. Things that, for the rest of us tamed people, would never work in a thousand years seem to just click, clack, klunk into place for this certain redhead.

Same for her toys. I've never known anyone to make those stupid little plastic/brass/etc. eggs work. I know several million (or so) Chinese can't be wrong but on this side of the Pacific, at least, no one I know has ever gotten off on Ben Wa balls.

Except for her – and, knowing her luck, the very first time. Now they are a staple of hers. That and her rocking chair that always squeaks. Many times I'd come to visit, wondering as she rocks back and forth, back and forth, in that squeaky chair, if the smile on her animated face was because a friend had dropped by or because of those uncertain, unpredictable, metal eggs rolling around inside her.

Me? I have to continue this hypothesis, I guess. Like mine I am long and thin. It's strange how you suddenly have your favorite.

I've tried a lot, over the years: things that oscillate and hum, buzz and expand, plastic and rubber, wood and metal. But then I found it and it's been on my nightstand ever since.

Long and thin, yes. For certain. Long and thin and leathery. Well, I ain't *that* old – so maybe we can supplant "leathery" (and all its tired, worldly connotations) with tough but flexible (lots better, don't you think?). I've tried other kinds, the rubber rings (watch out for pubic hair!), the steel ones (hard to get off but fun) and the Velcro ones (but they get loose) so mine has snaps.

Now for the personal details: I like the sensation, a lot, when I loop it around the shaft of my cock and my balls. I like the constriction, the strength it gives me when I'm hard. I like the way it also changes the way I feel – suddenly my skin feels less sensitive, like my cock belongs to someone else. I enjoy it – a lot.

So I guess I'm like my cock ring. In many, many ways – but, more than anything, I exist for fun. Lots and lots and lots of fun.

Like my friends.

Kissing on Concourse C

Susannah Indigo

There's this moment when you're first kissing your lover you haven't seen in a long time – weeks maybe months – where it's very tentative and your conscious mind is wondering who is this? but you keep kissing and kissing and kissing and then suddenly you're inside of it all just like a good story and it's flowing from beginning to neverending and all you can ask is don't stop and your body melts into the kiss and there is nothing but love and lust and touch and tongues and you know that if everyone kissed like this there would be no war no divorce no depression and you know that even though sex was always on the agenda now it is real and imperative and if you don't get out of this airport and into someplace where clothes can disappear immediately there will be a scene here in public that no one will ever forget.

That is how Carlos kisses Illona, *hello* and *goodbye*, with goodbyes sometimes wrapping back around into *hello* and *I love you* and *I can never leave*. She wears all the things he has given her when he is leaving so that he remembers, or maybe so that he'll think she's another possession of his and he'll pack her into his bag and take her wherever he goes. The silver necklace and earrings from Mexico, the thick black leather belt, the strappy heels, the Indian-beaded barrette in her long red hair, and always the sexy lingerie underneath, everything that he helped to create her with. *I never existed before you*, she often tells him, and even though she is a thirty-two-year-old lawyer and feminist to the core, she still knows that it is true. There were men and there was sex and there were words of passion and heat before him but she cannot recall a single detail from that time. *B.C. – Before*

Carlos – she jokingly calls that part of her life, but what she really means is *before submission, before kneeling, before dominance, before pain*. She had no idea she would like to be spanked – she would have laughed at the suggestion *B.C.* – and now she likes *hairbrushes and riding crops and paddles and whips* and most of all Carlos's hands all over her body, grabbing hard and controlling and circling her ankles and her wrists and her heart.

The first night they had dinner together he reached over and encircled her wrist with his big hand and, after watching her, he told her that he could always check on how submissive a woman was by how she reacted to this – *some pull away quickly, some only laugh when I don't let go, some get a look in their eyes that tells me everything I need to know.*

On the second date he spanked her, on the third he bought her a collar, and then there was never a question of where they were going to go. To a cottage for a weekend of being leashed and trained; to a club in a short skirt and cuffs to show off what he owned; to a dungeon and the cross, a trip into places that redefine your soul, the kind of trip that they never list on *travelocity* or mention in *frequent flyer polls.*

But in the final moment there is only Carlos and his leather bag and his arms around Illona and another plane that waits to take him away from her ... and they are *kissing and kissing and kissing* at the gate where she had to sneak through on an old ticket just to see him all the way to the plane, and she would not have cared if they tried to stop her because *nothing* can keep her from him, and anyway there aren't many redheaded terrorists wearing pink camisoles and kissing their lovers like they are *trying to climb up into their hearts.* When she pauses to catch her breath, he says *more* and he is holding her so tight that she can feel his hardness press against her belly, and with his hand tight in her hair and no breath left he says *come for me*, and she begins to melt into nothing but waves of love as he holds her while she shakes ... and then he must go, and she cannot possibly imagine that there will not be more time for this and that her very last memory of Carlos will be of herself as a fragile girl who stands by the window waving in a puddle of her own lust, a girl who will forever have to live with the memory of *kissing on Concourse C.*

Gravity

Helen E. H. Madden

"Let me tell you something, girl. Gravity sucks."

The fat woman spoke in a heavy voice that nearly rolled me flat with its declaration. The sound of it was a perfect match for her body. She was massive, no taller than 1.7 meters, yet she weighed over 200 kilos. At least she did on Earth, the woman confided. Here on the moon, she felt light as a feather.

"I had to leave," she rumbled as we rolled out of the space port. "Take-off *might* have killed me, but gravity definitely *would*. Couldn't move down there." She waved a bloated hand toward the glowing full Earth. "Couldn't even get out of the damned bed. They had to hoist me into the rocket by crane."

As we headed into the station, I marveled at how she moved. She bounced along the metal hallways with a slow, heavy grace, each ponderous step sending ripples through her distended form. Adipose overwhelmed her face, and she had more rings around her center than Saturn. She was a wonder to me, an icon of abundance and overindulgence from another world.

"What's your name?" she asked as I helped her check-in.

"Luna."

She chuckled. "Luna, the moon girl. You're thin."

"Born on the moon," I explained. "Never been planet-side. Everyone here is tall and thin."

She nodded. "Gravity doesn't weigh you down. Well, it won't weigh me down either, anymore."

We made love that night. My interest surprised her, I think, but I had never seen anyone like her before. The moon was a harsh place, full of dry dust and dead rock. Here, everything was rationed – the food, the water, the air. The people were as sparse and tenuous as the recycled oxygen, and we were all just a breath away from death. Not her though. I dug my fingers into the folds of her flesh, wallowing in the furrows and crevices of her landscape. I scaled her mountainous breasts and tumbled down the rolling hills of her belly. "Eat as much as you want," she laughed as I burrowed between her legs. "I got plenty to spare."

After that first night, I was bound to her, unable to escape her sphere. She wouldn't tell me her name. "Left it behind with the gravity," she joked. "Too heavy to carry around." So I called her Gaea. She had as much money as she did fat – how else could she have afforded the trip? – and she hired me to be her guide. "I want to go *everywhere*," she told me. "Now that I can, I want to *move*." So we bounced through the station, her leading the way, me trailing behind.

We didn't go far at first; she was unused to the exercise and the recycled air. Over the weeks though, Gaea's orbit expanded until she ran laps around the station. I was excited for her. She seemed so happy with her newfound freedom. But I soon noticed the laws of physics were wearing away my love. Without the full force of Earth's gravity to hold her in check, she had become an object in constant motion. As her velocity increased, her mass decreased. Like the Earth hanging in the endless night above, my beautiful Gaea began to wane.

In bed, I stumbled over the skeletal ridges of her once ample hips. Where were Gaea's mountains and hills? Where was the abundance of flesh? Gone. She had grown as flat and sparse as the lunar plains.

"You should eat more," I said, struggling to gain a handhold on her dwindling form. "You're rich. You don't have to starve."

Gaea scoffed. "One can never be too rich or too thin."

I tried feeding her more anyway, sneaking half of my rations into her meals. The sacrifice left me dizzy with hunger, but Gaea grew round and full once more. Overjoyed, I feasted on her bounty. Then the extra kilos began to weigh on her mind.

"I still feel it," she said one night as I suckled at her breast. "Even here, on the moon, gravity still has a hold of me. I'm heavy again."

"It's nothing. You've just acclimated to the moon. Don't worry—"

She jumped up, propelling me off the bed and into the nearest wall. As I struggled to right myself, she catapulted toward the observation port.

"I have to escape." She pointed to a blinking red light in the glittering sky. "The orbital supply station . . . Can you take me there?"

I shook my head. "It's dangerous. Besides, there's nothing up there; it's just an abandoned hulk of metal."

"Exactly. There's nothing, not even gravity. I'd be completely free. Make the arrangements tonight."

I did as she asked, but reluctantly. The orbital station had been closed for years. When we got there, we glided through its hollow corridors then went outside to walk along the cratered hull. A rocket lifted off from the moon below us and Gaea whooped with joy.

"Look at me!" she shouted over the comm of her EVA suit. "I can fly!"

She leapt into the starry night, sailing to the limit of her tether. The sight of her tumbling free fall chilled me to the bone.

"Gaea, come back! We should return to the shuttle."

"No." Her voice crackled in my ear. "I'm staying here."

"What? But—"

"I made arrangements. I'm staying." She drifted above me, cold and distant. "I know about the food, Luna. I know what you've been trying to do. You've become a stone around my neck. I need to cut you loose. Besides," she said, spinning away from me, "I'm not attracted to you anymore."

I felt as though someone had cut off the oxygen to my helmet. While I struggled to breathe, Gaea moved farther away. Without thinking, I reached for her tether and unhooked it from the anchor point. Gaea didn't notice until it was too late.

"Luna? Luna!" She jabbed at the controls of her jet pack, only to set herself further adrift.

"You were right," I said as she flailed around in the void. "Gravity does suck. It holds us down and crushes us in its grip. But it also holds us together and keeps us safely in our place. Too bad you never appreciated that."

Gaea fired her pack once more and hurtled away into space. I watched her go, and then I returned to the moon, alone.

Counterpane

Alison Tyler

"Take off the counterpane."

The boys were ahead of them. Not that the two couples were racing, but the blond stud was already on his back, head on the white-slipped pillow, slim hips arched. His dark-haired lover crouched between his thighs, licking that tender skin, working slowly to the blond's impressive hard-on.

Somehow Lia knew exactly how that would feel.

"Come on, baby. Help me with the counterpane." Ry was in a hurry to catch up. Lia could tell. Still, she turned to him, confused by his request.

"The what?"

"Bedspread," he said, his British accent stronger now that he was aroused. "Who knows how many people have shot their load onto those ugly watercolor flowers."

"How many do you think?" Lia asked as she helped him wrench back the heavy quilted comforter – abloom in gaudy burnt-orange and lemon-yellow blossoms. She was looking at the boys again. For the first time in her life, she wished she had a cock – and she wished that the dark-haired Romeo was sucking her, right down to the root. She could almost feel his full lips on her skin – pretty, cupid-bow lips.

Ry gripped her chin and forced her to face him, his own lips bending into a half-smile. "Slut." He elongated the word, really hitting the "l." "That's your favorite part, isn't it? Thinking about all the other people who have fucked in this bed."

"One of my favorite parts." She pulled her chin out of his hand and stared back at the other couple, who didn't appear to mind in the least – the blond was tall and fine-boned, the darker one well muscled, with tattoos scrolled over his skin. She'd hardly ever paused to notice gym rats before, but this guy did something to her. She watched the naked wrestling on the other bed – and she sighed out loud when the one with the chestnut hair hissed under his breath: "Roll over."

That was something Ry said to her, in just the same way: "Roll over. Show me that sweet fucking ass of yours."

Now, she watched as the top started to rim his lover. Fucking God. More than talking to Ry about who'd abused this hotel room before, she liked seeing what the two boys would do.

Her heart pounded at the way the brunet roughly pulled apart the blond's cheeks and licked in a tight circle around that tiny pink bud. She clenched her own thighs together. Ry had never done that to her. Nobody had. But she desperately wanted to own that experience, a tongue against her there. Wetness. Warmth. She thought that the sensation alone might make her come. Would it feel like Ry was suckling her clit? Would it make her feel like a boy?

The brunet didn't wait to see if rimming would make the blond come. He gripped a bottle of lube from the faux walnut bedside table and poured a shivering handful between the lean man's taut cheeks. Lia moved forward. She wanted to be as close to the action as possible. She watched hungrily as the dark-haired boy slid one hand over his own rigid cock, lubing himself up, before pressing just the head against the blond's hole.

Right then, Ry grabbed her.

It was as if he'd been waiting for this exact moment – as if he knew what was going to happen next. His touch made Lia groan. All morning, she'd been thinking of this situation. While working in her sterile little cubicle downtown, she'd fantasized about what Ry had told her, where he'd wanted her to meet him for lunch.

Not to eat. But to fuck.

From outside, she could hear the noontime traffic. Through a crack in the window, she could smell the fried calamari sizzling in the kitchen of the downstairs café. But all that mattered to her were the people in this room.

Ry pushed her down on the bed and ripped her pleated violet skirt to her waist. She wasn't wearing panties – he'd told her not to when he'd instructed her to meet him at this hotel, on a Thursday at noon. This was the sort of thing Ry did from time to time. Keeping her off guard. Keeping her guessing.

The boys had already been going at it when she walked into the room, and she'd looked from them to Ry and back to them again, catching the grin on Ryland's face – seeing that he knew how excited she already was.

They didn't know the boys' names. But names didn't matter. All that mattered was watching them – she and Ry on one bed, the dynamic duo on another.

With her skirt pulled up to her ass, naked skin beneath, her pussy pressed hard against the crisp white sheets. She focused intently on the men – oh, the noises that they made. Those were almost as sexy to her as what they were doing. But then Ry did exactly what she'd fantasized about moments before. He slipped a pillow under her hips to raise her, parted the cheeks of her ass and pressed his tongue to her hole.

Jesus fucking Christ.

Why hadn't she let him do this before? He made one spiral, and then another. She shut her eyes for a moment, because the wave of pleasure was almost too extreme – then opened her eyes and stared down at the forest green carpeted floor – speckled with bits of lint. Ry slid one hand under her waist and touched her clit.

"Oh, baby. You're so wet. Look how wet you get when I lick you here."

Her cheeks burned as shame flooded through her. She couldn't speak. Ry's tongue between her cheeks turned up so many different emotions inside of her. Is that why she'd never let him do that before?

He licked her again, then moved back and pressed the ball of his thumb to her asshole. He didn't push it in, he simply rested his thumb against her. She waited. He didn't move. She waited another second. He was as still as she was. Finally, Lia couldn't stand the tease. She was the one to push back, to thrust back, so that his thumb was inside of her and she was panting.

"You want it, don't you, you little slut," he said. She loved when he talked to her like that. His accent made her feel exceptionally dirty. She had no idea why. Her eyes went back to the boys. The top was fucking the blond now, and at a rapid speed. She saw things she hadn't noticed at the start. The blond's nipples were pierced, his chest was waxed, smooth and bare. The brunet had a tattoo of an anchor on one shoulder, a forties-style tattoo that made her want to trace the outline with her tongue.

"What are you thinking?" Ry asked, but she shook her head. He gripped on to her curls and pulled back hard. A shudder ran through her. His thumb was out of her ass now, and she could feel the head of his cock against her. Poised. Ready.

"What are you thinking, Lia?"

"That I'd like to lick him," she said. Her breath was coming faster now. "That I'd like to be him," she continued, unable to hold back as he pushed his cock into her. She wanted it all, and all at once. She wanted to be the boy on top, licking the blond's hole. Then fucking him. She wanted to be the blond, getting rimmed, getting fucked. She wanted to touch them, crawl into their bed, be a part of the game. Turned inside out by the way they moved, the way they fucked.

There was a picture on the wall. A sailing print. Gold frame. The room had that antiseptic smell of cheap cleaning products – but beneath the scent was the odor of so many other guests who had romped here before.

But they hadn't been doing this, Lia thought. They hadn't been fucking in tandem like she and Ry and the duo on the other bed.

It wasn't a race – she knew that – but now the couples were moving beat for beat. Ryland was deep in her ass. The brunet was fucking the blond to the same exact rhythm. Their groans were a background melody.

Their very breathing was in synch.

When the movie ended, Lia came. Ry's cock was deep in her ass, and his fingertips stroked her clit, stretching out her orgasm. She sighed and pulled off him, feeling dirty and used and clean and set free. Ry reached for the remote control and turned off the porn channel. Through the bathroom door, she could see those familiar cheap white towels, nearly threadbare. Too thin to be much use. She'd shower anyway, then head back to work – her ass sore, her body humming.

Ry said, "Next time, we'll take out an ad. Describe exactly what we want."

She looked at him, then at the dark box of the TV screen, and she nodded.

Because next time it was going to be for real.